Disney
365
Stories
A story a day
Parragon
Bath • New York • Cologne • Melbourne • Delhi
Hong Kong • Shenzhen • Singapore

This edition published by Parragon Books Ltd in 2016

Parragon Books Ltd
Chartist House
15–17 Trim Street
Bath BA1 1HA, UK
www.parragon.com

Researched and co-ordinated by Niamh Harkett

ISBN 978-1-4748-3498-8

Printed in China

January

1

New Year's Day

It was the first day of the new year, and Pongo and Perdita were out for a walk with their pets, Roger and Anita. The morning fog was beginning to part, and the air was clear and cold.

"Oh, Pongo," Perdita sighed happily. "What a wonderful year we've just had – 15 puppies to be thankful for!"

"Yes, darling, and just think of all we have to look forward to this year," said Pongo.

"Can you believe they all stayed up till midnight last night to ring in the new year?" Perdita cried. "And were still awake when we left! I do hope they don't tire out dear, poor Nanny."

"Yes, that was quite a party we had at the flat last night," Pongo agreed. "And Lucky would have spent the whole night watching television if we had allowed him to."

"Perhaps we should be getting home now," said Perdita. "I am so afraid that Cruella De Vil may come round while we're out. I dread the way she looks at our puppies."

"I suppose we should," said Pongo. "But I'm sure Nanny has been taking good care of them." Pongo and Perdita gently pulled on their leads to let Roger and Anita know it was time to go. The four of them walked towards home just as a sprinkling of rain began to fall.

"Nanny! Puppies! We're home!" called Roger as he and Anita took off their muddy boots, and Pongo and Perdy brushed off their paws on the mat in the hall. But no one answered.

"Pongo!" exclaimed Perdita, her panic rising. "Where are the puppies?"

Pongo raced up the stairs and began searching the rooms one by one. Perdita went to check the kitchen. Roger and Anita exchanged concerned looks, but tried to remain calm.

Pongo hurried into the sitting room to rejoin Perdita, who was on the brink of tears.

"Oh, Pongo!" she cried. "Where can...."

"Hush, darling," said Pongo, his ears pricked intently. The two dogs fell silent. Then they both heard it – a tiny snore coming from the direction of the sofa. There, nestled among the cushions, the puppies were sound asleep!

"I found Nanny!" Roger called. "She fell asleep in her chair!"

Perdita was busy counting the sleeping puppies. "... 12, 13, 14.... Oh, Pongo! One of the puppies isn't here!"

But Pongo had trotted into the next room. "Here he is, darling!" he called. "It's Lucky, of course. He's watching the New Year's Day celebration on television."

January

2

A New Talent

Pixie Hollow was getting ready to bring spring to the mainland, and a very special visitor was expected. "It's time for Queen Clarion's review!" Bobble told Tinker Bell.

Tink rushed home to collect the things she'd been making. This was her big chance to prove how important tinker fairies were!

The fairies gathered in Springtime Square, as the Minister of Spring announced, "The Queen is coming!"

Queen Clarion flew in gracefully. But before she could begin her inspection, there was a loud *RUMBLE*.... In raced Cheese the mouse, pulling a wagon laden with new inventions. Tink jumped down from the back.

"Queen Clarion!" she called.

Tink reached into the wagon and pulled out a nutcracker made from branches and stones. "This will help young squirrels to open acorns," she said. But as she pressed it down, the acorn shot out and hit a squirrel in the face!

Tink reached for another invention. "This is a flower painter. Look, Minister...." But as the Minister leaned forward to see, the purple paint squirted all over his face! "Oops, sorry!"

Queen Clarion interrupted. "Tinker Bell, dear, didn't anyone tell you? Tinker fairies don't go to the mainland."

Tink's face fell. "But I thought...." She could feel her eyes tearing up as she got back on her wagon. "It's okay, I couldn't make it anyway...."

Back in Tinkers' Nook, Fairy Mary explained, "Only when you can make flowers bloom or capture a sunbeam will you be allowed to go to the mainland."

Her words gave Tink a new idea! The next morning, she surprised her friends by announcing, "I'm no longer going to be a tinker fairy! I'm changing my talent!"

Iridessa, the light fairy, was doubtful. "I've never heard of a fairy changing her talent before."

Silvermist, the water fairy, felt sorry for Tinker Bell. "I'll help you! I'll teach you how to put dewdrops on spider's webs."

At the river, Silvermist cupped her hands in the water and flew to place the dewdrop gently on a nearby web. "See? Now it's your turn."

Tink reached into the water to gather up a drop – but it popped in her hands! She tried again, and again – but they all popped! And then ... success! Delighted, Tink threw her dewdrop as hard as she could at the web ... but it bounced backwards and soaked Silvermist from head to toe! "You know, you might consider becoming a light fairy," she grumbled.

Tinker Bell nodded. She'd try them all! Anything, to get to the mainland!

Disney Princess
The Little Mermaid

Dreams Under the Sea

Ariel's grotto was her favourite hiding place. It was where she kept all her secret things she'd found from the human world.

During Ariel's last visit to the surface she had met handsome Prince Eric by rescuing him from a storm. She knew he was the one her heart belonged to, but all she had to remember him by was a statue and the memory of his face.

"Swim away from that hunk of rock!" ordered Sebastian the crab, when he saw Ariel gazing at the statue. He didn't like to see Ariel dreaming of a life with humans and he was sure swooning over a statue was the start of many problems!

Ariel ignored Sebastian and rested her chin on the statue's broad shoulder. "Why yes, I'd love to marry you, Eric," she said playfully.

"Marry?" gulped Sebastian.

"I'm only pretending," insisted Ariel. "It's a fairy-tale wedding. We can have it here in the grotto." Ariel grabbed seaweed strands. "Help me decorate!"

Sebastian groaned loudly.

Flounder was excited. "Can I be head chef?"

Ariel clapped her hands in glee. "Oh, Flounder! Yes, that would be amazing!"

Wearing a chef's hat he'd found in Ariel's collection, Flounder made a beautiful wedding cake with six tiers and shells all around the outside. Ariel loved it.

"I can picture the ceremony," she said. "My sisters will be bridesmaids. Daddy will be proud."

"King Triton? No, he would be horrified!" scoffed Sebastian. "I can't take this anymore. I'm going."

"Then who will be the conductor of the grand orchestra?" Ariel cried. "You're my first choice...."

Sebastian paused and sighed. "Oh, fine."

Ariel found a veil and clipped it to her long red hair. Flounder gave her the gift of a pearl necklace. At last she was ready.

With Sebastian expertly playing his music, Ariel approached the statue with a smile. When the music had finished, Sebastian read the vows and Ariel said, "I do."

"You are imaginary husband and wife," Sebastian declared.

Ariel pretended the statue was really Eric and kissed him gently on the lips to seal the ceremony with love, but when she opened her eyes ... it was Flounder!

"See what happens when a mermaid thinks she can marry a human?" laughed Sebastian.

Ariel ignored the crab. She knew in her heart Eric was waiting for her – that he was the one she cared for and would really marry. Nothing could stand in the way of true love.

Disney · PIXAR
FINDING NEMO

Marlin's Story

"P. Sherman, 42 Wallaby Way, Sydney ... P. Sherman, 42 Wallaby Way, Sydney." Dory kept muttering the address. She and Marlin were searching for Marlin's missing son, Nemo. They had just escaped from an angry anglerfish, and now they were trying to find someone who could give them directions to Sydney. That's where Nemo probably was.

"P. Sherman, 42 Wallaby Way, Sydney ... P. Sherman, 42 Wallaby Way, Sydney," Dory continued to chant.

Marlin had the address memorized and thought he would go crazy if he had to hear it again. "Dory!" he said with a sigh. "I know you just want to be helpful, but do you really need to keep talking?"

"I love to talk," said Dory. "I'm pretty good at it. Hmm ... what were we talking about?"

"I just want to find Nemo," Marlin said.

"That's right, Chico," said Dory.

"One time, Nemo and I...." Marlin began.

"Go on," Dory said. "Is this going to be exciting?"

"Yes, it's an exciting story," said Marlin, relieved that he had got her to stop reciting the address. "Well," Marlin began, "one time, I took Nemo to the other side of the reef, to visit a relative of mine who was known as the fastest swimmer of all the clownfish, in his day. But when we visited him, he was getting on in years."

Dory yawned. "When's the good part?"

Marlin sighed. "I was just about to get to it!" he said. "So, anyway, on the way back home, guess what we ran into?"

"What?" asked Dory.

"A huge jellyfish! It was hovering in the water, blocking our way through two big tufts of sea grass."

"Uh-huh," said Dory. She seemed to be trying to remember something. "P. Sherman, 42 Wallaby Way ..." she muttered softly.

"For a moment there I thought we were goners," said Marlin. "But then ... a huge sea turtle swam up and swallowed the jellyfish in one gulp!"

"Did you say thank you to the sea turtle?" asked Dory, who seemed back on track.

"Well, no," Marlin replied. "I was afraid he would eat us, too, so Nemo and I hurried on our way. But, ever since then, I have been fascinated with sea turtles. And I hope I never have to meet another jellyfish!"

"Say, I've got a story too!" said Dory excitedly. "It takes place at 42 Wallaby Way, Sydney. At P. Sherman. Now, at P. Sherman, 42 Wallaby Way, Sydney, there was this, um, fish ... and ... well...."

Marlin just groaned and kept swimming.

January

5

Disney THE LION KING

Scaredy Cats

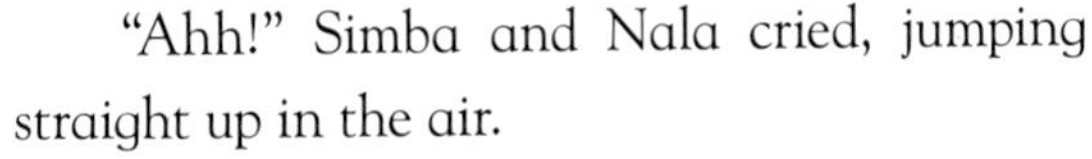

"Nala!" Simba whispered. "Are you awake?"

"Yes," Nala replied, stepping out of the dark cave where she slept with her mother. "Why are you here? You're gonna get us in trouble ... again."

Earlier, Simba and Nala had gone to explore the forbidden Elephant Graveyard, where they'd been trapped by hyenas. Simba's father, Mufasa, had rescued them.

"Come on," Simba hissed. "Follow me."

Soon the two cubs were on the dark savannah near the base of Pride Rock.

"What do you want, anyway?" Nala asked.

"I just wanted to make sure you weren't still scared," Simba said.

Nala scowled at him. "Scared?" she exclaimed. "I'm not the one who was scared!"

"What?" Simba cried. "You're not saying I was scared, are you? Because there's no way I'd be scared of a few stupid hyenas. I wouldn't have been scared even if we ran into 10 hyenas."

"Well, I wouldn't have been scared even if we found 20 hyenas and an angry water buffalo," said Nala.

"Oh yeah?" Simba said. "Well, I wouldn't have been scared of 30 hyenas, an angry water buffalo and a –"

"FURIOUS HORNBILL?" a new voice squawked from the darkness.

"Ahh!" Simba and Nala cried, jumping straight up in the air.

Just then, a brightly coloured bird stepped out of the shadows. It was Zazu, Mufasa's most trusted adviser.

"Zazu!" Simba cried. "You scared us!"

"I wasn't scared," Nala put in indignantly.

"Me neither!" Simba added quickly.

Zazu glared at both of them over his long beak. "Not scared, were you?" he said drily. "That certainly explains the shrieking."

"You just startled us, that's all," Nala mumbled.

Zazu fluffed his feathers. "Listen up, you two," he said. "There's no shame in admitting you're scared. Even King Mufasa wouldn't deny that he was terrified when he found out you were missing. And, if it's good enough for him, it's good enough for a pair of scrawny cubs like you. Right?"

"I guess so," Simba said as Nala shrugged.

"Everyone gets scared," Zazu went on. "It's how you respond to it that counts. That's where true bravery lies. Get it?"

"Got it," Simba and Nala said.

"Good." Zazu marched towards Pride Rock. The sun was coming up and it was time for breakfast. "Now let's get you back home ... or I'll really give you something to be scared of!"

Disney Princess
Beauty and the Beast

Winter Days

Winter had creeped into the castle and Belle felt the cold more than the Beast, who was covered in thick fur. Belle was lonely and winter was a hard time to feel sad and empty, so she decided she would try harder to be the Beast's friend.

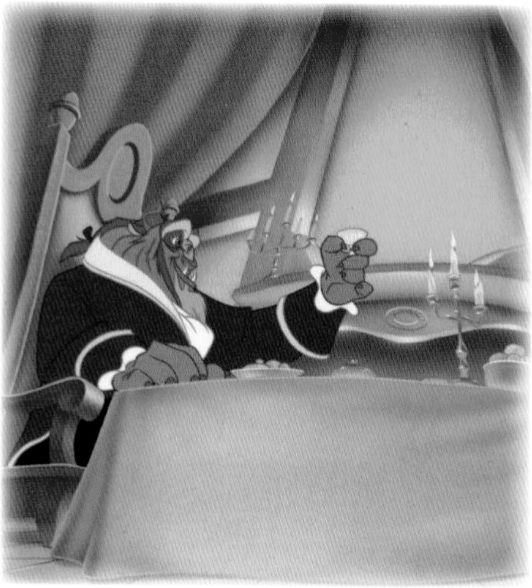

Nursing his poor arm that had been badly bitten when he rescued her from a wolf pack, Belle placed a blanket over the Beast while he napped by the fireplace. When he woke up, Mrs Potts insisted the Beast listen to Belle read from a book she'd selected from his library. But the Beast got bored quickly.

"A different story?" Mrs Potts suggested.

Belle found a story about brave knights and fire-breathing dragons. The Beast was enthralled by the tale. The wound in his aching arm was soon forgotten.

The next day, Lumiere and Cogsworth tried to encourage a friendly bond between Belle and the Beast. They suggested the two go for a walk. "It's beautiful outside!" insisted Cogsworth.

Belle and the Beast enjoyed a long trek through the snowy forest, but when the wind picked up and the snow started to come down heavy, they decided to head back to the castle.

"Stay close to me," the Beast said. Belle felt his hand protectively on her own as he led her safely through the blizzard.

That afternoon, Mrs Potts prepared a tasty meal for when they were both dry and warm again. The Beast got excited and stuffed his face with delicious snacks, until Lumiere reminded him that: "Young ladies appreciate politeness!"

The Beast understood and quickly behaved himself from then on.

When the drinks were served, a napkin slipped to the floor by accident. The Beast ducked down to retrieve it, forgetting how huge he was. Suddenly, the tablecloth slipped under his heavy paw and the whole table toppled over. A bread roll flew into the air and landed on Belle's head!

"I'm sorry!" the Beast blurted in panic.

But Belle was giggling. "It's fine!" she told him. "Come with me."

They left the messy dining room and Belle led the Beast to the dance floor.

"Here," she said, "let me show you."

Patiently, Belle taught the Beast to dance. Hand in hand, cheek to cheek, they waltzed around and around the dance floor, gliding majestically while Belle twirled and swished her gown.

From that day forward, they would always be friends. And they would never forget that the winter had helped bring them closer together.

Disney Princess
Cinderella

A Tiny New Friend

It had been a week since Cinderella's stepmother had forced her to move out of her bedroom and into the attic of the old house. But still Cinderella was not used to her new sleeping quarters. It was a cold, bare, lonely little room. The only other soul around to keep Cinderella company was a skittish little mouse who she had seen scurrying in and out of a hole in a corner of the room.

She had always been fond of animals, and mice were no exception. But how could she let the little fellow know that he shouldn't be afraid of her?

Well, thought Cinderella, *he must be cold and hungry....*

So one day, at suppertime, Cinderella slipped a piece of cheese into her apron pocket.

And that evening, when her work was finished, Cinderella hurried up to her room and pulled out her sewing basket. She used some scraps of fabric to make a mouse-sized suit of clothing – a red shirt and cap, a tiny orange coat, and two brown slippers.

"A tiny outfit for my tiny friend," she said.

Cinderella carried the clothes over to the mouse hole and kneeled before it. She pulled the cheese out of her pocket and placed it, with the clothes, in the palm of her hand. Then she laid her open hand just in front of the mouse hole.

"Hello in there!" she called.

A mouse cautiously poked his head out of the hole and sniffed the air. Seeing the cheese, he inched out of the hole and over to Cinderella's hand. He paused and looked up at her questioningly.

"Go ahead," she said kindly. "They're a gift just for you."

Seeming to understand, but still skittish, the mouse scampered onto her palm, picked up the cheese and the clothes, and hurried back into the mouse hole.

Cinderella chuckled, then waited patiently for a few minutes, still kneeling in front of the hole.

"Well," she called after a short while, "let me see how they look on you!"

Timidly, the mouse came out in his new outfit. Cinderella clapped her hands.

"Perfect!" she said. "Do you like them?"

The mouse nodded. Then he jumped, as if an idea had just occurred to him. He scurried back into the mouse hole. Cinderella frowned. Had she frightened him?

But her worries vanished when the mouse reappeared – along with several other mice, who followed timidly behind him.

"More friends!" Cinderella cried happily. She hurried to get her sewing basket, delighted to have found the warmth of friendship in the cold attic room.

January

8

The Fancy Dress Party

Bonnie was very excited. She'd been invited to her first fancy dress birthday party!

At the kitchen table sat all of Bonnie's favourite toys. They watched as she prepared her rucksack.

"Do you like my bows?" Bonnie asked her toys. She was wearing a dress covered in ribbons. "I can't wait to go to the party," she told them. She placed a bow on the table, smiling happily. "Look what I made for you. Isn't it beautiful?"

"Bonnie!" came a cry from the front door. "We're going shopping!"

"Can I keep my costume on, mummy?" she shouted back, running from the room.

The toys waited until Bonnie was out of sight and then came to life.

"Hey, who is this bow for?" asked Jessie.

"She was talking to me!" insisted Buttercup the unicorn.

"Wrong! Bonnie's taking me to the party," Mr Pricklepants the hedgehog told them firmly.

"Calm down, folks," said Woody. "Why don't we all try on the bow and see who suits it best?"

The toys agreed it was a great idea.

Rex tried it on first, placing it round his neck and twirling. "Do I look nice?"

"You're so funny!" giggled Jessie.

Next, Mr Pricklepants pinned the bow to his dungarees. "I look like a clown," he mumbled.

Jessie placed the bow on top of her cowboy hat. "Oh! It's too big for me," she admitted.

"I'm sure it'll be perfect on me though," said Buttercup, but the bow fell down over his eyes!

Finally, the Aliens wandered over and lifted the bow above their heads in fascination.

"No!" laughed Woody. "You're supposed to wear it!" he explained.

Eventually the toys gave up. The bow could be for any one of them.

"We just have to wait for Bonnie to tell us who the lucky toy is," Woody said, balancing the bow carefully on his head.

A door slammed and the toys hurried back into their seated positions – backs against mugs at the table.

"I'll be in the kitchen, mum!" Bonnie yelled.

The door swung open and she rushed in to find her beloved toys all sat waiting for her. She tipped her rucksack upside down on the table and a huge pile of multi-coloured bows tumbled out.

"I made bows for everyone!" she cheered. "You're all coming to the party. Mum's going to help me carry some of you in her handbag."

And with that, she fixed a different bow to every toy, so they could all enjoy the party without anyone being left behind!

The Magic in You

Tinker Bell was excited! Today, Iridessa was going to teach her how to be a light fairy, so she could go to the mainland with the others!

"We'll gather up the last light of day!" Iridessa caught a ball of light from the sun and dropped it into Tink's bucket. "Now comes the fun part!"

As the sky darkened, baby fireflies surrounded Tink and Iridessa. *Zip, zap!* Handfuls of light made them glow!

Tink grinned. "Are you ready?" But as she reached into the bucket, the light slipped through her fingers. "Oh no!" Frowning, she shook the bucket.

"Watch out!" cried Iridessa, as the ball of light zipped through the air, bounced off a flower – and crashed straight into Tinker Bell's bottom! "Fly!" yelled Iridessa, as a whole swarm of fireflies chased after the glowing Tink!

Perhaps she would have better luck with animals? The next morning, Fawn, the animal fairy, was teaching the baby birds how to fly. Tinker Bell went along to help.

"Hi there!" said Tink to a cute chick, putting on a baby voice. "Do you wanna do some flap-flap today?"

But the chick was too frightened!

Tink looked around for inspiration. "Oh, look at that bird flying up high. He'll help us!"

SCREECH!

"No, Tink!" cried Fawn. "That's a hawk!"

The other fairies pelted the hawk with acorns while Tink tried desperately to escape its outstretched talons! Finally, it gave up and flapped away.

Tink was disappointed. "Looks like I'll never go to the mainland!" Miserably, she flew off to be by herself.

But what was that? Pushing through the grass, Tink found a collection of lost things – cogs, screws, the figure of a ballerina and a large tin. Before she could think, Tinker Bell was putting them back together – and then the sound of tinkling music filled the air as the dancer twirled on top of the mended music box!

Tink's friends, who had been secretly watching, burst out to congratulate her. "It's beautiful! Tinker Bell, you have a very special talent for fixing things!"

"But I want to go to the mainland!" Tink said. "Rosetta, aren't you going to teach me to be a garden fairy?"

Her friends exchanged glances. "Tink, we want you to be happy...."

"Then help me change my talent!" cried Tink. "You promised!"

She might like fixing things, but that wouldn't get her to the mainland! Tink was determined to make it there, one way or another.

Disney · PIXAR FINDING NEMO

A Dory Story

Swimming through the beautiful reef, Dory was stopped by a smiling fish.

"Hey, Dory! Happy birthday!" the fish congratulated her.

"Birthday?" Dory said.

"Even you couldn't forget *that?*" the fish replied.

"Today is my birthday? Yay!" Dory cried, zooming through the water. "Hey, Marlin! Nemo! Today's my birthday. Oh ... and I remember that a birthday means presents."

Nemo and Marlin paled in colour. They had forgotten! But luckily, Dory was likely to forget any minute too.

"We've just got to go get your present," Marlin said, backing away slowly.

"Are you going somewhere?" Dory asked excitedly. "Can I come?"

"Oh...." Marlin floundered and changed the subject. "Happy birthday, Dory!"

"Today is my birthday?" She seemed surprised. "That means I get a present!"

"That's right," said Marlin, clutching Nemo's fin. "We'll be back with your present."

"Birthday present! Burpday pheasant!" Dory sang. "Gurby peanut. Guppy mean it." She froze. "The guppy meant it? What did it mean?"

Just then, a grey shark swam towards her.

"Hello, Mister Shark," she greeted. "Do you know what the guppy meant?"

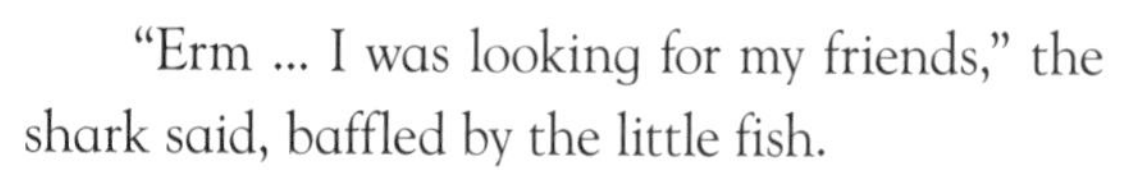

"Erm ... I was looking for my friends," the shark said, baffled by the little fish.

"Lots of my friends are just objects," admitted Dory, handing him a clump of kelp.

Little tiny fish hiding in the blades of the kelp darted in all directions, shrieking, "Shark!"

The shark swam after them. "Wait! I just want to be friends! I'm a vegetarian!"

As Dory turned, she spotted an orange flicker in the distance. Nemo and Marlin were returning.

Nemo had something dangling from his mouth.

"Do I know you?" Dory asked.

"Yes," promised Nemo.

"Today is my birthday!" she told him.

"Dory, this seaweed is soaked in cuttlefish ink," Nemo explained. "Now you can write on the rocks if you need to remember something."

"Wow! Thanks!" cheered Dory, clapping her fins. "I'll wear it on my back so I don't forget it." She draped the seaweed over herself like a scarf, but five minutes later she looked bemused. "Why am I wearing filthy algae on my back?"

"Dory!" Nemo sighed.

"Wait! I could wear this as a new fashion trend for my birthday!" she decided, twirling.

Nemo and Marlin shook their heads in defeat. Sometimes Dory could be hard work. But they wouldn't change her for the world.

Disney Lady and the Tramp

Spaghetti and Meatballs

Tramp had just escaped from the dogcatcher – again. He'd taught that dogcatcher who was boss! Tramp could smell wood burning in fireplaces, dinner cooking ... his stomach suddenly rumbled. Escaping from the dogcatcher always made him work up quite an appetite!

But where would he go for dinner tonight? Usually he stopped by the Schultzes for some Wiener schnitzel on Monday, he had corned beef and cabbage with the O'Briens on Tuesday ... but what he was really craving was some spaghetti and meatballs.

So, Tramp headed to Tony's Restaurant. He scratched at the back door, as was his custom.

"I'm coming! I'm coming!" Tony shouted. He appeared at the door wiping his hands on a towel. He pretended not to see Tramp, as he always did.

"Hey, nobody's here!" Tony shouted. "It must be April Fools' Day!" He pretended to think for a moment. "No, it's not the first. It's not even April ... it's January!"

Tramp couldn't take it anymore. He was so hungry! He barked.

"Oh, there you are, Butch my friend," said Tony. Tramp, aka Butch, jumped up and down. "I'll get your dinner," said Tony. "Relax, enjoy yourself."

Tramp sat down and looked around the cluttered alleyway. This was the life!

Just then Tony appeared with a plateful of pasta. He had given Tramp two, no make that three meatballs! This was quite a special night.

Tony stood and chatted with Tramp as he ate his meal, telling him about his day – the late delivery of fish, the customer who had complained that the tomato sauce was too garlicky, the trip that he and his wife were planning to take....

Tramp finished eating and gave the plate one last lick. It was sparkling clean.

"That reminds me," said Tony. "There's something I've been meaning to talk to you about. It's time you settled down and got a wife of your own."

Tramp gave Tony a horrified look and began to back out of the alleyway.

Tony laughed so hard his sides shook. "Goodbye, Butch!" he called. "But mark my words, one of these days, you're going to meet the dog you can't resist! And, when you do, I have a good idea – you bring her to Tony's for a nice romantic dinner!"

Tramp barked his thanks to Tony. He walked down the block, shaking his head. He was footloose and collar free! Settle down? That was never going to happen!

Disney Peter Pan

A Never Land Story

It was a cold winter night, and John and Michael just couldn't get to sleep – no matter how hard they tried. They climbed onto the bed of their older sister, Wendy.

"Oh, tell us a story, Wendy!" said Michael.

"Yes, please. A Peter Pan story!" pleaded John.

"Certainly," Wendy smiled happily. "Have I told you about the time that Peter Pan outsmarted the evil Captain Hook?"

"Yes!" said Michael eagerly. "And we want to hear it again!"

Wendy laughed and began her story. "Well, one night, Captain Hook moored his ship in a secret cove close to the island of Never Land. He and his men rowed ashore quietly, for he was intent on discovering the hiding place of Peter and the Lost Boys. Captain Hook hated Peter Pan because the boy had cut off his hand in a duel and fed it to a large crocodile. And now that crocodile was determined to swallow up the rest of him. Luckily for Captain Hook, however, this crocodile had also swallowed a clock, so the pirate would always be alerted to the crocodile's presence by the sound of the tick, tock, ticking clock.

"Fortunately for Peter Pan," Wendy continued, "his dear friend Tinker Bell learned of Captain Hook's evil plan ahead of time. She flew to Peter and warned him that the pirate was coming. 'Oh-ho!' laughed Peter. 'Well, we shall be ready for him then!' He found a clock just like the one the crocodile had swallowed. He whistled up into the trees, and a group of his monkey friends appeared. 'Here's a new toy for you!' Peter shouted, and tossed the clock up to them. 'Stay out of sight, now!' Peter told the monkeys, and then he and the Lost Boys hurried to their hiding places.

"When Hook came to the clearing, the first thing he heard was the ticking clock. The sound seemed to be coming at him from all sides! The monkeys were having a grand time, tossing the clock back and forth, and creeping up behind Hook. Seized with terror, Hook and his men raced to their boat and rowed madly back to their ship."

Just then, the Darling children's parents came in to check on them. "You're not telling more of these poppycock stories about Peter Pan, are you, Wendy?" their father asked.

"Peter Pan is real, Father!" cried the children. "We know he is!"

As the parents kissed their children goodnight, they didn't see that a boy in green was crouching just outside the nursery window. He had been listening to the story, and he would be back again – soon.

Disney Winnie the Pooh

Say Ahhh, Pooh!

"Christopher Robin says it's time for my animal checkout," said Pooh.

"Checkout!" cried Piglet. "Oh p-p-poor P-P-Pooh – you're sick!"

"Sick?" asked Pooh. "No – I'm fine. Though I must say I am feeling a bit rumbly in my tumbly."

"Let's go together," said Piglet. "It's so much more friendly with two." So, Pooh and Piglet climbed the ladder up to Owl's house.

"Christopher Robin, why do I need an animal checkout, anyway?" asked Pooh once they had arrived at Owl's house.

"Silly old bear," said Christopher Robin. "Not an animal checkout – an annual checkup. We need to make sure you are healthy and strong. And this time, Owl will give you a special injection to help keep you well." Pooh's tummy flopped and flipped.

"It's okay," said Christopher Robin. "It will only hurt for a few seconds, and the medicine in the injection will keep you from getting mumps and measles and things like that."

Rabbit called for Pooh to go into Owl's room. Piglet wished him good luck. Once Pooh and Christopher Robin were inside, Owl entered with a flourish. "Well, if it isn't Winnie the Pooh!" he exclaimed. "Splendid day for a checkup, isn't it? I say, how are you feeling?"

"A bit flippy-floppy in my tummy, actually," said Pooh. Then Owl felt Pooh's tummy. He felt around Pooh's neck and under his arms and said that everything seemed to be right where it should be. Pooh was glad. Then Owl pulled a small rubber hammer from his bag. "Reflex-checking time!" he said grandly.

"What's a reflex?" asked Pooh. Owl tapped Pooh's knee – and his leg gave a little kick. "Oh do that again," said Pooh. "That was fun." So Owl tapped Pooh's other knee, and that leg gave a little kick, too.

And it didn't bother Pooh in the least when Owl said to him: "Please sit right here in Christopher Robin's lap. It is now time for your injection."

"I know it will only hurt for a moment, and it will keep me from getting bumps and weasels," Pooh said bravely.

"That's mumps and measles, Pooh," said Owl.

Piglet came in and sat right next to Pooh while he had his injection. When Owl was done, Rabbit popped back in with a plaster.

"Wow," said Piglet. "You didn't even cry!"

"An annual checkup is no problem for a brave bear like Pooh," said Christopher Robin.

I'm just that sort of bear, thought Pooh with a smile.

January

14

Disney Princess

The Little Mermaid

Sebastian's Big Day

It was Sebastian's big day. As composer for the court of King Triton, he had been working very hard on a new piece of music, and that evening he was going to conduct the royal orchestra as they played his song before everyone for the first time. *At last*, thought Sebastian, *my true genius will be fully appreciated!*

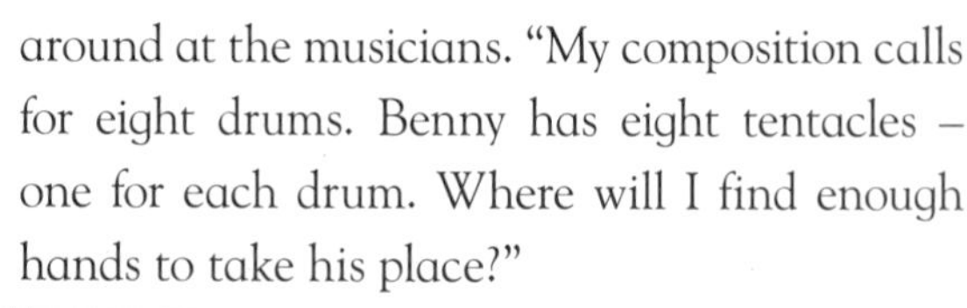

That afternoon, in preparation for the concert, Sebastian went over every detail. He perfected the positioning of the musicians' chairs on stage. He prepared extra copies of the music in case any of the musicians forgot theirs. He washed and pressed his bow tie.

Then, just before the curtain went up, the musicians began to gather backstage. Music filled the air as the trumpet fish and the conch shell players tuned their instruments.

Benny the octopus, the orchestra's drummer, was the last musician to arrive.

"Sebastian!" he exclaimed, rushing over to the conductor. "I – I can't play tonight!"

Sebastian stared at Benny in shock. "What do you mean? You *have* to play!"

"You don't understand," Benny replied. "I *can't*. I took a nap this afternoon and fell asleep on my tentacles, and now they're all tingly! I can't hold my drumsticks!"

The gravity of the situation hit Sebastian hard. "What am I going to do?" he asked, looking around at the musicians. "My composition calls for eight drums. Benny has eight tentacles – one for each drum. Where will I find enough hands to take his place?"

Just then, Ariel and her six sisters swam backstage to wish Sebastian luck.

"Ariel!" cried Sebastian. "I'm so glad to see you!" He explained his problem to Ariel and her sisters. "Could each of you help by playing a drum in the concert?" he asked.

"Of course!" the mermaid sisters replied.

Sebastian breathed a sigh of relief. "Okay, we have seven drummers. We just need one more!"

All the musicians stared at Sebastian.

"*Me?*" he said. "But I am the composer and conductor! This is the day my true genius will finally be appreciated. I cannot be hidden in the drum section. I must be front and centre!"

But, wouldn't you know it, when the curtain went up minutes later, there was Sebastian, drumming away. His day in the spotlight would have to come another time. As he played, he shrugged and smiled.

"Well, you know what they say," he whispered to Ariel, who drummed at his side.

"The show must go on?" Ariel guessed.

"No," Sebastian replied. "A true genius is never fully appreciated in his own lifetime."

Pongo Carries a Tune

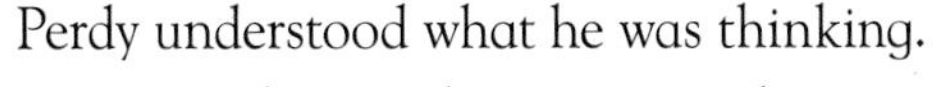

"I don't know what we're going to do," Roger Radcliffe told his wife, Anita. "We have all these puppies to feed, and I don't have one song to sell!"

"Don't worry," Anita told him. "I'm sure you'll be inspired soon."

"I'm glad you're sure!" said Roger. "Because all I've got is a pile of used paper." He pointed to the overflowing bin.

"Don't give up," said Anita. "I know that you can do it."

After Anita left, Pongo watched his pet pace in front of his piano.

"Pongo, old boy, I must have written 10 songs in 10 days. But they're all terrible," said Roger, pointing to the bin. "What am I going to do?"

Pongo wanted to help his pet, but he didn't know how.

That night, Pongo talked to Perdy about Roger's dilemma. They sat in the middle of the sitting room, surrounded by puppies.

"Roger has already written 10 songs," explained Pongo. "He just doesn't think they're good enough to sell. But I know they are – I've heard him play them, and you don't have a songwriter for a pet without developing a good ear for hit songs. The songs are right upstairs, stuffed inside his bin."

Perdy understood what he was thinking. "Do you know the way to the music publisher?" she asked.

Pongo nodded. "I've taken Roger for walks there dozens of times."

"I think you should try it," said Perdy.

After Roger and Anita had gone to sleep, Pongo padded into the music room and gathered up all the sheet music from the bin. Then he sneaked out of the house, carrying the music to the publisher's office. Pongo pushed all the pages under the door, then trotted back home.

The next day, the phone rang. Roger answered it.

"You what?" Roger said into the receiver. "You did...? But how did you...? Oh, I see.... Well, thank you. Thank you!"

Anita rushed over. "Who was that?"

"My music publisher," said Roger. "He's buying 10 of my songs."

"Ten songs!" cried Anita. "I thought you didn't even have one to sell."

Roger scratched his head in confusion. "I didn't think I did."

"So, what happened?" asked Anita.

Perdy looked at Pongo and barked. Her husband could carry a tune too – all the way across town to Roger's publisher!

January
16

Part of Our Talent

It was a beautiful day in Pixie Hollow and Tinker Bell was hard at work.

"Hey, Tink!" shouted her friend Fawn, the animal fairy, as she flew in. "I was in the neighbourhood and thought I'd stop by to say hi!"

An overpowering smell reached Tink. She dropped her hammer and clamped her hand to her nose.

Fawn blushed. "Sorry about how I smell. I was training the skunks."

"I could tell," said Tink, her hand still firmly in place. The smell was awful!

"I can't help it. It's part of my talent!" explained Fawn.

But Tink couldn't bear to be close to her friend. The skunk smell was making her dizzy! Eyes watering, she waved Fawn away.

When Fawn visited Rosetta later that day, Rosetta wouldn't come out. "What's the big deal?" asked Fawn. "I was just playing with stinkbugs!"

"That's fine," said Rosetta from inside a big pink flower, "but I'm staying in here!"

"I can't help it," Fawn said crossly. "That's just what happens when I use my talent."

Even Silvermist wouldn't face her friend. "Admit it!" said Fawn. "My smell bothers you!"

"Of course it doesn't," said Silvermist smoothly. "Why do you say that?"

Fawn pointed. "The water droplet covering your nose?" She sighed sadly. "I'm sorry, but I'm an animal fairy! I love playing with bugs!" She lifted into the air. "See you later at Tink's. I'm going to play with my friends, the skunks!"

Rosetta was disappointed to hear that Fawn was going to join them.

"I bet she's been playing with the stinkbugs again," she complained.

"Actually, I think she went to see the skunks," said Silvermist, grinning.

"My nose can't take it anymore!" wailed Rosetta.

"We might be able to overpower Fawn's scent," Tink said. "If we combine our talents...."

Fawn felt worried as she flew to Tink's house. She'd been playing with both the stinkbugs and the skunks and she smelled worse than ever! What if her friends wouldn't let her in?

WHOOOSSH!

Fawn was blasted backwards by a jet of water from Silvermist. Drenched, she sat on the ground, spluttering, as Tink used pumps to puff rose petals at her. Fawn was about to complain but then she sniffed. The skunk and stinkbug smell was gone – and instead, she now smelled of Rosetta's flower petals!

"This is for you," Tink said, presenting her with the bellows. "Odour-be-gone rosewater!"

Fawn laughed. "You guys are the greatest!" No matter how bad she smelled, her friends would never let her down!

Winnie the Pooh

A Winter's Tale

One bright, sunny January day, Winnie the Pooh was trudging through the Hundred-Acre Wood on his way to visit his good friend Piglet. Piglet was ill in bed with the sniffles. Overnight it had snowed heavily, and the woods were blanketed in beautiful, fluffy snow.

"Poor Piglet," Pooh said with a sigh. "What a shame he can't come outside to play in this lovely snow." His boots crunched on for a few more steps, and then the bear of very little brain came up with a perfectly wonderful idea. "I know!" he exclaimed. "I will bring some snow to Piglet!"

So he scooped up a mittenful of snow and formed a snowball. He dropped it into his pocket, and then he made another, and then another. Soon he had three snowballs in each pocket, and another on top of his head, underneath his hat. He hurried on to Piglet's house. When he was nearly there, he passed Tigger, Rabbit, Roo and Eeyore, heading the other way.

"Hello, Pooh!" called Roo. "Come and build a snowman with us!"

"I'm sorry, but I can't," said Pooh wistfully. "You see, I am bringing some snowballs to Piglet, who is sick in bed with the sniffles." He said goodbye and hurried on his way.

Piglet was indeed not well, but he was very happy to see his friend. "Hello, Booh," he said snuffily. "I'b glad you cabe. *AH-CHOO!*"

"Poor Piglet," said Pooh. "I'll make tea."

Pooh was just putting the kettle on when a large drop of icy water rolled out from underneath his hat and down his nose. This reminded Pooh of something he'd forgotten.

"Piglet, I brought you a present!" he cried, snatching off his hat. But there was nothing there. Puzzled, Pooh ran to his jacket, which he had hung on a hook near the door. There were no snowballs in the pockets! But there was a puddle of water on the floor underneath.

"I don't understand it!" Pooh remarked, scratching his head. "I brought you some snowballs, but they seem to have disappeared."

"Oh d-d-d-dear," Piglet said with a sigh. "Well, thanks for thinkig aboud be. I do wish I could go outside and blay. Could you bull back the curtains so that I can see the snow?"

Pooh hopped up and did what his friend had asked. Looking outside, both of them gasped.

There, just below Piglet's window, Tigger, Rabbit, Eeyore and Roo had built a beautiful snowman, just for Piglet!

"Oh, friends are wonderbul!" Piglet said happily. "*AH-CHOO!*"

Disney Princess
Snow White and the Seven Dwarfs

A Bedtime Story

It was bedtime in the little cottage in the woods. Snow White kissed each Dwarf goodnight and tucked them into bed.

"Wait! Wait!" called out Happy before she blew out the candle. "Please tell us a story!"

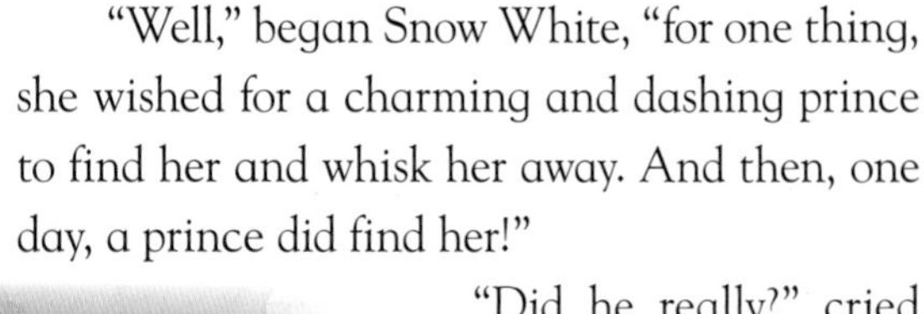

"Very well," said Snow White, smiling. She settled down at the foot of the beds and began....

"Once upon a time, there lived a happy little princess – or rather, a mostly happy little princess, but for a single person – her stepmother, the Queen."

"Bah!" grumbled Grumpy with a sneer.

Snow White sighed. "You see, no matter what the Princess did – no matter how hard she worked or how good she tried to be – the Queen did everything in her power to make her sad."

"Poor Princess," murmured Bashful.

"Oh, but don't worry," Snow White assured him. "Mostly, the Princess was jolly! She found that if she whistled and sang while she worked, her work would fly by and her mood would be sunny. And then, there were always her daydreams – for she truly believed that if she wished for something hard enough, it surely would come true."

"What did sh ... she ... *AH-CHOO!* ... wish for?" asked Sneezy.

"Well," began Snow White, "for one thing, she wished for a charming and dashing prince to find her and whisk her away. And then, one day, a prince did find her!"

"Did he really?" cried the Dwarfs.

"Yes!" Snow White told them. "He rode right up to her castle and scaled the wall to meet her. And, oh, he was ever so charming! But here is the sad part. The very next day, the Queen's huntsman took the Princess into the forest and told her to run far away and never return."

"Did she?" Sleepy asked.

"Yes," Snow White replied. "She ran until she could run no farther. Only then did she realize she was terribly lost and lonely – with no friend in the world and no place to go."

"Poor Princess," whispered Bashful.

"That's what the Princess thought too," Snow White said. "For just a minute. But then she discovered she wasn't alone at all. There were chipmunks and squirrels and deer and rabbits and birds ... all sorts of forest creatures there to help her. They took her to the sweetest little cottage you ever did see, and the most faithful friends a princess could ever have."

"And what happened next?" asked Grumpy.

"They lived happily ever after, of course!" Snow White replied. "What did you think?"

January
19

Disney
Bambi
The Race

"Good morning, young Prince," Thumper greeted Bambi one bright winter day.

"Good morning, Thumper," Bambi said.

"I have a great idea, Bambi. Let's have a race," Thumper said. "We'll start from here." He drew a line in the dirt. "And whoever makes it to that big pine tree over there first, wins the race."

"But it would be silly for us to race," Bambi told his friend.

"Why's that?" Thumper asked, confused.

"Because I'll win," Bambi replied confidently.

"What makes you so sure?" Thumper challenged, puffing up his chest.

"Because I'm bigger and faster than you," Bambi explained.

"If you're so sure you'll win," Thumper said, "why are you afraid to race me?"

Bambi paused to think about this. He didn't want to hurt the little rabbit's feelings. "Fine," he said at last. "Let's race!"

"Great!" Thumper exclaimed. "Ready?"

"Ready!" Bambi said.

"Okay," Thumper said, crouching down. Bambi crouched down too. "On your marks. Get set. Go!" cried Thumper.

They both took off as fast as they could. Bambi, with his long legs and big, wide stride, immediately took the lead. But Thumper's small size helped him to dart through the underbrush and slip through some tight groups of trees. When Bambi looked back, he saw that Thumper was right on his heels. Thumper took the opportunity to hop past Bambi. Bambi paused to jump over a tree that had been knocked down, blocking the path. Thumper was able to wriggle under it. He popped up in front of Bambi and took the lead.

Bambi took longer and longer strides, running faster and faster. Soon he had passed Thumper. But, in his hurry to go as fast as he could, he got tangled up in a bush. As Bambi struggled to free himself, Thumper hopped past him again.

They were quickly approaching the big pine tree. Bambi was running as fast as he could, jumping over logs and bushes. Thumper hopped as quickly as his bunny legs would carry him, ducking and weaving through whatever obstacles were in his way. As they crossed the finish line, they were in a neck-and-neck tie.

"See!" Thumper said, panting. "Little guys can keep up!"

"You are absolutely right!" Bambi said, also panting.

And the two friends, both winners, sat down together to catch their breath.

Disney Princess Cinderella

The Missing Slipper

"Oh, what a lovely morning!" cried Cinderella as she sat up in her bed in the royal palace. The sun was shining. The birds were singing. And the delicious smell of freshly baked cinnamon buns was drifting up from the royal kitchen.

"Mmm, breakfast," said Cinderella. She smiled down at the mice gathered on her satin bedspread. Then she stretched over and slipped on the dressing gown that lay at the foot of her bed. "Now, where are those slippers...?"

"Here's one of them, Cinderelly!" said Jaq, jumping down from the bed to drag a silvery bedroom slipper closer to Cinderella's foot.

"Thank you, Jaq, dear," said Cinderella as she slid her toes inside. "But ... where's the other one?"

Jaq turned and looked around. "I don't see it, Cinderelly!" Quickly, he bent down and peeked under the bed. Still nothing. Uh-oh!

"Mert! Bert!" Jaq shouted to his friends. "Has anybody seen Cinderelly's slipper?"

The other mice shrugged and shook their heads.

"Don't tell me I've lost my slipper," Cinderella said with a sigh. "Not again!"

"Don't worry, Cinderelly," a mouse named Suzy told her. "We'll find it."

Together, Cinderella and her friends searched her room from top to bottom. They peered under tables, behind bookcases, inside wardrobes and dressing tables – everywhere a missing slipper could possibly be.

"I'm beginning to think it walked away," Cinderella said sadly.

"Hmm," said Jaq. "That slipper was here last night...." Suddenly Jaq stopped. "Gus-Gus!" he exclaimed, smacking his forehead. "That's right!"

"What's right, Jaq?" wondered Cinderella.

"Follow me, Cinderelly," Jaq said.

With one slipper on, Cinderella followed Jaq as he tiptoed across the room and nodded towards a little mouse hole. "Look here, Cinderelly," he said.

Curious, Cinderella kneeled down and peered inside ... and sure enough, there was her missing slipper – with a soundly sleeping Gus nestled cosily inside.

"Oh," said Cinderella, "what a little dear."

"Wake him up, Cinderelly!" said Jaq.

"No!" replied Cinderella. "Let him sleep."

"But Cinderelly needs her slipper!" he cried.

Cinderella thought for a moment. "Actually, no!" she told her mouse friends as she kicked off her other slipper. "I've just decided it's the perfect day for breakfast in bed!"

Disney Princess Sleeping Beauty

Sleepless Beauty

"Oh, there, there, little Aurora. There, there," cooed Flora, trying to calm the crying, fussy baby princess. Flora and her fellow fairies, Fauna and Merryweather, stood huddled over the cradle of tiny Aurora and looked down anxiously and helplessly at their royal charge.

But Aurora's cries only grew louder. In fact, she had not stopped crying since the three fairies had arrived with the baby earlier that day at the secluded cottage in the woods.

"Oh, goodness!" cried Fauna. "What have we got ourselves into? We promised the King and Queen that we would hide Aurora out here in the woods, and raise her without magic. But we don't know the first thing about taking care of human babies!"

Flora gave Fauna a comforting pat on the back. "Now, now, don't panic, Fauna," Flora said. "It may be harder than we expected. But this is the only way to keep the Princess safe from Maleficent."

Merryweather and Fauna knew Flora was right. So, one after another, they tried different things to get the baby to stop crying and go to sleep.

"Well," said Flora, "fairy babies are soothed by a sprig of dandelion root placed in their cradle. Let's try that!" Flora hurried out of the cottage and returned minutes later with the sprig. She laid it at the baby's feet.

But the baby cried on. "Perhaps she needs to be entertained!" suggested Fauna.

So, Flora, Fauna and Merryweather locked arms and danced a little jig. They kept it up for quite a while, until they were out of breath. But baby Aurora took no notice and carried on crying.

"Come on," Fauna said to the others, "let's use a little magic. Just to help her sleep. I can't bear to see her so upset!"

"It's too dangerous!" cried Merryweather.

"Oh, fiddle-faddle!" shouted Fauna, who began to wave her wand over the sleeping child.

Just then, Fauna accidentally nudged Aurora's cradle, causing it to rock gently back and forth. Soothed by the rocking, the baby's cries slowly grew softer and softer.

"Fauna!" cried Flora. "You've done it!"

"Look how much she likes the rocking!" added Merryweather.

So, the three fairies continued to rock the cradle gently back and forth, and soon Aurora drifted off to sleep.

"Well," Fauna whispered to the others, once the baby was sleeping soundly, "that wasn't so hard, now, was it?"

Disney MINNIE

Where's Pluto?

"Minnie!" cried Mickey over the phone. "Goofy promised to walk Pluto while I'm at my dentist's appointment but he hasn't arrived yet. Can you come over?"

"Sure," Minnie said.

Minnie and Pluto were playing in the park when Daisy came along, then the three of them headed back to Mickey's house together.

Then there was a cry.

"Help! My cat is stuck in a tree!" cried Mickey's neighbour, dragging Minnie and Daisy away.

"Wait," Minnie cried. "What about Pluto?"

"Your dog?" said the neighbour. "He can't come – poor Fluffy will never come down!"

"We won't be long," Minnie promised Pluto, hooking his lead to a tree.

But when Minnie and Daisy got back a little later, Pluto was gone! He'd been dognapped!

Minnie and Daisy raced down the street, questioning everyone they met.

"I passed a dog with a man in a red hat," said an elderly man. "They went that way."

Minnie and Daisy raced away and found a man in a red hat walking a bulldog.

"That's not Pluto," Daisy cried. "We forgot to say that he's a golden-brown dog."

"You're looking for a golden-brown dog?" asked a girl. "One was tied to a postbox, over there."

Minnie and Daisy ran towards the postbox.

"It's got to be Pluto," Daisy cried. "How many golden-brown dogs could there be around here?"

Daisy and Minnie turned the corner and saw that the dog had golden-brown fur, but he wasn't Pluto.

"Well, there are at least two golden-brown dogs around here," said Minnie.

Minnie asked a passing postman if he'd seen a dog with golden-brown fur.

The postman nodded. "I saw one dog. The guy walking him was carrying a yellow ball and they were heading to the park."

"A yellow ball!" Daisy exclaimed. "The dognapper stole Pluto's toy, too!"

"I think I know who took Pluto," Minnie said to Daisy as they ran.

Sure enough, there was Pluto, with ... Goofy!

"Goofy was the dognapper," said Minnie.

"Dognapper?" Goofy asked.

"We thought someone had stolen Pluto from Mickey's garden," Minnie said.

"Gawrsh, sorry," Goofy said. "I saw Pluto tied to that tree and figured he was waiting for me. I promised to walk him, but I was late."

"How did you work it out?" Daisy asked.

"A dognapper wouldn't take the ball," Minnie said. "But a dog walker would!"

Pluto barked and Minnie laughed. "That's Pluto's way of saying that three dog walkers are better than one."

Disney
ALICE in WONDERLAND

A Tiny Tale

One day, Alice was sitting in the garden, listening to her older sister read a book out loud. It was lesson time and, as her sister's voice droned on about the ancient Greeks, Alice's mind wandered. She wondered if it was nearly teatime. She had smelled scones baking earlier, and her stomach rumbled in anticipation. She watched a little caterpillar climb a blade of grass, its tiny body scrunching and straightening as it moved up the leaf.

"What must it be like to be as tiny as that?" Alice wondered to herself.

The next thing she knew, she was that tiny! In an instant, the garden had grown higher and higher until the grass towered over her head, as tall as trees. The caterpillar, now half as long as Alice, waved its antennae at her and continued its climb.

"Oh, my!" cried Alice. "I must get back to the house. If I don't start out now, I shall never be back in time for tea!" She began to make her way through the forest of grass, until she arrived at the garden path. The path, which formerly had seemed to slope ever so gently, now appeared as a mountain in front of her, and the house was not even visible.

"I shall never get home in time for ... WHOOPS!" Alice felt herself suddenly on her back, travelling feet first up the path. She looked down and gasped. Three ants were carrying her on their backs! "Put me down at once!" she said to them crossly, but the ants took no notice of her. With a quick twist of her body, she managed to tumble to the ground. The ants appeared not to realize that their load had vanished, and continued up the hill.

"Well, at any rate I am now a good deal closer to home," said Alice, gazing up at her house.

She found herself standing at the edge of a huge puddle. "However shall I get across?" she wondered. Then a large leaf blew off a tree and landed in the puddle directly in front of her. She stepped onto the leaf and let the breeze blow her across. "I am nearly there!" she said triumphantly. But, a moment later, a huge blackbird swooped down and plucked her up by the sleeve of her dress. She felt herself airborne. "Oh, bother, now I shall never get home for tea," she said.

The next thing she knew, her sister was plucking her sleeve. "Wake up, Alice! You've fallen asleep again!" With an exasperated sigh, her sister stood up. "We may as well end the lesson for the day, as it's time to go in and have our tea."

Enormously relieved to be her usual size again, Alice followed her sister up the garden path and into the house.

January

24

A Far too Secret Secret

There was an air of secrecy in Pixie Hollow. Tinker Bell's friends were meeting without her to discuss something....

"Is everything ready?" asked Terence.

Silvermist nodded. "We're only missing the flower garlands. Rosetta's taking care of that."

Fawn clapped her hands in delight. "Perfect! Remember, this is a secret!"

"Hello!" Tink called, flying into the glade. "What are you all talking about?"

Her friends looked uncomfortable. "We were saying ... there's lots of work to do today," said Iridessa. "Better go!"

Terence nodded. "Me too! The fairies are expecting their pixie dust."

"Right," said Silvermist. "And we ... er...." She thought frantically. "We need to teach the tadpoles to make bubbles, right, Iridessa?"

Iridessa looked surprised. "Um.... Oh, right. Yeah! See you, Tink!"

"Hey!" called Tink, but her friends had gone.

How very odd! What was all that about? Curious, Tink followed Silvermist to see if she could find out why her friends were acting so strangely. "How are the preparations for the party going?" she heard Silvermist ask Rosetta.

"This is the last garland," replied Rosetta.

Party? What party? Tink didn't know anything about a party!

"See you down in the hollow," Tink heard Silvermist say. "Remember, don't tell Tink!"

Tinker Bell's heart sank. Why hadn't her friends invited her? Had she done something wrong? She could sometimes be impatient, and she had a bit of a temper. Didn't her friends love her anymore?

Tink trudged sadly through Pixie Hollow, trying to cheer herself up. "There probably isn't a party...." she said quietly, as she pushed a leaf aside ... and saw her friends setting up a table of delicious party food!

For a moment, nobody moved. Tink's friends looked at each other. She wasn't supposed to show up so soon! But now that she was here....

"SURPRISE!" they all shouted.

Tinker Bell couldn't believe it. "I-I don't understand! You want me here?"

"Of course!" said Rosetta kindly. "The party's for you, buttercup!"

"We didn't tell you so that it would be a surprise," Silvermist explained, smiling.

"But we didn't do a very good job," admitted Terence, "since you found us anyway!"

Tink beamed. "You're wrong! The most wonderful surprise is having friends like you!"

Tink's friends hadn't stopped loving her! And they were throwing her a party to prove it!

Disney · PIXAR
TOY STORY 3

The Fairy Pig

It had been a bad day for Hamm. Bonnie had decided he should be fairy pig, the sweet, cuddly friend of Buttercup the unicorn.

As soon as Bonnie left, Hamm began to complain. "I can't be a fairy pig," he grumbled. "I'm Evil Dr Porkchop!"

Hamm sighed when Buttercup whispered to him. "But now you can become a member of the Secret Unicorn Club."

"That's enough fairy tales for today, Buttercup!" Hamm said, but Buttercup kept talking.

"The SUC is for secret unicorn agents, and you have to take three dangerous trials to become one."

Dangerous trials? Hamm didn't believe it, so he was surprised when Buttercup led him up onto the roof of Bonnie's house.

"I thought the trials were about cuddles or something like that?" he said.

"You thought wrong," said Buttercup, then he tied elastic bands round Hamm's legs and shoved him towards the edge of the roof.

With a nervous cry, Hamm hurled himself off the roof. The elastic bands stretched like a bungee rope. He bounced madly for a while, before Buttercup lowered him to the ground.

Hamm's first trial was complete, but he still had a long way to go. "Next comes the obstacle course," Buttercup announced.

The obstacle course was even more difficult than the bungee jump. First, Hamm had to dodge falling acorns, then squeeze himself through a maze of plants and trees.

"Help!" he cried, getting stuck in a narrow gap. "I feel like a sausage!"

Hamm finally made it to the end of the course, puffing and panting. He had no idea it would be so hard to become a member of a unicorn club.

"You haven't seen the third trial yet," Buttercup said. "The Washing Loop the Loop!"

Hamm spluttered as he was spun around inside the washing machine, flipping and twirling as he went round and round. "Hold on, Hamm!" said Buttercup. "After a while it's like a merry-go-round!"

That night, when all the trials were complete, Buttercup gave Hamm his badge. "I officially name you a Secret Unicorn Agent," he said. "But it will have to be a secret. To other toys, you'll always be Evil Dr Porkchop!"

Hamm nodded and smiled happily. "I almost forgot our secret salute," Buttercup gasped. He wrapped his front legs round Hamm's neck. "The one hour hug!"

"I knew it," sighed Hamm. He pretended to hate the special salute, of course, but – secretly – he loved every minute of it.

January
26

Thunderbolt Patch

Every evening, Pongo, Perdita and their 15 Dalmatian puppies would gather around the television to watch the heroic adventures of Thunderbolt the dog. The puppies would stare wide-eyed as Thunderbolt saved the day from all sorts of thieves and villains. Patch wanted to be just like Thunderbolt!

After the programme, it was time for the puppies to go to sleep so Pongo and Perdita could go for a walk with their humans.

But one night, Patch had other ideas. "Can't we stay up longer?" he pleaded.

"It's time for sleep now," Perdita replied, as she and Pongo left for their walk.

But Patch didn't want to go to sleep. He wanted to go on a great adventure, just like Thunderbolt! And when the puppies heard a strange scurrying sound, Patch saw his chance.

"Look!" whispered Patch, pointing to a small mouse sitting near the puppies' basket. "It's a big bad bandit! We've got to catch him!"

The puppies all wanted to play pretend, so they scampered out of bed and sneaked upstairs after the fearsome outlaw.

"Follow me," Patch whispered, pretending to be Thunderbolt. "That nasty scoundrel is heading towards the music room."

Before the puppies could catch the bandit, they heard someone coming up the stairs. It was Nanny! If she caught the pups, they would be in big trouble.

"Hide," whispered Patch. The pups quickly scampered into the music room and found hiding places.

"Now, what's all this noise?" asked Nanny, looking around the apparently empty room.

As the pups held their breath, Patch spied the scoundrel slipping back downstairs. When the coast was clear, the puppies resumed their chase.

"That burglar must be in here somewhere," said Patch as the puppies searched the empty kitchen.

"There he is!" shouted Rolly, suddenly.

Rolly darted towards the bandit ... but he knocked over a bag of flour. The flour covered Rolly, turning him white!

"That pup doesn't have any spots," Patch said, pointing to his brother. "He must be the *real* intruder!" Patch pretended.

The puppies all pounced on Rolly, but soon Pepper saw Pongo and Perdita outside.

"Mother and Father are coming!" Pepper exclaimed. "Everyone back to bed!"

"Come along, chaps!" shouted the leader of the pack. "Thunderbolt Patch will save the day!"

When Pongo and Perdita peeked in on their precious puppies, they found them ... curled up in bed, just as they had left them!

Disney MINNIE

The Scavenger Hunt

One morning, Minnie found someone had slipped an envelope under her front door!

"What's this?" Minnie wondered, opening it. "A secret scavenger hunt! The first item on the list is a picnic basket."

Minnie opened the cupboard and pulled out a basket and a blanket.

Minnie headed outside and checked the list again. "Item number two – three cucumbers," she read.

Minnie picked the vegetables from her garden and put them in her basket.

Minnie read the next item on her list. "A long stick. There's only one place to go for that!"

Minnie was heading for the woods when she ran into Goofy.

"Hiya," Goofy said. "What are you doing?"

Minnie was about to show Goofy when she remembered that the scavenger hunt was a secret. Then she noticed that Goofy was hiding some blueberries behind his back. Maybe he was part of the scavenger hunt, too!

"Just out for a walk," Minnie replied. "See you later, Goofy!" She hurried off into the woods.

Soon Minnie had found the third item on her list. Then she heard rushing water. "I wonder what that is," she said.

A few minutes later, Minnie reached a stream. Nearby was a patch of plants.

"Strawberries! The next item!" Minnie cried.

The next item on her list was five smooth stones. Minnie waded into the stream and found them in no time.

Minnie had one item left – a yellow flower.

But Minnie had walked too far into the woods and now she was lost!

"I'll never finish the scavenger hunt if I can't get out of the woods!" she said.

Suddenly, Minnie saw something on the ground. "Blueberries! They must have fallen out of Goofy's bag."

Minnie followed the blueberry trail back to the path – and a daffodil patch!

"A yellow flower!" Minnie cried. "That's the last item on my list!"

Minnie added one to her basket.

As she arrived at the park, Minnie saw her friends appear with their own baskets.

"Surprise!" Mickey cried. "You each had a list of items to collect. Now we can combine them!"

Minnie laid down her blanket. Donald tied balloons to a tree. The friends added the flowers they'd picked to Daisy's vase. Mickey cut up the berries and vegetables for lunch.

Then they played in the park. Donald used Minnie's stick to hit the piñata Mickey had brought. They all played hopscotch with Minnie's stones and Daisy's chalk. Goofy made a funny hat from Donald's newspaper. It was a wonderful party!

January

28

Disney · PIXAR
FINDING NEMO

A Lucky Move

On weekends, Nemo was allowed to meet his friend Squirt. Squirt went to a different school to him, so it was nice to be able to share stories about what they'd learned and of their adventures in the evenings.

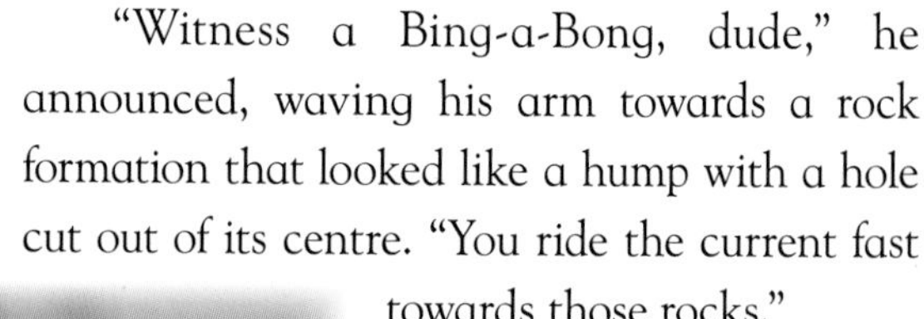

As the two friends giggled, a group of little sea turtles zoomed overhead.

"What's going on, dude?" Squirt blurted out.

"Hi, Squirt," said one of his turtle friends. "We're gonna hit this current for a major Bing-a-Bong run. You coming?"

"Totally!" Squirt replied.

Nemo marvelled at the turtles. Once in the current, they could gather immense speed and cross the ocean in no time! It was thrilling and fun, but also very dangerous.

"I want to go Bingo Bong," pleaded Nemo.

"Um. It's Bing-a-Bong, Nemo. And that is a screaming current. Do you think you can ride steady with that lucky fin of yours?" Squirt asked, nervously.

"Please don't leave me behind," said Nemo. "I can do anything a turtle can."

Squirt felt sorry for the little clownfish. "Don't get all bummed out on me, buddy. If you wanna rock, then let's rock."

Squirt led the way, rising in the water until they were at the brink of the current, which cut a choppy path through the ocean.

"Witness a Bing-a-Bong, dude," he announced, waving his arm towards a rock formation that looked like a hump with a hole cut out of its centre. "You ride the current fast towards those rocks."

Nemo felt his body slipping into the pull of the current. Squirt was leading the way, picking up speed....

"When you're inside, tuck into your shell and bing-bong-bounce off them sides until you can crank out of the current at the end."

"I don't have a shell!" Nemo cried in panic.

"Oh yeah," said Squirt. "Oops. Just hang tight and steer through!" he shouted as his little head disappeared inside his shell and he bounced his way through the rocks.

Nemo accidentally flipped upside down and found himself doing numerous loop-the-loops.

"I can't keep steady!" he wailed.

Spiralling through at top speed, he thought he'd never stop spinning....

"Woah! He's got killer moves!" cheered a sea turtle from above.

Nemo managed to slip safely out of the current. The sea turtles patted him on the back and couldn't believe how brave he was. Nemo had invented a new move!

From that point on, the Bing-a-Bong game was known as 'Nemo's Lucky Fin Flop'.

Disney Princess

Jasmine
A Magical Surprise

A rare desert breeze whistled through the palace gardens as Jasmine sat with Rajah, and enjoyed a morning cup of tea. The tiger purred happily like a kitten and lapped up some tea from his very own cup.

"I haven't seen Aladdin today," Jasmine told her tiger. "I wish I could spend the day with him." She had no idea where her husband could be. He hadn't mentioned anything important and yet, when she'd woken that morning, he had vanished.

As Jasmine stared at the sky, she noticed something coming towards her.... Magic Carpet zoomed above the trees and did a circle of the palace before coming to rest at Jasmine's feet.

"Carpet!" she said. "Shall we go for a ride?"

Magic Carpet waved his tassels in agreement and Jasmine hopped on.

They soared into the sky, flying over houses and the market, then over the vast expanse of desert, full of camels and travellers. But Jasmine soon started to think of Aladdin again. She really missed him and wished he was there too!

"Let's go back to the palace," she instructed suddenly. "Hopefully Aladdin is back."

Magic Carpet did a fantastic loop in mid-air and headed back towards the grandest building in the whole of Agrabah – Jasmine's home.

As they landed in the gardens, there came a burst of noise and energy.

"SURPRISE!"

Jasmine took a startled step back. "Oh my!" she gasped, as she watched Rajah and her father, the Sultan, jump out from behind the bushes. The Genie and Abu the monkey had been hiding behind the fountain, wearing colourful party hats! There were even decorations in the trees and tall flowers in gold pots.

But the best surprise of all was waiting behind her....

"Aladdin!" Jasmine cried.

He appeared from behind a giant cake with four gigantic layers and pink icing hearts.

"Happy anniversary," Aladdin cheered. He was dressed in clothes from the time he lived on the streets. "I wanted to celebrate when we first saw each other at the marketplace," he explained, bowing low in his purple waistcoat.

Jasmine blushed. It had been a very special day indeed. The beginnings of many special days with the man she loved.

They celebrated until the stars came out and the Sultan was too tired to dance any more! All the guests wished Aladdin and Jasmine a happy life together and waved goodbye as the happy couple took a ride on Magic Carpet.

"I'll never forget this anniversary," Jasmine promised Aladdin with a kiss.

January
30

The Acting Lesson

"Wow! I love this castle!" said Buttercup the unicorn, admiring the cardboard castle Bonnie and her mum had built.

"It looks so royal," Mr Pricklepants gasped. "I guess Bonnie will be playing knights and princesses today!"

Buttercup bowed his head. "I'll be the perfect prince unicorn."

"You'll be great in that role," Mr Pricklepants agreed. But as Buttercup looked over at the other toys, who were excitedly reading a space adventure, he wasn't so sure they were ready to take on their royal roles. "They all need a good acting lesson," Mr Pricklepants decided. "And I'm just the toy who can help!"

Buttercup and Mr Pricklepants rushed over to the other toys. "Hey! You know Bonnie's going to play with the castle, don't you?" shouted Mr Pricklepants.

"I'll be the tower dragon," roared Rex.

"Yes, but only after my acting lesson, Rex!" replied Mr Pricklepants.

Buzz was shocked. "We don't need any acting lessons. We are professional toys!"

But Mr Pricklepants wouldn't change his mind. "You're wrong!" he said. "A toy always needs to prepare, so he can give his best!"

Mr Pricklepants called the other toys when he'd set up an acting training session for them. He had one of Bonnie's fairytale books to read from, and watched as the toys acted out different parts of the story.

"Let's see the brave knight battle the terrible dragon!" called Mr Pricklepants.

Buzz, pretending to be the brave knight, rode in on Bullseye. Just then, Rex the dragon stormed in. Buzz fired his space laser at Rex. "You've lost, dragon!"

Mr Pricklepants sighed.

"Knights don't use space lasers," Buttercup pointed out helpfully.

Next, Jessie pretended to be a princess but then she started swinging from the castle turrets using her lasso.

"No!" cried Mr Pricklepants. "A princess doesn't move like that."

"But I'm a cool princess!" replied Jessie.

Later, all the toys acted out the final part of the story. But just as brave Buzz was about to rescue princess Jessie, Bonnie came home!

All the toys froze when she came into the room. Bonnie picked up the toys, ready to play. They had been preparing for knights and princesses all day, but Bonnie had another idea. "Let's pretend this castle is a space base!"

"All that work for nothing," sighed Mr Pricklepants.

Jessie giggled. "See, you should have read the space adventure with us!"

January

31

The Mysterious Intruder

Poor Rosetta was very upset. Someone had been eating the flowers in her garden! "Oh no!" she wailed as she saw yet more broken stalks and fallen petals. "The Flower Muncher! He's been here too!"

There was only one fairy who could solve this – Tinker Bell! "We've got to find out who's eating patches of my garden every night!" Rosetta begged. "First he ate my primroses, then the daisies and now the sunflowers ... those thistles over there will be next, I'm sure of it!"

"Hmm...." Tink looked around at the debris. "Maybe the best thing to do is try to capture him."

Iridessa flew in. "Need a hand, friends?"

Quickly, Tink explained what needed to be done, and soon the three friends were hard at work. "We'll hang this net from the tallest thistles," Tink said, weaving a net out of long grasses. "And when the big eater shows up –"

"We'll drop it on him and find out who he is!" finished Rosetta excitedly.

By the time evening came, everything was ready. The net was up, and the fairies waited.

Suddenly, the thistles started to tremble. "Now!" yelped Rosetta.

"Quick!" called Tink. "Untie the net!"

"Guys, wait!" called a voice from above. Fawn was flying in, waving for them to stop. "I've found out who the intruder is!"

Too late! "So have we!" cried Tink triumphantly. "It's...." She stopped, astonished. Below was a huge creature, with a wrinkled head and a domed shell. The woven net barely covered half of her! Gently she munched on a thistle leaf.

"It's Old Auntie Turtle," said Fawn fondly. "She's always lived on Never Land."

That was all very well, but they couldn't leave her in Rosetta's garden, eating through all of the beautiful flowers! After a quick discussion, the four friends sprinkled fairy dust over the turtle – who was suddenly lifted up into the air, much to her surprise!

Fawn waved a thistle. "C'mon, friend, this way!"

Tink flew ahead, and the other three helped to guide Auntie Turtle as she floated through the air. "Nearly there!" called Tink.

Below was a field full of long grasses and wild flowers. Gently, the fairies helped the turtle down to the ground, where she immediately reached out to grab a mouthful of cornflower – mmm, delicious!

Rosetta was very relieved! Her precious garden was safe once more – and Old Auntie Turtle was happy too, with all the yummy flowers she could wish to eat!

February

1

Disney 101 DALMATIANS

Rolly's Midnight Snack

"Time for bed!" called Pongo.

"Aw, Dad," complained Patch, "we're not tired!"

"No arguments," said Pongo. "Little puppies need their rest."

With a sigh, Patch joined the line of puppies climbing the staircase.

"I'm hungry," Rolly complained as the puppies settled down for the night.

"You're always hungry," said Patch.

"And you always want to stay awake and have adventures," said Rolly.

Patch sighed. "Too bad we never get what we want."

Hours later, Rolly felt a tap on his shoulder. "Is it morning?" he asked with a yawn.

"No," said Patch. "It's midnight. Wanna explore? I'll get you a snack."

"A snack!" cried Rolly excitedly.

"Shhhhh!" said Patch. "Come on."

Rolly followed Patch to the kitchen.

Patch nodded towards the table. "After dinner, I saw Nanny put some big, juicy bones up there. I think she's saving them for tomorrow's soup."

"Soup!" cried Rolly. "What a waste! Bones are for chewing on!"

So, Patch and Rolly came up with a plan.

First, Patch climbed onto Rolly's shoulders to reach the table.

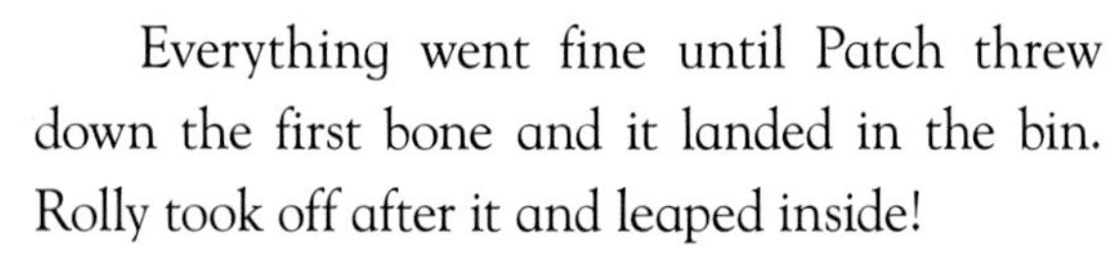

Everything went fine until Patch threw down the first bone and it landed in the bin. Rolly took off after it and leaped inside!

Rolly was stuck. Patch tried hard not to panic. He thought hard until he came up with another plan – a Rescue Rolly Plan!

Patch went upstairs and woke Lucky and Pepper. The two puppies followed Patch into the kitchen.

Then Patch found his father's long lead and tossed one end into the bin.

"Take hold of the lead!" Patch told Rolly.

"Okay," said Rolly.

Patch turned to the other puppies and said, "Now, let's all pull on this end of the lead, on the count of three."

The three puppies pulled and the bin fell over. Rolly tumbled onto the kitchen floor.

"Thanks!" said Rolly.

The puppies licked their brother, and they all returned to bed.

Before Rolly drifted off to sleep, he whispered to Patch, "Guess you finally got your adventure."

"Yeah," said Patch. "But I'm sorry you didn't get your snack."

"Sure, I did," said Rolly. "While I was waiting for you to rescue me, what do you think I was doing? I was eating that juicy bone. And, boy, was it good!"

Winnie the Pooh

Groundhog Day

Winnie the Pooh pounded on Piglet's front door. "Wake up! Wake up!" he called to his friend. "Today is Groundhog Day!"

Piglet dressed quickly and, moments later, the two friends were hurrying to the homes of their other friends who lived in the Hundred-Acre Wood.

"Today is Groundhog Day!" shouted Pooh and Piglet together as they woke Tigger, Rabbit, Owl, Eeyore, Kanga and Roo. Then the whole group proceeded to Christopher Robin's house to wake *him* as well.

But where are we going to find a groundhog? wondered Piglet. Soon, they arrived at the Thoughtful Spot, and everyone sat down to wait.

"Um, exactly what is it that we are waiting for?" asked Piglet after a few moments.

"Why, groundhogs, of course!" said Pooh.

"But what is it that is supposed to happen on Groundhog Day?" Piglet persisted.

Being a bear of little brain, Pooh was unsure how to answer. He looked expectantly at Christopher Robin.

"There is an old tradition," Christopher Robin began, "that says February 2nd is the day that the groundhog comes out of his hole after a long winter sleep, to look for his shadow. If he sees it, he decides that there will be six more weeks of winter and returns to his hole. If he doesn't see it, he decides that spring will soon be here, and stays above ground."

"I see," said Pooh, who, truth be told, did not really see at all.

A few more moments went by, and then Rabbit cleared his throat. "Pooh," he said, "do you expect that the groundhog will take much longer to appear?"

"Oh!" Pooh replied with a start, looking round at his friends. "I haven't got the faintest idea how long it will take to see a groundhog, as I don't know any groundhogs personally."

This news came as a bit of a shock to the group. But, all of a sudden, Gopher's head popped up from the ground in front of them.

"Aha!" shouted Pooh triumphantly.

"It's only Gopher," said Rabbit.

"I believe Gopher will do quite nicely today," said Christopher Robin. "Gopher, do you or do you not see your shadow?"

Gopher blinked in the sudden sunshine, then looked down at the ground. "I sssssay," he said. "I ssssuppose I do ssseee my ssshadow."

"Well, that's that, then," said Christopher Robin. "Six more weeks of winter. Thank you very much, Gopher."

"You're welcome," replied Gopher, who seemed a bit confused by the whole thing. "Happy ssspring, everyone!"

Disney Princess
Beauty and the Beast

Belle Takes Charge

One bright afternoon, Belle browsed the shelves of her favourite place in world – the Beast's Library. She had already discovered the books on the lower shelves, but there were still so many up high that she'd not yet explored. Even on the ladder and stretching as hard as she could, Belle couldn't reach the top shelves.

"Let me," said the Beast.

As he stepped on the ladder and reached upwards, there came an unsettling creak.

"Beast!" cried Belle.

In that moment, the ladder snapped and he landed on the floor among wooden splinters.

"Are you okay?" asked Belle.

The Beast grumbled. He was fine ... just a little embarrassed.

Later that day, Belle decided that she would build a replacement ladder herself. She'd watched her father build many inventions and knew that with the right book, she could do anything.

"Here we are!" she said to Chip, picking up a book on wood repair. "With the library to hand we can learn to fix lots of things."

Belle set to work. She read the book carefully and gathered lumber. She found a hammer and nails. After lots of measuring, sawing and nailing, she built a ladder far sturdier than the one before.

"You made that?" the Beast asked in surprise, as Belle presented it to her friends.

Word of Belle's cleverness spread through the castle. Soon, everyone needed her help. With the right books, Belle oiled the broken service bell for Cogsworth, she climbed the roof and cleaned the chimney for Lumiere and she tightened the pipe under the sink for Mrs Potts.

Her friends were so impressed and grateful for all she'd done, they threw Belle a party, with tea and biscuits.

"You're so clever," the Beast remarked, proudly.

"I knew we would find the answers in the library," Belle insisted, with a smile.

That night, in bed, Chip came to Belle. He was sad and in need of her help.

"My music box doesn't work," he explained with a little sniff of his porcelain nose. "I can't sleep without it."

"We just need the right book," Belle promised him.

Unfortunately, there wasn't a single book on music boxes in the library!

"I have a better idea," said Belle.

Together on her reading chair, Chip snuggled in as Belle read him a story and before long the little cup was fast asleep on her lap.

There truly was nothing a book, and a friend, couldn't fix together.

February

4

A Dazzling Delight

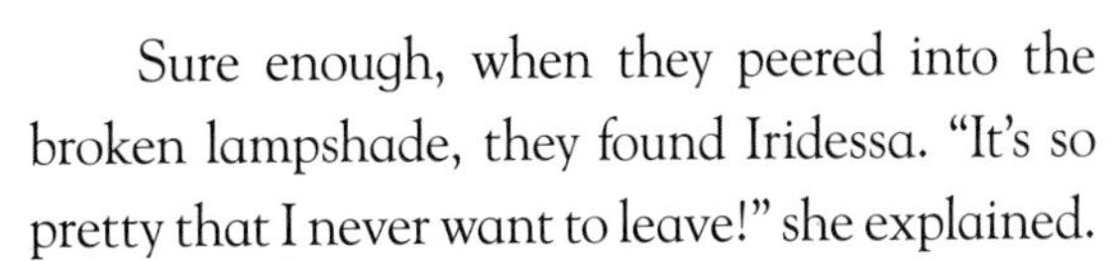

Iridessa was flying over the ocean, watching the sunlight shimmering on the water. "The waves are sparkling like diamonds today!"

A bright light was reflecting off something on the shore and it caught her eye. *Where is it coming from?* Iridessa wondered. She flew down to investigate and gasped. On the beach a broken lamp lay on its side. The lampshade was made of pieces of coloured glass, and when the sun struck it, rainbows were reflected all around!

"I've never seen anything like it!" breathed Iridessa in awe. "It's dreamy!" She ducked inside – it was like being in a palace of rainbows with colour and light everywhere you looked!

Back in Pixie Hollow, Tink was wondering where her friend had got to. "I haven't seen Iridessa since this morning," she said.

Rosetta carefully cleaned a speck of dirt off a flower petal. "She told me she was going to the beach, but she hasn't come back yet."

"We'd better go look for her," said Fawn.

The three friends flew to the beach and soon spotted the beautiful reflections coming from the lampshade. "I'm sure a light fairy couldn't resist all those lovely colours," commented Rosetta.

"You're right," agreed Fawn. "Let's go down and see."

Sure enough, when they peered into the broken lampshade, they found Iridessa. "It's so pretty that I never want to leave!" she explained.

The fairies stood inside the lampshade and marvelled. "It's like being in a different world," said Tink, gazing up at the beautiful colours. "Let's take it with us, as your new home!"

But Iridessa shook her head. "It wouldn't be the same. In Pixie Hollow there's no sea to make these wonderful reflections."

"Sugarplum, maybe you've grown too attached to something that's broken," said Rosetta sympathetically, looking at the jagged holes in the glass where sunlight was streaming through.

"Broken?" repeated Tink, interested. "Let me see." She picked up a piece of blue glass. "Thanks Rosetta, you've given me a great idea!" With Fawn's help, she pulled up some narrow roots. "Give me a sec," she told the others.

They watched and waited as Tink threaded the broken pieces of glass onto the roots. Then....

"Ohhh!" whispered Fawn, as Tink held up the mobile she'd made. The pieces of glass caught the sunlight and reflected it in all directions – just like the shade! Only this could be enjoyed anywhere.

Iridessa was overjoyed. "Thanks, Tink. With this, my house will be a real dream home!"

Disney Minnie

Cowgirl Minnie

Minnie was excited – she, Mickey and Goofy were going to the Lucky Star Dude Ranch for a few days!

Goofy was excited about riding a horse. As soon as they reached the ranch, he hopped on the first horse he saw. But he jumped on it backwards!

"Uh-oh!" Goofy cried as the horse bucked.

Luckily, Minnie had brought some carrots to feed the horses. She held one out and the horse happily trotted over to it.

"Thank goodness you were here!" Goofy gasped.

The owner of the ranch greeted them. "Howdy," he said to Minnie. "I'm Cowboy Bob. How 'bout we get you up on that horse?"

In no time Minnie was riding like a pro!

"Cowboy Bob, can you teach me how to lasso?" Goofy asked.

"Sure," Cowboy Bob said. "Just swing the rope over your head, aim and then let go!"

Goofy followed Cowboy Bob's instructions. "I'm going to lasso that post," he said.

Goofy whirled the lasso and let go. But he lassoed his foot!

Minnie giggled. "Mickey and I are going for a ride. See you when you get yourself untangled."

For three days, the gang learned how to be cowboys. On their last morning at the ranch, Minnie and Goofy watched a rodeo.

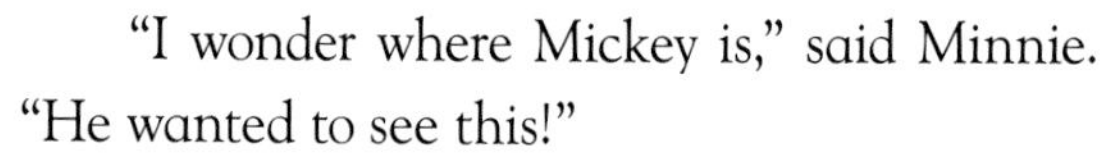

"I wonder where Mickey is," said Minnie. "He wanted to see this!"

But Mickey was asleep! Then the noisy crowd woke him up and he looked at the time. He had to hurry or he would miss all the fun!

Mickey raced across a field, jumped over a fence ... and landed on a bronco in the middle of the rodeo!

Everyone cheered as Mickey held on tightly. "This is sort of fun!" he cried.

As Mickey waved his hat to the crowd, the announcer called out, "Mickey has broken the ranch record for the longest-ever bronco ride!"

Then, the bronco bucked and Mickey slid off.

"We have to help Mickey!" Minnie cried.

"I'll lasso it for you, Mickey!" shouted Goofy. But he lassoed Mickey instead of the bronco!

Meanwhile, Minnie led the bronco safely back to his stall.

The crowd cheered as Cowboy Bob presented the rodeo ribbons.

Minnie won for taking care of the horses. Mickey won for his bronco riding. And Goofy won for trying to lasso everything in sight!

That night, the friends sat by the campfire. "This has been so much fun," Minnie said.

Just then, she spotted a shape against the moon. "Look, a coyote! Now I really feel like a cowgirl!"

February

6

The Induction

Nemo still had a satisfied smile on his face from the previous night's induction ceremony. *I'm part of the club!* he thought.

"So, Shark Bait, what did you think of the ceremony?" Gill asked.

"It was the best!" Nemo exclaimed excitedly.

"If only Flo could be part of the ceremony," Deb said, staring at her reflection. "But she never seems to want to come out at night."

"So, kid, what was your favourite part?" Jacques wanted to know.

"I think my favourite part was swimming to the top of Mount Wanna ... wannaha ... ha...." Nemo tried unsuccessfully to pronounce it.

"Wannahockaloogie," Bloat said.

"Yeah," Peach reminisced. "I have a soft spot for my first climb too."

"I wonder," Nemo said. "Who came up with that name?"

Bubbles pointed at Gurgle, who pointed at Bloat, who pointed at Peach, who pointed at Deb, who pointed at Flo.

Deb shrugged. "I guess we came up with it together," she said.

"Why do they call it the Ring of Fire if there's no fire?" Nemo asked.

"Well, you see, it's like this – I don't know," Peach had to admit.

"But who made it up, then?" Nemo asked.

"I think Bubbles came up with the Ring of Fire," Gurgle offered.

"Aren't they beautiful?" Bubbles mused.

"I find it very unsanitary to swim through others' bubbles," Gurgle complained. "Which is why I came up with the chanting part of the ceremony. It's very cleansing both for the body and the mind, and circulates carbon dioxide through the gills."

"That makes sense," Nemo agreed, although it really didn't.

"And don't forget about the kelp fronds," Peach piped up.

"Oh, there's no big secret there," Deb confided. "I just like giving a good whack with the old kelp fronds every now and then." And she demonstrated by whacking Bloat, who immediately began to swell up.

"Was that really necessary?" Bloat asked as he floated away.

"What can I do in the next ceremony?" Nemo asked eagerly.

"Hopefully, we won't have another one. Not if we break out of here first, Shark Bait," Gill answered.

"Well, you never know," Deb said forlornly. "Maybe Flo will come around."

Everyone rolled their eyes at that idea, including Nemo.

February

7

It's Party Time!

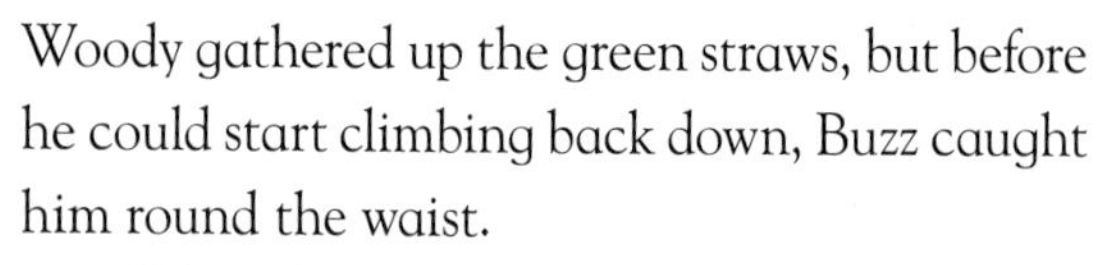

Andy was at school, and the toys had the house all to themselves. "Hey guys, how about we have an outer space party?" suggested Buzz.

Jessie loved the idea, but Woody wasn't so sure. "I'd prefer a western party," he said.

"Ugh," said Buzz, a little disappointed. He began to whisper to Jessie.

Jessie giggled. "Good idea," she said.

Before Woody could ask what they were up to, Buzz grabbed him by the arm. "Come on! We're on an intergalactic mission!"

Buzz dragged his friend all the way down to the kitchen. They stood under the table, looking up at its tall legs. "Is this going to be difficult?" Woody asked.

"Difficult, but very important," Buzz nodded. He pointed to a cup filled with straws sitting on the tabletop. "We need to bring back the alien green straws."

Woody gasped. Those straws were very high up. "Why alien green?" he wondered.

"We're making outer space decorations for our party," Buzz announced. Woody groaned. It looked like his dream of a western party wasn't going to happen any time soon.

Working together, the two friends climbed up onto a chair, then hopped onto the table. Woody gathered up the green straws, but before he could start climbing back down, Buzz caught him round the waist.

"To infinity and beyond!" Buzz shouted, leaping off the table. Woody screamed as Buzz opened his wings and swooped down low across the kitchen.

SPLASH!

They crash-landed in Buster's drinking bowl.

"Nice landing," a very wet Woody muttered.

Buzz looked at the bowl next to them, filled with smelly dog food. "It could have been worse," he said.

Carrying the straws under his arm, Woody followed Buzz to Andy's room. "We're back, folks," Buzz announced, pushing open the door.

Woody gasped as streamers rained down from above. All his friends were gathered together, dressed in their finest cowboy gear.

"Welcome to our wild west party, Sheriff Woody!" cheered Jessie.

"This is great," Woody cried.

"It was tough to pull off the surprise, but we did it!" Buzz said. "But what will I do with these straws?"

Woody had an idea. Bending a straw, he made it into an intergalactic cowboy belt, just for Buzz. The friends laughed. Cowboys and spacemen were both great on their own, but together they were even better!

Disney THE LION KING

Tag!

Early one morning, Simba woke up ready to find Nala and continue their game of Tag. The night before, when their mothers had made them stop ("Time for bed, Simba!" "Time for bed, Nala!"), Simba had been It – which is a terrible way to go to bed! – and he was eager to tag Nala and make her It as soon as possible. But, when he arrived at the pride's meeting place, everyone, it seemed, was there except for Nala.

"Where's Nala?" he asked his mother.

"Oh, I heard her mother say she wasn't feeling well," she replied. "So they're staying in the cave and resting until she's better."

"But she has to come out," protested Simba. "I'm It and I have to tag somebody!"

His mother smiled. "I'm afraid you'll just have to wait, little Simba," she said.

"But that's so boring!" Simba groaned.

"You can play by yourself, Simba," she reminded him.

"Aw, all right." Simba sighed. First, he tried hunting grasshoppers. But they jumped so high and so far – and so fast! – he soon grew tired and frustrated.

Then he tried climbing trees. But the birds didn't much like a lion cub messing around among their branches and shooed him away.

Finally, he tried just lying down and finding pictures in the clouds. But that was Nala's favourite game, and it made him miss her.

Simba rolled over and swatted a bright wildflower with his paw. "Tag, you're It," he said half-heartedly. Suddenly, an idea popped into his head. What if he picked some wildflowers and took them to his sick friend? It might even make her feel better!

With newfound energy, Simba picked as many flowers as he could carry in his mouth and made his way back to the pride's cave.

"Dees ah fur Nana," he said, dropping the flowers at Nala's mother's feet. "These are for Nala," he repeated. "I hope she feels better soon."

"Oh, thank you, Simba," the lioness said. "But why don't you give them to her yourself? She seems to be feeling much better. Nala!" she called. And out came Simba's friend, smiling and looking very glad to see him.

She sniffed at the pretty flowers. "Are these for me? Gee, thanks, Simba." Then she turned to her mother. "Can I go out and play with Simba now, Mama?"

"I don't see why not," said her mother.

"Grrreat!" said Nala.

"Yeah, grrreat!" said Simba. Then he reached out and gently tapped her with his paw. "Tag! You're It!"

February

9

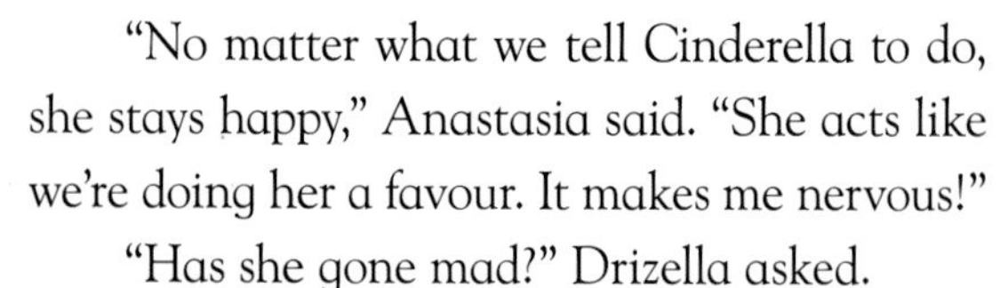

Dear Sisters

"I had the strangest dream," Cinderella told her mouse friends one morning while she was getting ready for another day of drudgery. "My Fairy Godmother sprinkled happy dust over Anastasia and Drizella, and they were so nice to me."

"But that was only a dream," Jaq warned her.

"I know," Cinderella told him, "but it was so nice, that I think I'll try to pretend it really happened. Whenever they're horrid to me, I'll pretend that they actually said something sweet and kind."

"They don't seem so sweet and kind to me," Jaq told Gus as the three went downstairs. Gus nodded in agreement.

"Wash my dresses." Drizella threw her laundry at Cinderella.

"And polish my shoes." Anastasia opened her wardrobe door. "All of them."

"Do the dishes!"

"And mop the floor!"

"Draw the curtains!"

"And clean the rugs!"

"Right away, sisters!" Cinderella sang out, as sweet as you please. "Thank you!"

All day long, Drizella and Anastasia barked orders at Cinderella. But, no matter what they asked her to do, Cinderella always sang back, "Right away, sisters!" or "You're too kind!"

Finally, Anastasia pulled Drizella aside.

"No matter what we tell Cinderella to do, she stays happy," Anastasia said. "She acts like we're doing her a favour. It makes me nervous!"

"Has she gone mad?" Drizella asked.

Anastasia looked worried. "Who knows just what she's capable of!"

Cinderella walked in, and was surprised to see her stepsisters looking at her as though she were crazy.

"Why, my dear sisters, whatever can be the matter? I hope you're not ill," she said.

"D-d-d-dear sisters?" quavered Anastasia. "You called us dear sisters?" She and Drizella edged towards the door.

"Of course," said Cinderella. "I adore you both. I'm the luckiest girl in the world to have such kind, caring siblings."

That did it. Convinced that Cinderella had lost her mind, the two stepsisters turned and ran. Cinderella listened as her sisters' doors slammed shut. Then she smiled at Gus and Jaq, who had been watching the whole time.

"They may not actually be caring," Cinderella said to the mice, "but they'll be too frightened to come out of their rooms for at least a few hours. Who's up for a game of hide-and-seek while we've got the run of the house?"

The mice squeaked happily, and the friends spent a lovely afternoon together while Drizella and Anastasia cowered under their beds.

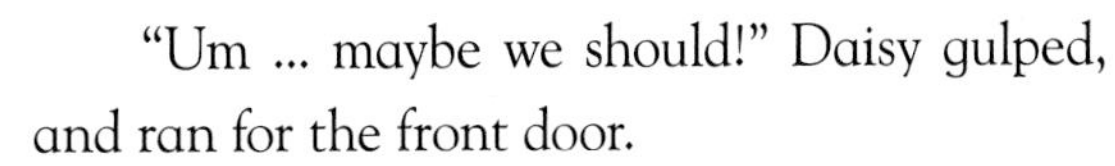

A Scary Sleepover

Minnie Mouse and her best friends Daisy, Konnie and Macy were looking forward to their pyjama party that night. All they needed to do was choose a film. "Anything's fine as long as it isn't scary!" said Macy as they headed out of school.

But someone was spying on them and had heard Macy's words....

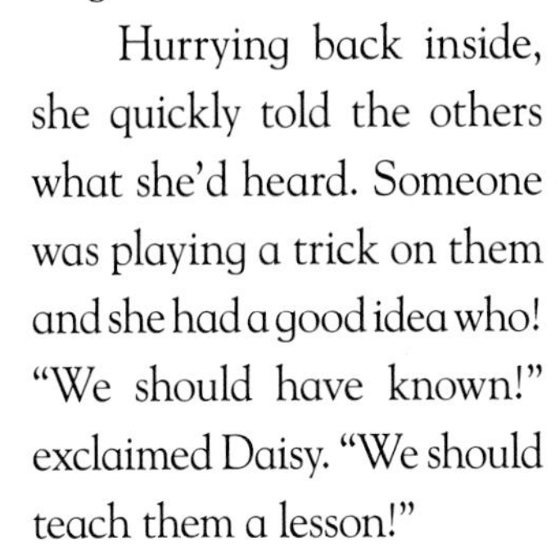

Later that evening, the girls were all ready for the film. "Do you like my new pyjamas?" asked Minnie. They were bright pink and covered in bows. "I think they're really cute!"

The others smiled. Minnie did like her bows!

"Let's watch the film," said Daisy.

But just as they switched on the TV, an eerie howl drifted in through the window. Macy jumped. "Did you guys hear that?"

"It's just the neighbour's dog," said Minnie.

"I know you're in there ..." a voice shouted.

All four of the friends jumped this time.

"Err, the neighbour's dog doesn't talk!" gulped Minnie.

Daisy was determined to take a look, so they went outside, Konnie brandishing a slipper in case she needed to hit a monster.

They couldn't see anything, but a nearby bush rustled, and then the scary voice shouted out again....

"Leave before it's too late!"

"Um ... maybe we should!" Daisy gulped, and ran for the front door.

Just as Minnie turned to follow, she stopped and frowned. She recognized that voice....

Hurrying back inside, she quickly told the others what she'd heard. Someone was playing a trick on them and she had a good idea who! "We should have known!" exclaimed Daisy. "We should teach them a lesson!"

A couple of minutes later, the front door opened again and the four friends came out. "Let's leave!" Minnie said loudly. "It's too dangerous here!"

And then, on the count of three, Macy, Daisy and Konnie threw buckets of water over the rustling bush! There were screams, then Abigail and her twin sidekicks appeared, soaking wet! "Hey, that's not nice!" Abigail said crossly.

"You guys almost scared us to death!" replied Macy.

"It was only a joke!" said Abigail. She looked so miserable in her dripping clothes that Minnie felt sorry for her.

"Join us," she said. "I'll lend you pyjamas."

Abigail hesitated. "Oh, all right," she said grudgingly. "Pass the popcorn."

Minnie smiled. Abigail might think of herself as the Queen of Mean, but everyone likes a pyjama party and popcorn!

February

11

A Fast, Fast Flight

"Hurry up, Cheese, we're late!" Tink called to the mouse. The two of them were bringing a cart full of paint pots to the animal fairies so they could paint the ladybirds – but they needed to get a move on!

Cheese scampered forwards, pulling the cart behind him. Tink guided him very carefully with the reins – she really didn't want to spill any of their precious paint!

Suddenly, something very fast whooshed past Cheese's nose. It gave him such a fright that he leaped forward and began running as fast as he could!

"Stop, or we'll fall!" yelled Tink, pulling hard on the reins. But it was too late....

CRASH! The cart hit a stone, the wheel came off – and Tink was thrown onto the ground as the cart broke into pieces, scattering baskets everywhere!

Tink, covered with splashes of paint, gulped as she looked around. What a mess!

"Haha! You look so funny, dearie!" called a snide voice.

Tink looked up to see Vidia, the fast-flying fairy, laughing down at her.

"It was you!" Tink cried angrily. Vidia had startled Cheese and caused the accident! "I ought to teach you a lesson."

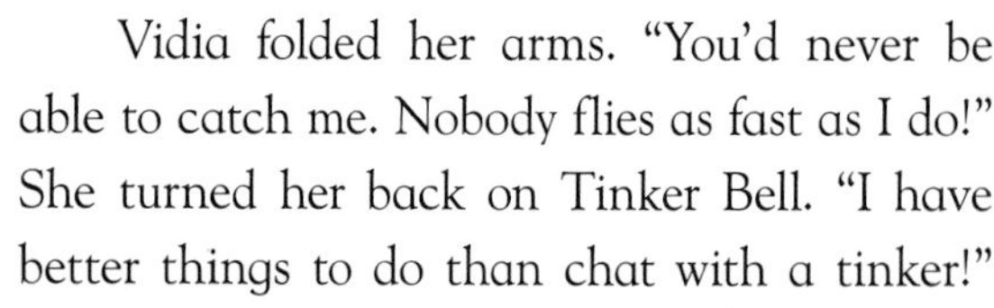

Vidia folded her arms. "You'd never be able to catch me. Nobody flies as fast as I do!" She turned her back on Tinker Bell. "I have better things to do than chat with a tinker!" She flew off, smirking.

Fawn had witnessed the whole thing.

"Vidia's mean!" she said, helping pick up the baskets.

"Yeah," agreed Tink. "It's her fault I'm covered with paint. I have to go back and get more baskets, too! She scared Cheese, and...." Tink stopped. An idea had come to her. Maybe it was time to get her own back!

Not far away, Vidia was using her wind to blow dry leaves off the trees. Piles of brown crackly leaves lay all around. "One more," Vidia said to herself. Then she could go and have a rest, while everyone else was still working! She flew to the nearest pile of leaves, and....

"BOO!" Tink and Fawn burst out of the pile, frightening Vidia so much that she flew backwards into a berry bush!

Tinker Bell and Fawn giggled helplessly. Vidia was covered in berry juice! Now Tink wasn't the only one who needed a bath!

Fuming, Vidia flew away as quickly as she could, dripping berry juice as she went.

Tink and Fawn grinned at each other. Maybe Vidia would think twice before playing a prank on Tink again!

Disney Lady and the TRAMP

A Lady's Touch

Late one night, Lady's ears perked up and her eyes flew open with a start. The baby was crying! Lady had grown to love the new baby in the house, and she was very protective of him. If he was crying, she was going to find out why. She climbed out of her basket, pushed open the swinging door with her nose and tiptoed up the front stairs.

Meanwhile, Jim Dear and Darling were trying to calm the baby. "Oh, Jim, I just don't know what's the matter with him!" said Darling. She was holding the baby in her arms, trying to rock him and soothe him, but his little face was a deep red and covered with tears. Jim Dear sat groggily at the edge of the bed and looked at his wife helplessly.

"Well, we know he isn't hungry," said Jim Dear, "since we've just given him a bottle." He massaged his temples as though they hurt. Then he noticed Lady, who had walked tentatively into the bedroom. "Hello, Lady," he said to her.

Lady took a few steps closer to the cradle, where Darling was laying the baby down. His little fists were closed tight, and his shrieks had turned to loud sobs.

"We just don't know what's the matter with the little guy," Jim Dear said wearily to Lady. "We've fed him and changed him, and I've sung him every lullaby I know. Maybe you can figure out what's bothering him!"

That was all the invitation Lady needed. She jumped up onto the bed and peered into the cradle. The baby's eyes were squeezed shut and his cheeks were wet with tears. His little legs were kicking the covers.

Lady reached in and tugged at the covers to smooth them out. The baby opened his eyes and looked at Lady. His cries dropped to a whimper, and he reached out to touch her. His tiny hand grabbed hold of her ear and tugged. Lady winced but held still. With her chin, she began to rock the cradle and, with her furry tail, she beat a rhythmic *THUMP, THUMP, THUMP* on the bedcover.

"Ga! Ga!" said the baby as he broke into a gummy smile, his big blue eyes looking like wet forget-me-nots. Still holding Lady's ear, the baby giggled.

"Oh, look, Jim Dear!" cried Darling delightedly. "Lady has got him to stop crying!"

"I just don't know what we'd do without you, Lady!" Jim Dear said gratefully.

Rock, rock, rock went the cradle.

THUMP, THUMP, THUMP went Lady's tail.

Soon the baby's eyelids grew heavy, and then his eyes slowly closed. Tears still streaking his little round cheeks, he relaxed his grip on Lady's ear, smiled and fell asleep.

Disney · PIXAR
BRAVE

On the Run

DunBroch Castle was alive with the sounds of giggles and little feet pattering across flagstones. Maudie the maid was at her wits' end, stomping around the place with her skirt hitched up around her ankles. Breathlessly she ran down corridors and cried out into empty rooms, trying to accomplish an almost impossible mission....

"Get back here!" she yelled, as she spied the triplets, Hamish, Harris and Hubert, darting from behind a curtain. "It's bath time you little rascals!"

The triplets split off in different directions. Maudie stamped her foot in outrage. They were just too quick!

It was always the same old story. When bath time came, the triplets played havoc.

Maudie peeked into the kitchen. Hamish was hiding beneath the stairs in darkness. "Where are they?" Maudie said. She hadn't seen him.

She made her way into the weapons room, not realizing Harris was hiding behind a big, stuffed bear. "No sign of them," Maudie sighed.

She sneaked into the tapestry room, where the Queen spent her days working on family heirlooms that would hang gracefully from the stone walls. But Maudie had no idea that Hubert was pressed against a tapestry, blending into a picture of himself and the other triplets.

"They've vanished into thin air," Maudie grumbled, leaving the room.

She searched high and low, far and wide. She looked in the most unusual places until the sun had moved across the sky and was setting behind the hills. Defeated, she made her way to the bathroom, deciding she would use the bath for her tired feet instead, only to gasp in surprise....

"You ... you ... little trouble makers!" she said, as bubbles filled the air.

The triplets had found their way to the bath on their own and were scrubbing each other's backs laughing.

Just then, Queen Elinor entered the room. "Maudie, you've done a great job!" she sang. "You know my little Princes love bath time."

Maudie dabbed her brow with a napkin.

Queen Elinor patted each triplet on the top of his fiery red head. "How do you manage to keep them so quiet?" she asked the maid. "They're usually such trouble."

The Queen left with a smile and Maudie glanced at the boys. She was just about to tell them off for making her run about all day, when they presented her with a flower.

Maudie's heart melted. "Such naughty boys," she said, "with hearts of gold.

And with that, she washed them and prepared them for bed, angry no more.

February

14

Disney Princess Snow White and the Seven Dwarfs

Happy Valentine's Day

"Whatcha doin', Doc?" Happy asked.

Doc was hard at work carving a heart out of a piece of wood. "I'm making a present for Snow White," he replied.

"A present for Snow White?" Happy exclaimed. "Oh, dear! Have I missed her birthday?"

"No, silly," Doc said. "It's Valentine's Day."

"Valentine's Day?" Happy turned to Dopey. "Have you ever heard of Valentine's Day?"

Dopey shook his head.

Doc cleared his throat. "Valentine's Day," he began, "is a very special tradition that gives people the opportunity to let loved ones know how important they are."

"I'm going to give Snow White these handkerchiefs," Sneezy said as he sneezed into one of them. "Well, maybe not *this* one."

"That's very thoughtful," Doc answered. "I'm sure she'll be able to use them."

"If he has any left," Grumpy moaned.

Then Bashful shyly held out a paper flower he had made.

"Wonderful! And you?" Doc asked Dopey.

Dopey held up a paper aeroplane he'd just made for Snow White.

"You know what I'm going to do? I'm going to juggle for Snow White for Valentine's Day," Happy offered.

"She'll love that!" Doc said.

Sleepy yawned as he held up a pretty card he had made.

"And you?" Doc asked Grumpy.

"Well, all right then," Grumpy confessed. "I wrote Snow White a poem."

"A poem! Really? Can we hear it?" Doc asked.

"Don't push your luck!" Grumpy snapped.

Just then, the cottage door opened. Snow White had arrived!

"Happy Valentine's Day!" the Seven Dwarfs sang, each holding up his gift for Snow White to see.

"What a wonderful surprise!" Snow White cried. She was holding a bundle of valentines. She handed them out to the Seven Dwarfs, placing a kiss on each of their cheeks. The Seven Dwarfs all thought they were the most beautiful valentines they had ever seen. Even Grumpy was pleased. Bashful blushed an especially bright shade of red as Snow White kissed him on the cheek, and Sleepy started yawning before Snow White could hand him his card. Then Sneezy sneezed, blowing his card high into the air. Happy began to giggle, while Doc and Dopey smiled at each other, and at their beautiful princess, Snow White.

If you asked any of them, he'd tell you it was the best Valentine's Day ever!

Disney·PIXAR
MONSTERS, INC.

Crash Course

A big award ceremony was taking place at Monsters, Inc. and Sulley had just been revealed as Monster of the Year. As Mr Waternoose presented Sulley with his trophy, he asked a favour. The son of one of the company's investors had been given a job at Monsters, Inc., and he needed help to turn him into an effective scarer.

Sulley was happy to take on the challenge. He quickly changed his mind, though, when he saw his new apprentice.

Edwin was short and skinny, with thick glasses and two buck teeth. He looked awkward and unsure, and Sulley realized he really had his work cut out for him.

Sure enough, when Sulley tried to teach Edwin how to roar, the skinny monster ran and hid under the table. "You aren't the one who should be scared," Sulley pointed out, but Edwin admitted he was afraid of everything!

Mike encouraged him to give roaring a try. Edwin took a deep breath, opened his mouth and ... wheezed. He coughed and spluttered, gasping for breath.

"Black Widow-flavoured liquorice?" asked Mike, holding a bag of sweets. All monsters loved them, they were great for soothing the nerves.

Edwin jumped back in fright. He was terribly allergic to the sweets, and didn't even want to be near them in case they brought on a reaction.

Sulley and Mike worked hard to turn Edwin into a scarer, but the boy just didn't get any more frightening.

In workouts, he managed just three push-ups and collapsed after running 10 metres. When they tried the scare simulator he had a friendly conversation with the robot kid, rather than trying to be scary. It was no use, Edwin would never be a real scarer.

But Mr Waternoose was demanding results. He arranged to come and see Edwin in action. Mike and Sulley groaned. Sulley's Monster of the Year title would almost certainly be taken away when Mr Waternoose saw how hopeless Edwin was at being scary.

As Sulley headed off to get Mr Waternoose, Mike made a plan to talk their boss to sleep before he saw Edwin in action. To prepare himself, Mike ate a Black Widow liquorice, and tossed one to Edwin. Without thinking, Edwin swallowed it whole.

When Sulley returned with Waternoose, they couldn't believe their eyes. Edwin was in the scare simulator, bouncing and roaring and sending the scare meter off the scale. Edwin's allergy had sent him crazy, but Mike decided to keep that as his little secret.

February
16

Disney Princess
THE LITTLE MERMAID

Fish-in-the-box

"Ariel?" Flounder called out timidly, poking his head inside Ariel's secret grotto. Ariel had told Flounder to meet her there, but she hadn't arrived yet. "I guess I'll wait for her inside," Flounder said to himself. He swam around slowly, gazing at Ariel's collection of things from the human world. The rock ledges were filled with various objects the Little Mermaid had found in sunken ships and up at the surface – everything from a clock to a music box to a knight's helmet. It was Ariel's favourite place.

But, without Ariel there, Flounder found the place lonely ... and quiet ... and ... creepy.

"Yikes!" Flounder screamed, startled by the sudden appearance of another fish as he swam past a piece of a broken mirror. When he realized it was just his own reflection, Flounder breathed a sigh of relief. "Oh, Flounder, don't be such a guppy," he told himself, repeating the line Ariel always used on him.

Flounder swam past one object that he had never noticed before – a square metal box with a handle on one side.

"I wonder what that thing does," said Flounder, staring at the handle. After a few moments' hesitation, Flounder summoned his courage. By flapping his tail fin and pushing the handle with his nose, he managed to turn it round once ... twice ... three times. Nothing happened. Flounder was halfway into the fourth turn when – *BOING!*

The latch to the top of the jack-in-the-box released and the spring-loaded jester inside popped out of the box and lunged at Flounder.

"Aaahhhh!" Flounder screamed as he raced backwards away from the jack-in-the-box and collided with the lid of an open treasure chest.

The force of the collision caused the lid of the chest to slam shut, trapping Flounder inside.

Moments later, Ariel swam through the door of the secret grotto.

"Flounder?" she called. "Are you here yet?"

From inside the chest, Flounder yelled to Ariel. "*Mm-nn-eer!*" came the muffled cry.

Ariel followed the sound of his voice and swam over to the chest. Lifting the lid, she found her friend inside. "What are you doing in there?" Ariel asked with a giggle.

Thinking quickly, Flounder replied, "I'm about to do my imitation of that thing." He pointed at the jack-in-the-box. Then Flounder sprang suddenly out of the chest, raced out of the door ... and kept on swimming.

He'd had enough of Ariel's secret grotto for one day!

Disney Princess
Snow White and the Seven Dwarfs

The Little Brown Bear

When the sun was shining at its brightest, Snow White loved nothing more than to go berry picking in the forest. Lots of berries meant one thing – jumble berry pie! It was one of the Dwarfs' favourite puddings.

Followed by her woodland bunny friends, Snow White smiled as they nibbled on the juicy fruits in the bushes. They ate the berries on the lowest branches, while Snow White gathered the berries from up high.

"My, my," she said, "these are the biggest I've ever seen! Our pie will be delicious."

When her basket was brimming, she decided to turn back, but was stopped in her tracks by a strange noise.

"What's that?" she wondered.

The bunnies' ears pricked up in curiosity.

"It sounds like someone's in trouble. We should help!" Snow White said.

The Princess and the rabbits followed the sound to a hollow log in the middle of a small clearing. Inside the fallen tree there was a brown bear cub – he looked sad and scared.

"Oh!" cried Snow White. "You're trapped. Poor little thing." She comforted the bear by stroking his soft, fuzzy head and then she turned to the rabbits. "Run to the meadow and bring the other animals," she instructed. "Hurry!"

The rabbits bounded away as fast as they could. They told the birds to spread the news of the bear cub and soon the sky was full of twittering. The deer and the squirrels heard and so did the raccoons, beavers and moles....

The animals rushed to Snow White's side, to help.

"Oh, my friends," said Snow White. "Thank you for coming." She soothed the bear with her hand, petting his velvety nose and singing gently to him.

The animals set to work. They measured the tree stump and pointed to a small hole at the top. Inside the hole they could see the top of the little bear's head. A bird started to peck at the wood. The beavers suddenly understood and together they chewed and chewed, making the hole bigger and bigger.

With a push and pull from the raccoons and moles, they nudged the bear along the log until the only way he could escape was up! The hole was now big enough to squeeze through. The frightened cub clambered out of the top of the stump, sighing with relief as he burst free.

"Well done!" Snow White clapped, as the animals chittered and chirruped in celebration.

All together, they shared Snow White's basket of berries, chomping the sweet fruits.

"I can always pick another batch of berries tomorrow," the Princess giggled merrily.

Disney Bambi

Growing Up

One day, Bambi and Thumper were playing in the meadow.

"Look, Bambi!" exclaimed Thumper.

A herd of stags was running towards them.

"I wish I could be a stag!" Bambi exclaimed.

"Well, you know what my father always says," said Thumper.

"I know," said Bambi. "'Eating greens is a special treat. It makes long ears and great big feet.'"

"No, not that!" said Thumper. "I mean, he does say that, but he also says, 'If you want to hop well, but your hop is all wrong, then you have to practise all day long!'"

"I have to hop all day long?" asked Bambi.

"No!" cried Thumper. "If you want to become a stag, you have to practise!"

Bambi glanced back at two big deer. They suddenly ran towards each other, locking horns to test their strength. They looked so powerful and majestic. Bambi wanted to be just like them!

"Okay," Bambi told Thumper.

"Okay," said Thumper. "Follow me."

Thumper hopped to the edge of the meadow. He stopped by a big oak tree. "Lower your head," he told Bambi.

Bambi lowered his head. "Now what?" he asked, staring at the ground.

"Run straight ahead," said Thumper.

Bambi ran straight ahead – towards the trunk of the old oak tree! But, before he got there, a voice cried, "Stop!" Bambi did, skidding to a halt only a few centimetres from the tree trunk.

Thumper and Bambi looked up. Friend Owl looked down at them with big curious eyes. "Bambi, why were you going to butt my tree trunk with your head?" asked Friend Owl.

"I'm practising to become a big stag," said Bambi. "Stags butt heads to show their strength."

Friend Owl laughed and said, "Bambi, the stags have antlers to protect their heads! And becoming a stag is not something you can practise. It's something that will happen to you with the passing of time."

"It will?" said Bambi.

"Of course!" Friend Owl assured him. "Next summer, you'll see. You'll be bigger and stronger. You'll also have antlers – and, I hope, enough sense not to butt heads with an oak tree!"

"Yes, sir," said Bambi.

"Now go on, you two," said Friend Owl. "And don't be in too much of a hurry to grow up. You'll get there soon enough, I promise you!"

"Okay," said Bambi and Thumper. Then the two friends returned to the snowy meadow to play.

A Kind Gesture

The garden fairies were hard at work in the Autumn Forest. Rosetta was painting a pumpkin a beautiful glossy orange. "You're just perfect," she said kindly as she finished.

Swish! Fawn flew in, trailing pixie dust behind her. "Ro! I've found you!"

Rosetta looked up in alarm. What was wrong?

"Why aren't the hazelnuts ripe yet?" Fawn asked Rosetta.

"Um ... it isn't their time yet," replied Rosetta, puzzled. "I'm busy with the pumpkins now, and it'll take me quite a while to finish."

Fawn looked around. There were lots of pumpkins still to be painted. She grabbed a brush and a paint pot. "I'll help you!" she shouted, and within a wingbeat had whizzed around four pumpkins, splashing paint all over them!

Rosetta clutched her hair in dismay. "What are you doing?"

"I'm helping you finish faster!" Fawn called back, splattering another pumpkin with paint. "This way you can ripen the – oops!" Tripping over, Fawn fell backwards. The paint pot sailed through the air....

SPLOSH! Rosetta, covered in splatters of orange paint, glared at Fawn. "I bet you were going to say hazelnuts, right?" she fumed.

"Those little nuts can't wait to be ripe!" pleaded Fawn. "You should make them happy!"

Rosetta sighed. Fawn wasn't going to give up – and Rosetta couldn't risk any more paint disasters! "Oh, all right," she said.

As they flew to the hazel tree, Rosetta asked, "Why are you so interested in the hazelnuts?"

"I think they're prettier when they're ripe," said Fawn, looking a bit guilty.

Rosetta was shocked. "Prettier?" Prettiness didn't usually concern Fawn.

"Yeah!" said Fawn, blushing. "Besides, when they're still green, you can't tell them apart from the leaves!"

Rosetta was baffled. Fawn was acting strangely today! But she got on with ripening the nuts anyway, and before long she was done.

Fawn cheered. "At last I can call them!" She put her fingers to her lips and whistled.

Rosetta put her hands over her ears. "Mind telling me who you just called?"

"With pleasure!" Fawn beamed. "Take a look down there!" She pointed to the bottom of the tree. Then she took hold of a nearby branch and shook it as hard as she could. Hazelnuts fell to the ground – and were quickly gathered up by a bunch of squirrels!

"I promised them a special snack," said Fawn. "Thanks to you, I didn't let them down!"

Rosetta laughed. "Trust you to promise something without checking first!"

Disney · PIXAR
FINDING NEMO

Hide-and-Seek

Nemo and his friends were bored. When they were bored, they liked to play games. One of the best games at the reef was hide-and-seek, because there were so many places to hide.

They were discussing who would be the seeker when suddenly a school of fish ploughed into them screaming: "Swim away!"

Nemo and his friends turned in panic to see a human invading their world, dressed in a black diving suit.

"We have to stop him!" Sheldon said.

"But we're so small," reminded Pearl.

"We need big help!" Nemo insisted.

"I'll get the sharks," offered Tad. "They'll soon scare him off!"

In the meantime, Sheldon and Nemo made a plan to distract the diver. They swam around and around his head, hoping to make him dizzy until *THWACK!* The diver's hammer struck the coral. Sheldon spiralled out of control. He fell to the ocean bed in a shower of pebbles.

"Are you okay?" asked Nemo, peeking through a gap in the stones. They had completely covered Sheldon.

"I'm stuck!" Sheldon cried.

Pearl and Nemo tried to budge the stones, but nothing worked. They needed a plan. They couldn't save Sheldon alone.

"Maybe the diver could dig him out?" Pearl suggested shyly.

Nemo thought about it. "I have an idea!" He looked for something shiny. Anything! He spotted a clam and tickled its shell. The clam opened its mouth with a giggle and inside was a glorious pearl. Nemo carried it away under his fin.

"Here," he said, passing it to Sheldon. "Keep this close. Humans collect shiny things. When the diver sees a sparkle, he'll investigate and set you free."

They waited patiently and as the pearl made rainbow lights reflect from Sheldon's enclosure, the diver came over. With curious fingers, he moved the heavy stones to get the pearl, freeing Sheldon in the process.

"Yes!" his friends cheered, just as Tad returned. Behind Tad was an army of vegetarian sharks but the diver didn't know the truth about their diet. He saw the sharks swimming a mean and scary path in his direction and, with a burst of bubbles, he shot to the surface like his life depended on it.

"That intruder won't show his face around here again," Bruce boasted.

Nemo thanked the sharks and followed his friends back home to safety. One thing was for sure: that had been the most intense game of hide-and-seek they'd ever played!

Disney Princess
Sleeping Beauty

Chaos in the Kitchen

"Now, now, dearie," said Aunt Flora to little Aurora, "it's time for your nap." Flora had just given the baby (who was now named Briar Rose) her bottle and settled her in her cradle.

"Time to make supper!" Flora said to Fauna and Merryweather, turning away from the snoozing baby princess and clapping her hands together purposefully.

Flora, Fauna and Merryweather gave each other uneasy grins. It was the first meal the three fairies had to prepare in the little cottage in the woods, where they would live until Aurora's 16th birthday.

The King and Queen had sent their beloved daughter into hiding to try to protect her from a curse laid on the princess by the evil fairy Maleficent.

In order to be sure to keep Aurora well hidden, the three fairies had vowed to give up their magic wands and live as ordinary humans. None of them had ever cooked, cleaned or cared for a baby before. This was going to be quite an adventure!

"Now, remember, dearies," said Flora firmly, "we're to use no magic when preparing this meal!"

The three fairies sighed. This was not going to be easy!

"I shall cook a stew," said Merryweather.

The others thought that was a wonderful idea. What a cosy meal for their first night in the cottage! Stew sounded hearty and delicious!

"I'll bake some blueberry biscuits and mash the potatoes!" said Flora.

"Are you sure you know how?" asked Fauna.

"How hard could it be?" said Flora. "Fauna, why don't you make a salad?"

"I'll try!" said Fauna.

So Merryweather chopped vegetables and meat, while Flora mixed flour and water for the biscuits, and Fauna chopped and diced the salad vegetables.

But, an hour later, dinner still wasn't ready. Merryweather's stew smelled like old boots. Flora opened the oven and pulled out her biscuits, which were as flat as pancakes. The mashed potato was terribly lumpy. And somehow most of the salad vegetables had ended up on the floor.

The three fairies looked at each other in dismay.

"Back to the drawing board, girls," said Flora. "But let's not be too hard on ourselves – after all, we've got 16 years to learn how to cook without magic!"

"And that's how long it's going to take!" replied Fauna.

Merryweather laughed heartily. Fauna was obviously joking – wasn't she?

Writing a Poem

One day in Wonderland, Tweedledum and Tweedledee decided to write a poem about writing poems. So, they put their heads together and set to rhyming. Soon they had quite an amusing poem composed. It even had a title – "So You Want to Write a Poem". The only thing they just couldn't agree on was how to end it.

"Read what we have so far, would you?" said Tweedledee.

So Tweedledum began:

So you want to write a poem.
You do? Is that true?
Writing poems is usually
Easy to do.
Sun rhymes with fun;
Dew rhymes with shoe;
End sounds like friend,
And other words too.
Breezy is easy;
It rhymes with queasy.
Pet sounds like net;
That one's no sweat.
Many a word
Will rhyme with day,
Like hay and say
And even bouquet.
Words with long 'e' sounds
Are always a cinch.
Bean tree and sweet pea
And flea, at a pinch.
But then there are toughies
Like cousin and buzzin'.
There are rhymes for them,
But they're not dime a dozen.
Also tricky is icky
And apple and stronger.
Although you can rhyme 'em,
It may take you longer.
There's whoozit and whatsit
And hogwash and hooey.
You try to rhyme those,
And your brain goes kablooey.
So, when writing a poem,
Keep one thing in mind:
Avoid all the hard words
And you'll do just fine!
This poem is over.
This poem is penned.
This poem is finished,
So this is the ...

Tweedledum looked up at Tweedledee. "That's it," he said.

Tweedledee racked his brain. "What rhymes with 'penned'?" he said. "'Bend'?" He tried it out. "'This poem is finished, so this is the *bend*.' No, no, that doesn't seem right."

Tweedledum took a stab at it. "There's 'pretend'. 'This poem is finished, so this is *pretend*.' Nah, I don't like it."

Tweedledee sighed. "We'll never think of a good rhyme for the end of this poem."

"You're right," said Tweedledum. "I guess we'll have to leave it unfinished."

So that's what they did.

And that was the end.

Disney Princess Cinderella

The Masquerade Ball

"Where could she be?" Cinderella asked. She looked around the ballroom. Hundreds of happy citizens were gathered there, each dressed in a splendid costume.

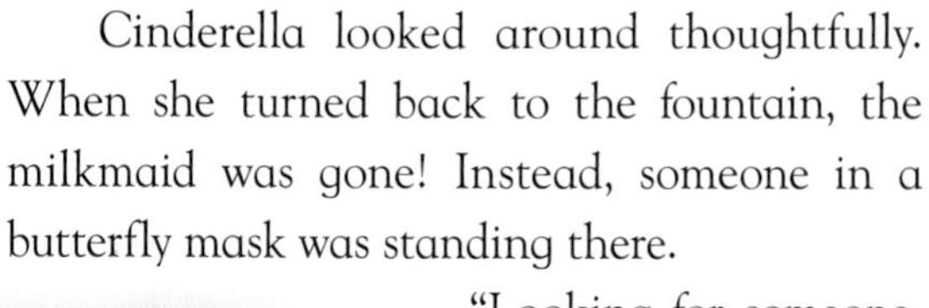

Cinderella and her husband, the Prince, were holding a Masquerade Ball. Cinderella had invited her Fairy Godmother, who had promised to come.

But the ball had started almost an hour ago, and there still wasn't any sign of the cheerful little woman.

"Don't worry, my love," the Prince said. "I'm sure she'll – what's this?"

A messenger handed Cinderella a note.

Never fear –
I'm here, my dear.
Just seek and you will find
Which mask I am behind!

Her Fairy Godmother was playing a trick on her! "I'll find you," Cinderella whispered.

Was her Fairy Godmother wearing that beautiful unicorn costume? Was she the princess with the pink mask? The dancing harlequin clown? The fuzzy brown bear? Cinderella felt a little dizzy as she turned round and round. How would she ever find her Fairy Godmother in the crowd?

Cinderella stared at a masked milkmaid with twinkling eyes standing near a fountain. *Could that be her?* she wondered.

Cinderella looked around thoughtfully. When she turned back to the fountain, the milkmaid was gone! Instead, someone in a butterfly mask was standing there.

"Looking for someone, Princess?" the butterfly said in a deep voice.

"No – never mind," Cinderella said.

She wandered away, still searching. But she kept thinking about the twinkling eyes behind the butterfly mask.

Then Cinderella remembered something – the milkmaid had the same twinkling eyes! Could it be...?

She hurried back to the fountain. But there was no sign of the milkmaid or the butterfly. The only person standing nearby was wearing a beautiful white swan costume.

"Oh, dear," Cinderella whispered.

She stared at the swan. Mischievous eyes twinkled behind the feathered white mask.

Suddenly, Cinderella laughed out loud. "Aha!" she cried. "I caught you!"

Cinderella pulled off the swan mask. Her Fairy Godmother smiled back at her. "You win!" she exclaimed. "How did you find me?"

"I almost didn't, the way you kept magically changing costumes," Cinderella said. "Then I remembered how you magically changed *my* outfit not too long ago – and I figured it out!"

February

24

THE JUNGLE BOOK

Go Fish!

"Today, small fry, I'm going to teach you to fish like a bear!" said Baloo the bear.

Mowgli was delighted. He loved his new friend Baloo. Unlike Bagheera the panther, who kept insisting that Mowgli should live in the Man-village for his own protection, Baloo made no such demands on Mowgli. Baloo was much more interested in having a good time living in the jungle, and so was Mowgli.

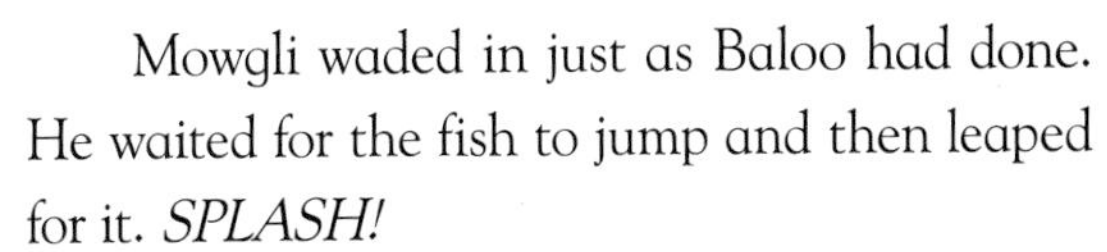

"Now, watch this, kid," said Baloo as they arrived at the riverbank. "All ya gotta do is wait for a fish to swim by and then...."

WHOOSH! Quick as a flash, Baloo held a wriggling silver fish in his paw. "Now you try it!" he said to Mowgli.

Mowgli sat very still, waiting for a fish to swim by. Then – *SPLASH!* – he toppled headfirst into the water.

"Hmm," said Baloo after he had fished Mowgli out and set him down, dripping. "Now I'll show you my second technique."

Baloo and Mowgli walked towards another part of the river. This time, the fish could be seen occasionally leaping out of the water as they swam down a little waterfall. Baloo waded a few steps into the water, waited for a fish to jump, then – *WHOOSH!* – he swiped a fish right out of the air. "Now you try, buddy."

Mowgli waded in just as Baloo had done. He waited for the fish to jump and then leaped for it. *SPLASH!*

"Okay, plan C," said Baloo, after he had fished Mowgli out a second time. "I'll take you to the big waterfall. The fish literally fall into your paws. All ya gotta do is reach out and catch one!"

Mowgli followed Baloo to the big waterfall. Sure enough, silvery fish were jumping all the way down the fall. Catching one would be easy!

In the blink of an eye Baloo held up a big fish for Mowgli to admire.

"I'm going to do it this time, you watch me, Baloo!" said Mowgli excitedly. He scrunched up his face with concentration. Then, for an instant, Mowgli actually had a silvery fish in his hands. But, a second later, the fish shot out of his grasp and jumped into the water again. Mowgli looked down at his empty hands with a sigh.

"You know what, kid?" said Baloo, clapping a huge paw on Mowgli's skinny shoulders. "I think you're working too hard. That's not how life in the jungle should be! It should be fun, happy and carefree. So, come on. Let's go shake a banana tree instead!"

And Mowgli cheerfully agreed.

February
25

The Moonstone

Pixie Hollow was abuzz with excitement! The fairies were preparing to celebrate the arrival of autumn, and Tinker Bell had been asked to make the sceptre that would hold the precious moonstone – which helped to make blue pixie dust and restore the Pixie Dust Tree.

Bursting with joy, Tinker Bell rushed to tell Terence the good news. He offered to help, but before long the little fairy began to get irritated with him getting in the way. Eventually, Tink lost her temper and accidentally broke the moonstone! Tinker Bell was in despair. She didn't know what to do.

That night, at the theatre, a fairy named Lyria told a story of lost treasure. Far away, on a forgotten island, there was a mirror, hidden in a boat, with the power to grant one wish. Tinker Bell decided to go in search of the mirror to put right her silly mistake. She set to work building a hot-air balloon and gathering her supplies.

Along the way, Tinker Bell met Blaze, a little firefly. One morning, the two new friends were surprised by a violent storm! When the fog cleared, they realized the balloon was stuck in a tree. Tink flew down to the ground, and the balloon drifted away and was carried far beyond their reach.

Tinker Bell was sad, but luckily Blaze and some new little bug friends were there to help her. Tink realized how much she missed Terence, her best friend who always did his best to be there for her.

Tink finally caught sight of the lost boat and discovered, at the bottom of the wreck, the magic mirror!

But, annoyed by Blaze's buzzing, Tinker Bell hastily asked for silence – instead of a new moonstone. And her wish was granted! Tinker Bell had just thrown away her last chance!

Tinker Bell started to think about Terence again, and she started to feel very bad about getting angry with him.

Then, as if by magic, Terence appeared behind her! He had flown all night long and had even found her balloon.

Back in Pixie Hollow, the Autumn Revelry was about to begin. They had no time to waste!

During the journey home, Terence helped Tinker Bell to make a new sceptre out of the shattered fragments of moonstone. They arrived for the ceremony just in time.

The blue harvest moon lit up the strangely beautiful sceptre, and blue pixie dust started to fall from the sky. Hurray! Tinker Bell had succeeded – with a little help from her friends!

Disney MINNIE

A Space Oddity

A poster had gone up on the board at Mouston School, and Minnie Mouse and her friends were excited. A film company was looking for background actors for a sci-fi film!

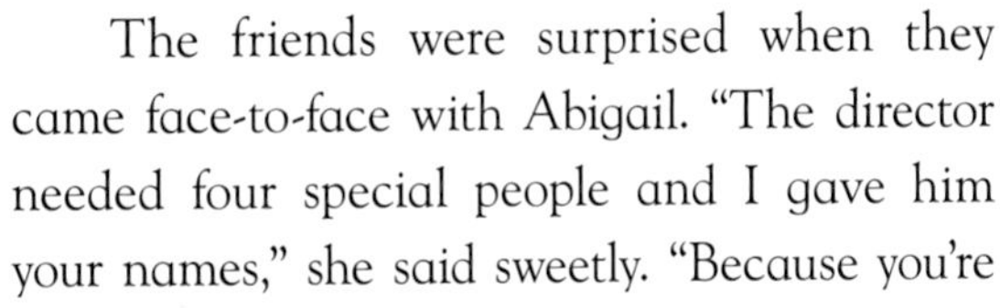

Abigail was boasting more than ever because her mum was starring in the film, and she'd got Abigail and her friends speaking roles! "You guys might as well give up," she told Minnie. "You're simply not cut out to be in movies!"

That did it! Minnie and her friends looked at each other. They absolutely had to try out for the film now!

Later that evening, Abigail was watching her mother get ready for a posh event. "We need four special extras," her mum said, admiring her long gown in the mirror. "Do you have any friends willing to play one-eyed aliens?"

Abigail's eyes lit up mischievously. She could definitely think of four people she'd like to see in alien costumes!

Minnie, Daisy, Leonard and Macy turned up the next day to try out for the film, but the queue was already really long! "By the time we get to the front, they'll already have chosen enough people!" sighed Minnie.

But then someone made an announcement: "Special background actors Minnie, Daisy, Leonard and Macy, follow me!"

Daisy and the others rushed to the front.

The friends were surprised when they came face-to-face with Abigail. "The director needed four special people and I gave him your names," she said sweetly. "Because you're my friends!"

Minnie's jaw dropped. They had never been friends with Abigail! Every time she saw them, she was mean to them! What was going on?

They soon realized. "She just wanted to make us look ridiculous," said Minnie, as they squashed into their costumes. They were completely covered from head to toe!

But Leonard didn't mind. "I quite like being a one-eyed alien!" he said, trying out a few moves.

Minnie wasn't impressed, but then Abigail and her twin sidekicks walked by, dressed in alien suits even sillier than the ones Minnie and her friends were wearing!

"What are we supposed to say?" asked one of the twins.

The other looked at the script. "Pzz," she read. "Zpt. What is this stuff?"

Abigail didn't say anything as she stormed past Minnie.

Minnie and Daisy couldn't help laughing. "This is going to be fun!" said Daisy.

"Yeah!" giggled Minnie. "In the end, Abigail actually did do us a favour!"

Disney · PIXAR
TOY STORY 3

Hair Clip Mission

Bonnie was getting ready to go out, but there was something missing.

"I've lost my hair clip with the flower," she said, hunting through a box of hair accessories.

Bonnie's mum fastened her hair back with a different clip. "We'll look for it later. Put this other one on for now."

Bonnie trudged out of the room behind her mum. "That hair clip is my favourite," she sighed.

As soon as Bonnie and her mum were out of the room, the toys jumped into life. "Did you hear that, folks?" said Woody. This was an emergency. Bonnie was their kid, and they knew they had to help.

They searched under the bed, in the toybox and all over the floor, but with no luck.

"Let's think this through," said Woody. "Where did we last see it?"

"Right here on this shelf we're on," said Buzz. He spotted a narrow gap at the back of the shelf. "The hair clip could have fallen back here! We'd better check."

Mr Potato Head snorted. "How do you plan to do that? It's really dark back there."

Woody smiled. "I have an idea!"

Moments later, he lowered one of Mr Potato Head's eyes down behind the shelf on a piece of string. The eye swung around in the gloom, before Mr Potato Head let out a cheer. "The hair clip is right there!"

He patted Woody on the back to congratulate him on a job well done, but Woody lost his grip on the string. Mr Potato Head's eye landed on the floor right beside the hair clip!

"Well, that's just great!" Mr Potato Head groaned. "Now we have to recover both the hair clip and my eye!"

Woody tried to force his way into the narrow space behind the shelf. "Maybe I can slip into this gap...."

With a sigh of effort, Woody squeezed into the gap – but then got stuck! Buzz tried to pull him out, but the cowboy was wedged in tight, and Bonnie was coming back up the stairs! The toys went limp just as Bonnie bounced into the room.

"Let's play!" she said, grabbing Woody by the arm. She tugged, but he was still stuck fast. "Mummy!" she cried. "I can't take Woody out."

Bonnie's mum moved the furniture, and Woody sprang free. At the same time, Bonnie spotted her missing hair clip and Mr Potato Head's eye!

She had no idea how everything had ended up behind the furniture, but she gave Woody an extra cuddle for helping to find her favourite hair clip.

Disney Princess
Beauty and the Beast

Together is Better

The Beast paced up and down his castle's long hallway. *Click, click, click* went his claws against the marble floor.

"It's been hours," he grumbled. "What on earth do you suppose she's doing in there?" the Beast asked Lumiere.

"Reading," Lumiere replied. "After all, monsieur, it is the library."

"I know it's the library!" bellowed the Beast. "I know my own castle!"

Suddenly, the library doors burst open. Belle stormed out. She looked around the hallway.

"What is going on?" she asked. "There's a terrible ruckus out here."

"It's the servants," complained the Beast. "They make too much noise."

"Don't blame them," said Belle. "You're the one who's been clicking your claws for hours."

"I have not," said the Beast, embarrassed.

"You have so!" insisted Belle. "It's been driving me crazy!"

"You were hearing things," said the Beast.

"And then you started bellowing," said Belle.

"So what if I was?" roared the Beast. "It's my castle!"

Suddenly, Mrs Potts rolled up on a serving cart. "Anyone care for tea?" she asked.

"Not me," huffed Belle.

"Me, neither," huffed the Beast.

"Oh, come now. Just a spot?" asked Mrs Potts, pouring two cups anyway. Humming merrily, she rolled her cart into the library.

Belle and the Beast followed her in and then sat down.

"So why were you so angry?" asked Belle, sipping her tea.

"I was bored," said the Beast. "And I guess I ... missed you."

"Why didn't you just say so?" Belle wondered.

"Because ... I didn't think you would miss me back," said the Beast.

"I've been reading," said Belle. "I just love to read."

"I know," said the Beast.

Belle thought for a moment. "I have an idea," she said. "How about we read together?"

Belle picked out a book about a princess and a dragon. First Belle read aloud to the Beast. And then the Beast read aloud to Belle.

"That was fun," said the Beast.

"Yes," said Belle. "Let's do it again tomorrow night."

"Tomorrow," he said, "and every night after that."

In the hallway, Lumiere sighed with relief.

"Maybe now we'll get some peace!" he said to himself.

Disney Princess
The Princess and the Frog

Cooking Up a Plan

Tiana had loved cooking since she was little. It had been her lifelong dream to own a restaurant that could be open to everyone.

She got a job at Cal's Diner and save, save, saved! In fact, she was so determined to open her own business that she went in search of a second job, too.

"Are there any jobs going, Mrs Johnson?" she asked at the dress shop. She quickly sewed the hem of a gown to prove she had the skills, but Mrs Johnson put a hand on Tiana's to stop her.

"I'm sorry, dear. I don't need a worker now."

Tiana did not lose heart.

At the handyman shop, she noticed the sign was wonky above the counter. "I'm pretty handy," Tiana told the owner, hammering the sign back into place. "And available for part-time work."

The owner shook his head. "I'm sorry, Tiana. I just gave my nephew the position here."

Marching onwards, Tiana visited Cora's Beauty Parlour.

"Hmm," said Cora, "let's see what you can do then." She sat down in front of a mirror and handed Tiana a hairbrush. But when Tiana had finished styling Cora's hair, it was as tall as a wedding cake and nowhere near as pretty.

She had failed the test.

Tiana went home and told her mother about her bad day.

"Oh, Tiana," Eudora said. "I'm sure you'll have your restaurant one day, where you'll serve your delicious beignets...."

Tiana had an idea! The next morning, she feverishly prepared some golden beignets. She stopped at Duke's café and placed a large tray of her baked goods on the counter.

Duke was curious.

"Homemade beignets," Tiana told him. "Try one!"

Duke thought they were delicious.

A customer wandered over, having smelled the beignets and asked to try one. In no time, Tiana's samples had gone.

"I'll bring more tomorrow," Tiana promised.

The following day, Tiana couldn't believe her eyes. Duke had a long queue of hungry customers outside his café, all waiting to taste her beignets.

"Can you teach me how to make them?" Duke pleaded.

"Sorry, but it's a secret family recipe," Tiana answered.

Duke sighed. "Then I guess I'll have to hire you to cook here. You've brought me so many extra customers! When can you start?"

When Tiana told her mother about her new job, Eudora congratulated her for being such a talented cook. And in the comfort of their home, they celebrated with tea and beignets!

Disney Princess
Tangled

Pascal's Painting

The moment the sun's rays landed against Rapunzel's cheek through the tower window, her eyes shot open in excitement. Today was the day she could create something with a bit of help from her friend....

"At last!" Rapunzel cried, hopping from her bed and dressing in a hurry. "Today I'm going to paint your portrait, Pascal! You promised you wouldn't change colours on me."

Pascal grinned. He had a habit of making his body shimmer into all the colours of the rainbow. It was how chameleons survived in the wild. They changed colour to suit their environment – hiding them from all kinds of big creatures who wanted to gobble them up.

As Rapunzel snatched up her pallette and paintbrush, Pascal leaped from the podium.

"Hey! Stop!" Rapunzel exclaimed. "We haven't got time for hide-and-seek!"

Pascal dived into the coils of Rapunzel's beautiful, long blonde hair, which was wound into a pile on the tower floor.

"If you think hiding is going to stop me painting you ... you're making a big mistake," she said, clambering after him. Pascal was so tiny and her hair was so very long, she couldn't see him anywhere!

Rapunzel snapped her fingers in thought. "I have an idea."

Using extra strong, extra-long bows, she tied her hair into a pile on top of her head – a pile so big it was difficult to carry. Rapunzel wobbled but smiled in triumph as Pascal emerged from the bundle onto her shoulder.

"Ha! There you are! Now it's time to paint!"

Pascal smirked at Rapunzel. She frowned in confusion. He reached up a little paw and tugged on one of her ribbons, making her hair tumble down around her in a humongous heap.

"Nice going Pascal!" Rapunzel grumbled. "You've knocked over my paints."

Paint had splashed everywhere. The pots lay on their sides oozing colourful puddles onto the floor.

Suddenly, Rapunzel gasped. "Wait a minute." She dipped her fingertip into a puddle of white paint and approached a green smudge on the wall. Pressing her finger against it, she created eyes in the splashes that had already formed a perfect likeness to Pascal's body.

"I didn't need to paint you after all!" Rapunzel announced.

Making the most of the mess Pascal had made over her wall, Rapunzel had created a splodgy version of her friend in mid-leap.

Pascal clapped in approval.

Rapunzel winked, patting him on the head. "We should play hide-and-seek more often."

A Question of Class

It was almost spring. Fairy Mary was checking the preparations for the changing of the seasons. Her wooden abacus under one arm, she watched as Fawn the animal fairy brought over another basket of berries.

"Here are the supplies for the little creatures coming out of hibernation," said Fawn, as she put down the basket with relief.

It was important that the fairies had enough supplies for all the animals on the mainland, so Fairy Mary was scrupulous with her checks. *Click, click* went the pebbles on her abacus, as she began looking over the baskets and adding up. "Walnuts plus acorns ..." she muttered. "Hazelnuts minus berries...."

It took a very long time, and Fawn was so tired of waiting that she fell asleep before Fairy Mary had finished!

Once Fairy Mary was satisfied with the animal supplies, she headed off to see Iridessa, who was working on the rainbows to be taken to the mainland. "This is the last one!" she announced as Fairy Mary arrived, carefully catching the end of a beautiful rainbow in a cone and packing it away.

"Perfect, my dear!" Fairy Mary said, smiling. *Click, click* went the pebbles on the abacus. "Make a thousand more, just to be safe!"

Iridessa gulped.

Fairy Mary sailed airily off to check the garden fairies' supplies. Baskets of every kind of seed were laid out for her inspection. *Click, click* went the abacus. "Fine! We've got the seeds." She dipped her finger in a bucket of paint. It was exactly the right shade of blue. "The paint for the flowers is ready." She looked around, frowning. Surely something was missing...?

"What happened to the sproutlings?" Fairy Mary called in panic. They couldn't have spring without the baby flowers!

Silvermist, who had been bringing drops of water to flowers nearby, jumped at Fairy Mary's shout. "They went that way with Rosetta," Silvermist reassured her.

Fairy Mary flew quickly to see for herself, and.... "For all the cracked kettles!" she exclaimed. She couldn't believe her eyes!

Rosetta was sitting in a clearing, surrounded by sproutlings. Each one wore a pink ribbon tied in a bow round its top, and Rosetta was gently powdering them with a little puff.

"What are you doing?" Fairy Mary asked.

"I'm giving the lil' fellas a makeover!" explained Rosetta. "They can't go to the mainland looking all scruffy!"

Fairy Mary sighed in despair as Silvermist giggled. There was no doubt about it – Rosetta was a fairy with class!

Disney THE JUNGLE Book

The Den of Doom

"Where are we going, Baloo?" Mowgli asked. He and Baloo had been travelling through the jungle for a while now.

"Have you ever heard of the Den of Doom, Man-cub?" replied Baloo in a hushed voice.

Mowgli gasped. "The Den of Doom? They say that the Den of Doom is a giant cave filled with bears who will eat anything – or anyone! They say that those bears can hear for miles and see in the dark! They say that even Shere Khan is afraid of them!" he exclaimed.

"Mmm-hmm," said Baloo. "They do say that. They *also* say that all of the bears in the Den of Doom are over three metres tall, that their teeth are green and razor-sharp, and that their battle cry is so loud that the whales in the ocean hear it and shake with fright. They say all that, and much, much more."

"And we're *going* there?" Mowgli squeaked. "We can't! Baloo, those bears aren't like you! They're dangerous!"

"Too late, Man-cub," Baloo said with a grin. "We're already there!" He picked up Mowgli, whose knees were knocking together so hard he could barely stand, and strode right into a thicket. The bear ducked under a huge palm frond and emerged into a large, sunlit clearing in front of an enormous cave. Baloo put Mowgli down. The boy looked around in complete and utter surprise.

Mowgli had expected to see hundreds of fierce, angry bears. Instead, he saw hundreds of relaxed, happy bears having a really good time. Bears were swimming in a small pond, splashing and laughing. Bears were resting in the cool shadows of the cave. Bears were playing tag out in the clearing and chomping on piles of ripe, delicious fruit. It was, in short, a bear party.

"I don't understand," Mowgli said to Baloo. "This is the Den of Doom?"

"Yep," Baloo said happily, grabbing a palm frond and fanning himself with it. "It used to be called the Den of Delights, but we had to change the name. See, everyone in the jungle knew that the Den of Delights was the most fun place around. We bears never turned anyone away from our party. But then it got so crowded that it just wasn't any fun anymore. So we spread a few rumours, changed the name, and *presto* – it's the Den of Doom! Now no one bothers us bears any more."

"But what about me?" Mowgli said anxiously. "I'm not a bear."

"You're an honorary bear, Mowgli," Baloo replied with a smile. "You sure have enough fun to be one!"

Disney DUMBO

Float Like a Butterfly

One day, Dumbo's best friend, Timothy Q. Mouse, found Dumbo looking sad. "What's the matter, little guy?" the mouse asked the elephant. "Have people been teasing you about your ears again?"

Dumbo nodded sadly. The little elephant looked totally miserable.

Timothy shook his head. The two were good friends and did everything together. He didn't mind one bit that Dumbo had large ears. In fact, he thought they were great.

Timothy was trying to think of a way to cheer up his dear friend. And then he saw something. "Look, Dumbo!" he cried, racing over to a nearby fence post. Hanging from the fence was a large cocoon. "It's a butterfly cocoon!" Timothy said excitedly.

Dumbo came over to examine it.

"And look – it's about to hatch into a butterfly," said Timothy. He looked thoughtful for a moment, and then he turned to Dumbo. "You know what? You are a lot like the little caterpillar that made this cocoon."

Dumbo looked at Timothy quizzically.

"It's true. You see, a caterpillar is something nobody really wants around. They think it's kind of plain looking, and it can't really do anything very interesting. But then one day, the caterpillar turns into a beautiful butterfly, and everyone loves it. And you know what? I think you're going to be that way, too. When you get older, everyone is going to admire you rather than tease you!"

Dumbo smiled at his friend, and wiped away a tear with one of his long ears.

Suddenly, it started to rain. "Oh no!" cried Timothy. "The butterfly is going to get its new wings all wet. It won't be able to fly if it gets rained on. What'll we do? We need an umbrella!"

As Timothy looked this way and that for an umbrella, Dumbo smiled and unfurled his long ears. He draped them over the fence post so that they made a lovely roof for the insect, protecting it from the falling droplets of rain.

"Great idea!" said Timothy admiringly. The two friends stood there during the downpour, which didn't last very long. While they waited, they watched the beautiful new butterfly emerge from its cocoon. When the rain stopped, the butterfly spread its wings (which were quite dry, thanks to Dumbo) and flew away.

"You know, my friend," said Timothy as they watched it fly away, "I think someday you're going to be a big success. You'll be like that butterfly – happy, carefree and floating along. Well, not floating for real, that's impossible. Imagine that, a flying elephant!"

Disney · PIXAR FINDING NEMO

Homesick

Nemo still couldn't believe everything that had happened to him. First, he'd been snatched up by a scuba diver in the ocean. Then, he'd travelled a long way in a big water cooler. Finally, he'd been dumped in a fish tank in a dentist's office. The other fish in the tank seemed nice, but Nemo missed his dad and his old home. He couldn't think about anything except getting back to the ocean. But would their plan to escape really work? It seemed hopeless....

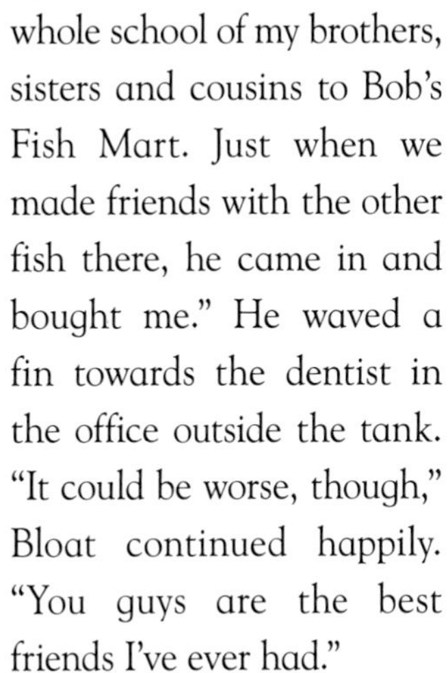

"Hey, kid." Bloat the blowfish swam over to him. "Are you okay? You look a little down in the gills."

"I'll say," said Nigel the seagull.

Peach the starfish glanced over from her spot on the tank wall. "He's just upset," she said. "It's only natural." She smiled kindly at Nemo. "It's okay, hon. We know how you feel."

"How could you know?" he muttered, feeling sorry for himself. "You weren't grabbed out of the ocean, away from your dad."

"Well, no," a fish named Gurgle admitted. "But we all had families back where we came from. We all miss them."

"Really?" Nemo blinked in surprise. He hadn't thought about that.

"Sure," Peach said. "The lady who sold me over the Internet kept lots of us starfish in her basement." She sighed sadly. "I still wonder where all my brothers and sisters ended up. I'd give two or three of my arms to see them again."

"I hear you," Bloat agreed. "I was hatched in somebody's garage. They sold me and a whole school of my brothers, sisters and cousins to Bob's Fish Mart. Just when we made friends with the other fish there, he came in and bought me." He waved a fin towards the dentist in the office outside the tank. "It could be worse, though," Bloat continued happily. "You guys are the best friends I've ever had."

A fish named Deb nodded. "I'm lucky he bought me and my sister together. Right, Flo?" She smiled at her own reflection in the glass of the tank. When the reflection didn't answer, Deb shrugged. "I guess Flo is too choked up to talk right now. But I can tell by her smile that she agrees. We don't know what we'd do without each other. But we still miss the rest of our family."

"Wow," Nemo said, looking around at his new tankmates. "I guess you *do* know how I feel."

Even though he was sad that the other fish had been taken from their families, it made Nemo feel a little less alone. At least they understood how much he wanted to find his way back to his father. Now, a little braver and more determined than ever, Nemo was ready to escape from the tank – no matter what.

Disney MICKEY & FRIENDS

The Pet Show

"Mickey! Morty! Ferdie!" Minnie cried, racing into Mickey's garden. "I'm chairperson for the Charity Pet Show. Isn't that exciting? We're raising money to build a new shelter for stray animals."

"We should enter Pluto in the pet show!" said Ferdie.

"We can teach him to do tricks," said Morty. "Can we, Uncle Mickey? Please?"

"All right," Mickey said. "It's for a good cause."

Mickey and Minnie watched as the boys started to train Pluto.

"Roll over, Pluto," said Morty. But Pluto just wagged his tail.

All week, Morty and Ferdie tried to teach Pluto new tricks. He fetched, he rolled over and he shook hands ... but only when he wanted to.

"At least he's doing *some* tricks," said Mickey.

Finally, the day of the pet show arrived. Minnie was at the ticket booth when Mickey and his nephews arrived.

"Guess what!" said Minnie. "We've already made enough money for the new animal shelter!"

"That's great!" said Mickey.

What wasn't great was Pluto's performance. He shook hands when he was told to sit. He rolled over when he should have jumped. And he barked when he was supposed to lie down.

Worst of all, when Police Chief O'Hara was choosing the Best Pet of the Day, Pluto growled at him! The chief was standing right where Pluto had buried a bone!

Chief O'Hara was about to announce the winner when the crowd heard Minnie scream from the ticket booth.

"Stop! Thief!" she cried.

"Oh no! The ticket money!" shouted Morty and Ferdie anxiously.

By the time Chief O'Hara, Mickey and the boys reached the booth, Pluto was sniffing around the scene.

"I turned away for just a minute," Minnie explained, "and someone ran off with the cashbox."

Suddenly, Pluto stopped sniffing and ran into the woods. A moment later, Minnie heard a shout and the thief came running out. He was holding on to the cashbox – and Pluto was holding on to him!

Pluto tugged the thief to Chief O'Hara.

Later that afternoon, Chief O'Hara presented Pluto with the Four-Footed Hero medal. "Thanks to Pluto, every animal will have a place to go – and a chance to find a good home," he said.

"You know," said Minnie later when they were back home, "it's okay that Pluto isn't a show dog. He's something better. He's a hero!"

Mickey, Morty and Ferdie agreed. And then, without being told to, Pluto shook hands with everyone because, this time, *he* wanted to.

Disney
THE LION KING

Just Like Dad

"Dad, when I grow up, I want to be just like you," Simba said to his father.

Mufasa nuzzled his son's head gently. "All in good time, son," he said.

Just then, Simba's friend Nala bounded up to them. "Come on, Simba!" she called. "Let's go play by the river!"

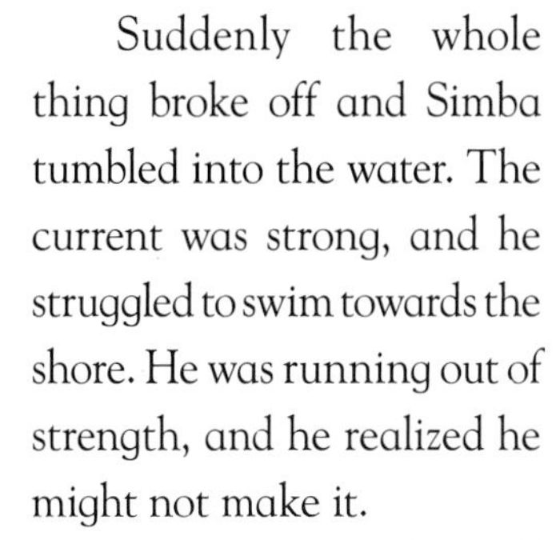

On their way, Simba stopped abruptly. "Listen to this," he said. He threw back his head and roared as loudly as he could. Then he looked at her expectantly. "Do I sound like my dad?"

Nala tried to suppress a giggle. "Not quite," she said.

Soon they reached the river. The waters were high as a result of the recent rains. Simba found a quiet pool at the side and stared down at his reflection. "Do you think my mane is starting to grow?" he asked Nala.

Nala sighed. "Maybe a little," she replied. "But, Simba, what's the big rush? Let's just have fun being young!"

Simba was eyeing a tree branch that stretched over the raging river. "Well, I may not be as big as my dad yet, but at least I'm as brave as he is!" he shouted, and raced up to the tree. Climbing its gnarled trunk, he began walking along the branch over the water.

Nala hurried over. "Simba!" she yelled. "Come back here! The branch is going to break!"

But Simba couldn't hear her over the loud waters. Nala bounded away to get help.

Simba felt the branch begin to sag. "Uh-oh," he said to himself.

Suddenly the whole thing broke off and Simba tumbled into the water. The current was strong, and he struggled to swim towards the shore. He was running out of strength, and he realized he might not make it.

Then he felt himself being lifted out of the water and tossed onto the bank. Dripping and coughing, he looked up – right into the angry eyes of his father.

"Simba!" thundered Mufasa. "There's a big difference between being brave and being foolish! The sooner you learn that, the better chance you will have of growing old!"

Simba hung his head. Out of the corner of his eye, he saw Nala, pretending not to overhear. "I'm ... sorry, Dad," he said softly. "I just wanted to be brave like you."

His father's gaze softened. "Well," he said. "As long as we're soaking wet, why don't we go to a quieter part of the river and do some swimming?" He looked over to where Nala was sitting. "Come on, Nala!" he called. "Come with us!"

"Yippee!" cried the cubs, and they all went off together.

Disney Princess
Cinderella

Chore de Force

Cinderella watched as a blue-and-pink-tinted bubble floated up from her bucket. "Isn't that pretty?" she said as she watched the bubble float higher and higher and finally pop into nothingness. Gus and Jaq and all the rest of Cinderella's mouse friends nodded in agreement.

"I bet it would be fun to float around in a bubble all day! I could see whole cities at a time, bounce on clouds and soar with the birds," Cinderella said dreamily.

Her bird friends chirped happily. They liked the idea of sharing the skies with her.

"What am I doing?" Cinderella suddenly said. "I should stay focused on my chores." She finished cleaning the windows and prepared to mop the floor.

Cinderella plunged the mop into a bucket of soapy water, then dragged it across the floor. At first, she felt worn out. Then it occurred to her, as the mop slid across the slippery floor, "This is like dancing! How I love to dance!" Gus and Jaq copied Cinderella as she twirled around the room with the mop. "What fun!" she cried happily.

"Oh, my," Cinderella caught herself. "Did I say that aloud?" *Maybe I just need to get away from all these bubbles,* she thought. *Ironing should do the trick!*

She was ironing away and humming merrily to herself when she realized how dark the sky had grown.

"Look at the time!" Cinderella exclaimed. "I've been daydreaming the day away and haven't even started dinner."

Cinderella hurried to the kitchen where she chopped and minced and grated and stirred. "I don't know where this day has gone," she fretted as she added ingredients to her stepsisters' favourite soup. "I've got absolutely nothing done!" And, just then, Cinderella's stepsisters, Anastasia and Drizella, barged into the kitchen.

"Where's my laundry?" barked Anastasia.

"Done," Cinderella said.

"And my ironing?" Drizella added.

"Done," Cinderella replied again.

"Did you mop the floors?"

"Wash the windows?"

"Make our dinner?"

"Done, done, done!" Cinderella said gaily.

The sisters marched out of the kitchen muttering with displeasure.

And there Cinderella stood, all alone in the kitchen once more. As she stirred the pot of soup, she thought, *I guess I did get a lot done, after all!*

Cinderella twirled across the room in celebration – and Jaq and Gus and the rest of her mouse friends joined her.

A Secret to Share

It had finally stopped raining in Pixie Hollow, and Silvermist and Rosetta were out in the meadow. "Oh, I love the smell of damp fields!" said Silvermist, twirling in the air happily.

"Lucky you," Rosetta said grumpily. "All dampness does for me is frizz my hair!" As the most stylish of all the fairies, Rosetta hated having her hair messed up!

PLOP!

"Stop worrying about that," said Silvermist. "Look over there!"

Rosetta turned and gasped. Not far away, a beautiful purple flower was splattered with mud. "That poor flower!"

"We need to clean it up," said Silvermist.

"I hate mud," grumbled Rosetta. "It's dirty!"

Silvermist couldn't believe her ears. "A garden fairy shouldn't say such things!" Everything Rosetta did depended on the earth. Silvermist flew down to help the flower but discovered she was soon knee-deep in mud! Yuck! This would take ages to wash off. And she hadn't even started on the flower!

"Don't worry, buttercup," Rosetta said. "I have an idea."

"What are you doing?" Silvermist called as her friend flew off to the closest tree, a weeping willow with long dangling branches.

"Wait and see!" Rosetta called back. Within a few minutes she'd returned, holding a leafy frond. Gently, she brushed the mud from the flower's petal. "Here you go, sweet thing. You'll be fresh as a daisy in no time."

Silvermist was astonished. Rosetta had cleaned the flower and managed not to get even a smidge of mud on her! "You were flitterific!" she told her friend admiringly.

"It's my little secret," Rosetta said, smiling. "I can do my job and end up smelling like a ro – eek!"

Something had landed nearby, splashing Rosetta with mud from head to foot!

"Sorry!" called Fawn from on top of a frog. "I didn't see you!"

"Umm ... we realized that," Silvermist said. She didn't dare glance at Rosetta, who was making a growling sound.

"Well, I'd better get going!" said Fawn cheerfully. The frog leaped out of the glade, splattering mud as it went. Silvermist and Rosetta dashed behind big leaves to protect themselves from getting another splashing.

"Maybe," said Silvermist hesitantly, "you should share your secret of staying clean with the animal fairies too!"

But one look at Rosetta's furious face was enough, and Silvermist flew hurriedly away. There was no point talking to Rosetta until she'd made herself clean and beautiful again. Fairies with style just didn't do mud!

March

11

Toy Story 3

A Very Good Idea!

Buzz, Woody and Rex strode through the streets of an old west town. "I sure like the easy life here in Bonnieville," said Buzz.

Woody nodded. "You can say that again."

But the friends had spoken too soon. A flying saucer swooshed by above their heads. "It's Dr Porkchop and the aliens," Woody warned, just as the spaceship began to fire laser blasts in their direction.

Rex ran away. "Ahhh! Every toy for himself!"

"Wait, Rex!" cried Buzz. "Not that way. That leads to the dark endless gorge!"

Bonnie dropped Rex in a toy box and slammed the lid shut. "Oh no! How are we going to rescue Rex, Buzz?" she gasped, moving Woody so it looked like he was the one asking the question.

Before Bonnie could start the rescue, her mum told her it was time for bed. The game – and Rex – would have to wait until tomorrow.

That night, as Bonnie slept, Woody and Buzz made plans on how they would rescue Rex. Little did they know, the toy dinosaur had clambered free on his own. He sighed sadly as he approached them.

"What's wrong, Rex?" asked Woody. "Aren't you happy with this adventure?"

Rex shrugged. "Yeah, but I always get the part of the scaredy-cat. At least once I'd like to be the brave hero! But I guess that's not the way things work for a dino in the wild west."

Woody and Buzz watched their friend walk off to bed. "You thinking what I'm thinking?" Woody whispered, and Buzz nodded.

Working quickly, the friends used Bonnie's craft materials to build something special. "Are you sure this is a good idea?" asked Buzz.

"Trust me, Buzz," Woody assured him. "When Bonnie sees our creation, she'll definitely make Rex the star of this adventure!"

The next morning, Bonnie swung her legs out of bed and cheered with excitement. Sitting on her floor was a home-made dinosaur island! "Thanks, Mum!" she cried. "This is the greatest island ever, and the great Rex can be its ruler!"

Bonnie grabbed her toys and began to play. Soon, her imagination was working at top speed as she created a new adventure.

"Rex! Buzz and Woody are in trouble," said Hamm.

Dressed as a brave adventurer, Rex pushed back his hat. "Don't worry, Hamm. I'll handle this one!"

Woody and Buzz had helped their friend be the hero he'd always wanted to be, but as they dangled above the island's volcano they wondered if they had made a very big mistake!

March
12

Disney Lady and the TRAMP

Don't Mock Jock

Aunt Sarah had only just arrived to look after the baby while Jim Dear and Darling were away, but already her Siamese cats, Si and Am, had caused nothing but trouble. When they made a huge mess in the living room, Lady had been blamed for it, and Aunt Sarah had taken Lady to be fitted with a muzzle!

Meanwhile, when they were left alone in the house, Si and Am had discovered the doggy door that led out to the garden.

"What works for doggies, works for kitties, too," hissed Si.

They slunk out to the garden. They dug in the flower beds, scared the birds at the birdbath and chased a squirrel up a tree.

Then they found a small hole in the garden fence. They poked their heads through the hole and spied Jock snoozing by his kennel.

"Time for a wake-up call?" said Am.

Si smiled and nodded. They squirmed through the hole and stole silently across the garden until they were sitting on either side of the sleeping Jock. Then, at the same moment, they let loose a shrill, ear-splitting yowl.

Jock awoke with a start. By the time he had identified the culprits, Si and Am were halfway across the lawn, heading for the fence.

Jock tore after them, barking. But, in a flash, the cats squirmed through the small hole and were out of Jock's reach. The opening was too small for Jock. He had to be content with sticking his head through and barking at the cats as they strolled casually up the back steps of Lady's house and through the doggy door. Then they collapsed in a laughing fit on the kitchen floor.

"Dogs are so very dimwitted." Si cackled.

They waited a while, then creeped out through the doggy door again, itching to try their trick once more. Peeking through the hole in the fence, they spied Jock, eyes closed, lying in front of his kennel. They squirmed through the hole and creeped towards him.

But, this time, Jock was ready for them. When the cats got within a metre of him, the feisty Scottie leaped to his feet and growled. The cats gave a start, wheeled round and raced for the fence, only to find the way blocked by Jock's friend, Trusty the bloodhound, who stood, growling, between the cats and the hole.

Jock and Trusty chased Si and Am around Jock's garden until Jock was confident they had learned their lesson. Then they allowed the cats to retreat through the hole in the fence.

This time, they didn't stop running until they were up the back steps, through the doggy door, and safely inside.

And inside is where they stayed.

Disney MINNIE

The Art of Innovation

Minnie and Daisy were at the Music Dome! They had gone straight there at the end of school and had been waiting in line for five hours – but now, finally, they had tickets to hear Spiky Triky, their favourite band!

"It's a dream come true!" said Daisy, clutching the ticket tightly. "I'll be seeing the legendary handsome-haired Andy Cool in the flesh!"

"And listening to Mike Guitar's wild solos!" sighed Minnie, picturing her hero on stage.

But in art class the next day, they were both in trouble. They'd spent so much time queuing for tickets that they hadn't studied at all, and neither of them could understand what the teacher was talking about.

"You both deserve bad marks for your lack of effort," the teacher told them sternly. "But I'll let you make up for this by presenting a report to the class tomorrow."

Minnie and Daisy were horrified. The concert was tonight! How would they have time to study for the presentation, unless they missed the concert?

"Mike Guitar and Andy Cool would never give up on their dreams," said Daisy miserably.

That gave Minnie an idea!

"Your phone takes videos, right?" she asked her friend.

"Yes," said Daisy, puzzled. How was that going to help?

Minnie smiled. "Perfect!" They would still be able to go to the concert!

Spiky Triky was on top form that night, and the crowd went wild! Minnie and Daisy sang along loudly to their favourite songs and danced their hearts out. Daisy held up her phone to video the concert, too!

In class the next day, Daisy and Minnie presented their project. "Today we're going to speak about a new area of art – rock music!" they announced. Then they played the video of Spiky Triky's concert.

"As you can see," said Daisy, "with each song, Spiky Triky expresses a new emotion! There's sadness for a lost love, happiness for a new love...."

"And then we have the visual elements of stage design," added Minnie. "There are laser lights and even a smoke machine!"

"A concert as an example of art, huh?" Miss Van Burlow clapped her hands. "How exciting! I think you two have brilliantly made up for yesterday."

Daisy winked at Minnie. "Well, it's just like Mike and Andy say in their song...."

Minnie grinned. "With a friend at your side, you can overcome any kind of trouble!"

March

14

Disney · PIXAR
MONSTERS UNIVERSITY

Silent Invasion

The members of Oozma Kappa were down in Squishy's basement, practising for the second event in the Scare Games – Avoid the Parent.

To win the event, they'd have to sneak past a robotic librarian and grab a flag, so Mike had come up with a great way for them to train.

"We'll sneak past Squishy's mum and grab a slice of cake," he said. "Be quiet and slow. Clear?"

"Yes, coach," said the other monsters, but Sulley just rolled his eyes. This was beginner stuff, and no challenge for someone like him.

A few minutes later, while Squishy's mum was busy knitting a new scarf, Mike tiptoed into the room. The cake was sitting on a table right next to her. This wasn't going to be easy.

Creeping across the floor, Mike squeezed under the table. He waited until just the right moment, then quickly stretched out an arm and snatched a slice of the cake. Mission accomplished!

After carefully making his way back to the basement, Mike told Terri and Terry to go next. The two-headed monster was too big to fit under the table, but they sneaked silently up behind Mrs Squibbles and grabbed two pieces when she turned to examine the scarf.

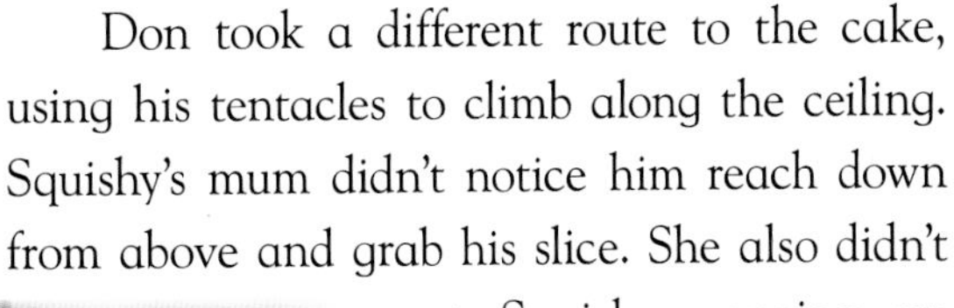

Don took a different route to the cake, using his tentacles to climb along the ceiling. Squishy's mum didn't notice him reach down from above and grab his slice. She also didn't spot Squishy popping up from behind her armchair to steal his piece, and even Art managed to collect some cake without being seen.

Then it was Sulley's turn. Mike tried to give advice, but Sulley ignored it. "I can do this blindfolded, Wazowski," he said.

Mike thought it would be good for the other monsters to see how Sulley did it, so they all sneaked up to watch him in action.

Sulley easily made it across the room without alerting Squishy's mum, but as he got closer to the cake one of his big feet tangled in the wool she was using to knit with. Sulley flapped his arms, trying to stay upright, but it was no use. He smashed into the table, sending the rest of the cake flying through the air.

The other monsters shut their eyes as the cake splattered down on them, covering them in sticky green icing. Mrs Squibbles gasped when she saw the mess. Sulley and the rest of the Oozma Kappa team had been well and truly spotted.

"Well, she caught us," said Squishy. He scooped a lump of cake off his head and ate it. "But at least we got a jumbo portion!"

Disney Princess
The Little Mermaid

The Wrong Gift

"Wow, Flounder, everyone's here!" cried Ariel. Mermaids and mermen had come from all over the ocean to wish Ariel's sister Aquata a happy birthday.

Unfortunately, Ariel still needed to pick out a gift for her sister. So, Ariel and Flounder left the party and swam to her secret cave.

Together they looked through Ariel's vast collection of bells, clocks, jewellery and other human knick-knacks she'd scavenged from shipwrecks.

"How about this?" asked Flounder, swimming around a ship's wheel.

"Too big," said Ariel.

"Or this?" suggested Flounder, nudging a single gold earring.

"Too small," said Ariel.

Then, out of the corner of her eye, Ariel noticed a music box.

"This is it!" she cried. "The perfect gift! I've listened to this one again and again, and it plays a really beautiful song."

Ariel swam back to the celebration. Beside King Triton, Aquata sat on a clamshell, and, one by one, the guests presented her with their birthday gifts.

While Ariel waited her turn in the queue, Sebastian the crab swam by. "Hello, Ariel," he said. "What gift do you have for Aquata?"

When Ariel proudly told Sebastian, his jaw dropped. "Are you out of your mind?" he cried.

Ariel's eyes widened. Sebastian was right! King Triton hated humans. And Ariel was not supposed to have anything from their world. That's exactly why she'd kept her cave a secret!

Just then, King Triton's deep voice bellowed, "Ariel, you're next."

Ariel hid the present behind her back.

"What gift do you have for your eldest sister?" asked Triton.

"Uh ..." Ariel began.

"A song!" Sebastian announced.

Ariel racked her brain for a song to sing, and then she hit on it! She opened her mouth, and sang the melody from the music box.

When she finished, Flounder swam behind her, replacing the gift in her hand with a beautiful starfish for Aquata's hair.

"It's beautiful!" said Aquata. "And so was your song!"

King Triton smiled approvingly, and Ariel sighed with relief. How she wished her father would change his mind about humans!

"I'd give almost anything to see what the human world is like," she told Flounder. "Do you think my father will ever understand?"

"Maybe when he finally sees what it means to you," said Flounder, "someday he will."

THE JUNGLE BOOK

Bagheera Bears Up

Mowgli danced around, humming happily to himself.

"What are you doing, Mowgli?" Bagheera asked from his perch in a nearby tree.

"Practising being a bear," Mowgli told him. "You should try it."

"Me?" Bagheera said, stunned. "I couldn't possibly do such a thing."

"Why not?" Mowgli wanted to know.

"Well, I'm a panther and I happen to like being one," Bagheera replied. "Why on earth would I want to be a bear?"

"Are you kidding?" Mowgli exclaimed. "Bears have the life! They hang out all day long, and they eat ants!"

"Eat ants?" Bagheera asked. "And that's a good thing?"

"Sure!" Mowgli said. "Well, truthfully, they tickle your throat at first. But you get used to it soon enough."

"Have you?" Bagheera asked.

"Not yet," Mowgli confessed. "But I will!"

"Whatever you say, Mowgli," said Bagheera.

Mowgli thought for a moment. "And if you were a bear, you would eat fruit and drink coconut juice, and you would relax, just like us!"

"If you ask me," Bagheera said, "I don't see anything so bad about being a panther. In fact, I like it very much."

"I think you're scared," Mowgli told him.

"Absolutely not!" Bagheera protested confidently. "What on earth would I have to be scared of?" He stood up, stretched and gracefully jumped out of the tree and onto the ground.

"Exactly," Mowgli said. "So, why not try it?"

"You've got to be kidding me!" Bagheera said.

"You know what your problem is?" Mowgli said.

"I'm afraid to ask," replied Bagheera.

"You're like a beehive," Mowgli told him. "You work too hard." He stared at Bagheera. "Come on, dance with me!" he cried excitedly, grabbing Bagheera's paw and prancing around the panther. After a bit, Bagheera began to dance too, moving his feet and twitching his tail.

"That's it!" Mowgli cheered.

"You know what?" Bagheera admitted. "This isn't so bad after all."

"Now you're getting it!" Mowgli exclaimed. "Now you see why being a bear is so great!" The Man-cub stopped dancing and threw himself on a soft patch of moss. "It's not so bad, is it?"

"Actually," Bagheera said, scratching his back against a rock, "it's sort of fun!"

"One more time!" Mowgli cheered, and they began dancing again.

March

17

Disney Princess

Jasmine

Jasmine's Treasure

Jasmine flipped through her parents' wedding album. She was happy to be marrying Aladdin but wished her mother were still alive to share the moment.

Jasmine studied every detail, and made a decision. "I want my wedding to be exactly like my mother's," she said. "Then she will be a part of my wedding!"

So she selected the same flowers her mother had chosen. She asked the chef to prepare the same menu and bake the same cake that her parents had. And she showed her mother's wedding dress to the royal seamstress.

"Your mother would be touched that you are honouring her like this," the Sultan said, handing Jasmine an envelope. "She wrote this letter to you many years ago."

My dear Jasmine,

I am writing this letter to give to you when you are to be married. I'm sure you are busy with the preparations. The most wonderful part of my own wedding was my treasure of all treasures. I am so happy that you have found yours!

All my love,

Mother

Jasmine imagined her mother dressed up, with her 'treasure of all treasures'.

"It must have been a truly breathtaking jewel!" Jasmine decided. She had to find hers. Jasmine studied the wedding album again, but her mother wasn't wearing a priceless jewel.

She found her father with the Genie. "Do you remember Mother's treasure of all treasures from your wedding day?"

The Sultan had never heard of it, but the Genie summoned diamonds, rubies and emeralds. "Choose your very own treasure of all treasures!" he exclaimed.

Jasmine knew none of the jewels was the treasure. "Thank you," she said. "I'll know it when I see it."

Jasmine shared her troubles with Aladdin.

"We'll find it, I promise!" he said.

Jasmine and Aladdin searched in all the store rooms, but they didn't find the treasure.

"I'll keep searching," Aladdin told her.

The day before her wedding, Jasmine read her mother's letter again and her eyes fell on a sketch of her father, drawn by her mother.

Suddenly, Jasmine understood. Her father was her mother's treasure of all treasures!

Aladdin entered. "I'm sorry," he said. "The treasure – I haven't found it."

"I had my treasure all along!" Jasmine said. "It's *you,* Aladdin!"

Their wedding was perfect. Jasmine's dress was lovely and the food was delicious. But, most importantly, Jasmine had Aladdin, her treasure of all treasures, by her side.

Disney Winnie the Pooh

A Blustery Day

"Oh dear," said Pooh as the wind whipped around him. "It's very windy. Are you sure this is a good idea, Tigger?" He and Tigger were carrying Pooh's kite out into a clearing in the middle of the Hundred-Acre Wood.

"Don't be silly, Pooh Boy," Tigger responded. "Today is the perfect day to fly your kite. After all, what else is wind for?"

"Yes," Pooh replied. "I suppose you're right." He leaned into a particularly strong gust to keep it from blowing him over as they walked on. Winter was on its way out of the Wood, and spring was on its way in – and it seemed the wind was rushing in to fill the space in between, for it was one of the blusteriest days Pooh could remember.

At last, struggling against the wind, Pooh and Tigger reached the middle of the clearing and got ready to launch the kite. Pooh unrolled some kite string while Tigger held the kite.

"Okay, Pooh," said Tigger. "Get ready! You hold on to the string, and I'll toss the kite up into the wind. One ... two ... THREE!"

With that, Tigger tossed the kite and it was immediately seized by the strong wind and carried high into the air where it danced and darted this way and that.

Meanwhile, Pooh struggled to hold on to the roll of kite string.

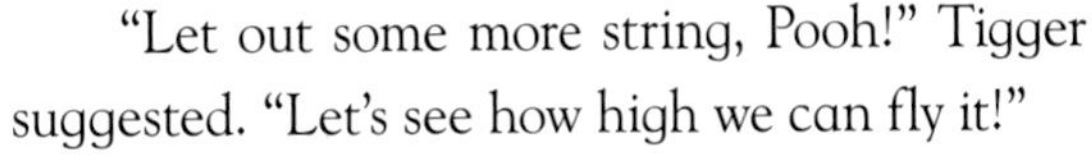

"Let out some more string, Pooh!" Tigger suggested. "Let's see how high we can fly it!"

So Pooh let out some more string. The kite sailed higher into the air and, blown around by stronger and stronger gusts, it tugged harder and harder on Pooh's end of the line.

"Fly it higher, Pooh!" exclaimed Tigger.

So Pooh let out more and more string until he had let it all out. He clung tightly to the end of the line as the kite soared, seeming almost to touch the low clouds.

Then, all of a sudden, a tremendous gust of wind blew through the clearing. At the end of the kite string, Pooh felt his feet leave the ground as the wind grabbed hold of the kite and carried it sharply upward.

"My goodness!" said Pooh, realizing that he was being lifted up. Then, before he could be carried too high, he let go of the kite string and tumbled gently to the ground.

But the kite sailed on – up and away, dancing on the breeze for what seemed like forever, until it came to rest at last in the high branches of a very tall tree at the edge of the clearing. Pooh wondered how he would ever get it down.

"Oh well," said Tigger, patting his friend sympathetically on the back. "Guess you flew it just a little too high there, Pooh Boy."

March

19

A Question of Taste

The fairies had a special job today. Rosetta, the most stylish garden fairy of all, was choosing a new dress and wanted their opinion.

"I'll try," said Silvermist, "but I don't know anything about fashion!"

Rosetta was delighted that Tinker Bell, Iridessa and Silvermist had all come to help. "Welcome, sugarplums!" she said. "I'll go put on the first outfit."

"Hurry up," called Iridessa, reclining on a large leaf. "We're curious."

Rosetta had unique taste, but her friends weren't expecting such a large first dress! The pink fluted flower began at Rosetta's neck and flared out into a frilled hemline around her feet. It was quite a sight! Tink, Iridessa and Silvermist glanced at each other, unsure what to say. Eventually Tink ventured, "I don't think it suits you."

Rosetta picked up another large pink flower and perched it on her head, the green stem pointing straight up to the sky. "What if I wore it with this delightful hat?"

"I'm not so sure," said Iridessa tactfully. "Why don't you show us another dress?"

To the girls' relief, Rosetta simply nodded and went to change. While she was away, Fawn arrived, carrying a wriggly green friend. "How cute!" exclaimed Silvermist, reaching out to pat the creature. "Where did you find him?"

"These days I'm taking the caterpillars out to pasture," Fawn told them. "It's a big job and I have to keep a constant eye on them."

"So that's why you brought him along!" grinned Tink.

But the petting of the caterpillar was interrupted by Rosetta in the next dress. "Here it is!" she cried, doing a twirl. "Isn't it flitterific?"

Her friends stared, momentarily at a loss for words. The dress had a huge pink skirt with yellow pompoms around the hem. The bodice was green and the puffed sleeves were so large that they reached up to Rosetta's cheeks. She was wearing another hat, too, made of green leaves bent up and out at the brim, with a spray of yellow pollen on the top.

"For special occasions ..." tried Iridessa.

"With a few changes ..." added Fawn.

"Or maybe we just don't have an eye for fashion," Silvermist said hurriedly.

Luckily Rosetta could see the funny side. "No, you're right!" she said, giggling. "These dresses are terrible!"

CHOMP! Fawn's caterpillar had taken a big bite out of Rosetta's skirt! Everyone burst out laughing. "At last, the opinion of someone with great taste!" giggled Fawn.

"Well," said Rosetta, smiling, "at least somebody likes my dresses!"

Disney Bambi

Spring Has Sprung!

Spring had come at last to the forest. *Sniff, sniff* – Bambi could smell the change in the air. The days were growing longer. The nights were getting shorter. The ice and snow were quickly melting away. Crocuses and daffodils were pushing new green shoots out of the ground.

And the forest didn't feel quite as lonely as it had during the cold weather. In just the last few days, Bambi had noticed that there were more animals peeking their heads out of their holes and burrows and dens.

As he took a walk through the forest very early one morning on the first day of spring, Bambi came upon Mrs Possum and her children hanging upside down by their tails from a tree branch. She and Bambi had not seen one another in a long while. But Mrs Possum recognized him just the same.

"Well, hello, Bambi," said Mrs Possum.

"Hello, Mrs Possum," Bambi replied. "I haven't seen you since autumn. Where have you and your family been all winter long?"

"Oh, we like to spend most of our winter indoors," Mrs Possum replied. "But now that spring is here, it's so nice to be out in the fresh air again." Then Mrs Possum and the rest of her family closed their eyes and dozed off, because they liked to spend most of their days sleeping, you know.

Walking on through the forest, Bambi stopped by a tree filled with twittering birds.

"Hello, Bambi," said one of the birds.

"Hello," Bambi replied. "And where have you birds been all winter long?"

"Oh, we fly south for the winter, to warmer places where we can find more food," the bird explained. "But we are so happy it is spring once more. It is lovely to be back in the forest."

Then the bird joined her voice with her friends' twittering tunes. After so many months without it, the chirps and tweets were sweet music to Bambi's ears.

Bambi walked farther, meeting old friends at every turn. He came upon mice moving from their winter quarters back into their spring and summer homes. He noticed the squirrels and chipmunks snacking leisurely on nuts, no longer storing them away in their winter stockpiles. He heard a woodpecker rapping at a pine tree. And he spotted the ducks out for a swim on the pond.

Yes, thought Bambi, *it had been a long, cold, difficult winter.* But somehow the arrival of spring made him feel that everything would be all right. Everywhere he looked there was life, there were new beginnings ... and, most importantly, there was hope.

Disney Princess
Snow White and the Seven Dwarfs

Home Sweet Home

As the sun rose above the Seven Dwarfs' cottage, Snow White was already thinking about what to make for supper that evening.

She had arrived at the cottage just the day before, after her evil stepmother, the Queen, had driven Snow White from the palace and the Queen's huntsman had left her alone in the forest. Luckily, a group of helpful woodland creatures had befriended Snow White and led her to the Dwarfs' little cottage. Now, for the first time in a long while, she felt safe and happy.

She was so grateful to the Dwarfs for sharing their cosy home with her, she wanted to give them a special treat.

"Perhaps we'll have berry pie for supper tonight!" she said to her furry woodland friends after the Dwarfs had gone to work. The little animals nodded in agreement. Together they left the cottage and headed to the forest to pick berries. With all her friends helping, Snow White quickly filled her berry basket. Then she sat down among the sweet-smelling flowers with a sigh.

"How different life has become," she said to her friends. "I don't miss the grand castle at all. I love living in this funny little cottage. A home does not need to be grand to be a happy one. Remember that!"

The animals exchanged looks with one another. They began tugging at her skirt to pull her to her feet.

"What is it, dears?" she asked them. "Oh! Do you want to show me where all of *you* live? I would love to see!" she cried.

Two bluebirds were first. Twittering excitedly, they fluttered around their nest, which had been built in a cosy nook of a nearby tree.

"What a lovely nest!" cried Snow White. The birds looked pleased.

The fawns were next. Pulling at her skirt, they brought Snow White to a sun-dappled clearing in a warm glade.

"How cosy!" exclaimed Snow White. The fawns flicked their tails happily.

Next, the chipmunks and squirrels showed her the hollow in an old tree where they lived. Then the rabbits proudly showed her the entrance to their burrows.

"You all have such pretty little homes," said Snow White, as they made their way back to the Dwarfs' cottage. "Thank you for showing them to me. We are all lucky to live where we do, aren't we?" she said with a smile.

And with that, she skipped the rest of the way back to the cottage to start preparing her pie. She could hardly wait until the Dwarfs got home!

March

22

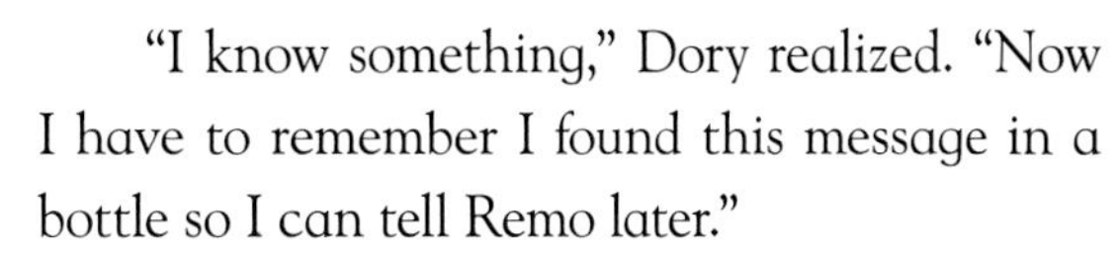

Massage in a Bobble

On the edge of the reef, with its beautiful plant life of every colour imaginable, Nemo and his friends waited to ride to school on the back of their favourite teacher, Mr Ray. In the distance, they could just make out Mr Ray's long barbed tail trailing behind him as he swooped through the water.

Dory had come to visit the night before and was keeping the children company as they prepared to board.

"See you later Fido, Earl, Chad and Milton. Have fun at school!" she said with a wave of her yellow and blue fins.

"It's Nemo, Pearl, Tad and Sheldon," Nemo corrected his forgetful friend, "but thanks Dory!"

Mr Ray ushered the children onto his back. "Come on kids, this way to knowledge."

Dory overheard the word knowledge and was intrigued. "That sounds like fun," she said. "I bet if I swim around long enough, I just might learn a thing or two as well."

She wandered through the seaweed and coral formations, casting her eyes down for something interesting. "Hey what's that?" She paused in front of her discovery. "Oh I know what that is! It's a message in a bottle!"

How exciting! The message could hold the secrets to the ocean. Or be a long lost love letter!

"I know something," Dory realized. "Now I have to remember I found this message in a bottle so I can tell Remo later."

She thought hard, trying to lock it into her memory. "What helped me remember before?" she asked herself. "A song! No, no that never works." She thought harder. "Aha! I know. A song! I'll sing a song!"

Dory swam back home, humming and singing to her heart's content. "I found a message in a bottle ... messy eggs and nooooodles! Massage in a bobble ... bottom oodle poodle...."

Later that day, Dory caught up with the children. "Nemo, Pearl, Tad, Sheldon!" she called.

"Hey, you remembered our names!" squeaked Pearl in surprise.

"Yes! And I know this too," Dory insisted. "I found a massage in a bobble. No wait, an egg in a poodle. Wait ... a giraffe and a beetle! No, no ... a message in a bottle!"

"Wow!" The children gasped.

"What did it say, Dory?" asked Tad.

Dory's smile melted and her face formed a bewildered expression. "Err ... I don't know," she admitted. "I forgot to read it!"

The children laughed together. They may not know the secret of the message, but it was certainly a victory for Dory ... she'd actually remembered she'd found it in the first place!

Disney Minnie

All For an Autograph

Minnie and Daisy's favourite band, Spiky Triky, were in town to shoot a music video – and the two girls were desperate to meet their idols! They'd come up with a secret plan to get into the hotel where the band was staying – they disguised themselves as news reporters!

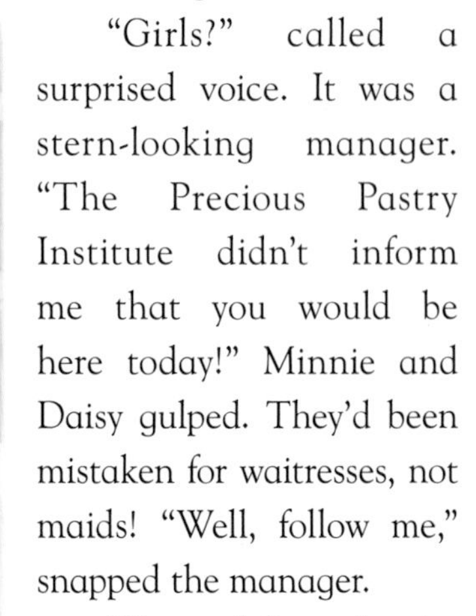

The Diamond Palace Hotel was extremely fancy and Minnie felt scared. What if they were kicked out? What if someone realized they were just kids, not real reporters at all?

But to her surprise, the doorman waved them in. And the scary-looking security guard pointed them in the direction of the main hall. "Go in and wait your turn," he said.

Minnie and Daisy couldn't believe their luck. They were going to meet their rock idols at last! But their hopes were dashed when one of the other reporters told them that Spiky Triky hated giving interviews and always sent their manager instead.

Minnie and Daisy walked out of the hall, feeling disappointed. "We've got to come up with a plan B," said Daisy. "We could climb up to their window ... or hide in their lunch!"

Just then, two maids came out of a door up ahead. Minnie brightened. "I've got a better idea!" Through that door was the maids' changing room!

"I get it!" said Daisy. Quickly, the two of them ditched their reporters' outfits and changed into maids' uniforms. They were off to find Spiky Triky without being noticed!

"Girls?" called a surprised voice. It was a stern-looking manager. "The Precious Pastry Institute didn't inform me that you would be here today!" Minnie and Daisy gulped. They'd been mistaken for waitresses, not maids! "Well, follow me," snapped the manager.

They followed the manager into a huge room decorated with ribbons, flowers and chandeliers. She pointed to a table covered with hundreds of cupcakes still to be decorated. "You can help prepare for Spy Tie's reception ... or whatever they're called," she said.

"I guess we overdid it," said Daisy miserably as they started work. "So long, autographs!"

But as they carefully iced and decorated each cupcake, Minnie and Daisy heard a familiar sound....

It was Mike and Andy from Spiky Triky, rehearsing in the room next door!

Minnie and Daisy couldn't believe it! "It's like they're singing just for us." This would make the work fly by.

Who wanted an autograph when you could have a private concert!

Disney Princess
Sleeping Beauty

Berry Picking

Once upon a time, in a forest far away, there lived a lovely princess who did not know she was a princess, and three good fairies who pretended to be mortal. (Of course, you know exactly to whom we are referring ... so let's get right to the story of Briar Rose and her three 'aunts'.)

One morning, Flora called the group together to suggest they go out to search the forest for berries.

"What a wonderful idea," said Briar Rose.

"Yes, indeed," said Merryweather. "If we pick enough, we can make a berry pie."

"If we pick enough," declared Fauna, "we can make enough jam to last us through the whole year."

"Well, we'll never have enough if we don't get started now," said Flora. And so they gathered their berry baskets and set out.

They followed a shady path through the forest until they came upon a thicket bursting with berry bushes. And, without delay, the four berry-pickers got to work. But, as you will see, just because they got to work, doesn't mean their baskets actually got full.

Merryweather, for one, had a terrible time keeping her basket upright. Every time she bent to pick another berry, her basket tipped and out spilled all but two or three.

Fauna, on the other hand, had an entirely different problem keeping her berries in her basket – somehow they kept finding their way into her mouth!

And as for Briar Rose, her heart and her mind were miles away from her berry basket ... dancing instead in the arms of a handsome stranger.

"All right, dearies," Flora called as the sun began to sink. "It's time to start back to the cottage. Let's see what you've got."

"Um, well," said Merryweather. "I don't seem to have many berries in my basket."

Flora rolled her eyes and moved on to Fauna. "Let me guess ..." she said as she looked from Fauna's empty basket to her purple mouth.

"Ah, yes," Fauna said as she guiltily dabbed at a drop of juice on her lips. "Berries are delicious! Don't you think?"

Flora sighed. "And you, Briar Rose?" she asked hopefully.

But Briar Rose just looked down at the empty basket in her hands sheepishly. "I'm sorry, Aunt Flora," she said. "I guess I got a little bit distracted."

"Well," said Flora, shaking her head, "no berry pie for us this week, I guess." Then she shrugged. "But we can always have chocolate cake instead!"

March
25

The Mysterious Treasure

Sheriff Woody was playing cards with Jessie and Buzz when Slinky ran up, panting excitedly. “Woody! Come and look!”

Following Slinky, Woody was amazed to find a carefully drawn treasure map!

“Andy drew this a long time ago, after hiding something in the garden,” Woody remembered.

“Do you think the treasure is still there?” asked Slinky.

There was only one way to find out. With Jessie at his side, Woody carefully folded the map and then climbed out onto the window ledge. Woody and Jessie slid down the drainpipe as Buzz and Slinky watched from Andy’s window.

Down in the garden, Woody unfurled the map. “It should be easy to find this treasure,” he said.

Jessie gulped. “Um ... I’m not so sure!” she said. “B-behind you!”

Woody spun round to see a large, mean-looking cat approaching. Its eyes were narrow and its fur stood up on end. It was getting ready to pounce!

Woody and Jessie backed up against the wall as the cat let out an angry hiss. Up at the window, Slinky and Buzz watched on. “What can we do?” Slinky asked.

Luckily, Buzz had a plan. Grabbing a nearby megaphone toy, he held it in front of Slinky’s mouth. At once, the stretchy toy dog knew what to do. He barked and growled into the megaphone as loudly as he could.

Startled, the cat let out a loud “Meoooow!” then ran off with its tail between its legs.

After shouting a thank you to their friends, Woody and Jessie set off to find the treasure. With help from the map, they found their way to a pile of bricks. “It must be under here,” Woody said.

He and Jessie pushed the bricks out of the way. Beneath them was a hole, and sitting at the bottom was a shiny gold tin.

“Yee-ha! There it is!” Jessie cheered.

Climbing down into the hole, the toys pushed open the tin’s lid. Inside was a folded up piece of paper. “Huh. What’s this?” Jessie wondered.

“We’ll soon find out,” said Woody, carefully unfolding the paper.

When they saw what was on the paper, Woody and Jessie both gasped. “Oh, it’s beautiful!” said Jessie.

Woody looked down at the page, which showed a drawing of him and Andy together, holding hands and having fun in the sunshine. “Now that,” said the cowboy, wiping a tear from his eye, “is a real treasure!”

Disney Princess
The Little Mermaid

Sealed With a Kiss

In the ocean, Ariel and Flounder were playing a game of hide-and-seek. Ariel loved trying to find the little yellow and blue fish, but after a while they decided it might be fun to get a friend to join in too.

"Let's ask the baby seal we met the other day," Ariel suggested, swimming quickly towards the surface.

They found the baby seal lazing on a rock.

"I'd love to play!" he said, wriggling his tail. "Thanks for inviting me!"

Ariel and Flounder clapped in glee and dived back into the water with the baby seal in tow.

"One ... two ... three...." Ariel started to count, as Flounder and the baby seal rushed off to hide.

Flounder knew exactly where he was going, but the seal had nowhere to hide as he swam off.

"Ready or not, here I come!" Ariel cried.

She found Flounder in no time at all, hidden among the tall seaweed.

"How did you find me so soon?" Flounder asked, feeling a little grumpy.

"I always know how to find you. You're my best friend!" Ariel giggled. "Plus I know this is your favourite hiding place."

Together Ariel and Flounder went in search of the baby seal, but they couldn't seem to find him anywhere.

They heard music playing in the distance and went to investigate. "Perhaps he's hiding among the musicians?" Ariel suggested.

As Flounder danced to the sound of the music, Ariel had a good look around, but there was no sign of the baby seal.

They decided to swim back to where they had first met the baby seal ... the rock at the surface of the sea. Scuttle the seagull was perched there, enjoying the breeze ruffling through his feathers.

"Haven't seen him," said Scuttle, when Ariel explained who they were looking for.

Back under the water, they heard a distressed squeak. Ariel and Flounder raced off to find out where the noise was coming from and there, stuck in a giant shell, was the baby seal!

"Help!" he pleaded, trying to wiggle free.

"We'll free you," Ariel promised, lifting and tugging and pulling with all her might. The giant shell opened with a groan and the baby seal squirmed free with a swish of his tail.

"Thank you, Ariel," he said, relieved.

Ariel gave him a kiss on the cheek. "You're a real good hider," she laughed. "But next time you can be the one that counts and finds us."

"No problem," the baby seal agreed, but that was enough fun and games for one day!

March

27

Disney ALICE in WONDERLAND

The Silent Treatment

The Queen of Hearts loved to shout orders at her royal subjects. She shouted so much, in fact, that it wasn't surprising when she came down with a very sore throat.

"There, there," said her husband, the King. "Rest your voice and let me do the ruling for you, my dear." Usually, the Queen hardly let the King get a word in at all, so he was looking forward to being in charge for a change.

As they walked through the royal garden, the Queen noticed that the fence was painted pink instead of the required red. "Off! Off!" the Queen croaked. She wanted the King to punish the royal gardeners with her favourite order, "Off with their heads!"

Instead, the King said, "The Queen decrees that you may have the day off!" The gardeners cheered as steam escaped from the Queen's ears. "You must relax, sweetheart," the King warned her, "or you simply won't get well."

Soon the couple paused to play a game of croquet. The Queen hit the hedgehog ball with the flamingo mallet, and the hedgehog rolled willy-nilly across the lawn. The playing-card hoops knew better than to let the Queen make a bad shot. They jumped all over the grass, making sure the ball passed underneath them. "I'm undefeated!" the Queen rasped triumphantly.

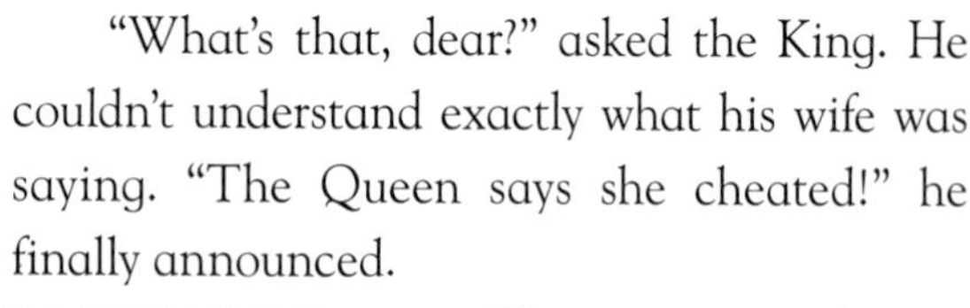

"What's that, dear?" asked the King. He couldn't understand exactly what his wife was saying. "The Queen says she cheated!" he finally announced.

The entire royal staff gasped. Those nearby ducked as the Queen swung a flamingo at the King's head.

"That's enough croquet for today," said the King soothingly. "You don't want to tire yourself out."

He led his wife over to a bench. The Queen sat down, pointed to the servants hovering nearby and acted out drinking a cup of tea.

The King stood up and announced, "You're all invited to have tea with the Queen!" Of course, this was not what the Queen had in mind at all.

A table was laid with tea, fancy cakes and sandwiches. Everyone ate, laughed and had a wonderful time. The Queen, ignored by everyone, seethed with anger.

She grabbed one of the flamingo mallets, then charged the table. Unfortunately, she didn't see the croquet ball in her path. As she tripped, the flamingo's beak plunged into the ground, causing the Queen to pole-vault up and over the table of guests and through her open bedroom window.

"A splendid idea, my dear!" called the King. "A nap will do you good!"

Disney The Jungle Book

Dance, Daddy-o!

Deep in the jungle at the temple ruins, the monkeys and their ruler, King Louie, were always looking to have a swingin' time.

"Let's have a dance-off!" King Louie suggested to the monkeys one evening.

"Hooray! Hooray!" the monkeys cheered.

"What's a dance-off?" one monkey asked.

"You know, a contest," said King Louie. "An opportunity for everyone to get down, strut their stuff, cut a rug! And whoever lays down the smoothest moves is the winner!"

"Hooray!" cheered the monkeys.

King Louie rubbed his chin. "The first thing we need is some music," he said, pointing at the monkey musicians. "Hit it, fellas!"

The musicians blasted out a jazzy tune, blowing through their hands like horns, knocking out a beat on some coconuts and drumming on a hollow log. Soon, all the monkeys were gathered around the musicians, tapping their toes and shaking their tails.

"Now," said King Louie, "who will dance?"

All the monkeys raised their hands. King Louie looked around. "Let's see," he said scratching his head, "I choose ... me!"

"Hooray!" the monkeys cheered. They were disappointed not to be chosen. But, after all, King Louie *was* their King.

So King Louie moved his hips from side to side. He waved his arms in the air. Then he closed his eyes so he could really feel the beat.

"Dance, Daddy-o!" one monkey cried.

King Louie boogied and bopped like he had never boogied and bopped before. Then, when the song was over, King Louie stopped dancing and scrambled onto his throne. "Now it's time to choose the winner!" he said.

"But King Louie ..." one monkey began to object. All the other monkeys were thinking the same thing – didn't you need more than one dancer to have a dance-off?

"Oh, silly me," said King Louie with a chuckle. The monkeys looked at each other and smiled, expecting that the King had realized his mistake. But, King Louie said, "Of course, we need a judge! Who will judge?"

Everyone raised their hands. King Louie looked around, then said, "I choose ... me!"

"Hooray!" the monkeys cheered.

"And as the judge, I will now choose the winner of the dance-off," King Louie continued. He looked around at all the monkeys. "Now, let's see. I choose ... me! Let's hear it for the winner!"

"Hooray!" the monkeys cheered, because, after all, King Louie was their King – and a pretty swingin' dancer, too!

Dangerous Pearls

One day, when Bonnie had gone out with her mum, the toys found a box of multi-coloured beads in her room.

"Hey guys, come look at this!" Dolly called, opening the box for everyone to see. "They're pearls to create treasures."

"I've always loved necklaces," swooned Mrs Potato Head, trying on one of the brightly coloured strands of beads. "How does it suit me?"

"Very well," replied Mr Potato Head. "You look like the Queen of Potatoes!"

"They are just so fashionable!" said Jessie, as she attached some of the beads to her cowboy hat to add a touch of glamour.

"And funny too!" laughed Woody. "You can even use them to play football." He grabbed a red bead from the box and kicked it towards Mr Potato Head.

"Mine!" called Mr Potato Head, as he caught the bead. "Are you ready? I'm going to pass it to ... Buttercup!" He launched the bead into the air, but as Buttercup the unicorn leaped into the air to get it ... *CLONK!* The bead got stuck on his horn!

When the bead didn't land on the floor, Buttercup got confused. "Huh? Where has it ended up?" he asked. He couldn't see that the bead had got stuck!

Mr Pricklepants started giggling. "It's on your horn!"

Buttercup shook his head from side to side, trying to get the bead free, but it was stuck tight. He started to worry it would never come off.

"Take it away from me," he said sadly.

Mr Pricklepants thought if they pulled hard enough the bead would come off, but even when he and the aliens pulled together, it still wouldn't budge! The toys eventually collapsed in a heap on the floor. "Nothing is working," sighed Woody.

"Wait!" said Buzz suddenly. "There is a better way." Holding a bead between his fingers, he explained, "We can thread something into the opposite hole of the bead to push Buttercup's horn out!"

"We could use my tail," Rex suggested.

Buzz thought that this was a great idea. Carefully, he threaded Rex's tail into the bead and *POP!* The bead came off.

Buttercup was delighted. "Hurray, I'm free!" he cheered, galloping around in celebration.

"Well done, you did it!" shouted Buzz. All the toys whooped and cheered, except Rex ... who was staring at the bead that was now stuck on the end of *his* tail.

He let out a big sigh. "So who's going to free me?"

A Slick Solution

In Pixie Hollow, the time had come to make the sleeping flowers open up again. Silvermist, Iridessa and Vidia flew over a field of beautiful pink flowers, all still tightly closed.

"All they need," Iridessa said, "is a little beam of light from the rising sun." She guided the light to fall directly onto a flower, and as it felt the warmth, the petals opened.

"And now, a little dew to help them wake up too!" added Silvermist.

Summoning a small whirlwind, Vidia declared, "Now let's scatter their pollen around with some...."

WHOOOSH!

"Watch it!" a voice called.

Vidia turned to see a furious Iridessa and Silvermist, covered in pollen. "Cut it out, Vidia," scowled Iridessa, as Silvermist sneezed.

Vidia smirked at them. "All this fuss over a little pollen!"

There was no time to argue though – they still had a lot of work to do. One by one, the flowers opened to the morning sun. Well, nearly all of them....

"This flower refuses to open up!" shouted Iridessa, frustrated.

"Have you tried tickling her a little?" asked Silvermist. She tickled the flower, but it didn't budge.

"I'll go call Rosetta," said Iridessa.

But Vidia didn't like to be beaten, especially by a flower! "Forget that," she said. "I'm not going to let Miss Precious Petals get the better of me! C'mon, open up!" She started forcing the petals apart. "I've almost got it...!"

"I don't think that's such a good ..." said Silvermist.

SNAP! The flower had snapped shut, trapping Vidia inside! Now she was hanging upside down with only her head sticking out. "This isn't funny!" she snarled. "Get me out of here!"

"What do we do now?" asked Iridessa.

Silvermist looked around for inspiration. "Maybe the answer is down there!" Smiling, she picked up a snail. "He'll help Vidia."

Together, they stroked the snail along the petals. Slime dripped into the flower. "This will make the petals slippery enough for you to slide out," Silvermist told Vidia.

Suddenly, Vidia slid out of the flower and landed with a bump on the ground. "Look!" smiled Iridessa. "The flower opened up."

"And you're free," Silvermist said to Vidia. "Wasn't that a great idea?"

Vidia blinked slime out of her eyes. Every part of her was covered in the stuff. She was going to need a bath! "Yeah," she said sarcastically. "Just perfect."

Disney MINNIE

The Missing Daffodils

One spring day, Daisy went over to Minnie's house to help in the garden. But when the two got outside, they found a big surprise.

"My daffodils are gone!" Minnie shrieked.

"It must be a flower prowler!" Daisy cried.

Minnie and Daisy searched for clues.

"What's this?" Daisy asked, pulling a few strands of fuzzy white hair off a bush near the daffodil patch.

"Maybe the flower prowler left it," Minnie said.

A moment later, Minnie's doorbell rang. Mickey was standing there with a big bunch of daffodils tied with a fluffy white ribbon!

"Mickey!" Minnie cried. "How could you cut down my daffodils?"

"What do you mean?" Mickey asked, confused. "I bought these at the flower shop!"

Minnie put the flowers in a vase. She was glad that Mickey wasn't the flower prowler.

Minnie, Daisy and Mickey decided to look around town for the thief.

They headed to the park and found Goofy. He had a daffodil pinned to his waistcoat.

"Hiya," Goofy called. "Do you like my flower? Mr Power has a daffodil sale on today!"

"Hmmm ..." said Minnie. "That's quite a coincidence."

They peeked through the window of Power's Flowers. The shopkeeper had a fuzzy white moustache and his shop was full of daffodils!

The friends burst inside. "Where did you get these daffodils?" Minnie demanded.

"From Mrs Pote, the farmer," Mr Power replied. "She delivers daffodils every day, but today she brought dozens of extras!"

Mr Power pointed the way to Mrs Pote's farm. "You can't miss her," he said. "She has fuzzy white hair."

Mrs Pote's farm was called Pote's Goats.

"Yes, I delivered extra daffodils today," Mrs Pote told Minnie. "My favourite goat, Flower, eats a lot of them as soon as they bloom but she must not have been very hungry today."

Mrs Pote led the friends to Flower's pen but there was no goat inside!

"She must have escaped!" Mrs Pote cried.

"There's a hole in the fence," Mickey said.

"Not only are Minnie's daffodils gone, but so is Mrs Pote's goat!" Daisy said.

"These two mysteries are connected," said Minnie. "I know who the flower prowler is!"

She pointed towards a trail of footprints.

They followed the footprints to Daisy's garden. There was Flower, happily munching away on Daisy's flowers.

"There's our flower prowler," Minnie said. "If we could only train her to like weeds!"

Disney · PIXAR

BRAVE

Princess Prankster

In the early hours of the morning, when the sun had barely peeked over the hills, DunBroch Castle echoed with the sounds of little feet on the flagstone floor. The triplets, Hamish, Harris and Hubert had been plotting a prank and had woken each other up before even the maids were awake.

They sneaked into their sister's bedroom, where Merida was fast asleep – her wild red hair spread across her pillow. The triplets stifled a giggle and carefully spread thick honey over her face. Next came the fur. The castle was full of stuffed animals from their father, the Bear King's, hunting trips. It wasn't hard for the triplets to find thick, fluffy bear hair to make their plan come to life!

As the sun finally revealed itself, with the triplets in hiding, there came a very loud scream.

"Ahhhh! I'm a bear! The witch's spell has caught me too!" Merida shouted. Her face was covered in thick fur. "But I don't feel like a bear. And I didn't eat any strange cakes." She touched her face with shaking hands and noticed the honey that was gluing it into place.

She wasn't a bear! This was a trick.

The triplets laughed loudly.

"You three!" Merida yelled. She started to run after them, but her brothers vanished in a heartbeat.

"I'll get you back for this," Merida promised angrily, wiping the mess from her skin.

The next night, when the triplets were fast asleep in their beds, there came a loud *CLANG, CLANG, CLANG.* They awoke with a start and looked up to the shadows above them, to find a ghost hovering there with a gaping, hungry mouth and big, black pits for eyes.

Outside their room, Merida hid. She had rigged her 'ghost' up with rope and was making spooky noises through a broken jug to scare her brothers. It seemed to be working too, until the sound of banging met her ears.

Merida gasped. What on earth were they doing?

She peeked into the room and found her brothers armed with their wooden swords, slashing the 'ghost' to ribbons. Bits of the 'ghost', which had actually been Merida's bedsheet, fell to the floor in tatters as the boys swished and jabbed and pounded the prank to smithereens!

Merida took off at a run, letting the rope go and leaving her brothers to fight their ghostly visitor to their hearts' content.

One thing she'd learned that night – her brothers were fearless. And it would take a whole lot more than that to scare them!

Disney · PIXAR TOY STORY 3

Bath Time

Bonnie loved creating exciting new adventures in the garden with her toys, but as a dark cloud passed overhead her mum appeared from inside the house.

It was going to rain, so Bonnie grabbed Hamm while her mum gathered up all the other toys.

Or so she thought! As Woody was carried inside, he realized Dolly had been left out on the grass!

In Bonnie's bedroom, the toys made a plan. "If it rains, Dolly will get soaked," said Woody.

"We've got to rescue her," gasped Buttercup, the unicorn.

Luckily, Woody and Buzz had lots of experience of leading rescue missions. Together, they lowered Slinky Dog out of the window, just as the rain began to fall.

Slinky's spring stretched all the way to the ground. The brave little pup caught hold of a clump of grass to stop himself springing back up and called over to Dolly.

"I knew you wouldn't leave me outside in the rain," Dolly cheered.

"Quick, take my paw," Slinky began, but just as Dolly took hold, the grass Slinky was holding broke.

Slinky sprang upwards, dragging poor Dolly across the ground and through a bush, before catapulting her into Bonnie's bedroom.

Dolly fell through the air, then landed in a messy heap on Bonnie's favourite chair.

"Nice to have you back, Dolly," said Woody, tipping his hat. Dolly flipped herself the right way up and smiled. It was nice to be back.

Suddenly, the toys heard the sound of footsteps outside the bedroom door "Quick, someone's coming!" yelled Jessie and the toys dropped just as Bonnie's mum walked in.

"Oh no, look Bonnie," said Mum, stooping to pick up the messy-looking doll. "I hadn't realized how dirty Dolly got outside." Mum shrugged as she took Dolly out of the room. "No big deal. We'll give her a bath!"

"Poor Dolly," whispered Buzz.

Woody nodded. "Uh-oh! She's gonna be soaked after all!"

Sure enough, just a few minutes later, Mum and Bonnie returned, carrying a dripping-wet Dolly. They made a little washing line from string and pegged the doll to it, then went downstairs for dinner.

Dolly looked at her friends and folded her arms, crossly. "As you can see, guys, I avoided the shower," she said. "But not the bath!"

Try as they might, the other toys couldn't help but laugh. Maybe a little bit of rainwater wasn't so bad, after all!

Disney 101 Dalmatians

The Good Thing About Rain

"Rise and shine!" cried Pongo. One by one, he nudged each of his 15 Dalmatian puppies with his nose.

The puppies yawned and stretched.

But Rolly just rolled over and slept on.

"Come on, Rolly," Pongo whispered in the pup's ear. "It's morning! Don't you want to go out?"

At the mention of the word 'out', Rolly was instantly wide awake!

Rolly was not alone. As if by magic, the sleepy group had become a pack of jumping, barking puppies. They raced together through the kitchen to the back door, where they jumped up and down, waiting for Nanny to let them out into the garden.

"Okay, here I come," said Nanny, as she made her way across the kitchen. Then she flung the door open wide and stepped out of the way to let the puppies race past.

But they didn't move. It was raining!

"Oh, go on," said Perdita, trying to nudge the pups out the door. "It's only a little water."

But they wouldn't budge.

The next morning, Patch awoke with a start. With a few sharp barks, he helped Pongo wake the other puppies. Within seconds, all 15 were crowding around the back door.

Nanny rushed to open the door again.

And once again, the puppies were very disappointed to see raindrops falling.

"Well," said Pongo with a sigh, "April showers bring May flowers!"

The next morning, the puppies weren't in any hurry to go outside. After all, it was probably still raining. They thought that all they had to look forward to was another whole day spent inside.

So, when Nanny opened the door on a sunny morning, the puppies were so surprised that they didn't know what to do.

Then, springing into action, they tumbled over one another in their rush to get out the door. They raced off in different directions, ready to sniff, dig, roll and explore.

But then, almost at once, all 15 puppies froze in their tracks. They looked around at each other, then down at themselves. What was this stuff getting all over their spotted white coats? It was brown. It was wet. It was squishy. It was mud! And it was fun!

From the doorway, Pongo and Perdita looked out at their muddy puppies and laughed.

"You know what this means, don't you?" Pongo asked Perdita.

Perdita nodded. "Baths."

Pongo smiled, watching the frolicking puppies. "Let's not tell them – just yet," he said.

Disney MINNIE

Minnie's Easter Bonnet

It was a perfect spring day and Minnie was spending it in the perfect spring way – she was making a new Easter bonnet!

"Not bad," Minnie said, admiring her new hat in the mirror. "But it's not quite right."

Minnie searched through her wardrobe and her dresser until she found an old bag of balloons. Minnie quickly blew up two – one pink and one yellow. Then she removed the feathers from her Easter bonnet and tied the balloons to it with pretty lavender ribbons.

As Minnie was putting the final touches to her creation, she spotted Mickey through her window. "Yoo-hoo, Mickey!" she cried, running outside. "I want to show you something!"

Suddenly, a gust of wind took the balloons and Minnie's bonnet up into the sky!

Minnie quickly jumped into Mickey's car. "Follow that hat!" she cried.

Mickey and Minnie drove through town, keeping their eyes on the floating bonnet.

"Oh no!" Minnie cried. She watched as a curious crow flew towards her bonnet! The bird began pecking at the pink balloon and ... *POP!* The startled crow flew off.

There was only one balloon left, but the bonnet was still floating high in the air.

Mickey and Minnie drove to the edge of town, following the bonnet as the wind carried it farther and farther away.

Soon they reached a farm and Mickey spotted a rope hanging from a fence post. Mickey grabbed the rope and made a lasso.

One .... two ... three times he tossed the lasso into the air, but the bonnet was still out of reach.

The hat zigged and zagged over the farm until the yellow balloon snagged on a weather vane on top of a barn. *POP!*

Minnie watched the bonnet drop into the branches of a tree. "Help me with this ladder, please!" she cried.

While Mickey held the ladder, Minnie carefully climbed up and found ...

... a robin sitting in her hat!

"Shoo! That's not a nest!" Minnie said.

But the robin was comfortable and wouldn't budge. Then it was joined by another robin.

"Oh, I see," Minnie said, smiling at the happy couple. She tried to be very quiet as she climbed back down the ladder.

"I should have suspected that it would end this way," Minnie sighed.

"What do you mean?" Mickey asked.

"After all," Minnie said with a laugh, "what's an Easter bonnet without a few Easter *eggs?*"

April

5

A Sleepless Sleepover

Bonnie was sleeping over at her mum's friend Betty's house and she had brought her toys to keep her company. "Oh, I love your nightcap, Sheriff!" she said, playing with her cowboy toys, Woody and Jessie.

Just then, Bonnie was called up to bed. "Let's go Jessie! The others will sleep here," said Bonnie, carrying her cowgirl toy upstairs. She left Woody, Buzz, Mr Pricklepants the hedgehog and Trixie the triceratops downstairs.

After Bonnie had left, the toys came to life.

Mr Pricklepants began to yawn and stretch. "I think it's time to go to sleep," he said. Woody agreed, but Trixie wasn't ready for bed yet.

"I can't sleep if I don't look at a computer," she complained.

"Betty doesn't have a computer," Buzz pointed out.

But Trixie already knew that. "I know!" she cried. "That means we can stay up and chat all night long!" The other toys grumbled – they wanted to go to sleep.

"Hmm, maybe we can find a way to make you feel sleepy, Trixie," wondered Woody.

"I'll read a nice book for you!" offered Mr Pricklepants. Unfortunately, the only book they could find was a recipe book and that made everyone feel hungry!

So Woody suggested another idea. "We can play a card game!" But Trixie thought that would be boring. "Exactly!" Woody laughed. "That's why it'd make you fall asleep. Let's get the cards out and see."

But the playing cards were on the top shelf of the bookshelf, out of reach of the toys. Luckily, brave Buzz and Woody were ready to accept the challenge.

"Don't worry," Buzz called down, when they had climbed halfway up. "We'll save your night's sleep!"

Finally, Buzz and Woody reached the top shelf. They pushed the playing cards towards the floor, where Mr Pricklepants had placed a cushion to catch them.

"Phew! That was a hard mission," said Buzz, climbing down from the final shelf.

"Shh!" whispered Mr Pricklepants, pointing to where Trixie was curled up on the floor. "While you were climbing, Trixie was staring at the swaying pendulum and she fell asleep!"

Buzz couldn't believe it. "All that climbing for nothing!" he moaned.

"No," smiled the hedgehog. "Now we can go to sleep too!"

But Woody and Buzz were too excited to sleep now – they wanted to explore!

Mr Pricklepants sighed ... it was going to be a long night.

Disney
DUMBO

You're Gonna Be Huge!

Dumbo sat in the corner with a big frown on his face.

"What's the matter, kid?" Timothy asked.

Dumbo just shook his head.

"You've got nothing to be sad about," Timothy continued. Dumbo didn't say anything.

"Well, if you're not going to tell me what's bugging ya, I guess I'll just have to figure it out for myself," Timothy said. "I know!" he shouted. "You're hungry?"

Dumbo shook his head.

"Thirsty, then?"

Dumbo shook his head again.

"Concerned about the June-bug population in Saskatchewan?" Timothy suggested.

Dumbo shook his head doubly hard.

"Well, then," Timothy concluded. "It can only be one thing. It pains me to say it, but I think you have a case of 'feeling sorry for myself-itis'."

Dumbo's large ears pricked up.

"Yes," Timothy continued. "It's a dangerous disease that has affected many of us. Even the strongest cannot avoid it."

Dumbo looked to his left and to his right, then pointed to himself.

"Yes, that's right – you!" Timothy said. "And I bet I know what's got you down – your above-average ear size."

Dumbo nodded.

"And the fact that people make fun of you," Timothy continued.

Dumbo nodded even more.

"And, on top of all that," Timothy said, "you've been separated from your mother."

A tear started to form in Dumbo's eye.

"Don't feel sorry for yourself!" Timothy ordered. Dumbo looked up, surprised.

"You know why?" Timothy asked his friend. "Because one day you're gonna be huge!"

Dumbo was surprised.

"We're talking autographs, your name in lights. They're gonna eat their hats for the way they treated you," Timothy predicted.

Dumbo looked nervous.

"I don't mean eat their hats for real," Timothy explained. "It's just a figure of speech. Not that some of them wouldn't deserve having to eat their hats. But that's not what we're talking about. They're gonna be really sorry they treated you so bad, understand?"

Dumbo nodded his head.

"All right then," Timothy said, with a smile. "Feeling better?"

Dumbo smiled back at Timothy, then nodded his head doubly hard as visions of success, happiness – and being with his mother again – filled his head.

A Special Apple

Rosetta was busy sprucing up some flowers when she heard a familiar voice. It was Chloe, another garden fairy – one who loved getting muddy and usually got everyone else around her muddy too! "There you go!" she was saying. "Now you're all bright and shiny."

That wasn't the sort of thing Chloe usually said! Curious, Rosetta flew over to see what Chloe was doing. Then she gasped. Chloe was painting a red apple – the glossiest and shiniest apple Rosetta had ever seen! "One last touch and then you'll be perfect," Chloe said, tenderly dabbing the last patch with paint.

"Chloe!" Rosetta flew down. "What are you doing?"

Chloe laughed. "Why, my job, of course!"

"Since when have you acted like a real garden fairy?" Rosetta asked.

Chloe laughed. "I know it must seem strange. Normally I'm not as organized as you guys, and my clothes are splattered with mud."

"You mean covered with mud," Rosetta corrected, smiling.

Chloe patted the apple. "But today I'm going to do impeccable work and do it with style." She let loose a stream of magic that made the apple sparkle in the sunshine. "Just like you!" she told Rosetta.

Rosetta was flattered. "Well, I sure am happy to hear you say that, rosebud. After all, you couldn't choose a better role model."

"Well, I'm off to work," Chloe said, giving the apple one last pat.

"Bravo," Rosetta told her, impressed. "You've done a great job on this apple. Its peel is so red and smoo –" Then she gasped. "A hole!" True enough, there in the side of the beautiful shiny red apple was a small hole. "How could you have overlooked it?"

"Um ..." said Chloe, looking guilty. "Actually –"

But she didn't get a chance to finish. "Don't worry. I'll teach you how to cover it up," Rosetta said kindly.

"Wait!" cried Chloe. "There's no need!"

"Are you kidding?" Rosetta laughed. "All it takes is a pinch of pixie dust...." She dabbed the dust over the hole. "Then...."

POP!

Suddenly, a long green worm popped out of the hole, right in front of Rosetta's face! She shrieked and fell backwards.

"Umm ... I forgot to tell you ..." admitted Chloe. "This apple is the home of my good friend!" She tickled the worm under its chin and it wriggled happily.

Rosetta couldn't help smiling. "Now I understand all that special attention!"

Disney · PIXAR
FINDING NEMO

A Change of Scenery

Dr Sherman had left for the day when Gill called everyone together for a Tank Gang meeting.

"We need to make some changes around here," Gill began. "We've all been living in this glass box for how long now? And every day we stare at the same scenery – the same volcano, the same sunken ship, the same treasure chest and tiki hut. Well, seeing as how we can't change what's in our tank, I propose we rearrange things a little. Who's with me?"

"Great idea!" cried Peach the starfish.

"I'm with you," said Deb. "And Flo is too," she added, pointing at her reflection.

Everyone agreed. "We can completely transform the place," said Bloat.

"All right!" said Gill. "Then how about we start with the tiki hut? Bloat, you hoist it up. Gurgle and I will help you move it. The rest of you guys tell us where you think it should go."

Gill, Bloat and Gurgle swam over to the tiki hut. Bloat wriggled his body underneath it and blew himself up, hoisting the hut a few centimetres off the gravel. Meanwhile, Gill and Gurgle stationed themselves on either side of the hut and prepared to push.

"Let's try it over there," said Peach, pointing to a far corner of the tank.

With blown-up Bloat acting as a cart underneath the hut, Gill and Gurgle pushed the tiki hut into the corner.

"Oh, no," said Deb, "that's all wrong. Can we see what it looks like over there?" She pointed to the opposite corner of the tank.

So Gill, Gurgle and Bloat worked together to move the tiki hut again.

"That's a disaster!" cried Jacques.

"Yeah, he's right," agreed Nemo.

Gill, Gurgle and Bloat were getting worn out by all the moving. "Can we all just agree on where it should go?" said Gill. "And quickly?"

"Ooh! I know!" said Deb. "Bring it over this way." She led Gill, Gurgle and Bloat over to a shady spot next to some plastic plants. "Put it down here," she said. So they did.

"I like it!" exclaimed Peach.

"The perfect spot," said Jacques.

"Mmm-hmm," said Bubbles.

Gill stepped back and looked around. "Guys, this is where it was in the first place!"

"Is it?" asked Peach.

Deb giggled. "Well, no wonder it just seems to fit here!"

The other fish nodded – except for Gill, who sighed in frustration. And that was the end of the tank redecoration for the evening.

Disney
THE
LION KING

Pictures in the Stars

Ever since Mufasa had died and Simba had left the Pride Lands, Timon and Pumbaa had been Simba's only friends – but what fun the three of them had together. One of their favourite things to do after their evening meal was to lie on their backs in the tall grass and gaze up at the night sky, looking for shapes in the stars.

"Okay, okay, I got one," said Pumbaa, lifting a foreleg to point to one area of the sky. "See, over there, that long, thin, curving outline? It's a big, juicy, delicious slug!" Pumbaa licked and smacked his lips, imagining the taste of a slug snack. "Mmm-mmm!"

Simba chuckled. "Pumbaa, how can you still be hungry? We just ate!"

Pumbaa shrugged. "It's a gift," he said.

Timon cleared his throat. "I hate to disagree with you, Pumbaa my friend, but that's no slug you see up there. That's an elephant's trunk. If you follow that curving line of stars, you see it connects with the elephant's head at one end. And there are the ears," Timon said, tracing it all out with his finger, "and there are the tusks."

Simba chuckled again. "Somebody still has his mind on that elephant stampede we almost got flattened by this afternoon," he said.

"Hey ..." Timon said defensively, "what's that supposed to mean?"

"Oh, no offence, Timon," Simba replied. "I just think it's funny that the things you and Pumbaa see in the stars just happen to be the same things that are on your mind at the time."

"Ooh! Ooh! I've got another one!" Pumbaa interrupted. "A big bunch of tasty berries right over there," he said, pointing at a grouping of stars.

"See what I mean?" Simba said to Timon.

"All right, all right, Mr Smarty-Pants," Timon replied. "So what do you see in the stars?"

"Well, now, let's see," said Simba, gazing intently at the tons of tiny lights twinkling down at them. There were so many that you could see practically any shape in them that you wanted to. It all depended on how you looked at them. But just to annoy Timon, Simba wanted to find something really bright and clear. Something Timon couldn't deny that he saw too.

Just at that moment, a shooting star streaked the entire length of the night sky.

"I see a bright streak of light rocketing across the sky!" exclaimed Simba.

"Ooh! Me, too!" said Pumbaa. "Timon, do you see it?"

Timon had to admit that he did. "Yeah, yeah, I see it," he muttered grudgingly. "Ha-ha. Very funny, Simba."

Winnie the Pooh

Piglet's Pink Eggs

Winnie the Pooh had dropped in to visit Piglet, who was busy dyeing Easter eggs. "Easter is coming up, you know," Piglet explained.

On Piglet's kitchen table were six little cups. Pooh peered inside them. Each one held a different-coloured dye – blue, green, red, yellow, orange and pink.

Then Pooh noticed a basket filled with some eggs Piglet had already dyed. Every one of them was pink.

"Would you like to dye the last egg, Pooh?" Piglet asked.

"Oh yes," Pooh replied. "I would like that very much."

So Piglet showed him how to place his egg in the wire dipper, and how to use the dipper to dip the egg into the cups of dye.

"What colour should I dye my egg?" Pooh asked.

Piglet smiled. "That's the fun of it, Pooh," he said. "You can choose any colour you want!"

Pooh looked over at Piglet's basket of pink eggs. Then he looked back at the cups of dye.

"You don't seem to have a yellow egg yet," said Pooh. "So I think I will dye mine yellow."

"Good idea!" Piglet exclaimed.

Pooh dipped his egg into the cup filled with yellow dye. He let it sit in the dye for a few minutes, then lifted it out again.

"It worked!" cried Pooh. "Piglet, look! What do you think of my yellow egg?"

"Oh Pooh, it's great," Piglet said. "It's b-bright ... a-and it's sunny ... and i-it's very, very yellow, isn't it?"

Piglet was quiet for a moment. Then he cleared his throat.

"D-do you think ... I don't know for sure, mind you. But do you think it could maybe use a little bit of, say, pink?" Piglet said.

"I think you're right," Pooh said. So he dipped his egg into the cup filled with pink dye. He let it sit there for just a few seconds before lifting it out. The little bit of pink dye on top of the yellow dye made the egg look pinkish-yellow.

"Hmm," said Piglet. "That's very pretty. But – if you don't mind my saying so, Pooh – I think it could use just a little more pink."

"Okay," said Pooh. So he dipped the egg back into the pink dye. This time he let it sit for five whole minutes before lifting it out. More pink dye on top of the yellow-and-pink colour made the egg look as pink as pink could be.

"Well, what do you think?" asked Pooh.

"Perfect!" Piglet exclaimed.

They let Pooh's egg dry. Then Piglet put it in the basket with all the other pink eggs.

"Well, what do you know," said Piglet. "It fits in so nicely!"

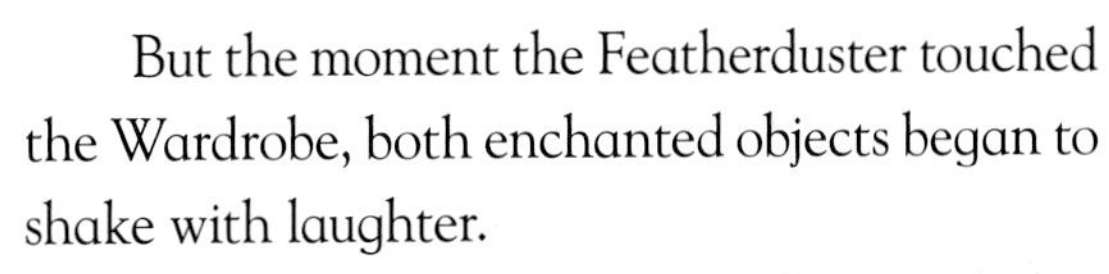

Castle Cleaning

It was a particularly warm and sunny April morning, and Belle and Chip the teacup were gazing out of a castle window at the blue sky and the budding trees and plants.

"Well, Chip," Belle said, "it is definitely spring at last. And you know what that means, don't you?"

Chip hopped up and down in excitement. "It means we get to play outside?" he asked.

Belle laughed. "Well, yes, that too," she replied. "But first it's time to do some spring cleaning."

So Belle got together a few cleaning supplies. "I think I'll start in the dining room," she said. Belle pulled the silverware out of the silver cabinet and began polishing a fork.

"Ooh!" exclaimed the enchanted fork. "Careful! Ouch! Not so hard around the tines!"

"Oh, dear!" said Belle. "I'm sorry." She gently polished the rest of the utensils.

Next, Belle gathered all the dishes. But when she dipped the first enchanted dish into the soapy water in the sink, it cried out, "Ahh! Too cold! Too cold!"

Belle gasped ... and hurried to add more warm water to the sink.

After finishing the dishes, Belle moved to her bedroom, where she began dusting the Wardrobe with the Featherduster.

But the moment the Featherduster touched the Wardrobe, both enchanted objects began to shake with laughter.

"Hee, hee! Ha, ha!" said the Wardrobe. "That tickles!"

"You've got that right!" the Featherduster said.

Belle went to the library to take a break from her cleaning. Chip hopped in.

"Oh, Chip," she said wearily, "spring cleaning in this castle is a challenge. I'm not used to cleaning enchanted objects!"

Chip giggled. "And I guess we're not used to it either. We always just clean ourselves!"

"Clean yourselves?" said Belle.

That gave her an idea. If the enchanted objects could clean themselves, they could clean other objects too!

Belle called the enchanted objects together. "I wonder if I could ask your help with a little project," Belle began.

Soon Belle had a small army of enchanted objects cleaning everything else in the castle. In a few short hours, the entire castle had been cleaned, and Belle and Chip were relaxing in the library.

"Well," Belle said as she sank into a comfortable chair, "you know what they say – 'Many hands make light work.' And a little enchantment never hurt either!"

Disney Princess
MULAN

The Magic of Girls

After brave Mulan saved China from the Huns, she returned to her village. But as time went by, the villagers forgot how courageous she had been. To them it seemed that Mulan was just a girl whereas the men in the village were the warriors – the heroes.

One day a group of children rushed to Mulan at the village wishing-well.

"Jin is trapped in a cave!" they cried.

Mulan dropped her bucket of water instantly. "Let's hurry to him!"

At the cave, there were already men gathering.

"A rock fell," explained the blacksmith. "It's blocking the boy's way out. But you should leave, Mulan. This is no place for a girl."

Mulan didn't leave. She wanted to help. As the men tried dislodging the rock they told her to fetch some water. But Mulan had a better idea. She hurried back to the village and found her spade. With Mushu the dragon riding on her shoulder, she returned to the cave.

Ignoring the men, Mulan began digging a hole near the cave entrance. The men were confused about what she was doing....

"I'm going around the rock," she said. "It's too heavy for anyone to push aside!"

The men frowned as she shovelled piles of dirt to one side. Soon, she had made a hole big enough to crawl through. Mushu led the way, his little flames lighting up the cave within.

"Mulan! Mushu!" squealed Jin, no longer hiding in fear of the dark. "Look what I found!"

Jin took Mulan by the hand and guided her to a mountain of gold pieces and beautiful gems.

"Wow!" gasped Mulan. "Jin, this will be a fortune to our village!" She picked Jin up and swung him around in celebration.

When they left through their little tunnel, the men were still on the other side waiting for news.

"Everything's okay!" Mulan declared. She was carrying handfuls of sparkling jewels alongside Jin. Handing them to the blacksmith, she looked him straight in the eye and said, "Now I'll go back to the village and fetch water."

The blacksmith felt foolish. Of course Mulan was helpful and brave! Girls were courageous too.

"I'm sorry," he said, bowing his head.

Mulan accepted his apology and went back to the village, where a massive celebration was thrown in her honour. She had saved them from the evil of the Huns and now she had brought them riches.

One thing was for sure – Mulan was special and from that day on, the people remembered just how magical girls could be.

Disney · Pixar Toy Story 3

King of the Rodeo

Jessie bounced on Bullseye's back, holding his reins with one hand and waving her hat with the other. "Yippeeee!" she cheered, giggling as Bullseye bucked and kicked.

"What are you doing?" asked Dolly.

"It's a rodeo," Woody explained. "Jessie has to ride Bullseye for as long as she can, while Bullseye tries to throw her off."

Dolly's eyes went wide. "Looks like fun!" she said. "Can I try?"

Mr Potato Head and Mr Pricklepants scurried up behind her. They wanted to join in with the rodeo, too.

"It's not as easy as it looks," Woody warned.

"We know all about rodeos, sheriff," Mr Potato Head said.

"I can play this part to perfection," Mr Pricklepants insisted.

Mr Potato Head pointed an accusing finger at Woody. "Maybe you're afraid we'll ride better than you!"

Woody shrugged. Oh well, they'd asked for it!

A few moments later, Dolly gasped as she shot off Bullseye's back and thumped against the wall. Mr Pricklepants was hobbling away, while Mr Potato Head hunted around for his missing nose and eye. Woody was right – the rodeo really wasn't as easy as it looked!

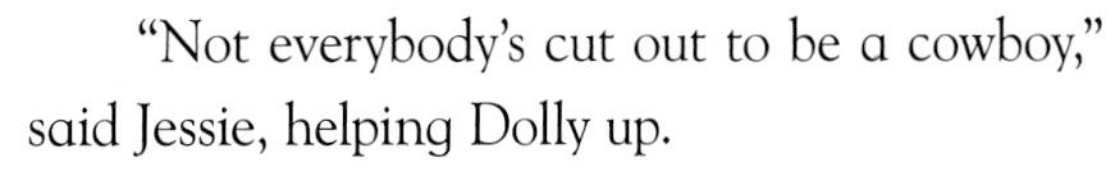

"Not everybody's cut out to be a cowboy," said Jessie, helping Dolly up.

It looked like the rodeo adventures were over for the day, until a voice rang out behind Woody. "Can I try, too?"

Woody turned to find Slinky Dog looking up at him. "Dachshunds can't ride horses!" Woody said, but Slinky shook his head.

"That's not quite what I had in mind," the springy pup said. "I want to take Bullseye's place!"

Woody wasn't sure. He'd never tried rodeo with a dog before! Still, he climbed onto Slinky's spring and held on. "Climb on, Jessie," Slinky said. "There's room for both of you!" Jessie hopped on behind Woody.

"Ready?" asked Slinky. The cowboy and cowgirl nodded. "Here we go!"

BOING! Slinky kicked, stretching his spring out. Woody and Jessie yelled in fright as they were shot upwards into the air at incredible speed.

Woody and Jessie crashed down on the floor just as the other toys started laughing. "Now who's king of the rodeo?" Slinky said, smiling proudly.

Jessie took off her hat and gave it to Slinky. She and Woody both giggled. When it came to being a rodeo star, no one could compete with their stretchy pup pal!

April

14

The Feeble Fireflies

The sun was setting on another day in Pixie Hollow. Iridessa smiled as she flew over the field of sunflowers where the baby fireflies slept. In her arms she held a bucket of light, gathered from the last rays of the sun. "Come on, little fellas!" she called. "Fly and shine!"

But the field was silent.

Iridessa frowned. "Hey! Where'd you all go?"

Flying down for a closer look, she was surprised to see the baby bugs fast asleep and snoring! "Wake up!" she said, tapping gently on one of them. "It's time to shine!" But the firefly simply turned over in its sleep!

"But ... look at all this lovely light!" Iridessa couldn't believe it. The fireflies were always keen to get up and receive the light that made them shine! But tonight all they wanted to do was sleep! What was going on?

"Iridessa!" Tinker Bell flew to meet her friend. "Why aren't the fireflies glowing?"

Iridessa didn't want to admit she didn't know the answer! "Everything's under control!" she fibbed.

"It looks like they're tired," said Tink, examining a firefly as it slept on the yellow petals of the flower.

Iridessa sighed. "They don't want to glow, and I can't figure out why."

Tinker Bell felt sorry for her friend. Then a thought struck her. Back when she had been determined to change her talent, Iridessa had shown her how to bring light to the fireflies. But Tink's clumsiness had resulted in a ray of light attaching itself to her own bottom! And the baby fireflies had been so excited, they'd chased her for miles! Maybe Iridessa could try doing that?

Quickly, Tinker Bell explained her idea. Iridessa blushed. "Thanks, but I'll try and come up with a more dignified solution!"

Tink shrugged. She flew off, leaving Iridessa with the bucket of light still in her hands.

ZZZ ... SNORE ... the baby fireflies were determined to sleep!

Iridessa felt desperate. She didn't want to try Tink's idea, but it was the only one she had! Looking around to make sure there were no other fairies to see, she scooped out a handful of light from the bucket, and stuck it to her bottom – *ZAP!*

Instantly, there was a stirring from the fireflies below as they saw the light. In an excited flurry, they set off after Iridessa, who shared the light from her bucket as she flew.

Iridessa was delighted! Once again the fireflies would light up the night in Pixie Hollow. She just hoped nobody would see her glowing bottom!

April

15

Disney Lady and the TRAMP

Tony and the Tramp

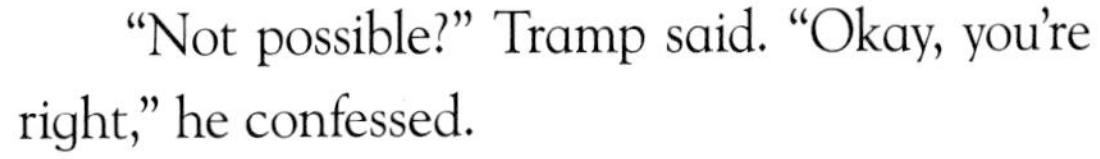

Tramp licked the last of the tomato pasta sauce from his chin. "So, what do you think, Pidge?" he asked Lady.

"That was the most wonderful meal I've ever had," Lady gushed.

"What did I tell ya?" Tramp boasted. "There's no one in the world who can cook up a meal like Tony!"

"I couldn't agree with you more," Lady said. "Can I ask you a question?"

"Sure thing," Tramp said. "Ask away!"

"I was just wondering," Lady began, "how you and Tony met."

"How I met Tony?" Tramp laughed. "Now that's a story!"

"I bet!" Lady said.

"Well, see, it goes like this," Tramp began. "It was a cold and snowy night. I don't think it had ever been that cold before, and I know it hasn't been since. I had been walking uphill for miles. Icicles were hanging from the tip of my nose."

"Wait a minute!" Lady interrupted. "You were walking for miles – uphill? In this town?"

"That's right!" Tramp said. "You've never seen the likes of it."

"Exactly!" Lady told him. "You know why?"

Tramp shook his head.

"Because it isn't possible! There are no big hills around here!" Lady said.

"Not possible?" Tramp said. "Okay, you're right," he confessed.

"So, then, what's the truth?" Lady asked.

"The truth is," Tramp began, "I wasn't always the slick, handsome devil you see before you."

"Is that right?" Lady was amused.

"And this one afternoon I was being harassed by a group of mangy mutts who outnumbered me ten to one. So, I took off as fast as my paws could carry me. And as they were chasing me, along came this dogcatcher!"

"Oh, no!" Lady cried.

"Exactly!" Tramp continued. "The mutts scattered out of sight, so I didn't have *them* to worry about anymore. But now the dogcatcher was closing in! I thought I was a goner!"

"What happened?" Lady asked.

"Then Tony came running out with a bowl of steaming hot pasta," Tramp explained. "He told the dogcatcher I was his dog. The dogcatcher didn't believe him. But, when Tony put the bowl of pasta down in front of me, he had no choice. Let me tell you, I thought I'd died and gone to heaven."

"I can relate to that," Lady said, recalling the meal.

"And the rest," Tramp said, "as they say, is history!"

"And a tasty one at that!" Lady concluded.

April

16

Peter Pan

Should I Stay or Should I Go?

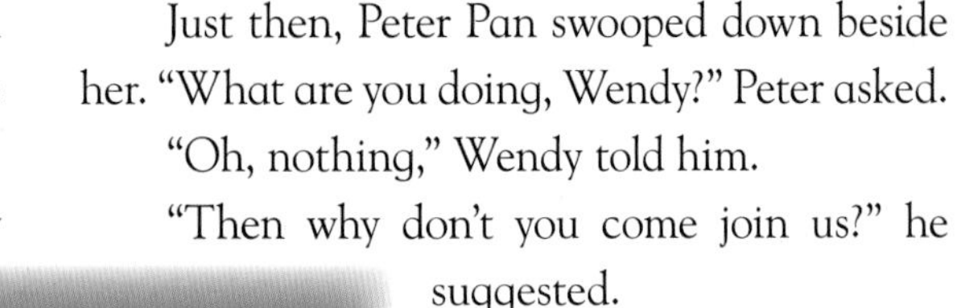

Wendy sat watching Michael and John play with Peter Pan and the rest of the Lost Boys.

"John and Michael seem so happy," Wendy said to herself. "And why wouldn't they? Never Land is such a beautiful place, and the flying is so much fun!

"Still," she had to admit, "it is also dangerous. Who knows what sort of trouble we could get into, especially with Captain Hook running about?

"And," Wendy said, "I don't think that Tinker Bell likes me very much."

Wendy considered this, then burst out, "What am I talking about? I'm making it sound like it's an awful place, but the truth is, Never Land is the most wonderful place on Earth!

"Perhaps that explains it!" Wendy suddenly realized. "Maybe I really want to stay in Never Land, but in my heart of hearts I know I shouldn't. After all, Mother and Father must miss us terribly. And we miss them too! Oh, and what about Nana?" Wendy began to fret. "She must worry about us endlessly!

"That settles it!" Wendy stood up abruptly. "We must leave for home immediately.

"But if I stay –" Wendy stopped herself. "I'll never have to grow up!

"Then again, I always wanted to be an adult someday," she concluded.

Just then, Peter Pan swooped down beside her. "What are you doing, Wendy?" Peter asked.

"Oh, nothing," Wendy told him.

"Then why don't you come join us?" he suggested.

"I will," Wendy told him. "In a minute."

"All right! But last one there is a rotten –" Peter took off before he could finish his sentence.

"How can I ever leave Peter and the Lost Boys?" Wendy wondered. "They need me so much.

"But so do our parents," she quickly reminded herself. "Should I stay?" she wondered out loud. "Or should I go?"

Wendy's eyes fell upon a daisy. She bent over and pulled it out of the ground. If she couldn't decide on her own, maybe the flower could help. "Should I stay?" she asked as she pulled a petal from the daisy. "Or should I go?" she asked as she pulled a second petal from the daisy.

Wendy did this over and over again until there was only one petal remaining on the daisy.

"Well," she said, "this flower says we should go back home. And I suppose it's right. We'll go back ... but maybe not just this minute."

Wendy stood up. "Hey, Peter, wait for me!"

And with that, she flew off after Peter, her mind at ease at last.

Disney Princess The Little Mermaid

Ariel Changes the Tune

Sebastian tapped his claw on a piece of coral and cleared his throat. But the mermaids kept talking as if the little crab were not even there. With a heavy sigh, Sebastian grabbed a huge conch shell. After a lot of effort he managed to hoist it to his mouth and blow.

The shell sounded like a giant horn. The mermaid princesses looked startled, and, to Sebastian's relief, they stopped talking.

"Shall we begin?" the small crab asked calmly. He was anxious to start rehearsing. King Triton's daughters had amazing singing voices, but they still had not decided on the right song to sing for their father's birthday. And there were just a few days left before the celebration!

Sebastian raised his claw and was about to bring it down to start the vocal warm-up when Aquata interrupted him.

"Ariel's not here," she said.

"Oh, Ariel!" Sebastian cried. Ariel was constantly swimming off on her own and holding things up.

"Do you want us to find her?" Arista asked.

"No." Sebastian sighed dramatically. "Then you will all be lost, and I don't know what I would tell your father."

"We wouldn't get lost," Attina protested.

"We *always* show up right on time," Adella added. The other sisters nodded their heads in agreement.

"Why do we have to sit around and wait for her?" Alana grumbled. The rest of her sisters nodded angrily.

"Girls, girls!" Sebastian said, trying to calm them down. He wished they could go ahead without Ariel, but her voice was by far the most beautiful.

Suddenly, Ariel swam up with Flounder.

"I hope you weren't waiting for me," she said.

"Ariel!" cried Sebastian. He didn't know whether he should be angry or relieved.

"Where have you been?" Aquata put her hands on her scaly hips.

"We still don't have a song for father!" Attina added.

"We do now!" Ariel said cheerfully. She couldn't tell them, but she had been to the surface. It was forbidden. But she had got something very special from her seagull friend Scuttle today. A new song! Ariel began singing the human tune. After only a moment, Ariel's sisters began to sing along.

Sebastian closed his eyes and listened. The song was perfect! "Where did you learn it?" he asked when they were done.

Ariel looked at Flounder. "A little bird told me," she said with a wink.

April

18

A Question of Colour

One bright, sunny day, Fawn and Rosetta were hanging out at Fairy Camp.

"Rosetta," Fawn asked, turning to her friend. "Would you do me a favour?"

Rosetta was sat on a toadstool, powdering her nose. "Of course!"

Fawn showed her a beautiful white butterfly perched on a table. The rest of the table was filled with paintbrushes and acorn cups full of paint. "Would you look after this butterfly for a while? I need to go get something."

"Sure thing, buttercup," she smiled.

"Thanks," said Fawn as she flew off. "I'll be back in a wingbeat!"

Rosetta went over to the table where the white butterfly was waiting patiently.

Fawn must be planning to paint its wings, thought Rosetta. Well, she had lots of experience in painting flowers. Surely painting butterflies wasn't any different?

Rosetta picked up the paintbrush. "It'll be a surprise for Fawn," she told the butterfly, who looked alarmed. As soon as the first drip of paint touched the butterfly's wings, it started flapping wildly. "Eeek!" cried Rosetta as the paint splatted her dress!

After a moment, the butterfly calmed down, but Rosetta was cross. "That was so rude!" she scolded, wagging her finger at it. Then she realized. "Wait a sec! Maybe you don't care for these colours!" If there was one thing Rosetta was good at, it was style. "Don't worry," she told the butterfly, "I'll find just the right shades for you."

Curious, the butterfly flew down to watch Rosetta mixing paints on the table. "Periwinkle lilac and bellflower pink," she announced. "They're soft and elegant."

The butterfly nodded enthusiastically.

"I'm so glad you like them," Rosetta smiled. She dipped her paintbrush into the pink paint and reached towards a white wing....

Flap, flap, splash!

"What's got into you?" cried Rosetta. "My colours were perfect!"

"Rosetta!" Fawn flew into the clearing. "Don't tell me you tried to paint that butterfly!"

"Yes!" said Rosetta, dripping with paint. "I wanted to do you a favour, but that naughty little creature ..."

"... suffers from ticklish wings," finished Fawn, trying not to smile. She showed Rosetta the thing she had fetched. "That's why I got the flower-sprayer!"

Rosetta couldn't help laughing. She looked down at herself, splattered with paint. "Well, at least I picked colours that look good on me!"

Disney Princess

Jasmine

A Rich Friendship

In the streets of Agrabah, three orphans felt their stomachs rumbling with hunger.

"I'll go find something to eat," said Jenna to her brother and sister, Raf and Salima.

Jenna walked around until she found herself outside the palace grounds. "Imagine living there. I bet you'd get to eat whatever you wanted."

She noticed a tree towering above the palace wall. It was full of fruit!

"Lunch!" said Jenna excitedly. When she'd plucked all the fruit from the lower branches, she climbed higher ... and higher ... until she slipped and tumbled into the palace gardens.

Jenna clambered up and turned to find the Princess standing there.

"I'm Jasmine," she said. "Are you okay?"

Jenna was struck by Jasmine's beauty and grace as she whispered her own name. She then started walking away embarrassed, but felt a pain in her ankle.

"You're hurt!" gasped Jasmine. "Please, come with me."

The Royal Doctor checked Jenna's ankle carefully. "You need two days' rest," he declared.

"My brother and sister are waiting for me!" Jenna explained, as Jasmine put her in bed.

"They can come here," promised Jasmine.

"But I don't want to be a burden on you," Jenna insisted, feeling out of place in such a grand palace.

Jasmine told her it would be fine and sent the magic carpet to fetch Jenna's siblings.

At dinner they ate with joy. There were so many delicious things to try, and they didn't waste a bite. But Jenna was aware the luxuries could all be over soon.

Jasmine told the orphans the story of how she had met Aladdin on the streets before they'd married. He had been just like them, so there was hope yet!

The next day, Jasmine took Jenna to the palace menagerie and showed her all the animals. They warmed to her instantly – particularly a baby elephant the Princess had adopted, who had lost his parents.

"He's always sad," Jasmine said softly. "We think he's lonely."

Jenna wrapped her arms round the elephant's neck and hugged him. "Poor boy."

Days later, when Jenna's ankle had healed, she knew it was time to leave.

"Will you stay?" Jasmine asked her. "You and your family? I think the animals need you."

Jenna's heart did a somersault. "Oh yes!" she cried.

And from that day forward, the orphans always had a safe place in the world, at Jasmine's palace, and delicious food in their bellies.

April

20

Disney Princess Snow White and the Seven Dwarfs

The Prettiest Flower

One morning, Bashful went out to pick the prettiest flower he could find. Suddenly, he heard a noise just over the hill.

"*AH-CHOO!*"

Bashful climbed the hill and saw his friend on the other side.

"These darn flowers are making me sneeze," said Sneezy. "But it's worth it – because I've picked the prettiest flower for Snow White's hair." He showed Bashful the white orchid he'd picked.

"That sure is pretty," said Bashful. "But I've got a flower for her too. It's even prettier."

Bashful showed Sneezy the rosebud he'd picked. Then he blushed pinker than its petals.

"*AH-CHOO!* Yours is pretty too," said Sneezy. "Let's go home and see which one Snow White likes best."

On the path back to their little cottage, Sneezy and Bashful came upon Doc, Happy and Sleepy. They were all arguing about something.

"Snow White bikes liolets," insisted Doc. "I mean she likes violets!"

Happy laughed. "No. She likes daisies!"

"I think she likes muuuuums," said Sleepy with a yawn.

"You would think that!" grumbled a voice behind them. It was Grumpy. He held a long stem with small pastel blossoms.

"That's the perfect flower for you, Grumpy," said Doc. "Snapdragons!"

"Very funny!" Grumpy snapped.

When they all arrived at their house, they saw Dopey.

"Dopey, what's behind your back?" Doc asked.

Dopey showed them a single yellow tulip.

"Another flower!" cried Happy.

When the Seven Dwarfs went inside, they found Snow White in the kitchen.

"We all wanted to thank you for being so good to us," said Doc. "So we each picked a flower for your hair."

"Now it's your turn to pick the flower you like best," said Grumpy.

Snow White felt terrible. She loved all the Dwarfs and she didn't want to hurt any of their feelings by choosing one flower over another.

"I have an idea," she told them. "Put all of your flowers down on the table, and go outside for five minutes. When you come back in, I'll be wearing the flower I think is the prettiest."

The Dwarfs went outside. When they came back in, they gasped in surprise. Snow White had made a flower crown.

She'd found a way to wear all their flowers!

"I love every one of your flowers!" she told them. "Just like I love each and every one of you!"

Disney MINNIE

The Self-Fulfilling Bad Luck

Minnie Mouse was watching her best friend Daisy Duck perform her routine in the rhythmic gymnastics competition. Miss Wellness, her gymnastics coach, gave Daisy a thumbs-up – Daisy was doing a great job! The crowd held its breath as the final move, a daring somersault, approached....

Meanwhile, on the road outside the sports hall, a lorry turned to avoid hitting a skunk, making the back doors burst open and releasing a flock of exotic birds into the air!

Just as Daisy was performing her final move, a toucan flew in through the open window and crashed into her! Daisy fell in a tangle of feathers.

She was furious. "Disqualified!" shouted the judge. Daisy had two more rounds to go, but she hadn't scored a single point for her routine!

"It's not your fault," Minnie told her.

"With such bad luck," Daisy muttered, "I don't think I have any chance."

Two days later, Daisy's friends were worried about her. "She's convinced she's jinxed!" Minnie said. "Yesterday, a fox cut her off when she was crossing the street, making her bump into an ice-cream vendor and miss the bus!" She sighed. "She's even stopped going to gymnastics practice."

They had to do something. But when they went round to Daisy's house, she wouldn't even open the front door! The friends needed a new plan, and luckily Minnie had an idea....

The next day, Minnie persuaded Daisy to take a walk with her to see a very special person. "Dr Lucky is an expert in jinxology," she told her friend.

Daisy wasn't sure it was a good idea, but Dr Lucky listened to her worries and then told her, "This is a serious case of self-fulfilling bad luck!" He gave her a good-luck charm to help reverse the problem. Daisy was thrilled – but something about Dr Lucky seemed familiar....

Daisy went back to the gymnastics competition for another try at her routine. This time it went perfectly! The judges awarded her 10 out of 10! Daisy was sure it was because of her good-luck charm – and then she realized there was a message inside. She opened it and read, "Bad luck only happens when ..."

"... you stop believing in yourself," finished Miss Wellness, with a twinkle in her eye. She had been disguised as Dr Lucky!

"You mean there is no Dr Lucky?" asked Daisy, amazed.

"The important thing is that your bad luck is gone," smiled Miss Wellness. "Now, go off and celebrate!"

April

22

Disney

Bambi

First Impressions

Bambi was just discovering the wonders of the forest. His mother had brought him to a little clearing in the trees. The sudden sunshine and bright green grass surprised and pleased him, and he bounded around on his still-wobbly legs, feeling the warm sun on his back and the soft grass under his hooves. While his mother grazed nearby, Bambi began to explore.

He found a patch of green grass and clover, and he bent down to eat. This was not an easy feat, as his long legs made it difficult for his little neck to reach the ground. When his nose was a few centimetres from the tips of the grass, he suddenly leaped backwards in alarm. A leaf had just sprung up from the patch of grass and had landed a few feet away. *A hopping leaf?* he wondered. He followed it and, as soon as he drew close, the leaf hopped away from him again!

Bambi looked around at where his mother stood, still grazing. She seemed to think they were in no great danger. So, he followed the leaf all the way to the edge of the clearing, where a wide brook babbled over craggy rocks.

Bambi's fascination with the hopping leaf faded as he approached the brook. Water cascaded over the rocks, bubbling and frothing in shallow pools. He took a step closer and felt his foot touch a rock at the edge of the water.

Suddenly, the rock moved! It shuffled towards the water and then – *PLOP!* – jumped right in and swam away.

Bambi was dumbfounded as he watched it dive beneath the surface and vanish. He stared at the spot where the rock had been for a moment, and then stooped down to have a drink, widening his stance in order to do so.

Suddenly, he jumped back in alarm. There in the water, staring right back up at him, was a little deer! Cautiously he approached again, and there it was!

Bambi turned and bounded back across the clearing to his mother.

"Mama! Mama!" he cried breathlessly. "You will never guess what I have seen!"

His mother lifted her head and gazed at him with her clear, bright eyes.

"First," he said, "first I saw a jumping leaf. Then, I saw a rock with legs that walked right into the water and swam away! And then," he continued in amazement, "and then I saw a little deer who lives right in the water! He's right over there, Mama!"

His mother nuzzled her son, thinking over what he had said. Then she laughed gently.

"Darling," she said, "I think you have just seen your first grasshopper, your first turtle and your very own reflection!"

April

23

Sweet Dreams, Rosetta!

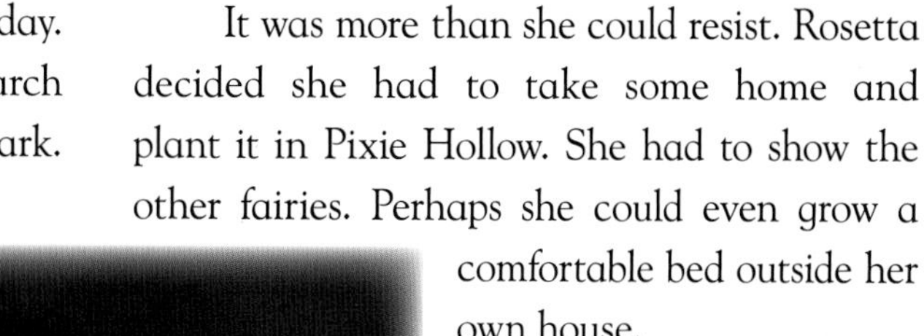

Rosetta was tired! It had been a busy day. She'd flown all over Never Land in search of plants for her garden, and now it was dark. Time to sleep!

"I'm going to sleep outside tonight," she decided. Sleeping outside, among the flowers and leaves of her beloved plants, was one of her favourite things to do. Baby mice creeped out of their nests to watch the tired fairy fly slowly by.

But where would be a comfortable spot to rest her head? Rosetta felt her eyes closing as she looked around for somewhere suitable. There – below! That small hill looked like a good place! Happily, Rosetta snuggled down. Goodness, it was soft! And warm, too, probably from the rays of the sun during the day.

As the stars twinkled in the sky, Rosetta pulled the long, soft grass over herself and slept.

She didn't wake until the morning sun was shining brightly. Rosetta stretched and rubbed her eyes. "I slept so well!" Her bed had been so comfy – but she'd been so tired, she hadn't even looked at it properly.

Rosetta reached down to grab a handful of grass. "That's strange!" It was long and brown and soft and she didn't recognize it at all. "I'm a garden fairy," she said, shaking her head, "but I've never seen grass like this before."

It was more than she could resist. Rosetta decided she had to take some home and plant it in Pixie Hollow. She had to show the other fairies. Perhaps she could even grow a comfortable bed outside her own house.

She pulled hard on the handful of grass. How tough it was! The roots must be very deep.

Rosetta was determined to have a sample of the grass. She pulled again on the strands, but, as she did so, Rosetta was knocked off her feet. The hill was moving! "Eeek!" she yelled as she fell backwards.

The hill was no hill – it was a wild boar! And the soft grass wasn't grass at all, it was fur!

The boar grunted angrily as it got to its feet. Who had been pulling on its fur? It swished its tail, sending Rosetta flying through the air and landing on the ground with a bump. Then it galloped away, hoping to find a safer place to rest!

"Ouch!" said Rosetta, as she got to her feet and dusted herself off. "Well, now I know why I'm not an animal fairy."

She stared after the disappearing boar. To think she'd been snuggled into it without even knowing!

"Next time," she decided, "I'll be more careful about where I rest!"

Disney Princess
Cinderella

The Heart of a Champion

Life at the palace was a dream come true for Cinderella. She particularly loved that her dear old horse, Frou, lived there too. He had been her faithful friend since she was a child.

One day, an invitation arrived. "You are hereby invited," read the Grand Duke, "to attend this year's annual Royal International Horse Show, to be held exactly one week from today. Please choose one member from your royal household to represent you in the competition."

Everyone decided that Cinderella should compete!

Although there were lots of fine horses to choose from, Cinderella wanted to ride her old friend, Frou.

"My dear," said the king, turning up his nose at the idea. "If none of my horses suit your fancy, I can have another hundred champions here by morning!"

"Frou may be old," said Cinderella, "but he has the heart of a champion!"

And with that, she saddled Frou and swung herself up. "Come on, Frou," she told him. "Let's show them what you've got."

Every day for a week, Cinderella and Frou trained for hours, but Frou kept making mistakes. No matter how sweetly Cinderella urged him, he missed every jump.

At last, it was the night before the royal horse show. "Please don't worry," Cinderella told Frou. "You're going to be wonderful."

But Frou didn't quite believe her.

Just then, Cinderella's Fairy Godmother appeared! "My dear," she whispered, "you know Frou can win, and I know Frou can win, but our friend Frou doesn't know it at all. What he needs is a reason to feel confident."

And with that, she raised her magic wand and waved it at Frou. To Frou's amazement, a glass horseshoe appeared on each of his hooves!

"With these horseshoes, you'll never miss a step," she told Frou, winking at Cinderella. "And while I'm at it," she added, waving her wand again. Instantly, a golden saddle appeared on Frou's back and Cinderella's simple dress became a beautiful riding outfit.

The next day at the horse show, Frou looked like a true champion! He held his head up high and cleared every jump with ease. And it was all thanks to the magical glass horseshoes – or so Frou thought. Cinderella knew better, though. The horseshoes just gave Frou the confidence he needed to be the great horse he always had been.

Cinderella and Frou came first, and the Princess was very proud of her oldest friend.

Disney Princess Sleeping Beauty

Fairy Medicine

Deep in the forest, in a humble cottage, the three good fairies had been secretly raising Briar Rose for many years. One morning, the girl woke up with a terrible cold.

"We must nurse her back to health," said Flora.

Merryweather and Fauna agreed. So, while Briar Rose stayed in bed, Flora brought her a bowl of warm soup. Fauna fetched her a cup of tea. And Merryweather gave her a dose of medicine.

"Ooooh!" said Briar Rose, wrinkling her nose. "That tastes awful!"

"Most medicine tastes awful, dear," said Merryweather. "Just drink it down."

"Would you like anything else?" Flora asked.

The princess blew her nose and gazed out her window at the beautiful spring day. "What I really want is to get out of bed," she said.

"Oh, no, dear," said Flora. "You're far too sick for that."

Then the fairies left Briar Rose to rest and went downstairs.

"I feel bad for the sweet girl," said Fauna. "Staying in bed all day is boring."

"What can we do?" asked Merryweather.

"I know!" cried Flora. "We'll entertain her!"

"Splendid!" said Merryweather. "I'll fetch my wand and conjure up some fireworks, a puppet show, and –"

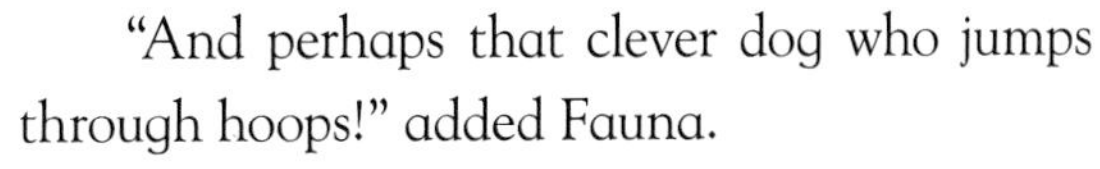

"And perhaps that clever dog who jumps through hoops!" added Fauna.

"No!" Flora cried. "We all agreed to give up our fairy magic until Briar Rose turns 16 and she's safe from Maleficent's curse."

"Not even a little magic?" asked Fauna. "Just a few fireworks?"

"No!" Flora said again, stomping her foot.

"Well," said Fauna, "how do mortals entertain themselves when they're sick in bed?"

"I know!" cried Flora. She brought out a pack of cards. "We'll play card games! That will be fun!"

The three fairies then went up to Briar Rose's room and played card games with her all afternoon. Briar Rose won almost every game, too, which really cheered her up.

After a while, Briar Rose yawned and said she was ready to have a sleep. So the fairies went back downstairs.

When Flora went outside to do some gardening, Fauna approached Merryweather. "Tell me the truth," she whispered. "Did you use magic to let the princess win?"

"I just used mortal magic," confessed Merryweather. "No harm in a little sleight of hand. After all, you must admit, if you're feeling down, winning is the best medicine!"

Disney · PIXAR
FINDING NEMO

Safe Swimming

In the deep blue ocean, Marlin the clownfish emerged from his sea anemone home, ready for a day of adventure with his son, Nemo.

"Nice to see you're up early," he said, finding Nemo already outside.

"I've been waiting for this all week!" Nemo cried. "Let's go!"

"Nemo, wait!" Marlin shouted as his son dashed off. He caught Nemo by his littlest fin. "What are you doing? You can't swim off into the ocean willy-nilly. It's dangerous!"

"Aww c'mon, Dad," said Nemo. "I've been lost in the ocean before and came home fine."

"Just because you were trapped in a fish tank doesn't mean you know how to survive the ocean," Marlin warned him. "We can still have fun together. Safe fun ... Nemo!" His eyes bugged out of his head when he realized his son had left him again.

Nemo swam upwards towards a pair of orange legs swishing in the water. Pelican legs! Marlin powered after him and snatched him from harm's way, just as the pelican ducked its beak into the water to swallow Nemo whole.

"Just because you've met a friendly pelican before and had a ride in his mouth, doesn't mean others won't try and eat you," Marlin scolded.

"That was so cool," marvelled Nemo.

"This is no laughing matter!" said Marlin, losing his patience. Nemo needed to be clever in the ocean. Everything could be an enemy....

"Hey, Dad! I've found something."

In the brief moment Marlin had looked up to see if the pelican's legs were gone from above them, Nemo had swum off again.

"This is awesome," Nemo declared, rubbing a fin across the shiny glass surface of a discarded bottle from the human world.

"Stay away from that. It could be dangerous!" snapped Marlin, rushing over. He glanced at the surface of the object. His jaw fell open. In the reflection, bolting towards him and his son was a....

"Barracuda! We'll never out swim him!"

Thinking on his fins, Nemo dived into the narrow opening of the bottle.

"Follow me!" he yelled.

"But we'll be trapped," worried Marlin.

"I know," said Nemo.

The barracuda swam directly at the bottle and slammed its face into the glass as it tried to eat the little clownfish inside. Realizing it couldn't get in, the barracuda swam off into the ocean with a few teeth loose and wobbling.

"You did it!" Marlin high fived Nemo.

Nemo hoped his Dad had learned his lesson ... that sometimes being trapped in a glass tank could have its advantages!

Disney
ALICE in WONDERLAND

Sillying the Blues Away

"Oh, me, oh, my!" the White Rabbit said as he rushed past Alice.

"Wait! Excuse me!" Alice called to him. But he was gone.

Alice sat down. "I'm never going to get out of here," she said worriedly.

"What's the matter?" a voice asked. "You seem blue."

Alice looked all around, but she didn't see anyone. "Where are you?" she asked.

"Is that better?" the Cheshire Cat asked as he suddenly appeared out of nowhere, sitting on a tree.

"Why, yes," Alice replied cautiously.

"Would you like some help?" the Cheshire Cat asked.

"You'll help me?" Alice cried.

"Absolutely!" the Cheshire Cat said with a grin. "But you have to do exactly as I say."

"Okay," Alice agreed.

"First," the Cheshire Cat told her, "you have to put on this winter coat."

"But it's spring," Alice protested.

"You promised to do as I say," the Cheshire Cat reminded her.

"Okay." Alice started putting it on.

"Backwards!" the Cheshire Cat ordered.

"But ..." Alice began. The Cheshire Cat started to disappear. "Wait, don't go!" she pleaded. "Here, I'm putting it on."

Once the coat was back on, the Cheshire Cat reappeared. "Let's go for a walk," he said, grinning at Alice.

"But I'm feeling a little silly," Alice said.

"Don't worry," the Cheshire Cat told her. "No one's looking."

But the truth was, Alice could have sworn she heard the bread-and-butterflies laughing at her.

"Now, drink this cup of apple sauce," the Cheshire Cat said.

"Don't you mean apple juice?" Alice asked.

"No, I mean apple sauce," the Cheshire Cat said. "Drink it while walking round in a circle – three times."

Alice hesitated. "Are you sure about this?"

"It's always worked for the bread-and-butterflies," the Cheshire Cat told her.

"All right, then," Alice said. But, by the time she started her second circle, her doubts grew stronger. "I think you're playing a trick on me," she said. "You're having me do all these things to make me look silly."

"True," the Cheshire Cat agreed. "But it's awfully hard to feel blue when you look this silly!" His smile hung in the air a moment before he entirely disappeared.

Alice thought for a second, and she had to agree. She was still lost, but now she didn't feel quite so sad about it!

April
28

Disney Princess

Tangled

Flying Stars

At the top of Mother Gothel's tower, Rapunzel spent her days gazing out of the window and dreaming about what adventures were out there. On this particularly special night, the sky was clear, perfect for what was to come....

Rapunzel had read about it in one of her books – a night where the stars would shoot across the sky.

"Come on, Pascal!" Rapunzel sang excitedly. "It's almost time."

She placed her book on the window ledge. Pascal clambered onto its pages and snuggled in close to Rapunzel's arm.

"I hope we see as many as we did last year," Rapunzel said. "Or even more! I love the night sky, full of its bright stars and constellations."

Pascal glanced at Rapunzel, confused.

"What?" she asked him. "You don't know what constellations are? They're groups of stars that form patterns in the sky...." Rapunzel pointed upwards for Pascal to understand. "Tonight I can see the great hero Perseus!"

Pascal grinned and nodded. He could see him too.

"And over there is the winged horse Pegasus. Oh, Pascal!" Rapunzel gasped suddenly. "A shooting star!"

As she said it, a streak of light blossomed and sped across the inky black sky.

"I wonder if they're really stars?" she said. "The book doesn't say. But it does say that if you make a wish when you see one...."

Rapunzel closed her eyes tight. She tried to think of the perfect wish but Pascal was making a squeaky racket next to her ear. "Hold on! I'm not finished," she told him.

When Rapunzel had finished wishing, she peeled open her eyes to see two ... three ... no, wait, four shooting stars!

"Oh my!" Rapunzel gasped as she stepped away from the window ledge. "There shouldn't be that many at once! And they shouldn't be coming this way!"

Racing through the sky, the stars approached her tower. Rapunzel ran from the window and grabbed a frying pan. Raising it to her face protectively, she waited for the stars to strike her....

Until she realized they weren't stars at all!

BUZZ! BUZZ!

"Oh!" she exclaimed, lowering the frying pan from her face. "They're bugs! The most beautiful bugs I've ever seen, Pascal."

Rapunzel danced around the tower and the bugs lit the way with a gentle buzzing. She would never forget that night – the night of the falling stars and the dance of the friendly fireflies.

Disney Winnie the Pooh

Pooh's Neighbourhood

"I say, it's a splendid day in the neighbourhood!" cried Owl.

"Which neighbour wood are we talking about?" asked Pooh.

"Neighbour*hood*," said Owl. "The place where we live and where all our neighbours live and are neighbourly."

"Oh," said Pooh, "it is a splendid day in it, isn't it?"

"Now I'm off for an owl's-eye view!" said Owl. He flew up and circled once round Pooh's house. "I can see the Hundred-Acre Wood spread out below me, and it's a fine place indeed."

As Owl flew off, Pooh began to think about what it means to live in a neighbourhood, and he thought perhaps he would bring a neighbourly present to his closest neighbour, Piglet. Pooh went inside his house and took a honeypot out of his cupboard. He tied a nice blue ribbon round it.

When he reached his Thoughtful Spot, Pooh suddenly had a thought – *I could take the path straight to Piglet's house. Or – I could go up the path and around the whole neighbourhood. And sooner or later the path would take me to Piglet's house, anyway.*

So that's what he did.

As he walked the long way to Piglet's house, Pooh came across each of his neighbours in turn. He joined Kanga and Roo for a snack at the picnic spot, and collected some carrots from Rabbit. After lunch and a longish snooze at Christopher Robin's house, he soon reached Eeyore's Gloomy Place, which was where Eeyore lived.

Eeyore was feeling sad, so Pooh offered him a nice lick of honey. Pooh put the jar down, and Eeyore peered in. The honeypot was empty! Pooh walked away glumly and, before long, Owl flew over.

"I've seen our whole neighbourhood today," Pooh told him. "But now I have no neighbourly present left for Piglet."

"The bees have been quite busy at the old bee tree lately," said Owl. "Perhaps you can get a fill-up there."

So they walked together until they came to the old bee tree. Up, up, up Pooh climbed. Then Owl had a thought – he told Pooh to go to the very top of the tree and look around.

"Our neighbourhood!" cried Pooh. "Our beautiful home!" The Hundred-Acre Wood was spread out below him.

"That's the owl's-eye view," announced Owl grandly.

Then, Pooh filled up the honeypot once more, and he and Owl went to Piglet's house for supper.

April

30

The Lost Button

Bonnie was off to the daycare centre, leaving the toys to have fun on their own.

"Good morning, Woody," said Dolly, hopping down from her spot on the bed.

Woody pointed to Dolly's dress. "Hey! You're missing a button," he said.

Dolly looked down. "Oh no! You're right," she gasped. "Where could it be? My dress isn't the same without it!"

Woody rested a hand on her shoulder. "I can help you look for it," he said.

That cheered Dolly up. She knew with Woody on the case her button wouldn't stay lost for long.

"Okay, let's start looking!" she smiled, grabbing him by the hand and pulling him out of the room.

They raced downstairs and out to the garden. "Yesterday, Bonnie took me to play outside," Dolly said. "My button could be somewhere out here. You have to find it."

Woody looked at the jungle of tall grass and sighed. "Me? I knew it."

The sheriff wrestled his way through the jungle. There was no button to be found – but there was an angry bee which chased him all the way round the garden!

The nimble Woody managed to escape the insect, but not before falling and landing in a puddle of thick, gloopy mud!

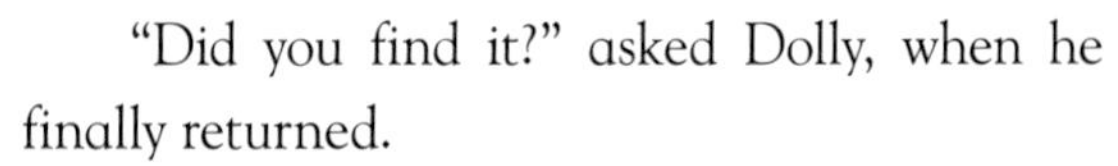

"Did you find it?" asked Dolly, when he finally returned.

"No," Woody wheezed. "I sure could use a nice warm bath, though."

Dolly's eyes widened. "Good idea! Let's head straight for the bathroom."

Woody was suspicious. Dolly seemed oddly excited.

In the bathroom, Dolly pointed to a basket of brushes, bows and other hair products. "Yesterday, we played with these," Dolly said. "Look in there."

Woody groaned. "I wish I would learn to keep my big mouth shut."

In the basket, Woody was jabbed by combs, pricked by hair clips and caught in a hair net. There was no sign of the button anywhere.

"Wait, I remember!" said Dolly. "My button's in Bonnie's room."

Woody untangled himself from the net. A spotty red bow was hooked on his hat. "What?" he spluttered.

Sure enough, they found the button on Bonnie's pillow. "It fell off and Bonnie put it here so she wouldn't lose it," Dolly explained. She smiled. "You know, it was actually fun looking for this button, wasn't it, Woody?"

Woody looked at the new bow on his hat and sighed. Dolly was a good friend, but her idea of fun was very different to his!

May

1

A Starless Night

It was a beautiful clear night and Tinker Bell was sitting on a cloud watching her friend Iridessa dive across the sky.

"Watch this, Tink!" shouted Iridessa. "I'm going to leave behind a beautiful glimmering streak!" Being a light fairy, Iridessa could create a bright, shining trail through the darkness.

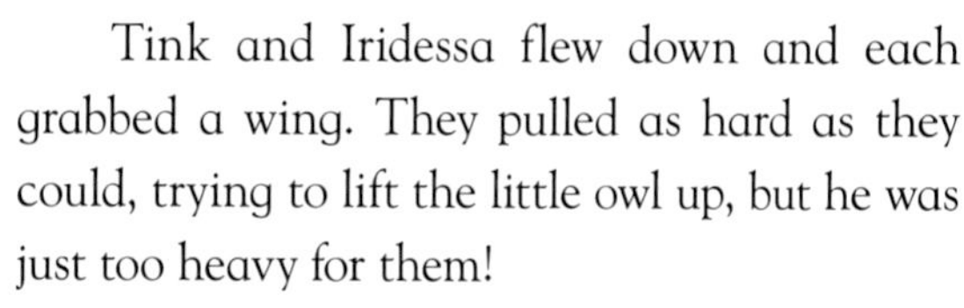

Tink clapped her hands in delight. "How wonderful!" she cried. "You look almost as bright as a shooting star! And speaking of stars...." Tink looked up and frowned. Where were they? "On such a clear night, the sky should be filled with stars, but I can only see one star – the second star to the right, the one that leads the way to Never Land. What's happened to the others?"

"An old legend has it that stars don't shine when someone in Never Land is in trouble," Iridessa said.

Tink gasped. "Do you think...?"

Someone needed their help! But who – and where? Never Land was so big!

It took a lot of searching, but as they flew through the woods, the two friends heard a faint hooting noise. "Look Iridessa!" called Tink.

Below them, a baby owl had fallen into the river! Hooting in distress, it flapped uselessly against the current.

Tink and Iridessa flew down and each grabbed a wing. They pulled as hard as they could, trying to lift the little owl up, but he was just too heavy for them!

"What do we do now, Tink?" asked Iridessa, looking worried.

This was a job for a tinker fairy! Tink glanced around in search of something that could help them. "Hmm, that tall grass might come in handy," she said, as she started to form a plan. "Follow me, I've got an idea!"

By weaving together lots of blades of grass, Tink managed to make a sturdy rope. "Let's give it a go!" called Tink.

Together, she and Iridessa threw the rope lasso over the owl – and pulled it to safety! The baby owl sat on the bank, soaked, but hooting in gratitude to the two fairies.

As soon as he had dried out, Tink and Iridessa took the baby owl home to his nest in a tree trunk, where his mother tucked him under her wing.

"Take care!" Tink called, and the owls hooted back.

As they flew home, Tink and Iridessa looked up at the sky – to see it full of stars again! The creatures of Never Land were safe again, thanks to the two fairy friends and Tink's tinkering skills!

May

2

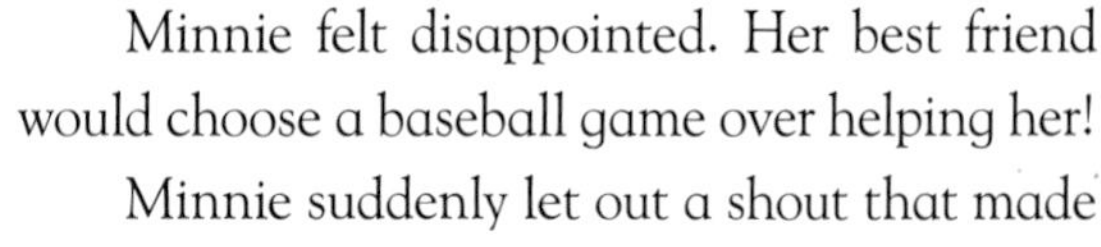

The Field of Fashion

Daisy Duck was giving her best friend Minnie Mouse a lift to school on her bicycle. Minnie was finding it difficult to hang on. "Daisy, if we go any faster, we'll start flying!"

"It's your fault!" Daisy called over her shoulder. "You spent an hour choosing your bow." As she came to a halt, Minnie jumped off.

"Sorry," said Minnie, "but today's art lesson is the most important one of the year."

She ran into class just in time to hear Miss Van Burlow announce the topic for the final project – "I want you to design outfits and put on a fashion show for Principal Van Arm."

Minnie was overjoyed. Fashion was her passion! Despite what her classmate Abigail might think. "That bow totally clashes with your top," she sneered as she looked at Minnie.

"She thinks she's the coolest girl around!" Minnie complained to Daisy after school. The two of them were sipping milkshakes at the local cafe. "I'd love to win the fashion show and teach her a lesson." Then she had the best idea. Daisy could be her model!

Daisy was shocked. "Who, me? Forget it! What if something went wrong and I made a total fool of myself? Besides, I've got a baseball game tomorrow. In fact, I have to go practise right now."

Minnie felt disappointed. Her best friend would choose a baseball game over helping her!

Minnie suddenly let out a shout that made the waitress next to her jump and spill juice everywhere. "I've got it!" she shouted, and started sketching designs ... and the spilled red juice gave her an idea too!

Meanwhile, at baseball practice, Daisy was feeling guilty about her decision. Best friends should support each other – and what did a little embarrassment matter? She threw down her bat and ran to find her friend. "I want to help!" said Daisy, when she found Minnie.

Minnie smiled. "You won't look like a fool, I promise." She showed Daisy her designs.

"They're gorgeous!" Daisy cried. "I can't wait to try them on!"

On the day of the fashion show, Minnie led everyone out to the field.

"Here's my project," said Minnie. The whole baseball team was there, led by Daisy – and they were all wearing new bright red uniforms!

"Amazing!" said Principal Van Arm admiringly. "Our team will look great at the next championship. This is without doubt the best project."

Minnie and Daisy hugged each other in delight. Friends took risks for each other – and that made winning all the sweeter!

May

3

Patch and the Panther

One dark night, 15 Dalmatian puppies sat huddled around a black-and-white television set. They watched intently as Thunderbolt, the canine hero, creeped through a deep, dark jungle.

Suddenly Thunderbolt pricked up his ears. The puppies held their breath. Two yellow eyes peered out of the bushes beside him. It was a panther!

"Thunderbolt, look out!" Penny barked at the television.

"Will Thunderbolt escape the panther?" the TV announcer asked. "Don't miss next week's exciting episode!"

"Aww!" the puppies groaned, disappointed that their favourite show was over.

"I'll bet Thunderbolt tears that ol' panther to pieces," said Patch.

"I'd be scared to fight a panther," said his brother Lucky.

"Not me!" cried Patch.

"All right, kids. Time for bed," Pongo said, shutting off the television with his nose. He watched as the puppies padded upstairs and settled down in their baskets.

"Goodnight, pups," Pongo said.

"Goodnight, Dad," the puppies replied.

Pongo switched off the light. Moments later, the sound of soft snores filled the room. The puppies were fast asleep.

All except for one. Patch was wide awake. He was still thinking about Thunderbolt.

"I wish some ol' panther would come around here," Patch said to himself. "I'd teach him a thing or two."

Just then a floorboard creaked. Patch pricked up his ears. Then he crawled out of his basket to investigate.

The floorboard creaked again. *What if it's a panther?* Patch thought. *But I'm not scared of any ol' panther*, he reminded himself.

Suddenly Patch saw a shadow flicker across the doorway. The shadow had a long tail. Panthers have long tails. Just then two yellow eyes peered out of the darkness.

"Aroooo!" Patch yelped. He turned to run, but he tripped on the rug. In a flash, the panther was on top of him. Patch could feel its hot breath on his neck. He shut his eyes....

"Patch, what are you doing out of bed?" the panther asked.

Patch opened his eyes. It was Pongo!

"I – I was just keeping an eye out for panthers," Patch explained.

Pongo smiled. "Why don't you get some sleep now," he suggested. "I can keep an eye out for panthers for a while."

"Okay, Dad," Patch said with a yawn.

Pongo carried Patch back to his basket. And in no time at all, the puppy was fast asleep.

Disney · PIXAR
BRAVE

Tapestry Trouble

It was raining outside DunBroch Castle, giving Queen Elinor an opportunity to stay indoors and make progress on her tapestry piece. But the tapestry wasn't looking as good as she imagined it would.

The door clanked open as she worked, revealing her husband Fergus, the Bear King, in his fur cloak and iron helmet.

"My love," he called. "How's the tapestry going?"

Queen Elinor shook her head. "Not very well. It's impossible to get you, or the children to pose for me. I have to sit here and picture you all in my mind."

King Fergus frowned. "But we've posed a lot already," he said.

"Yes, but you never stood still!" snapped Queen Elinor.

She reminded King Fergus of the last time they had posed for her. The dogs had wrestled with one another. Fergus had petted and played with the hairy hounds distractedly. Not to mention that the triplets had stolen Merida's favourite bow and run circles around the room, just before the dogs had snatched the bow and took off out the door.

"I really don't know if I'll ever finish the tapestry," Queen Elinor admitted sadly, leaving the room for a much needed break.

The following morning, Queen Elinor woke up to an empty bed. King Fergus was nowhere to be seen and it was hard to miss such a tall, round man in all his furs and finery.

The Queen placed her crown upon her head and left the room in a hurry, wandering down corridors in search of her husband. Or her children for that matter. Or even the dogs!

"Fergus, where are you?" she called, feeling a little concerned.

"We're in the tapestry room!" replied a deep, echoing cry.

Queen Elinor knew that voice well.

She quickly entered the tapestry room....

"SURPRISE!" a cheer rang out.

Queen Elinor gasped. Her whole family waited proudly before her, standing as straight as arrows and looking as fresh as daisies. Even the dogs were sitting statue-still – not even their tails were wagging.

"We are ready to pose for you," said the King with a bow, "for as long as you need us to."

"I can't believe it! How did you get them to pose?" Queen Elinor wondered.

Fergus grinned. "It wasn't hard, love."

Behind Fergus's back, balanced in one big hand, was a pile of delicious cakes, waiting to be eaten by the triplets and Merida – and the dogs of course. But not until Queen Elinor had finished her tapestry.... It seemed like a fair deal.

Disney Princess
Sleeping Beauty

Lakeside Adventure

It was impossible to resist a trip across the pond when the sun was shining so brightly. Aurora and the good fairies, Flora, Fauna and Merryweather, had packed a little basket of cucumber sandwiches and some juicy, ripe strawberries. They even wore their best outdoor gowns.

Together, they climbed aboard a wooden sailboat and set off to enjoy a relaxing outing. There was no telling how long good weather would last and it was always best to make the most of every minute!

Aurora wanted to visit a family of swans she had befriended at the beginning of the summer. But when she arrived, their babies were missing!

"Don't worry," she said to the swans, soothingly. "We'll find your little ones."

"They were probably hungry," Flora suggested, looking under the berry bushes. But swans don't eat berries and the babies were nowhere to be seen.

Fauna looked high up in the treetops, searching among every bright green leaf. She pushed aside branches and almost fell when a twig came free in her hand.

"Eeeep!" she squealed.

Luckily, she righted herself in the space of a heartbeat and dusted off her gown with a little cough of embarrassment.

But, sadly, she found nothing up in the trees ... because swan babies can't climb!

Merryweather stuck to the ground in her search. She traipsed through muddy puddles, pushing aside reeds and turning over rocks. Her dress was filthy and her socks were soaked right through! But unfortunately, there was no sign of the little ones there either.

Aurora stopped and thought carefully. "If I were a baby swan, where would I seek comfort and safety?" She looked around and was suddenly struck by an idea.

Running to the edge of the lake, she found a clearing where the earth was softer and cooler to the touch. The baby swans were curled up in a huddle, dreaming of lazy summer days, and unaware of how much trouble and worry they had caused everyone!

Aurora scooped the little birds into her arms and carefully took them to their home on the lakeside, surrounded by daisies and moss. She presented the sleeping babies, all fluffy with eyes tightly shut, to the happy swans who bowed their heads in thanks.

At last the family were reunited and there was nothing Aurora and the fairies loved more than to see friends and family so fond of one another – safe, warm and deeply loved in a world so full of wonderful things.

May

6

Mickey & Friends

Prize-winning Pooch

One day, Minnie was walking her dog, Fifi, when she saw a poster.

"Look, Fifi," she said. "A dog show – with prizes! You should enter!"

Minnie and Fifi went straight home to practise.

"Fifi, sit!" said Minnie.

Fifi sat.

"Shake. Good girl!" said Minnie, shaking the paw Fifi held up. "Roll over."

Fifi sat up. "Arf!"

"No," said Minnie. "You're supposed to bark when I say 'speak'."

Fifi rolled over.

"We've still got some work to do!" sighed Minnie.

On the morning of the show, Minnie gave Fifi a bath and dressed her in a red dotted bow.

Fifi pulled at the lead as they walked towards the town square. She'd seen a squirrel!

Minnie held on tight, but Fifi slipped from her collar. Minnie watched the squirrel disappear round a corner – followed by a red dotted bow!

"Fifi!" cried Minnie. "Come back!"

Minnie raced after Fifi but when she turned the corner her dog was gone. Minnie searched and searched, then she called Daisy.

"I'll be right there!" announced Daisy. "And I'll bring Mickey!"

"Don't worry, Minnie," said Mickey when he and Daisy arrived, "we'll help you find her."

Minnie and her friends made posters that read: *Missing! Tan and cream dog. Name of Fifi. If found, please call 555-5736.*

Then they went all around town, calling for Fifi and putting up the posters.

"Now let's go back to your house, Minnie," suggested Daisy. "Fifi may have found her way home."

But there was no little dog at Minnie's house.

"I'm sending a message to my friends – *Lost: tan and cream dog with a red dotted bow. If you see her, please send a message!*" said Daisy.

Within minutes, Daisy started getting messages and a picture came up on her phone. It was of a dog with a red dotted bow – and a big blue rosette!

Daisy sent back: *That's Fifi! Where is she?*

The answer came. "She's at the dog show!" Daisy said.

The three friends raced to the park.

Fifi barked when she saw Minnie.

"Fifi, I was so worried!" said Minnie. "How did you win a blue rosette?"

"Your dog is so well behaved," one of the judges explained, overhearing Minnie. "When we said 'sit', your dog sat. When we said 'shake', your dog held up her paw. We just had to give her the prize."

Minnie couldn't help giggling. "You're lucky none of the judges asked her to 'roll over'," she said, smiling at Fifi.

Disney Princess
The Little Mermaid

A History Lesson

"Ariel, what am I going to do with you?" King Triton asked with a sigh. He looked wearily at his daughter. "You know you're not allowed to visit the surface. None of us are – it's just too dangerous!"

Ariel hung her head. She had been caught going to visit the surface – again – to visit her seagull friend, Scuttle. King Triton couldn't understand Ariel's interest in the human world. It made him sad that most of his conversations with his daughter involved him yelling and her storming off. Suddenly, the King had an idea.

"You know, Ariel," he said thoughtfully, "you're so interested in learning more about the human world, but I bet you don't know that much about the world you live in!"

Ariel looked up. "What do you mean, Daddy?" she asked, looking confused. "What's there to know?"

"Well," said Triton, "for starters, do you know about the first Queen of the Merfolk?"

"I guess not," Ariel replied.

Ten minutes later, Ariel and her father were swimming slowly through the Royal Merseum, and Ariel was discovering that merfolk history was much more exciting than she had ever imagined.

"This is a portrait of Queen Fluidia, the first Queen of the Merfolk. She was my Great-great-great-great-great-great-great-great-great-great-great-great-grandmother," said King Triton. He pointed at a sandpainting of a regal mermaid holding a pearl sceptre. "That would make her your Great-great-great – well, you get the idea. Anyway, Fluidia united all the merfolk into one kingdom many years ago, to fight an invasion of sharks. The Shark Army was the greatest, fiercest army the ocean had ever seen, but Fluidia was more than a match for them! She used that pearl sceptre as a club – she was so strong that she could start whirlpools just by swinging it round."

"Wow," said Ariel. "She sounds fierce."

"She was. She drove those sharks off almost single-handedly, and in gratitude the merfolk made her Queen," King Triton said.

"You know, you come from a pretty interesting family," he continued. "And you remind me a lot of Fluidia, Ariel. You have her strength of will. I think you'll do great things – even if we won't always agree on *how* you'll do them."

"Thank you, Daddy," said Ariel. She decided not to mention to her father how much his trident looked like a human object Scuttle had once shown her. Maybe she would tell him some other time!

May

8

A Stinky Surprise

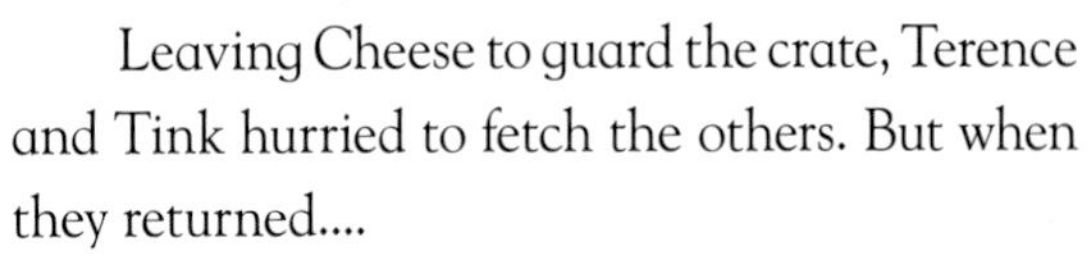

Tink, Terence the dust-keeper fairy and Cheese the mouse were searching for lost things on the beach – one of Tink's favourite places. Today she was delighted to find a big red pebble. "Ooh, how pretty! It looks like a giant cherry!"

"Shame it isn't real food," Terence laughed.

Tink picked up the pebble to smell it. No, it was definitely not edible. But ... hold on ... she sniffed again. A strange smell reached her nose. "Do you smell that?"

Terence wrinkled his nose. Yes, he could smell something too – and it wasn't the pebble. "It's coming from over there," he said, pointing to where the waves lapped at the sand.

A large wooden crate had been washed up on the beach! "Let's go see what it is," Tink said, always up for going on an adventure and finding something new.

The closer they got to the crate, the stronger the smell became. "A poor skunk must have become trapped inside!" gasped Tink. "We've got to get it out of there!"

Together, the two friends heaved at the side of the crate. The nails were long and deep, and although they pulled with all the strength they had, Tink and Terence were soon worn out.

"We can't do this alone," Tink panted. "Let's go get Fawn and the other fairies."

Leaving Cheese to guard the crate, Terence and Tink hurried to fetch the others. But when they returned....

"Where did Cheese go?" wondered Tink. She couldn't see the little mouse anywhere.

"I think I just heard him squeak," said Fawn, with her ear pressed to the side of the crate.

Tink was shocked. "Cheese? How did you get in there?"

SQUEAK! SQUEAK!

Now there were two poor animals trapped inside! There was no time to waste – they had to rescue Cheese and the skunk!

"Faith, trust and pixie dust!" chanted the fairies as they worked together to get the lid open. The smell grew stronger and stronger ... and then finally, the lid popped up, revealing what was really inside!

Cheese the mouse ... and cheese! A lot of cheese! The crate was brimming with all different sizes, colours and types.

Rosetta clapped a hand to her nose. "It's as stinky as a whole family of skunks!"

"Well done, Cheese," Terence laughed. "You found a treasure!"

Tink couldn't help laughing too. Inside the crate, Cheese was waist-deep in a huge yellow cheese, nibbling contentedly. This mouse was well-named indeed!

May

9

Disney · PIXAR TOY STORY 3

Dressed to Thrill

It was Sunday, and Ken had spent most of the weekend preparing for a party he was throwing. He had hung up decorations and the Sunnyside Daycare centre looked amazing!

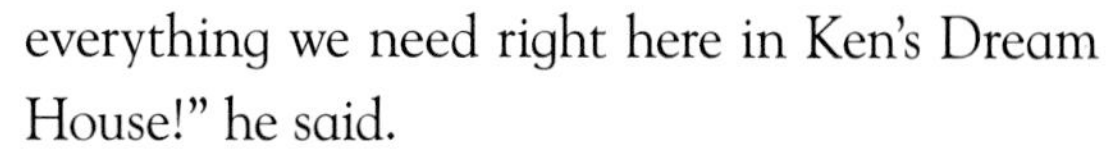

"Really cool, Ken," said Jessie, as she and Woody admired the place.

"Please save your compliments for tonight," Ken said. He handed them two love-heart-shaped cards. "Here are your magical invitations."

Woody read his invitation. "What does 'dress to thrill' mean?"

Ken looked Jessie and Woody up and down. "It means you can't come to the party wearing your old cowboy outfits," he said. Turning to the aliens, he added: "And those space suits are definitely out of style."

Buzz puffed out his chest. "Of course, my Space Ranger uniform will be fine for your party, right pal?"

Ken raised his perfect eyebrows. "It's not exactly in keeping with the party's theme, Buzz. You've got to be elegant, stylish and chic," Ken said. "In short, you've got to dress like me!"

As Ken hurried off to continue the preparations, the other toys discussed their problem. None of them had any other clothes they could wear.

Luckily, Woody had an idea. He knew just where to find lots of different outfits. "We'll find everything we need right here in Ken's Dream House!" he said.

Jessie's eyes widened as she studied the rows and rows of outfits. "Wow! Look at all these clothes!"

Buzz picked up a shirt. It was covered in pink flowers. He quickly put it back down again. "Are you sure Ken won't get mad?"

Woody pulled on a cap. "Well, he's the one who asked us to change."

Buzz smiled. "Then he's in for a surprise all right!"

That evening, as he welcomed guests to the party, Ken couldn't believe his eyes. Jessie, Buzz, Woody and the aliens were wearing a mish-mash of some very familiar clothes.

"Hey! Those are my absolutely precious outfits you're wearing!" he spluttered.

"Right you are!" beamed Jessie, twirling to show off her new hat, and the pink poncho she had turned into a skirt.

Buzz tugged on the lapels of his suit jacket. "You said you wanted us to dress like you!"

Woody tightened his colourful tie. "And we've done just that."

Ken couldn't really argue. The toys had certainly dressed to thrill, but as he watched them stretching his valuable outfits out of shape, he decided that at his next party he'd let guests wear whatever they liked!

Disney · PIXAR
FINDING NEMO

Finding Ne-who?

"The coral reef is falling down, falling down, falling down."

Nemo was home, brushing up against the anemone, when the most awful singing he ever heard in his life made him cringe. He swam deeper into the anemone, but it didn't help. The song went on.

"My fair octopus!"

And there was something familiar about it.... Still cringing, Nemo poked his head out of the golden tentacles to see who was making the awful racket.

"Dory!" Nemo should have known. How could he have forgotten that voice? Nemo swam as fast as he could towards the regal blue tang fish. "Dory! Where have you been?" It seemed like a whale's age since Nemo had seen the fish that helped his dad rescue him from the dentist's fish tank. And he couldn't wait to give her a big hug!

When Nemo got closer Dory stopped singing. That was good. But when she looked at him her face was blank. That wasn't so good.

"Did you say something, kid?" she asked.

"Dory, it's me. Nemo," he replied.

"Ne-who?" She looked at Nemo blankly. "Sorry, kid, don't know you. I was just swimming by, minding my own business, singing a song. Hey, why was I singing? Am I famous? Maybe that's how you know me."

"Dory! We're friends, remember?" Nemo had been missing Dory a lot. She just had to remember who he was.

"Friends? I just made friends with a hermit crab ... I think." Dory swam in a circle looking for the crab, but got distracted and started chasing her tail.

"Please try to remember, Dory," Nemo asked again. "You helped save me. You helped me find my dad. You know my dad. Big orange guy? Three white stripes? Looks kind of like me?"

"My dad? Looks like you? Sorry, kid, you don't look anything like my dad." Dory looked at Nemo like he was crazy and began to swim away.

Nemo swam after her. "Just think about it for a second," he pleaded. She had to remember something. "I'm Nemo!"

Dory did not turn round but she slowed down. Swimming in a wide circle, she came back. She looked at Nemo sideways, and then started laughing so hard bubbles came out of her nose.

"Had you going, huh?" Dory gave Nemo a big hug and smiled at him slyly. "That was just my little joke. You know I could never forget you!"

Nemo giggled and swam circles around his friend. "Good one, Dory!" He grinned.

Dory smiled back. "Good one, who?"

Nemo groaned. That Dory!

Disney THE LION KING

Simba's Thank-you Present

Simba lounged in the jungle, feeling happier than he'd felt in ages. After the terrible stampede near Pride Rock, he didn't think he'd ever be happy again. But his new friends Timon and Pumbaa had helped him feel better.

"I should do something to thank them," Simba told himself as he watched his friends in the river nearby. "Something really special!"

He decided to make them a present. When he saw a piece of bark lying on the ground, he had an idea.

"Ta-da!" he exclaimed a while later, leading his friends to the gift.

Pumbaa blinked. "Thanks," he said. "Er, what is it?"

"A scratching spot," Simba said, flexing his claws. He'd used vines to attach it to a thick tree trunk at shoulder height.

"Gee," Timon said. "Nice thought and all, Simba. But it's a little high for me." He stretched to his full height but could barely reach it.

Pumbaa nodded. "And I don't scratch." He held up one foot. "Hooves, you know."

"Oh." Simba hadn't thought of that.

"Thanks anyway, kid," Pumbaa said.

Simba decided to try again by building them a nice, soft bed to sleep in. He dug a cosy hole in the ground, then filled it with soft things like feathers, sand and bits of fur.

"Ta-da!" he cried, showing his friends.

Timon sighed. "What are you trying to do, kill us? Prey animals here, remember? If we sleep on the ground, we become somebody's midnight snack!"

Simba sighed as they left again. Why couldn't he think of a present they would like?

"I would've loved that scratching spot," he mumbled. "The bed, too."

Suddenly he sat up straight, realizing what he'd just said. All this time he'd been thinking of presents *he* would like – but the presents weren't for him.

"I've got to think like they think," he whispered. Slowly, a smile spread across his face....

A little while later he called them over. "I've got something for you." He pointed to a pile of palm fronds. "I think you're really going to like it. Ta-da!"

He pulled back the leaves. Underneath was a mass of wriggling, squirming, creeping, crawling creatures – bugs and grubs and worms of every shape, size and flavour.

Timon and Pumbaa gasped with delight. "Simba!" Timon cried. "You're a prince! It's just what we always wanted!"

"Yeah, thanks," Pumbaa mumbled through a mouthful of grubs. "You're a real pal!"

Simba smiled. "No," he said. "Thank *you*. Both of you. *Hakuna matata!*"

Disney Princess
Cinderella

A Birthday Surprise

"Get up, Jaq! Get up!" Gus cried, trying to nudge a sleepy Jaq awake.

But Jaq just mumbled and rolled over.

"No, no, Jaq. Get up. It's a special day." Gus pulled on his tail. "It's Cinderelly's birthday."

Jaq sat up. "Today?" he asked, wide-eyed. "Today is her birthday?"

Gus smiled and nodded vigorously.

"Well, come on! We haven't got much time!" Jaq cried. "We have a lot to do if we're throwing a surprise party!"

Soon the birds and mice were gathered on the windowsill for a secret meeting.

"We can make a cake!" Suzy and Perla volunteered.

"Watch out for L-L-Lucifer," Gus stuttered. Baking would mean stealing eggs and butter from the kitchen!

"We'll take care of that cat," Mert and Bert said, crossing their arms.

The birds whistled that they would decorate the room.

"But we still need a present," Jaq said.

"Something pretty!" Gus cried.

"I've got it!" Jaq sat up straight. "I saw some slippers in the bin last night when I was looking for food. There's a hole in one toe, but the bottoms were okay."

"We can fix them," the mice chorused.

"And I have a bit of ribbon I've been saving. We can use it on the slippers to pretty them up." Jaq pulled a rose-coloured silk ribbon from his small bag. "Now, let's get to work. We have lots to do!"

It took the mice all day to get ready, but everything turned out beautifully. The sun was setting when the mice and birds heard Cinderella's soft steps coming up the stairs.

"Here she comes!" Gus whispered.

Jaq took a match and lit the candle stump that was stuck in the iced cake. Beside it the slippers were mended and wrapped. The ribbon was twirled into two pink roses, one at each ankle.

The door opened slowly.

"Surprise!" the mice squeaked. The birds twittered and dropped confetti.

"Oh, my!" Cinderella gasped. "This *is* a surprise!"

"Happy birthday," Gus said shyly.

"It's all so lovely," Cinderella said. "But I'm afraid it's not my birthday."

"It's not?" Jaq's smile vanished. The rest of the mice and birds were silent.

"I'm afraid not, but that's what makes this such a special surprise." Cinderella beamed. The animals laughed and they all sat down to share the delicious cake together.

Disney Mickey & Friends

A Perfect Picnic

Mickey and his friends were planning a picnic!

"We can all make our favourite foods and then swap baskets!" Mickey suggested.

"Sharing our lunches sounds like fun. I can't wait!" said Minnie.

The friends raced home and each began to pack a lunch.

Donald made a sandwich. He chose his favourite drink and a piece of fruit. But as Donald looked at the food, he realized he didn't want to share them!

Over at Minnie's house, things were not going well either. Minnie had packed all her favourite foods. But she started to wonder if she would like the lunches her friends had packed.

Daisy was excited about sharing her lunch. She hummed to herself as she packed her basket. But when Daisy picked up a banana, she thought about someone else eating it and began to frown. Maybe she didn't want to share her lunch after all....

Meanwhile, Goofy was making lemonade to take to the picnic. Covered in lemon juice, Goofy tasted his lemonade. It was delicious and he wanted to drink it all himself!

Mickey didn't know that his friends had changed their minds. As he walked to the park, he grew more excited about the picnic.

When Mickey got there, he found his friends waiting for him. They all had baskets of food, but they didn't look happy.

"What's wrong?" Mickey asked his friends.

Donald explained that everyone wanted to eat their own food.

"Oh," Mickey said, disappointed. "I guess we don't have to share...."

Minnie looked at Mickey. He looked so sad. She didn't want to be the reason he was upset!

Minnie handed Mickey her basket. "I'll trade lunches with you, Mickey," she said.

"Really? Thanks, Minnie!" Mickey said.

Mickey's friends saw how happy Minnie had made Mickey and swapped baskets, too.

Mickey laid out a blanket, sat down and opened his picnic basket. When he saw what was inside, he started to laugh.

"What's so funny?" Minnie asked. She looked in her basket and started to laugh, too.

Everyone had packed peanut butter sandwiches and lemonade! The only difference in the baskets was the fruit. There was an orange, a banana, an apple, grapes and a pineapple.

"I have an idea," said Mickey. While his friends ate, Mickey made a big fruit salad.

As Mickey's friends ate their pudding, they realized that Mickey had been right. Sharing was fun, after all!

May
14

A Colourful Style

The sun rose over Pixie Hollow, awakening all its inhabitants. While the birds on the branches chirped sleepily, the water fairies were already hard at work sprinkling dew on the flowers.

Up on a cosy branch, Rosetta opened her eyes and stretched. "Good morning, Pixie Hollow!" Who knew what wonderful sights she might see today?

Instantly, something caught her eye – a beautiful brown bird sitting on a branch not far away. On its tummy was a bright red splash.

Rosetta gasped. "That little bird has such a wonderful style! The fairy who painted it that way had such an original idea!"

It gave Rosetta an idea too! Gathering everything she would need, she set off....

Later that day, Tinker Bell was helping Fawn to feed the baby bluebirds.

"Funny," she commented. "I haven't seen Rosetta yet today."

"Me neither," said Fawn. "Let's go find her."

But on their way to Rosetta's garden, the fairies were startled when they saw a squirrel run past, sporting a bright red tummy!

"What strange colours for a squirrel," remarked Tink, confused.

"Yeah," agreed Fawn. "Somethin' funny is goin' on here!"

Rounding a corner, they finally saw what was happening. A whole line of animals were queuing up – and at the front of the line was Rosetta, holding a paintbrush and a pot of red paint! "Stay still, buttercup," she was saying to a squirrel, as she painted its tummy. "I'm almost done." Then she looked up. "Oh, hi girls!"

"What are you doing?" asked Fawn.

Rosetta told them about the bird she had seen earlier with its beautiful red tummy. "I want to paint them all that way," she said. "To make them all beautiful and special."

Fawn laughed. "The robin redbreast is naturally that colour! We can't paint all the creatures the same way!"

"Right!" said Tink. "It would be like all the fairies having the same talent. That would be so boring!"

Rosetta thought for a moment. Would she like it if everyone dressed exactly the same way? Or if all fairies were garden fairies? Of course not! "You're right, girls. Differences are what make us special." She smiled at her friends.

Fawn patted her shoulder. "Exactly. And now let's clean up all these 'redbellies'!"

Tinker Bell smiled. Rosetta loved to decorate the world ... but sometimes, the world was beautiful enough just the way it was!

Disney Princess
Beauty and the Beast

The Perfect Pearl

Belle and Chip were in the library. "My library is your library," the Beast had told her. "Read and enjoy any book you find." Belle took him at his word. She spent hours there, reading book after book. To her, books were priceless treasures.

One morning, Belle noticed the Beast had left the only book he ever read lying open on a chair.

She picked it up and turned it over. Although the leather cover was worn, it was a beautiful volume with a decorative brass clasp containing three pearls.

"Chip, look!" she said to the enchanted cup, pointing at the clasp. There was an empty hole where a fourth pearl should have been.

They looked around on the floor nearby, in case it had fallen out.

"I found something!" called Chip. There by the library door was a single, perfect pearl.

Belle dropped the pearl into the empty hole in the clasp to see if it fit.

"Just right!" said Chip.

"I have an idea," Belle said. "As this book is your master's favourite, I'll fix it up for him."

"Then you can surprise him!" Chip cried.

Belle borrowed some polish from Mrs Potts to clean the leather cover. Then she put the book back on the Beast's chair so that he wouldn't miss it. But when the Beast came into the library, he didn't pick it up. He seemed to be looking for something.

"Can I help?" Belle asked him.

"No!" he bellowed. "I mean, no. Excuse me." And without another word, he left the room.

In the evening, Belle passed the Beast in the hall. She smiled at him but he simply snapped "Goodnight!" and carried on walking.

The next morning, Belle was about to add the pearl to the clasp when the Beast burst through the library door.

"You?" he cried. "I've been looking for that pearl!"

"Well, why didn't you say so!" Belle shouted, throwing the pearl onto the table. "I've been fixing up your book as a surprise."

The Beast looked at the book. Then he picked up the pearl and began to laugh.

"I've been working on something for you, too," he said, holding up an antique pin. "I wanted you to have it, but first, I had something to add."

He placed the pearl on the pin and it fitted perfectly.

"I removed the pearl but dropped it. I'm sorry I blamed you," said the Beast.

Now it was Belle's turn to laugh. They still had so much to learn about one another!

May
16

Disney Lady and the TRAMP

Howling at the Moon

Lady had been having a really bad day. First, she'd had a run-in with two nasty cats. Then, she'd been put in a horrible muzzle. But, because of Tramp, everything had changed.

"It's amazing how a day can start off terribly but end wonderfully," Lady told Tramp as they trotted through the moonlit park. "Thank you for helping me escape that terrible muzzle and for dinner at Tony's."

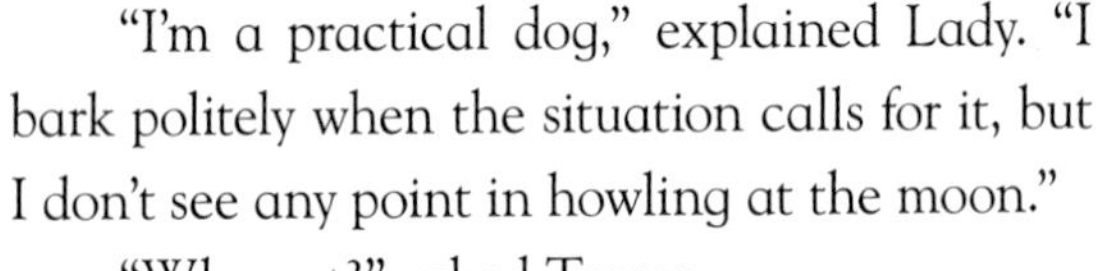

"Aw, shucks, don't mention it!" said Tramp. "Hey, you wanna have some real fun?"

"I don't know," Lady said cautiously.

While she was very fond of Tramp, she also knew they were very different dogs. Tramp was used to life on the streets. So his idea of 'fun' might be very different from hers.

"Don't worry," Tramp teased. "This is something I think you'll enjoy."

"What is it?" asked Lady.

"Well, for starters, you have to look up," said Tramp.

Lady did. The sky was filled with stars and a big, bright moon.

"What am I looking for?" she asked.

"The moon, of course!" cried Tramp. "Haven't you ever howled at the moon?"

Lady laughed at Tramp's suggestion.

"What's so funny?" asked Tramp.

"I'm a practical dog," explained Lady. "I bark politely when the situation calls for it, but I don't see any point in howling at the moon."

"Why not?" asked Tramp.

"Well," said Lady, "what's the use of it?"

"You know, Lady," said Tramp, "a thing doesn't have to be useful to be fun. You like to chase a ball, right?"

"Right," said Lady.

"So, there you go," said Tramp. "Sometimes it's good to chase a ball. And sometimes it's good to just let go and howl at the moon, even for no reason."

Lady thought it over. "Okay," she said. "What do I do?"

"First, sit up real straight," said Tramp. "Then, look up at the moon, take a deep breath, and just let all the troubles of your day disappear in one gigantic howl!" He demonstrated – "*Ow-ow-OWWWWW!*"

Lady joined Tramp and howled as loudly as she could.

"You're right!" she cried. "It does feel good to howl at the moon!"

"Stick with me, kid," said Tramp. "I know what's what."

Lady suspected Tramp did know what was what, but there was an even better reason for her to stick with him. He'd become the very best friend she'd ever had.

Disney Peter Pan

The Lost Boys Get Lost

The Lost Boys were walking single file through the woods of Never Land, on their way home after an afternoon of adventures, when Slightly, who led the way, stopped in his tracks on the bank of Mermaid Lagoon.

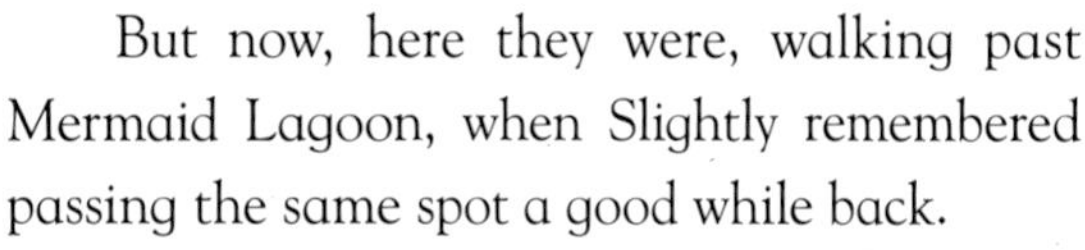

The others – Rabbit, the Raccoon Twins, Cubby and Tootles – came to an abrupt halt behind him.

"Wait a minute," said Slightly. "We already passed Mermaid Lagoon. What are we doing here again?"

Behind a bush, Tinker Bell giggled as she watched the Lost Boys looking around in confusion.

Tink had spotted them on their march and had not been able to resist playing a joke. So, she had flown ahead of them and used her fairy magic to enchant various landmarks on their route home. She had made Bald Rock look like Spiky Rock, causing the Lost Boys to make a right turn where they should have turned left.

Then she had enlisted the help of the sparrows, convincing them to move from their usual perch in the Sparrow Bird Grove to another group of trees, thus tricking the Lost Boys into making another right turn too soon.

Finally, she had enchanted the Towering Elm Tree to look exactly like the Weeping Willow, and the Lost Boys had made yet another wrong turn, thinking they were nearly home.

But now, here they were, walking past Mermaid Lagoon, when Slightly remembered passing the same spot a good while back.

"I think we're walking in circles!" Slightly proclaimed. "Lost Boys, I think we're ... lost!"

Tinker Bell overheard and tried desperately to stifle her laughter. But, before she could contain it, one giggle exploded into a fully fledged laugh and –

"Hey!" said Cubby. "Did you hear that?"

He darted over to a bush growing alongside the path and moved a branch to one side. There was Tinker Bell, hovering in mid-air, shaking with laughter.

"Tinker Bell!" cried Tootles.

It didn't take them long to work out that Tinker Bell was laughing at *them* – and that she was the cause of their confusion.

Still laughing, Tinker Bell flitted away, taking her normal route home to the fairy glade – left at the Weeping Willow Tree, right just before Sparrow Bird Grove, right again at Spiky Rock, and on towards the Sparkling Stream, which led to Moon Falls and the fairy glade entrance.

But – wait a minute! After turning right at Spiky Rock, Tinker Bell saw no sign of the Sparkling Stream anywhere. Where was she? She had got completely lost. Do you know how?

May

18

Disney Princess The Little Mermaid

Shark Surprise

At the surface of the ocean, Ariel found Scuttle with something he'd salvaged from a shipwreck.

"It's a wing-tapper!" he explained, pounding against the surface of a drum.

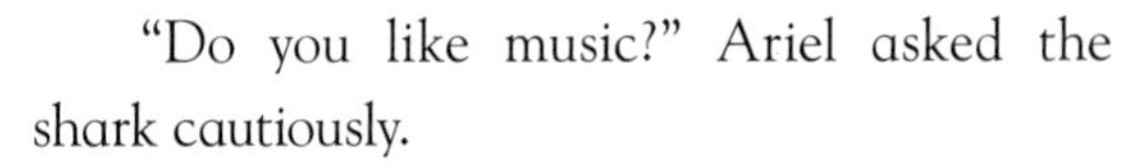

Ariel wanted to find the shipwreck herself, but as she rushed home for her bag, her father stopped her.

"A shark has been seen. I want you to stay close today," King Triton told her.

Ariel seemed to agree, but when she had the chance, she slipped away against his wishes.

"Didn't you hear about the shark?" asked Flounder, nervously.

"Don't worry, we won't go far," she said.

At the shipwreck, they found a room full of musical instruments. Ariel blew hard on a tuba and out of the funnel flew Sebastian the crab!

"What are you doing here?" Ariel cried.

"Chasing after you!" snapped Sebastian. "You're coming home this instant."

"Ariel!" Flounder interrupted them. "Look!"

A giant shark was staring through the ship's window, his big scary nose pressed against the glass. Suddenly he smashed through! Ariel used her tail to knock a large drum at it. The shark burst through the drum's skin and got stuck. He wriggled uselessly and then became still, unable to free himself. He eyed a tambourine sadly.

"Do you like music?" Ariel asked the shark cautiously.

The shark nodded.

Ariel started to sing to soothe the creature while Flounder tapped on the tambourine. Sebastian played a happy tune on the violin and before long, the shark was cheering, "Bravo!"

When they finished, Ariel and her friends bowed.

"I love music," said the shark. "I wanted to join you earlier but you swam off. I'm actually very friendly."

Ariel believed him. He seemed very sweet. "We have an orchestra at the palace," she said. "Do you want to join us, perhaps?"

"I wish I could," sighed the shark. "But my fins are too short to play an instrument."

Ariel picked up two mallets. "Smile please," she instructed.

The shark grinned, flashing his teeth, and Ariel played them like a xylophone!

Later that day, she introduced the shark to her father. He was astonished to begin with, until he heard the beautiful music Ariel made with the shark's sharp teeth. They celebrated with a concert for all the merfolk, who marvelled at the new orchestra member and cheered to their hearts' content when the music was over.

Overjoyed, the shark smiled at Ariel. "Thank you for making my dream come true."

Disney THE JUNGLE BOOK

Baloo's Secret Weapon

Mowgli and his pal Baloo were taking a lazy afternoon stroll through the jungle. Suddenly, Mowgli stopped in his tracks. "Did you hear that?" he asked.

"Hear what, little buddy?" Baloo asked.

"It sounded like twigs snapping," Mowgli said. "I think somebody might be following us!"

"That was just your old Papa Bear's stomach growling," Baloo told him. "It's time for some lunch."

"And I know just where to get it," announced Mowgli. He climbed up a tree, plucked a bunch of bananas and tossed them down to the bear.

"That's my boy!" Baloo cried proudly.

But, as he was scrambling back down, Mowgli spotted a flash of orange and black.

"Shere Khan!" Mowgli whispered to Baloo. "We've got to get out of here!" The tiger had been after Mowgli ever since the boy had first set foot in the jungle.

The two friends didn't know which way to turn. Now that Shere Khan had their scent, it would be hard to lose him. Then they both heard a lively beat drumming its way through the jungle.

"Oh, no," said Mowgli. "King Louie and his crazy band of monkeys. That's all we need!"

Baloo's eyes suddenly lit up. "That's *exactly* what we need, Little Britches!"

Still clutching the bananas, Baloo and Mowgli ran towards King Louie's compound. When they arrived, Baloo disguised himself as a monkey. The monkeys were so busy dancing and singing they didn't notice his disguise.

Then the bear quickly found an empty barrel, and filled it with the bananas.

"Look!" cried Baloo, peering into the barrel. "Lunch!" The monkeys ran over and jumped right into the barrel! They greedily ate the feast, tossing peels out as they made their way through the bunch.

Baloo signalled to Mowgli, who came out of hiding. "Come and get me, Shere Khan!" the Man-cub taunted.

Within seconds, the tiger appeared in the clearing, a fierce gleam in his eye. "Hello, Stripes," Baloo greeted him cheerfully. Then the bear picked up the barrel, heaved it, and sent King Louie's troop flying at Shere Khan. The monkeys landed on the tiger's back, where they frantically jumped up and down, pulling on his tail and ears. Mowgli and Baloo watched as Shere Khan raced back into the jungle, trying to free himself from his shrieking passengers.

"Like I always say," Baloo declared as he grinned at Mowgli, "there's nothing more fun than a barrel of monkeys!"

Disney · PIXAR TOY STORY 3

Space Comedy

One night, while Bonnie was fast asleep, Jessie and some of the other toys set to work making a movie!

Jessie wanted to make a thrilling space adventure film for Buzz, and Ken and Chunk, the rock-like toy, had come all the way from Sunnyside to help her out.

Ken and Chunk used the camera, while Mr Pricklepants directed. Jessie and the aliens were the stars of the show, with Rex dressed up as a scary alien monster for them to battle.

The stage was set for the most amazing space adventure story ever – but things didn't quite go to plan.

"Space Ranger Jessie is in danger!" Jessie announced, as Ken pointed the camera her way. "We need the help of our hero...."

"The Claw!" chimed the aliens.

"Stop!" cried Mr Pricklepants. "Who is this Claw? It's not in the script! You have to say 'Buzz Lightyear'."

The aliens smiled. "The Claw!"

Jessie gave a sigh. "Let's move on to the next scene," she suggested.

Ken raced excitedly out from behind the camera. "Did you say next scene? Stop! Change of costumes!"

"Already?" frowned Jessie. "But we only just started filming."

Ken explained that a professional never wore the same costume in two different scenes. He and Chunk brought out a rack of outfits they'd taken from Sunnyside. There were dozens of them – and those were just for the first three scenes!

"We have to wear all these?" Jessie asked. "But we'll never make it!"

Just then, Rex came charging onto the set, wondering if it was his turn in front of the camera. His swinging tail knocked part of the set, bringing it crashing down on Mr Pricklepants.

As Jessie pulled the hedgehog out from under the set, the aliens raced up to the camera holding a sign which read: 'The End'.

"The Claw!" they said again, giggling into the camera lens. Jessie shook her head sadly. Her movie was terrible!

The next day, she decided just to go ahead and show Buzz the movie anyway. "I'm so sorry," she said, when the film had finished. "I wanted to give you an adventure movie, and instead –"

"It's the funniest comedy I've ever seen!" Buzz laughed. He planted a kiss on Jessie's cheek. "Thanks, Jessie," he said. "I like it a lot!"

Buzz had loved his present. Jessie blushed, making a note to thank her friends – for being such disasters!

Disney Princess
Snow White and the Seven Dwarfs

Good Housekeeping

Snow White and the Prince were going to be married. Her dear friends, the Seven Dwarfs, were overjoyed to see Snow White so happy. But they knew they were going to miss her – not to mention her wonderful cooking and how she kept their cottage so clean and tidy.

Snow White was also worried about how the little men were going to get along without her. She decided it was time they learned how to cook and clean for themselves.

"First, let's see you sweep out the cottage," she said. "Remember to push the dirt out of the door and not just move it around the floor." The men all grabbed brooms and set to work.

"AH-CHOOO!" boomed Sneezy as a huge cloud of dust rose into the air.

"Don't forget to open the door first," Snow White added. She moved on to the next task. "Now we'll wash the dishes. First you dunk the plate, then you scrub it, then you rinse and dry it," she said, demonstrating as she went.

Doc stood, holding a dirty plate. "Let's see," he mumbled. "Scrub, dunk, dry, rinse? Or is it dunk, rinse, dry, scrub? Or ... oh, dear!"

"Never mind," giggled Snow White. "Now, laundry! First you heat the water, then you scrub the clothes with a bar of soap, rinse them and then hang them on the line to dry."

Dopey was first in line. He jumped into the tub and rubbed the bar of soap all over the clothes he was wearing.

"Dopey," said Snow White, "it's easier if you wash the clothes after you've taken them off."

A bit later, the Dwarfs trooped into the kitchen for a cooking lesson.

"Today we're going to make stew," said Snow White. "You take a little of everything you have on hand, throw it into a pot, and let it simmer for a long time."

As Snow White was leaving, Doc tried to reassure her. "Don't worry, Snow White. We're going to be fust jine ... I mean, just fine."

The next night, the Dwarfs invited Snow White and the Prince for dinner – which the Dwarfs had made themselves. When their guests arrived, Dopey led them over to a large pot simmering over the fire and grandly lifted the lid. An old boot, some socks, a bunch of flowers and a bar of soap were floating on the top. "We made it with a little of everything we had on hand, just like you said," Sleepy said.

"Perhaps we should go over that recipe again," Snow White said gently. Then she brought out four gooseberry pies from her basket. Ordinarily, Snow White didn't believe in eating pudding before dinner, but this time she would make an exception!

May

22

Disney

Bambi

Rain, Rain, Go Away

RUMBLE, RUMBLE, BOOM! The loud clap of thunder startled Bambi and his friends.

"I hate thunderstorms!" cried Thumper, looking a little scared.

"I don't like them either!" cried Flower.

"Bambi!" called his mother as the clouds grew dark and the rain began to fall. Bambi followed his mother out of the open meadow and into the woods. From their warm, dry thicket, Bambi watched sheets of rain pour down through the trees.

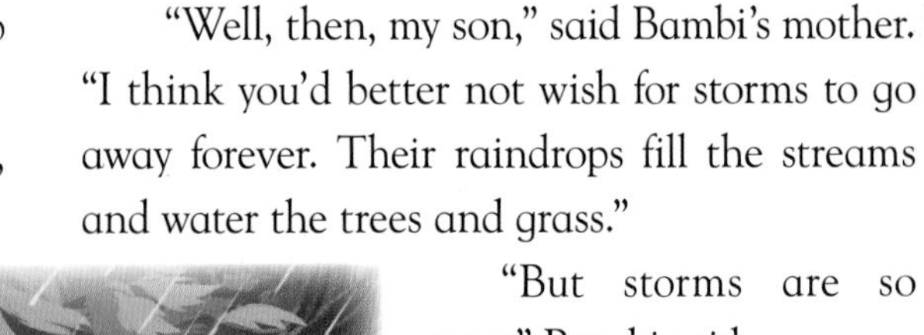

"I hate thunderstorms," he told his mother, echoing Thumper's words. "I wish the storm would go away and never come back again."

"Oh, my," said his mother. "Do you mean you never again want to drink the cool, fresh water from the forest stream?"

"Well, no," said Bambi.

"Then, do you want the big trees to go thirsty? Their leaves to wither and branches to become brittle?" asked his mother.

"No! Of course not!" cried Bambi. "The trees give us shelter, and their branches give the birds a place to make their nests."

"Then, do you want the sweet grass to turn brown?" asked his mother.

"No," said Bambi. "We eat the grass. We'd go hungry if that happened!"

"Well, then, my son," said Bambi's mother. "I think you'd better not wish for storms to go away forever. Their raindrops fill the streams and water the trees and grass."

"But storms are so scary," Bambi said.

Just then, the rain began to let up, and Bambi's friends scampered through the underbrush and into Bambi's thicket.

"Look at the pond!" cried Flower.

Bambi peered through the thicket. The pond was alive with activity. The frogs were leaping and playing. And a family of ducks were shaking their feathers and waddling into the water.

"Uh-oh," said Thumper. "That old bullfrog's gonna get a surprise."

Bambi watched the lily pad with the big bullfrog drift closer and closer to the line of ducklings. The last duckling wasn't paying attention. The sudden collision sent the frog toppling off its lily pad with a startled croak and surprised the duckling so much it did an underwater somersault!

Bambi, Thumper and Flower laughed.

"I guess I like thunderstorms after all," Bambi told his mother.

"You didn't like thunderstorms?" said Thumper. "That's silly! Why would you ever say a thing like that?"

Disney Princess
Cinderella

Springtime Celebrations

Spring was on its way. The frosty mornings had become warmer and the flowers were starting to bloom. Cinderella wanted to have a party to celebrate the beginning of her favourite season!

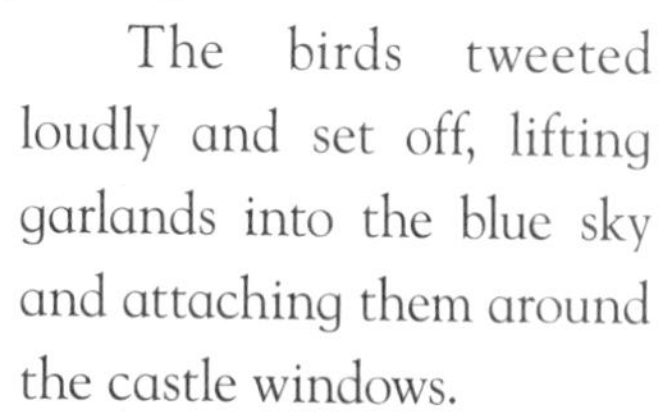

"It will be perfect," she told the Prince, as they sat on the balcony, overlooking the beautiful garden.

The Prince loved to see Cinderella excited for spring and couldn't wait to see what she had planned.

Cinderella soon left to take care of every detail. Her first visit was to the kitchen.

"We need a royal menu!" she declared to the head chef. Together, they tried a variety of cakes, breads and fancy pies. Then they made a list of all the delicious things that the head chef could bake for her special party.

"We have such a long list of tasty treats!" Cinderella smiled, when they finished tasting. "The guests will be so happy!"

Cinderella left the kitchen and met with the royal gardener, who showed the Princess his bouquets of glorious red and pink roses.

"They're magnificent!" Cinderella cried. "And will you make garlands to hang?"

"Of course, Princess," the royal gardener promised with a bow.

But when the day of the party arrived ... there was a problem.

"Your majesty!" said the royal gardener. "My ladder has broken. I can't put up the garlands."

Cinderella tried not to panic. She signalled to the birds. "Will you help us?" she asked.

The birds tweeted loudly and set off, lifting garlands into the blue sky and attaching them around the castle windows.

"Perfect!" Cinderella cheered, clapping her hands.

Now the only thing left to do was get dressed for the big event.

Cinderella disappeared into the castle and fetched her new gown from the wardrobe. It shimmered and sparkled in all shades of pink. But would the Prince like it?

When she entered the garden, with her hair styled upwards, just like the day she'd first met the Prince at the palace ball, the guests gasped and applauded. What a beautiful young woman Cinderella truly was and so pretty in her glittery dress.

"You're beautiful," said the Prince, taking her by the hand. He twirled her so everyone could see the pink dress shimmer in the light. It was the perfect spring colour for a perfect spring party and the kingdom celebrated deep into the night.

Cinderella certainly knew how to bring happiness to the castle. That was just one of many reasons the Prince loved her so much.

May

24

Disney DUMBO

The Best Gift Ever

Apart from Dumbo's mother, Mrs Jumbo, all the elephants at the circus made Dumbo feel like a nobody. They laughed at Dumbo's large ears and said that he would never amount to anything.

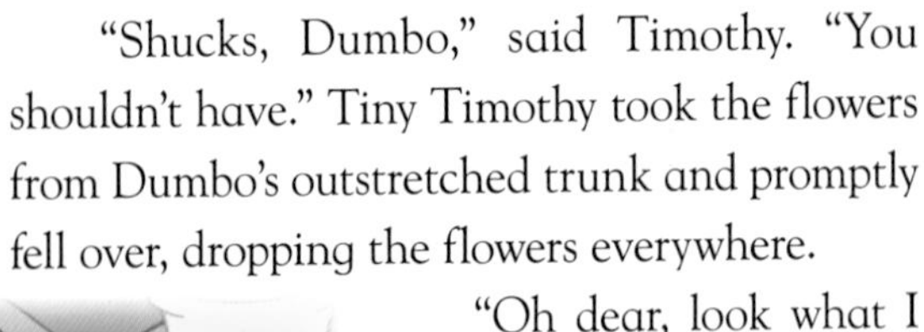

But Timothy Q. Mouse was different. Since the day he and Dumbo had met, Timothy had encouraged Dumbo. Dumbo was so happy to have a friend like Timothy. He wanted to do something nice for him.

So, one afternoon, Dumbo decided to give Timothy a gift. At feeding time, Dumbo put aside a bale of hay. Then he lugged the hay behind the Big Top and looked around for Timothy. Dumbo found him lounging in the shadow of the lion cage and plopped the hay bale down.

"Hiya, Dumbo!" said Timothy. "What's with the hay?"

Using his trunk, Dumbo nudged the hay bale closer to Timothy.

"For me?" Timothy said. "Wow. Uh ... thanks. I, uh, wonder what I'll do with it all."

Dumbo's heart sank as he realized that mice didn't eat hay. And he wanted to give Timothy something he'd really like.

The next day, Dumbo came upon a patch of flowers growing just outside the elephants' tent. He picked a nice big bouquet and took it behind the Big Top to Timothy.

"Shucks, Dumbo," said Timothy. "You shouldn't have." Tiny Timothy took the flowers from Dumbo's outstretched trunk and promptly fell over, dropping the flowers everywhere.

"Oh dear, look what I did," said Timothy.

But Dumbo thought *he* was the one who should feel bad. The bouquet was too heavy for Timothy to enjoy.

The next day, under the Big Top, Dumbo spotted a bunch of balloons tied to a seat, left behind by one of the children. *Balloons!* thought Dumbo. *Why, those wouldn't be too heavy for Timothy. They stay up all by themselves.* So Dumbo untied them and brought them to Timothy.

But, when Timothy took hold of the balloon strings, the helium-filled balloons lifted him right off the ground! Quickly, Dumbo reached out with his trunk, grasped Timothy round his waist, and placed him gently on the ground.

Then, with a disappointed sigh, Dumbo took the balloons back. *Will I ever find a good gift for Timothy?* he wondered.

"Dumbo," Timothy said, "I wanted to thank you for giving me the best gift ever."

Dumbo's eyes widened in surprise. What could Timothy mean? Every gift he had tried to give him had been all wrong.

"You're my best friend," Timothy said. "And that's the best gift I could ever ask for."

May

25

The Long, Long Night

It was night time in Pixie Hollow. Birds snuggled up in their nests, and the only lights to be seen were the stars in the sky and the fireflies chasing each other around the trees.

All the fairies were fast asleep in their beds....

Or were they?

In Tinkers' Nook, a light flickered in the window of Tinker Bell's house.

Bleary-eyed and cross, Tinker Bell sat up in bed. She was exhausted, but somehow she just couldn't fall asleep!

Maybe she should try a different position?

She turned onto her front and pulled the sheet over her head. But ... "Nope, it's no use!" she sighed, slumping onto her pillow. Sleep still wouldn't come!

Outside, the fireflies flew past Tink's window, shining bright against the dark night sky. "I'll try what Fawn does," said Tink to herself. "I'll count fireflies! One, two, three...."

Half an hour later, Tink was still counting. "751, 752, 753...." It was no good! "I have to find a way to relax," said Tink. "Otherwise I'll never fall asleep!"

Maybe doing something she enjoyed would help Tink relax.

Fixing things was fun! And there was a broken music box that needed her attention too. Tink worked on it for a long time. When it was finally mended, she got back into bed, pleased with her achievements. Now, surely, sleep would come....

No! Still her eyes remained open!

"It's impossible!" Tink sat up in bed, frustrated. "This bed's uncomfortable! I need something softer...." And then an idea struck her. "Of course! Why didn't I think of it before?"

Grinning, Tink got out of bed again. But this time she'd find the answer to her troubles outside her house.

The next morning was clear and bright, and Rosetta the garden fairy was flying her usual route over the cotton puff field.

"Good morning, Rosetta!" called Iridessa, the light fairy.

But Rosetta put her finger to her lips. "Don't shout!" she whispered.

Iridessa was puzzled. "What's going on?"

Smiling, Rosetta pointed behind her. There, stretched out on a cotton puff and snoring gently was Tinker Bell.

Rosetta giggled. "We should let her sleep."

"Okay," said Iridessa, stifling a laugh, "but later she'll have to tell us how she ended up there!"

Tink slept on, blissfully unaware of the confusion she had caused. This cotton puff was the softest bed she'd ever had!

Disney Princess Sleeping Beauty

How Rose Dozed

The moon hung high in the sky, and the stars twinkled around it. It was late at night, and Briar Rose was supposed to be sleeping. But, with all those owls hooting and the frogs in a nearby pond croaking, who could sleep? So, after tossing and turning for hours on end, Briar Rose woke up her three trusted aunties, Flora, Fauna and Merryweather, to see if they could help.

"I've got the solution!" Fauna exclaimed. "You need to count sheep."

"Lie down now, dear," Flora joined in, "and picture a fence. Then imagine sheep jumping over it one by one, and don't lose count!"

Briar Rose lay back and did as they said. But, when she got to sheep 544, she knew it wasn't working. Briar Rose went back to her aunts. "No luck," she said.

"Oh, dear," said Flora. "We'll have to think of something else instead."

"Sleep, schmeep!" Merryweather chimed in. "The night has its own brightness, twinkle and shine. It's such a shame to sleep through it all of the time!"

"You really think so?" Briar Rose asked.

"Absolutely!" Merryweather exclaimed. "Look at the stars burning bright and the moon sending down its own special light."

"That's all well and fine," Flora interrupted. "But if Briar Rose doesn't sleep at night, she'll be tired during the day."

"Good point," Briar Rose agreed.

"Well, then, try reading a book! Reading always puts me to sleep," Merryweather said with a yawn.

"But I *like* reading," Briar Rose protested. "I'll never fall asleep."

There was a pause, as each of the aunts thought and thought about how to help Briar Rose.

"I know a way to help you sleep!" Fauna said suddenly. "All you have to do," she explained, "is think good thoughts about the day that's passed, and hope for the happy things that tomorrow may bring."

"Is that true?" Briar Rose asked.

"Absolutely!" Flora agreed.

"Now, close your eyes," Merryweather instructed, "and we'll see you in your dreams."

Briar Rose wasn't sure at first, but Flora, Fauna and Merryweather had never let her down before. So she lay back down and closed her eyes. She remembered her favourite things from that very day, then thought about the wonder tomorrow would bring. Just as she was drifting off, she thought, *I hope that never happens to me again. I need my beauty sleep!* And wouldn't you know, pretty soon, she was lost in her dreams.

Disney·PIXAR TOY STORY 3

A Big Surprise

The toys were having an emergency meeting in Bonnie's room. "Buttercup and Bullseye have been missing since yesterday," Woody announced. "And the Potato Heads have been gone since this morning. We have to find out where they are before Bonnie gets home."

The other toys agreed. Splitting into three groups, they set off to explore the house. Each group had a walkie-talkie so they could keep in touch with the others as they searched for their missing friends.

In the hall, Woody, Buzz and Jessie couldn't see any sign of the missing toys.

Team two – made up of Rex, Hamm and Trixie – had nothing to report in the kitchen, either, but there was something going on right next door.

"This is team three," Dolly whispered into the walkie-talkie. "Something's moving in the sitting room. We're checking it out."

Out in the hall, Buzz gasped as Dolly's voice was silenced. There was a crackle over the radio, as if someone was struggling. "Team three, what is going on?" Buzz barked. "Dolly?"

Suddenly, Rex's voice crackled out of the walkie-talkie. "It's Bonnie's mother," he whispered. "She's come to take us away!"

Before Buzz could answer, Rex's voice became a hiss of static. "Rex?" Buzz said, turning the dial. It was no use. The other two teams were no longer answering.

"Why would she be toynapping us?" Woody wondered.

"Maybe she wants to throw us away," said Jessie.

The hall door creaked open and Bonnie's mum stepped into the room.

The terrified toys dropped and kept very still as Bonnie's mum stuffed them into a dark bag.

When the lights came back on, Woody recognized a friendly face. "Bullseye! Glad to see you," he said, studying their odd surroundings. "Even if I don't know where we are."

All the toys huddled together. "Are they really throwing us away?" Jessie wondered.

Just then, they all heard Bonnie's voice getting closer. Part of the wall peeled away, letting in the light.

"Surprise, dear!" said Bonnie's mum. Bonnie looked at her toys and jumped with joy.

"A bouncy castle!" she cheered, admiring her new gift. "Full of all my favourite toys!"

Bonnie's mum hadn't been throwing the toys away, she'd been gathering them up as a surprise. Little did she realize, she gave the toys a pretty big surprise, too!

Disney Princess
Pocahontas

Chief Mischief-maker

Like all raccoons, Meeko was curious – and that often got him into trouble. And though Pocahontas had a lot of patience when it came to her small furry friend, other members of the tribe were not as understanding.

"Pocahontas, you must teach that animal how to behave!" Chief Powhatan told her.

"Not him again!" cried the women when Meeko knocked over the baskets of grain they had spent the whole morning collecting.

"Don't you worry," Pocahontas told her friend. "They can't stay mad at you for long. Tomorrow is your birthday, after all!"

Meeko chattered excitedly. He loved birthdays – especially opening presents!

"Now stay out of trouble," Pocahontas warned. "I'll be back soon."

Meeko sat outside the hut Pocahontas shared with her father. He wondered what gift his friend had chosen for him this year. Soon, unable to resist temptation any longer, he slipped inside and spied a parcel. He wasted no time unwrapping it and discovered ... a feather headdress just his size!

Meeko couldn't wait to try it on. He didn't want to be discovered, so he grabbed his gift and scampered off towards the river. There, he put on the headdress and gazed at his reflection. As he was admiring himself, the headdress fell into the water.

The raccoon fished it out, dragging it through the mud as he pulled it ashore. Meeko's heart was pounding. He rinsed the feathers as best he could and headed back to the village. On the way, the headdress caught on the bushes. By the time he reached the village, all the feathers except one had fallen out.

Meeko knew what he had to do. He found Pocahontas and showed her what was left of the present. Pocahontas looked at Meeko sternly, but after a moment her face softened.

"Meeko, I am proud of you. You had the courage to admit what you have done," she said. "But you must try to do better. No more getting into places where you shouldn't!"

All day on his birthday, Meeko behaved perfectly. That night, Pocahontas presented him with a gift. It was the headdress, but now it had two feathers instead of one. "For every day that you are able to stay out of other people's belongings, we'll add another feather," she said.

Meeko was grateful to Pocahontas for being so understanding, and he was determined to make her proud. He would do his best to fill the headdress – but he knew it would probably take him until his next birthday!

Disney THE JUNGLE BOOK

A Bear-y Tale

It was time for Mowgli, Bagheera and Baloo to go to bed.

"Goodnight, Man-cub," purred Bagheera.

"But I'm not sleepy yet," protested Mowgli. "I need a bedtime story."

"Bedtime story?" said Bagheera. "At this hour?"

Mowgli turned to the big bear. "Please, Baloo?"

"A bedtime story, huh?" said Baloo. "Now, how do those things begin?"

"Once upon a time ..." purred Bagheera.

"Oh, right.... Once upon a time, in a house not far from this very jungle, there lived a clan of men," Baloo began.

"Real men?" asked Mowgli.

"Yep," said Baloo. "A father and a mother, and a little cub, just like you. Well, now, this clan, they cooked their food, and one day, they made a mighty tasty stew ... only thing was, when they sat down to eat, it was just too hot. So the mother got an idea. They'd go for a walk in the jungle and, by the time they got back, their stew would be nice and cool. But do you know what happened next?"

"No," Mowgli said.

"Well, that family had barely been gone a minute, when an old bear came wandering up, and stuck his nose into the Man-house."

"He did?" gasped Mowgli.

"Well, now, can you blame him? That stew just smelled so awfully good. And the next thing you know, he was tastin' it – startin' with the biggest bowl, but that was still too hot. So next he tried the middle bowl, but that was too cold. So – he tried the littlest bowl, and, don't you know, it was just right! That old bear didn't mean to, but he ate the whole thing right up!"

"What happened next?" said Mowgli.

"Oh, well, after that, this bear, he started to get tired. Real tired. And, don't you know, Little Britches, that right there in that house, looking so soft and comfortable, were three cushy-lookin' pads ... I think men call them 'beds'. Anyway, that bear, he had to try them, too. Naturally, he laid down on the biggest one first. But it was too hard. So he tried the middle one, but that was much, much too soft. So, he tried the littlest one, and, son, let me tell you, that thing was so comfortable, he fell asleep right then and there! And he would have slept clear through the next full moon ... if only that family hadn't returned and...."

"And what?" Mowgli asked breathlessly.

"And startled that bear so much, he ran back into the jungle ... full belly and all."

Mowgli smiled and tried to cover a big yawn. "Is that a true story, Baloo?"

The bear grinned. "Would I ever tell you a tall tale, Little Britches?"

Disney Princess
Jasmine

Jasmine the Matchmaker

Every morning, Jasmine enjoyed a trip through the busy streets of Agrabah in her royal coach. Rajah the tiger would sit proudly beside her for protection and the merchants all waved from their shops.

One day the street was closed off for a travelling show. "I can't wait to tell Aladdin!" Jasmine said. The circus was one of her favourite pastimes.

On opening night, Jasmine and Aladdin took the coach to the end of the street. Rajah swished his tail when he saw the circus poster with a tigress jumping through fire.

"Rajah is excited too!" smiled Jasmine.

At the circus, they were given the best seats in the house as they watched the marvellous acts unfold. Jasmine was thrilled. Aladdin cheered. But Rajah seemed sad until ... the lights dimmed!

"Ladies and gentlemen," the circus ringmaster bellowed. "I now present Mallika, the star of the show!"

Out strutted a beautiful tigress. Rajah's face lit up instantly.

"He's in love!" Jasmine realized.

Mallika dived through rings of fire. She did back flips and even walked a tightrope. But before they knew it, the show was over and Mallika went backstage.

Jasmine felt sorry for Rajah as he watched the tigress disappear, so the Princess hurried backstage. Behind the curtains, she found Mallika resting in her grand cage.

Jasmine pleaded with the ringmaster. "Could I perhaps take Mallika back to the palace?"

"Your Highness, there would be no circus without her!" he replied.

Rajah returned home that night feeling miserable.

"Poor Rajah," Jasmine said to Aladdin. "I know how he feels. I remember when we fell in love and couldn't bear to be apart. I need to talk to the circus owner again."

Suddenly there came a knock at the palace door ... and, as if he had heard her speaking, the ringmaster walked in with Mallika.

"Your Highness." He bowed. "Since your visit, Mallika has been so very sad. She would love to spend time with another tiger. I want her to live a happy life. So I have come to give her to you. Even if it means the end of my show. She means everything to me."

Rajah bounded over to Mallika and nuzzled her neck with his nose. They were truly in love – there was no denying it.

From that day forward, the circus took place in the palace grounds and the two tigers lived happily ever after.

Disney · PIXAR
FINDING NEMO

Bravest of the Bunch

"Come on, Nemo," said Gill, swimming through the fish tank. "You have to move faster, like this." He rapidly swished his black and white tailfin.

"Okay!" said Nemo. "Can I try again?"

"Of course you can! But let's see you put some more effort in this time," coached Gill.

Nemo wriggled his tailfin this way and that with all his might.

"That's better! You'll be in shape for my next escape plan in no time," Gill praised.

The other fish swam over to find out what was happening. They watched in fascination.

"But I'm in great shape already!" insisted Nemo, flexing both his big and little front-fins like a weightlifter with muscles.

"It's not all about strength, Nemo," Gill explained. "You must be brave! It's a dangerous world out there."

"Here we go again," said Gurgle, putting a purple fin to his eyes and shaking his head.

Bloat, on the other hand, was puffed up in excitement. He loved a survival story! Even if he'd heard it before.

"I approached the tank's north wall with my goal in sight," began Gill, his scarred face shimmering in the sunlight. "When a child's hand came and slammed me against the glass."

Nemo gasped. "Then what?"

"I didn't give up because nothing scares me," Gill said, with a proud smile. "I turned round suddenly and ... AAHHH!"

Nemo flinched. Just as Gill moved dramatically to demonstrate the final part of his story, a pirate skull appeared with a grisly expression and a patch over one eye. Gill had never screamed so loud before!

"Surprise!" cried Bloat, swimming out from behind the skull.

When Nemo got a closer look he realized the skull was just a plastic ornament. Gurgle and Bloat had dropped the skull behind Gill right at that crucial moment in the story ... having heard it so many times before they wanted to make it more exciting.

"So nothing scares you huh, Gill?" laughed Bloat.

"Very funny guys," Gill said, blushing with embarrassment.

The fish giggled and set the plastic skull back in its rightful place on the tank's bed.

"Of course I knew it was them all along, Nemo," whispered Gill, in private. "I was just showing you what not to do."

Nemo smiled, secretly happy to see that even Gill got scared sometimes. "Sure thing, Gill," he replied. "Whatever you say!"

June

1

The Forces of Nature

Tinker Bell was fixing the wheel of the wagon. "A few more swings of my hammer and...."

BOING! BOING! BOING!

"Done!" Tink sat back on her heels to survey the result. "It's just like new!" she decided.

"A masterpiece ..." came a voice. It was Vidia, the fast-flying fairy.

Tink was about to say thank you, when Vidia continued. "... for a tinker, that is."

Tink frowned. "What do you mean by that, Vidia?"

"I'm just noticing the difference between our talents," said Vidia rudely. "I make forces of nature. You make pots and fix wheels!"

"Think what you want, Vidia," Tink said hotly. She had work to do! Vidia was always trying to put her down – well, this time Tink was going to ignore her! She flew off to weave some baskets instead.

But Vidia wouldn't leave her alone! "You're so committed, sweetie!" she called, as Tink finished her last basket. "But no matter how hard you try, the results are always the same...."

Suddenly, Tink was blown off her feet and the baskets sent spinning as Vidia unleashed a strong gust of wind. Vidia laughed, "I make forces of nature and you weave flying baskets."

"Why don't you cut it out, Vidia?" snapped Tink, but Vidia had already gone.

"Right," Tink said to herself as she started to mould a pot. "Vidia wants to get on my nerves, but she isn't going to!" She felt quite pleased with herself for not losing her temper.

"What are you doing, Tink?" came the voice Tink was dreading to hear. Vidia flew down, sending the leaves on the nearby tree whirling into Tinker Bell's face. "As always, I make forces of nature," Vidia said gleefully, "while you make pots, pots and more pots!"

"That's not all, Vidia!" muttered Tink to herself as Vidia flew away. There was no way she was going to let Vidia get the better of her again!

The next time Vidia came visiting, Tink was ready. "Look, Vidia!" she called. "I made all these myself!"

"Pots and baskets as usual," Vidia sneered. "While I make forces of nature." Just to prove her point, she sent a small whirlwind up the tower of baskets.

But Tink knew Vidia would do that, so she had set up the whole tower to come crashing down on Vidia when she did!

Tink smiled sweetly at Vidia, buried under a pile of inventions. "You do," she agreed, "but sometimes my pots and baskets are real forces of nature too!" Giggling, she flew off, leaving Vidia fuming under the mess she had caused herself.

Disney Princess

Jasmine

Runaway Rajah

Agrabah was full of joyous cheers as the kingdom came together for the biggest parade of the year. Even Princess Jasmine and Aladdin had arrived to watch the magic unfold.

A group of talented tigers caught Jasmine's eye.

"They're magnificent!" she gasped, watching as a girl from the parade made the tigers jump through hoops. Jasmine could do a clever trick with Rajah too. Grabbing a basket of fruit, she showed Aladdin a watermelon and tossed it into the air. Before the melon hit the ground, Rajah sliced it into juicy segments with his claws.

"Amazing!" Aladdin clapped. "Hey, why don't you and Abu go and walk along the parade with the other animals and make friends?" he suggested to the tiger.

Abu jumped onto Rajah's back and together the two of them set off through the excitable crowd.

Later that day, Abu found Aladdin and Jasmine at the palace. He tugged on Jasmine's outfit in desperation.

"What's wrong?" she asked him.

Abu pointed at the gates leading outside the palace. He walked on all fours like a lion and screeched loudly.

Jasmine realized what he was trying to say. "Something is wrong with Rajah!"

Quickly, Aladdin whistled for his magic carpet. Carpet flew over and scooped them up.

As the magic carpet travelled at great speed over the kingdom, it didn't notice the washing line between two houses and got caught like a fly in a spider's web!

Jasmine, Aladdin and Abu fell off the carpet and landed with a bump on a rooftop. But they didn't waste a moment. Grabbing a wooden pole, Jasmine vaulted onto the next house, and the next, and the next! Aladdin and Abu followed close behind her.

Finally they reached the end of the parade. They jumped off the roof into a pile of hay.

"There are the tigers," Aladdin said.

Jasmine spotted Rajah and rushed to cuddle him.

"What are you doing?" a man asked. "I'm the parade master and these are my animals."

"This is my tiger, Rajah," Jasmine insisted. "Watch this."

Jasmine picked up a melon and tossed it into the air. Rajah sliced it into segments before their very eyes.

"Incredible!" said the parade master. "None of my tigers can do that!"

The parade master apologized for the mix up and as a reward, his people stayed for one more day – making Rajah the star of the show!

Disney Princess
Beauty and the Beast

Sweet Surprises

On a sunny morning, Belle strolled to the Jolie Bakery with her wicker basket piled with books. She always stopped there on the way to the library to see the baker's daughter, Claire.

"Are those new books?" Claire asked.

"They're the ones I'm about to return," Belle replied. Usually she would read a story to Claire but this time she had a new idea. "Shall I make up a story instead of reading one?"

Claire was happy to listen to Belle's enchanting fairytale as she iced a cake for her father's shop.

"I wish I could make up stories," Claire said.

"Have you ever tried?" Belle asked.

"Yes. I just can't do it," she grumbled.

When Claire had finished icing the cake, Belle accompanied her to deliver it. Along the way, they saw a beautiful dress in a window.

"How lovely!" Claire pointed out. "Whoever made it is so talented. I could never make a dress like that."

"But Claire, look at the cake you just made. It's magnificent!" Belle reassured her.

Claire sighed. "I'd rather make something unique and special."

The following morning, when Belle popped into the Jolie Bakery, she found a gift waiting for her. It was a dress made from mismatched materials, with a sleeve sewed at the waist.

"I designed it myself," Claire explained shyly. "But it went a bit wrong!"

Later, Claire tried to write her first poem.

"While a cake bakes, a rolling pin drops on my toes and my foot aches," she read from a sheet of parchment. But she knew it wasn't exactly a masterpiece.

Still in search of a talent, Claire tried painting, but her pictures were a disaster. When Belle visited, Claire quickly put her paintings out of sight in embarrassment.

"It's my father's birthday," Belle said. "I want to bake a cake for him."

Claire grabbed the mixing bowls, but no matter how hard Belle tried, she simply could not get the cake mixture right and the icing bag split and shot icing over the floor.

"Oops!" Belle cried, blushing.

"Don't worry!" Claire said. "I'll make you the perfect cake!"

Determined, Claire set to work and baked a cake in the shape of a miniature version of one of Belle's father's inventions, which she'd seen at his workshop.

"Wow!" cried Belle when it was finished. "That's where your creativity blossoms!"

Claire smiled. Belle was right. She did have a talent – an incredible talent for cake making. The entire town admired her cakes and no one could deny they tasted divine!

Disney MINNIE

Friends on Ice

"An ice-skating competition!" gasped Minnie Mouse. She showed her friends the poster. "First prize is a golden ice skate!"

Macy shivered. "That ice blade is so sharp! If you even touch the blade on a skate, you could be seriously injured."

Minnie and Daisy were determined to enter. But the competition was only open to trios – who could be the third member of their team?

Konnie had an injury, and Leonard couldn't skate, so that left only Macy. "But aren't you afraid of the blades?" Daisy asked.

"Well," replied Macy, "I'll just try not to look at them or touch them."

Minnie was thrilled. They had a team! And what with Daisy's choreography ideas and her own costume design talents, they were in with a great chance of winning the golden skate!

Except that, at their first practice, Macy wouldn't let go of the side. "If I slip, I'll fall!" she gasped in panic. "And then I'll see the blades!"

Abigail skated by with her twin sidekicks. "Look, girls," she called. "A koala on skates!"

Minnie and Daisy rolled their eyes. How typical that Abigail was entering too! Now they had to win! But how were they going to get Macy to learn to skate in time?

Daisy switched on some music. Macy brightened up. "Wow! This beat really makes me want to dance!" She let go of the side and boogied around.

"Come on then!" called Daisy. "Follow me!"

But dancing on the spot was one thing and skating quite another! Macy grabbed hold of Daisy for reassurance. "We can't skate like this!" protested Daisy, nearly losing her balance.

So Macy hung onto Minnie's hair bow instead. But pulling Macy along just slowed Minnie down!

"Macy's a disaster," Daisy said to Minnie later, as Macy was changing. "She's going to make us lose!"

Unknown to Daisy, the sneaky Abigail was listening to the conversation and went to tell Macy everything. When Daisy and Minnie realized what had happened, they felt awful.

They went round to Macy's house and apologized. "Nothing is more important than our friendship," said Daisy sincerely.

Macy forgave them – and they came up with the perfect way to make their routine work!

On the day of the competition, Minnie, Macy and Daisy glided onto the ice in perfect synchronicity – linked together by beautiful ribbons! The routine was a triumph, and the judges awarded them the golden skate for "The Most United Trio"!

The three friends beamed at each other. True friendship could withstand anything!

June

5

Lucky's Last Laugh

It was getting quite late at Pongo and Perdita's house, but their darling little puppies were still not asleep. It wasn't that they didn't want to go to sleep. At least most of them. No, the problem was that one of them wouldn't let them go to sleep – and that puppy was Lucky!

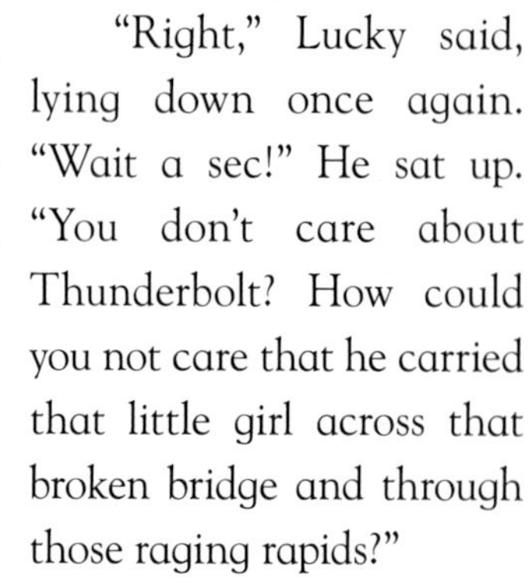

"And then, don't you remember, you guys, the part at the very beginning, when Thunderbolt jumped across that canyon? Whoosh! Like a rocket! Clear to the other side!" Lucky said, recounting his favourite TV show.

"Yes, Lucky, we remember," his sister Penny groaned. "How could we forget? You've reminded us 101 times!"

"Yeah! It was so great! And then there was that part when –"

"Lucky!" wailed Rolly. "We all watched the same episode of Thunderbolt tonight. You don't have to tell us about it."

"Yeah, I know, but I just wanted to tell you about the part when Thunderbolt found the little girl, then ran back to tell the sheriff –"

"Lucky! It's late! We want to go to sleep!" barked Patch.

Lucky laid his head on his paws. "Okay," he said. "I'll be quiet."

All the puppies closed their eyes.

"Oh! But what about the part when the sheriff told Thunderbolt to climb up that cliff, and he got to the top, and he grabbed that rope with his teeth, and he pulled up the little girl –"

"Lucky!" yelped Pepper. "We don't care about Thunderbolt. We want to go to bed!"

"Right," Lucky said, lying down once again. "Wait a sec!" He sat up. "You don't care about Thunderbolt? How could you not care that he carried that little girl across that broken bridge and through those raging rapids?"

"We mean," said Freckles, "we want you to be quiet so we can go to sleep!"

"You mean," said Lucky, "you don't want me to tell you about the last part where Thunderbolt ran back to the mountains and into that cave, and found that amazing thing?"

"Yes!" Lucky's siblings shouted together.

"Why didn't you say so?" replied Lucky, closing his eyes. "Goodnight."

For a minute, everyone enjoyed the silence. Then Penny sat up.

"Hey, wait a minute," she said. "What thing did he find?"

"Yeah," said Patch. "I missed that part."

"Me, too," said Rolly. "What was it exactly that he found, Lucky? Tell us."

But there was no answer. Lucky was fast asleep. And now the other Dalmatian puppies were wide awake!

Tinker Bell's Discoveries

It was a beautiful sunny day and Tinker Bell was out hunting for lost things. Being a tinker fairy meant that Tinker Bell loved to fiddle and fix, craft and create, with anything that she found.

"Why do so many things get thrown away?" she wondered. Other people might call it junk, but Tink believed that every object from the mainland that wound up in Never Land could be useful to the fairies. Nothing was more exciting than making a new discovery!

A large, round glass object caught her eye as it glinted in the sun, and she hurried over to investigate. "Oh, look! A Whatchamacallit!" It had a frame with a handle, but Tink had no idea what it was. "I wonder what it's for...."

Curiously, she peered into the glass ... and suddenly, a huge, terrifying monster appeared in front of her! "Argh!" Tink yelled, falling backwards in shock. "Blazing bolts!"

The monster opened its big jaws at her. It was green, with red horns and was at least three times her size! Was it going to eat her?

Tink got to her feet, ready to flee. But she hated running away, even from danger. How dare this monster threaten her! She had every right to be here, looking for lost things for her work! She made her hands into fists.

"Put up your dukes if you've got the guts!" she said, trying not to let her voice wobble. "You don't scare me!"

The monster hesitated – and then vanished.

Tink was astonished. Where had it gone? "Come here!" she called, feeling braver already. "I'll ... where are you?"

A small green caterpillar with cute red horns crawled out from behind the magnifying glass. It looked at Tink in surprise.

"Huh?" Tink looked from the caterpillar to the glass and back again. It looked just like the monster she'd seen ... only smaller. And then she realized – the glass object made everything look bigger! It hadn't been a monster at all!

Tinker Bell burst into laughter. The caterpillar was annoyed – it thought Tink was laughing at it!

Tink went round the other side of the glass and pulled a funny face at the caterpillar. The shape of the glass made her face look even bigger and sillier – and soon the caterpillar was laughing too! Tink stuck out her tongue and waggled her fingers, and before long they were both helpless with giggles. What a great new game they had discovered!

Tink was delighted with her new find – and her new friend!

June

7

Disney Princess Snow White and the Seven Dwarfs

A Windy Adventure

Snow White awoke and decided it was the perfect day to visit the Dwarfs at their cottage. She picked some berries on her way through the woods, so she could bake a delicious pie for them.

"It'll be a wonderful surprise when they return home after a hard day at the mines," she told her woodland friends, as she walked along.

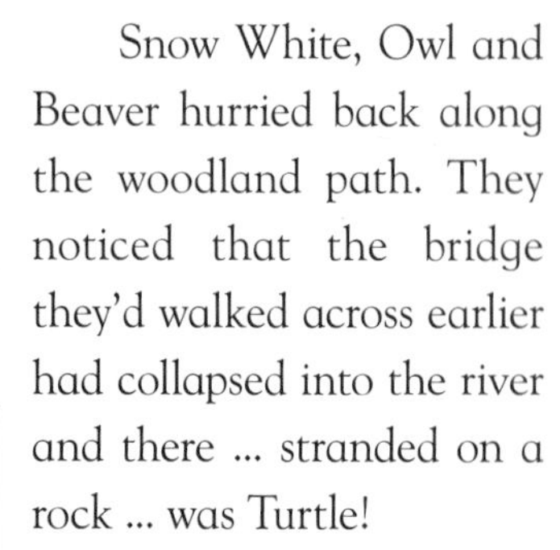

Soon, she reached a fork in the path. "I've never taken the trail to the right before," she said, curiously. Then suddenly a strong gust of wind blew her towards the mysterious trail. "I think that's a sign," she said to Turtle, who was slowly plodding behind her. The other woodland animals nodded in agreement.

The trail opened into a sunny clearing with trees full of nuts. Snow White was overjoyed, she started gathering them in her basket. But as she busied herself, a gust of wind snatched the cape right off her shoulders! She chased the cape until finally it stopped, when it caught on a tree branch.

"Oh my," she said, retrieving it and looking around. "I think I'm lost."

She couldn't remember which way she'd come. Then she spotted her footprints in the mud. "I know, I'll follow my tracks!" she realized, with a sigh of relief.

When she was back at the clearing, she collected her basket and smiled at the animals. But Turtle was missing. "Oh my, did he get lost too?" she worried.

Snow White, Owl and Beaver hurried back along the woodland path. They noticed that the bridge they'd walked across earlier had collapsed into the river and there ... stranded on a rock ... was Turtle!

"Owl!" Snow White called. "If you fly to the other side and pick up the broken rope, Beaver can chew some new wooden stakes. Then I'll hammer them in place and together we can rebuild the bridge!"

The three friends set to work. Snow White used a rock to hammer Beaver's freshly chomped stakes into place and attached them to Owl's rope. Soon, there was a crowd of animals working together to save Turtle, and Snow White's bridge was finished in no time.

"I'm here!" she called to Turtle, scooping him safely into her arms.

When Snow White and her friends finally made it to the Dwarfs' cottage, she baked a lovely gooseberry-nut pie.

"Did you have any problems today?" the Dwarfs asked.

"Nothing we couldn't handle," she replied, with a happy wink to her friends.

DISNEY
DUMBO

Ears a Job for You, Dumbo!

It had been a hard day for little Dumbo. It was bad enough that everyone made fun of his ears except his mother, but then they had put his mother in a cage, so Dumbo couldn't even be with the one person who loved him and treated him kindly.

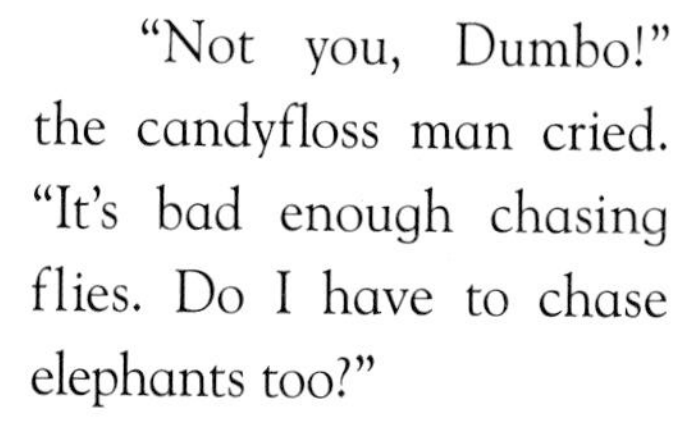

What made things even worse was that Dumbo didn't have anything to do. It seemed that he was the only creature in the circus who didn't have a job. Everyone had a purpose except Dumbo. All he could do was feel sad and be laughed at.

Dumbo heaved a sigh and went for a walk through the circus tents. Soon, he found himself among the refreshment stalls. Everyone here had a job too. Some were squeezing lemons to make lemonade. Others were popping popcorn or roasting peanuts. Wonderful smells filled the air.

Finally, Dumbo came to a little candyfloss wagon. The puffy cloud of sugar looked tempting, and Dumbo wanted a taste, but there were so many customers crowded around the wagon that he couldn't get close enough.

Suddenly Dumbo heard a loud buzzing. Then all the customers waved their hands over their heads and ran away.

The smell of sugar had attracted a swarm of nasty flies!

"Scat!" cried the candyfloss man. "Go away before you scare off my customers."

Dumbo reached out his trunk to smell the delicious candyfloss.

"Not you, Dumbo!" the candyfloss man cried. "It's bad enough chasing flies. Do I have to chase elephants too?"

Poor Dumbo was startled. With a snort, he sucked candyfloss right up his nose.

AH-CHOO! When he sneezed, Dumbo's ears flapped, and something amazing happened.

"Remarkable!" the candyfloss man cried. "All the flies are gone. They think your ears are giant fly swatters!"

The candyfloss man patted Dumbo's head. "How would you like a job?"

Dumbo nodded enthusiastically and set to waving his ears. Soon, the candyfloss stall was the most popular refreshment stall in the circus – and had the least flies. But, best of all, Dumbo now had something to do to take his mind off his troubles. He was still sad, but things didn't seem quite so bad. And, who knows, perhaps soon he'd have his mother back.

"I wonder what other amazing things those big ears can do?" said the candyfloss man, giving Dumbo a friendly smile. "I'll bet they carry you far...."

Hide, Dude!

"Come on, Squirt!" Nemo cried happily. "Race you to the coral shelf!"

Nemo took off, pumping his fins as hard as he could. His sea turtle friend laughed and swam after him.

Squirt was visiting Nemo at his home on the reef. "This way, dude!" Squirt yelled, flinging himself through the water. "I'm catching some rad current over here!"

Nemo hesitated, watching as his friend tumbled past some stinging coral. Squirt was so brave! Even after all that Nemo had been through – being captured by a scuba diver, then escaping from a tank to find his way home again – he still got scared sometimes.

With a deep breath, he threw himself into the current. He tumbled after Squirt, fins flying as the water carried him along. Finally, he came out the other end, landing in the still ocean beside Squirt.

"That was fun! Let's do it again!" Nemo giggled, but Squirt looked worried. "Squirt? Squirt, what's wrong?"

The sea turtle was staring into the distance, his eyes wide. "Hide, dude!" Squirt cried.

Before Nemo could respond, Squirt's head and legs popped into his shell and he landed on the sea floor with a flop. Nemo started trembling. What had scared Squirt so much?

Nemo looked around, expecting to see a shark. But all he could see nearby were a few pieces of coral with a lone Spanish dancer floating along above them. He swam down and tapped on Squirt's shell. "Hey," he said. "What is it? There's nothing scary here."

"Whew!" Squirt's head popped out. He looked around, then gasped and hid again. When he spoke, his voice was muffled. "It's totally still there!"

Nemo blinked and looked around again. Still, all he could see was the coral and the Spanish dancer.

"Hey, wait a minute," he said, suddenly realizing something. "Haven't you ever seen a Spanish dancer before?"

"A – a Spanish wha-huh?" Squirt asked, from inside his shell.

Nemo knocked on his friend's shell again. "It's a kind of sea slug," he explained. "Don't worry, Spanish dancers are nice – you don't have to be scared. I promise."

Finally Squirt's head popped out again. He smiled sheepishly at Nemo.

"Sorry, dude," he said. "I never saw one of those before. It totally freaked me out."

"It's okay." Nemo smiled back. He already knew that new things could be scary – and now he knew he wasn't the only one who thought so. "Come on, let's go play," he said.

Disney THE LION KING

The Best Fisherman of All

Simba and his friends Timon and Pumbaa were hungry. They wandered through the forest until they came to an old, rotten tree. Timon knocked on the trunk.

"What's it sound like, Timon?" Pumbaa asked.

"Like our breakfast!" Timon replied. He pulled at the bark and hundreds of grubs slithered out.

Timon offered Simba one of the grubs.

"No, thanks." Simba sighed. "I'm tired of grubs."

"Ants are tasty," said Timon. "They come in two flavours. Red and black."

Simba shook his head. "Don't you eat anything other than bugs?"

"Fish!" Pumbaa declared.

"I love fish!" Simba exclaimed.

"Why didn't you say so?" said Timon. "There's a pond at the end of this trail." The three friends started off down the trail.

"What now?" asked Simba when they arrived at the pond.

"That's the problem!" said Timon. "We're not the best fishermen in the world."

"I'll teach you!" Simba said.

The lion climbed up a tree and crawled onto a branch that hung over the water. Then he snatched a fish out of the water.

"See!" Simba said, jumping to the ground. "Not a problem. Fishing's easy."

"Not for me!" Timon cried. He dangled from the branch, just like Simba had shown him, but his arms weren't long enough to reach the fish.

Simba laughed. "Better let Pumbaa try."

"What a joke!" cried Timon. "Pumbaa can't even climb this tree."

"Want to bet?" Pumbaa said to him.

"Stay there," Timon warned. "I don't think this branch is strong enough for both of us."

With a hop, Pumbaa landed on the branch next to Timon. The limb started to bend.

"Yikes!" Timon cried as he leaped to another tree.

CRACK! The branch broke under Pumbaa. With a squeal, he landed in the pond. The splash was enormous!

Simba, sitting on the bank, was soaked. Timon was nearly blasted from his perch. Pond water fell like rain all around them.

Simba opened his eyes and started to laugh. So did Timon.

Pumbaa was sitting in a pool of mud where the pond had been. He'd splashed so much of the water out that dozens of fish squirmed on the ground, just waiting to be gobbled up.

"Wow!" Timon cried. "I think Pumbaa is the very best fisherman of all!"

Disney Princess Cinderella

Dressed to Scare

Cinderella worked from morning until night doing the bidding of her stepmother and stepsisters. In return, they treated her unkindly and dressed her in tattered old clothes. It wasn't a very fair deal.

Luckily, Cinderella had the friendship of the animals in the manor, including two mice named Jaq and Mary.

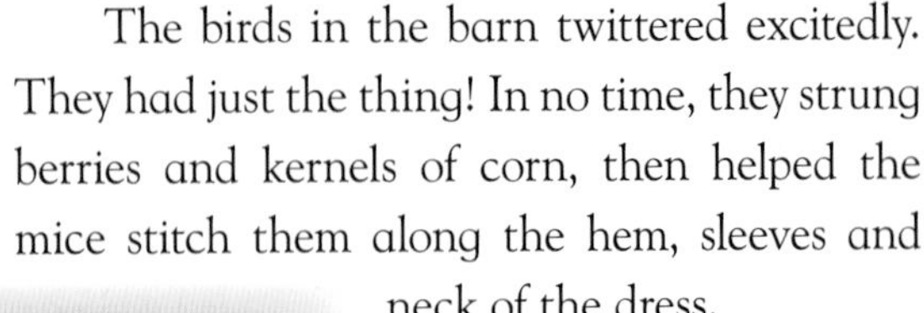

"Poor Cinderelly," said Jaq as he and Mary watched their dear friend scrubbing the floor. "She deserves a present."

"Hmm," Mary replied. She led Jaq out to the farmyard so that Cinderella wouldn't hear them planning. "Let's make a new dress!" she suggested.

"Good idea!" Jaq replied. But he wondered what they could use for cloth. Jaq looked around, then scurried over to a sack of feed and gnawed it open with his teeth.

"Jaq, no!" Mary scolded. "You can eat later."

"No-no," Jaq explained. "This cloth is for Cinderelly's new dress. See?" He gestured towards the sack.

The other mice joined to help. They cut out the dress in no time, sewing it together with some thread they had borrowed from Cinderella's sewing kit. They stepped back to admire their work. "Too plain!" Gus announced.

"Yes," Jaq agreed in a disappointed voice. "What should we do to fix it?"

The birds in the barn twittered excitedly. They had just the thing! In no time, they strung berries and kernels of corn, then helped the mice stitch them along the hem, sleeves and neck of the dress.

"There!" said Perla the mouse. "Much better!"

With the birds' help, the mice hung the dress on a post in the garden where Cinderella kept her straw hat. "Cinderelly's gonna love it!" Jaq proclaimed.

The mice went inside to fetch Cinderella, then told her to close her eyes as she walked out into the garden.

"Open your eyes now, Cinderelly!" Jaq instructed.

"Surprise!" the mice shouted.

Cinderella gazed at the sackcloth dress on the post with her hat perched on top. "Oh, thank you!" she exclaimed. "I've been needing a scarecrow for the garden!"

Jaq opened his mouth wide to explain, but Mary clamped her paw over it.

"You're welcome, Cinderelly," Mary said.

After Cinderella had gone, Jaq frowned. "We sewed a bad dress."

"But we made a good scarecrow," Mary told him, trying to look on the bright side.

"Yes!" Jaq agreed. "And Cinderelly's happy!" And to the mice, that was the most important thing of all.

Disney MICKEY & FRIENDS

Goodbye, Hiccups!

Mickey sighed. No matter what he did, he couldn't stop hiccuping.

"What's wrong, Mickey?" Minnie asked, peering over the fence.

"Oh, hi – *hic* – Minnie," Mickey said. "It's these hiccups. They won't – *hic* – go away."

"Maybe Daisy and I can help," said Minnie.

"Help with what?" asked Daisy, walking up.

"Mickey has the hiccups!" said Minnie.

Leading Mickey into the kitchen, Minnie poured him a glass of water.

"Take a tiny sip," she said. "Then another."

Mickey did as Minnie said.

"I think it worked!" he said. "Thank – *hic!*"

"Hmmm," said Minnie. "I think we need another idea!"

"It sounds like you need my tried-and-tested hiccup cure!" said Daisy. "This may seem silly, but just do what I do."

Daisy did two high kicks, a little tap dance, then spun round once and took a bow.

Mickey started to do the same, but halfway through – "*Hic!*"

"Maybe Donald knows a cure for the hiccups," said Minnie.

They went to find Donald, but Minnie and Daisy raced ahead. When Mickey arrived at Donald's house, they were waiting by the door.

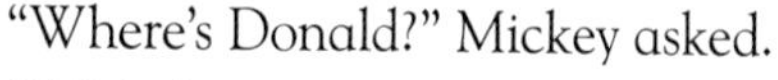

"Where's Donald?" Mickey asked.

"BOO!" Donald jumped out at Mickey.

"Aaah!" Mickey cried.

"Sorry," Donald said. "I thought I could scare your hiccups away. Did it work?"

But poor Mickey just hiccuped again.

Mickey tried everything he could think of to get rid of his hiccups.

He stood on his head while saying the alphabet backwards. "*Hic!*"

He held his nose and whistled a tune. "*Hic!*"

"It's no use," he told his friends. "I think they're – *hic* – here to stay."

Minnie led Daisy and Donald to the side of the garden. "I have one last idea," she told them.

The friends whispered to one another. Then Donald went inside and returned with a big sack.

Minnie pulled out some blocks. She balanced three of them on her nose.

Daisy and Donald pulled out two rings. They hung one on each of Minnie's arms and she began to twirl them.

"Your turn, Mickey!" Minnie said.

All Mickey could do was laugh. "I'm sorry, Minnie," he giggled. "You just look so ... silly!"

When Mickey finally stopped laughing, he realized his hiccups were gone!

"You cured me," said Mickey. "I guess laughter really is the best medicine!"

Disney · PIXAR TOY STORY 3

A Smile for Chuckles

Chuckles the clown stared glumly out of Bonnie's bedroom window. *Poor Chuckles,* thought Jessie. *He always looks so sad.*

The clown's big frown gave Jessie an idea. "We'll each try to get Chuckles to smile," she said, to her friends. "The first to succeed will be crowned 'The Funniest Toy'!"

After taking some time to prepare, the toys began their acts. Buttercup was up first. "Look, pal!" he cried, standing on one leg as he balanced a spinning ball on his horn. "I'm a juggling unicorn!"

Chuckles frowned. "Um ... right," he said.

Buttercup trudged back to the others, disappointed. "I thought a clown would enjoy a good circus number," he said.

Jessie hopped onto Bullseye's back. "Maybe he prefers the rodeo!"

She twirled her lasso as Bullseye hopped and bucked around the room. It was quite a show, but Chuckles didn't look impressed.

Next it was the turn of Mr and Mrs Potato Head. They were barely recognizable as they stumbled out from below the bed. Their arms were where their eyes should be, their mouths were poking out of their earholes and their noses were on top of their heads!

"Oops, I feel a little mixed up!" Mrs Potato Head said.

They really were a funny sight, but not funny enough to amuse Chuckles.

Jessie gathered her friends beside the house of cards Bonnie had built that morning, out of sight of Chuckles. "It sure is tough to get a smile out of him," Jessie said.

Suddenly, something whizzed over Jessie's head. "Run for cover!" she cried, as three little green balls bounced into the house of cards, knocking it flat.

"Comin' through!" the little green balls giggled.

The cards toppled down on Jessie and her friends, sending them sprawling onto the floor.

"What was that?" asked Buttercup, climbing out from underneath the cards.

"Maybe an earthquake," said Mrs Potato Head, looking worried.

Mr Potato Head knew better, though. The mess had been caused by the peas-in-a-pod toys, who loved bouncing around Bonnie's room. Mr Potato Head was about to give them a telling off, when he heard a sound he'd never heard before.

Chuckles was laughing! "You peas are really funny," he giggled.

Jessie was happy. The funniest toys had been found – but tidying up the mess they had made before Bonnie got home was going to be no laughing matter!

Disney Fairies

Water Games

It was a hot, hot day, and Tinker Bell decided to go to the pond to cool down and visit her friend Silvermist, the water fairy.

But when she arrived, a strange sight met her eyes. Silvermist was riding on a spoon as a hummingbird pulled it across the pond! "What are you doing?" called Tink.

Silvermist waved back from the pond. "Hi Tink! I'm skiing on the water with the help of my hummingbird friend!"

"That sounds fun," Tink said. "Can I try?"

"Sure!" said Silvermist. "Hop in!" She held the spoon still while Tink climbed into its curved bowl. It wobbled alarmingly. "The trick is keeping your balance!" Silvermist told her.

From the opposite side of the pond, Vidia lay on a leaf and watched. "You might as well give up, Tink!" she called. "You're too clumsy!"

Tink fumed. Vidia said the meanest things sometimes! But that only made her more determined to succeed! "We'll see about that!" she shouted back.

The hummingbird picked up the handle of the spoon in its claws and prepared to take off.

"I can do it!" Tink told herself confidently. "Here I go!"

The spoon whizzed across the surface of the pond as the hummingbird flapped its wings very fast. It was hard for Tink to stay upright – but it was so exciting! The plants and flowers on the bank flashed past – and there was Vidia, lying lazily on her leaf....

"Look out!" yelled Vidia.

SPLASH!

Tink stepped off the spoon, beaming with delight. "What a ride!" she cried. "I want to go again!"

Silvermist, who had flown over to meet her, lowered her voice. "I don't think everyone wants you to go again...."

Stomping towards them was Vidia, soaked from wing to toe. "Just look at what you've done!" she shouted at Tink.

"I'm so sorry," Tink said. "I didn't mean to get you wet."

"Tink didn't do it on purpose," Silvermist said, backing her friend up. Vidia looked as though she were about to explode! "Besides, look on the bright side!"

"Which would be...?" growled Vidia.

Silvermist smiled. "We were all trying to cool down, but you're the only one who actually managed to!"

Vidia opened her mouth to protest, but instead a smile spread over her face, and soon all three of them were laughing together. Silvermist was right! On such a hot day, getting wet was the only way to cool down!

THE PRINCESS AND THE FROG

Happy Birthday, Mama Odie

Princess Tiana and Prince Naveen had a very special celebration to get to ... it was Mama Odie's 198th birthday!

As they entered Mama Odie's big house at the edge of the bayou, she welcomed her friends with open arms. "It's so nice to see you!" she cried.

"We wouldn't dream of missing your birthday, Mama Odie!" Tiana said.

"Not for anything in the world," agreed Naveen.

"We invited our friends the fireflies as well!" Tiana told her, as the beautiful, glowing bugs flew into the house excitedly.

"Oh! What a brilliant idea," smiled Mama Odie. Then she noticed someone was missing. "Isn't jabber jaws coming?"

"Oh I'm here! I'm here!" came a call from the door. Louis the alligator blundered in with his trumpet in hand. "I love parties."

"Perfect," said Mama Odie. "Let's have some music then!"

"You got it," winked Louis. He raised his trumpet to his lips, but a strange sound came from the instrument as he blew.

"That's it?" asked Mama Odie. "I remember jazz sounding different...."

Louis stared into his trumpet in confusion. "Hang on. Hang on." He banged the end and a firefly tumbled out into the palm of his hand.

"Edmund!" cried the other flies. "What were you doing in there?"

"Sleeping!" the little bug admitted, feeling a bit dizzy from the vibrations.

After some dancing and singing, it was time for cake. But something seemed to be missing....

"Did you forget the candles?" Tiana asked.

Naveen looked guilty. "I didn't forget them ... I just didn't bring them."

"Why?" Tiana pressed.

"Because 198 candles can't fit on one cake," he explained matter-of-factly.

"What's a birthday without candles?" asked a hovering firefly.

Tiana frowned. "Don't worry. I may know how to fix this...."

Finally, Tiana was ready and Naveen helped Mama Odie into the kitchen, where the smell of cake filled their noses. Mama Odie couldn't believe her eyes. The cake was glowing!

"How did you manage to fit all those candles on?" she asked, mesmerized.

Tiana and Naveen chuckled. As they got closer to the cake, Mama Odie spotted what made the flickering of the candles so special....

"They're fireflies," she realized in glee.

When the firefly lights were all blown out, the only thing left to do was gobble the cake up ... and party all night long!

Lady and the TRAMP

In the Doghouse

"Good morning, Tramp," said Lady, with a yawn and a stretch. She rolled over on her silk cushion. "Wasn't that just the most wonderful night's sleep?"

But Tramp's night's sleep had been far from wonderful. In fact, he hadn't had much sleep at all.

The past night had been Tramp's first sleeping in Lady's house ... or in any house, come to think of it.

"How do you do it?" he grumbled. "That bed is so soft, I feel like I'm sinking in a feather pool. And between Jim Dear's snoring and the baby's crying, I could barely hear the crickets chirping."

"Oh, dear," Lady said, feeling truly sorry for him. "Well, Jim Dear and Darling love you so I'm sure they'd let you sleep up on their bed tonight. There's nothing in the world better than that!"

But Tramp didn't agree. "I'm afraid it's the outdoors I need," he explained. "I mean, I know you grew up this way and all ... but it's so much fun to sleep under the moon and the stars. There's nothing to howl at in this bedroom."

"You can see the moon out of the window," Lady told him.

"It's not the same," said Tramp, shaking his head. Then he had a thought. "You know, we've still got that fine doghouse in the garden. What do you say we go back out there tonight? It'll be like a honeymoon!"

Lady looked at poor Tramp's tired eyes. "Well ... okay."

And so that night, as soon as the sun set and the moon began to rise in the sky, Lady and Tramp went out to the garden.

Happy at last, Tramp turned three times and then plopped down. "Oh, how I love the feel of cool dirt on my belly!" he said with a dreamy smile, while Lady gingerly peeked into the dark kennel. The stars were not even out, and already she missed the comforts of Jim Dear and Darling's room.

Tramp watched as Lady stretched out on the kennel floor, then got up and moved outside, then back in once again. It was plain to see – try as she might, Lady just could not relax on the cold, hard ground.

"Don't worry," Tramp announced, "I have an idea."

And with that, he ran into the house. In seconds, he reappeared with Lady's cushion in his teeth. Carefully, Tramp swept the kennel with his tail, and laid the cushion down just the way Lady liked it.

Lady smiled and lay down. And, do you know what? That night, they both had the sweetest dreams either one had ever had.

June
17

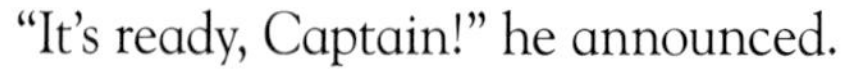

A 'Snappy' New Ship

"My ship, my beautiful ship!" Captain Hook moaned. It had not been a good day for the pirate. Peter Pan and the Darling children had stolen his ship. And now, Hook was stranded on an island with Smee and the other pirates, after their rowing boat had been destroyed by the crocodile.

"It's a nice island, Captain," said Smee, trying to cheer up his boss. "And you could use a holiday."

Captain Hook turned to Smee with a furious look on his face. "Pirates don't take holidays! Pirates seek revenge! Which is precisely what we are going to do, as soon as we have a new ship to sail in."

Smee looked around. "Where are we going to find a ship around here, Sir?" he asked.

"We aren't going to find one," Captain Hook answered. "You and the rest of this mangy crew are going to build one! And I don't mean a little one either. I mean a big, menacing, fit-for-a-magnificent-pirate-like-me one!"

For weeks, the pirates chopped trees and cut them into planks for the ship. They made thousands of pegs to use for nails, and crushed countless berries to use for paint. "You're not moving fast enough!" Hook complained as he sat in the shade, sipping juice out of a pineapple.

Finally, an exhausted Smee fetched Hook as he awoke from his afternoon nap.

"It's ready, Captain!" he announced.

Even Hook had to admit the ship was magnificent. Shaped like a gigantic crocodile, it was painted a reptilian shade of green.

"No one will dare come near this ship. Not even that pesky crocodile. He won't want to fight with anything this terrifying," Smee assured him.

Captain Hook was delighted. "We set sail tomorrow!" he announced.

That night, Smee couldn't resist putting one more finishing touch on the ship. He painted a row of eyelashes on the crocodile's eyelids.

The next morning, Captain Hook and the crew climbed aboard and pushed off. The ticking crocodile soon appeared.

"Smee!" yelled a terrified Captain Hook. "I thought you said he wouldn't come near us!"

"But look how calm he is," said Smee, puzzled. "He's even smiling!"

Smee leaned over the side of the railing. "You know, it might be those eyelashes I painted. Maybe the croc thinks the ship is its mother."

Hook lunged at Smee. "You made my ship look like a mother crocodile? This vessel is supposed to be terrifying!"

"Mothers can be terrifying, sir," said Smee. "You should have seen mine when I told her I was going to become a pirate!"

June

18

Disney Princess

Jasmine

Jasmine and the Star of Persia

Princess Jasmine loved stories about the stars. Every night, she and Aladdin would gaze up at the sky and he would tell her about them.

"What's that star?" Jasmine asked Aladdin one evening.

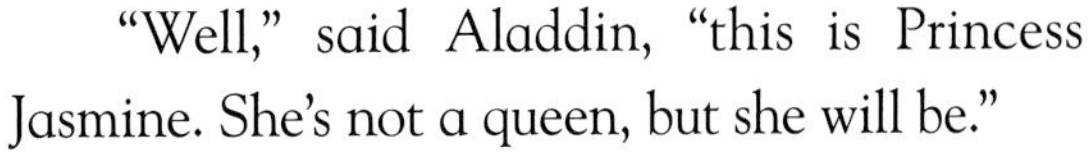

"The Star of Persia," he replied. "It belonged to a kind and beautiful queen. When she died, they hid the jewel away in a tower, sure that no one would be worthy of its beauty again."

Jasmine's eyes shone. "Is that story true?"

Aladdin shrugged. "I don't know. But there is one way to find out."

The next morning, Jasmine and Aladdin set off on the Magic Carpet. Before long, a tall tower rose from a square in a tiny kingdom – it was the tower from Aladdin's story.

"Let's fly down and see if there's a way in," Aladdin said.

But they discovered that the tower was locked. Without a key there was little chance of getting in.

All of a sudden, a guard spoke up. "What do you want?" he demanded.

"We've heard about the Star of Persia," Jasmine explained, "and we've come to see the famous jewel."

"That's impossible," the guard said. "No one can see the jewel except a queen as lovely and worthy as our own."

"Well," said Aladdin, "this is Princess Jasmine. She's not a queen, but she will be."

"I'm very fair," Jasmine assured him.

The guard's eyes searched the square. "Fair enough to solve the argument happening over there?" he asked.

Jasmine made her way across the square and solved the argument.

"You did well," said the guard. "But the answer is still no. For our queen was also kind."

Jasmine turned to Aladdin. "Let's not bother the guard anymore," she said. "I'll go and get him a drink from the fountain, then we'll leave."

Jasmine found the fountain dry. However, as she held a jar under it, a stream of water came out. Everyone in the square stared.

"The fountain!" blurted the guard. "It hasn't had water since our queen was alive!"

The people bowed and the guard unlocked the tower door. He led Jasmine to the highest room where the gleaming Star of Persia sat.

The guard offered the jewel to Jasmine. "You have proved you are worthy enough to keep it. But promise to come and visit us whenever you can."

"Oh, I will!" smiled Jasmine.

And because she was not only fair and kind, but also honest, she most certainly did.

Disney Princess The Little Mermaid

Love Letters

"Ahhh," Ariel sighed dreamily.

"Oh, no," Sebastian fretted. "A sigh like that can only mean one thing."

"What?" said Flounder.

"She's obviously writing love poetry for that human she's so obsessed with," Sebastian said.

"Oh," said Flounder.

Ariel was hard at work writing in her seaweed notebook. "How do I love thee ..." she said out loud.

"Oh, yuck!" cried Flounder, when he heard.

"You're telling me," Sebastian agreed. "Terribly trite and overused."

"What would you write?" Ariel asked.

"Me? Well, this is just off the top of my head." Sebastian ceremoniously cleared his throat. "But I would write something like, 'Oh, crabby crab, Oh, crab of my heart, My crabbiest crab, May our claws never part!'"

"Double yuck!" Flounder exclaimed.

"What do *you* know?" Sebastian snapped.

"But he's a total stranger!" Flounder cried, turning back to Ariel.

"What's that supposed to mean?" Now Ariel felt offended.

"How can you be in love with someone you don't even know?" Sebastian said, joining in.

"I know him," Ariel protested. "Besides, haven't you ever heard of love at first sight?"

"Oh, please!" Flounder moaned.

"You're such a guppy!" cried Ariel.

"Hey! Who's being a guppy?" Flounder said defensively.

"Flounder is right," Sebastian interrupted. "This human doesn't even know you exist!"

"You don't know that!" Ariel cried, and went back to work on her poem. She wrote and wrote....

Finally, when she had finished, she cleared her throat dramatically.

"How's this sound?" she asked Sebastian and Flounder, and began reading:

"I'm always thinking of you,
It sets my heart a-twitter.
But I'm also easily distracted – ooh!
By things that shine and glitter.
Do you remember me?
Of me have you thunk?
Sorry, I've just got to go see
This boat that has just sunk.
(Now I'm back)
I love you more than anything,
Even more than my snarfblatt.
I wish this was a song to sing.
I'm really much better at that."

"Wow –" Sebastian exclaimed.

"– that's pretty bad!" Flounder finished.

"True love, indeed!" Sebastian concluded.

June
20

The Twilight Bark

Rolly, Patch, Lucky and the rest of the puppies were watching the end of The Thunderbolt Adventure Hour. As the credits began to roll, Pongo turned off the TV.

"Aw, come on, Dad!" Patch complained.

"We let you stay up late to watch the whole show," Pongo said.

Lucky sat staring at the blank television screen, hoping it would magically turn itself back on.

Perdy licked his face encouragingly. "Sit down, children," she said. "Your father and I need to speak with you."

"Uh-oh," Penny said worriedly.

"Oh, it's nothing like that," Pongo assured her. "We just think it's time to tell you about the legend of the Twilight Bark."

"Sounds cool!" Pepper cheered.

"What's the Twilight Bark?" Freckles asked.

"Legend has it," Perdy began, "that there's a special way that dogs can send each other messages. It stretches from the farthest side of the city all the way to the countryside."

"Wow!" Penny gasped. "Why would you need to do that?"

"Sometimes," Pongo began, "you need to communicate information from one place to another quickly, and you don't have time to go to the other place yourself."

"I don't need any Twilight Bark!" Patch said. "I can take care of myself."

"Fat chance!" Lucky said under his breath.

"What do you know?" Patch barked back at him.

"If you ever get into any trouble," Perdy told the pups, "just go to the top of the highest hill you can find and bark out your message, and the members of the Twilight Bark will pass it along until someone can come and help you."

"That sounds like a bunch of baloney," Patch told his parents.

"Patch!" Pongo scolded his son. "That isn't very nice."

Just then, Lucky started howling at the top of his lungs.

"What's got into you?" Perdy asked.

"I'm trying out the Twilight Bark," Lucky said. "To get us rescued from Patch."

"Lucky," Perdy scolded him, "apologize to your brother."

"That's okay," Patch said. "I don't need his apology. I was right anyway. All that howling and no word from the Twilight Bark."

Just then, the doorbell rang. All of the puppies gasped and turned to look at Patch.

Perdy and Pongo smiled at each other, knowing it was actually Roger returning from the shop with milk for tomorrow's breakfast.

Disney Fairies

Pixie Style

It was early morning and Tinker Bell was the first to arrive at the well to receive her daily cup of pixie dust. Terence, the dust-keeper, grinned as he sprinkled the dust over his new friend. "I can tell you haven't been in Pixie Hollow very long," he said.

"What do you mean?" Tink was puzzled.

"You haven't found your style yet, that's all," Terence replied. "Each fairy has her own special way of receiving her pixie dust. Stick around a little while and you'll see!"

Rosetta was the next fairy to arrive at the well. Daintily, she dabbed a dust-covered leaf on her cheeks. Rosetta was always so stylish!

Terence had just scooped another cupful of dust from the well when a frog leaped into the glade! Fawn, the animal fairy, was riding on its back. With a cheer of delight, she took the cup right out of Terence's hand as the frog leaped across the well!

Tink laughed as Terence got back on to his feet. Being a dust-keeper wasn't an easy job – she could see that now!

Iridessa was next. As Terence poured the dust into Iridessa's outstretched hands, the light fairy glowed so brightly that Tinker Bell had to cover her eyes. "Wow!"

Then Silvermist arrived, and Terence knew exactly how she liked her dust too. "One pixie waterfall coming up!" he said as he tipped a stream of dust onto Silvermist's head.

"For all the hammers in Tinkers' Nook!" said Tink. She was impressed – each fairy really did have her own way of receiving the dust!

"Just a moment," Terence interrupted. Vidia, the fast-flying fairy, had arrived. Extending one finger towards the cupful of dust, she made a mini whirlwind to spin the dust over her.

Tink flew back home very excited. She knew now she needed to come up with her own special way of receiving her dust – one linked to her talent!

The next morning, Terence was baffled to see Tink carrying what looked like an acorn cup with a handle. "What's that?"

"Pour in a little pixie dust and you'll find out!" said Tink, holding her invention above her head.

Terence shrugged and did what she asked. To his astonishment, the dust streamed out of the hollowed-out stem straight onto Tink's head. "And there's also a rain effect!" said Tink, turning the handle to release the dust through lots of tiny holes instead.

Terence couldn't help laughing. Trust Tink, the most creative fairy in Pixie Hollow, to come up with not one but two styles of her very own!

A Beastly Makeover

One evening, the Beast was heading towards the dining room when Lumiere suddenly stopped him.

"You can't go to dinner looking like that!" Lumiere said.

"Why not?" the Beast demanded. "I'm wearing my best outfit!"

"But clothes aren't enough," Cogsworth chimed in. "You have to make a good impression."

"You always told me looks don't matter, anyway," the Beast said.

"There's a difference between looks and style," Lumiere told him.

"And you may have no control over your looks," Cogsworth added, "but you certainly can do something about your style!"

"What's wrong with my style?" the Beast said, looking a bit hurt.

"Okay," Cogsworth began, "let's talk about your hair."

"What's wrong with my hair?" the Beast cried, offended.

"Women like hair long, but it has to be neat. Not straggly," Cogsworth explained. "When was the last time you combed it?"

"I –" the Beast began.

"You've got it all wrong," Lumiere interrupted. "Women like hair short, closely cropped." He brandished a pair of scissors.

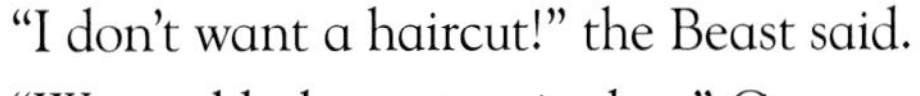

"I don't want a haircut!" the Beast said.

"We could always try ringlets," Cogsworth offered, nodding wisely.

"Or plaits," Lumiere suggested. At this, the Beast climbed onto a bookcase that swayed under his weight.

"How about a French roll?" Cogsworth said.

A low growl began in the Beast's throat. Just then, Belle hurried into the room, and this is what she saw – the candelabra and mantel clock brandishing combs and ribbons at the snarling, cornered Beast, who was scrabbling to stay on top of the bookcase. Belle burst into laughter.

"What's going on?" she asked.

"We were just trying to fix his hair," said Lumiere. "It's a dreadful mess!"

"Actually," Belle said, "I happen to like it just the way it is. Beast, are you going to stay up there all night?"

And at that, the Beast leaped off the bookcase and strode towards her. "Do you really like my hair?" he asked.

"It looks just fine," Belle reassured him. "Now, would you escort me to dinner?"

"I would be honoured," the Beast replied.

Cogsworth and Lumiere looked baffled as the two headed off to the dining room.

"Kids these days!" Cogsworth said.

A Dance with Snow White

No one could remember a more wonderful day. The sun was shining, the sky was blue, and the Prince was holding a glorious ball for his true love, Snow White. Nearly everyone in the land had come to join in the fun, including seven rather short men who loved Snow White very much. They had never been to a royal ball before!

After a great banquet, the guests entered the ballroom, and each was announced. "Doc, Happy, Sneezy, Bashful, Grumpy, Dopey and Sleepy!" the announcer shouted into the great room as the Seven Dwarfs tripped over one another, dazzled by the grand surroundings.

"Gawrsh," Bashful said, hiding behind Doc, amazed by the marble and chandeliers.

Then, as the orchestra began to play, the Prince took Snow White in his arms and they waltzed across the dance floor.

The Dwarfs sighed. They could not take their eyes off Snow White.

"Wouldn't it be wonderful to dance with Snow White?" Happy sighed.

That gave Doc an idea. He led the other Dwarfs into the cloakroom and borrowed a few things. "Sneezy, stand here. Bashful, you stand on his shoulders. Dopey, do you think you can make it to the top?"

When Dopey was balanced on Bashful's shoulders, Doc wrapped a cloak around the tower of Dwarfs and buttoned it up around Dopey's neck.

Wobbling precariously, the makeshift Dwarf prince stumbled towards the dance floor and Snow White.

"May we have this dance?" Bashful asked from within the cloak.

"Of course!" Snow White giggled when she saw the familiar faces peeking out at her from beneath the cloak.

As the music began, Snow White and the Dwarf prince lurched and swayed into the middle of the room.

"Yikes!" Sneezy squeaked. "This cloak is tickling my nose!"

Above them all, Dopey was having the time of his life, when suddenly the Dwarfs heard a sound that made them freeze.

"Ah ... ah ... ah ..."

"Hang on, men!" Doc shouted.

"... *CHOOO!*" cried Sneezy.

The cloak billowed. The Dwarf prince was knocked off balance!

"I got you!" The Prince caught the Dwarfs just before they all came toppling down. After steadying them, he turned to Snow White and held out his hand.

"May I cut in?" he asked, with a smile.

Disney
Bambi

Sweeter than Clover

"Hi, Bambi," said a soft voice. Bambi looked up from the grass he was eating, and his friend Flower stopped searching for berries. Standing in front of them was the pretty young fawn Bambi had met that spring.

"Hi, Faline," Bambi said. "It's nice to see you!"

"It's nice to see you too," Faline said shyly.

"Faline!" a young male deer called across the meadow. "Come over and play with me!"

Bambi's eyes narrowed. He didn't like the idea of Faline going off to play with someone else.

Faline blinked in confusion. "Do you want me to go?" she asked Bambi.

"No, don't go," said Bambi. *But what can I say to make her stay?* he wondered. Suddenly, Bambi had an idea.

"I want to show you something special," he told her.

"Something special?" asked Faline.

"I know where to find the sweetest clover you'll ever taste," Bambi bragged. Thumper had shown him exactly where to find it.

"Where?" asked Faline.

"Just follow me!" exclaimed Bambi.

He led Faline across the meadow to the babbling brook. Then he followed the brook all the way up a steep grassy hill.

Finally they came to a big waterfall.

"The sweet clover is right here by this weeping willow tree," said Bambi.

Bambi couldn't wait to share it with Faline. But, when he got to the tree, there wasn't one single clover blossom left.

"Oh, that Thumper!" complained Bambi.

"What's the matter?" asked Faline.

Bambi shook his head. He felt very silly. He'd brought Faline all this way, and now he had nothing special to share with her! Just then, Bambi looked up.

"Look," he whispered. "In the sky."

Faline looked up and gasped.

Shimmering bands of colour had formed an arch over the waterfall.

"It's so beautiful," whispered Faline. "I've never seen anything like it."

"Neither have I," said Bambi. "But I remember hearing my mother talk about it. I think it's called a rain ... bow."

"It's wonderful!" cried Faline.

"I'm glad you think so," said Bambi, a little relieved. "But I'm sorry you came all this way for no clover."

"Oh, Bambi," said Faline. "I came because I wanted to be with you. And, besides, a rainbow is a much sweeter surprise than some silly old clover, anyway!"

June
25

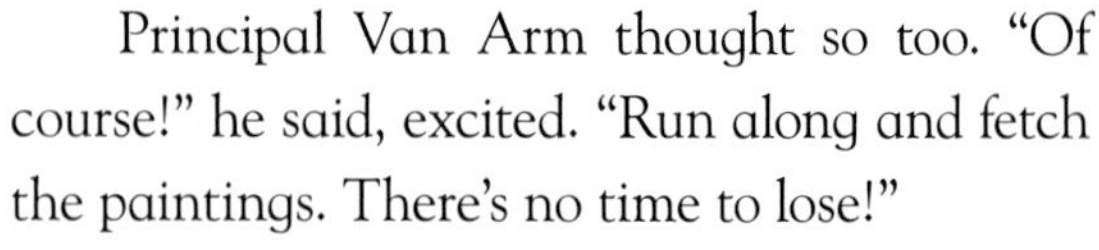

Miss Van Burlow's Secret

Minnie Mouse and her best friend Daisy Duck were on their way to meet Leonard when they spotted something odd. "Isn't that Miss Van Burlow?" asked Daisy.

Their art teacher was peering in through the windows of a gallery, which was hosting a special exhibition of paintings by the famous artist Theresa Glittershine – but she didn't look at all happy.

"I wonder why she looks so upset," said Minnie.

Daisy's imagination went into overdrive. "Maybe she's in love with a painting she can't have. Or maybe she doesn't like the artist and wants to teach her a lesson!"

Leonard had another idea. "Maybe our teacher's jealous!" he exclaimed. "Glittershine is a famous painter whose works are shown all around the world. But Miss Van Burlow gave up painting to become a teacher!"

"She must really regret it," said Minnie, feeling sorry for her.

"Yeah," agreed Daisy. "We're not exactly ideal students."

Leonard had an idea. "Why don't we put on an exhibition of Miss Van Burlow's paintings?"

Minnie and Daisy brightened up immediately. What a great idea! And the school assembly hall would be the perfect place to host the exhibition!

Principal Van Arm thought so too. "Of course!" he said, excited. "Run along and fetch the paintings. There's no time to lose!"

Minnie, Daisy and Leonard ran straight to Miss Van Burlow's house to tell her the good news. She was touched. "How sweet! What gave you the idea?"

They explained about seeing her outside the exhibition, looking sad. Miss Van Burlow laughed. "I wasn't sad – I was bored!" She waved an arm towards the front room. "Meet my friend Theresa Glittershine!"

The three friends gawped at the sight of the famous artist. "It was my fault!" she admitted. "She was waiting for me, but I was talking, and there were so many people, and time just flew...."

Minnie blinked. Theresa Glittershine certainly was talkative! She could see why Miss Van Burlow might have been bored waiting for her friend!

"Your idea was so kind," Miss Van Burlow said. "But I'm not interested in exhibiting my old paintings. I love my teaching job! In fact, why don't you kids paint the pictures? That way the principal will see how talented my students are!"

Minnie's good deed had turned into a whole weekend of work for them all! "Next time you have an idea," Daisy whispered to her friend, "remind me to run away in advance!"

Disney Princess
Cinderella

The Great Cat-astrophe

Once a year, the King hosted the Royal Flower Show. Cinderella loved seeing all the beautiful, unusual flowers.

"I heard you want to go to the Royal Flower Show?" said her stepmother. "I see no reason why you shouldn't go ... as long as your chores are finished."

"Oh thank you!" Cinderella cried.

Just then, the front doorbell sounded.

"I forgot to mention," added her stepmother. "Lady DuPont is visiting with her two cats, Precious and Treasure. You must take care of them and prepare dinner."

Cinderella put the cats on a soft sofa and set to work on her chores. "How much trouble could two kitties be?" she said, as Lucifer, the family cat, entered the room.

Cinderella gasped in shock as the three cats suddenly started wildly misbehaving – clawing at the cushions and swinging on the curtains. Not to mention leaving dusty paw prints everywhere.

Cinderella hurriedly re-stuffed the cushions and fixed the curtains. Then she had an idea! She carefully sewed tiny mop-shoes onto the cats' paws. Finding a ball of yarn, she tossed it onto the floor for them to chase. As the cats ran around, the floors were clean in no time.

Satisfied, Cinderella checked the dinner.

"All I have to do is keep an eye on those naughty cats until everyone goes home," she muttered. "Then I can go to the flower show."

Returning from the kitchen, she found the cats napping on the windowsill, except for Lucifer who was swishing his tail and watching something.

Glancing out of the window, Cinderella saw her friends, Jaq and Gus the mice, huddled on the roof.

"You chased them out there, didn't you?" she scolded Lucifer. Bravely, she climbed onto the roof to gather her friends in her arms.

Then Cinderella heard a *SLAM!* The cats had closed the window so she couldn't get back in, and sat grinning at her through the glass.

Cinderella frowned and put the mice in her pocket. "I'll show them," she insisted.

Grabbing onto the clothesline that was attached to the roof, she swung down into the garden and landed gently on the grass. She then hurried to the kitchen and prepared dinner.

"Have my cats been good?" Lady DuPont asked Cinderella, later on.

"Very good," Cinderella lied.

"I guess you can go to the Royal Flower Show then," said her stepmother reluctantly.

Cinderella didn't wait around in case her stepmother changed her mind. She knew she had truly earned a fun day out.

Winnie the Pooh

Rabbit's Frightful Garden

Rabbit woke up bright and early. He had a lot of work to do in his garden. There were weeds to be pulled up, vines to be trimmed and lots of delicious vegetables waiting to be picked. The only problem was that Rabbit had lent all his tools to his friends – and they hadn't returned them.

In the meantime, Pooh and Piglet were enjoying breakfast at Kanga and Roo's house when Roo bounced in with a bunch of wildflowers for his mother.

"Thank you, Roo!" Kanga exclaimed, giving him a kiss. "Let me just trim these and put them in some water." She rummaged around in a kitchen drawer, where she came across Rabbit's gardening shears. "Oh, no," Kanga said. "I never returned these to Rabbit after I borrowed them."

"That reminds me," said Piglet. "I still have Rabbit's rake. And, Pooh, I'll bet you still have Rabbit's spade."

The friends decided the neighbourly thing to do would be to return Rabbit's tools right away. When they arrived at Rabbit's house, though, their friend was not at home. He was on his way to their houses to get his tools back.

"Rabbit's garden could use some work," Kanga said. "Why don't we take care of it for him as a way of saying that we're sorry for keeping his tools for so long?"

Everyone agreed that this was a splendid plan. Pooh set about weeding while Piglet raked. Kanga snipped ripe tomatoes, peppers and cucumbers off the vines. Then Roo gathered them into big baskets.

When they'd finished, they spotted some birds hungrily eyeing the harvest.

"This garden needs a scarecrow!" cried Roo.

The work crew sprang into action, and soon a towering scarecrow was planted right in the middle of the garden. They propped the tools against the scarecrow, placed the baskets of food in front of it and started heading home. "Rabbit is going to be so surprised!" Piglet said proudly.

When Rabbit returned home a few minutes later, he couldn't quite believe his eyes. First he looked at the vegetables, all neatly picked. Then he looked at his garden tools, which had mysteriously reappeared. Finally, he looked at the strange scarecrow, which seemed to be looking right back at him! "D-did you do this?" he stammered to the straw man. Just then, a gust of wind knocked over the rake resting on the scarecrow's arm.

Convinced his garden was haunted, Rabbit turned and ran for his life. "Ahhhh!" he screamed as he rushed past his friends.

"I told you he'd be surprised," giggled Piglet.

Disney Fairies

Invisi-Bell

It was snack time in Autumn Forest, and Iridessa and Silvermist were helping Fawn deliver nuts to the squirrels. "These little fellows are so cute!" Silvermist smiled. The glade was buzzing with squirrels and fairies, and all was going well until....

"It's flitterific!" yelled Tinker Bell, flying in so fast that she blew over the piles of nuts and scattered the squirrels in a panic!

"Watch out, Tink!" shouted Silvermist.

Tink was too excited to apologize. "I've been working for days and have finally come up with ..." she paused dramatically, "... a hawk-proof hiding place!"

The others gasped. Hawks were such a danger to fairies and small animals. A hawk-proof hiding place would be amazing! "You sure it'll work?" asked Fawn.

Tink winked at them. "Let's try. If you can't find me, it means my idea's perfect." She took off, calling over her shoulder, "Count to 10 and then come find me!"

The fairies looked at each other and shrugged. The nuts and squirrels would have to wait! All three of them shut their eyes and counted to 10.

Then the search began! Iridessa spotted a hole in a tree trunk. "Tink, I know you're in there," she said, reaching in a hand to grab her friend. Instead, she got a handful of fur! "So sorry!" she stammered to an annoyed beaver.

Meanwhile, Silvermist was investigating a patch of branches covered in crisp, brown leaves. But she became tangled in the branches, and the leaves covered her face so she couldn't see where she was going!

Fawn giggled as she creeped up on a fir cone that was wobbling by itself. "Found y –"

"Eek!" Iridessa, on the other side, jumped in fright.

The friends searched for a long time with no luck, and as the sun began to set they gave up. "You win!" called Fawn, sliding down the side of a tree trunk and landing with a weary thump. "Come out, Tink!"

"Here I am!" To their astonishment, a door opened in the side of the trunk – and Tink stepped out! "Ta-dah!" she said proudly. "Not even a hawk could have found me!"

It was true! The door in the trunk was the exact shape of Tink herself – no wonder she fitted so perfectly behind it!

"Now all you need to do is make one for every fairy in Pixie Hollow," Iridessa giggled.

"Right!" said Fawn, looking at the door. "This shape only works for you!"

Tink gulped. "I hadn't thought of that!" Oh well – back to the drawing board!

Disney Princess Snow White and the Seven Dwarfs

Where is Astor?

Snow White was surrounded by her woodland friends as she made her way along the dirt path to the stables.

She carried a bucket of water for her beautiful white horse Astor, but when she arrived at the stable's wooden gate, Astor was nowhere to be seen.

Snow White rushed to speak with the Dwarfs at their little cottage.

"Astor isn't in her stable. Where could she be?" she asked them, worriedly.

"I'll help you look, Princess," offered Doc.

Together, Snow White and Doc made their way into the forest followed by their woodland friends. The twittering birds looked from high above as the squirrels searched down below. Doc checked behind every tree, behind every mushroom and inside every hollow tree stump.

"Where are you, Astor?" Snow White cried.

Doc peered through a patch of tall grass and found a field mouse. But not Astor.

"She's not here," Doc said.

Snow White and Doc went to see Grumpy at the diamond mines. With his pick balanced on one shoulder, Grumpy shook his head from side to side. "I'm sorry. She hasn't been through here," he told them.

"Oh no!" said Snow White. "I hope she's not lost."

"I'll help you look," Grumpy said.

On the hills at the edge of the forest, Snow White, Doc and Grumpy searched for signs of Astor. She loved to chew grass as a tasty snack, so they thought they might spot her in a field.

"She's not there," Snow White sighed.

"There are still a lot of places we can look," Grumpy assured her.

They set off again on their search and came to one of Snow White's favourite places – the Wishing Well. Happy was there collecting water in a bucket.

"Hello, Happy," said Snow White. "Have you seen my horse, Astor?"

"I'm sorry, Princess," said Happy. "But there's been no horse around here. I can help you look though!"

Snow White, Doc, Grumpy and Happy all started searching through the palace gardens. They looked through the rose bushes, and then they wandered over to the vegetable patch....

"Oh, Astor!" Snow White giggled. "There you are!"

Astor looked up with a big juicy carrot between her teeth. Snow White petted her on her warm, fuzzy neck.

"You silly thing! I've been on a long journey trying to find you ..." she said and gave her a big, happy hug. She was glad to see her safe!

Disney Princess
Sleeping Beauty

Cherry Pie Surprise

Briar Rose picked up a large basket and stepped out of the door. It was a beautiful afternoon, and she couldn't help but sing a little song as she headed into the forest.

Rose had spent many afternoons in the forest and knew exactly where the cherry trees grew. She put her basket down by her favourite tree and began to fill it with juicy cherries. A pair of bluebirds came and landed on her shoulder while she picked. Soon the basket was heavy with fruit.

"That should be more than enough for a pie," she told the bluebirds. She was going to bake her aunts a delicious, surprise pudding. Still humming to herself, Rose carried the cherries back to the cottage.

Rose put down the basket and looked around the cosy kitchen. She felt nervous. She had never baked a pie by herself! She wasn't even sure where to find all the ingredients.

"It can't be that hard to find the butter, flour and sugar," she told herself.

Taking a deep breath, Rose searched the cupboards. Then she set to work mixing the butter into the flour for the crust. After adding a little cold water, she gently shaped the dough into a ball.

"And now for the tricky part," she said to the bluebirds, who had followed her home.

Rose put the dough on the worktop and began to roll it out into a large, flat circle.

"Here we go," Rose said as she folded it in half and lifted it into the pie tin. After unfolding it, she crimped the edges. It looked perfect.

"And now for the filling," Rose said. She washed the cherries and pitted them. Then she mixed in some spice and sprinkled on spoonfuls of sugar.

The pie was just coming out of the oven when her aunts arrived home.

"What is that delicious smell, dear?" Flora asked as she took off her pointed hat.

Rose beamed. "It's a cherry pie," she said. "I baked it myself!"

Fauna clapped her hands together proudly. "How wonderful!"

After dinner, Rose cut four pieces of pie. Smiling, everyone dug in. But their smiles soon turned to frowns.

Then Rose burst into tears. "Salt!" she cried. "I used salt instead of sugar!"

"There, there, dear," Flora consoled her. "I once made the same mistake with an entire batch of fruitcake – 20 cakes! It took a while before anyone would touch my cooking again!"

Rose wiped the tears from her eyes and started to giggle. At least, she had ruined only one pie!

The Black Venus Panther

Buzz dashed for safety. "Run," he cried. "The Dino-Aliens have found us!"

He and some of the other toys were the heroes in Bonnie's latest game. The dinosaurs, Rex and Trixie, were the villains, who stomped and roared as they chased them.

Soon, Bonnie ran in for lunch, leaving the toys alone on the grass. Rex was upset – he was having great fun being the Dino-Alien.

"Don't worry, Rex," Buzz assured him. "Bonnie will be back soon."

Woody gulped. "Uh, guys? Do you feel like someone's watching us?"

Slowly, the toys turned round to see a fearsome-looking black cat staring at them, hungrily licking its lips.

Screaming, the toys ran in all different directions as the cat pounced at them. "Jessie, bring them home safe," Buzz barked, pointing to Dolly, Trixie and some of the others. "We'll draw the cat's attention."

Buzz, Woody and Mr Pricklepants ran past the cat, waving and shouting. While it raced after them, Jessie got the others to safety.

"Quick! Climb the tree," Buzz ordered. Working together, the three friends frantically clambered up onto a low branch.

Finally they were safe – or so they thought! Then the cat started to climb up after them!

Suddenly, Mr Pricklepants lost his grip on the branch. "Help!" he cried tumbling from the tree and landing in a heap on the grass.

The cat dropped to the ground and slowly approached, like a tiger stalking its prey.

Mr Pricklepants gulped nervously. "Please, don't eat me." The hedgehog toy closed his eyes. He could feel the cat's breath on his face. Any second now, it would –

SLURP! The cat gave the toy a friendly lick on the cheek. Mr Pricklepants opened his eyes, then laughed with relief.

"Um, guys? I think it's safe. Come down," he called.

The friends soon realized that the cat just wanted to play. They called Jessie and the others back out, and took turns tickling the cat's tummy.

Woody smiled at Buzz. "Are you thinking what I'm thinking?" he asked.

Buzz nodded. "I think so, Woody!"

The toys went back to playing their game again, but this time when the Dino-Aliens attacked, they were in for a big surprise.

"We've brought our new friend, the Black Venus Panther!" said Mr Pricklepants.

The Dino-Aliens took one look at the huge beast, then turned and ran away! The cat miaowed happily. Being a toy sure was fun!

July

2

Disney Lady and the TRAMP

Lost and Found

Lady stretched and rolled over. It was so cosy up on the window seat. Sunlight shone through the glass and glinted on her diamond-shaped name tag. Lady sighed contentedly. The tag was her most prized possession. Besides her owners, of course.

Jim Dear and Darling were very good to her. Just last night, they had given her and Tramp steak bones to munch on. There were so many, they had not been able to eat them all.

The bones! Lady had almost forgotten them. Leaping off the window seat, she hurried to the kitchen. Luckily, they were still right next to her food bowl.

Lady began to carry the bones into the garden. It took three trips, but soon the bones were lying in a heap on the grass.

Then she started to dig. The soil piled up behind her. At last, she carefully nosed the final bone into the hole and covered it with soil. After prancing delicately on top to pat down the soil, she collapsed in an exhausted heap. Burying bones was hard work!

Rolling over, Lady let the sun warm her belly. The garden was the perfect place for a late-afternoon nap. She was just dozing off when, suddenly, her neck itched.

Sitting up, Lady gave it a scratch. But something was missing.

Lady stopped scratching and gingerly felt her neck. Her collar! It was gone! Panicked, Lady searched the garden for the collar. But it was nowhere to be found.

"I must have buried it with one of my bones!" Lady realized with a jolt. She looked at all the freshly dug holes. It would take her all night to dig up the bones. But she just had to find her collar!

She knew she would need some help. She ran inside to find Tramp. He was playing with the puppies, but ran outside as soon as he heard what was wrong. Soon the two dogs were busy undoing all of Lady's hard work.

"I see something shiny!" Tramp called. Lady was by his side in an instant, but it wasn't the collar. It was just an old bottle cap. Lady dropped her head sadly.

Lady and Tramp got right back to digging. They had to find the collar!

Just as dusk was falling, Tramp found a thick blue band with a golden tag. Lady's collar!

Lady let out a happy bark. Then she carried the collar into the house and sat down at Jim Dear's feet.

"Did your collar come off, Lady?" Jim asked as he fastened the collar round Lady's neck. "It's a good thing you didn't accidentally bury it with your bones!"

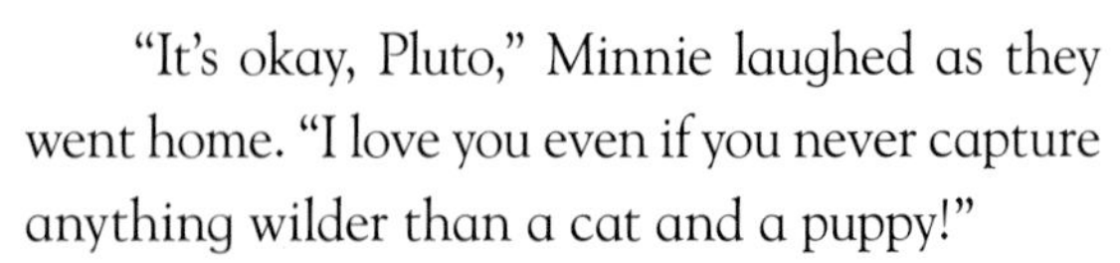

The Bravest Dog

Minnie was in her garden when she saw Mickey run to his car. "Where are you going?" she asked.

"A circus train was going through town and some animals got lost!" Mickey replied. "The sheriff asked me to help find them."

Pluto tried to follow, but Mickey stopped him. "You stay here with Minnie," he said and drove away.

Soon, Pluto began to tug at Minnie's skirt.

Minnie knew he wanted to go for a walk. "Okay," she said. "We're not likely to run into any of the animals."

So Minnie followed Pluto down the path to the river. Suddenly, they heard a hissing sound coming from behind a log.

"Snakes!" Minnie cried. "They must have escaped from the circus train!"

But Pluto wasn't afraid. He pounced into the grass ... and found a small cat and her kittens.

Minnie giggled. "Come on, Pluto, let's not disturb them."

Minnie stayed close to Pluto. If there were snakes around, she didn't want to run into them.

"It would be fun to find a seal," said Minnie.

Just then, they heard a splashing sound coming from the river. Pluto dashed down a hill and plunged into the water.

But it was not a seal splashing around in the water. It was a puppy!

"It's okay, Pluto," Minnie laughed as they went home. "I love you even if you never capture anything wilder than a cat and a puppy!"

When Minnie and Pluto walked into Mickey's kitchen, they found that milk had been spilled, all over the floor, dishes had been broken and one of the windows was open!

"Oh, Pluto!" Minnie cried. "Someone has been in here! What if it was one of the circus animals?"

Pluto sniffed around. Then he leaped through the open window and raced over to the shed.

"Be careful!" Minnie called. Just then, Mickey pulled up.

"Oh, Mickey," Minnie said, "something broke into your kitchen! Pluto is tracking it!"

Minnie pointed to the shed, where Pluto had disappeared inside. What would Pluto find?

The shed door opened and Pluto came out – and he was not alone. On his back was a monkey dressed in a little hat and waistcoat.

"The last missing animal!" Mickey said.

The monkey jumped into Mickey's arms. "This little guy isn't so wild," he said, "but it took a lot of courage to go into the shed."

"Pluto's been brave all day," Minnie said.

Pluto and Mickey returned the monkey.

"Thanks, Pluto," the circus ringmaster said. "The show couldn't have gone on without you!"

July
4

A Strange, Strange Star

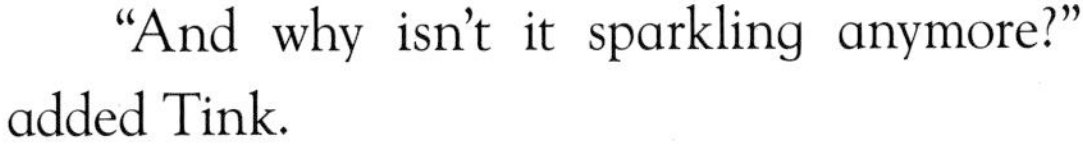

Tinker Bell and Terence were out in a boat on the ocean, searching for lost things on the sea floor. Tink was peering through her telescope when suddenly she spotted something.

"There's something sparkling in the water!" she cried excitedly.

Terence guided the boat closer so they could see it better. "It looks like a star!" gasped Tink.

"How'd it get down there?" wondered Terence.

"I don't know, but we've got to save it," said Tink.

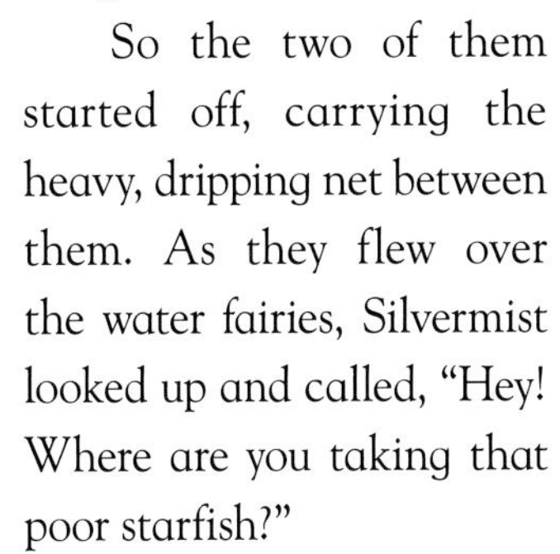

Leaping to the back of the boat, she grabbed the controls and sent it speeding over the waves to shore. Terence hung on for dear life! When Tink had an idea, nothing could stop her!

Once they were back on the beach, Tink quickly set about finding everything she needed to build a star-catcher. In no time at all, she had built a large woven net.

They got back into the boat, and sailed over to where they had spotted the star. Tink leaned out over the water and scooped her net as deep as it would go.... "Got it!" she shouted, as the star emerged from the water.

Terence helped her pull it into the boat. "It's so heavy!"

Not only was it heavy, it was ... blue? Terence scratched his head. "I didn't think stars were blue!"

"And why isn't it sparkling anymore?" added Tink.

"Let's take it to Iridessa," Terence suggested. "She knows all about light and stars."

So the two of them started off, carrying the heavy, dripping net between them. As they flew over the water fairies, Silvermist looked up and called, "Hey! Where are you taking that poor starfish?"

Tink and Terence exchanged glances.

"Starfish?" repeated Tink, feeling confused. "But earlier it was sparkling like a star in the sky!"

"Some little starfish light up when they move across the dark sea floor," Silvermist explained to them.

Tink gulped. "We've got to get it back into the water!"

Silvermist came to help, and together the three friends gently lowered the starfish back to its home on the sea bed. "Look at it glow!" exclaimed Tinker Bell.

"It's saying goodbye," said Silvermist, waving at the starfish.

"I promise we won't fish for you anymore!" Terence called, laughing.

What a mistake to make! The natural world was full of surprises, and today Terence and Tink had discovered a brand new one!

Disney Princess
Tangled

Rapunzel's Challenge

The day Flynn Rider climbed into Rapunzel's tower to hide was the beginning of some unexpected, yet wonderful adventures. Rapunzel had never met a man like Flynn before – a thief on the run for stealing a jewelled crown!

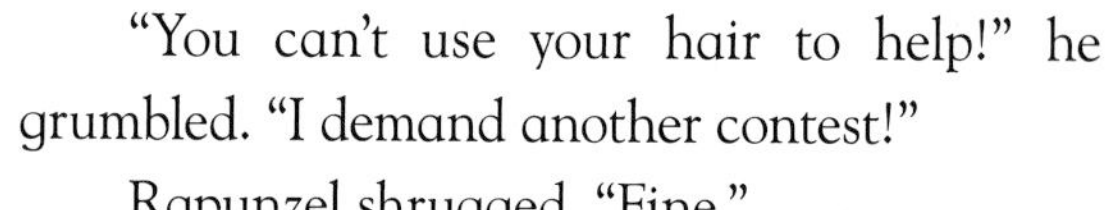

She had taken the crown from Flynn and told him she would return it only if he showed her the kingdom that lay beyond her tower.

Free at last, Rapunzel hopped, skipped, jumped and ran around the forest, madly in love with the world and its beauty.

"You know Blondie, this is no place for you," Flynn told her.

Rapunzel frowned. "Why not? Anything you can do, I can do better!"

"Let's have a contest then," Flynn said. "If I win, I get the crown back."

Rapunzel wasn't so easily fooled. "No. The crown can't be part of the bet." She pulled out her frying pan. "Whoever loses cooks dinner for the winner."

"You're on," agreed Flynn. He pointed to a tree. "Who can climb the fastest I wonder?"

Rapunzel threw her long hair onto a low branch and swung gracefully as Flynn used arrows to stick into the trunk, yanking himself up. When he'd almost reached the top, he gasped as Rapunzel waved at him from above.

"You can't use your hair to help!" he grumbled. "I demand another contest!"

Rapunzel shrugged. "Fine."

They decided to have a race to the river. As Flynn bounded through the grass he noticed a WANTED poster with his face on, pinned to a tree. "Not again!" he moaned. They always drew him with a crooked nose.

While he was staring angrily at the poster, Rapunzel sped past. Flynn tried to catch up, but tripped over her golden hair.

"I win!" Rapunzel cried gleefully at the river's edge.

"That's not fair – you used your hair again," Flynn complained. "Let's see who can cross the river first!"

Rapunzel had no idea how to swim. As Flynn dived into the water and swam, she pulled a vine from a tree and swung to the embankment.

"What?" Flynn choked in surprise. "You got here first and you're not even wet...."

He hated to admit it, but Rapunzel had beaten him every time.

"You owe me a snack," she said, pulling out her frying pan.

Flynn laughed and started a fire. Together they sat and enjoyed a delicious meal. It was the tastiest treat Rapunzel had ever eaten.

Disney Princess
Cinderella

Of Mice and Rice

"Cinderella! Help!" shrieked Drizella.

"And hurry!" yelled Anastasia.

Cinderella dropped the broom she was holding and rushed down the hallway. "What is it, stepsisters?" she called.

"We're stuck!" yelled Anastasia, angrily.

Cinderella ran to the parlour. She had to suppress a giggle at what she saw. Her two stepsisters were stuck in the doorway, so hasty had they both been to leave the room first. Their grand hoop skirts were wedged tightly in the doorway! With a bit of tugging and pulling, Cinderella managed to free the sisters. Smiling to herself, she headed back to the kitchen.

"*Meeeoowww!*" came a cry.

"What on earth ..." said Cinderella. She hurried into the kitchen. Lucifer the cat was howling at the top of his lungs. "What is the matter, Lucifer?" she said, running over to the fat feline. "Oh! You silly thing! You've got yourself stuck too!" Cinderella laughed and tugged him out of the mouse hole he had wedged his paw into. With a haughty look at Cinderella, the cat strode away.

"Oh, that naughty cat!" she said. "He got himself stuck chasing after you poor little defenceless mice, didn't he?" She peeked into the tiny mouse hole.

The mice cautiously crept out.

"You little dears," Cinderella said softly. "Why, you're all shaken up! Well, do you know what I do when I feel sad or afraid? I find happiness in my dreams." She picked up her broom. "You see this broom? I like to pretend that it is a handsome prince, and the two of us are dancing together!" She and the broom began gliding around the room.

The mice squeaked with delight, and then they suddenly dashed for their hole. Someone was coming!

It was Cinderella's stepsisters. "What on earth are you doing, Cinderella?" said Drizella.

"I was just, uh, sweeping," Cinderella replied quietly, blushing.

"Well, you looked as though you were having too much fun doing it!" snapped Anastasia. Then a nasty smile appeared on her face. Picking up a bowl of rice from the table, she dumped it onto the floor. "Perhaps you need something else to sweep!" she said with a mean laugh. The two sisters left.

Cinderella's mouse friends rushed out and began to pick up the grains of rice. That gave Cinderella an idea. "Why don't you take the rice for yourselves?" she said. The mice squeaked happily, and Cinderella smiled. "You know," she said, "I think we'll be just fine if we all look out for each other."

Disney Princess Sleeping Beauty

A Moment to Remember

Aurora loved being a Princess, but life at the castle was so busy! Special visitors were to arrive that night and everyone was frantic with arrangements. Even the fairies had spent the afternoon arguing over what colour dress Aurora should wear.

"Your majesty," said a servant, approaching her. "We've made the swan sculpture you requested. It needs your approval."

"Where would you like these flowers put?" asked another servant.

"Your approval of the seating arrangements is needed, your majesty!" pleaded the royal steward.

Aurora sighed – there was so much to do. She felt relieved when Prince Phillip came into the room unexpectedly. "I'm so glad to see you!" she said. "What are you doing here?"

"I came to see you," he replied. "And I've just decided to rescue you from this room. Let's go where no one can ask you anything."

Soon the royal couple were on their horses and riding towards the woods. It was just what they needed – time to be alone. But as they raced towards freedom, Prince Phillip's horse got carried away and galloped too fast, throwing the Prince from his saddle and into a shallow stream. *SPLASH*!

"No carrots for you tonight," Phillip scolded the horse, soaked in water.

Aurora caught up with them. "Do you remember this place?" she asked, as she helped him to his feet.

"I remember. I'll never forget the day we met." He smiled, taking her by the hands. "No matter how crowded our lives become at the palace, when we're together, everyone else just disappears."

Aurora decided she wanted to bring a little of the glade's peace and quiet back to the palace. The glade was a special place they could always visit when they needed to.

"We should go back now," Aurora said. She was concerned people would start to worry.

As she took off on her horse, the Prince remained behind, having thought of a gift he could make his true love.

That night, back at the castle, the fairies helped Aurora into her dress and Prince Phillip arrived with something hidden behind his back.

"Here," he said, "I made you this...."

It was a beautiful crown made of flowers from the glade!

Aurora had a surprise for him as well. The party would be held in the courtyard – flowers and trees blowing in the breeze and candles flickering like stars. She smiled at Phillip and said, "Now we have a little part of the glade at our palace." He was delighted!

Disney MINNIE

Precious Gifts

Daisy Duck was over the moon. She had won the annual Super School Competition! Not only did she still have the applause of the audience ringing in her ears, but she also had a handful of prize money. "At last I can buy that fantastic swimsuit I've had my eye on," she sighed happily. "It'll be perfect for the big surfing competition!"

She and her best friend Minnie Mouse set off to the sports shop. Daisy was skipping with delight, and Minnie was so pleased for her. "You deserve it after all that hard work."

Daisy smiled. It certainly had been hard work! Take art, for example ... all those hours sitting in class while her teacher explained the basic techniques yet again.

"It's only thanks to Miss Van Burlow that I passed art," Daisy said. "And Maths was much harder!" She thought fondly of the kind members of the Maths and Science club, who'd helped her understand all the really hard ideas she had been struggling with.

"Thanks to them you didn't make a single mistake," Minnie pointed out. "They were so proud of you." Then another thought struck her. "The most generous help you got was from Principal Van Arm."

Daisy smiled. The head teacher had helped her identify a rare species of toad while she'd been doing work outside. "Without his help, I'd never have passed my science test."

The two friends had reached the sports shop, but Daisy hesitated. "Minnie, you won't believe it ... but I'm not sure I still want that swimsuit. I mean, I've already got loads of swimsuits anyway...."

So many people had helped her to win the competition – surely it wasn't fair to spend all the prize money on herself? "I have a better idea!"

Minnie turned round confused, as her friend ran off. What was Daisy up to?

The next day at school, Daisy's grand plan was revealed....

She had bought brand-new T-shirts for the members of the Maths and Science club. The T-shirts had mathematical symbols all over them! And Miss Van Burlow was almost tearful as she thanked Daisy for her year's subscription to the exhibitions at the museum. Even Principal Van Arm had a present – a unique explorer's hat!

"You were very generous," said Minnie to her friend after school, giving Daisy an extra special hug.

Daisy beamed. "It was a pleasure for me to do it. When it comes down to it, what's a swimsuit compared to thanking those who helped you when you needed it most?"

Disney 101 DALMATIANS

One Lucky Pup

"Where are we going?" Penny asked. "Why do we have to get in the car? We're going to miss Thunderbolt!" The puppies all hated missing their favourite dog hero TV show. They groaned in disappointment.

"This will be even more fun," Perdy said soothingly as she coaxed the puppies into the car. "I promise."

Roger and Anita got into the front seat. It didn't take long to leave the city. Soon the car was winding down a country lane. The puppies smelled all kinds of good things. They smelled flowers and hay. Then they smelled something sweet – peaches!

"Here we are!" Anita opened the car door.

"Where's here?" Freckles asked Lucky.

"It looks like an orchard!" Lucky barked. He loved to eat fruit.

Roger stretched. "You dogs run and play," he said. "We'll call you when it's time for our picnic."

"Don't eat too many peaches," barked Pongo, but the puppies were already running off.

All morning, the puppies ran around and played on the grass until Pongo and Perdy came to get them. "Time for lunch!" Pongo barked.

"I'm not hungry," Rolly said, rolling over in the grass.

"I hope you didn't eat too much," Perdy said.

The big dogs herded their puppies up the hill towards the spot where Roger and Anita were laying out a picnic.

Perdy scanned the group. "Wait a minute," she said to Pongo. "Where's Lucky?"

The black-and-white pack stopped in its tracks. Pongo counted them. Lucky was definitely missing!

Perdy sighed and began to whimper.

"Don't worry, Mother," Pepper said sweetly. "I have an idea." Then he turned to his brothers and sisters. "Hey, everyone. Let's play Thunderbolt!" he barked. "We have to find Lucky!"

All of the puppies yipped excitedly and tumbled over one another to find Lucky's trail. Soon every nose was sniffing the ground.

Penny sniffed around a tree and behind a patch of tall grass. She'd caught the scent! "Here he is!" Penny barked.

The rest of the dogs gathered around to see the puppy asleep in the grass.

Lucky's ears covered his eyes, but there was no mistaking the horseshoe of spots on his back, or the pile of peach stones by his nose!

"Lucky is lucky we found him," Perdita said with a relieved sigh.

"And," Pepper joked, "he'll be really lucky if he doesn't wake up with a tummy ache!"

Disney · PIXAR
MONSTERS UNIVERSITY

The Glove Challenge

One morning at Monsters University, Mike Wazowski was leaving his room to go to his first lesson of the day, when suddenly something stopped him in his tracks. Right there, on the floor in front of him, was a bright pink human glove!

Mike screamed in fright. Monsters were not supposed to touch anything that belonged to a human because they were told it could contaminate them. If any item from the human world entered the monster world, the Child Detection Agency had to destroy the item and decontaminate any monster that touched it.

Hearing Mike's scream, the other monsters rushed out of their rooms.

They all gathered round the glove, staring at the strange object. It wasn't very often they got to see a real human belonging! Everyone started to wonder what would actually happen if they touched it....

The monsters began nudging each other, wondering if anyone would be brave enough to take on the glove challenge.

"I can touch it ... I'm not afraid!" shouted Mike, trying to sound confident.

"Easy there, little guy,' grunted Sulley, moving to the front of the crowd. "Let a monster with real scare potential take care of this!"

Mike brought himself face to face with Sulley. "So touch it," he said. "I dare you!"

"And I double dare you!" replied Sulley.

"Gentlemen," called a voice from the crowd. "Are you not up to the challenge?" It was Mike's rival, Johnny "The Jaw" Worthington. Johnny was the leader of the top fraternity at Monsters University, Roar Omega Roar, and had refused to let Mike join because he didn't think he was scary enough.

Mike was not going to let Johnny tease him in front of all the other monsters. He was determined to prove that he was brave enough to touch the glove. "Okay then," Mike said. "I'm gonna do it."

But Sulley wasn't going to let Mike take on the challenge on his own. "Let's do it together."

Slowly, they approached the glove. But just as they were reaching out their hands to touch it ... a voice calling out made them stop. "You've found it!" it shouted.

Mike and Sulley froze. Who could that be?

Suddenly a small, green monster with five eye stalks, like the shape of a hand, ran across the floor.

"My hat!" the monster said. "I was looking for that everywhere!" Then it picked the glove up, put it over its head and left. Leaving behind a very confused bunch of monsters.

Disney
DUMBO

Pass It On!

"Did you hear the news, my dear?" one of the circus elephants said to another.

"What is it?" the second elephant asked.

The first elephant looked around carefully to make sure that no one was listening. "Well," she whispered to the second elephant. "You know Mrs Jumbo's son, Dumbo, right?"

"Of course," the second elephant replied. "The small fellow with the big ears. The one who became a ..." she shuddered with distaste, "... a clown."

"That's right," the first elephant said. "Well, a little bird told me that the first show was a hit! Everyone loved the 'Building on Fire' act. Dumbo leaped off a platform 20 feet high. And they're going to raise it up much higher next time!"

"Oh, my!" the second elephant said.

"But you musn't tell a soul!" the first elephant warned.

But, as soon as the first elephant turned away, the second elephant turned to another of her friends. "Listen, dear," she said. "You'll never believe what I just heard!"

"What is it, dear?" the third elephant asked.

The second elephant lowered her voice to a whisper. "Oh, you'll never believe it!" she began. "It's Dumbo – 20 clowns had to hit him with a tyre to get him to leap off a platform!"

"Oh, my!" the third elephant gasped. "That is big news!"

"But don't breathe a word to anyone!" the second elephant exclaimed.

"Certainly not!"

Soon, the third elephant was whispering to another friend. The fourth elephant gasped with amazement as she listened.

"... and so Dumbo set the platform on fire, and it took 20 clowns to put out the flames," the third elephant told the fourth.

The fourth elephant told a fifth, and a fifth told a sixth. Soon, the whole circus was buzzing with the news of Dumbo's first clown show.

A bird was flying over the Big Top when he saw a pair of elephants chattering below.

He flew down to see what was going on, landing on one elephant's trunk. "Good day, ladies," he said. "What's the word around the circus this evening?"

"It's about Dumbo," one elephant said excitedly. "It seems he fell off a platform in the last show, and hit 20 clowns. Now they're talking about setting him on fire next time!"

The bird didn't stick around to hear the end of the discussion. "I can't wait to spread this news!" he squawked, fluttering back up into the sky. "Wait until everyone hears – they'll never believe it's true!"

Sleep Tight, Nemo

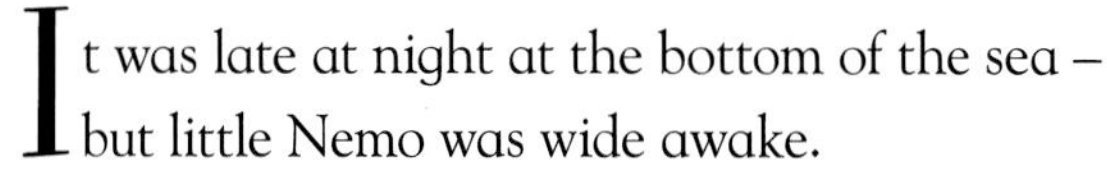

It was late at night at the bottom of the sea – but little Nemo was wide awake.

"Nemo," said Marlin, poking his head into the anemone, "you should be asleep!"

"But I can't sleep," said Nemo. "I need another story."

"No more stories," Marlin replied. "I have told you five already."

"Then maybe another snack?" said Nemo.

But Marlin rolled his eyes. "No, Nemo. You just had a plankton snack five minutes ago. What you should do now, young clownfish, is go to sleep!"

"Okay, Dad," said Nemo. Then he did as his dad told him and closed his eyes. But, seconds later, they popped open again.

"Dad!" Nemo called out. "Daaaad!"

"Nemo!" Marlin groaned. "I'm beginning to lose my patience!"

"But, Dad," said Nemo, "I ... I ... I think I heard a noise."

"What kind of noise?" Marlin asked.

"Um ... it ... it was a spooky noise," answered Nemo.

"Hmph." Nemo could tell Marlin did not like this reason for being awake either. But still, Marlin stopped and listened ... and listened ... and listened.

"I don't hear anything, Nemo," he said after a moment.

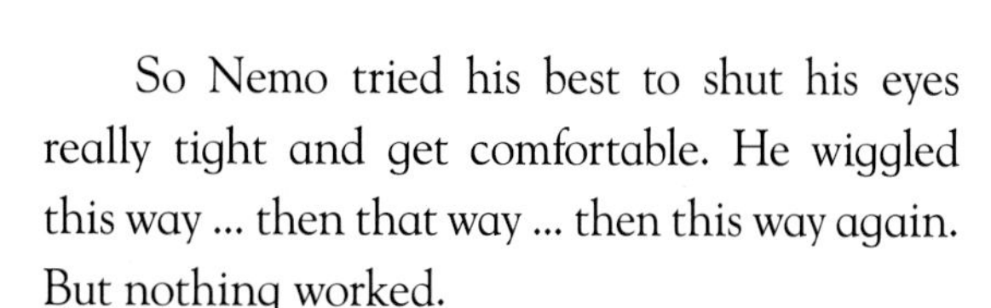

So Nemo tried his best to shut his eyes really tight and get comfortable. He wiggled this way ... then that way ... then this way again. But nothing worked.

"Dad!" he called out.

"Nemo," Marlin said. "For the last time, it's time to go to sleep. If you call for me again, it had better be for a good reason or ... or ... or else. Goodnight!"

Now, Nemo knew his father well, and he knew when Marlin was just a teeny, tiny, itsy, bitsy bit angry with him. But Nemo also knew that when you can't go to sleep, you can't go to sleep. And no matter how many moonfish or angelfish or sea stars you count, no matter how tightly you close your eyes, no matter how mad your dad gets – you'll never go to sleep until you're absolutely, positively, no-doubt-about-it ready. And Nemo wasn't. But why not?

Suddenly, Nemo bolted up. "Dad!" he shouted. "Dad! Oh, Daaad!"

"All right. That's it, Nemo!" Marlin said.

"But, Dad," Nemo said. "There's one more thing I really, really, truly need. Then I promise, I'll go to sleep."

And with that, he snuggled into Marlin's fins for a great big goodnight hug.

"I love you, Dad," he said, smiling. "See you in the morning."

Disney Princess
Snow White and the Seven Dwarfs

Two Hearts as One

Snow White's stomach fluttered with excitement as she made her way through the forest. In a few days, it would be her first wedding anniversary with the Prince and she needed her friends, the Dwarfs, to help her with something.

When Snow White arrived at the little cottage, the Dwarfs gathered around her in curiosity. "I'd like to make dinner at your cottage for the Prince," she asked. "And give him a special gift."

"How about a diamond?" suggested Doc.

"What a great idea," Snow White agreed. "The Prince can use it to decorate his shield."

Snow White went home, leaving the task in the hands of her friends.

The next morning, the Dwarfs set off for the diamond mines ... except for Grumpy, who had accidentally overslept. When he woke up, he bolted from the cottage, but in his haste, slammed into the belly of the Prince who was coming along the path!

"I'm glad I found you. I have a favour to ask," chuckled the Prince. "I want to give Snow White a precious gift," the Prince said. "Could you help find me the perfect diamond?"

Grumpy swelled with pride, the Prince needed his help! He promised he wouldn't fail the Prince, then ran off.

Deep in the mine, Doc had spotted a giant diamond buried deep in the wall. As he left to get his pickaxe, Grumpy, who had just arrived, noticed the same magnificent gem.

"We can't both have it," Doc pointed out.

Dopey had overheard them bickering and quietly came up with a plan. Taking the perfect diamond back to the cottage, he cut the gem into two pieces.

"Oh gosh!" said Doc.

Had Dopey made a terrible mistake?

Later that day, Snow White arrived with the Prince. The Dwarfs nervously sat with them.

"This is for you," announced the Prince, handing Snow White the velvet sack with the diamond segment hidden inside.

Snow White opened it. "Oh! Look how it sparkles!" she gasped.

"And this is Snow White's gift to you," Doc said, handing the Prince his velvet sack.

The Prince smiled as a diamond piece rolled into his palm.

Dopey unexpectedly took both diamond pieces and slotted them together for all to see. They formed the exact shape of....

"A love heart!" cheered the Dwarfs.

And the Prince kept the heart-shaped diamond on display at the castle for Snow White, to shine like their love, forever.

Disney THE LION KING

Runaway Hippo!

One morning Simba, Timon and Pumbaa were eating breakfast.

"Mmm, crispy, crunchy bugs," said Pumbaa.

"Try the big red ones," said Timon. "They have lots of legs. They come with their own toothpicks!"

Suddenly, they heard a sad cry from the jungle.

"Sounds like somebody is in trouble," said Simba.

"The sound is coming from over here," said Pumbaa. He led them to a muddy pond full of thick vines. In the middle of the swamp was a baby hippo. He was tangled up in vines and half buried in mud.

"Help!" the hippo cried as he struggled against the vines. The more the hippo squirmed, the more tangled he became, and the deeper he sank into the mud.

When the little hippo saw Simba, he became very frightened. "Oh, no, a lion! He's going to eat me!" he cried.

"Take it easy," Simba replied. "These guys have got me on an all-bug diet."

Timon grabbed a vine and swung over to the hippo. He began digging the little hippo out of the mud.

Meanwhile Simba jumped onto the hippo's back and began tearing at the thick vines with his teeth.

That made the hippo even more afraid!

"You *are* trying to eat me!" he shouted.

Finally, Simba and Timon got the hippo unstuck. Free at last, the hippo started to cry. "P-p-please don't eat me," he said to Simba.

"I'm not going to eat you, I promise," said Simba. "I just want to know how you got stuck in the mud."

"I was angry at my little brother and I bit his tail and made him cry. I was afraid my parents would be upset so I ran away from home," said the little hippo.

"I'll bet your parents *are* upset," said Simba. "Because you're gone and they're worried about you."

"They won't care," the hippo said.

"Come on," said Simba. He led the little hippo to the edge of the river. When they got there, they could hear the other hippos calling.

"Oyo! Oyo! Oyo!"

"Listen," said the hippo. "Oyo's my name. They're calling me! They miss me!"

"Sure," said Simba. "You can't just run away without being missed. When you're part of a family, no matter what you do, you'll always belong."

"What about *your* family, Simba?" Timon asked as they watched the little hippo rejoin his family. "Do you think they miss you?"

"I didn't use to think so," Simba replied thoughtfully, "but now I wonder...."

Disney Princess
Cinderella

Fit for a Princess

Cinderella hummed to herself as she slipped the silver needle through the colourful fabric. She had been working hard on her new quilt for weeks, and it was finally almost finished!

Though it was made of scraps of fabric from her stepsisters' old gowns and other rags, Cinderella knew the quilt would be fit for a princess. The worn fabrics were colourful and soft, and with the cotton wadding she'd found in the attic, the quilt would be wonderfully cosy. No more shivering under her threadbare blanket!

Gus agreed. He couldn't help but climb between the sewn-together quilt fabric and snuggle into the cotton filling.

"This is very cosy, Cinderelly," he called from deep inside the quilt. "I think I'd better see how it is for sleeping...."

Suzy and Perla, the mice who were helping Cinderella with the sewing, giggled.

"Go and get us some more thread, sleepyhead," they called. But Gus was already dozing off. The sound of his snores drifted out from between the layers of quilt.

"Gus!" Jaq called. But the snores only got louder. "That mouse hasn't helped with this quilt one bit!" Jaq sighed and went to get the spools of thread himself.

Cinderella, the mice and the birds worked all evening. They were just sewing together the last edge when loud footsteps echoed on the attic stairs.

"Cinderella!" called an angry voice. It was Anastasia, her stepsister. A moment later she stormed into the room, carrying a fancy blue gown. "My dress was not ironed properly!" she shouted. "Can't you do anything right?" Then she spotted the quilt.

"It's beautiful!" she cried. "And it will look wonderful on my bed!"

Cinderella looked at Anastasia in shock. Would her stepsister really steal her quilt? Cinderella knew Anastasia and Drizella could be mean, but that would be very cruel!

Suddenly the quilt began to move. A moment later Gus's quivering nose poked out from between the unsewn pieces of fabric.

"A rodent!" Anastasia screamed. She dropped her dress in fright and leaped onto a small wooden chair. "Why, that quilt isn't fit for use in the stable!" she cried.

Cinderella tried not to laugh as her stepsister leaped off the chair and fled down the stairs. Yawning, Gus climbed the rest of the way out of the quilt.

"Well, Gus," Jaq said admiringly, "I guess you did end up helping with the quilt, after all!"

Disney Princess
Snow White and the Seven Dwarfs

A Royal Visit

Snow White was very happy. She had married her true love and she lived in a beautiful castle. But she missed her good friends from the forest, the Seven Dwarfs, very much.

"Well, why don't we go for a visit?" the Prince said.

"That would be lovely!" Snow White cried.

Snow White wrote a note to tell her friends that she was coming, and asked a bluebird to deliver it.

At the Dwarfs' cottage, Doc read the note then ran downstairs to tell the others. "Hooray!" Happy cheered. "Snow White is coming!" But then the Dwarfs looked around their messy cottage. "We have a lot to do, men!" Happy admitted.

"She'll want lunch," Grumpy huffed. "Someone's gonna have to cook!"

"Why don't you and Happy fix somethin' suitable for Snow White to eat?" Doc suggested. The Dwarfs started to work on their chores right away. It didn't go very well. Sleepy got tired and lay down. Sneezy kept sneezing as he dusted. And Dopey knocked furniture over as he swept. Meanwhile, Happy and Grumpy couldn't agree on what kind of sandwiches to make.

"Snow White likes peanut butter and jam, I know," Happy declared.

"She likes ham and cheese," Grumpy grumbled. "Everyone knows that."

By the time Doc finally got them to agree on something, the clock struck 12 and there was a soft rap on the door. Their beloved princess was here! They smiled as Snow White hugged each of them and kissed their foreheads. "How I've missed you all!" she cried.

"Please forgive the mess, Princess," Bashful whispered to her. "We didn't quite get it cleaned up."

"Oh, please," Snow White said with a laugh, "forgive me for giving you such short notice! Besides, I've come to see you – not your cottage."

"Would you care for a ham-and-jam sandwich?" Doc offered, holding up a platter. "Or peanut butter and cheese?"

"How sweet," Snow White kindly replied. "If I had known you'd go to all this trouble, I wouldn't have brought a picnic with me."

"Picnic?" the Dwarfs exclaimed.

"Well, yes. I remembered how much you liked it when I cooked, so I brought some of your favourites. But let's eat your sandwiches first."

The Dwarfs looked at one another and Doc cleared his throat.

"We can have ham and jam any time," he said. "Let's enjoy your picnic and have a great visit." And that's exactly what they did.

Disney · PIXAR
TOY STORY 3

Garden Guardians

Bonnie had brought Woody with her to Sunnyside, but when it was time to go home she had accidentally left him behind.

Woody stared out of the window. It was Friday, so Bonnie wouldn't be back at the daycare centre until Monday.

"Bonnie hasn't left you on purpose, Woody," said Chunk the rock-like action figure.

Woody smiled. "I know, Chunk," he said, brightening up. "It'll just be like a little holiday."

It was a beautiful day, so Woody decided to head outside to take a relaxing stroll in the garden. The place sure was quiet without any kids around, but as Woody passed the climbing frame he heard something rustle in the long grass nearby.

"Hey!" he said. "Is anybody there?"

When no one replied, Woody stepped into the grass. "Come out, friend," he began, pushing aside the long blades. Before he could say any more, a piece of string went tight around his foot. He gasped as he was pulled up into the air.

"Hands up!" shouted a voice from the grass, as Woody dangled helplessly from a tree branch above.

Meanwhile, back inside, the bug-like action figure, Twitch, was wondering where Woody had gone. When Chunk told him Woody had gone into the garden, Twitch started to worry.

"What? Didn't you warn him that they are out there?" he gulped. "He might fall into one of the traps they built to stop intruders."

Chunk's face fell. "Oops!" he said.

Along with Stretch, the rubbery purple octopus, Chunk and Twitch raced out of the daycare centre and into the garden. They searched the sandpit and crawled under the picnic tables, searching for the missing sheriff.

"Woody! Woody!" cried Stretch.

"Where are you?" yelled Chunk. He was feeling guilty. He should have warned Woody what was in the garden.

The toys were about to call for help, when Twitch spotted something. "Look!" he said, pointing over to near the climbing frame.

Chunk and Stretch sighed with relief. Woody was standing in the grass, laughing and chatting happily with a group of tiny green army men. "It was a pleasure to meet you again, sir!" said the sarge, saluting.

"We got worried for nothing," said Twitch.

Woody smiled. It was nice to catch up with Andy's old toys, the army men, again, but he had to admit that dangling from that trap had got him a little worried, too!

Disney Princess
Beauty and the Beast

A Little Help

"This is bad," fretted Cogsworth the clock, pacing at the bottom of the castle's staircase. "Bad, bad, bad!"

"What is wrong, my friend?" asked Lumiere the candelabra.

"The Beast hurt Belle's feelings," said Cogsworth. "Then Belle hurt the Beast's feelings. Now they're sulking in their rooms."

"Ah, that *is* bad," said Lumiere. "We will never be human again unless the spell on the Beast is broken. And the spell won't break until Belle falls in love with him."

"Well, there's no chance of that happening now!" cried Cogsworth.

"Nonsense," said Lumiere. "Sometimes love just needs a little help."

After Lumiere told Cogsworth his plan, they got to work. When everything was ready, Lumiere knocked on Belle's bedroom door.

"*Mademoiselle*," he called sweetly. "I am here to tell you that the Beast is very sorry about what happened."

"He is?" asked Belle.

"Oh, yes," said Lumiere. "Now do you wish to see your surprise?"

The door slowly opened. "My surprise?" asked Belle.

"*Oui, mademoiselle*," said Lumiere. "Just follow me."

At that very moment, Cogsworth was standing outside the Beast's bedroom door, his gears quaking with fear. "Darn that Lumiere," muttered Cogsworth. "Why do *I* get the Beast?"

Gathering all his courage, Cogsworth finally knocked.

"Go away!" came a roar from inside.

Cogsworth wanted to! But, instead, he called, "Master, I am only here to tell you that Belle is very sorry about what happened!"

After a long pause, the Beast said, "She is?"

"Oh, yes indeed," said Cogsworth. "Now follow me to see your surprise."

The door slowly opened. "My surprise?" asked the Beast.

"Yes, Master," said Cogsworth.

Both Belle and the Beast were led into the large drawing room. The room had been filled with fresh flowers from the greenhouse. And there stood Plucky the golden harp.

"Ohhhhh," said Belle and the Beast when they heard the beautiful harp music.

"You're sorry?" asked Belle.

"I am," the Beast admitted.

"I am too," said Belle.

They smiled at each other.

Lumiere and Cogsworth sighed. "You see, my friend," whispered Lumiere, "in their hearts, each really was sorry. They just needed a little help to admit it!"

July
19

A Very Special Friendship

Rosetta, the garden fairy, was busy using her talent. "The time to bloom is here! Now, bloom!" she cried, and flower buds opened all over the woodland glade. Pink and purple flowers turned their heads to the sun in a beautiful display. Rosetta smiled happily. She loved being a garden fairy!

But then, something caught her eye. Down below, on the very edge of a pond, a flower was still closed in a bud. Rosetta flew down.

"Why haven't you blossomed?" she asked the flower. A little goldfish, watching from the water, smiled up at it. "Bloom!" Rosetta tried again. "Bloom! Bloom!"

The flower remained stubbornly closed.

"Oh, it's no use," she sighed.

"Need a hand, dewdrop?" called Silvermist, the water-talent fairy, as she came skimming over the water.

"I can't get it to blossom," replied Rosetta in frustration. What could be wrong?

Silvermist thought for a moment. "Maybe the flower just needs a little more time?" Then she spotted the goldfish, swimming at the base of the flower. "Hey, look! The flower seems to have a friend down here!"

"The flower isn't blooming because of the fish?" Rosetta couldn't believe it. She'd never heard of a fish and a flower being friends before!

"Not exactly!" Silvermist giggled. "Get ready to use your talent."

She turned to the little goldfish. "Are you ready to fly inside a bubble?" Using her magic, Silvermist conjured a large bubble of water out of the pond – with the fish safely inside!

Rosetta stared in astonishment. What was Silvermist planning? And then, as her friend carefully flew the water bubble above the flower bud, she suddenly realized what she was doing!

"Now, Rosetta!" called Silvermist. "Do your thing!"

"With pleasure!" Rosetta reached towards the flower. "Bloom!" she urged.

And slowly, very slowly, the petals began to unfurl. The flower tipped its head up to the sky as it finally blossomed – and right above it, the little goldfish grinned and turned somersaults of delight inside its bubble.

The two fairies smiled as they looked on. "The flower wanted its little friend the fish to be able to see it blossom," said Silvermist, feeling all warm inside.

"They're so cute," said Rosetta, wiping away a tear of happiness. "That's the nicest pair of friends I've ever seen!"

That day, the fairies realized everyone needs a friend – even flowers and fish!

Disney Princess
Beauty and the Beast

The Mysterious Book

"What are you looking at, Belle?" Chip asked. Belle smiled at the little teacup.

"Oh, you caught me daydreaming, Chip," she said. "I was just looking up there."

She pointed to the highest shelf in the Beast's library. The only thing on the shelf was a single book.

Belle had wondered about that book since the Beast had first shown her the library. The trouble was, none of the ladders quite reached the shelf. So the book had remained a mystery ever since.

Belle's curiosity had grown until she could hardly stop thinking about the book. What could it be about? Surely it had to be the most magical, unusual, wonderful book in the world!

She explained the problem to Chip. He went straight to his mother, Mrs Potts.

Mrs Potts called a meeting of all the enchanted objects. As soon as she told them about the book, they wanted to help Belle.

"What we need is a plan," Cogsworth said.

"Yes!" Lumiere cried. "And I've got one!"

That evening the enchanted objects gathered in the library. First the Wardrobe stood at the base of the shelves. The Stove climbed on top of her, then the Coatrack climbed up next. Soon a whole tower of enchanted objects stretched almost to the top shelf.

Finally Lumiere started to climb. When he reached the top, the book was still a few centimetres away. He stretched as far as he could....

"What are you doing?" Belle exclaimed from the doorway.

"Oh, *mademoiselle*!" Lumiere cried. "You're just in time – *voilà*!"

With that, he finally managed to reach the book, knocking it off the shelf into Belle's hands.

A moment later, the tower collapsed in a heap.

As soon as Belle made certain that everyone was all right, she opened the book. She couldn't wait to see what new wonders lay within its covers....

"Oh!" she said when she saw the first page.

"What is it?" Chip asked breathlessly.

Belle smiled sheepishly. "I can't believe it! I've already read this one."

The enchanted objects sighed. Had their plan been for nothing?

"But thank you anyway!" Belle said quickly. "It's so nice of you to get it for me." She hugged the book to her. "Even though I've read it before, it's one of my favourites – it's full of far-off places, magic spells ... well, let me show you...."

Soon all the enchanted objects were gathered around as Belle read the book to them. And, wouldn't you know, it became one of their favourite books too!

July

21

Disney *Lady and the* TRAMP

A Tramp Tale

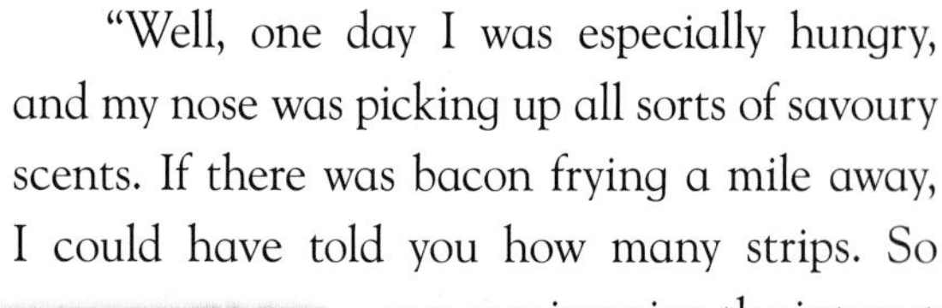

It was a warm evening, just about the time that the first star comes out to shine, and *long* past the time for Lady and Tramp's puppies to go to sleep.

"Just one more story, Dad," begged Scamp.

Tramp rolled his eyes.

"Well ... okay," he said, "but just one."

Happily, the puppies snuggled down onto their cushion. Tramp stretched out beside them.

"Did I ever tell you kids about the time I stole my very first sausage?" he asked.

"Tramp!" Lady warned him from her seat across the parlour. "That hardly sounds like a proper story for the children to hear."

"Oh, tell it, Dad!" Scamp urged him.

"Well, maybe 'stole' isn't exactly the right word," Tramp reassured his wife. "And besides, it's got a great moral!" And with that, he began his tale.

"Now this all happened way back when I was just a little pup, already living on my own in the big city. I hope you puppies know just how good you have it living here in this nice house, with Junior and Jim Dear and Darling. Your old dad, though, was not so lucky. Oh, sure, I had a lot of friends. And I had a lot of fun. But I'd be lying if I said I wasn't hungry – just a little – nearly every day.

"Well, one day I was especially hungry, and my nose was picking up all sorts of savoury scents. If there was bacon frying a mile away, I could have told you how many strips. So you can imagine the interest I developed in a certain, spicy smell coming from the butcher shop. Well, I followed my trusty nose, which has still never let me down and, sure enough, there was a heaped tray of steaming sausages. Can you believe it?"

"So you jumped up and gobbled them all up! Right?" Scamp broke in.

"That's my boy!" Tramp laughed. "But no. Don't forget, I was just a little guy. Couldn't reach the tray. All I could do was think about how to get that sausage ... when up walked a lady with a kid in a pram. Well, at first I was irate. Competition! But then I noticed the crumbs all over the pram. Hey! I thought to myself. This might be the ticket – this kid obviously can't hang on to anything. Sure enough, when the lady handed the kid a piece of sausage, the kid dropped it, and down it fell into my waiting mouth! Delicious!

"See," Tramp said with a grin, "no stealing!"

"And what exactly is the moral of that story?" Lady asked.

Tramp laughed. "Why, good things come to those who wait, of course!"

Disney · PIXAR TOY STORY 3

Bonnie's Birthday Surprise

Bonnie's mum had been hard at work, busily preparing the food for Bonnie's birthday party. While she and Bonnie went out for some last-minute supplies, the toys admired the delicious-looking spread.

"It's gonna be a great party," Woody whistled.

Rex and Trixie, the dinosaur toys, pushed past. "Hey! I wanna see the cake," said Rex. Trixie agreed, and they both began to scramble up the table.

"Well, I don't think that's a good idea guys," began Woody, but it was too late. Rex and Trixie had already made it onto the table top and were racing towards the box containing Bonnie's birthday cake.

"I can't wait to see it!" Rex cheered.

Woody was nervous. Rex had a habit of being clumsy. "We'd better go after them," he said, so he and Dolly hurried to catch the dinosaurs up.

"Be careful, Rex," Woody warned, climbing up onto the table beside the cake box.

Rex nodded. "Don't worry, I'll be super careful," he said, as he slowly lifted the lid of the box.

The cake was beautiful! There was pink and white icing, sweet sprinkles, and Bonnie's name written across it. Bonnie was sure to be delighted with it.

"Let me see it, let me see it!" demanded Trixie, shoving Rex out of the way. Rex flapped his stubby arms as he lost balance and – *SPLURT!* He landed face-first in the cake.

Rex pulled his head free of the icing and gasped. "What will we do now?"

The toys couldn't let Bonnie's birthday be ruined, so they quickly set to work. Trixie searched the internet for cake decorating tips, but they were all too difficult for them to even attempt.

Woody had an idea. "What about using jelly beans and sweets?" he suggested. Bonnie loved jelly beans, and the toys quickly agreed. The only problem was, the icing was still a mess. No amount of sweets would fix that.

Rex waggled his tail. "Maybe I can do something about that."

In no time, Rex used his long tail to smooth over the pink icing, and the toys set to work decorating. They finished just as Bonnie and her mum returned from shopping.

Bonnie cheered when she saw her cake. "Wow! This is the best cake ever!" she said.

Her mum nodded. "Yes ... it's even better than I remembered," she said.

Down on the floor, Dolly whispered quietly to Rex. "Well done. Everything turned out fine, thanks to you and your dinosaur tail!"

Disney Peter Pan

A Feather in His Cap

Peter Pan and Tinker Bell were off on an adventure and the Lost Boys were bored.

"Never Land is a dull place without Peter Pan," Slightly complained.

Then Rabbit spoke up. "We can play Pirates! That's always fun."

"Can't," said Slightly. "I lost the feather off my pirate hat."

"We could find another feather," Tootles suggested.

"An extraordinary feather," Cubby said. "Like Captain Hook's."

"That's it!" Slightly cried. "I'll steal Captain Hook's feather!"

A short time later, the Lost Boys were sneaking aboard Hook's pirate ship. Luckily for them, the pirates were taking a nap!

There, hanging from a peg on the mast, was Captain Hook's hat.

"There it is," whispered Tootles. "Get it!"

"M-m-m-me?" stammered Slightly.

Smee, Hook's first mate, awoke with a start. He thought someone had said his name. "Smee you say! That be me. But who be calling Smee?"

He opened his eyes and spied the Lost Boys. "Ahoy!" he cried, waking up the others. Quick as a flash, the Lost Boys were caught.

Captain Hook burst from his cabin. "Lash them to the mast!" he commanded. "We'll catch Peter Pan when he comes to save his friends."

Floating high on a cloud, Peter Pan and Tinker Bell saw their friends being captured.

They flew down to Pirates' Cove and landed on the ship's mast. Peter cupped his hands around his mouth and made a most peculiar sound.

"Tick tock," Peter went. "Tick tock!"

Down on the deck, Captain Hook became very frightened. "It's that crocodile!" he cried. "The one that ate my clock and my hand! Now he's come back to eat me!"

"Tick tock ... tick tock," went Peter.

"Man the cannons!" Hook cried. "Shoot that crocodile!"

The Lost Boys, tied to the mast, were forgotten. As the pirates ran in circles, Tinker Bell began to flap her wings. Fairy dust sprinkled down onto the Lost Boys. Soon they floated out of the ropes and up into the clouds. On the way, Slightly snatched the feather from Hook's hat and stuck it in his own.

Peter Pan, Tinker Bell and the Lost Boys met on a drifting cloud.

"Thanks for saving us!" exclaimed Tootles.

"You helped me scare old Hook!" Peter Pan cried. "That's a feather in all your caps."

"But the best feather of them all is in mine," Slightly said, as he showed off Captain Hook's prized feather!

Disney Princess
The Little Mermaid

A Hair-raising Experience

Ariel looked at her hair in the mirror and sighed. *Ugh!* It was so straight ... and red ... and boring! Ordinarily, it wasn't such a big deal. She'd run a dinglehopper through it, and that would be that. She had more important things to think about, you know. But today, for some reason, she felt like a change.

Ariel was still staring in the mirror when her six mermaid sisters arrived.

"What are you doing?" the oldest, Aquata, asked.

"Oh, nothing," said Ariel. "Just trying to figure out something new to do with my hair."

"Just parting it on the other side can make a big difference," said Aquata. "Shall I try?"

"Sure!" said Ariel.

But, when Aquata had done it, Ariel's sister Andrina shook her head. "Not enough," she declared. "What you need, Ariel, are some curls."

"Okay," Ariel shrugged. She sat patiently as Andrina rolled her hair in curlers and took them out half an hour later.

"Oh, my," said Ariel, gazing into the mirror.

"Still not enough," said another sister, Arista. "Imagine how great your hair would look if we coloured it black with squid ink!" And, just to prove her point, that's exactly what she did.

"Well it certainly is different," said Ariel, looking at her new inky-black hair.

"Different, yes," said her sister Attina, "but if you want *better*, you should really put your hair up. You know, a ponytail or two ... no! I know, three!"

And soon Ariel's new hair was in not one, not two, but three curly black ponytails – all sticking straight up from her head.

"You know what you need?" said her sister Adella, looking at the finished product. "Plaits! Girls, come and help me."

And, before she knew it, Ariel's ponytails had been divided into 99 tight, twisty plaits.

Ariel looked in the mirror ... and then looked away twice as fast!

"What if we just cut it all off?" said her sister Alana.

"Hold it!" said Ariel, suddenly jumping up. "You're *not* cutting off my hair! I wanted a change – not a total reconstruction!" She reached up and began to unplait her hair.

"Suit yourself," said her sisters. They helped her undo their hard work. Soon Ariel was back to normal, to her great relief. Still, she thought, it had been an interesting experiment. Changing her hair hadn't worked out so well, but what about changing something else? She shook her head and sighed. She was a redheaded mermaid princess, and that was that.

Winnie the Pooh

A Bouncy Babysitter

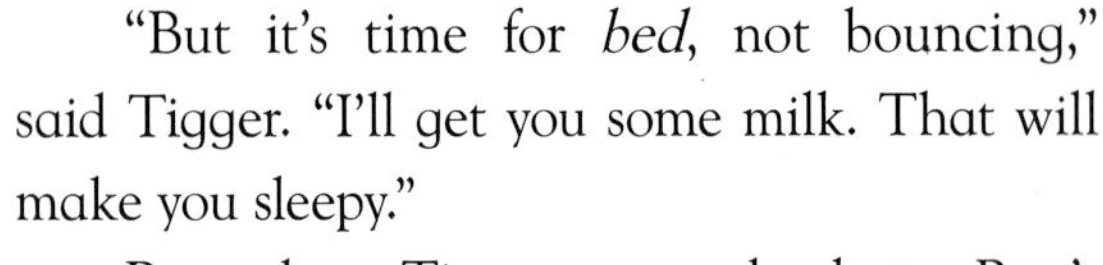

"Roo, I have to go out tomorrow evening," said Kanga. "So you'll need a babysitter. Who would you like?"

"Tigger!" shouted Roo.

Kanga was not surprised. Tigger was the only animal she knew who liked to bounce more than a baby kangaroo!

The next day, Tigger came over to Kanga's house.

"Now, Tigger, I know you and Roo like to bounce," said Kanga. "But a good babysitter must know when to put the bouncer to bed."

"Don't worry, Kanga!" said Tigger.

For hours, Tigger and Roo had a fine old time bouncing around. Then Tigger looked at the clock and said, "Time for bed!"

Roo hopped right into his room.

"That was easy," Tigger said to himself. "Now I'll just tuck you in and – hey! I said bounce *into* bed. Not *on* it!" cried Tigger. But Roo wouldn't stop. So Tigger gave up and started bouncing too.

Then Tigger remembered Kanga. "Wait a minute! I'm the babysitter!" said Tigger. "I'm supposed to be tucking you in!"

"I don't want to be tucked in!" said Roo.

"What if I read you a story?" asked Tigger.

"No," said Roo. "I'm not even sleepy. I could bounce all the way to Pooh's house!"

"But it's time for *bed*, not bouncing," said Tigger. "I'll get you some milk. That will make you sleepy."

But when Tigger came back to Roo's bedroom, Roo was gone!

"Uh-oh!" said Tigger. He rushed to Pooh's house.

"I'm sorry, Tigger," said Pooh, "but Roo isn't here."

Then Tigger rushed to Piglet's house. But Roo wasn't there either.

And he wasn't at Owl's or Rabbit's.

Finally, Tigger returned to Kanga's house. Where could Roo be? Just then, Tigger passed Roo's room – and saw Roo in his bed!

"Where were you, Tigger?" asked Roo.

"Where was I?" replied Tigger. "Where were *you*?"

Roo explained that when Tigger had gone to get the milk, Roo had decided he did want to hear a story. But his favourite book was under the bed.

"You were *under* the bed?" cried Tigger.

"I'm home!" called Kanga at the front door.

Tigger sighed with relief.

"How did it go?" she asked Tigger.

"Kanga," said Tigger, "the wonderful thing about Tiggers is bouncing – and from now on I'm sticking with that. Babysitting just has too many ups and downs!"

Disney · PIXAR
BRAVE

The Legend of the Emeralds

The Rites of Summer Festival had arrived at last. A time to celebrate the friendship between DunBroch and the Macintosh clan with a day of games!

Merida wasted no time in luring Young Macintosh away towards the forest. They had both agreed they wanted to have an adventure before the welcoming ceremony began. So, at the Fire Falls, they raced each other to the top of the cliff.

"Let's discover where this water comes from!" Merida said, but as she turned, she tripped and stumbled into some vines that parted and swallowed her whole.

"Merida!" Young Macintosh cried. He pushed the vines aside and found a deep cave.

"I'm okay!" insisted Merida. "You'll never believe what I found!" Kneeling next to a pool of water, Merida pointed at two glorious emeralds.

"Emeralds mean power," said Young Macintosh, grabbing one.

Merida grabbed the other.

Back at DunBroch castle, the welcoming ceremony was about to begin. Queen Elinor was furious, but Merida ignored her questions and instead asked one of her own. "Did you know there are two emeralds at the Fire Falls?"

"According to legend," said her father, King Angus, "Kings from each clan placed something they cared about at the Fire Falls to represent friendship and peace between DunBroch and Macintosh – two emeralds worth great riches."

Suddenly, a guard raced into the hall. "The Fire Falls!" he shouted. "They've gone dark."

Merida and Young Macintosh jumped on their horses and raced off to investigate. They found the water from the falls had turned as black as night.

Then Merida realized. "We have to put the emeralds back!"

Young Macintosh and Merida clambered up the rock face as fast as they could. But as they neared the top, Young Macintosh slipped and his emerald fell into the forest below them.

"We have to keep going!" he cried.

The two friends found the cave and placed the remaining emerald in the water but nothing happened.

"Wait!" said Merida. "The legend said that the kings put something they cared about at the falls."

Young Macintosh quickly unclasped the family crest from his kilt and put it with the emerald. A golden light appeared around the items and the water ran clear once more.

"We did it!" they cheered in triumph. Together, Merida and Young Macintosh had saved the Fire Falls and their clans' friendship.

Disney Mickey & Friends

Minnie's Summer Day

It was a hot summer day and Minnie and her friends were relaxing in her living room. The friends were just deciding what they could do that day when *POP!* Minnie's air-conditioning broke!

"Let's all go outside," Minnie suggested. "Maybe there will be a breeze."

But there was no breeze at all.

"What are we going to do now?" asked Daisy.

Minnie looked around. "Maybe we could make fans. Or we could try sitting in the shade under a tre...." she said.

"Those sprinklers look nice and cool!" said Goofy, pointing at Minnie's lawn.

Donald nodded. "But there isn't enough water coming out of those sprinklers to keep all of us cool!" he said.

Minnie had an idea. "I've got it!" she shouted. "Let's go to the lake! There's always a breeze there and there's so much to do!"

"It is the perfect day for a swim, as well," Daisy added.

Minnie's friends were so excited! They quickly raced to the lake.

"What should we do first?" Minnie asked, turning to her friends.

Everyone had a different idea. Daisy wanted to play basketball. Mickey and Pluto wanted to play fetch. And Donald wanted to go fishing!

Before anyone could stop him, Donald had raced off towards a little boat.

Donald was about to hop into it when Minnie called to him. "Donald, I don't think we can all fit in the boat. Why don't we all do something together! We could go for a swim?" said Minnie. "Everyone can do that!"

Donald wanted to go fishing, but finally he agreed.

The friends jumped into the water....

"Aah," sighed Donald, feeling much cooler already. "You were right, Minnie. This was a good idea!"

Minnie smiled. She was glad she and her friends had found a way to cool off.

"I could stay in this water all day!" Daisy said. And, do you know what, that is just what they did.

As the sun set and the day started to get cooler, Minnie and her friends got out of the water and Minnie had one last surprise for her friends ... marshmallows!

"Minnie, you really do know how to plan the perfect day!" said Mickey as they roasted marshmallows over a campfire, which they had all built together.

Finally, it really was time to leave.

"That was so much fun!" said Donald as they drove home. "We should do it all again tomorrow!"

Disney Princess
Snow White and the Seven Dwarfs

A Relaxing Picnic

"What a lovely day for a picnic!" Snow White cried as she arrived at the Dwarfs' cottage for a visit one morning.

"We can't have a picnic," Grumpy said. "We have to work."

"But we have been working so hard in the diamond mine." Sleepy yawned. "Can't we take a day off?"

The other Dwarfs all cheered – except for Grumpy. He just folded his arms and frowned.

"Please don't worry, Grumpy," said Snow White. "A relaxing picnic will cheer you up."

"I doubt it," he grumbled.

"Now, what shall we rake – I mean take – on our picnic?" Doc asked.

"How about some porridge?" suggested Sleepy with a yawn.

"That is not a very good picnic food," said Snow White. "It's much more fun to pack food you can eat without spoons or forks."

"Gosh, like s-s-sandwiches?" stammered Bashful shyly.

"Exactly!" cried Snow White.

"How about fruit?" asked Doc.

"And biscuits!" suggested Happy.

"Wonderful!" exclaimed Snow White.

The Dwarfs helped Snow White pack.

"After lunch, we'll want to play," said Snow White. "So you should pack up some things to play with."

They did, and then they were off, hiking through the forest. When they came to a clearing with a babbling brook, Snow White spread a blanket on the grass, and they all sat down to eat.

After lunch, Doc and Happy played draughts, Bashful and Sneezy tossed a ball back and forth, Sleepy took a nap and Dopey launched an enormous blue kite.

Snow White watched Dopey as he ran through the meadow. She clapped when the wind took the kite up in the air. Then the kite lifted Dopey off the ground too!

"Oh, my!" cried Snow White. "Someone help! Dopey is flying away!"

Grumpy, who had been pouting by the brook, jumped to his feet. He raced after Dopey. Huffing and puffing, he followed the kite up one hill and down another.

Finally, Grumpy climbed all the way up a tall oak tree and grabbed Dopey as he flew by. Snow White cheered.

Still huffing and puffing, Grumpy collapsed on the blanket.

"Jiminy Cricket!" he cried. "I can't wait to get back to the diamond mine tomorrow. Relaxing picnics are way too much work!"

July

29

An Excellent Sculptor

Clank and Bobble were hard at work in Tinkers' Nook building a new carriage for the Minister of Autumn. "Wow!" gasped Tinker Bell when she saw it. "Nice carriage!"

But Clank and Bobble weren't entirely happy with it. "We want to decorate it with something special," explained Clank.

"But all we found are the same old leaves," added Bobble.

"Don't worry," Tink said, smiling. "I'll help you find special decorations!" She flew off to start looking.

Not far from the Nook, Tink heard a familiar sound.

The woodpeckers were learning how to peck holes in trees! Tink waved to her friend Fawn, but Fawn looked so sad Tink had to fly down and see what was wrong.

Fawn shook her head. "I taught the baby woodpeckers to drill holes to make nests."

Tink looked around at the birds that were practising. "They look good to me."

"Yeah, the little fellas did a great job," said Fawn with a sigh, "all except one." She pointed to where a baby woodpecker sat on his own. Fawn picked up a fallen tree branch next to him. "This isn't how you make a hole for a nest!"

Tink gasped. The branch had been pecked and carved into a beautiful leaf pattern! And it gave her an idea.... "I think our friend here has a special talent," she said. She beckoned to the little bird. "Let's go to Tinkers' Nook and I'll show you."

Clank and Bobble looked hopeful when Tink arrived with Fawn. "Did you find something to decorate the carriage with?" asked Clank.

"I found something better!" Tink said, showing them the woodpecker. "A friend who'll help us!"

The bird puffed out his chest, looking very proud. Then he set to work on the carriage. Bits of wood flew into the air and clouds of dust whirled up around it.

Clank turned pale. "He's going to ruin our carriage!"

"Just wait and see," Tink reassured him.

And sure enough, when the dust cleared ... the carriage had been decorated from front to back with elegant carvings. Flowers, leaves and curling branches were etched into the wood. This was now a carriage like no other! The Minister would be delighted!

Clank, Bobble and Tink cheered. "Hooray for our sculptor friend!"

The baby woodpecker may not have been able to drill holes, but he could do something else – something very special indeed.

Trust Tink to discover his true talent and make him feel proud of it!

Disney

Bambi
A Manner of Speaking

Bambi and his mother were out for a summer's walk. As always, they stopped by the rabbit den where Thumper lived.

"And how are you today, Thumper?" asked Bambi's mother.

"I'd be better if my mum didn't just give me a dumb old bath," he said.

"Thumper!" his mother scolded him. "Please, mind your manners!"

"I'm sorry, Mama," Thumper said. He looked back at the doe. "I'm fine, thank you," he replied.

Bambi and Thumper were given permission to play, so they headed off into the woods.

"So, what do you want to play?" Bambi asked Thumper.

"How about hide-and-seek?" Thumper suggested. "I'll hide first, okay?"

Bambi turned his back to Thumper, closed his eyes, and started to count. "One ... two ... three ... four ... five...."

"Save me! Help! Bambi, save me!" Thumper cried. Bambi whirled round to see Thumper hopping towards him with a terrified look on his face. A moment later, a mother bear emerged from a nearby cave with three small cubs toddling behind her.

Though he was terrified, Thumper *still* managed to make a rude comment. "That's the meanest-looking creature I ever saw!"

"I beg your pardon?" the mother bear said. "First, you come into my home and disturb my children while they're sleeping. And then you have the nerve to call me mean? I think you owe me an apology!"

"Do it!" whispered Bambi. "Apologize."

"I'm sorry you're mean," Thumper stammered.

"Thumper!" Bambi cried. "That isn't funny."

Thumper was confused by Bambi's outburst. "I wasn't trying to be funny," he said.

"Try again!" the mother bear boomed.

"Um," Thumper tried again. "I'm, um, sorry I disturbed your cubs ... and, um, you look just like a bear mum should look ... which is big. And nice. Yup, you sure look nice."

Before the mother bear let Thumper and Bambi go, she said, "Like I always tell my children – manners are important!"

Bambi and Thumper ran home as quickly as they could. When they arrived at Thumper's, his mother said, "Just in time for a nice lunch of greens." Thumper was about to tell his mum how awful he thought the greens tasted, then changed his mind. "Thank you, Mama. That sounds wonderful," he said.

Thumper's mother beamed. "What lovely manners! I guess you have been listening to me, after all!" she said, as pleased as could be.

The Secret of Skull Cove

In a quiet corner of the reef, there was a twisted coral formation that looked like the open-mouthed skeleton of an angry clownfish.

"My dad said Mean Old Man Crab lives in there. He's been chasing kids away for an eternity!" said Nemo.

"No one has seen Mean Old Man Crab in years. Let's go explore! It will be an adventure," said Tad, fins wiggling in excitement.

Nemo and his three friends cautiously entered the mouth of the cove.

Sheldon sneezed loudly, startling Pearl. She rounded on him in annoyance, but froze when she saw something emerging from a dark corner.

"Ahh!" she screamed, as a giant crab with pincers as big as her body came bursting out.

"What are you kids doing?" the crab screeched with a click of his claws. "Maybe one or two pinches will teach you a lesson!"

"It's Mean Old Man Crab!" shouted Nemo. "Swim for your lives!"

Pearl squirted ink in the crab's scary face as they dashed off, tearing up the seaweed garden in their haste.

"You're trampling my plants!" the crab wailed. "Wait until I get my claws on you!"

Back home, Marlin was wondering where his son could be, when Nemo came racing up with his frightened friends in tow.

"Dad! A crab!" he screamed.

"Crab?" everyone at the reef choked in fear.

"Use the coral as camouflage!" Marlin called to them.

"I'm sorry I went to Mean Old Man Crab's cove," Nemo apologized, as they hid.

"That's the crab that's chasing you?" asked Marlin. He seemed less afraid now.

Mean Old Man Crab scurried over the hill, with his pincers raised.

"Hey! Keep those claws to yourself, crabby!" Marlin yelled. "Remember me? You chased me from Skull Cove when I was little, but I went back anyway and warned you about the shark. You were almost dinner until I saved you!"

Mean Old Man Crab's angry frown melted. He lowered his claws thoughtfully. "That was you?"

Marlin nodded.

Later, the sea creatures emerged from their hiding places to find Mean Old Man Crab smiling at them.

"Swim by the cove tomorrow," the crab said. "We can talk about old times!"

"You got it crabby, my man," Marlin promised him.

"Dad's a super-fish." Nemo grinned in pride, as Mean Old Man Crab waved goodbye.

Woodland Washing

"La, la, la, la, la," Briar Rose sang as she hung the sheets on the washing line. She could feel the sunshine on her back and it felt good. It had been raining for days, and the change in the weather was a welcome surprise. She could catch up on the washing and spend some time outdoors.

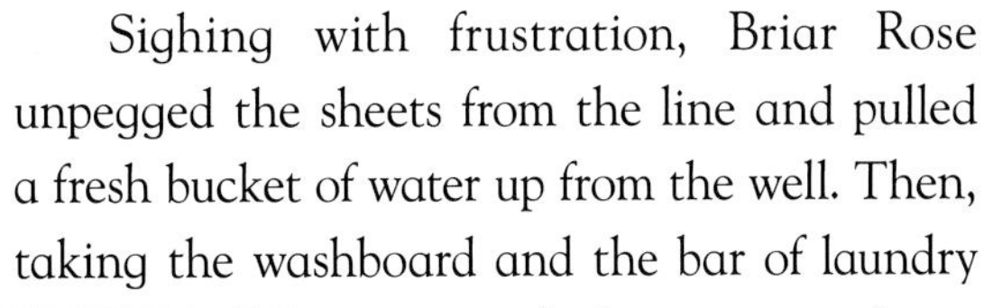

"Doesn't the sunshine make you want to sing?" she asked a bluebird who was chirping along with her. The bird chirped a new song in response, and Briar Rose laughed as she pulled her Aunt Flora's red dress out of the basket of clean laundry. Once she was finished, she could take a nice walk through the forest.

Aunt Merryweather's blue dress was next. Briar Rose was just pegging the shoulder to the washing line when suddenly a pair of cheeky chipmunks leaped onto the line from a tree branch and raced down the length of it, covering the dresses and the sheets with muddy footprints.

"Look what you've done, you naughty chipmunks!" Briar Rose scolded, shaking a finger at the wayward creatures. "It took me two hours to get those dresses and sheets clean!"

The chipmunks leaped up to a tree branch and twittered guiltily at her in response. Then they turned and scampered off into the forest, their striped tails waggling.

Sighing with frustration, Briar Rose unpegged the sheets from the line and pulled a fresh bucket of water up from the well. Then, taking the washboard and the bar of laundry soap, she began to scrub out the muddy prints. It looked as if she wouldn't get a walk in today after all.

Suddenly, a chattering noise caught her attention. Looking up, she saw the chipmunks hurrying out of the forest with several other forest animals at their heels! There were two rabbits, four chipmunks, three bluebirds, a deer, a skunk and an owl.

Briar Rose laughed. "Why, you've brought all your friends!"

The chipmunks chattered excitedly while everyone got to work. The bluebirds lifted the sheet into the air so the edges wouldn't get dirty while Briar Rose scrubbed. The deer, the skunk and the rabbits brought fresh water from the well. And the chipmunks scampered across the laundry soap to get their feet all soapy, then walked across the muddy parts of the sheets until they were clean. Then everyone helped hang the newly washed laundry on the line for a second time.

Briar Rose smiled at her animal friends and gave the chipmunks a little pat. "Finished at last," she said. "Now we can all take a walk in the forest ... together!"

Disney Princess
Cinderella

Princess in Disguise

Cinderella felt as if she'd been made a Princess overnight and it was a lot to take in! She'd gone from being a miserable servant at her wicked stepmother's house to marrying a Prince and becoming royalty.

It felt strange to have the palace staff waiting on her hand and foot. She was so used to doing everything. Cinderella wanted to help and be able to get to know everyone, but the palace staff were always too busy to talk to.

One morning, at breakfast with her beloved Prince, Cinderella shared her thoughts. "I want to know if the servants are happy to work here."

The Prince smiled. "Well, do whatever you think is right."

Cinderella placed a wig on her head to conceal her blonde hair and dressed in the clothes of a maid. It was the perfect disguise!

"Now I'll find out if they're happy," Cinderella said to her mice friends.

She found maids cleaning the entrance.

"Are you new?" one asked.

Cinderella nodded.

The maid sighed and whispered. "I wish this heavy bucket had wheels on the bottom."

Later Cinderella found some servants polishing silver.

"These are already done," said Cinderella.

"We know," said a servant. "But the rules are we have to polish the silver every day. And the backup silver too."

"That's just silly," Cinderella admitted.

Next she went to the sewing room. The maids were working away on Cinderella's dresses.

"We have to finish all these gowns by tomorrow!" explained a seamstress. "I just wish we had better light in the room."

Cinderella saw that the work conditions could easily be improved.

When the maids and servants gathered for lunch, there was plenty of food to go around, but as soon as a royal bell rang, they had to take it in turns to leave their bowls of soup to attend to the royal members. Cinderella thought this was unfair.

The staff were clearly happy to be working at the palace, but they could be even happier.

That evening, Cinderella revealed her disguise to everyone.

"I worked alongside you and listened to every word," she announced. "Heavy buckets will have wheels, silver polishing will happen only when necessary, the sewing room will have more candles and meal times will be quiet."

The servants and maids cheered. The Princess had proven how big her heart was – and everyone loved her for her kindness.

Disney · PIXAR TOY STORY 3

A Sandy Adventure

The Sunnyside Daycare kids had gone home for the day, and the toys were getting ready to relax. When, suddenly, Jessie realized something terrible.

"Bullseye's been left in the playground all by himself!" she fretted.

Buzz flexed his muscles. "Don't panic. Buzz Lightyear will save him!"

Stretch the octopus volunteered to join him. She'd been at the centre longer than most of the other toys, and knew her way around the place better than anyone.

Leading Jessie and Buzz through the dusty air ducts, Stretch swung open a vent which led to the outside. Buzz and Jessie fell out, getting themselves tangled in the octopus's long rubbery arms on the way to the ground.

"Wasn't there an easier way out?" Jessie panted.

"Or one with no tentacles in the way?" grumbled Buzz.

The toys looked around the playground, but there was no sign of Bullseye. Then, from over by the sandpit, Jessie heard the thunder of tiny hooves. "He must be inside," she said. "Let's go!"

The friends rushed to the sandpit. Sure enough, Bullseye was racing around inside it. He was trying to climb out, but the sides of the pit were too steep.

"He can't get out," Jessie realized.

"Don't worry! I have a plan," said Buzz. He pointed at Jessie. "We'll make a chain."

Stretch tried to interrupt, but Jessie and Buzz had already leaped into action.

Taking one of Jessie's hands, Buzz lowered the cowgirl into the pit. She stretched out, trying to reach for Bullseye. "Just a little more ..." she called.

"I can't hold on!" Buzz yelled. His fingers slipped and Jessie tumbled down into the pit beside Bullseye.

Stretch tried to make a suggestion, but Buzz was deep in thought.

"We need a new supergalactic plan," he said. Buzz clicked his fingers. "That's it! I'll get a rope, lower myself inside the sandpit and ... are you getting all this, Stretch?"

Buzz looked at the octopus in time to see her reaching two long tentacles down into the pit and lifting Jessie and Bullseye to safety.

"We're almost there, guys," Stretch said. Jessie laughed and Bullseye whinnied loudly with relief.

In no time, the toys were safely out of the sandpit. Stretch used her long arms to dust them down. "Great job, Stretch!" Jessie said.

Buzz agreed. He had to admit, Stretch had been the one to save the day. Maybe all those tentacles weren't so bad, after all.

Disney MINNIE

The Magic Four

Daisy Duck was hanging out in her room, when her phone buzzed to show that she'd received a text.

It read: 'On our way! Surprise for you!'

"Oh no, not now!" She sighed.

Within seconds the doorbell rang and Daisy went to open it. Her best friends Minnie, Macy and Leonard were waiting outside, looking very pleased with themselves.

"We bought you a wand!" they cried. The four of them were planning to go to a party dressed as the characters from their favourite TV show, *Wizards & Fun*. They'd been planning their costumes for ages!

But Daisy had some bad news. "I'm not coming with you," she said and shut the door.

Her friends were confused. Why had Daisy backed out? But more to the point, what were they going to do now? *Wizards & Fun* had four main characters – and now there were only three of them!

Then Macy, glancing at Minnie's dog Dante, had a brilliant idea....

Dante was very well-behaved as the other three dressed him up in a cape and hat. Minnie was thrilled. "We're the coolest wizards ever seen," said Leonard, "and we're sure to win the prize for the best costumes!"

But at the party, the man on the door wouldn't let them in. "No dogs allowed," he said, frowning.

"He's no dog, he's a wizard!" Leonard fibbed, but the man wasn't having any of it, and the friends turned sadly away. "This is rubbish," sobbed Leonard.

Minnie was about to reply when she suddenly saw Daisy – in a costume of her own! "Daisy! What are you doing here?"

"And dressed as Elf Queen of the Crystal Forest!" added Macy.

Daisy looked sad. "I wanted to win best dressed," she confessed. "But it's not as fun getting ready on your own, I wish I'd stayed with you.... I'm sorry."

"Hey, don't worry," said Leonard, smiling. "We're still a group."

"But I don't have a wizard's costume," Daisy said.

"No, you don't," said Macy.

Everyone looked at Dante. "But he does!"

Quick as a flash, they swapped Daisy's elf queen costume for a wizard's cape and hat. "Now we can get in and win!" Leonard cheered.

Daisy beamed. How lucky she was to have such kind and understanding friends! "This afternoon is going to be magic!" she cried. "Let's go and have fun!"

Disney Princess
Beauty and the Beast

Belle and the Castle Puppy

Belle was strolling through the castle garden one day when she saw a puppy huddled outside the castle gates. He looked cold and dirty.

"Oh, you poor thing!" Belle cried. "Let's get you warmed up and fed!"

Once inside the castle, Belle gave the puppy a bath. When he was clean and dry, the puppy ate a bowl of warm stew.

"I hope we can keep him!" Chip exclaimed.

All the enchanted objects were happy to have a guest. But the Ottoman remembered when he had been a real dog. What if Belle liked this dog more?

"Do you want to play?" Belle asked, letting the puppy outside. As Belle and the others followed, the Ottoman slinked out behind them.

A while later, the Beast walked up to Belle. "Someone has dug up my roses!" he exclaimed. Then the Beast saw the puppy. "Get rid of him – NOW!" the Beast roared as he stomped away.

Just then, the Ottoman ran past Belle and chased after the Beast – his legs were muddy. Belle suddenly understood.

"The Ottoman dug up the roses! He just wanted some attention, too!" Belle realized.

The puppy raced after the Ottoman, barking playfully.

"What if they get lost?" Belle worried. "I have to bring them both back safely."

"I'll come and light your way," Lumiere called to Belle.

Belle, with Lumiere in her hand, walked along a dark path. "Puppy! Ottoman!" she called.

Suddenly, Belle heard barking and followed the sound to a clearing where she saw the Ottoman and puppy – who was barking loudly. Belle gasped. A large wolf was sitting nearby.

"Look at that, the puppy is protecting the Ottoman!" Lumiere exclaimed.

Quickly, Belle put Lumiere on the ground and lit a large stick she'd found.

"Get away! Get away!" she shouted, swinging it towards the wolf.

Just then, the Beast showed up, roaring loudly. The wolf yelped with fear and quickly scampered away.

Later that night, everyone settled by the fireplace. Belle watched the Beast stroke the Ottoman and feed biscuits to the puppy.

"May the puppy stay until I can find him a home?" she asked.

The Beast cleared his throat. "His home is here – with us," he answered gruffly.

Belle smiled. She loved the Beast's gentle, caring side that he was starting to show.

Disney Princess
The Little Mermaid

The Purple Pearl

Ariel was stopped in her tracks outside her sister Adella's bedroom, when she heard wailing noises coming from inside.

"You have a bad case of the Bubbles!" Aquata told Adella, whose face was covered in polka dots! "The cure is a lotion made from a purple pearl, which grows inside oysters known to eat merfolk!"

Adella wailed again. There was no hope for her.

Ariel decided to go looking for the purple pearl because she loved her sisters dearly and would do anything to help them.

"You'll have to cross the thorny sea kelp," said Flounder, worriedly.

Ariel ignored the little blue-and-yellow fish and continued on her way. Swimming through the thorny kelp gave her cold fins, but she was determined to make it through. When she noticed a strong current making the kelp strands part, she urged Flounder to ride the rip tide with her, slipping through quickly and safely.

On the other side of the thorny sea kelp, there was a clearing. Scattered like flowers in a strange underwater garden were shells holding glistening pearls of the deepest purple.

"They don't look very scary," said Flounder.

"They're actually quite pretty," Ariel added. "Maybe sea oysters eating mermaids is a myth?"

Flounder tossed driftwood at the giant shell to check and it chomped the whole thing in two!

Ariel gulped. This was going to be tricky.

She emptied her bag and found only a feather ... which gave her an idea. Tying the feather to a stick, she ran it along the oyster's pink underbelly.

"*Ah-choo!*" it sneezed. The purple pearl shot from its mouth and Ariel caught it in both hands. "Wow!" she said, admiring it.

Using the light of the pearl to guide her through the thorny kelp and home to the castle, Ariel found her sisters at last. They were brushing their long hair and giggling about mermen.

"Oh Ariel!" said Adella in surprise. Her eyes widened as she spotted the purple pearl. "You're so brave and kind ... but ... my Bubbles illness went away on its own."

Aquata joined them. "I was joking about the pearl," she admitted. "I wanted Adella to think she'd always be spotty."

The girls looked sadly at Ariel.

"It's okay," Ariel insisted and swam back to her room with Flounder following.

"Never mind," she said, petting her friend on his back. "There's a much better place for the pearl than in a lotion bottle!"

Ariel placed the purple pearl in her treasure grotto, where it glowed brightly forever more.

Beignets for Everyone

Tiana's new restaurant, 'Tiana's Palace', was the talk of the town. News had spread of her delicious meals and wonderfully friendly service and everyone wanted to visit. It was the place to be in New Orleans.

"Hey, what are you fellas waiting for?" asked a tourist, curious about the huge queue of people outside the restaurant.

"To taste Tiana's mouth-watering specials, of course," replied one man.

"You have to try her gumbo!" another insisted.

"And the scrumptious beignets," piped up another hungry, waiting customer.

"Are they that good?" the tourist wondered.

"Just smell that aroma!" they all insisted, as their noses picked up the scent on the breeze.

"Okay, you've convinced me," said the tourist. "I'm staying!" He wandered to the back of the line, salivating at the thought of a hearty meal. But the queue was so long ... it went around the corner of the building!

"Let's step on it guys!" cried Tiana, inside the restaurant, to her busy chefs. "Big Daddy just ordered a giant-sized serving of beignets!"

The chefs nodded and set to work.

A news reporter wandered over to Tiana and peeked his head into the kitchen's hatch, where plates were served. "So tell me, Tiana. What's in the dough?"

"It's a secret," she replied. Everyone wanted to know how she made her food so irresistible.

More and more people asked her how she made her cooking the best they'd ever eaten.

"It's a secret," she told them all, weaving around the room serving dinners. They scoffed their meals and sighed in satisfaction.

Later on, Tiana left the kitchen with a tray of steaming beignets for Big Daddy. The beignets were piled so high, she found it difficult to get through the masses of people.

"Excuse me! Coming through! Pardon me! Thank you!" she cried, over the noise of happy customers. "Here you go, Big Daddy." She lowered the tray ... but it was empty!

"What happened to all the beignets?" she asked the crowd.

The people in the room shrugged, wiping crumbs from around their mouths.

"It's a secret," they each said in turn.

Big Daddy laughed. "Oh, Tiana!" he said. "I hope there are more of your delicious beignets in the kitchen because this time ... I'm coming with you!"

She smiled and nodded, linking arms with her friend. If he wanted to get his order of beignets, he'd just have to eat them out the back where no one could steal them ... in secret!

Disney Mickey & Friends

Pluto's Surprise

One sunny morning, Mickey looked out of the window. "This is perfect building weather!" he cried.

"What are you going to build?" asked Morty and Ferdie.

"A tree house!" he said.

"Can we help?" the boys asked excitedly.

"You would be great helpers," Mickey replied, "but there will be lots of tools and it might not be very safe. Why don't you take Pluto to the park?"

"Sure!" they replied.

Mickey called his friends and soon Minnie, Donald, Daisy and Goofy arrived to help.

"It's a big job," Mickey told his friends. "So, let's split up the work. Why don't you saw the boards, Goofy? Then Donald and I can hammer them together."

"I have an idea," Minnie said. She showed Mickey a drawing she had made.

"Good thinking, Minnie!" Mickey replied. "That'll be one of the most important jobs of all."

Goofy dumped his toolbox in the garden and began sawing the boards.

"Goofy, I was wondering if you would cut some boards for me, too?" Minnie asked him.

"Sure!" Goofy said. "What do you need?"

Goofy looked at Minnie's drawing then started cutting.

Donald and Mickey worked together to make a rope ladder, then Mickey attached it to the thickest tree branch.

"Once we finish building, we can use this ladder to climb into the tree house," Mickey said.

Goofy brought them a stack of boards. "I still have to saw boards for the roof, but you can use these for the floor and walls," he said.

"Thanks!" Mickey said.

Mickey and Donald pulled the boards into the tree and started building.

"Do you have any extra nails?" Minnie called up.

"Here," Donald said, passing them down.

On the way back across the garden, Minnie stopped to watch Daisy mixing up some paint.

"Wow," Minnie said. "That's a lot of paint!"

"Too much!" Daisy giggled. "Need any?"

"Great, thanks, Daisy," Minnie said.

Mickey's garden was a very busy place!

When Morty, Ferdie and Pluto came home they couldn't believe their eyes. "Wow!" the boys cried as they scrambled up the rope ladder.

But Pluto couldn't climb it like the others.

"Come round here!" Minnie called.

Pluto trotted round to the other side of the tree and found a set of stairs that was just right for him!

"Minnie made them for you," Mickey explained. "Come on up and join the fun!"

Pluto thought it was the best tree house ever!

August

9

Colourful Excuses

In Springtime Square, Tinker Bell, Rosetta and Fawn were having a wonderful time sliding down a rainbow.

"Wheee!" laughed Rosetta, as she whizzed down to the ground.

"Gangwaaay!" shouted Fawn as she slid down behind her, flat on her back.

"This is a flitterific game!" panted Tink.

"Especially if Iridessa doesn't catch us!" Fawn agreed. The light fairy wouldn't like her rainbow being used as a slide!

"Don't worry," said Rosetta, waving away the suggestion. "She won't notice a th –"

"Where's the rainbow you want to roll up, Iridessa?" came Silvermist's voice suddenly.

The three friends panicked. "Forget I said anything!" gasped Rosetta.

"Let's move – quick!" exclaimed Fawn.

The fairies dashed out of sight just as Iridessa and Silvermist flew in.

"There it is," Silvermist said. Then her mouth fell open in horror. "I've never seen a rainbow in such terrible shape before!"

"Who could have done this?" Iridessa wailed as she examined the rainbow, all jagged and bent out of shape.

Just then, Silvermist caught sight of the others. "Maybe the girls saw something," she said hopefully.

Tink, Fawn and Rosetta, who were pretending to be busy, froze. "Who ... um ... us?" asked Fawn nervously.

"Do you have any idea who made that mess?" asked Silvermist.

Rosetta powdered her nose with her mirrored compact. "Sorry, buttercup. We were all busy."

"Yeah," nodded Tink. "Really busy!" She and Fawn burst into giggles. It had been such fun!

"Oh?" said Silvermist suspiciously. She and Iridessa looked at each other.

"Um ... we really need to go now," Rosetta said, and Tink and Fawn eagerly agreed. But as they turned to go....

"I can't believe it!" gasped Silvermist.

"So that's who did it!" Iridessa cried.

Tinker Bell, Fawn and Rosetta's backs were covered in rainbow dust! The three fairies didn't realize as they walked away.

Tink glanced back and wondered what Silvermist and Iridessa were laughing about, but decided it would be better not to stop – they might be discovered! Little did she know, they had already been found out!

"They look so silly I can't be mad at them!" chuckled Iridessa. Silvermist nodded, wiping tears of laughter from her eyes.

Sliding down rainbows was fun, but you should at least try to clean up the evidence!

August
10

Disney Peter Pan

Tiger Lily

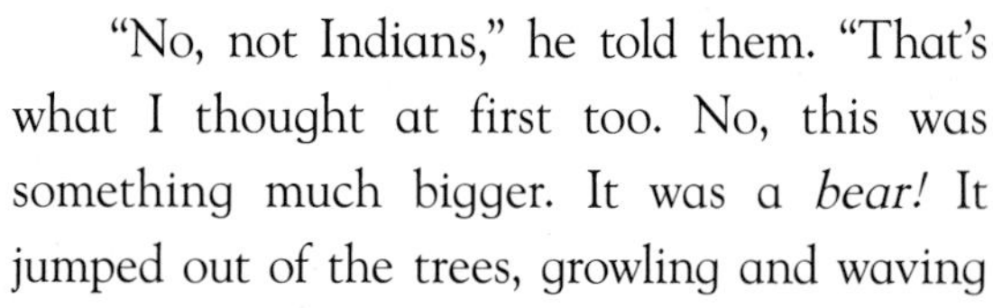

It was a hot summer night in Never Land – so hot, in fact, that the poor Lost Boys couldn't sleep. And so it was decided that instead of trying to stay in their hideout in Hangman's Tree, Peter Pan and the Lost Boys would camp out for the night in the wild wilderness.

They thought that the woods would be cool and shady, and the trees would catch any breeze kind enough to blow through. But little did they know how mysterious – and spooky – a forest could be once the sun went down.

"It's dark out here," said Cubby.

"And awful quiet," said Tootles.

"Won't you tell us a story, please, Peter?" asked Slightly, who was shivering in his fox suit despite the sticky heat.

"Very well," agreed Peter. "If it will make you all be quiet! I will tell you the story of the very first time I ever camped out in the wilderness – which, by the way, was the first time I met Tiger Lily....

"I had made myself a fire, a great big one, 'cause it was autumn and the nights were getting cool. I'd just laid my head down on a patch of nice, soft moss, when all of a sudden I heard a rustling in the shadows."

"*Indians?*" the Lost Boys gasped.

But Peter shook his head.

"No, not Indians," he told them. "That's what I thought at first too. No, this was something much bigger. It was a *bear!* It jumped out of the trees, growling and waving its big paws in the air like Captain Hook swattin' blue flies. I've never seen such a mean, angry beast, before or since!"

"So w-w-what did you do?" asked the Lost Boys.

"Told him to get lost, of course. To *scram!* But, apparently, he didn't understand English, 'cause he just kept charging.

"Well, I'm not going to lie to you – I started to get nervous. And then, there she was – Tiger Lily – as quiet as a mouse. Without even a 'hi' or 'how do you do', she grabbed a stick from my fire and waved it at the bear. The next thing I knew, the bear had turned round and was running off crying! I suppose Tiger Lily saved my life that night," said Peter. "And it wasn't the last time either. The end."

"Um ... Peter," said Cubby, peering out into the darkness, "do you know what ever happened to that bear?"

Peter thought for a moment. "Nope," he said and shrugged. "Probably still out there, wandering around, I guess." He yawned a big, mischievous yawn. "Now stop yer yammerin' and close your eyes and go to sleep!"

Disney Princess

Jasmine

The Beauty of True Love

Jasmine and Aladdin were strolling through the streets of Agrabah when, in a puff of smoke, the Genie appeared.

"I'm back!" he announced with a bow. In his hand was a suitcase and he was wearing sunglasses.

"Genie!" yelled Aladdin happily. "How was your trip around the world?"

"Amazing," the Genie told them cheerfully. "I saw the Egyptian pyramids, went skiing in Sweden and got a tan in the Caribbean!" He showed them his arms, which were a darker shade of blue than usual.

The Genie gave his friends some souvenirs, including a bouncy kangaroo from Australia.

"I'd better go catch him," cried Aladdin, as the kangaroo jumped away down the street.

When Aladdin had left, Jasmine had a chance to sit with the Genie alone. The Genie seemed sad now that he'd finished talking about his adventures.

"The travelling was great," the Genie told her glumly, "but I got a bit lonely. I wish I had another genie to share my life with."

Jasmine sighed. "I know how that feels. I wanted to marry for love, but my father wanted to pick a husband for me! I met so many suitors...."

Jasmine told the Genie about Prince Achoo who sneezed constantly because of her flowery perfume. There was also the horrid Prince Macho who expected her to cook and clean all day. And not to mention Prince Wishy-Wash, who agreed with everything she said like a performing monkey with no brain.

"I almost lost hope," Jasmine admitted. "But then, I met Aladdin ... and, even though he pretended to be Prince Ali Ababwa in the beginning, when I discovered his true self and gave him a chance, he won my heart."

The Genie started crying. "That's the sweetest story ever!"

"You'll find a special genie," Jasmine promised. "There's someone out there for everyone."

The Genie nodded and decided he would go in search of his one true love. When Aladdin returned with the kangaroo, the Genie did a fashion show for the Prince and Princess. He tried on several different styles of clothes.

"One thing I've learned is just to be yourself," said Aladdin. "True beauty lies within and someone should like you for what's inside."

The Genie understood and switched back to his normal clothes before jetting off on another adventure.

Then Aladdin and Jasmine were alone at last, with their new kangaroo of course, remembering the time they had met and how grateful they were for the gift of true love.

August
12

Care for Some Tea?

"I'm not sure about this!" said Fawn. Tinker Bell had invited her round for tea, but now it turned out she had a new invention to show her friend. There was a giant tank with three spouts underneath, and a container of sugar with a huge spoon. Fawn had no idea what it was, but Tink's habit of causing a mess made her suspicious!

"Are you kidding?" said Tink. "It's perfect!"

Fawn edged away. "Have you even tried using this ... this...."

"Multi-cup teapot!" Tink cheered. "But, no...."

Fawn's heart sank. "You've never used it before?" she fretted.

"Not yet!" said Tink. "That's why you're here!" Gently, she guided her reluctant friend closer to the table. "You'll be the first one to taste the tea from the multi-cup teapot!"

"Um, I just remembered I forgot to do something ..." said Fawn. She opened her wings. "Now you'll have all the time you need to try it out. And then I'll be very happy to taste your – yikes!" Something had grabbed her foot. It was an angry Tinker Bell!

Tink tugged Fawn back to the ground. "Have I ever doubted your talent as an animal fairy?" she asked.

"Um ... no," admitted Fawn, feeling guilty. "But I've been practising it a long time...."

Tink looked hurt. "The truth is you don't trust me!"

Fawn tried to explain. "It's just that you're so enthusiastic, you can get carried away." Tink looked even sadder, so Fawn added hastily, "But I completely trust you and your incredible Talent!"

"Prove it then!" said Tink, brightening up. "How do you like your tea?"

Fawn knew she couldn't leave now! Sighing, she sat down. "Very sweet," she said. "But are you sure...."

"Don't worry!" Tink flew up to her invention. "I'm flitterific at gadgets!" She turned the handle to start up her invention. "Extra sugar," she muttered, as the machine began to whirr.

Suddenly, steam shot out of the spouts underneath. "Oops!" called Tink.

Before Fawn could escape, she was buried under an avalanche of sugar!

Oh no! And Tink had so hoped that this invention would be a success! She flew down to help her friend, but Fawn sat in the snowy mountain with a furious expression. "Flitterific?" she growled. "I hope you're flitterific at escaping, too, because if I catch you...!"

Without waiting to hear the end of the sentence, Tink took off. She'd better hide until Fawn calmed down! Tinkers were always being misunderstood.

Disney Mickey & Friends

A Nice Day for a Sail

One lovely summer day, Mickey Mouse asked Minnie if she'd like to go for a boat ride.

"I would love to," Minnie said with a smile.

Mickey and Minnie were preparing to set sail when Goofy came running by on the shore.

"Hiya," he said. "What a great day for sailing!"

But Goofy didn't see a squirrel in front of him and he accidentally stepped on its tail. The squirrel squealed, then leaped up and landed in the boat! Mickey and Minnie were so startled that they jumped, making the boat rock.

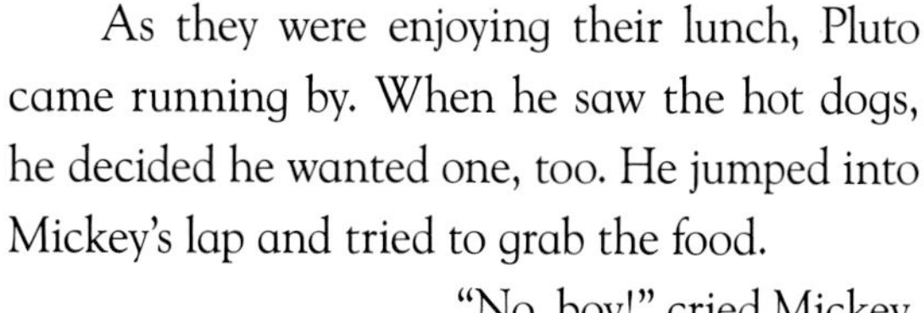

Mickey tried to stop the rocking, but the boat tipped over, and Minnie shrieked as she and Mickey fell into the water.

Donald Duck came up in his speedboat and helped Mickey and Minnie on board.

"Why don't you ride with me?" Donald suggested kindly.

Relieved, Mickey and Minnie sat back and started to relax. But moments later, the boat's engine suddenly stopped.

"What do we do now?" Minnie asked.

"I have an idea," Donald said. He took off his hat and started to paddle with it. Mickey and Minnie did the same. Huffing and puffing, they made their way back to shore.

"How about lunch while we dry off?" Mickey said. So they ate hot dogs in the sun.

As they were enjoying their lunch, Pluto came running by. When he saw the hot dogs, he decided he wanted one, too. He jumped into Mickey's lap and tried to grab the food.

"No, boy!" cried Mickey, a second too late. Pluto knocked Mickey and Minnie into the water again!

Mickey and Minnie swam to shore and climbed out of the lake. Coughing and spluttering and really fed up, they settled on the grass to dry off yet again.

Not long after, Huey, Dewey and Louie came by in their sailing boat.

"Would you like to borrow our boat?" called Dewey. "There's a good wind today."

"Yes, please!" said Mickey. He and Minnie hopped into the boys' sailing boat and took off.

"Aah, this is the life," Mickey said.

Just then, the wind stopped blowing.

"Oh, no!" Mickey groaned. "Not again!"

Mickey and Minnie tried to paddle with their hands, but it was no use. The boat just kept going round in circles. As they huffed and puffed, Mickey saw Goofy and Donald coming towards them in rowing boats.

"We thought you might need some help," said Donald.

As Donald and Goofy towed the sailing boat, Mickey and Minnie sat back and relaxed. They had finally got their nice, easy boat ride!

August

14

DISNEY PRINCESS

MULAN

Looks Can Be Deceiving

Yao, Ling and Chien-Po missed Mulan. They had become friends in the army – even though, when they had first met her, Mulan was disguised as a young man. They forgave her for tricking them, because Mulan went on to bravely save China from Shan-Yu and the rest of the Huns. Mulan was famous – even the Emperor himself had bowed to her!

Now, her three friends decided they would go to her village and follow Mulan in whatever adventure she might embark on next.

"But what if Shan-Yu seeks revenge?" Ling said. "He might be looking for us. After all, we did help Mulan defeat him."

Yao thought they should disguise themselves. So the friends donned kimonos, wigs and makeup, and set out for Mulan's village, looking like a trio of women.

When they arrived, the Matchmaker instantly approached them. "And who would you lovely ladies be?" she asked. The Matchmaker was desperate. There weren't many single women in the village, and she had a list of bachelors a mile long to marry off!

"Visitors from far away," said Chien-Po, speaking in a high voice.

"And are you unmarried ladies?" the Matchmaker asked.

Ling said, "We're unmarried, all right!"

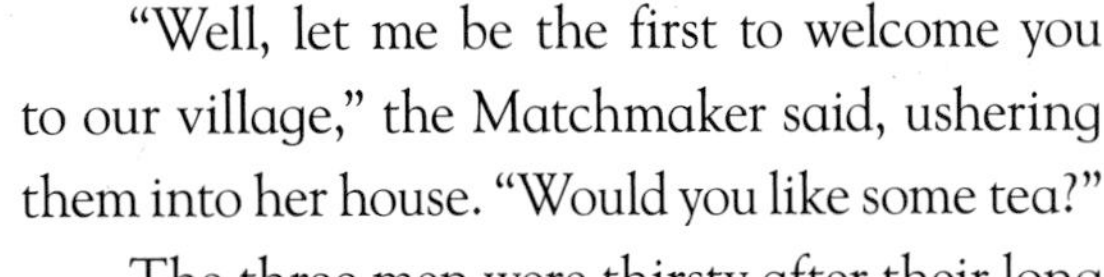

"Well, let me be the first to welcome you to our village," the Matchmaker said, ushering them into her house. "Would you like some tea?"

The three men were thirsty after their long journey. They didn't realize the Matchmaker wanted to see if they would make suitable wives.

"Perhaps you would like to pour?" she asked Yao. He tried to remember the way his mother served tea at home. Yao set out the cups and poured as daintily as he could.

"Cookie?" the pleased Matchmaker asked Chien-Po, holding out a plate.

Chien-Po resisted the urge to grab a fistful of cookies. Instead, he chose one, stuck out his little finger and took small bites.

Perfect! The Matchmaker was delighted.

Next she asked Ling what his favourite pastime was. "Wrestling," he answered.

Then, seeing the shocked look on the Matchmaker's face, he added quickly, "Yes, I find that *resting* keeps my complexion lovely." He batted his eyelashes.

The Matchmaker led the three back outside, just as Mulan was riding into the village. "Stop! You can't marry them off!" Mulan cried, seeing her friends with the woman.

"I certainly can," said the Matchmaker. "Unlike you, Mulan, these three are real ladies!"

Disney
DUMBO

Lend Me Your Ears

"I think I can, I think I can, I think I can," chugged Casey Jr, the circus train. The train moved slowly around a bend. "I think I can. I think I ... *ah-choo!*" he sneezed.

Suddenly, he came to a halt. "I know I can't," he admitted finally. The animals and the performers poked their heads out, wondering what was wrong.

"Well?" asked the Ringmaster.

"Casey Jr here has a cold," the engineer replied. "He's going to need some rest before he can take us any further."

The Ringmaster frowned. "But we're due at the fairground in a few hours. What will we do? After all, the show must go on!"

The engineer just shrugged and turned his attention back to the sneezing, coughing and spluttering little engine.

The Ringmaster went down the train, swinging open the doors to all the cages and cars. "Come on, everyone," he said. "Might as well stretch your legs."

The animals lumbered, scampered and pranced onto the wide open field. Next, the clowns, acrobats and animal trainers sauntered out. Some set up crates like tables in the grass and played cards, others rehearsed and a few pulled out packed lunches and sprawled on the ground.

Dumbo the elephant and his mother, Mrs Jumbo, took a drink from the bucket of water the Ringmaster had set out.

Mrs Jumbo gazed around. "Looks like we're in the middle of nowhere," she said. "I do hope poor Casey Jr is feeling better soon."

"Me too," Dumbo's friend Timothy Q. Mouse said hopefully.

Just then there was a loud clap of thunder. Rain began to fall from the sky. The animals and performers ran for the shelter of the circus wagons. Dumbo held on to his mother's tail, but just then, the wind picked up. The gust caught Dumbo's huge ears and sent him flying backwards.

"That's it!" yelled the Ringmaster over the howling wind. "Dumbo, come with me!" He led Dumbo over to the train, climbed onto the front wagon, and motioned for the little elephant to join him.

"Now spread out those great ears of yours!" the Ringmaster instructed.

Dumbo's ears billowed out, catching the wind like giant sails and pushing Casey Jr along the tracks. "The show will go on!" the Ringmaster shouted happily.

"I know I can. I know I can. I know I can," chanted Casey Jr. And then he added, "Thanks to Dumbo!"

Disney · PIXAR
FINDING NEMO

Nemo's Best Shot

"Come on, Dad! We're going to be late!" cried Nemo.

Nemo and Marlin were hurrying through the busy swimming lanes of the colourful Great Barrier Reef, towards Sea Urchin Stadium.

"Are you sure you want to play pearl volleyball?" Marlin asked nervously. "There are lots of other things you can do. Sponge jumping, for example. Or maybe reef dancing."

"Reef dancing!" cried Nemo, horrified. "No way! That's for babies! I want to play pearl volleyball!"

At the stadium, Mr Ray made the opening announcements. "Hello and welcome, everyone! Before we get started, let's give a big thank you to Ms Esther Clam for donating today's ball."

Everyone applauded as Esther opened her shell and spat out the pearl.

"Let's play pearl volleyball!" cried Mr Ray.

"Good luck, son," said Marlin. "Just remember what I told you –"

"I know! I know!" said Nemo, rolling his eyes. "When you give it your best shot, even if you lose, you win."

The players lined up on either side of the sea fan net. Ray's Raiders were on one side, and Nemo's team, the Fighting Planktons, were on the other.

Marlin watched anxiously. He was sure that Nemo wouldn't be able to play as well as the other fish because of his small fin. And Marlin wasn't the only one who had doubts. Turbot Trout came up to Nemo on the court.

"Coach may be letting you play today," Turbot snapped, "but you better not mess up the Planktons' winning streak."

Turbot didn't know Nemo had spent hours smacking around pebbles in a dentist's fishtank.

"Just watch and learn," murmured Nemo.

Suddenly, the pearl came right to Nemo. *SMACK!* Using his good left fin, Nemo sent the pearl flying right over the net. The pearl flew so fast, the other team couldn't return it. Nemo scored his first point for the Planktons!

Nemo played like a pro. He scored again with his good fin, then with his tail. And, just to show his father and Turbot Trout, he scored the winning point with his little fin.

"Go, short fin!" cried Turbot Trout. "With a player like you, we're going to go all the way to the Lobster Bowl Clam-pionship!"

"Wow, Nemo," said Marlin after the game. "That was amazing."

"Thanks, Dad," said Nemo. "I gave it my best shot, just like you said. And we actually won too!"

The Hic-hic-hiccups

"What a day!" Pumbaa said as he led Simba and Timon through the forest.

"What a day, indeed," Timon agreed.

"Hic!" said Simba.

"What was that?" Timon cried.

"Don't be scared. It's just that I have the – *hic!* I just have the hiccups," Simba explained.

"I'll tell you what to do," Timon assured him. "Forget about it! They'll go away – eventually."

"Forget about it? *Hic!* But I can't roar when I have the hiccups," Simba explained. And to demonstrate, he opened his mouth really wide. But, just as he was about to roar, he hiccupped!

"See?" he said sadly.

"Have you tried licking tree bark?" Pumbaa asked.

"Licking tree bark?" said Simba.

"It always works for me," Pumbaa explained. "That or closing your eyes, holding your nose and jumping on one foot while saying your name five times fast – backwards."

Timon watched Simba hop around on one foot, holding his nose with his eyes closed. "Abmis, Abmis, Abmis – *hic!* It's not working!" Simba cried.

"Maybe there's something caught in his throat," Timon offered.

"There's nothing caught in his throat," Pumbaa said.

"How do you know?" Timon asked.

"I just know about these things," Pumbaa answered confidently.

Suddenly, right on cue, Simba interrupted their argument with the loudest hiccup of all.

And, wouldn't you know, just then the biggest fly you've ever seen came soaring out of Simba's mouth. It flew right into a tree and crashed to the ground.

The fly stood up groggily and shook itself off.

"It's about time, buddy!" the fly called up to Simba.

Simba was about to reply, but he was interrupted by two voices, shouting in unison –

"DINNER!"

The fly gave a frightened squeak and flew off, as Timon and Pumbaa both pounced on the spot where it had been just a moment earlier.

Disney Princess Cinderella

Lucifer's Bath

Cinderella's stepsisters didn't like the idea of Cinderella going to the Prince's ball.

"But Stepmother told me I could go," said Cinderella.

"*Only* if you finish your chores," sneered Drizella. "Which includes giving our cat, Lucifer, his bath."

"And that reminds me," said Anastasia. "I'll be needing a bath myself."

"Me, too," said Drizella.

"You heard my girls, Cinderella," her stepmother said. "Get their baths ready at once!"

Cinderella already had far too many jobs to do. But she didn't argue.

Once Anastasia and Drizella were soaking in their bubble baths, all Cinderella had to do was mend their clothes, clean the house, wash the curtains and give Lucifer his bath – then she could get ready for the ball.

Unfortunately, her stepsisters wouldn't leave her alone.

"Cinderella! Bring my face cream!" cried Drizella.

"And my bath salts!" cried Anastasia.

Each time her stepsisters called, Cinderella had to stop whatever she was doing and take care of them.

When Drizella called for tea, Cinderella went down to the kitchen and put the kettle on. Then she let Bruno the dog in for a snack.

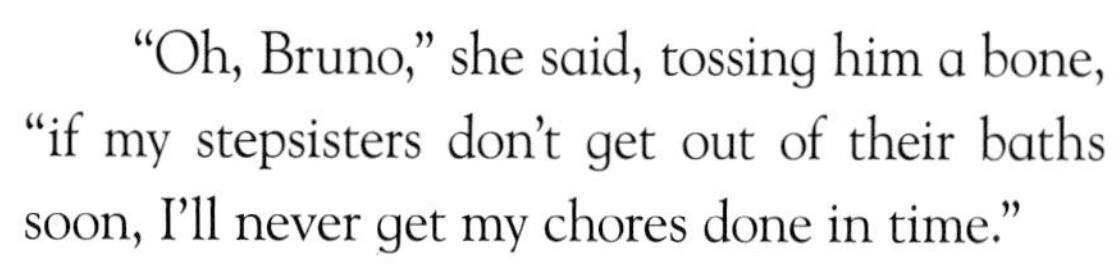

"Oh, Bruno," she said, tossing him a bone, "if my stepsisters don't get out of their baths soon, I'll never get my chores done in time."

Bruno narrowed his eyes. Those stepsisters were the most selfish, lazy, nasty girls he'd ever known and their cat was just like them. He wanted to help Cinderella. So, when the tea was ready, Bruno followed her up the stairs and down the long hallway.

Just as Cinderella walked up to Drizella's bathroom door, Bruno saw Lucifer sleeping nearby.

"Woof, woof!" Bruno barked loudly. "Woof, woof!"

With a screeching yowl, Lucifer ran into Drizella's bathroom.

SPLASH! Bruno chased the cat right into Drizella's tub! Then Bruno jumped in himself!

Drizella screamed. Lucifer jumped out. And Bruno chased the cat down the hall and into Anastasia's bathroom.

SPLASH! Lucifer was now in Anastasia's tub. And Bruno jumped right in after him!

"Get out of your baths this instant!" Cinderella's stepmother cried. "You don't want to smell like that dog, do you?"

Cinderella sighed in relief. Although she still had many jobs to finish before the ball, at least one job was now done. Thanks to Bruno, Lucifer had had his bath!

Disney Winnie the Pooh

Tigger's Moving Day

After breakfast, Tigger likes to bounce. *SPROING! SPROING! SPROING!* He likes to bounce all day long, but he is always bumping into things.

"Tigger, you don't have enough bouncing room in this little house," said Rabbit. "We've got to find you a bigger house. That's all there is to it!"

By evening, everyone was excited about the big new house they had found.

"It *is* a bouncy house," said Tigger. "The kind of house tiggers like best!" He bounced, and he didn't bump into anything. "But," he said, sighing, "I won't live next door to little Roo anymore."

"I know you'll miss being neighbours with Kanga and Roo," said Christopher Robin, "but now you'll live much closer to me. We can have fun being neighbours."

Kanga told Tigger she would bring Roo to visit. Tigger felt better and invited everyone to stay awhile. Rabbit put his paws on his hips. "We aren't finished yet. We need to move all your things from your old house to this house," he explained. Rabbit told everyone to bring all the boxes they could find to Tigger's house. Then he told Eeyore to get his donkey cart.

"Wow! Boxes are fun!" cried Roo as he and Tigger bounced in and out of the boxes everyone brought.

"There'll be time for fun later, you two," grumbled Rabbit.

Tigger packed all his games and his stuffed toys in a box. He took his favourite lion out and hugged him. Rabbit packed Tigger's dishes. Kanga packed Tigger's hats and scarves. Pooh and Piglet packed Tigger's food. Soon Eeyore arrived with his donkey cart. Christopher Robin and Owl hoisted Tigger's bed and table and chairs onto the cart.

"Now my new home will be perfect," Tigger said, as they unloaded the cart and carried everything inside. "Thanks for your help, everyone!"

After his friends had gone, Tigger put all his things just where he wanted them. When he was finished, he sat down to rest.

Hmm, seems like an awfully quiet house, Tigger thought. He tried out a few bounces, but decided he wasn't in such a bouncy mood, after all. But just then, he heard a little voice.

"Hallooo!" it called.

"Roo!" Tigger cried happily. "Kanga! Come on in!"

"Hallooo!" Tigger soon heard all his friends calling outside his new door. Everyone had brought housewarming presents!

"Our work's all done," said Rabbit. "Now it's time for fun!"

Flying Lessons

Tinker Bell sat by the side of the pond, surrounded by all kinds of lost things, and felt totally uninspired. "I just don't know what to make!" she sighed. "Maybe a leaf-curler, or a petal-polisher, or...." She sighed again. She didn't really want to make any of those things!

Then she heard a familiar voice. "Spread open your wings, lil' fella! C'mon, move those feathers!"

It was Fawn. She was trying to teach a baby bird how to fly. Tink headed over to see if she could help. Fawn was standing on the end of a branch, a leaf in each hand, flapping for all she was worth. "It's easy!" she said.

But the bird was having none of it! He shook his head and crouched down further in the nest. Fawn drooped in despair. "Lazybones here doesn't want to fly!" she told Tink.

"Let me try," suggested Tink. "Maybe a new face will inspire him." She leaned into the nest. "C'mon, birdie, it's flap-flap time!"

But the bird simply rolled his eyes and ignored her.

Tink didn't like being ignored. "Enough! Outta that nest!" she ordered.

The bird turned his back on her. Tink couldn't believe it!

Then Fawn had an idea. "I think I've got it. He's really little...."

"So?" said Tink huffily.

"Maybe we need to find something fun to convince him," said Fawn.

Tink thought for a moment. She was a tinker fairy – surely she could come up with something to help? She clicked her fingers. "I've got a flitterific idea!"

Quickly she flew back to her collection of lost things. "Finally, I know what to build!" She set to work, sewing leaves on to a frame made of twigs. A wingbeat later, it was finished, and Tink carried it back to Fawn and the baby bird. "Here I am!" Tink shouted.

Fawn realized straight away what Tink had made – a kite! With a tow-rope and a long tail threaded with berries! She jumped up and down excitedly. "This'll work, I know it will!"

And it did! The little bird couldn't wait to take hold of the kite's tail with his beak and play catch-up with it as Tink steered the kite high into the sky. He was learning to fly without even realizing – and it was fun!

"Thanks Tink," called Fawn, following on behind. "You're a real pal!"

"I should be thanking you!" Tink called back. "Without you two I never would've found my inspiration!"

Sometimes, helping out a friend in need is the best use of your own talent!

Disney Princess
Beauty and the Beast

The Missing Vegetables

Of all the things Belle loved about the Beast's castle, the thing she loved best was the garden at the back. She had read every one of the Beast's books about gardening, and every season she experimented with something new. This summer, she'd decided to try growing vegetables. And now they were ready to be picked.

"Don't tell the Beast," she whispered to Mrs Potts, "but today for lunch I'm going to make him a salad."

"Oh, really," replied Mrs Potts.

"Mmm-hmm." Belle nodded proudly. "Yesterday, I saw so many things ready to be harvested. Lettuce, carrots, cucumbers, peas ... even tomatoes! Can you believe it? The Beast is going to be so surprised!"

"Indeed," Mrs Potts smiled. "Lunch is definitely going to be a surprise."

Belle slipped on her gardening gloves and her sun hat, grabbed her biggest basket and happily skipped out into the garden.

"First," she said out loud, to no one in particular, "let's get some lettuce!"

But, when she bent down where the lettuce should have been, she found a bed of empty soil.

"My lettuce!" she cried. "Where did it go?"

Rabbits? Deer? Bewildered, Belle moved on to where her tender, sweet, young carrots had been growing.

"Oh, dear!" she cried. "There's nothing here now either!"

There wasn't a single pea to be found. "I don't understand," she said.

But facts were facts. The garden was empty and there was nothing she could do ... but go back to the castle and look for a book about building fences for next summer's garden!

As she walked back inside, empty-handed and disappointed, Belle passed Mrs Potts and Chip.

"What's the matter?" asked Mrs Potts.

"Oh, everything!" Belle sighed. "My whole garden has been robbed." Then she shrugged. "So much for my salad idea."

"Don't feel sad, Belle," Chip said. "Come and have some lunch."

"I'm not hungry," Belle replied, smiling sadly.

"Oh, I don't know," said Mrs Potts, steering her into the dining room. "You might be...."

"SURPRISE!" called the Beast.

"What?" Belle gasped. There, laid out upon the table, was what looked like every possible vegetable from her garden, washed and sliced and arranged, just so, on fancy dishes.

"You've worked so hard in the garden," the Beast explained, "I thought it would be nice if I did something for you. I hope you like it."

Belle smiled. What a treat!

August

22

Winnie the Pooh

Eeyore Beats the Heat

One day, when it seemed the sun was shining even more sunnily than ever over the Hundred-Acre Wood, Eeyore sighed and wished that autumn – if it wouldn't be too much trouble – would hurry itself up and get there.

"Something the matter, Eeyore?" asked Roo.

"Oh, it's just that it's so terribly hot," replied Eeyore. "If I weren't stuffed with sawdust, I think I would melt."

"Come with me! I'm going to cool off in the swimming hole," said Roo.

Eeyore shook his head. "Can't do, Roo," he said glumly. "Not with my sawdust and all ... I'd probably sink. And that's if I'm lucky."

And so Roo, who felt sorry for Eeyore, but who was also keen to swim, continued on his way.

Soon, another friend came along. And this friend was Winnie the Pooh.

"You're looking a little warmish, Eeyore," Pooh said.

"Same to you," said Eeyore with a sigh. "Same to you."

"Ah," said Pooh, "but I am off to catch a breeze – and pay a call on some bees – with my trusty balloon here. Care to join me?"

"No, thanks, Pooh," said Eeyore. "I never did like feeling like the ground was missing.

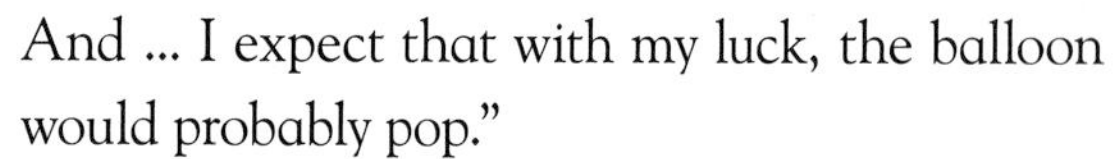

And ... I expect that with my luck, the balloon would probably pop."

"Well, Eeyore, I understand completely. Wish me luck, then, won't you?" Pooh replied.

"Good luck, Pooh," said Eeyore. "As if anything I ever wish for comes true...."

The next friend to come upon Eeyore was little Piglet.

"Hello, there, Eeyore," said Piglet. "Whoo! Are you as uncomfortably hot as I am?"

"Oh, no," said Eeyore. "I'm sweltering. Parched. Smouldering. Torrid. Yes – 'uncomfortably hot' would be an understatement."

"Poor Eeyore," said Piglet. "Why don't you come play in the cool mud with me?"

But once again, Eeyore shook his head. "Afraid mud is not an option, Piglet," he said. "Once I get dirty, I'll never get clean. No. Go enjoy yourself on this hot day like everyone else. All except me. As usual. I'll just suffer."

And suffer poor Eeyore did ... until not too much later when his friends all returned with something sure to cool even Eeyore off.

"Guess what we've brought you, Eeyore!" Roo squealed with delight.

"It's ice cream," whispered Pooh.

"Ice cream, huh?" Eeyore sighed. "I suppose I'll have to eat it all before it melts."

And do you know what? He did!

Disney Princess

BRAVE

The Missing Gem

"Och!" Merida complained. "I spent all month working on a brooch for Mum's birthday tomorrow but it's still not right!"

Maudie clucked in sympathy, but as cook and nursemaid at Castle DunBroch, she was more worried about her muffins.

"Mm! Who are those for?" asked Merida.

"For the DunBroch Brownie, the wee elf that lives outside the gate," Maudie replied.

"Have you ever seen him?" asked Merida.

"Brownies don't like to be seen by humans," explained Maudie. "But every day I leave him muffins, milk – and thistles for good luck. If the Brownie isn't happy, who knows what mischief he could make."

Merida sighed, thinking about the brooch again. It had started as a good idea. She had chosen a beautiful quartz, her mother's favourite gem, but couldn't get the setting right.

Merida went to take another look at the gem ... but it was gone!

Then Merida saw her mischievous little brothers with a glint in their eyes.

"What did you do this time?" Merida asked.

She quickly discovered that her brothers had 'borrowed' the brooch because it had looked so royal on their capes, but they had dropped it somewhere when they were playing.

Merida looked closely at Hubert's shirt. "Is this a thistle?" she asked. Then she looked at the others. "Crumbs on your shoes. Milk on your face!"

Suddenly, Merida knew where the triplets had been playing that morning. She led the boys to the large flat rock under the bridge.

"You ate Maudie's treats for the DunBroch Brownie!" Merida said.

They looked all around the clearing ... but they couldn't find the brooch. "What if the Brownie took it because you ate his treats?" said Merida. "Maudie said he makes mischief if he isn't taken care of."

They ran to get more muffins, more milk and more thistles and set up the tray again.

They waited but nothing happened.

Then Merida remembered that Brownies don't like humans to see them. So they closed their eyes and Merida whispered into the air, "We're sorry," she said, "but we've tried to fix everything. Could you help us in return?"

But when they finally opened their eyes, Harris spotted something shiny beneath a tree. The brooch! Had it been there the whole time?

When Merida examined it she saw that the gem was now set in a beautiful silver thistle! Merida thought it was perfect, and the Queen was delighted, too.

Disney *Lady and the TRAMP*

Trusting Trusty

"Tramp!" cried Lady one morning. "One of our puppies is missing!"

"Don't worry," said Tramp with a yawn. "Scamp is always getting into mischief."

"It's not Scamp," said Lady. "It's little Fluffy! She never gets into trouble. Tramp, what should we do?"

"You look inside. I'll look outside," Tramp told her. He searched their back garden. Then he went to the next garden, and the next.

From a neighbour's garden, Trusty the bloodhound called, "Hey! Whatcha looking for?"

"My daughter, Fluffy! She's missing," replied Tramp.

Trusty's long, floppy ears pricked up. "A missing puppy – now that's serious! And I should know. I used to help my grandpa track down missing persons through the swamps!"

"I know," said Tramp. He'd heard Trusty tell that story 100 times.

"Have you found a trail yet?" asked Trusty.

Tramp shook his head.

"Well, let me at it!" Trusty loped back to Tramp's garden. He put his big nose to the ground. *Sniff, sniff, sniff....*

"Tramp, have you found Fluffy?" Lady called from the dog door.

Tramp ran over. "No," he replied. "But Trusty offered his ... uh ... services."

"He can't smell anymore," Lady whispered. "I know he tracked that dogcatcher's wagon and saved you – but he hasn't tracked anything since then."

"He helped us once," said Tramp. "I think we should trust him again."

Just then, Trusty shouted, "Look at this!"

He had spotted a bluebird's feather below a window. "That's the window the puppies look out from," said Lady.

"Look! A bit of puppy fur," said Trusty. "And footprints!" Trusty followed the trail of footprints to the back of a shed.

And that's where Trusty found the missing puppy! Fluffy was fast asleep under a big tree.

"Fluffy! What happened?" Lady cried.

"I woke up and saw a pretty bluebird," said Fluffy with a yawn. "And I didn't want Scamp to bark and scare it away, like he always does. So I didn't wake anyone. I followed the bird all the way to this tree. Then I guess I got sleepy."

Lady walked over and gave Trusty a kiss.

"Thank you," she told the bloodhound.

"Aw, shucks," said Trusty, blushing. "It weren't nothin'."

As the bloodhound trotted home, Tramp turned to Lady. "See that," he said with a grin, "I told you we should trust Trusty!"

Disney Princess Sleeping Beauty

Buttercup the Brave

On a lovely summer day, with not a cloud in the sky, Aurora and Prince Phillip visited the stables to admire the royal horses.

"Which horse would you like to ride today?" Phillip asked.

Aurora looked at all the soft fuzzy faces staring back at her over their stable doors. "From now on, I'd like to ride the same horse every day."

Phillip smiled. "What a wonderful idea. You can have a horse of your own just like I have Samson!"

Aurora found it difficult, but when at last she'd picked a palomino horse as her future companion, she knew she'd made the right choice. In fact, she loved him even more when she rode him.

"I'll name him Buttercup," she decided.

The horse snorted in approval.

Aurora put Buttercup through his paces, urging him over a high stone wall. He cleared the wall effortlessly. "What a beautiful, brave horse!" she congratulated him proudly.

The next day Aurora set off for the fairies' cottage, but the moment Buttercup entered the woods his trot became a slow walk.

"What's the matter?" Aurora asked him.

A squirrel wandered over and Buttercup panicked and tried to run away. Aurora could hardly believe how much he'd changed.

Riding at a snail's pace, she couldn't wait to ask the fairies for help. Perhaps some magic would settle the poor creature?

"My dear, I'll try and help you," promised Flora, when Aurora had explained the fear that had developed in her lovely horse.

Merryweather and Fauna joined them, but no matter how many spells they tried, nothing made a difference. Buttercup was afraid in the woods!

Aurora decided magic wasn't the answer. "I'll just head back," she said.

As she rode home, she wondered what she could do for Buttercup. Lost in thought, she wasn't prepared for the mountain lion that appeared, with sharp teeth and claws.

Buttercup rose up onto his hind legs and whinnied angrily, pounding his hooves against the earth repeatedly. The mountain lion scarpered away with a yowl and at last, Buttercup became calm and steady.

"So that's why you've been on edge!" Aurora realized. "You knew we were in danger."

Buttercup nodded.

"You were so brave," Aurora said.

On their journey home, Buttercup behaved fearlessly, with his head held high. He knew that if he could face a mountain lion, he could face anything! It was the perfect end to his first real adventure.

Disney MINNIE

Roughing It

Abigail groaned. "I can't believe Principal Van Arm has planned a trip for us!"

For once, Minnie Mouse and Daisy Duck agreed with her. "This is the last thing we need!" sighed Minnie.

The class was not looking forward to the weekend. Camping – with no video games, or fun, or shops! And sleeping in the dark woods filled with scary animals! *Why would anyone want to do that?* they wondered.

But Principal Van Arm was determined that they should experience the great outdoors – and so they set off early in the morning to walk to the campsite. Macy was scared. "What was that?" she said for the 100th time as they heard a noise. "And that?"

Abigail complained her feet hurt, and Paul Poser said he was hungry. But Principal Van Arm was almost bouncing with delight when they reached the campsite, which had a waterfall leading down to a clear pool. He made them drink water from the pool and gather berries from the bushes.

"I could really go for a snack at Donkey Donuts right now," moaned Daisy. But Principal Van Arm had other ideas – it was time to pitch their tents!

By the time night fell, the friends were all exhausted – but Principal Van Arm wanted them all to get up at dawn to listen to a special kind of bird!

"Emergency meeting!" called Leonard. "Time to plan our escape!" They weren't going to put up with this any longer!

That night, the friends stuffed their sleeping bags with grass, so that it looked like they were still sleeping inside them. Then as dawn broke, Abigail did her best acting and pretended she'd heard the Principal's special bird. He dashed off into the forest to find it!

Now was their chance!

"Are you sure you know the way?" Macy asked as they all set off together.

"Don't worry!" said Leonard. "Follow me!"

But after hours of walking through the forest, they had to admit they were completely lost. "I'm sorry," Leonard said.

Strangely, the others weren't as bothered as they might have been. "The woods aren't so scary after all," said Macy. And Abigail even offered Minnie her jumper to keep herself warm!

Just then, Principal Van Arm turned up to guide them back. But far from being angry, he was smiling. They'd overcome their fears and discovered the importance of teamwork!

"Actually," admitted Minnie, "I've never had a more exciting weekend!" They all laughed. Who'd have thought that a camping adventure would be so much fun?

Disney Princess
The Little Mermaid

A Working Holiday

Sebastian the crab loved his busy job as court composer to King Triton. He wrote songs, ran rehearsals, consulted with the King – and he even watched out for Ariel to make sure she stayed out of trouble.

One day, King Triton burst into the rehearsal hall and announced, "Sebastian! You need a holiday! I want you to relax and forget about work for a few days. And that's an order."

"Yes, sire," Sebastian said glumly. He wasn't very good at relaxing.

After Sebastian had gone, King Triton gathered his daughters and the court musicians.

"Sebastian has been my court composer for many years," he said, "and I've been wanting to honour him with a grand concert. Now that he's away, we can finally prepare a wonderful surprise for him." Triton smiled. "I can't wait to see the look on Sebastian's face!"

Meanwhile, Sebastian was at the Coral Reef Resort. "Well, here I am at the most beautiful spot in the sea," he said to himself. "But I am bored out of my mind!"

When he couldn't sit still any longer, Sebastian decided that he would sneak back to the palace for a few minutes just to see how everything was going. He wandered into the concert hall, where he found the orchestra and Triton's daughters about to start rehearsing.

"Sebastian!" cried Ariel. "What are you doing here?"

"Oh, nothing," he said. "I forgot my conducting baton. I never go on a holiday without it." He looked at Ariel. "And what are *you* doing here?"

Thinking quickly, Ariel told Sebastian that they were preparing a last-minute concert for her father. It was all Sebastian had to hear! He immediately set to work rehearsing the musicians.

He worked harder than he had in weeks. And he loved every minute of it.

After the three days were up, Sebastian made a big show of returning to the palace.

"I feel so refreshed!" he announced to King Triton. "Thank you, sire, that was just what I needed."

"That's grand, Sebastian!" replied the King. "Now follow me."

Triton led Sebastian to the concert hall, where the King gave a glowing speech about the crab's many contributions throughout the years. Then the elaborate programme of music began. The orchestra played beautifully, Ariel and her sisters sang exquisitely, and the King beamed proudly.

"What do you think?" Triton asked.

"It's perfect!" said Sebastian. "I couldn't have done a better job myself!"

Good for Something

Bobble and Clank, the tinker fairies, were hard at work. There was always so much to do in Tinkers' Nook! And where was Tinker Bell?

"Hey, guys!" Tink flew in with a bulging bag.

"What's in your sack?" asked Clank.

Tink smiled happily as she pulled out a large shiny blue button. "I found this on the beach!" she said. "Isn't it a pretty colour? I don't know what it is, but I'm going to use it to build something flitterific!"

Bobble was not impressed. "I say it's useless," he grumbled.

But Tink wasn't easily put off. "Well, I'm sure I'll find something useful to do with it." She got straight to work.

Half an hour later.... "What do you think?" she asked her friends, showing them the beautiful stool she'd made with the button as a seat.

"It doesn't look very sturdy to me," said Clank.

"Well it is!" said Tink, annoyed. "Look!" She sat down heavily on the stool, and the button tipped right over and dumped her on the floor!

Bobble and Clank burst out laughing. "Oh, poor Tink!" said Bobble unsympathetically.

"I told her so!" chortled Clank.

All of a sudden there was a crash of thunder from outside. "Sounds like it's about to rain in Pixie Hollow," Clank remarked.

Tink brightened. Pushing a stick through the hole in the button, she said, "Cover up and let's go try out my new invention!"

Within moments, the three of them were walking along in the pouring rain. Bobble and Clank shared a large leaf to shelter under, while Tink walked along holding her button as an umbrella. "See?" she said smugly. "It's a lot more protective than leaves!"

But the raindrops gathered on the top of the button and weighed it down ... and again it tipped over, emptying the water all over Tink!

"This thing really is useless!" she snapped.

Angrily, she kicked the button, sending it spinning up into the air ... where it bounced off a rock and hurtled back towards her, scooping her up as it went!

Tink grinned. She'd had her best idea yet!

Some time later, Bobble and Clank heard a strange noise – and into the Nook whirled Tink! With a flower for a seat and branches for pedals, she'd turned the button into a unicycle! "You've got to try!" she said. "It's so much fun!"

Bobble and Clank shook their heads in amusement. Trust Tink – give her enough time and she could find a use for anything!

Disney · PIXAR
TOY STORY 3

A Pea Problem

The Peas-in-a-Pod were having fun bouncing around Bonnie's room, chasing after each other and laughing.

Buzz and Woody were having almost as much fun watching them, when Woody noticed one of the peas was missing! Then something suddenly landed on Woody's head.

BOING!

"There she is," laughed Buzz, as the pea landed in front of them.

Woody turned to the pea. "You should be more careful about where you bounce, Peatrice," he said, rubbing his head. The pea looked upset.

"I'm Peanelope!" she corrected him. The other peas landed either side of Peanelope, looking equally upset.

"You keep getting our names wrong!" one of them complained.

"Yeah! It's so annoying," added another.

"Huh? I'm sorry," Woody apologized. "But you look so similar...."

"It's not fair!" said one pea, turning to another. "I can't help looking exactly like you."

Buzz overheard the peas and wanted to help. "Can I tell you a story?" he asked.

The peas were happy to have something to distract them, but Woody wasn't sure it was the best thing to do. "Maybe we should apologize," he suggested.

"Don't worry!" replied Buzz. "I've got a plan."

When the peas were settled in front of him, Buzz began his story. "I was exploring the dangerous planet Zurg, it seemed to be deserted ... but suddenly I heard a strange humming. In a minute, I found myself surrounded by Emperor Zurg's army of robots!" The peas gasped!

Buzz continued. "They kept humming and closing in around me – they wanted to capture me! But then I heard a different noise ... it sounded like singing! The Zurgrobots didn't like the sound of that so they ran away. I realized it was another Zurgrobot making that noise. It turned out that this Zurgrobot, who was called Zenny, didn't like humming and so he saved me! You see, even though Zenny looked exactly like the other Zurgrobots ..."

"... He was different from them!" finished Woody, with a cheer.

"You too!" Buzz said to the Peas-in-a-Pod. "You look the same, but each of you is unique!"

"And we know it even though we get your names wrong!" Woody added.

The peas looked pleased. "Wow! You're great guys," they smiled.

Happy in the knowledge that even though they all looked the same, each pea was different, they bounced off to play some more.

Disney Princess
Snow White and the Seven Dwarfs

The Good Old Summertime

The Seven Dwarfs were on their way back home after a long, hard day at the diamond mine. Each swung a spade in one hand and a bucket in the other.

As they marched through the forest, Happy enjoyed the sounds of the birds singing and the warmth of the summer sun on his face.

"Summer is such a wonderful time of year!" he exclaimed cheerfully.

"Oh, yeah?" snapped Grumpy. "And what's so wonderful about it?"

"Well ... the days are longer," said Happy.

"The days are hotter," complained Grumpy.

Doc spoke up. "I like the summertime too. It's a very healthy season."

"Healthy?" said Grumpy. "This heat?"

"Look at all the fresh vegetables and fruit you can eat all summer long," said Doc.

"Like what?" asked Grumpy.

"Like peaches," Sleepy said with a yawn. "I like them with cream before I go to bed."

"And just look at the size of the melons on those vines over there," said Doc. "They're as big as Dopey's head!"

Dopey grinned and nodded.

Grumpy rolled his eyes and said, "Dopey's a melon head, all right!"

"Don't be such a grump!" scolded Doc.

"Yes, cheer up! Summer's a great season," Happy said with a grin.

"It's too hot, I say," Grumpy insisted. "And all those plants make Sneezy sneeze even more!"

"Yes," said Sneezy. "Sorry, but ... *AH-CHOO!* I think Grumpy's right."

"No, he's not," said Happy. "Summer's the very best time of year."

"It's too hot, I say!" repeated Grumpy.

By this time, the Seven Dwarfs had reached a small bridge running over a brook.

"Well, if it's too hot for you, Grumpy, then I have a special warm-weather remedy," said Doc, stopping in the middle of the bridge.

"Yeah?" snapped Grumpy. "What is it?"

Doc motioned for the other Dwarfs to gather around him. They blocked Doc from Grumpy's view as he leaned over and filled his bucket with cool water from the stream.

"Well?" said Grumpy. "Are you going to give me your special remedy?"

"Of course," said Doc.

With a big "Heave-ho!" Doc dumped his bucket of water over Grumpy's head.

SPLASH!

"That should cool you off," said Happy.

Grumpy spluttered with surprise. But he had to admit, the soaking actually did cool him off!

Disney
Bambi
Flower's Power

It was a warm summer afternoon in the forest, and a shy little skunk named Flower was playing a game of hide-and-seek, searching for his friend Thumper. He had been looking for quite a while.

"Come out, come out, wherever you are!" Flower called. "I give up."

"*Surprise!*" shouted Thumper, bursting out of a thicket. "Here I am! *Ugh!*" Thumper wrinkled his nose. "What's that *smell?*"

Flower blushed bright pink. "Sorry," he said miserably. "I sprayed. It happens when I get scared."

"*Whew!*" Thumper waved his paw in front of his face. "You should warn us before you let out that kind of stink!"

"Well *you* should warn *me* before you jump out like that," Flower said. "Anyway, it'll go away ... in a day or two."

But a day or two was too long for his friends to wait. The smell was just too strong!

"Sorry," Bambi told Flower. "I, uh, think my mother's calling me," he said.

"Me, uh, too," Faline gasped. "See you later, Flower ... in a day or two."

"Or three!" Thumper added, giggling.

And the next thing he knew, Flower was all alone.

Poor Flower. *If only I weren't a skunk*, he thought. If only he didn't *stink* so much whenever he got scared. What was the point? It only drove his friends away. But now it seemed he couldn't even play hide-and-seek!

No matter what his mother and father said, being a skunk stunk!

And that's why Flower wouldn't have been very surprised if, two days later, his friends had still stayed away. But, to his bashful pleasure, there, bright and early, were Bambi and Faline – with Thumper hopping close behind.

"Want to play?" Bambi asked Flower cheerfully.

"Sure! Anything but hide-and-seek!" said Flower.

"How about tag?" said Thumper. "Ready or not, you're It!"

But before the game could begin, a soft *crunch* of leaves made the friends turn.

"Wh-wh-what's that?" Bambi stuttered, staring straight into a hungry-looking, red face.

"That's a fox!" said Thumper.

"A fox?" shrieked Flower. "Oh no!"

He spun round and lifted his tail and buried his head in fear ... and the next thing the friends knew, the hungry fox was running away, whimpering and rubbing his nose.

"Sorry," Flower sighed, blushing.

"Don't be!" said Bambi and Thumper.

And do you know what? Flower wasn't!

Disney 101 Dalmatians

Patch's Plan

"Whoa!" Patch said. "Look at all these other puppies!"

His brothers and sisters were whimpering with fear. They had just been dognapped, and after a long, bumpy ride in a car, they had arrived at a big, draughty house. But Patch was already trying to work out a way to get back home. He looked around the large, shabby room. "Hey," he asked the closest stranger. "Where are we?"

The spotted puppy smiled at him. "Oh, you must be new!" he said. "Which pet shop did you come from?"

Patch scowled at the strange new puppy. "We're not from a pet shop – we were stolen from our house."

Several other puppies heard Patch and moved closer. "Stolen? Really?" they exclaimed.

The first puppy shrugged. "Well, bought or stolen, we're all stuck here now."

"Maybe *you're* stuck here," Patch said boldly. "Our parents and their human pets will be here soon to rescue us, just see if they don't!"

"I hope so," Patch's sister, Pepper, said. "I wonder why someone would want to steal us, anyway?"

Patch didn't know. But he was sure that their parents would find them soon. In the meantime, he wanted to make sure he and his siblings stayed well away from all the pet shop puppies, so there wasn't any confusion.

"We don't know why there are so many of us," the strange puppy told Pepper. "I guess Cruella really likes puppies."

Patch gasped aloud. "Cruella?" he cried. "Do you mean Cruella De Vil?"

His brothers and sisters shuddered. Their parents had told them scary stories about that nasty woman. Could it be true?

"Yes, she's the one who bought us," several of the other puppies spoke up, while others nodded their heads.

This changed everything! "We have to get away," Patch declared.

Rolly sighed. "We know," he said. "Mum and Dad will be here soon. I just hope we get home in time for breakfast...."

"No, you don't understand!" Patch shook his head. "Cruella is bad news – that's what Dad always says. We have to get away from her now – all of us!" He gestured to the entire group of puppies, bought and stolen. It didn't matter where they'd come from. What mattered was they were in this mess together. "We have to work as a team."

The first puppy smiled at him. "I'm with you!" he exclaimed. "When we're done with her, Cruella will be seeing spots!"

September 2

Disney · PIXAR FINDING NEMO

First Day of School

It was the first day of a brand-new school year for Nemo and his friends.

"Hey, Tad! Hey, Pearl!" called Nemo as he swam into the playground. "Isn't it great to be back at school?"

"Well," said Tad, "I wouldn't go *that* far."

"What do you mean?" asked Nemo. "It's gonna be awesome! I heard this year we get to learn how to subtract and speak Prawn."

"Sure," said Tad, "but did you hear who's gonna be teaching us all that?"

"Who?" asked Nemo.

Just then, up swam Sheldon, Jimmy and Jib.

"Hey, Sheldon," Tad called out. "Why don't you tell Nemo here about our new teacher, Mrs Lobster?"

"Mrs Lobster?" said Nemo.

"Yeah," said Sheldon. "Ooooh, they say she's the worst!"

"Who says she's the worst?" asked Nemo.

"Well, Sandy Plankton, for one. He says his cousin, Krill, had her last year – and that she was so mean, he'll never go to school again!"

"And you know what I heard from Sandy," said Tad. "I heard she has these great big claws, and that she uses them to grab students real hard when they give the wrong answer!"

"Oh!" said Pearl. "Don't say that. You're going to make me ink!"

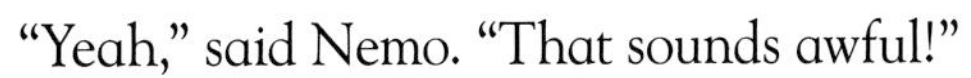

"Yeah," said Nemo. "That sounds awful!"

"I know," said Jimmy. "Sandy says Mrs Lobster never goes on field trips like Mr Ray did. And she sends you home with tons of homework, and makes you stay after school if you forget to bring it in the next day!"

Oh, no! Nemo thought. All summer long he'd been looking forward to this day. And now school hadn't even started yet and already he wished it would end!

"Don't look now," Sheldon whispered, "but I think she's coming!"

"I'm gonna ink!" whimpered Pearl.

Nemo shut his eyes and wished with all his might for his dad to come and take him back home....

"Hello there," said a warm voice. "You must be my new pupils! I'm Mrs Lobster."

Huh? thought Nemo. Surely this wasn't the Mrs Lobster the kids had been talking about. And yet, when he opened his eyes, there she was, taking the register.

"Jib, Jimmy, Nemo, Pearl, Sheldon, Tad ... my, what a smart-looking class. I do hope you kids are ready to have fun."

Nemo sighed. Silly Sandy Plankton – they should know by now not to believe everything he said. Because Nemo was pretty sure this was going to be a great year, after all!

Ask Nicely

"Steady, Samson," Prince Phillip said absentmindedly, tightening the horse's reins. "No need to hurry. We'll get there soon enough – and I need some time to think."

Phillip had a lot to think about. He was riding through the forest towards the castle of King Stefan and Queen Leah. Phillip's father, King Hubert, would be meeting him there. So would the girl Phillip was destined to marry ... Princess Aurora.

Phillip had heard her name since her birth 16 years earlier. Their parents had long planned their marriage. But Aurora had been cursed by the evil Maleficent at birth, and had been forced to go into hiding until her 16th birthday, when the curse would end.

That meant Phillip had never set eyes on his bride-to-be, nor spoken with her. He had always wondered what she might be like.

"I hope I like her," he murmured to his horse. Then another thought occurred to him. "I hope she likes me!" he added. "I'd better make sure I impress her." *But how?* he wondered.

"I know!" he exclaimed suddenly. "I'll make a dramatic entrance. We'll gallop in and slide to a stop right in front of her. That will impress her for sure!" He whistled and gave Samson a little kick. "Come on, Samson! We've got to practise."

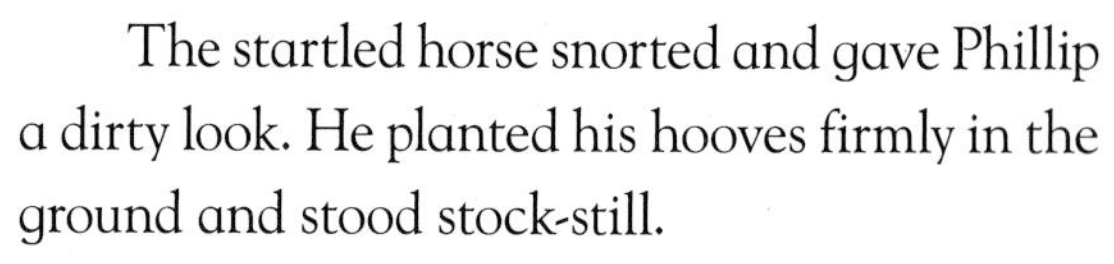

The startled horse snorted and gave Phillip a dirty look. He planted his hooves firmly in the ground and stood stock-still.

Phillip frowned impatiently. "Come on!" he urged his horse. "Go, Samson, go!"

But Samson refused to budge.

"It's like you don't even *want* to help me," he moaned. Suddenly, Phillip blinked in realization. "Wait a minute," he said. "Why would you want to help me when all I do is yell at you?" He patted the horse's shoulder. "Sorry, old boy."

He reached into his pocket for a carrot. He fed it to the horse, still patting him.

Samson finished the carrot and snorted. Suddenly, he galloped forward, then leaped up and kicked out his heels. Phillip hung on tightly, gasping with surprise as the horse skidded to a halt.

Phillip laughed. "Wow!" he exclaimed. "Thanks, Samson. That was perfect – I guess all I had to do was ask you nicely! Now if we can just repeat that for the princess...."

Suddenly, he stopped short. He heard the faint sound of beautiful singing. He listened carefully. Who would be out in the forest singing like that?

"Come on, Samson," he said. "Let's go see – if you don't mind, of course!"

September

4

The Missing Butterfly

In a few hours, the big party celebrating the changing of the seasons would begin! Everyone was busy with preparations. Fawn, the animal fairy, had a very important job. She was in charge of the 21 butterfly salute – and they were having one more practice to make sure they got it exactly right!

"On three, you all fly into the air together," Fawn told the butterflies perched on a bush. "One ... two...."

Then she gulped.

There was one butterfly missing! You couldn't have a 21 butterfly salute with only 20 butterflies! "How embarrassing!" Fawn muttered to herself, hoping that Fairy Mary, who was checking the preparations nearby, hadn't noticed. She needed to find the missing butterfly – and quickly!

"Maybe the butterfly is hiding in one of those?" Fawn wondered as she noticed Iridessa hanging up strings of orange lanterns. She tugged on the end to bring them closer, peering into each lantern. Not in this one, or that one....

"What a mess!" cried Iridessa as she saw the piles of lanterns on the ground. She was cross with Fawn. "Are you going to help me hang them back up?"

"Of course I will," replied Fawn. But as she helped Iridessa, she couldn't help worrying. Where could the butterfly be?

Just then, Rosetta flew past with a basket of flower petals. Wait! Wasn't that a butterfly wing poking out? Eagerly, Fawn plunged her hands into the basket, scattering petals everywhere. "Gotcha, you little rascal!"

But her hands came out empty – there was no butterfly hiding inside!

"My petal decorations!" gasped Rosetta in dismay.

Fawn had to help tidy up again! Sadly, she went back to her butterfly bush. What could she do? The salute would be no good without the missing butterfly!

She heard Silvermist calling. "Hey, Fawn, maybe I can help you!"

Fawn followed her friend round the corner to where three tadpoles were practising blowing bubbles for the party.

"Look what I found!" Silvermist smiled.

Fawn gasped. Sitting on the bubble branch was the missing butterfly! As Fawn watched, one of the tadpoles blew a perfect bubble – and the butterfly flew into the air and popped it!

"She's spent the whole afternoon playing with bubbles," Silvermist laughed.

"You could've let me know," Fawn said fondly to the butterfly. "If I'd known you were here, I wouldn't have caused so much trouble!"

Together they flew back to the other butterflies. Fawn was relieved. Now that she had all 21, this salute was going to be perfect!

Disney Princess
Tangled

An Artistic Adventure

When Rapunzel had finally escaped from her tower to see the delights of the real world, she couldn't wait to go into the nearby village. Her friends Flynn, Pascal the chameleon and Maximus the horse could barely keep up with her, she was so excited.

Rapunzel squealed, darting all over the street to look into windows. "There's even a whole shop of books."

"It's a village." Flynn rolled his eyes. "Villages are full of shops."

Rapunzel raced ahead and found an art shop. She'd always dreamed of seeing one. Mother Gothel had delivered her painting supplies in the past....

"May I help?" asked a man with a paint brush behind his ear.

"I've never met another artist before, or seen a shop like this!" Rapunzel said.

The man laughed and admired her enthusiasm. "Are you an artist too?"

"I'm self-taught," she admitted with a blush.

"And I'm a model!" piped up Flynn, winking in a nearby mirror.

Pascal copied Flynn and posed in front of a painting, his scales turning different colours.

"You're a true master of colour, Pascal," Rapunzel said, petting him on the head.

"My name is Roberto," the man told them. "I'd love to give you a free art lesson outdoors?"

Rapunzel accepted and together they went to a beautiful clearing illuminated by the sun.

"I want to paint everything!" Rapunzel declared, putting her paintbrush to paper.

Roberto was amazed with Rapunzel's technique. "You have a real talent!"

As Rapunzel painted, Flynn fell asleep in the grass with Pascal curled on his shoulder. Rapunzel painted away merrily, until Flynn finally woke up. He rubbed his eyes and laughed when he realized what Rapunzel had been working on....

"I painted what I saw," she told him, pointing at an image of Flynn asleep with a fly on his nose.

"It's brilliant!" he said.

When it was almost time to leave, Pascal was nowhere to be seen. Rapunzel was sure he was lost, until at last, he emerged from a bush.

Rapunzel instantly understood why he'd hid. He'd been jealous that she'd painted Flynn and not him!

"Silly," she said. "You're my best friend."

Pascal cuddled up to her in response.

Roberto was so impressed with Rapunzel's artwork that later that day he threw a party! The townsfolk came to marvel at her painting and asked how she'd painted it so life-like.

It was a wonderful experience. Rapunzel hoped she would have many more in the future....

Disney·PIXAR
MONSTERS, INC.

Occupational Hazard

Mike strolled in through the front doors of Monsters, Inc., whistling happily. Today was the anniversary of his first day working for the company, and he was sure his friends would all want to celebrate with him.

When he arrived, though, Sulley and the others just looked at him in surprise. "Everyone forgot?" he gasped. He threw down his lunch box and turned round. "I can see I'm not appreciated here. I quit!"

Sulley tried to stop him, but Mike had made up his mind. He stormed off, determined to find a job where he would be recognized for his hard work and dedication.

As Mike went in search of a new career, he felt excited. The world was full of thrilling new opportunities, and a monster of his talents would have no difficulty finding work.

Even he was amazed, though, when he landed a job as a model. He was dressed from head to toe in elegant clothes, and told to parade up and down a catwalk. On Mike's stubby frame, the outfit looked anything but stylish, though, and as Mike flopped around in his too-large shoes his boss called him over to tell him it wasn't working out.

"I'm too handsome, that's it, isn't it?" said Mike. Being a model clearly wasn't for him, but there were plenty of other roles for him to fill.

Next, Mike got a job wrapping parcels at a gift company. On his very first package he managed to completely cocoon himself in tape and wrapping paper. Only his one big eye was visible in the colourful tangle, and when the boss told him he was fired, Mike hopped out the door.

A little later, Sulley was sitting in a café, wondering how he could get Mike to come back to Monsters, Inc. He accidentally knocked his coffee onto the floor, and the waiter called for a cleaner. The kitchen doors flew open and Mike emerged, running.

He slipped on the floor and slid straight into Sulley's table, smashing it to pieces. This time, he didn't even wait to be told he'd been fired. Instead, he trudged back to Monsters, Inc. with Sulley. Nobody else wanted him, so what other choice did he have?

When he reached Monsters, Inc. Mike gasped in surprise as all his co-workers jumped out at him. They handed him an enormous cake and all hurried to shake his hand.

"Happy Anniversary!" they cheered.

"You planned a party all along?" Mike said. "Why didn't you tell me?"

Sulley explained that Mike had run off before they could reveal the surprise. Mike smiled happily. His friends did appreciate him, but he appreciated them even more.

Disney · PIXAR
TOY STORY

Kung-fu Cowboy

Andy was curled up in bed, reading a comic with Woody by his side. Woody loved hearing the tales of the comic's high-kicking kung-fu hero, and was disappointed when Andy fell asleep.

Still, Woody was pretty sleepy, too. As the little cowboy doll snuggled under the covers, he soon began to dream....

In his dream, Woody found himself back in the old Wild West. He sat behind a desk in the sheriff's office, waiting for trouble to arrive. He didn't have to wait too long.

"Sheriff Woody!" cried a townsperson, rushing into the office. "Black Hat and his bandits have shown up!"

"No outlaw's gonna rob the citizens of Ricestone with me here to protect them!" Woody promised, leaping to his feet.

Instead of reaching for his cowboy hat, Woody reached for a kung-fu headband! He tied it round his head just as the mean-looking Black Hat and his gang of outlaws arrived in town.

"Hand over all the money, sheriff!" Black Hat ordered. He and his gang were some of the roughest, toughest villains around.

Woody narrowed his eyes. "I've got one thing to say to you, Black Hat," he said, ducking into a fighting stance. "Take that! Hai-ya!"

With a series of flying kicks and a few well-aimed chops, Woody took down the whole gang. The townspeople cheered. "Thanks, Woody! You're our hero!"

Suddenly, Woody was awoken by a real cry for help. He blinked his eyes. He'd been so caught up in his dream he hadn't noticed Andy leaving for school.

"Emergency!" called Slinky from the floor. "Red monkeys on the loose!"

Woody peered over the edge of the bed and saw Rex racing by chased by a gang of crazed red monkeys.

"This is a job for the kung-fu sheriff!" Woody announced, but as he jumped up he tripped on the bedcovers. Flapping his arms, he fell off the bed, bounced on a ball, then smashed into Andy's dressing table with a *THONK!*

"Woody, are you all right?" gasped Bo Peep, rushing to his side.

"Aw ... I'm so bad at flying kicks," Woody groaned. The others had no idea what he was talking about. "If bandits come, you'll need a real kung-fu cowboy, and I'm not one of them."

"You don't need flying kicks to be a good cowboy," Bo said, and Woody realized she was right. Snatching up his lasso, he raced to help Rex. He may not be able to do kung-fu, but the other toys knew that when it came to being a sheriff, Woody was the best in the business.

Winnie the Pooh

Playing School

Now, it just so happened that when the wind changed ever so slightly, and the leaves began to turn scarlet or golden, depending on their preference, and the days grew ever so much more keen to be over and done, this was also the time that Christopher Robin returned to school, as well as the time, not so surprisingly, when his friends in the Wood felt as if they should really do the same.

But *playing* school, as you might suspect, is not as similar to real school as perhaps it should be. First of all, there's no teacher to tell you what to do. And, after sitting at their desks for what seemed like a good three and a quarter hours (but was really just five or so minutes), Winnie the Pooh and his friends came to the conclusion that something rather important in their game of school was missing.

"Perhaps it's time we had a snack," suggested Pooh.

"I don't think that's it, Pooh," said Piglet.

"Our problem," announced Owl, "is that we do not have a teacher. No classroom is complete – and this is a well-known fact – without a teacher. Which is why I'm quite happy to offer my considerable expertise."

"Just a minute, Owl," Rabbit broke in. "And why is it, exactly, that we should let you be the teacher? Some might say – myself included – that I'm better suited to the job."

"You?" Owl scowled.

"Perhaps we should have a vote," said Piglet. "I nominate Pooh."

"Me?" Pooh said. "Why, thank you, Piglet. I gladly accept. Now ... what's a 'teacher' again?"

"Really!" said Owl, with no small amount of scorn. "A 'teacher', my dear Pooh, is the someone who stands before the class."

"To give out snacks?" asked Pooh, hopefully.

"No," said Owl. "To give out knowledge."

"Oh," said Pooh. "I don't think I'd enjoy that nearly so much."

"Well, if it's all the same to you, I'll be the teacher," Eeyore said glumly. "I probably wouldn't have made a good student anyway."

"That will never do!" exclaimed Rabbit.

"Hi-ho!" said Christopher Robin, returning from a thoroughly enjoyable, and well taught, day at school. "Whatever are you up to?"

"Playing school ... I think," said Pooh.

"Only we don't have a teacher," Piglet told him.

"I could teach you. I learned ever so many things today," said Christopher Robin.

"Hooray for Christopher Robin!" cheered Roo. "Let's start right away!"

September

9

Misunderstood Style

It was morning at the Pixie Dust distribution depot, and Terence the dust-keeper was yawning. "You look a little tired today, Terence," Fairy Gary told him.

Terence nodded. "My wings are dragging."

Fairy Gary beckoned. "Come with me. Some hot tea with chestnut honey will do the trick!" He came out from behind the counter.

Terence burst out laughing. "I don't think I need it anymore!"

Fairy Gary looked around, puzzled. What was Terence laughing at?

"Your skirt's really funny!" Terence went on. "It's already perked me up!"

Fairy Gary was offended. "It's a kilt!"

"Then your kilt's really funny," Terence said. He flew off, still chuckling.

"Dust-keepers don't understand one speck about fashion!" complained Fairy Gary.

"Hello!" It was Fairy Mary, flying in with the abacus she used to make her calculations. "How are the deliveries coming along?"

"Everything's fine," Fairy Gary assured her.

Fairy Mary gave a wink. "Not everything, I'd say. Your skirt is so odd!"

"But ... but...." Fairy Gary spluttered.

"You're the only sparrowman in Pixie Hollow who wears clothes like that!" Fairy Mary flew off with a tinkling laugh.

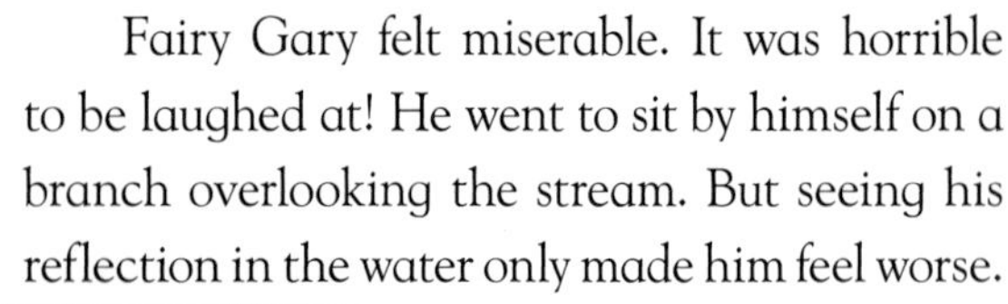

Fairy Gary felt miserable. It was horrible to be laughed at! He went to sit by himself on a branch overlooking the stream. But seeing his reflection in the water only made him feel worse. Was his kilt really that silly?

"Hey, Fairy Gary!" It was Tinker Bell and Fawn. "Why the long face?"

"Tell the truth," Fairy Gary said fiercely. "You don't like my kilt either!"

Hastily Tink clapped a hand over Fawn's mouth to stop her friend agreeing. "Well," she said, "it's not bad, but you could use a little change of style. How about a pair of flitterific maple-bark trousers!"

Fawn wriggled away from Tink. "Yeah!" she said enthusiastically. "They're really comfy!"

Trousers, eh...? Fairy Gary thought.

The next day, he was proudly standing beside his counter in a pair of green trousers. He felt very uncomfortable, but at least no one was laughing at his clothes.

"Oh no!" Rosetta was staring at him, aghast. "You gave up your dashing kilt for a pair of ordinary old trousers! What a shame!"

Fairy Gary was astonished. Rosetta, the most stylish fairy in Pixie Hollow, actually liked his old kilt! "That's just what I was thinking!" he exclaimed. "Thanks, Rosetta!" Humming, Fairy Gary flew off to change. Because without his kilt, he just wasn't Fairy Gary, was he?

Disney Princess
Beauty and the Beast

Enchanted Stew

Belle hummed to herself as she strolled through the castle. She had been living in the castle for a few months now and was finally beginning to feel at home. The enchanted inhabitants were truly good to her, and even the Beast seemed to be softening a bit.

Finishing her song, she stepped into the kitchen for a chat with Mrs Potts and the Stove. They were always pleased to see her, and Belle enjoyed talking to them while she learned new recipes.

"Well, hello dear!" Mrs Potts and the Stove called out together as Belle stepped into the large kitchen. The smell of roasting meat and vegetables greeted Belle as well, and her mouth watered. She could tell dinner would be delicious, as usual.

"Hello," Belle replied.

"You're just in time for a spot of tea," Mrs Potts said.

Belle smiled as Chip hopped across the counter, stopping right in front of her. "I'll be your teacup," he said. "And no bubble tricks, I promise," he added seriously.

"All right," Belle agreed. Mrs Potts filled Chip with tea and dropped in a sugar cube.

"How was your morning in the library, dear?" Mrs Potts asked.

"It was wonderful!" Belle exclaimed. "I finished my book about knights in shining armour and started one about a prince who's disguised as a frog."

"A frog!" the Stove exclaimed. "Oh, my!"

Suddenly, black smoke began to billow out of the sides of the oven door.

"Oh, my!" the Stove said again, throwing open the door. Smoke poured into the room. When it finally cleared, Belle spied a scorched roast and crispy black vegetables inside.

"Oh, my!" the Stove exclaimed again.

"What are we going to feed the Beast for supper?" Mrs Potts fretted.

The kitchen door opened, and Lumiere rushed into the room. "What is that awful smell?" he asked. A moment later, he spied the roast. "It's absolutely scorched!" he shouted. "We can't possibly feed that to the Beast! What will we do?"

Belle got to her feet. "Enchanted Stew," she said calmly. Taking down a large stew pot and a few vegetables, she began to chop and simmer. The last ingredient was the scorched roast.

"It adds the perfect smoky flavour," she explained. Just then the Beast came into the kitchen. "What smells so delicious?" he asked.

"Supper," Belle replied with a smile and a wink at the Stove and Mrs Potts. "It's called Enchanted Stew, and we cooked it together!"

September

11

Shampoo Time

The toys were having fun playing in Bonnie's room when – oh no! – a glass of orange juice spilled all over Mr Pricklepants the hedgehog.

"Look at me! I'm soaked!" he groaned.

Buzz grabbed a towel. "Don't panic. I'll dry you up in a minute," he promised.

After Buzz had finished drying him, Mr Pricklepants looked even worse! The orange juice had made his hair sticky.

"You need a shampoo to wash it away," said Buttercup the unicorn.

Mr Pricklepants raised an eyebrow. "A shampoo?" he said, quizzically. He'd never had a shampoo before, but before he knew what was happening, the other toys had dragged him to the bathroom and put him in the sink.

"The shampoo's coming," announced Buzz, glugging the sweet-smelling green goo over the hedgehog's head.

"And here's the water," added Dolly, turning on the tap.

The basin quickly began to fill with water and bubbles. Soon, Mr Pricklepants was struggling to stay afloat.

"Heeelp!" he spluttered.

Buzz got ready to jump in and save their friend, but Dolly had a better idea. Thinking fast, she pulled out the plug, letting the suds drain away. Mr Pricklepants was safe but he was covered from head to toe in frothy white foam.

"I've got a super plan!" Buzz said. He turned on the shower, blasting Mr Pricklepants with a jet of icy-cold water. The force of the water almost knocked him off his feet.

"It's too powerful!" he spluttered.

"Hold on. Almost done," Buzz promised, rinsing away the last of the soap.

When he was clean, Dolly used the hairdryer to give the hedgehog a blow dry. Mr Pricklepants could only sigh as the hot air hit him in the face, swishing his hair all around.

At last, it was over.

Mr Pricklepants looked at himself in the mirror and gasped. He looked like an enormous ball of fuzzy fluff! Still, at least he was clean, and he wouldn't have to be washed again for a very long time.

Or so he thought!

That night, when Bonnie was called for bath time, she grabbed Mr Pricklepants and tucked him tightly under her arm.

"Let's pretend I'm a hairdresser!" she said, carrying him through to the bathroom.

Buzz and the others giggled quietly. Something told them that Mr Pricklepants would be having another shampoo session very soon indeed!

Disney Princess
The Little Mermaid

Ariel and Beau, the Royal Colt

Prince Eric had given Ariel many beautiful things – silk bows for her hair, fine gowns she could twirl around the dance floor in and beaded slippers from lands far, far away. But the gift she cherished most dearly was the gift of a colt named Beau.

"He's beautiful!" she gasped, when Eric surprised her with the shy creature on four wobbly legs.

"He'll be a great companion," Eric assured her, petting Beau on his soft neck as Ariel kissed the animal on his warm snout.

Ariel took Beau everywhere. They were inseparable! His wobbly legs became strong and sturdy and he pranced about with his head held high. Ariel liked to groom him too, with his very own jewelled brush that made his brown fur gleam and shine.

Beau's favourite food was delicious carrots. Ariel made a point of bringing him a bowlful every evening as a yummy treat. He would nuzzle against her side in thanks and then chomp the carrots up.

"Be careful in the palace," Ariel warned Beau. He liked to be indoors with her, just like the palace dogs. Beau tried to behave, but he was just so clumsy....

His swishing tail knocked a precious vase from a podium causing it to smash into little pieces. He dashed into the hall, where a fresh coat of soapy water had been used to wash the tiles and left hoof marks on the floor. And when he was hungry, he ate the gardener's prized tomatoes by mistake!

One night, there was to be a grand party. The King and Queen from a nearby kingdom arrived for the royal dance.

Suddenly, Beau burst in and galloped through the throne room, knocking over the guests of honour.

"I'm so sorry your majesties!" exclaimed Ariel, calming the colt down.

The King and Queen were not upset in the slightest.

"It's quite all right," said the Queen with a titter. "We love horses. In fact we've brought you a special gift."

They entered the grand gardens together to find another colt!

"She's gorgeous. Oh, thank you!" Ariel cried, watching Beau trot over to investigate.

Beau instantly became friends with the new colt. They frolicked about together and even napped at the same time. Thanks to the Queen's special gift, Beau learned how to behave properly without causing trouble indoors!

Ariel loved Beau with all her heart. He'd been a good house pet ... sort of ... but she loved him all the more for being a proud and wonderful horse in the safety of the palace grounds.

Disney Princess
Mulan

Invincible Mushu

After helping Mulan defeat the Huns and restore the Fa family honour, Mushu had been given back his old job as family guardian. He was supposed to help guard the temple of the Fa ancestors.

One day Mushu was sunning himself on the temple roof, when a big lizard waddled up. He seemed to be staring right at Mushu.

Mushu frowned. "Who you lookin' at?" he said to the lizard.

The lizard flicked out his tongue.

Mushu was offended. "Oh, yeah?" he said. "Stick your tongue out at me, will you? Well, get a load of this!" Puffing out his tiny chest, Mushu spat out a miniature burst of fire, no bigger than the flame of a match.

The lizard just blinked.

"Not good enough for you, eh?" Mushu said. "All right, tough guy. Try this on for size!" Mushu cleared his throat dramatically. Taking a deep breath, he opened his mouth and spat a bigger flame at the lizard.

The lizard crouched, lowering his chest to the ground. Then he straightened his legs. Then he crouched again. The lizard was doing push-ups, as lizards will do.

"Oh-ho!" Mushu shouted. "Think you're tough, do you? Well, Scales for Brains, I didn't spend time in the Imperial Army for nothing!" And with that, Mushu crouched down on all four legs and began to do push-ups, too.

"... 98 ... 99 ... 100!" Mushu counted, panting. He leaped to his feet and began to run circles around the lizard. "Just ask anyone," he told the lizard. "I'm the dragon that defeated hundreds of Huns. I could eat you for lunch, small fry."

The lizard just sat there.

Huffing and puffing, Mushu stopped in front of the motionless reptile. He began to box at the air, bouncing around on his hind feet. "Think you can take me on, do you? Well, watch out. I'm a three-time champion in the featherweight division. 'Float like a dragonfly, sting like a bee', that's me all ri –"

Suddenly – *SNAP!* – the lizard snatched up a fly that landed on Mushu's nose.

"Ahhhh!" Mushu screamed. He was so startled, he leaped backwards ... and fell off the roof. He landed on the ground in a puff of dust.

"Ha-ha-ha-ha-ha-ha!" The air filled with the sound of roaring laughter. The ancestors had seen everything.

"Cheer up, Mushu," one ancestor said. "It looks like you have a new friend."

Sure enough, the lizard had followed Mushu down from the roof. "Well," Mushu said, "I always did want a pet."

September

14

DISNEY 101 DALMATIANS

Cruella Sees Spots

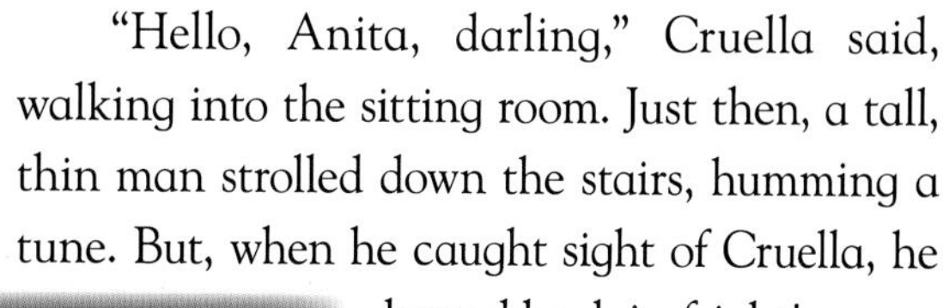

Cruella looked around the living room of the old De Vil mansion and rubbed her hands together. The room was full of Dalmatian puppies. Everywhere Cruella looked she saw spots, spots, spots! At last, her dream was coming true! Cackling with glee, Cruella thought back to the day this had all started....

It had begun as a perfectly miserable day. Cruella had been shopping for fur coats all morning and she hadn't found a single thing she liked.

"Too long! Too short! Too black! Too white!" she screeched, knocking an armload of coats out of the shop assistant's hands. "I want something unusual! I want a coat that has never been seen before!"

Cruella stormed out of the shop, slamming the door so hard that the glass cracked. She needed something to cheer her up. Just then she remembered that her old school friend, Anita, lived nearby.

Soon Cruella stood at the door, ringing the buzzer impatiently. She could hear cheerful piano music coming from an open window.

Just then, a pretty brown-haired woman answered the door. Her eyes opened wide when she saw the skinny woman, covered in fur, standing on her doorstep. "Oh, Cruella!" she cried. "What a surprise!"

"Hello, Anita, darling," Cruella said, walking into the sitting room. Just then, a tall, thin man strolled down the stairs, humming a tune. But, when he caught sight of Cruella, he leaped back in fright!

"Ah, Prince Charming," Cruella said, smirking at Anita's new husband, Roger. Suddenly something else caught Cruella's eye. Two black-and-white spotted dogs were sitting in the corner of the room.

"And what have we here?" Cruella asked.

"Oh, that's Pongo and Perdita," Anita explained. "They're wonderful pets." But Cruella wasn't looking at the dogs. She was looking at their coats. Their glossy fur wasn't too long or too short. It wasn't too black or too white. Cruella had never seen anything like it. It was perfect.

"And soon we'll be even happier," Anita went on. "Perdita is going to have puppies!"

"Puppies!" Cruella shrieked. Suddenly she had an idea that made her smile an evil smile.

"Oh, Anita, you have positively made my day. Now, you must call me just as soon as the puppies arrive. I think they are *just* what I have been looking for."

Pongo snarled, but Cruella didn't notice.

"What a perfectly *marvellous* day," Cruella said to herself as she strode out of the door.

... And *that* was how it all started.

September

15

One for All, All for One!

It was a special day at Cavendish Stream. Silvermist was very excited. "Tonight I'll show you my new dancing water fountains!"

Her friends were looking forward to it. Silvermist's water displays were always beautiful!

"I just hope you won't get our wings wet like last time," commented Vidia.

It was true – the last time the fairies had seen the dancing fountains, there had been lots of splashing and as everyone knew, wet wings meant no flying! Luckily Tink had an idea. "I'll make leaf umbrellas for everyone," she said.

Rosetta clapped her hands. "Good idea!"

Silvermist nodded. "Perfect! That way you'll all stay dry!"

Tink got to work straight away. She collected the right kind of leaves and took them to her workshop, but then a new idea struck her. She could make them personalized! Each fairy would have an umbrella to match her talent! Blaze the firefly looked up in alarm as Tink flew off again to collect even more items. Blaze knew perfectly well how carried away Tink could get at these moments – would she finish in time?

Tinker Bell collected scented petals for Rosetta, feathers for Vidia and acorn cups for Fawn. She even managed to find some sparkly gems for Iridessa. It was late in the day by the time she finally started assembling the umbrellas. Blaze watched, just hoping that Tink would get everything done....

"Wow!" cried Fawn in delight as she saw her umbrella that night.

"They are beautiful!" said Rosetta, twirling her flower-decorated umbrella from side to side to admire it.

Even Vidia was pleased with hers! Tink felt proud of her work – these umbrellas would keep her friends dry during the water display!

"But where's yours, Tink?" asked Iridessa.

Tink gasped. "Cracked kettles! I forgot to make myself one!" She'd spent so long making the others, she'd run out of time to make her own! Laughing, Tink shrugged. "Oh well, I'll just get a little wet."

"No you won't," said Vidia. She pulled Tink under her own umbrella. The other fairies stood close, using their umbrellas to make a canopy big enough for them all.

The display started, and as Tink watched Silvermist conjure up incredible shapes and patterns in the water, she felt blessed to have such good friends. "Thank you," she whispered.

"One for all," smiled Fawn.

"And all for one!" finished Rosetta.

Faith, trust and pixie dust would get you through most scrapes – but friendship made everything worthwhile!

Disney Princess

BRAVE

Merida's Wild Ride

Merida sat in the stables reading from an old book of Highland tales. She and her horse Angus wanted to go for a ride, but it was a wet afternoon.

"Look, right there," Merida said to Angus, pointing to a picture in her book. "Magical horses. That one there is called a kelpie. It's a water horse."

Angus snorted at the book. He wanted nothing to do with magic.

The raindrops slowed and the clouds scattered. When the sun finally came out, Merida said, "Come, lad. Let's go for a ride."

They galloped down the hill to the woods. Suddenly a flash of grey caught Merida's eye.

"What was that?" she cried. "Let's follow it."

But Angus didn't want to follow it – whatever it was.

"Don't be a ninny," Merida teased him. "I'm sure it's not a bear."

She guided a reluctant Angus to a clearing and there stood a grey horse. Its coat shimmered and its mane was like silk.

Merida jumped off Angus and approached the horse. Angus blocked her path.

"Don't be jealous, lad!" she said. "This horse must be lost. We need to help him."

Merida talked to the grey horse and it responded with a whinny, so she swung on to its back. She didn't have a spare bridle, but she thought she could guide him by his mane. But the horse bolted!

Merida wasn't scared. She had been around horses all her life. But as she tried to calm the horse, she realized her hands were stuck to the horse's mane.

When the horse brushed against some tree branches, rainwater fell on her hand and it came free. She tried to grab hold of a tree branch, but they were all out of reach.

"Angus, help!" she called. The grey horse was racing towards a cliff's edge!

Merida pulled on the horse's mane but nothing worked. Suddenly, Angus galloped up next to them and tossed his bridle at Merida. She caught it and slipped it over the horse's head. She was able to guide the horse to safety.

When they reached a loch, the horse stopped. Merida jumped off and looked into the horse's eyes. Something made her remove the bridle, and the horse galloped down to the shore. Was he really racing into the water, or was it the fog playing tricks on Merida's eyes?

Back at the stable Merida read more about the legend of the kelpie. "Once a bridle is put on, the water horse will do your bidding," she read. She looked up at Angus. Had she really been riding a kelpie?

Disney · PIXAR
FINDING NEMO

What a Crab!

Nemo was having trouble at school – and its name was Ruddy. The big crab was mean to Nemo and the other kids whenever he got the chance. The trouble was, he was crafty and he never did it when the teachers were looking.

One day, he shoved Nemo into a tide pool and made him late for their coral lesson. Another time, he taunted Nemo by saying, "My dad's bigger and stronger than your dad!"

"Ignore him," Marlin told his son. "And just so you know, his dad *may* be bigger and stronger than I am, but he's certainly not as smart or good-looking."

"My friends and I have tried everything," Nemo complained to his shark friends, Bruce, Chum and Anchor. "But he won't leave us alone. What do *you* think we should do?"

"Just leave it to us!" said Bruce. "We're experts in behaviour modification."

The next day, three huge shadows fell over Nemo's classmates as they played in the school playground.

"Hello," Bruce said, putting a fin round the crab. "You must be Nemo's new little friend."

While Ruddy trembled, Bruce snarled, "We just wanted you to know that any friend of Nemo's is a friend of ours. You are a *friend* of Nemo's, aren't you?"

Everyone looked at Ruddy. "Oh, yeah!" he spluttered, throwing a claw round Nemo. "You bet! Nemo and I are buddies. Yessiree!"

"Good!" Anchor said. "Because you don't want to know what happens to anyone who's not nice to our little pal here."

Chum cleaned a piece of seaweed from between his razor-sharp teeth with a spiny urchin. "You should stop by for lunch sometime," he said to Ruddy with a wink.

When Mrs Lobster arrived to pick up the class, the sharks said goodbye and swam away.

Ruddy sidled up to Nemo. "You're friends with three sharks?" he said. "Wow! That's pretty cool! I wish I had friends like that. In fact, I wish I had any friends at all."

"How do you expect to have friends when you're so, well, *crabby* all the time?" Nemo said.

Ruddy admitted that he hated being the new kid. He had decided to pick on everyone else before they had a chance to pick on him.

"If you promise to stop acting mean, I promise to be your friend," Nemo said.

"Deal," Ruddy agreed. "Besides, I guess I'd better be your friend if I don't want your shark pals to eat me."

Nemo didn't say a word. Bruce, Chum and Anchor were vegetarians, but Ruddy didn't need to know that – at least not today!

Disney Princess
Snow White and the Seven Dwarfs

Snow White's Special Day

And with one kiss, Snow White awoke. The Prince lifted her onto his horse, and together they rode towards his castle. Just before they arrived, the Prince helped Snow White down from the saddle.

"There's something I must ask before we go through those gates," he said. "Will you do me the honour of marrying me?"

Of course, Snow White said yes!

Just then, the gates to the castle opened wide. It seemed all of the kingdom's people had gathered to meet them!

Soon the Prince's staff was bustling around Snow White, making preparations for the wedding. She glanced at the Prince nervously, but his smile put her at ease. She knew he would always be there to help her.

Soon Snow White was at the royal dressmaker's, trying to choose a style for her wedding dress. It was a difficult task.

Later that evening, Snow White went to her room. It seemed very large – and quite lonely! She missed her friends. Just then, there was a knock at her door....

"Hello, my dear," the Prince said. "I'm not sure about you, but I'm having some trouble planning this wedding – especially finding the perfect ring for you. So I thought I should bring in the best helpers I know...."

The Prince opened the doors to the balcony outside of the room. There stood the Seven Dwarfs, along with all of Snow White's animal friends from the forest! She was so happy to see everyone!

The next day, as Sneezy, Doc and Sleepy helped Snow White with the dressmaker, Dopey and Happy helped the Prince find his own diamond in the mine for Snow White!

When the wedding day arrived, Snow White's friends helped her to get dressed in her wedding gown. The royal dressmaker couldn't help but smile – the little animals' special touches did complete his work perfectly.

As she stood ready to walk down the aisle, Snow White looked at her seven dear friends. "You know," she said, "I do need to be walked down the aisle. Would you do that?"

The Seven Dwarfs were overjoyed! They walked their beloved Snow White down the aisle to her prince. Dopey even stood on top of Sneezy so that they could be a bit taller.

Thanks to a little help from her friends, Snow White had the most wonderful wedding day she could have imagined. And as day turned into night, the royal couple rode off in a carriage decorated with flowers. Everyone knew that Snow White and the Prince would live happily ever after.

Disney Princess Sleeping Beauty

The Gift Horse

"I can hardly wait to see her!" Prince Phillip told his horse, Samson. He had just met the woman of his dreams singing in the forest. And she had invited him to her cottage that very evening.

Suddenly, the Prince pulled his horse's reins up short. Samson jerked to a stop and chuffed angrily.

"Sorry, boy," said the Prince. "But I just realized that I should bring her a gift tonight – something to show her how much I love her. Let's go to the village."

Samson shook his mane and refused to move a hoof. Shopping wasn't his idea of fun. He was tired and wanted to go back to the castle for some oats!

"C'mon, boy," pleaded the Prince. "I'll give you some nice crisp apples."

Apples! Samson's eyes widened. Suddenly, he wasn't so tired any more! With a whinny, he kicked up his hooves and took off.

When they reached the village square, the Prince scratched his head in thought. There were so many shops.

"What sort of gift do you think she will like?" he asked.

As a horse, Samson didn't care all that much. Yet he did his best to answer.

"Red roses?" asked the Prince, passing a flower shop.

Samson shook his head.

"Yes, you're right," said the Prince. "She lives in the forest. She must see flowers every day."

They passed a dress shop and the Prince peered in at the window.

"How about a new dress?" he asked Samson.

Samson shook his mane in irritation.

"No?" said the Prince. "Girls like to choose their own dresses, don't they?"

They passed more shops – a bakery, a hat shop and a blacksmith's.

Samson sighed. If he didn't help the Prince find a gift soon, they could be here all day! With a whinny, Samson took off down the street.

The Prince yelped in surprise. By the time he'd taken back control of the reins, Samson had stopped in front of a jewellery shop.

"Samson, you're a genius!" the Prince cried at the sight of the gems glittering in the window. "That sapphire ring sparkles as beautifully as her blue eyes."

The Prince bought the ring, slipped it in his pocket, then mounted Samson again.

"To the castle!" said the Prince. "I've got to tell my father I've found the girl of my dreams."

Samson whinnied and took off at a gallop. He didn't know what the King would say to the Prince, but one thing he was sure of – he had certainly earned those apples!

Disney THE LION KING

Timon and Pumbaa Tell It All

It was a very hot day on the savannah. Simba, Timon and Pumbaa were lying in the shade, barely moving. It was too hot for the three friends to do anything except talk. Pumbaa had just finished telling a story about the biggest insect he had ever eaten (to hear him tell it, it was the size of an ostrich) and a silence fell over the little group.

"I know," said Simba. "Hey, Timon, why don't you tell me the story of how you and Pumbaa met each other?"

Timon looked at Pumbaa. "Do you think he's ready for it?" he asked.

"Knock him dead," said Pumbaa.

"It all started in a little meerkat village far, far away," began Timon.

"No," interrupted Pumbaa. "You've got it all wrong. It all started near a little warthog watering hole far, far away."

"If I recall correctly, Simba asked *me* to tell the story," said Timon. "And this is the story as told from *my* point of view."

"All right," said Pumbaa sulkily.

"And in that little meerkat village there was one meerkat who didn't fit in with the rest. All the others were content to dig, dig, dig all day long," said Timon. "*I* was that isolated meerkat. How I hated to dig! I knew I needed to go elsewhere, to find a home of my own, a place where I fitted in. So I left. Along the way I ran into a wise old baboon who told me what I was seeking – *hakuna matata* – and pointed me in the direction of Pride Rock. So I boldly set off towards this rock of which he spoke. And on my way there, I –"

"Met me!" Pumbaa loudly interrupted.

Timon gave him a dirty look and continued. "I heard a strange rustling in the bushes. I was scared. What could it be? A hyena? A lion? And then I found myself face to face with a big, ugly warthog!"

"Hey!" said Pumbaa, looking insulted.

"We soon realized we had a lot in common like our love for bugs and our search for a home to call our own. So we set out for Pride Rock together. A lot of bad things happened along the way – hyenas, stampedes, you name it. But before long we managed to find the perfect place to live. And then we met you, Simba!"

"That's a nice story," Simba said with a yawn. "Now I think I'm going to take a nap...."

Pumbaa cleared his throat. "It all started near a little warthog watering hole far, far away," he began.

"You always have to get the last word, don't you?" said Timon.

"Not always," said Pumbaa. And then he continued with *his* side of the story.

Disney Princess
Cinderella

The Prince's Dream

The Grand Duke was a little worried about Prince Charming. At tonight's ball, the Prince had finally met the girl of his dreams. But, at the stroke of midnight, she'd run away. And now it was impossible to reason with the Prince.

"You must bring her back!" the Prince told the Grand Duke.

"Of course, Your Highness!" said the Duke. "I've already sent the royal guards after her carriage ... as I told you four times already!" he added under his breath.

But the guards had no luck. The captain bowed to the Prince. "I'm very sorry, Your Highness," he said. "I don't understand what happened. I could see her carriage ahead of us – and an extraordinary carriage it was. It actually seemed to shimmer."

The Prince remembered how the girl's gown and tiara had shimmered too. The Duke sighed as he watched Prince Charming's eyes glaze over. The Prince would clearly be distracted until they found this mystery girl.

"Then what happened?" asked the Duke.

"We turned a corner and the carriage simply ... vanished," said the captain.

"I don't even know her name," said the Prince, in a daze.

"Well, for now, you must try to focus on your duties as the host of the ball," the Duke advised the Prince. "The ballroom is still filled with eligible maidens."

The Prince shook his head. "There is no other maiden. Not for me. If only she had left some clue!" he cried despairingly. "Some token to remember her by!"

The Duke rolled his eyes. "Your Highness might try investigating your right jacket pocket, then."

Startled, the Prince stuck his hand into his pocket and withdrew a glass slipper! He had been so distracted by his newfound love for the mystery girl that he had completely forgotten about the tiny glass slipper she had left behind on the stairs. He looked at the slipper, then at the Duke.

"I ... I ..." the Prince stammered.

"I suggest you allow me to see to the arrangements," the Duke said kindly, taking the slipper. "We shall find your mystery lass, Your Highness."

The Prince nodded gratefully, then turned towards the window and gazed out into the night. Somewhere out there, his princess was waiting for him. "Dreams can come true," he murmured. "After tonight, I'm sure of it."

Little did he know that on the other side of his kingdom, Cinderella was standing by her own window, holding the other glass slipper – and saying the very same thing!

Remember Me

Tinker Bell had just returned from a trip to the beach, her arms full of exciting treasures. "Look, Blaze!" she called to her special firefly friend. "I found lots of lost things!" She couldn't wait to get working with them!

But Blaze wouldn't come over to say hello. Instead, he buzzed quietly in the corner, his light dim and miserable.

"Hey, what's wrong?" asked Tink as she put down her collection. Then she realized. "Oh, cracked kettles! I forgot to ask you to go with me!"

Tinker Bell felt really bad about leaving her friend at home. She gave Blaze a big cuddle. "I'm sorry! Next time, I'll try to remember!"

That night Tink was so tired from collecting all her treasures – she yawned and said, "Goodnight, sweetie!" to Blaze then fell asleep as soon as her head touched the pillow.

But Blaze was worried. He knew how busy Tink was – and she wasn't always very good at remembering things. How could he make sure she didn't forget him again?

BZZZ! An idea came to him! Blaze buzzed off to collect the things he would need....

The next morning, Tink awoke to find a blue flower petal on her pillow, right in front of her nose! Puzzled, she sat up to examine it. "How'd this get here?" she wondered.

CHIRP CHIRP! went the bird in her clock, but as it popped out, so did a shower of more flower petals! Tink ducked, and then smiled. "Hmm ... I think I know who pulled this prank on me!" Leaving the petals strewn across her floor, she flew off.

But when she brought her friend Rosetta, the garden fairy, back to her house, Rosetta didn't have a clue what Tink was talking about. "It wasn't me!" she exclaimed when she saw the mess.

Then she took a closer look at one of the petals. "These flowers are forget-me-nots," she told Tink. "I think someone wants to remind you of something."

Tink was baffled – who could it be? But then she heard a buzzing sound, and suddenly it all made sense.

"Blaze!" she cried, turning to her friend. "Don't tell me it was you!"

The little firefly nodded nervously. Was Tink cross with him?

Of course not! She caught him in another big hug.

"Don't worry," she told him. "I'll never forget to take you with me again!"

Blaze buzzed happily. Tinker Bell might be a bit forgetful sometimes, but she was still a great friend!

Disney Princess
Beauty and the Beast

Lessons at Hide-and-Seek

"Belle," Mrs Potts called. "Oh, Belle!" Belle was sitting in the library, surrounded by a pile of books.

"There you are!" Mrs Potts cried.

"Hi, Belle," Mrs Potts' son, Chip, chimed in.

"Hello to both of you. Were you looking for me?" Belle asked Mrs Potts.

"As a matter of fact, I was," Mrs Potts told her. "I was just stopping by to enquire as to whether or not you would like some tea."

"Thank you," Belle said. "I would love some."

Mrs Potts poured Belle a piping hot cup of tea. Belle drank it, and thanked her.

"You're welcome, Belle," Mrs Potts said. "Come along now," she called to Chip.

"But Mama," Chip whined. "I want to stay here with Belle!"

"Belle is busy," Mrs Potts explained. "You'll just get in the way."

"That's all right," Belle said. "I was just about done for today. I'd love to spend some time with Chip."

"All right," Mrs Potts said. "But Chip, you come right back to the kitchen when Belle tells you to."

"Okay, I promise," Chip said.

"So," Belle began when Mrs Potts had left, "how about a game of hide-and-seek?"

"How do you play that?" Chip asked.

"It's simple," Belle said. "One person hides and the other person tries to find them."

"I can do that!" Chip said.

"Of course you can," Belle told him. "So, do you want to be the hider or the seeker?"

"I want to be the hider," Chip told her.

"Okay," Belle said. "I'll close my eyes and count to 10. One, two, three...."

Chip took off, darting behind the curtains just as Belle called, "Ten! Ready or not, here I come! Hmm, now where could he be?" she wondered aloud.

Belle looked under the table. "He isn't there," she said. Then she looked in the corner. "He isn't there, either," Belle continued. She looked high and low. But she just couldn't seem to find Chip anywhere. "I give up," Belle said. "Come out, come out, wherever you are!"

Chip silently giggled from behind the curtain, but he was careful not to make too much noise. He was having fun!

"It seems that Chip doesn't want to come out from his hiding place," Belle said. "I guess that means I'll have to eat a slice of Mrs Potts' chocolate cake all by myself."

And, upon hearing that, Chip jumped out from his hiding place and called after Belle, "Here I am! Wait for me!"

September
24

Disney Princess The Little Mermaid

Stackblackbadminton

After dinner at Prince Eric's castle, Ariel, Eric and Grimsby went into the drawing room to relax.

"My dear, do you play?" Grimsby asked Ariel. He pointed to a table. On it sat a red-and-black chequered board.

Of course, Ariel could not answer because she had exchanged her voice for legs. But she nodded.

"I'll go first," Eric said, as he slid a black disc from one square to another.

That seems simple enough, thought Ariel. The game seemed similar to a merpeople game called 'Conch'. She pushed the same black disc to a third square.

Eric laughed. "No, no. I'm black. And you're red. *You* move the *red*. Understand?"

Ariel gazed at Eric and sighed.

"Perhaps I should show the young lady?" suggested Grimsby.

He took Ariel's seat, and the two men moved the discs all over the chequered board. But Ariel still didn't understand what they were doing – this game wasn't like Conch at all!

Suddenly, she heard a flapping sound on the windowsill. It was Scuttle the seagull!

Ariel pointed at the men and mouthed, *What are they doing?*

"They're playing Stackblackbadminton, a popular human game," said Scuttle.

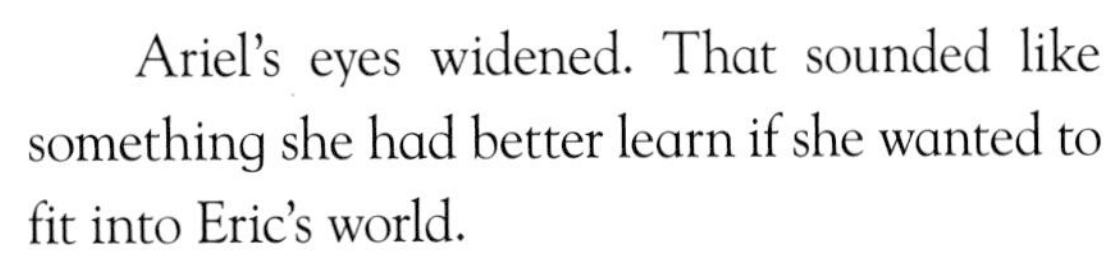

Ariel's eyes widened. That sounded like something she had better learn if she wanted to fit into Eric's world.

"You see those discs?" asked Scuttle. "Those are *chips*. At the end of the game, players stack their chips. Then the dealer – the person *not* playing –"

Me? mouthed Ariel.

Scuttle nodded. "Yes. It's up to you to end the game by collecting all the chips off the board."

Ariel smiled. She would show Eric she *did* know how to play.

She walked right over to the two men. They seemed to have finished playing. They were staring hard at the board – and there weren't many chips left on it. So she bent down and swept all the pieces off the board.

Eric and Grimsby yelped in surprise. The little mermaid grinned. Eric didn't think she knew how to play his game but, from the stunned look on his face, she'd given him quite a shock!

Ariel smiled and began to lay the 'chips' out as if they were shells in a game of Conch. This 'Stackblackbadminton' game was all right, but she couldn't wait to teach Eric and Grimsby how to play a *really* good game.

She picked up the first 'shell' and showed Eric how to move it. He smiled at her, and her heart fluttered. Things were starting to go well at last.

September

25

Disney · PIXAR TOY STORY 3

A Sunnyside Weekend

Mr Pricklepants was feeling upset after Bonnie had left him and Dolly at Sunnyside Daycare for the weekend.

"Why, oh why, did she leave us in this messy, crowded place?" Mr Pricklepants asked Dolly.

"Come on! It's not that bad!" said Dolly, trying to cheer him up.

"Yeah, we can do lots of things!" Stretch the octopus added, as the other Sunnyside toys gathered round to help.

But it wasn't working.

"I miss our cosy house," Mr Pricklepants said with a sigh. "I miss my books, my poems, our cute tea-table with its little chairs...." He wandered away from the other toys, listing everything he missed.

Dolly knew she had to do something to make Mr Pricklepants feel better, so she came up with a plan and asked the other toys to give her a hand. "Just give us some time!" she called after him. "We'll organize a special programme for you!"

Later, Dolly found Mr Pricklepants sitting alone, reading a book. He looked happy to see her. "At last! You're back!"

"Please, follow me to the Caterpillar Gallery," she said, smiling and leading him to the Caterpillar Room. As they arrived, she announced, "Welcome to our art exhibition!"

"It's amazing!" Mr Pricklepants cheered.

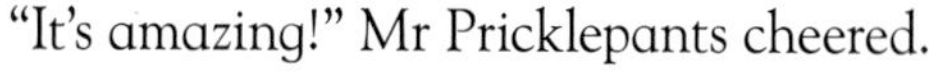

"I'll be your guide!" said Stretch, showing him the children's colourful drawings of flowers and houses taped to the walls.

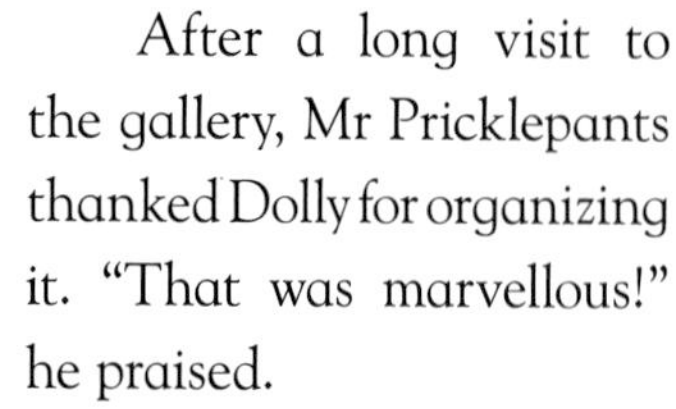

After a long visit to the gallery, Mr Pricklepants thanked Dolly for organizing it. "That was marvellous!" he praised.

But the fun wasn't over yet.... "The best is yet to come!" beamed Dolly. "As we prepare for the next event, you can enjoy a relaxing beauty treatment."

"Fantastic! This is just what actors like me love!" replied Mr Pricklepants, as he settled down ready to be pampered.

When the beauty treatment was finished, Dolly led Mr Pricklepants to a posh tea party where Ken was waiting to greet them. "Please, be our guest!" he said, handing Mr Pricklepants a toy teacup.

"Isn't this the poshest tea party you've ever had?" asked Dolly.

"It is indeed!" he cried.

Afterwards, the Sunnyside toys put on a dramatic play for Mr Pricklepants to enjoy. Dolly turned to him when it finished. "So ... have you changed your mind about Sunnyside?" she wondered.

"Definitely!" he said happily. "I can't wait to see what you've got in store for tomorrow!"

September

26

Disney Princess
THE PRINCESS AND THE FROG

Just-right Gumbo

Tiana loved to cook, but she especially loved to cook with friends. It was so much more fun to have people around her, enjoying the smells that came from delicious meals, watching the recipes come together before their very eyes and best of all – tasting the dish at the end!

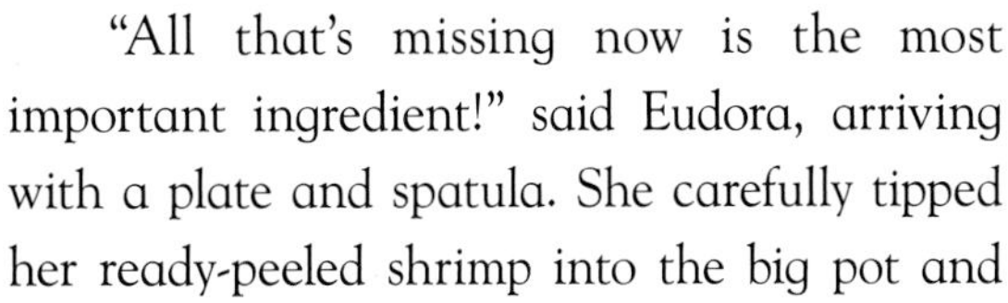

One day, Tiana asked her friends and family to help her make gumbo as she wanted each of them to add their own special touch to one of her favourite dinners!

Naveen was more than happy to help. With a glorious chef's hat on top of his head, he cut tomatoes in neat little slices. "These tomatoes are absolutely delicious," he told them all happily.

Charlotte helped by cutting the onions. With her apron tied round her waist, she sat at the table and diced away.

"I love onions," she said, with tears streaming from her eyes. But rest assured, Charlotte wasn't crying because she was unhappy. Onions just have a habit of making your eyes water terribly as you cut them!

When it was Big Daddy's turn, with his pointy moustache oiled to perfection, he tossed chopped green peppers into a great big pot ... it was almost as big as Tiana! "The special taste of the peppers will give the gumbo just the right flavour. I'm sure of it," insisted Big Daddy.

"All that's missing now is the most important ingredient!" said Eudora, arriving with a plate and spatula. She carefully tipped her ready-peeled shrimp into the big pot and watched them sink into the mixture with the vegetables.

The smell that filled the kitchen was divine.

With everyone's special ingredients in the pot, Tiana added the final touch.

"Hot sauce is what this needs!" she announced. She watched the sauce mix into the pot and smiled with satisfaction.

As Tiana, her friends and family waited for the food to cook, they talked about their morning and how much their bellies were starting to rumble in hunger.

Tiana was the first to take a spoon in her hand and check that the gumbo was just right....

"It smells so good!" said Charlotte.

"What's it taste like?" asked Naveen, impatiently peering over Tiana's shoulder.

"Delicious!" Tiana cried.

There was only one thing left to do ... and that was to enjoy it together! Gathering around the pot they each filled a bowl and sat at the table, admiring their delicious gumbo soup before tucking in ravenously.

"*Bon appetite*!" Tiana said, with a wave of her spoon.

"*Bon appetite*!" everyone laughed.

Disney Lady and the Tramp

A Rainy Night Out

"Yip!" Scamp barked at the squirrel nibbling on an acorn in the grass. His brother and sisters were taking a nap under the big oak tree, and there was nobody else around to have fun with.

Scamp barked again, and the squirrel darted across the lawn. Scamp chased after it. The squirrel zipped up a lamp post and leaped onto a nearby tree branch. With a whimper, Scamp sat down and thumped his tail on the pavement. That was the problem with squirrels. They always got away too easily.

Disappointed, Scamp trotted along the pavement, stopping when he got to an open space. The grass here was tall, and butterflies flitted from wild flower to wild flower.

"Yip! Yip!" Scamp raced through the tall grass. He chased the butterflies to the end of the open space and back again.

It was getting dark. Scamp decided it was time to head home. He hadn't caught a single butterfly, but he'd had fun trying. He couldn't wait to get home and tell his brother and sisters about the new game he'd invented. They'd be so impressed!

Scamp trotted up to the front porch and tried to get through the doggie door. *THUNK!* His nose hit the wood, but it didn't move. The door was locked!

"Yip! Yip! I'm home!" he barked. "Let me in!"

Scamp sat there for several minutes, barking. Nobody came to the door. Suddenly – *BOOM!* – thunder echoed overhead. Lightning flashed and rain began to fall.

Scamp bolted over to the big oak tree, sat down and covered his eyes with his paws. Thunderstorms were scary!

"I'm not going to cry," he told himself as his eyes started to water. He shivered in the dark. He'd probably catch a cold by morning!

Scamp let out a little whimper and moved even closer to the tree trunk. He buried his wet nose in his wet paws and closed his eyes.

Scamp was just falling asleep when a sound suddenly startled him. Somebody was coming up the drive!

By the time Jim Dear and Darling were out of the taxi, Scamp was dashing across the lawn as fast as he could go. He bolted through the door just as it opened.

"Scamp, you're soaking wet!" Darling declared as the puppy found his brother and sisters napping in front of the fire. And, as he lay down among them, Jim Dear came over with a warm towel to dry him off.

Home, sweet home, Scamp thought happily, as he drifted off to sleep.

Disney Peter Pan

We're Going on a Picnic

"Cap'n?" Mr Smee knocked softly on Captain Hook's door. There was no answer. He pushed his way inside, carrying a breakfast tray. "I've got breakfast, Cap'n."

"I'm not hungry!" Captain Hook replied angrily. "Go away!"

"But, Cap'n. You have to eat." Smee was getting worried. The Captain hadn't eaten in days. In fact, he hadn't even got out of bed! "I know you feel bad about Pe –" Smee stopped himself from saying the dreaded name just in time, "– that flying boy. And the croc – I mean – that ticking reptile, too." Captain Hook was really angry about being beaten by Peter again. Even worse, Peter had set the crocodile right back on Captain Hook's trail. "But we haven't seen hide nor scale of either of them for a week. I think the coast is clear."

There was no reply from Captain Hook.

Smee thought for a minute. "I know how to cheer you up!" he cried. "We'll have a nice old-fashioned picnic! Won't that be lovely!"

Again, silence from Captain Hook.

"Ah-ah-ah! No arguments!" Smee left the breakfast tray and hurried down to the galley. A picnic on Mermaid Island was just what the doctor ordered!

Smee whistled merrily as he made herring-and-pickle sandwiches (Captain Hook's favourite) and packed them in a wicker basket. This was Hook's day! Smee carefully folded a gingham tablecloth and placed it in the basket with his tin whistle. He was going to make sure that Hook had a good time, whether he wanted to or not!

Once the picnic basket was packed, Smee called down to Hook, "It's time to go, Cap'n!"

After a while, Captain Hook finally appeared on deck, blinking in the sunlight. "Fine," he said grumpily. "But I know I'm not going to have fun!"

Smee let the rowing boat down into the water and Hook began to climb down the rope ladder. Once he was safely in the boat, Smee picked up the picnic basket.

TICK TOCK. TICK TOCK. TICK TOCK.

"Smee!" cried Hook. "Help me!"

Smee peeked over the side of the ship. The crocodile was about to take a bite out of the boat!

In a panic, he threw the only thing he had on hand – the picnic basket. It landed right in the crocodile's open mouth. The crocodile stared at Smee in surprise. Then, without a sound, it slipped back under the water.

"My picnic!" cried Smee. "My tin whistle!"

"Next time you have any clever ideas about cheering me up," said the Captain, glaring at his first mate, "keep them to yourself!"

September

29

The Bad-Mannered Blossom

Tinker Bell was keeping Rosetta company as she painted sunflowers in the meadow. Rosetta chatted happily as she moved from petal to petal, but Tink was starting to become bored. "This is the perfect shade, see?" said Rosetta, finishing another petal.

"Uh-huh," said Tink, not really listening. When would Rosetta finish so that they could go play? She gazed into the distance, wondering if more lost things had been washed up on the beach today. Maybe she could just sneak off....

"Oh no!" Rosetta shouted, sounding suddenly alarmed.

Tink sat up. "What's wrong?"

"This poor petal's so pale!" Rosetta said, stroking a petal that had faded to a pale grey. She reached into her bag of pixie dust. "Don't worry," she told the petal. "With a lil' pinch of pixie dust, you'll be just fine!"

Tink lay back again with a sigh. "Don't you think you're overdoing it?" she asked.

"No!" said Rosetta indignantly. "My little flowers need to be perfect!"

Just then, Tink heard a strange noise.

ZZZZ ... ZZZ....

"Um ... does being perfect include snoring?"

"Flowers don't snore," Rosetta said, tutting.

"This one does," Tink said, pointing at a large sunflower, its head tilted up to the sky.

Rosetta gasped. "It can't be! It's unheard of!"

"Maybe it's a new, really sleepy species," giggled Tink.

"Enough of that noise," Rosetta frowned at the flower. "I'll teach you some manners!"

Offended, the sunflower folded up its petals and turned away from Rosetta. But the snoring continued....

"I don't understand!" said Rosetta.

Tink looked down. "Maybe it's not the flower's fault...." She pointed down to where Blaze, her firefly friend, was asleep at the base of the stalk. The snoring was coming from him!

"I knew it!" exclaimed Rosetta. "My flowers don't do such things!" Then she clapped her hands to her face in sudden horror. "Withering willows! I called that innocent sunflower rude."

"You'll have to find a way to make up for it!" laughed Tink.

She was teasing, but Rosetta agreed. "You're right. I'll offer it a special petal-lift treatment!"

Tink groaned. This would be even more boring than painting petals!

"Come watch, Tink!" Rosetta called, as she flew up to the tightly-closed flower. "It'll be fun!"

"Yeah, fun!" replied Tink, sinking to the ground next to her sleepy firefly friend. There was no chance of going off to play for ages yet! "Sometimes I should keep my big mouth shut!"

Disney · PIXAR
MONSTERS UNIVERSITY

Child Invasion

It had started off as a day just like any other at Monsters University. Students and staff had spent the morning going about their business, learning and teaching and discovering new ways to scare.

All that changed when a piercing alarm began to ring loudly across the campus. The monsters yelped and gasped in panic. They began to run, waving their arms and tentacles, and screaming at the tops of their voices.

It was the child alarm, and that meant only one thing – a human kid was loose in the university!

"We're doomed!" wailed one fearsome fanged creature, running around in panicky circles. He and the rest of the monster stampede raced past the Dean and Professor Knight, who watched with growing concern.

"It's coming from that direction," said the professor, pointing across the campus. "We must call the CDA."

The Child Detection Agency was made up of a fearsome bunch of experts, trained to capture, contain and dispose of any human children who managed to find their way into the monsters' world.

"Wait! You can't do that!" cried Mike, hurrying over to the staff. Sulley grabbed him by the arm and pulled him in the direction Professor Knight had pointed. "I can't explain now," Mike cried. "Just don't call the CDA!"

Mike and Sulley shoved their way through the fleeing crowds until they spotted a little boy wandering towards them. He wore thick gloves and thicker glasses, and had a mop of curly brown hair.

Without hesitating, Mike and Sulley dived for the boy, arms outstretched. The Dean and the Professor watched in disbelief. "They just touched a human kid!" Professor Knight gasped.

Meanwhile, Mike and Sulley wrestled with the boy. Sulley's big paws pinned him to the ground, while Mike's fingers searched in the child's curly hair. "Where is it?" Sulley cried.

After a few panicked moments of searching, Mike and Sulley found what they were looking for. There was a zip on the boy's head, and it was stuck fast. Taking hold of the material, Sulley tore it apart, revealing the child's head to be just a mask.

Squishy let out a deep breath as the mask was pulled away. "Thank you, guys," he wheezed. "I got it stuck and couldn't breathe."

Mike and Sulley both smiled, relieved they had managed to save their friend. Squishy smiled, too.

"This is the last time I wear a kid costume to practise our scaring skills," he laughed.

Disney THE LION KING

Hot on the Trail

"Over here!" Simba said, sniffing the trail. "It's going this way!"

"Yup, this way," Nala said with a nod, sniffing a stick. "And not long ago."

"I saw that stick first," Simba said. Nala was a good tracker, but Simba had learned from an expert – his mum. She was one of the best hunters in the pride.

"So what do you think we're following then, master tracker?" Nala asked. "Can you tell me that?"

Simba was silent. They had seen some footprints, but they weren't clear enough to read. They'd also seen some dark, wiry hair on a log, but that could belong to lots of animals.

"Something that isn't very graceful," Simba said. They had seen lots of crushed grass and broken sticks.

"Mmm-hmm." Nala nodded impatiently.

"A rhino!" Simba said confidently.

"A rhino?" Nala rolled onto her back, laughing. "Simba, you crack me up!"

"What?" Simba couldn't hide the hurt in his voice. It *might* be a rhino!

"The footprints aren't big enough," Nala said. "It's Rafiki, the baboon."

Now, it was Simba's turn to laugh. "Rafiki likes the trees, he doesn't use trails like a hyena!" The giggle died in Simba's throat and he felt the fur on the back of his neck stand up. Hyenas were clumsy and had dark, wiry hair....

Nala didn't say anything, but her fur was standing up a little too.

The two lions walked in silence. Ahead of them they heard noises – thrashing and grunting.

"Hey, Simba," Nala whispered, "maybe we should turn back."

"Just a little farther," Simba whispered. They were almost there!

The young lions creeped through the grass on their bellies as quietly as they could. The grunting and thrashing grew louder. They could see a dust cloud rising. Simba stifled a growl. Something about the smell and the sound was familiar, but Simba could not put his paw on it.

As they creeped closer, two bodies came into view by a termite mound. Simba pounced!

"Pumbaa! Timon!" he shouted, landing between his friends.

"Simba!" the warthog said. Termites dripped out of his muddy mouth. "Want some?"

Timon held a handful of wriggling insects towards Nala. "There are plenty to go around."

"Uh, no thanks," Nala said as she came out of the grass, giggling. She shot a look at Simba. "I think I'll wait for the master tracker to hunt me up some lunch!"

Disney Princess Snow White and the Seven Dwarfs

A Thank You Present

"I don't know how I can ever thank them," Snow White said to her new husband, the Prince. The two of them were on their way to visit the Dwarfs and give them a special present – a meal fit for seven kings!

Snow White looked at the dishes and hampers filled with delicious food. "It just doesn't seem like enough," she said with a sigh. "They saved my life!"

"I'm sure seeing you happy is thanks enough," the Prince said, putting his arm round Snow White. "They don't want riches, and they seem quite happy living the way they do."

Snow White had to agree and, as the cosy Dwarf cottage came into view, she perked up. She could not wait to see her friends!

"Yoo-hoo!" she called as she dashed from the coach. "Sneezy? Happy? Bashful?"

Snow White knocked on the door, but there was no answer. "They must not be home yet," she said to the Prince. "We'll have just enough time to get everything ready."

Snow White went inside and set the table and tidied the house, humming while she worked. She was so excited to see her friends, that she couldn't help checking the windows for a sign of them every few minutes. As the sun set, the Princess began to worry.

"They're awfully late!" she said.

The Prince agreed. It was getting dark. "Perhaps we should go and find them," he said.

The Prince strode outside and unhitched one of the horses from the coach. Together the Prince and Princess set off to find the Dwarfs.

At last they reached the mine. Holding up lanterns, they saw at once what the trouble was. A tree had fallen over the mine entrance. The Dwarfs were trapped!

"Snow White, is that you?" Doc called through a small opening.

"Are you all right?" Snow White asked.

"We're fine, dear. Just fine," Doc told her.

"No, we're not," Grumpy said, rather grumpily. "We're stuck!"

"Don't worry," the Prince said. "We'll have you out in no time."

Hitching his horse to the big tree, the Prince pulled it away from the mine so the Dwarfs could get out.

Snow White embraced each dusty Dwarf as he emerged. She even hugged Dopey twice! "Now let's get you home," she said.

Back at home, the Dwarfs were thrilled to see the fine meal laid out on their table.

"How can we ever thank you?" Doc said, wringing his hat. "You saved our lives."

"Don't be silly." Snow White blushed. "Seeing you happy is thanks enough."

October

3

Disney Bambi

Winter Nap

Bambi nosed under the crunchy leaves, looking for fresh grass. There was none. He looked up at the trees, but there were no green leaves there either. Food was getting scarce in the forest.

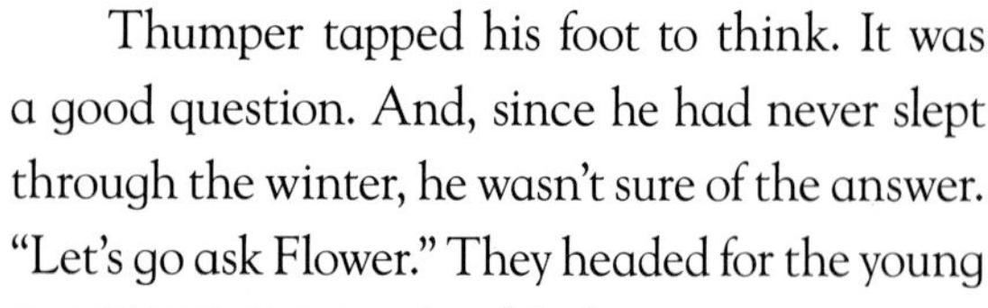

"Don't worry, Bambi," Thumper said when he saw the confused look in Bambi's eyes. "We'll get through the winter. Dad says we always do. We find what we can when we can, and we always make it until spring."

Bambi sighed and nodded. Thumper's dad was smart. He knew lots of things about the forest.

"Besides, it's better to be awake than napping all winter. Yech!" Thumper hated to go to bed, even at bedtime.

"Napping?" Bambi didn't know that some animals slept through the winter months.

"Sure. You know, like Flower, and the squirrels, and the bears. They hole up for months. Haven't you noticed the chipmunks putting their acorns away the past couple of months?" Thumper pointed towards an oak tree.

Bambi nodded.

"That's their food for the winter. As soon as it gets cold enough, they'll just stay inside and sleep," Thumper explained.

"But how will they know when it's time to wake up?" Bambi couldn't imagine life in the forest without all the other animals.

Thumper tapped his foot to think. It was a good question. And, since he had never slept through the winter, he wasn't sure of the answer. "Let's go ask Flower." They headed for the young skunk's den.

"Hello," Flower said.

"Hello Flower, you sleep all winter, right?" Thumper asked curiously.

"It's called hibernation." Flower yawned a big yawn. "Excuse me," he said, his cheeks blushing.

"So, Bambi wants to know who wakes you up in the spring," Thumper said.

"You'll be back, won't you, Flower?" Bambi asked worriedly.

The little skunk giggled. "Oh, we always come back. Just like the grass and the flowers and the leaves," Flower explained. "I never thought about what wakes us up before. It must be the sun, I guess."

Bambi smiled. He didn't know the grass and leaves would come back in the spring too! He was feeling much better about the forest's winter nap.

Suddenly, Thumper started laughing. He rolled on his back and pumped his large hind feet in the air.

Bambi and Flower looked at each other in confusion. "What is it?" they asked together.

"You really are a flower, Flower!" Thumper giggled. "You even bloom in the spring!"

The Brightest of Them All

Another day drew to a close in Pixie Hollow, and Iridessa was busy lighting up the fireflies as usual. "Happy flying, sweeties!" she called as the last firefly received her light and took off into the night sky.

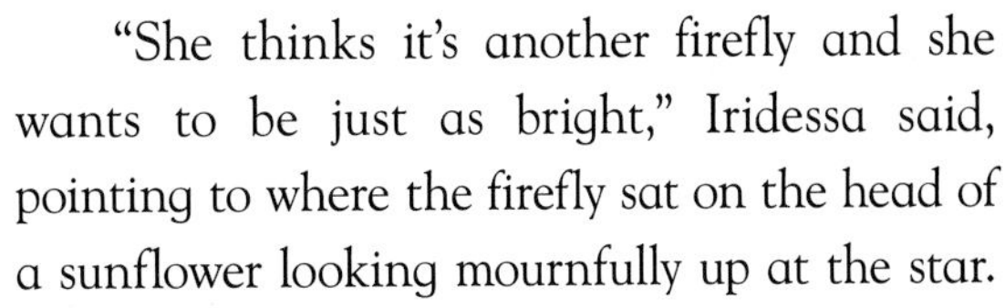

Tinker Bell, who was keeping her friend company, smiled at the cloud of dancing lights. "Have fun!" she shouted up.

But one firefly didn't look like she was in the mood for fun at all. In fact, she looked distinctly cross! "What's wrong, sweetie?" Iridessa asked.

The firefly buzzed angrily, glancing at her own glowing light.

Iridessa was baffled. "What are you trying to tell me?"

The firefly pointed up at a star, which shone very brightly in the sky.

"Oh, I get it!" Iridessa exclaimed. "You want more light!" She scooped the last handful of sunlight from her bucket and gave it to the firefly, making her glow even more brightly. "Here you go."

The firefly was delighted, and zipped back and forth in the sky. But then she glanced up at the star again, and her wings drooped.

"I think she's jealous of that star," Iridessa whispered to Tink.

"Of the star?" Tink was taken aback. Why would a firefly be jealous of a star?

"She thinks it's another firefly and she wants to be just as bright," Iridessa said, pointing to where the firefly sat on the head of a sunflower looking mournfully up at the star. "Unfortunately, I can't make her shine that much!"

"I think I have the answer," smiled Tink. In a wingbeat, she had fetched Silvermist, the water fairy. "She can help us!"

Silvermist flew up into the sky and nudged a cloud towards the star. "C'mon! Just a little farther...."

Soon the cloud was covering the star – and dimming its light! The star could hardly be seen now. Would it make the firefly feel better?

Tink giggled as the firefly blew a raspberry at the sky. "She's already getting back at the star for outshining her!"

"See?" Iridessa said to the small creature. "Now you're brighter." The firefly gave her a big kiss. "Oh, thank you! Now, off you go."

The firefly happily flew off to join the rest of her friends.

"You were flitterific!" Tink told Silvermist.

Iridessa agreed. "Yeah, we couldn't have done it without you."

Silvermist smiled. "Let's just hope the star isn't offended!"

That would be all they needed – a grumpy star! One firefly was quite enough to deal with!

October

5

Disney Princess

Cinderella

The Lost Mice

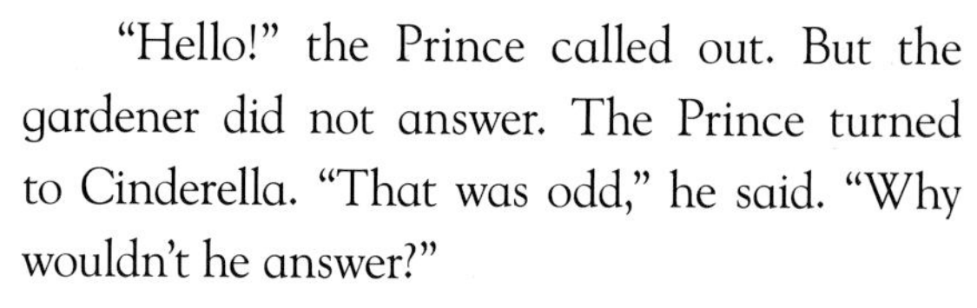

One chilly winter night, the Prince led Cinderella out to the balcony. "I have a surprise for you," he said, handing her a box. Inside was a beautiful new coat.

"Oh, it's lovely! And so warm!" Cinderella cried, trying it on.

Next morning, the princess showed her new coat to Suzy, one of her mouse friends.

A few minutes later, Jaq went into Cinderella's room. It had been a chilly night in the attic.

"Cinderelly!" Jaq called. If he told the princess how cold the attic was, she would be sure to help them. But she was on her way out and didn't hear. Jaq sighed. He was sure she wouldn't mind if they sat in front of the blazing fire in Cinderella's room.

Soon, the new housekeeper came in. When she saw the mice, she shrieked. She didn't know that the mice were Cinderella's friends. She chased them with a broom and the mice ran straight into the castle gardener. Before they knew what was happening, he had trapped them. "Take them outside!" the housekeeper said.

Meanwhile, Cinderella and the Prince were out riding. As their horses trotted through the countryside, they saw the castle gardener in one of the fields.

"Hello!" the Prince called out. But the gardener did not answer. The Prince turned to Cinderella. "That was odd," he said. "Why wouldn't he answer?"

"Perhaps he was lost in thought?" said Cinderella.

Cinderella was right. The gardener was thinking. The housekeeper had told him to let the mice go, but he was worried about them. Finally, he took the mice to the stables. "Don't tell the housekeeper," he said to the stable workers. "These poor mice need warmth and food." The mice were very grateful.

Later that night, Cinderella was starting to worry. She hadn't seen the mice all day. She was searching for them when she ran into the Prince.

"I am looking for our new housekeeper. Apparently she threw the mice out of the castle today!" said the Prince.

"Oh, no!" Cinderella cried. "Poor dears. They'll freeze outside!"

"Don't worry," the Prince said. He told Cinderella what the gardener had done.

Together, Cinderella and the Prince went to the stables. They thanked the gardener and the stable workers. Cinderella was relieved to see her little friends safe and sound. From then on, the mice always had a warm place of their own – in one of the main rooms of the castle.

Disney Princess Sleeping Beauty

The Helpful Dragon

Princess Aurora went riding on her horse, Buttercup, with Prince Phillip close behind. As they rounded a bend, a small dragon popped out from behind a tree.

"Oh, he's so cute!" Aurora exclaimed.

But Phillip looked worried. "Dragons can be dangerous!" The little dragon shook his head.

Aurora laughed. "Let's take him home. I'm going to call him Crackle!"

"He does seem like a harmless little fellow," Phillip agreed.

When Phillip and Aurora rode into the courtyard, the three good fairies were hanging banners for a ball. King Stefan and the queen were coming to the castle.

Flora gasped when she saw Crackle. "Dragons can be dangerous!"

"Remember the last one!" Fauna warned.

"Oooh, I think he's sweet," Merryweather spoke up.

Just then, Crackle noticed a cute, little kitten in a basket of wool. Crackle listened to it purring. Then he tried to purr. "Purrgrr, purrgrr!" Clouds of smoke streamed from his nose and mouth.

Crackle looked sad. "Oh, Crackle," Aurora said gently. "You're not a kitten. You're a dragon."

Aurora noticed that Crackle looked unhappy, so she took him to the castle.

But King Hubert heard Crackle and rushed into the room. "Oh, my! How did a dragon get in here?" he shouted. Frightened, Crackle ran to the garden.

Aurora found the little dragon sitting beside a fountain, watching a fish. *SPLASH!* Before Aurora could stop him, Crackle jumped into the water.

"Crackle, you're not a fish!" Aurora exclaimed. "You're not a kitten either. Do you think no one will like you because you're a dragon?" she asked. Crackle nodded sadly.

"You can't change what you are," Aurora said to him kindly. "But you can learn to be a helpful dragon and then other people will see how wonderful you are."

Suddenly thunder boomed and rain began to pour down. Everyone was gathered in the grand hallway, watching the storm.

"I'm afraid King Stefan and the queen might lose their way," Prince Phillip said.

Aurora looked at Crackle. "Please fly to the top of the tower and blow the largest, brightest flames to guide my parents to the castle."

Soon after, gold and red flames lit up the sky, like a beacon to guide King Stefan and the queen. Crackle had done it! And thanks to Crackle's flame, the king and queen arrived home safely.

Disney·PIXAR TOY STORY 3

One Too Many

Bonnie was having a birthday party, and her friends were having fun playing with her toys in the garden. There was only one thing better than playtime – birthday cake!

When Bonnie and her friends ran inside to eat, the toys chatted excitedly about the party.

There were dozens of brightly coloured helium balloons tied with string all around the garden. Mr Potato Head took a few strings in each hand. "I love balloons," he said. "They're so light...."

"Look out!" gasped Mrs Potato Head, as her husband lifted off the ground and began to drift higher and higher into the sky.

"We need to do something!" Woody cried.

Buzz quickly leaped into action. Snatching more balloons, he tugged the strings free and rose quickly into the air. "I'm coming, my friend!" he called.

Mr Potato Head gulped. "And then what?"

"You'll see!" said Buzz. He waited until his balloons were level with Mr Potato Head's, then he jumped.

For a moment, it looked like Buzz would fall, but he wrapped his arms around Mr Potato Head and they both swung wildly on the breeze.

"We're heavier together," Buzz explained. "So now we'll come back to the ground softly."

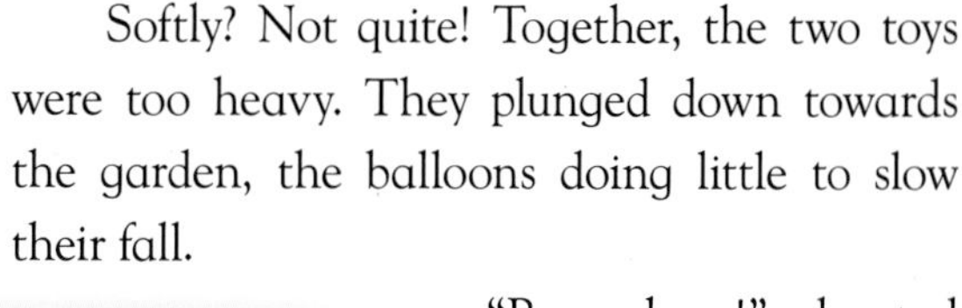

Softly? Not quite! Together, the two toys were too heavy. They plunged down towards the garden, the balloons doing little to slow their fall.

"Buzz, here!" shouted Woody, pointing to a large bucket of water Bonnie and her friends had been using in their games.

"Roger, sheriff!" Buzz called. He knew just what to do. His wings opened, knocking the balloons out of Mr Potato Head's hands.

"What are you doing?" Mr Potato Head gasped. "You can't fly!"

"Perhaps not to infinity and beyond," Buzz admitted, swooping towards the bucket. "But enough to make a perfect splashdown!"

With a splash, Buzz and his passenger landed safely in the bucket – and not a moment too soon. Bonnie and her friends came racing out, still munching on slices of cake.

"My balloons!" Bonnie gasped, as she watched them all float off into the sky.

"Don't worry, we have plenty more!" said her mum.

Unnoticed, Buzz and Mr Potato Head climbed out of the bucket and onto the grass.

"The most important thing is that all the toys are here," Buzz said.

Mr Potato Head smiled. "With their feet firmly on the ground!"

Winnie the Pooh

A Yummy Dream

Winnie the Pooh stepped into his house and sat down with a sigh. He and Piglet had been out on a long walk through the woods. Now Pooh was tired. And, more importantly, he was hungry.

"My tummy feels very rumbly," Pooh said aloud.

Pooh got to his feet and went over to his honey cupboard. There was only one pot of honey inside.

"Oh dear," Pooh said. One pot of honey was not very much. He sat down and began to eat. He ate every last sticky drop. But when he was finished, his tummy was still feeling a tiny bit rumbly.

"Well, I suppose there's nothing left to do but go to bed," Pooh said sadly. He put on his nightshirt and his nightcap and climbed into his cosy bed. A minute later Pooh's snores filled the air. And dreams began to fill his head – dreams of honey, of course.

Pooh stood in front of the honey tree. It was so full of honey, it was oozing out of the trunk!

"Yummy, yummy," Pooh said. He began to fill his honeypots.

Then, suddenly, a purple heffalump appeared behind him.

"Mmm," the heffalump said, licking his lips. The creature stuck his long trunk into one of Pooh's honeypots and gobbled up all the honey.

"Those are my honeypots!" Pooh cried. He tried to sound brave, even though he was just a little bit scared. The heffalump looked very big and very hungry.

The heffalump just stared at Pooh.

Pooh looked at the honeypots. There were a lot of them. Some were full, but most were empty. Pooh looked at the honey tree. It was overflowing with honey.

"I have an idea," Pooh said to the heffalump. "Let's fill the honeypots together, then share a nice snack."

The heffalump nodded excitedly. He picked up a honeypot with his trunk and carried it to the tree. Pooh did the same, and the sweet honey dripped into the pots.

When all of the pots had been filled, Pooh and the heffalump sat down together. They ate and ate until all the pots were empty and their tummies were full.

"Thank you, Pooh," the heffalump said as he got to his feet. "That was fun. We should do this again soon."

Pooh nodded in agreement and watched the heffalump walk away. Getting to his feet, he patted his tummy.

When Pooh awoke the next morning, to his surprise, his tummy wasn't the slightest bit rumbly. Then he remembered his strange dream. It had been a dream, hadn't it?

The Bubbly Bath

Tinker Bell had found a new lost thing and it had given her a great idea! Silvermist and Rosetta were very enthusiastic when she told them. "Fawn will be so happy!" cried Silvermist.

Fairy Mary was passing by and came over to them. "What are you doing with that tea cup?" she asked.

"We're going to turn it into a bath cup for the birds!" Tink explained with a smile. Then she turned to her friends. "Let's get to work, girls!"

"You can't take a bath without water," giggled Silvermist. Within minutes, she had used her water talent to fill the cup to the brim and added something special.

"Wow!" Tink was impressed. "These bubbles are great, Sil!"

Then Rosetta flew down with her arms full of flower petals. When she added them to the water, a delicious fragrance filled the air.

Fairy Mary, who had been watching with interest, closed her eyes and breathed in the perfume. "Mmm, that smells nice!"

Tink hugged her friends. "Now it's a flitterific bath cup!" she said. Fawn was going to love it – and so were the birds!

"Where are you going to put the cup?" wondered Fairy Mary.

"I'll leave it here in Sunflower Meadow," Tink said. "So that Fawn's little bird friends can use it to keep their feet nice and cool." She opened her wings. "I'm going to call Fawn!"

"Yes ... um ... of course!" said Fairy Mary, as the other three flew off. She'd had an idea of her own...!

Tink couldn't wait to show Fawn her surprise. "You're going to love it," she told her friend.

Fawn smiled. "I'm sure I will!"

But as they reached the spot in Sunflower Meadow where the cup should be, Tink gasped. "What's going on?"

A screen of leaves now covered the cup from view ... and from behind it came the sound of singing! "I think someone's back there," said Fawn.

Tink was taken aback. "Yeah, and they sound really cheerful too!" Who was using her special bird bath?

The two fairies creeped closer and then slowly pulled back the leaves....

"For all the pots and pans!" cried Tink.

Sitting in the tea cup bath and playing with the bubbles was Fairy Mary! "Why all the fuss?" she said. "I just wanted to make sure your bubble bath cup was a good invention!"

Fawn burst out laughing, and even Tink couldn't help smiling. "How was it?" she asked.

Fairy Mary got out of the cup and wrapped herself in a leaf towel. "Truly relaxing!" she said as she flew away. "The birds will love it!"

October

10

Disney · PIXAR
FINDING NEMO

Sports Day

The reef was teeming with vibrant fish and crustaceans, all sensing the excitement in the water. Sports Day was here – a chance for the kids to have fun and take part in competitions, while their proud parents watched and applauded.

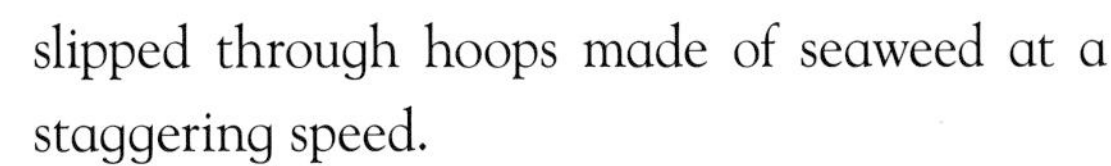

"Hooray! I love sports day. Don't you, Nemo?" asked Tad the seahorse, Nemo's closest fishy friend. "Which events are you in?"

"I don't know. I'm not sure what I'd be good at," confessed Nemo.

"What do you mean?" wondered Tad.

Nemo looked sad. "I'm not very good at sporty things," he said timidly.

"Come on," said Tad, "I'll find you something to take part in."

He took Nemo on a tour of the events that were taking place all over the reef. Lots of sea creatures were practising, ready for their moment to compete and the ocean bubbled with the anticipation of it all.

Tad brought Nemo to the football pitch. "What about football?" he suggested.

"Err, I'm not sure," he admitted, as Pearl expertly head-butted a ball into the back of the net. "I haven't got anything on her."

"Okay," said Tad, leading him away. "What about the obstacle course?"

Nemo watched as Squirt and his turtle friends dodged incoming bubble blasts and slipped through hoops made of seaweed at a staggering speed.

"I'll leave that to Squirt," Nemo said quietly.

"Hey! Weightlifting! That could be your thing!" Tad beamed at him.

Nemo studied the fish lifting rocks above their heads, five times their own weight. There were gasps and clapping all round.

"Well, maybe not," said Tad, before Nemo could open his mouth. He didn't like to see his best pal so deflated. Then, he had a brain wave. "Actually, I know just the thing. Come on, Nemo!"

Tad found Nemo the perfect race ... so perfect, even Nemo couldn't believe his luck!

Stretching his littlest fin, Nemo focused on the finish line. Tad smiled in encouragement at his side. When the signal came for the fish to start the race, Nemo and Tad swam neck-and-neck the whole way round the sandy track.

"We won!" cheered Tad.

"And I'd never have thought to enter the three-finned race without you," Nemo laughed.

Tad and Nemo high fived each other and accepted their medals with puffed up chests and smiles as big as a pelican's grin.

Sports Day wasn't so scary after all. And Nemo couldn't wait to put his medal on the wall at home, to remember his unexpected but well-earned victory.

Disney Princess

Jasmine

The Desert Race

Jasmine and Aladdin were enjoying a walk through the palace grounds when, from a balcony above, the Sultan cried, "This dratted Desert Race! Prince Fayiz will be riding with his horse, Warrior. They've won three years in a row!"

"I could ride my fastest horse, Midnight. We'd win!" Jasmine said.

"My daughter in a race? No, no," the Sultan replied.

"What if I ride Midnight?" Aladdin said.

The Sultan agreed.

But there was one problem. Aladdin hadn't ridden Midnight before and when he tried to practise, the horse misbehaved. Midnight threw Aladdin off!

"I'll try," said Jasmine. Confidently, she hopped onto Midnight's back and he allowed her to trot gracefully across the sand. Aladdin was very impressed.

Jasmine tried to convince her father to let her ride in the race but he refused.

The Desert Race soon arrived and the riders paraded around. Fayiz was there on his impressive stallion called Warrior, as well as a mysterious rider wearing a veil.

They went to the start line. Aladdin was there too, riding a horse that no one recognized.

"Where's Jasmine?" the Sultan wondered. Her seat was empty. Fed up of waiting for his daughter, he signalled for the race to begin.

The riders galloped into the desert. As soon as they were out of the Sultan's view, the mysterious rider took off their mask.

Aladdin rode close behind the rider. He had no idea it was his beloved Princess until their horses came neck-and-neck.

"Jasmine!" he gasped.

Jasmine had been in the lead from the start, but Fayiz and Warrior were catching up. When they edged ahead, Fayiz boasted: "That trophy will belong to Zagrabah!"

"We'll see!" Jasmine said, flying over a ditch.

Fayiz didn't see the ditch and Warrior skidded to a halt, throwing him out of his saddle.

Nothing could stop Jasmine from winning… until Aladdin caught up on his mystery horse.

It was a thrilling dash to the finish line and both Prince and Princess crossed at the same time.

"Agrabah wins twice over!" announced a jolly Sultan.

Jasmine hugged Aladdin. "Where did you find such a fast horse?" she asked him.

Suddenly, his horse vanished in a puff of smoke and Genie appeared!

"Well!" said Sultan. "If he wasn't really a horse that means the true winner is Jasmine!"

Jasmine smiled and accepted her trophy. She'd known she could win all along, and now everyone else knew it too.

October
12

Disney · PIXAR
MONSTERS UNIVERSITY

The Fear Party

Randy had found a half-torn invitation for a party some other students had organized, and was trying to convince Mike to go with him.

"We're not invited," Mike said. "Besides, I have to study."

"But we have half of the invitation, and we know the dress code," Randy insisted, pointing to where it said guests should wear red fur. "The only thing we don't know is the location."

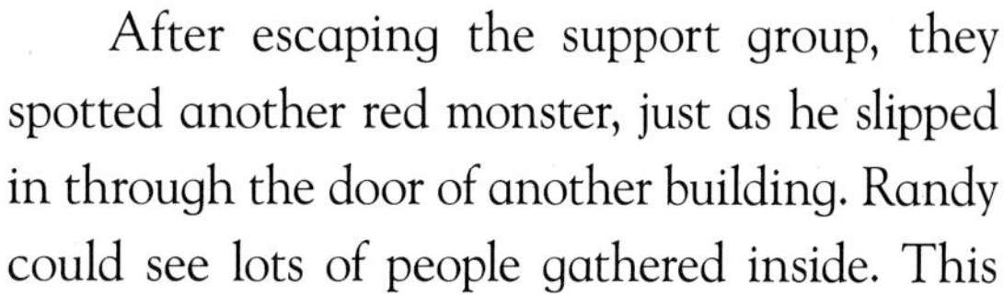

Randy reminded Mike that there would be senior scare students at the party, who could know some secret scaring tips.

That was all the convincing Mike needed. If there was a chance he might learn some new scare techniques, he was willing to give it a try.

When Randy dressed him up in red fur, Mike felt like a walking carpet. Still, Randy realized, the fur was the trick to finding their way to the party. They just had to find another monster with red fur and follow it.

Soon, they spotted a furry red monster striding towards one of the fraternity houses. This had to be it! They scurried after him and raced in the door before he could push it closed.

Instead of finding the most exclusive party of the year, though, they found a support group for homesick students. Before they knew what was happening, the big slug-like group leader gave them a big hug, smearing them in slime.

After escaping the support group, they spotted another red monster, just as he slipped in through the door of another building. Randy could see lots of people gathered inside. This had to be it.

Or maybe not....

As they entered, Mike and Randy were given a warm welcome to a Recycled Cooking Course. A bin full of rubbish was dumped on top of them. "Choose your ingredients," the teacher encouraged.

Mike and Randy spluttered as the smelly rubbish rained down on them, but then they spotted something among the litter – a party invitation, and this one showed the location!

The two monsters raced to the party and threw open the door ... only to find it had already finished. They were too late. They had missed the most exclusive event of the year.

Randy seemed to be taking it very hard. He kneeled down, staring at the floor.

"Randy ... are you okay?" Mike asked gently.

"I can't believe it," Randy said. He held up another torn-up invitation. This one was for an even more exclusive party next week.

As Randy tried to convince him they should go, Mike rolled his eye. He turned and walked off. After tonight, his partying days were well and truly over.

October

13

Disney Princess Snow White and the Seven Dwarfs

To The Rescue

Snow White and her Prince spent nearly every day together. But one morning, the Prince told Snow White that he had an errand to take care of. The Prince saddled his trusty steed, Astor, and bid Snow White farewell.

That afternoon, Snow White spotted a cloud of dust on the road. A horse was rapidly approaching. She was excited that the Prince was home early. But imagine Snow White's surprise when she saw that Astor was alone! "Why, where's the Prince?" she wondered out loud. But the horse could not say.

Snow White's tender heart filled with dread. *Surely the Prince is in trouble*, she thought. She bravely decided she must go and find him. Astor stamped her hoof on the ground and nodded towards her empty saddle.

"Do you want me to get on?" Snow White asked. Again, Astor nodded. *Goodness!* Snow White thought. *Maybe Astor can tell me where the Prince is after all!* The Princess barely had time to sit down before Astor was racing down the road towards the forest!

Astor ran deeper into the woods with Snow White tugging uselessly at the reins. If only she knew that the Prince was safe! Then, suddenly, Snow White spotted a piece of red cloth caught on a sharp thorn. Could it be? It was! A scrap torn from the Prince's very own riding cloak! And that wasn't all. As they continued through the forest, Snow White spotted petals from the rose she had given the Prince. Then she found his hat dangling from a tree!

Snow White gripped the reins with one hand. She clutched the Prince's hat and concentrated on thinking hopeful thoughts.

Finally, they emerged into a sunny clearing, and Astor slowed to a stop.

Snow White spotted the Prince, lying on the ground. She slipped out of the saddle and raced across the clearing. Breathless, Snow White reached the Prince just as he sat up and stretched.

"What a nice nap!" he said, with a grin. "I hope you're hungry!"

Snow White was bewildered. Next to the Prince lay a lavish picnic spread out on a soft blanket, and the Prince was as happy and healthy as ever!

"I knew Astor would get you here quickly," he said, beaming. "Tell me, are you surprised?"

Snow White paused for a moment to catch her breath. "Oh, yes, very surprised," she said at last, smiling. She picked up an apple and offered it to Astor.

"And," she added, "I'm very glad you have such a dear and clever horse!"

Disney Princess
Beauty and the Beast

The Birthday Surprise

On a cosy evening in front of the fire, Belle was very quiet as she sat deep in thought. The Prince encouraged her to share her thoughts and Belle sighed. "It's my horse Phillipe's birthday soon. I'd like to make him a special present this year but I'm just not sure what to do."

"What about carrots?" asked Chip as he lay on his belly doodling pictures on some parchment. "If you plant some now, they'll be ready by his birthday."

"What a lovely idea!" Belle agreed.

The next day, Belle bought some carrot seeds. She went to the garden with Chip to plant them. The Prince carried a heavy bucket into the garden and made sure the seeds were thoroughly watered.

In the days that followed, Belle checked her seeds every morning.

"They're growing so slowly," she sighed, feeling disappointed.

"Will they be ready in time?" asked Chip.

"Don't worry, my dears!" said Mrs Potts. "All will work out fine!"

When Belle took Phillipe from his stable to stretch his legs, the horse galloped straight towards the garden.

"Oh no! He can smell the C-A-R-R-O-T-S," Belle cried, spelling out the word 'carrots' so as not to ruin the surprise.

The Prince had an idea and rushed to the kitchen. On his return, he placed some apple slices on the ground for Phillipe to sniff out.

"A perfect distraction," Belle laughed.

"This will keep him away from your garden," the Prince promised.

On the day of Phillipe's birthday, Belle rushed to the garden and found that her carrots had grown big. She picked a dozen of the largest and tied them with a ribbon.

Joined by Chip and the Prince, they took the gift of carrots to the stable and cheered together. "Happy Birthday, Phillipe!"

Phillipe was excited! He neighed as he sniffed the carrots. As he started gobbling them up, Mrs Potts appeared.

"Belle, you were so worried about Phillipe's birthday you forgot something ..." she said.

Belle was puzzled.

"It's your own birthday tomorrow!" the Prince reminded her. "So we decided to celebrate today with Phillipe. It's a double celebration."

Mrs Potts presented Belle with a large carrot cake, covered in white icing and red sugar rose petals. It was the tastiest cake Belle had ever eaten and everyone agreed.

"How nice we can celebrate together," Belle smiled as she fed Phillipe some carrot cake.

It was the best birthday ever!

October

15

The Far Too Popular Poppy

BUZZ! BUZZ! Two bees were busy fighting over the same poppy.

Fawn, the animal fairy, was desperately trying to stop them. "The mainland's full of flowers," she tried to point out. "You could look for others instead of bothering this poor little thing."

But the bees took no notice of her. *BUZZ! BUZZ!* The petals of the poppy were becoming bruised as the bees bumped into it.

"Don't fight over it!" pleaded Fawn, but the bees just got cross with her as well as each other!

When one of the bees tried to drag the other off the poppy, Fawn knew she had to try something new. "All right!" she said. "I'll take care of this!"

Placing her fingers in her mouth, Fawn let out a piercing whistle. In seconds, her friends Rosetta, Iridessa, Vidia and Silvermist were flying towards her.

"Did you call us, dewdrop?" Silvermist asked kindly.

"Yes!" cried Fawn in relief. "I need your help!" She showed them the problem.

One of the bees had managed to tie up the petals of the poppy tightly and was sitting on it, while the other buzzed angrily round and round. The poor poppy couldn't take much more of a battering!

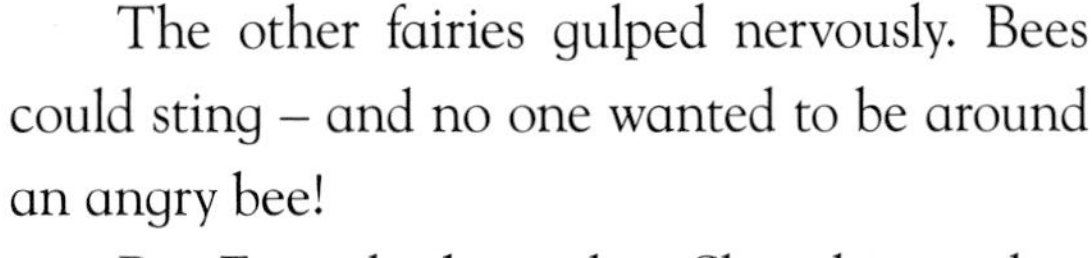

The other fairies gulped nervously. Bees could sting – and no one wanted to be around an angry bee!

But Fawn had an idea. She whispered to the others, and as everyone heard the plan, they began to smile. This could work! But it would require all of their talents....

First, Vidia whipped up a wind that pulled the seeds out of the middle of the poppy, while also blowing the bees backwards in surprise.

"Now let's plant them!" Rosetta said, sprinkling the seeds on the dry earth.

"And water them," added Silvermist, creating a fine rain to fall on the ground. The bees watched suspiciously.

"All we need now is a little sunshine," said Iridessa, diverting a ray from the sun to fall exactly in the right place.

WHOOSH! Stalks sprouted from the ground, leaves unfurled, and hundreds of poppies bloomed in the sun! The bees couldn't believe their eyes! It was a dream come true!

"Now let's see who wants to argue!" Fawn laughed.

As the bees dived into the beautiful new flowers, the five friends put their hands together. Any problem could be solved with faith, trust and pixie dust!

Disney Princess
The Princess and the Frog

The Jewel of the Bayou

One morning, Tiana, Naveen, Eudora and Charlotte were discussing Tiana's birthday party, which was happening later that day. Prince Naveen was worried – he still hadn't found the perfect gift for his princess!

Nothing had seemed special enough for Princess Tiana. But luckily, Naveen had overheard Tiana and Charlotte in the kitchen.

"When my daddy and I used to go fishing in the bayou, we'd sometimes find a piece of swamp amber," Tiana said. "It was the most precious thing!"

"That's it!" Naveen whispered to himself.

Naveen met with Louis, the jazz-loving alligator. They were going to find Tiana some swamp amber!

As the birthday party was about to begin, Tiana couldn't find Naveen anywhere. A guest said he saw the Prince down by the old, mossy tree in the bayou. Tiana was afraid Naveen was in trouble.

She ran to the river and climbed into a rowboat. She saw Naveen in the distance. He dived into the water by the old tree.

"Naveen!" Tiana called out. When the prince didn't reappear, she dived into the water!

She found Naveen in a tangle of roots. Tiana grabbed his hand and pulled him up to the surface.

Naveen reassured her that everything was fine and gave her a hug. He opened his hand to reveal a plain, muddy rock. "I was expecting a sparkling jewel, but this is just...."

"Swamp amber!" Tiana exclaimed happily. "Oh, Naveen, what a wonderful birthday surprise!"

Later, when Charlotte saw the birthday gift she screamed in fright. But Tiana explained that the rock brought back loving memories of her father.

"And that is the most precious gift of all," said Tiana, smiling at Naveen.

Mama Odie picked up the swamp amber. "Hmm, a little sparkle couldn't hurt," she said, tossing the rock into a pot of gumbo. "Gumbo, gumbo in the pot, we need some sparkle. What you got?"

In a puff of magic, the plain swamp amber became a dazzling golden jewel set in a fine necklace.

"Mama Odie!" Naveen exclaimed. "How did you do that?"

Mama Odie winked at Tiana.

"Oh, it's just a talent we have down here in the bayou. We like to take things that are a little slimy and rough around the edges and turn 'em into something wonderful!"

"Like turning a frog into a prince!" Naveen agreed, as he and Tiana danced the night away.

Disney Princess
The Little Mermaid

Ariel's New Move

"Whoa." Prince Eric brought the carriage to a stop. Beside him, Ariel barely managed to keep from sliding off the seat. She had been human for just a short time, and she wasn't used to her legs yet.

"Are you hungry?" the Prince asked. Eric gestured towards a restaurant and looked at Ariel expectantly.

Ariel smiled and nodded. She could not speak, having traded her voice for legs, and she was a little wary of eating. Humans ate fish, and she could not help but think of her best friend, Flounder, whenever she saw something scaly lying on a plate. But she wanted to please the Prince.

The restaurant was nearly empty. Eric and Ariel sat at a table for two as the owner approached them.

"What'll it be?" asked a woman with white hair, looking kindly at Ariel.

"She'll have ... the soup?" Eric looked at Ariel for confirmation. Ariel nodded. "And I will have the speciality of the house."

Ariel was glad that Eric didn't seem to mind talking for her, though she desperately wanted to speak for herself and tell him how much she enjoyed being with him.

When the owner walked away, the silence in the room seemed to grow. Ariel tried to communicate with gestures, but Eric didn't seem to understand and, after a few minutes, the poor girl started to feel foolish.

With a sigh of relief, Ariel noticed the owner coming back with their food. Eric seemed relieved too. After she set down the plates, the white-haired woman walked over to a tall wooden piece of furniture near the wall. She sat down in front of it and placed her hands on the black and white keys.

Ariel had never seen a piano before. And she had never heard one either. She was enchanted by the music. She let her spoon drop into her bowl. The song was lovely – happy and sad at the same time. She wanted to sing along! But, of course, she could not. Still, she could not break away. The music reminded her of the rhythms of the ocean. She stood and began to sway, but her new legs were so awkward, she stumbled.

Suddenly, Eric's strong arm was round Ariel's waist. With his other arm, he took Ariel's hand in his. Ariel looked startled. "Haven't you ever danced before?" the Prince asked.

Ariel shook her head shyly.

"I'll show you," the Prince said, smiling at her. He whirled Ariel around the floor. The Little Mermaid was a natural. She spun and smiled, glad that they had found a way to communicate without words.

October

18

DISNEY 101 DALMATIANS

A Helping Paw

The dairy barn was warm and cosy, and 99 exhausted, hungry pups were taking turns to drink warm milk from the motherly cows.

"We'd nearly given up hope that you would get here," the kindly collie said to Pongo and Perdita, who had just arrived with the puppies.

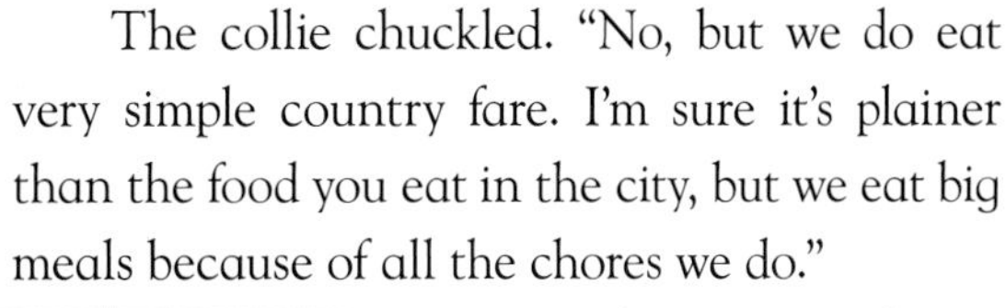

"We're so very grateful to you for your hospitality," Perdita murmured wearily.

"Just look at the little dears," said one of the cows. "I've never seen so many puppies in one place before!"

Pongo, Perdita and the puppies had just come in from a long and weary march in the cold. It was very late, and the pups waiting for a drink of milk could barely keep their eyes open. The puppies had recently managed to escape from the dreadful old house owned by Cruella De Vil. They had been held prisoner there, guarded by two villains named Horace and Jasper. Cruella was planning to make a fur coat out of their lovely spotted fur. Luckily Pongo and Perdita had rescued them all just in the nick of time.

After the pups finshed their dinners, they gathered around the collie to thank him for his hospitality.

"Not at all, not at all," the collie replied.

"Do you have warm milk for supper every night out here in the country?" asked Rolly.

The collie chuckled. "No, but we do eat very simple country fare. I'm sure it's plainer than the food you eat in the city, but we eat big meals because of all the chores we do."

"And is it always this cold in the country?" asked Patch.

"Well, now," replied the collie. "I suppose most of you come from the city. No, it isn't always this cold, but there are plenty of differences between living in the country and living in the city. Take leads, for instance. We don't keep our pets on leads here, the way you do in the city, since our pets have a lot of wide-open space to roam around in. There aren't as many dogs nearby, but there are certainly other sorts of animals that one doesn't see in the city. Take cows, for instance. And then there are sheep and horses and geese, and...."

Suddenly, the collie stopped talking. A tiny snore escaped one of the pups he had just been talking to. He looked around and realized that every one of the pups, as well as Pongo and Perdita, had fallen into a deep sleep.

"Poor little things," he said quietly, as he trotted outside to stand guard. "They've been through so much. I do hope they get home safely soon."

October

19

Disney · PIXAR TOY STORY 3

Rescue Mission

Up in her bedroom, Bonnie was playing with the toys. They were having an outer space adventure, and Bonnie laughed as she swooshed and looped Buzz around and around.

When Bonnie was called downstairs, she put Buzz on the windowsill, next to Woody – and right beside the open window! A gust of wind pushed the spaceman backwards, knocking him out of the window!

As the other toys raced up onto the windowsill, Woody leaned out and looked down. "Don't worry. He's holding onto the house," Woody said. He reached a hand down to his pal, who was clinging tightly to a plank of wood. "I've almost ... got him!" Woody said, but then he lost his grip and he tumbled out of the window, too!

Buzz and Woody grabbed hands, and both fell towards the hard stone path far below!

"There's a snake in my boot," said Woody's voice feature as the string on his back caught on a nail sticking out of the house, stopping their fall.

"Pull us up!" Woody shouted, as he and Buzz dangled helplessly in mid-air.

But before the other toys could organize a rescue mission, they heard Bonnie coming back.

The toys ducked for cover as Bonnie raced into the room. When she saw that Woody and Buzz were missing, she realized what must have happened. She flew down the stairs calling for her mum, then they both ran outside.

"Are you sure they fell out the window?" Bonnie's mum asked, searching the flower beds.

"Yes, I left them on the windowsill. The wind must have knocked them out," Bonnie insisted. "I hope they're not broken!"

Bonnie's mum stood up and looked around. "Where are they? I don't see them."

High overhead, Woody was starting to worry. All those batteries meant that Buzz was a heavy toy and Woody wouldn't be able to hold him forever. "She'll never find us up here," he groaned.

"We've got to get her attention," said Buzz.

"How?" asked Woody. "We can't just say 'Hey, we're up here!'"

Buzz shook his head. "No, but there's something else we can say." He cupped a hand to his mouth took a deep breath and shouted, "There's a snake in my boot!"

That did the trick! Buzz sounded almost exactly like Woody. Bonnie and her mum looked up. Bonnie cheered as she realized her toys were safe and sound.

As Bonnie's mum went to get the ladder, Woody winked at Buzz. "Good job, pal," he whispered. "I loved that imitation!"

Disney Princess Sleeping Beauty

Trouble in the Forest

In their cosy little cottage, Aurora and the good fairies sat at the table to eat breakfast.

"Do we have to have raspberries again?" complained Merryweather. "I'd rather eat blueberries instead."

"There aren't any blueberry bushes for miles," Flora replied.

After they'd eaten, the fairies noticed something.

Fauna asked, "Where is Merryweather?"

"She might have gone off to get blueberries," Flora realized worriedly.

Quickly wrapping their capes round their shoulders, Flora and Fauna set off to find her. "Wait here, Aurora, in case she comes home," said Fauna.

Aurora waved from the cottage door.

Several hours passed and Aurora started to grow concerned. She put on her cloak and left the cottage to look for her friends. "Do you know where the blueberries grow?" she asked the woodland animals. The forest looked the same to her and she had no idea which way to go.

The animals led Aurora along a shady path. She spotted a piece of Merryweather's blue cape dangling from a sharp branch and gasped. "We're on the right track!"

Suddenly, she heard two familiar voices. "Aurora? Is that you?" they called.

Aurora looked up to find Flora and Fauna dangling from a tree ... caught in a net!

"I'll get you down!" Aurora exclaimed, climbing up the tree as quickly as possible.

"Be careful," the fairies warned her.

Aurora untied the knots and lowered the fairies safely to the forest floor, where they untangled themselves. As they brushed leaves off their gowns, Aurora saw a hole nearby.

"Help!" came a squeak.

They rushed to the hole and found Merryweather at the bottom, covered in mud.

"Grab the net," Aurora instructed. The fairies pulled the net over and lowered it into the hole so Merryweather could use it as a ladder.

"You rescued us all," Merryweather cried.

Just then, hooves sounded in the forest.

"Hunters!" hissed Fauna. "Hide!"

Aurora and the fairies hid behind a blueberry bush as two hunters arrived. They inspected their traps and scratched their heads. Then an owl friend flew down from a tree and started pecking at the hunters' heads.

Aurora stifled a giggle and soon the men were chasing after the bird, deep into the woods.

"Let's go," Fauna whispered.

Back at the cottage, Aurora pulled Merryweather's basket from behind her back as a surprise. It was full of fresh, ripe blueberries.

It had certainly been an adventurous day but it had been worth it!

Following a Dream

It was a sunny day in Never Land, and Tinker Bell's friends were hard at work. Iridessa scooped sunlight into her hands, Silvermist gathered dewdrops from the pond, Fawn was teaching a baby squirrel how to collect nuts and Rosetta was painting flowers.

Tink flew down to meet them, smiling. "You seem pretty happy today," said Silvermist.

Tinker Bell whirled in the air. "Just before dawn, I had a wonderful dream!"

Her friends gathered around her excitedly. "You're really lucky!" Rosetta said.

Silvermist nodded. "Yes! According to an ancient legend, the last dream a fairy has before waking up always comes true!"

"Ooh," replied Tink. "That's flitterific!"

The others laughed. "What did you dream about?" asked Rosetta.

Tink hesitated. "I ... I don't ... I don't remember anymore."

"What a shame," sighed Rosetta. "Then your dream won't come true."

Iridessa saw Tink's face fall. "Don't worry," she said. "We'll help you remember it."

"After all," added Fawn, "we're your best friends, aren't we?"

The fairies tried to guess what Tink's dream might have been. "You might have dreamed of drifting on a water lily," suggested Silvermist.

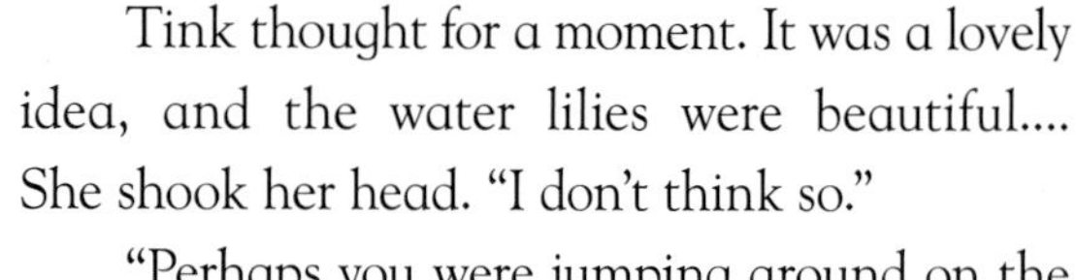

Tink thought for a moment. It was a lovely idea, and the water lilies were beautiful.... She shook her head. "I don't think so."

"Perhaps you were jumping around on the clouds?" called Iridessa, from high up in the sky.

Tink smiled up at her. "Not that either."

Maybe she had dreamed about flowers? Rosetta took Tink over to the tallest pink flowers, just blossomed, and got her to take a big sniff. Had that jogged her memory?

But no, Tink was sure she hadn't dreamed about flowers. That was a garden fairy dream!

Fawn's suggestion was a chorus of chirping birds. She got a friendly bird to sing a song, in case it helped Tink remember her dream.

But it wasn't that either! Sadly, she shook her head. Her dream wouldn't come true!

Her friends felt sorry for her. "We've tried everything," Silvermist said. "Sorry, Tink."

"Thanks anyway," Tink said gratefully. "You're good friends."

Good friends.... That was it!

"I remember!" Tink exclaimed. "I dreamed I spent a wonderful morning with my best friends!"

They all burst out laughing. "You were right!" Tink said, as they all flew into the air to celebrate. "My wonderful dream really did come true!"

Disney · PIXAR
FINDING NEMO

A Whale of a Tale

"Hop aboard, explorers!" called Mr Ray. Nemo, Tad and the rest of the class jumped on the back of the big manta ray. It was 'special guest' week and they were going to the Drop-off.

When they reached the edge of the reef, a royal blue tang fish swam up to meet them.

"And here is today's special guest," announced Mr Ray.

"Hello, everyone," said the blue tang. "My name is Dory ... um ... is it? Yes! Just kidding! I'm Dory, and I'm very happy to be here!"

"Dory, can you teach us something about whales today?" asked Mr Ray.

"Well, let's see ... whales are very big, but they eat little creatures called krill. And I should know. One whale I met *almost* ate me –"

"So it's not true!" blurted Tad.

"What's not true?" Dory asked.

"Sandy Plankton said Nemo made up that story about how you and Nemo's dad got eaten by a whale!" said Tad.

"I did not make it up!" cried Nemo.

"Well," said Dory, "technically, Sandy Plankton is right. We weren't actually *eaten* by the whale –"

Tad smirked, until Dory added, "We were just in the whale's mouth for a mighty long time!"

"Whoa!" said the class. They were quite impressed. Tad frowned.

"You see, the whale was just giving us a ride to Sydney. I find if you talk to a whale beforehand, you can clear up most ingestion issues," Dory explained.

"Excellent lesson!" said Mr Ray. "Now teach us a few words in whale."

"Oh, okay," said Dory. "Now repeat after me. Haaaaavvve aaaaaaaaa nnnniiiiice daaaaayyyy!"

"Haaaavvve aaaaaa nnnniiiice daaaayy!" the class repeated.

"Very good!" said Dory.

"This is stupid," said Tad. "You didn't...."

Suddenly, Tad stopped talking. Everyone just stared at Dory in horror.

Slowly, Dory turned round. A blue whale was right behind her!

Dory simply shrugged and told the whale, "Weeeee weerrrrre juuuuuuuussst praaaaactisinnnng!"

With a loud bellow, the whale wished her a nice day anyway, then swam off.

"So, Tad, do you believe Dory now?" asked Nemo.

"Wow, that was *so* cool!" cried Tad. "I can't wait to tell Sandy Plankton how I was almost eaten by a whale!"

Nemo and Dory just sighed.

Disney MINNIE

Scaredy-Cat Sleepover

Minnie was having a sleepover at her best friend Daisy's house!

"I've got lots of stuff planned!" Daisy told her. "First, we're making cupcakes!"

The friends got right to work mixing, baking and decorating.

"Yummy!" Daisy said.

Next it was time for a fashion show. Minnie looked at the fancy, sparkly dress she was wearing. "I look just like a Christmas tree!" she laughed.

Minnie and Daisy then changed into pyjamas. It was time to watch a film.

They settled on a scary film called *The Invisible Monster with Three-metre Claws.* Minnie and Daisy watched as an actress entered a spooky mansion, the door slamming shut.

"You'll never get me, monster!" the actress cried. The monster chased her all over the house.

"Eeek!" Minnie and Daisy watched the rest of the film with the lights on.

When it was over, the friends got ready for bed. But an hour later, they were still awake.

"That film scared me," Minnie admitted.

"Me, too!" replied Daisy.

Minnie suggested they drink some warm milk to make themselves sleepy. After two big mugs, they were back in bed ... and still awake.

"It's not working," Daisy groaned.

"Let's try counting sheep," Minnie replied.

They closed their eyes and began picturing a meadow full of them.

Finally, the girls started to drift off. Then, suddenly, they heard a loud *SCRATCH!*

"What was that?" Daisy cried.

"Maybe it was just a branch scraping against the window?" Minnie said, huddling under her blanket.

"Yes, that must be it," replied Daisy.

A few minutes later, they heard more scratching and a loud *SCREECH!*

"Aaah!" yelled the girls.

"What if it's the monster?" asked Daisy.

Minnie took a deep breath. "We have to investigate," said Minnie.

They tiptoed towards the scratching sound, which was coming from outside the front door.

"Let's peek out of the window," said Daisy.

Minnie pulled aside the curtain and gasped.

"Kittens!" cried Minnie, throwing open the door and bringing them inside.

"They must be lost," Daisy said.

"We'll ask around town tomorrow and find out who they belong to," Minnie replied.

"Who would have guessed that our monster would turn out to be cute?" Minnie asked as she snuggled back into her bed.

Just a few minutes later, Minnie, Daisy and the not-so-scary kittens were all fast asleep!

Disney
THE
LION KING

Hakuna Matata

"Why are you so sad?" Pumbaa asked Nala.

"I'm not sad," Nala said. "I'm just a little more on the serious side than the two of you."

"I think you could use a little *hakuna matata*," Pumbaa said.

"A whona mawhatta?" Nala asked.

"You really think she can handle it?" Timon whispered to Pumbaa out of the side of his mouth.

"Of course I can handle it!" Nala said, raising her voice. "I just need to know what it is first."

"Ahhh, *hakuna matata*," Pumbaa said dreamily. "It's the problem-free way of dealing with all of life's inconveniences."

"It means, 'No worries'," Timon explained.

"Oh, I get it," Nala said. "Instead of dealing with your problems, you just ignore them and pretend they don't exist."

"*Hakuna matata* helps you relax," Pumbaa tried to point out.

"It sounds like your *hakuna matata* is just another way of saying 'uninspired and lazy'," Nala continued.

"I think she might have just insulted us," Timon whispered to Pumbaa.

"There you are," Simba called as he came walking towards them. "What are the three of you up to?"

"I was just learning about a strange little notion called *hakuna matata,*" Nala explained.

"Isn't it great!" Simba said with a grin.

"Well, sure," Nala said. "If you don't ever want to get anything done."

Simba frowned. "It's not like that. *Hakuna matata* will help you get through things."

"Yeah, sure," Nala replied. "*Hakuna matata* – I don't have to worry. I don't have to try."

"I guess you could look at it that way," Simba said. "But, for me, it means, 'Don't worry about it right now. It's okay.' It gives me the strength to get through the bad times."

"Wow, I hadn't thought about it like that," Nala said.

"So, are you ready to join us now?" Timon asked.

"Absolutely!" Nala smiled.

"Then bring on the crunchy beetles!" shouted Pumbaa.

"And let's go tease some elephants!" cried Timon.

"Everyone to the mudhole for a mud fight!" Simba yelled, and the three of them started off.

"Oh, dear," murmured Nala, "this isn't exactly what I had in mind." But she smiled, and ran after her carefree friends. "Last one to the mudhole is a rotten egg!" she cried.

Disney Princess
Cinderella

A Sweet Royal Visit

On a school day that started like any other, the children suddenly heard horse hooves outside and rushed to see. A carriage halted outside the gates and whispers spread like wild fire as to who it could be.

"The Princess is coming!" the girls cried, when they spotted a flash of Cinderella's blue dress. She was paying them all an unexpected visit.

The headmistress greeted the Princess. "Welcome!" she said. "Such a wonderful surprise!"

The school children lined up and curtsied as Cinderella entered.

"I've come to tell you that in one week's time, there will be a grand ball at the castle ... to be held in your honour. I'm having dresses made for each of you as well!" said Cinderella.

The girls clapped in joy, but one girl in particular was over the moon! Her name was Emma and she loved Cinderella.

That afternoon, Emma gazed at the castle from the playground. She couldn't wait to see what it was like inside. In fact, she was so curious that when she spotted a group of royal dressmakers she hid among them and sneaked into the palace grounds.

Luckily for Emma, the dressmakers thought the little girl had been sent to them to try on all the dresses that were being made for the ball.

"Oh my!" said Cinderella, as she entered the room and saw Emma parading around in a beautiful new gown. "You look beautiful!"

Later that day, Cinderella invited Emma to tea after all her hard work modelling outfits.

"It must be wonderful to be a Princess," said Emma.

Cinderella laughed. "There's more to being a Princess than parties," she said. "I'll show you...."

Cinderella busied herself around the castle, making sure everything was running smoothly and preparing supplies for the poor and hungry. She put baskets together containing food, books and clothing for schools and orphanages.

Emma was so amazed with Cinderella's kind heart and how she managed all her duties that Emma visited the palace to help every day!

When at last the ball arrived, Emma and her school friends swirled on the dance floor in their magnificent dresses.

"I still wish I could be a Princess," said Emma to Cinderella.

"Well, because you've worked so hard for me," said Cinderella, "I'm making you an honorary princess for the evening."

Emma was thrilled. "Thank you!" she cried.

And for one perfect, magical night, Emma felt like royalty.

Disney Princess Sleeping Beauty

The Crown of Diamonds

It was Aurora's 17th birthday, and she had some surprises awaiting her.

Her mother, the Queen, came in to wish her happy birthday. She led Aurora to a huge portrait hall.

"Why, Mother! Is that you?" exclaimed Aurora, pointing to a portrait. The Queen was wearing a crown with a beautiful pink, heart-shaped diamond.

"Indeed, I was 17," said the Queen. "It's a tradition that on a princess's 17th birthday, this crown is to be passed down by her mother, and worn until the princess becomes queen. However, she must answer three riddles," her mother said with a smile.

The three fairies, Flora, Fauna and Merryweather, flew in. "Happy birthday, Princess!" said Merryweather. "We're here to give you your clues!"

Flora recited the first riddle. "To the eyes, it's a treat – to the nose, a delight. To the hand it can be quite a fright. Though few think to taste it, its sweetness still shows. To this first riddle, the answer's a...."

"Let's see," said Aurora. "'To the eye, it's a treat. To the nose, a delight.' So it's pretty and smells good. 'To the hand quite a fright.' Like a thorn – on a rose. That's it!" She hurried off to the garden, and picked the biggest rose.

"Very good!" exclaimed Fauna. "And now for the second one – 'Some plant it, some blow it away. Some do it several times in a day. Some may blush getting this on their cheek.' Can you guess?"

"It's a kiss, isn't it?" Aurora laughed. She kissed each fairy, causing them to blush.

"Now it's my turn!" exclaimed Merryweather. "What only gets stronger the longer it lives? Some say it's blind, some say it's true, some simply say, 'I feel this for you.'" Aurora thought hard. Just then Prince Phillip walked by.

"Happy birthday, my love!" he called. Instantly, Aurora knew the answer. She hurried up to her mother's sewing room.

"I've solved the riddles!" Aurora exclaimed. She handed her the pink rose and gave her a kiss on the cheek.

"Very good!" declared the Queen. "And the answer to the third riddle?"

"It's love," said Aurora.

The Queen proudly placed the crown on Aurora's head.

That afternoon, Aurora had her portrait painted, so it could be hung in the portrait hall alongside her mother's.

"Happy birthday, Aurora," her mother warmly told her. "May you have many more!"

October
27

A Perfect Hiding Place

Tinker Bell and her friends were playing hide-and-seek with their human friend Lizzy. No one could beat Lizzy at hide-and-seek because she was just too good!

"Nineteen ... twenty! Ready or not, here I come!" called Lizzy. She looked around her bedroom. Fairies were tiny ... but Lizzy had sharp eyes!

"I see you, Fawn!" she cried, spotting the animal fairy hiding behind a toadstool on a shelf.

"How'd you find me?" exclaimed Fawn.

Lizzy grinned and kept looking. Over on another shelf there was a toy kangaroo.... "Hi, Tinker Bell," Lizzy giggled.

Tink climbed out of the kangaroo's pouch. She'd been sure it was the perfect hiding place!

"Caught you, Iridessa!"

The light fairy climbed out of the bedside lampshade. "I was so well hidden!" she sighed.

Lizzy kept looking. Not behind the curtains ... not among her books ... something caught her eye. Her sewing box lid was open! "Found you too, Bobble!" she laughed.

Bobble tugged on Lizzy's plait fondly. "You're a great fairy-finder," he said.

Lizzy hadn't finished. "The only one left is Clank...." Carefully, she looked through the rest of her bedroom. Under the rug, inside her drawers ... but no! There was no sign of Clank.

Lizzy felt disappointed. She was usually so good at finding the fairies! "Would you all help me find him?" she asked the others.

"Sure!" Tinker Bell and her friends joined in. But after some serious searching, they were baffled!

"He isn't under the bed," said Iridessa.

"Or in the wardrobe," added Tink.

Fawn shook her head. "He's disappeared!"

They tried calling him. "Claaaank! Come on out!"

THUMP!

"What was that?" Iridessa asked, alarmed.

"I don't know," said Tink, "but it came from in there!" It was the fairy house Lizzy had made in the hope of finding a fairy. And now the home-made fairy house lived in her bedroom – but no one had thought to look inside it!

Tink pushed open the door, and saw Clank lying on the floor next to the fairy bed, rubbing his head. "Clank! Why didn't you answer us?"

"I hid," said Clank, dazed, "but the bed was so cosy that I fell asleep! Then your shouts startled me and...." He rubbed his head again.

"You bumped your head!" Tink realized.

The other fairies chuckled at Clank's misfortune. "Next time," suggested Fawn, "you'd better pick an uncomfortable hiding place!"

Hide-and-seek was lots of fun – as long as no one fell asleep!

October
28

Lady and the Tramp

Like Father, Like Son

Tramp had a whole new life. He had gone from being a stray to becoming a member of the Dear household. And now, he and Lady were proud parents.

But Tramp was finding it difficult to change some of his old ways.

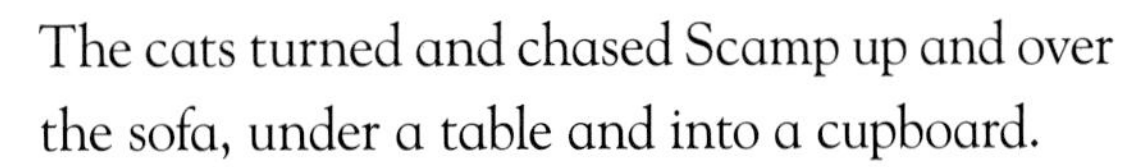

"Tramp," Lady said gently, "you need to set an example for the puppies – especially Scamp."

Scamp had an adventurous side, just like his dad. So, it wasn't surprising that father and son often got carried away when they played together. They couldn't resist the urge to roll in a puddle of mud – and then chase each other across the clean kitchen floor.

Soon, Aunt Sarah and her two troublesome cats, Si and Am, were going to be visiting. Lady was worried.

"Don't worry. I promise to keep Scamp away from those troublemakers," Tramp said.

"And?" replied Lady.

"And I promise to stay away from them, too," Tramp added.

When the big day came, Lady and Tramp herded their pups into a bedroom and told them to stay. But Scamp was curious. He slipped out of the room and hid behind the sitting room sofa. Then he sneaked up behind the cats and swiped at their tails as they flicked back and forth. The cats turned and chased Scamp up and over the sofa, under a table and into a cupboard.

Well, Tramp thought, *I suppose I'm going to have to chase those nasty old cats whether I want to or not!*

He enthusiastically dived into the cupboard. Seconds later, Tramp and Scamp emerged. Much to Aunt Sarah's horror, Si and Am were later found inside, tied together with a scarf. When no one was looking, Tramp and Scamp shared a victory wink.

Tramp and Scamp were banished to the garden for their antics. When Lady came out that evening, she found that they had dug up the entire garden looking for bones. Father and son saw the look on Lady's face and knew that they were about to get a lecture.

Tramp looked at Lady innocently. "You want him to get exercise, don't you?" he asked.

"Try it, Mum!" Scamp cried. "It's fun."

"What am I going to do with you two?" Lady said, laughing.

Tramp and Scamp dragged a huge bone out from behind the kennel.

"Join us for dinner?" Tramp replied.

"Well, all right," Lady said. "But, as soon as we're done, we're cleaning up this garden."

"Yes, ma'am!" chorused Tramp and Scamp, looking very pleased with themselves.

A Thorny Rescue

Rex leaned over Andy's video game controller, hitting the buttons as fast as his little arms could. Andy's new video game was great fun, but it sure was tricky!

"Go, buddy! Hit that alien!" Buzz cheered, but Rex knew better.

"No! I'm trying to avoid him. See? It's written here," Rex said, holding up a list of tricks Andy had written down on how to complete the game.

Rex cried out in shock as a sudden gust of wind snatched the page of notes from him and carried it out of the window!

"The notes have blown away!" he yelled.

"Well, shoot my pistols," said Woody, rushing to join Buzz and Rex at the window.

"They've landed in the neighbour's front garden," Buzz said, pointing to the page. "Getting 'em back will be child's play."

But Woody had spotted a problem. The postman was strolling up the path, right towards the instructions! The toys watched in horror as the postman picked up the note, then stuffed it into the neighbours' postbox.

"Oh no!" Rex groaned. He had no hope of completing the game without those instructions.

"We'll go get 'em," smiled Woody.

Sticking his fingers in his mouth, Woody let out a shrill whistle. A moment later, Buster the dog came running into the room. Woody and Buzz jumped onto Buster's back, then held on tightly as he raced down the stairs and out into the neighbours' garden.

"Up we go," said Woody, as they arrived at the bottom of the postbox.

Buzz frowned at the tangle of spikey thorns which had grown all around the postbox's post. "Those thorns might tear my space suit."

Woody agreed. The thorns were a problem. Luckily, he was an excellent problem-solver.

"Up on your hind legs, Buster!" he cried.

Panting happily, Buster did as he was told. On his back legs, the dog was still not quite tall enough to reach the postbox, though, which meant it was time for some acrobatics!

Very carefully, Woody and Buzz climbed up onto the pup's head. Woody braced himself as Buzz clambered onto his shoulders.

"Ugh, you weigh more than Hamm with a full belly," Woody gasped. They all wobbled unsteadily as Buzz stretched up and....

Yes! With a final stretch, Buzz caught the edge of the note. They had done it. Woody and Buzz had saved the day. There was no mission they couldn't handle together, but Woody really hoped they wouldn't have to tackle another adventure any time soon!

Disney Princess
Beauty and the Beast

The Mysterious Message

On a cosy autumn evening, Belle found a dusty book in the library and settled down to read to her friends. But there was a problem....

As Belle neared the end of the book, she discovered that the last chapter was missing! "Someone has ripped it out!"

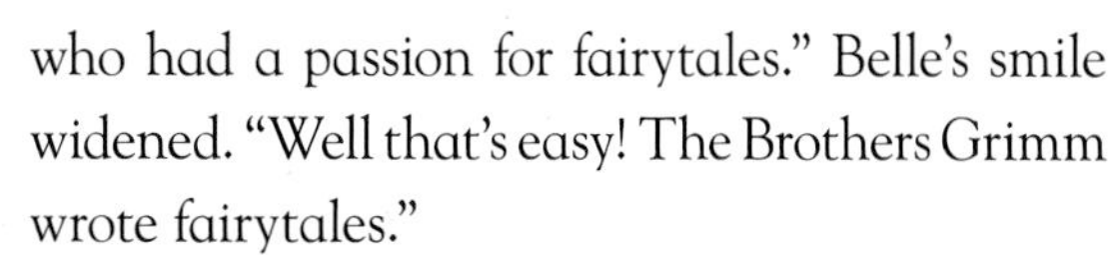

Her friends sighed. They were enjoying the tale of a brave Knight who fought dragons. Now they'd never know if he won the heart of the Princess.

"There's a note sticking out," said Cogsworth.

The note spoke of a young master mistreating the book and explained that the final chapter could be found by answering three riddles.

"The young master is the Beast! This was his favourite book as a boy," Lumiere realized.

Belle read the clue out loud. "It does not fight when empty. It makes a metal sound. His footprint holds a clue...."

She thought deeply.

"I think it's the piano!" cried Chip.

They rushed to the piano and lifted the lid, but there was nothing inside.

"Wait!" said Belle. "I think I know!"

Wandering along the corridors, Belle checked under the feet of every suit of armour until she found an old sheet of paper.

"That's it!" she cheered. "The note says that you'll get the next clue from two brothers who had a passion for fairytales." Belle's smile widened. "Well that's easy! The Brothers Grimm wrote fairytales."

Again, they marched through the house until they reached the library. Belle located the book quickly and found the next clue tucked safely between its pages.

"The final clue!" she read aloud. "You're almost home. You'll find it underneath the elf."

Belle looked at her friends expectantly. They stared back in confusion.

"We have no idea," Cogsworth admitted. "There are no elves in the castle. Not even garden ornaments."

Belle heaved a great sigh. She had no choice but to ask the Beast for help.

Finding the Beast in his armchair, she explained her quest and showed him the book.

"I remember this!" Beast's face lit up. "And I know what my old tutor means by 'under the elf'. Come with me!" The Beast took Belle by the hand and led her outside. "My favourite hiding place was by a rock shaped like an elf."

They dug holes around the rock until they found a box. In the box was the missing chapter!

"We did it!" Belle cheered. "We solved it!"

And that night, huddled around the fireplace, everyone listened to Belle reading the final chapter ... even the Beast!

Disney MINNIE

A Monstrously Fun Party

It wasn't long till Halloween, and the students of Mouston School were getting excited. Minnie Mouse and her best friend Daisy were talking to the foreign exchange student Augustus. "How do you like it here?" Minnie asked.

Augustus beamed. "There are so many new things to learn about your country – like Halloween! What an interesting tradition that is."

"We're arranging a party," Minnie told him. "Then you'll see what Halloween is all about!"

"That's what you think!" someone shouted. It was Abigail, the meanest girl in the school. "To see the real Halloween, you'll have to come to the coolest event of the season – my party!"

"Daisy and I are planning a huge party!" Minnie replied.

Abigail snorted. "Let Augustus judge whose party is the most fun."

"Okay!" Minnie accepted the challenge, but later confessed to Daisy that she didn't even know where to hold her party! Daisy pointed across a field to the old abandoned school building on the cliff top. It was the perfect place!

The race was on to create the perfect party. Minnie and Daisy carved out pumpkins and hung ghostly pillowcases up to scare their guests – but preparations took so much time that they forgot to pick up their Halloween costumes! "Oh no!" groaned Minnie as the shopkeeper showed them all he had left – two not-at-all-scary monster costumes!

But that wasn't the worst thing. Abigail had hired a tent in the shape of a castle and parked it right next to the abandoned school building!

"It looks like a film set," Minnie sighed. Was their party going to be a disaster?

Their school friends started arriving – but Abigail took one look at a kid dressed as a large blue Yeti and kicked him out of her party! The Yeti headed over to Minnie and Daisy's party instead – where he was met with quite a sight! The friends' monster costumes were so big and lumbering that they kept knocking over sweets and decorations! The Yeti started laughing ...

... and then the lights went out! Abigail had switched off the electricity!

It was time to light the pumpkins – and suddenly Minnie and Daisy's party was spooky, scary and way more fun than Abigail's! Everyone poured into the school building. Then the Yeti took off his costume – it was Augustus! "I had a great time," he said happily.

Abigail fumed. She had lost the bet!

Minnie and Daisy high fived each other. Friendship would always win in a competition!

Disney · PIXAR
BRAVE

The Royal Contest

In DunBroch forest, the earth rumbled with the sounds of heavy hooves galloping.

"No need to run, Merida," teased her father, the King. "Just try and beat me!"

Merida squinted her eyes, nudging her trusty horse faster. She let an arrow fly at the same time as her father and watched as it whizzed through the air. It struck the target hanging from a tree.

"Oh no!" Merida complained, scowling at her arrow. It was a few centimetres away from her father's, which had hit the target dead centre. "I was sure I'd made it."

"You just get distracted," said the King. "You must act as if no one is around you. Even in the noisiest chaos."

Merida gripped her bow in one hand and reins in the other. "Let's try again," she insisted.

"Oh, Merida ... again?" groaned the King.

"Yes!" Merida urged him determinedly. "But this time we'll shoot at that old clawed trunk growing from the cliff." She pointed to a tree emerging from a rocky wall.

"Are you joking?" the King wondered. "We can't get that from here. It's impossible."

"Dad!" cried Merida. "Same bet as before."

"Fine." He nodded.

Father and daughter aimed their arrows at the clawed trunk and set them loose. Slicing a straight line through the air, Merida's struck the trunk with ease, but the King's arrow arced over the tree and landed among the rocks.

"Yes!" cried Merida. "I did it!"

"No!" yelled the King. "It's not possible!"

Back at the castle, Merida couldn't wait to tell her mum, the Queen, the news of her victory.

"Can you believe it? I hit the clawed trunk!"

Her mum frowned. "A Princess does not place weapons at the table. When will you learn?"

Merida quickly slipped her bow onto the floor.

The triplets started making a scene, battling each other with bread rolls on forks.

"You three, sit properly!" the Queen scolded.

ROARRRR!

Everyone at the table snapped to attention at the strange noise and turned their heads slowly towards the King.

"Fergus?" said the Queen, in confusion.

The King was wearing a bear skin and raising his hands like clawed paws.

"It's part of the bet I made with Merida," he explained. "I have to be a bear for a day, because I lost."

Laughter filled the great hall, but the Queen put her head in her hands. Sometimes Fergus could be just as bad as the children!

Disney Fairies

A Tricky Tool

Tinker Bell was at the fairy camp on the mainland, hard at work. Today she was finishing a very complicated invention that she hoped would help the garden fairies to do the watering. Tink stood back and looked proudly at her achievement. The watering machine was ready!

Now to test it out!

It was already full of water. All Tink needed to do was lift the lever to start the water running....

"Hooray!" cheered Tink. It worked! The water was sucked up through a straw and sent flowing down a spout on the side of the machine. This invention would water the flowers much quicker than anything the garden fairies already had!

Satisfied, Tink pushed the lever back down to stop the water. But as she let go, the lever sprang up, and water again flowed down the spout! "Oh no." Tink grabbed it. "The lever won't stay down. When I let go of it, the water keeps running."

She thought for a moment. What she needed was something heavy to hold the lever down while she fixed the problem. She looked around to see if she could find ... aha! That small round rock would do!

"I'll put this rock on the lever to stop it moving," she said, picking it up and balancing it on the handle. Now the lever couldn't spring up.

Tink bent down to look underneath the machine. "I just need to tighten this up a bit...." She reached for one of the grass bindings that held the structure together.

SPLASH!

"Eeek!" cried Tink as water splashed all over her head. "What's going on?"

The rock had rolled off the handle! Tink grabbed it. "Get back here. I need you!" She put it back in place, but as she bent down....

SPLASH!

"Again?" cried Tink, shaking water from her wings. By this time she was soaking wet and getting quite annoyed. "What kind of rocks move around on their own?" she fumed. She reached for it – but then stopped in astonishment. "And what kind of rocks have eyes?"

"The kind that look like rocks but aren't!" answered Fawn, the animal fairy, as she flew into the glade. "I've been looking for that prankster all day!" She reached for the rock – and it uncurled to reveal a cheeky face! Fawn chuckled and held it up for Tink to see. "Meet the pill-bug, Tink. He likes to play hide-and-seek and pretend he's a rock!"

The pill-bug grinned at Tink. She couldn't help laughing. "Well, he sure fooled me!"

She'd certainly be more careful what she picked up next time!

Disney Princess
Snow White and the Seven Dwarfs

Rise and Shine!

"All right, Dwarfs!" Doc called one morning. "Is everyone ready to leave for work? Let's see. We've got Happy, Dopey, Sneezy, Bashful, Grumpy and Sleepy." Doc looked around. "Sleepy?" No answer. Sleepy was nowhere to be found.

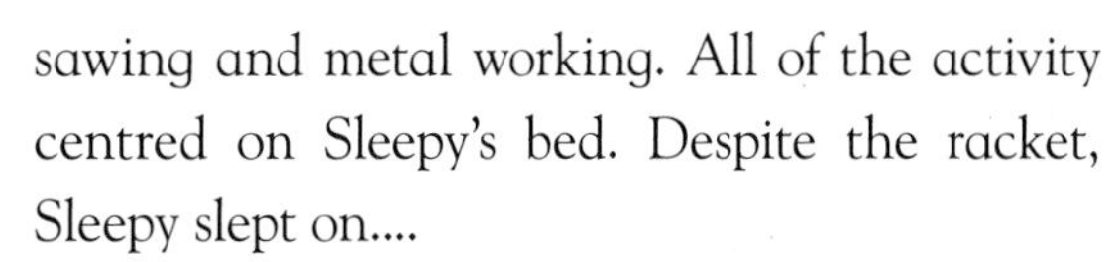

"Oh no, not again," Doc complained, leading the other Dwarfs up the stairs to their bedroom. There, just as Doc expected, they found Sleepy, dozing peacefully in his bed.

Doc walked to Sleepy's bedside. He pulled the covers off the sleeping dwarf. "Come on, Sleepy! Rise and shine!" Doc called. But Sleepy just rolled over and dozed on.

"Oh, this is ridiculous!" exclaimed Grumpy. "We go through this every single morning, dragging Sleepy out of bed, and I'm tired of it."

"Me too!" said Bashful.

"Me three!" said Sneezy. *"AH-CHOO!"*

The Dwarfs stood around Sleepy's bed, looking down at him, wondering what to do.

"I have an idea!" said Doc. "We'll have to take the day off from the diamond mine and stay here today to work on my plan, but I think it will solve our problem – once and for all!"

The Dwarfs gathered into a huddle around Doc as he outlined the details. Then they got their tools and set to work. Soon the bedroom was filled with the sounds of hammering, sawing and metal working. All of the activity centred on Sleepy's bed. Despite the racket, Sleepy slept on....

He slept all morning. He slept all afternoon. He slept all evening. He slept through the night.

Then, bright and early the next morning, an alarm clock perched on top of Sleepy's bedside table sprang to life – its bell jangled noisily, shaking the clock.

With a rope tied to its handle, the clock bounced across the top of the table until it fell off the edge. The falling clock tugged on the rope, yanking a broomstick at the other end. When the broomstick moved, the large weight it was propping up dropped to the floor, activating a pulley that pulled up sharply on Sleepy's headboard. The head of Sleepy's bed lifted off the floor, and Sleepy slid down and off the foot of the bed, onto a smoothly carved wooden slide that carried him out of the window, down to ground level and – *SPLASH!* – right into a wooden tub filled with cold water.

Wide awake, Sleepy sat in the tub, blinking and wondering what had just happened.

The other Dwarfs crowded around the bedroom window and peered down at him, grinning cheerfully (except Grumpy, of course).

"Good morning, Sleepy!" cried Doc. "Do you like your new alarm clock?"

Disney Princess The Little Mermaid

Ariel to the Rescue

"Oh, Eric! This is wonderful!" Ariel said excitedly as she twirled around the ballroom with her prince. "I can dance with you and see the ocean!"

"Do you miss your sea friends?" he asked.

"Sometimes," Ariel replied. "But I love being with you."

A few weeks later, Eric took Ariel to the lagoon. Ariel noticed that a big wall had been built around it. The wall would keep out dangerous sea creatures, but it also had a gate for Ariel's friends to enter the lagoon. In fact, Flounder, Scuttle and Sebastian were already there to greet her.

Ariel was so excited that she waded into the lagoon to greet her friends. Then she saw something in the water.

"Look!" she exclaimed. As they watched, a small dolphin leaped out of the water!

"He's just a baby. I wonder where his mother is," Flounder said. He swam across the lagoon, but the baby dolphin raced away.

"Poor little guy," Flounder said. "He seems scared of me."

But the Princess wouldn't give up. Soon she had coaxed the baby dolphin to swim over to her.

"I wish there was something we could do," Ariel said.

"I bet his mother is on the other side of that wall," Flounder said. "We'll find her!"

But a few days later, Sebastian and Flounder still hadn't found her. Tomorrow, Ariel would ask more of her friends from under the sea to help with the search.

Later, Ariel awoke to the booming sound of thunder. When she and Eric arrived at the lagoon, Flounder was trying to calm the frightened baby dolphin.

Ariel climbed onto the lagoon wall and called to the sea creatures. "Help me, please! I am Ariel, princess of the seas. I need my father, King Triton."

Below the surface, sea creatures raced to find King Triton. Suddenly there was a flash of light! King Triton had arrived.

The storm quietened down. The baby dolphin's mother was at the lagoon gate, frantically trying to get in.

"Oh, dear!" Ariel exclaimed. "The gate won't open! She can't get in!"

Eric looked at King Triton. He raised his trident and blasted down the wall. The dolphins swam to each other, then the baby went to Triton to thank him.

That night, the moon rose. But there was no royal ball at the palace. Instead, Eric and Ariel returned to the lagoon and enjoyed a wonderful night with all of their ocean friends.

Disney
Bambi
First Frost

Slowly, Bambi opened his eyes. Curled up next to his mother, he was toasty-warm in the thicket. Bambi blinked sleepily, peering past the brambles. Something was different. The forest did not look the same. The air was crisp and cold, and everything was frosted and sparkling.

"Jack Frost has been here," Bambi's mother explained. "He's painted the whole forest with glittering ice crystals."

Bambi was about to ask his mother who Jack Frost was and how he painted with ice, when he heard another voice, an impatient one.

"Get up! Get up! Come look at the frost!" It was Thumper. He tapped his foot impatiently. "We haven't got all day!"

Bambi stood and looked at his mother. When she nodded approvingly, he scampered out of the thicket. Bambi looked closely at the colourful leaves on the ground. Each one was covered in an icy-white pattern. He touched his nose to a big orange oak leaf. "Ooh, it's cold!" he cried.

"Of course it is!" Thumper laughed.

"I think it's beautiful," said Faline, as she stepped into the clearing.

"Me too," Bambi agreed.

"Well, come look at this!" Thumper hopped away and the two young deer followed, admiring the way the sun sparkled on the frost-covered trees and grass.

Thumper disappeared under a bush. Then Bambi heard a new noise. *CREAK. CRACK.*

Faline pushed through the bushes with Bambi right behind her. There was Thumper, cracking the thin ice on a puddle with his feet.

Bambi had never seen ice before. He pushed on the icy-thin puddle-covering with his hoof. It seemed to bend. Then it shattered!

Soon the three friends were stomping on the ice-covered puddles. When all the ice was broken, Faline had an idea. "Let's go to the meadow!"

Bambi thought that was a great idea. The grass would be sparkling! They set out at a run, bounding and racing each other through the forest. But when they got to the meadow's edge, they all stopped.

They looked, sniffed and listened quietly. They did not sense danger – no, the trouble was that in the meadow, nothing was different. There was no frost.

"What happened?" Bambi asked.

"Frost never lasts very long," Thumper explained. "It melts as soon as the sun hits it. But don't worry. Winter is coming, and soon we'll have something even better than frost. We'll have snow!"

Winnie the Pooh

Orator Owl

On their way home from a leaf-collecting excursion on a cold, blustery autumn afternoon, Pooh, Rabbit, Piglet and Eeyore made their way past Owl's house. They couldn't help but notice the cheerful light glowing in all the windows – a light so warm and so inviting that the chilly group seemed to thaw just looking at it.

And so it happened that they soon found themselves warm and cosy in Owl's sitting room.

"Owl, thank you for having us in to warm up," said Pooh. "It's awfully windy and cold outside."

"Well, it is getting on towards winter," Owl replied. "Naturally that means it will only get colder before it gets warmer." Owl went on to explain the difference between the blustery autumn cold that they were experiencing and the winter sort of cold that was to come. He explained it in very great detail, using words like frost, frosty and frostily. It turned out to be quite a long explanation. Owl was just beginning to expound on the particular subject of frostbite when Rabbit interrupted, hoping to give someone else a chance to talk.

"Yes, Owl," he said. "I know Piglet was glad to have his scarf on today, weren't you, Piglet?"

"Oh yes," Piglet said. "Kanga knitted it for me."

Owl cleared his throat. "Ah yes, knitting," said Owl. "An admirable hobby. Did you know that knitting is done with knitting needles? But they aren't sharp, as one might assume. They are not, for example, as sharp as sewing needles. Or cactus needles...."

Owl continued with a comparison of many, many different types of needles. An hour later, when Owl seemed ready to jump into a discussion of pins, Rabbit again tried to change the subject.

"Speaking of pins," Rabbit began, "how is your tail today, Eeyore? Suitably secure and well attached?"

"Seems secure," Eeyore replied with a shrug, "but it always falls off when I least expect it. And I certainly wouldn't expect it to fall off now, when it seems so secure. So I suppose that could mean it's about to fall off."

Rabbit saw Owl sit up in his chair and take a deep breath – a sign that he was preparing another speech about tails or expectations – so Rabbit decided it was time to go.

Goodbyes and thank-yous were said, and soon the four visitors were outside, making their way home through swirling leaves.

And all the way home, Rabbit tried to decide who was windier – the great autumn wind ... or long-winded Owl!

The Great Jewel Hunt

The Prince was leaving the palace for a business trip and Snow White and the Dwarfs rushed to send him on his way.

"I've left an envelope in the well!" the Prince called. "It's the first clue to a treasure hunt. At the end is a gift!"

Snow White waited until the Prince was out of sight and then turned to the Dwarfs. "The well is where I first met the Prince!"

She found the envelope and opened it. "Can't leave you a kiss or even a hug, so here is a clue – Look under the...." The missing last word was part of the riddle!

"Under the bug!" insisted Happy. The Dwarfs followed him to the garden to check under all the ladybirds, butterflies and bees.

"It would be hard to hide a clue under a bug," laughed Snow White, watching the Dwarfs scurrying among the plants.

"Could be a jug or a mug," said Grumpy.

The Dwarfs went into the castle and headed for the kitchen first. As they began lifting jugs and mugs, Grumpy tripped over Dopey. Dopey had been looking under the rug instead, and pulled out an envelope.

"You're a genius, Dopey!" Snow White opened the envelope and read: "Smile, it's no time to frown. The next clue is in your royal...." She paused in thought. "Gown, perhaps?"

The Dwarfs followed Snow White to her wardrobe upstairs and searched through every gown she owned, but not a single clue was found!

"Hey!" said Grumpy, as Bashful picked up Snow White's crown from the dressing table. "You can't wear that!"

Underneath the crown was an envelope.

"Oh! The answer to the riddle!" said Snow White, clutching the letter. "The gift is almost yours! My, my ... this game has flown! There's one thing left to do. Go look upon your...."

"Stone!" yelled Sneezy.

"Cone!" said Doc.

"Trombone!" shouted Grumpy.

"I think I know!" said Snow White. "Quickly, follow me!"

She led the Dwarfs through the palace to the grand hall, where they found Sleepy dozing dreamily on Snow White's....

"Throne!" she cried. "The answer to the riddle!"

Sleepy woke with a start and from the top of the throne – two birds flew out from behind it with a necklace in their beaks. The pendant was a heart-shaped ruby – a symbol of true love. With it, there was another note.

Snow White read aloud. "This hunt ends, but remember – the best gifts are...."

"Friends!" everyone cheered at once.

November

8

Disney Princess
THE PRINCESS AND THE FROG

Tiana's Royal Wedding

After many adventures and a ceremony in the bayou, Tiana and Naveen were finally getting married properly! They welcomed Naveen's parents, the King and Queen, for the wedding.

But all too soon, the royal helpers cornered Tiana, announcing their plans for her wedding.

"We'll do this ... and this," they told her. Tiana's head was soon spinning!

"I don't want to upset the King and Queen, but their helpers' wedding plans aren't right for me!" Tiana told her friend Charlotte.

"It's your wedding! You should do what you want," Charlotte said. So Tiana made her first wedding decision – she asked Charlotte to be her maid of honour!

Just then, Tiana's mother arrived. "I'd like to make your dream gown for you," she said.

"Oh, Mama! That's perfect!" Tiana exclaimed when she saw her mother's sketch.

After everyone else had gone to bed, Tiana sneaked into the La Bouffs' kitchen to work on the menu with Charlotte.

"I want a taste of New Orleans," Tiana said. "Let's start with gumbo."

Later, Charlotte said, "Tia, every bride needs something old, something new, something borrowed and something blue. So here's your 'something blue'."

Charlotte handed Tiana a beautiful blue necklace.

The next day, Tiana told the royal helpers that she had everything she needed. Though surprised, they agreed – Tiana should have her dream wedding!

Just then Naveen's mother, the Queen of Maldonia, walked into the room. Would she be upset?

"Tiana dear, I am glad you are planning the wedding you want, but would you do me the honour of wearing the tiara I wore when I wed the King?"

Everything seemed perfect.

But Tiana missed her father. The night before the wedding, as she gazed at the Evening Star, Tiana realized that her father would always be part of her.

On her wedding day, Tiana carried her father's favourite old spoon inside her bouquet. She wore her new gown from her mother, the tiara borrowed from the Queen and Charlotte's blue necklace under her veil.

As she kissed Naveen, Tiana knew that *love* was what made her wedding – and her life – perfect.

The wedding guests loved Princess Tiana's cooking. And as Tiana and Naveen took the first nibble of their cake, they shared the sweetness of their new life together.

November

9

Disney Princess Sleeping Beauty

Small Fairies in Big Packages

Princess Aurora's wedding to Prince Phillip would take place in a few days. The three good fairies, Flora, Fauna and Merryweather, wanted to give Aurora the perfect gift. They stood in front of a huge box, trying to decide what to put in it.

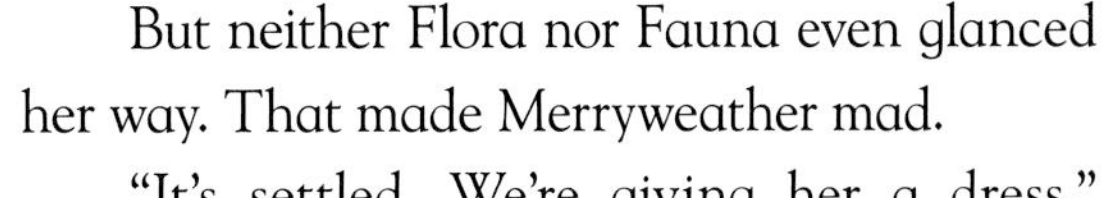

"How about a pretty dress for Princess Aurora to wear on her honeymoon. Something pink!" Flora said decisively.

"What about a grand carriage?" Fauna suggested with a smile.

Flora shook her head. "King Stefan is already having a carriage made for them. No, let's give her a dress."

"I've got it!" Fauna cried. "A flock of doves that we'll release just as Aurora and Phillip come out of the church. Perfect!"

"A tiara to wear with her wedding gown – that's what Aurora needs," Merryweather piped up. "With three jewels – one red for Flora, one green for Fauna and one blue for me. It will remind our sweet Briar Rose of how much we love her."

"A dress is much more practical than a flock of doves, dear," said Flora firmly.

"But a flock of doves is much more romantic than a dress," Fauna insisted.

Merryweather put her hands on her hips. "A tiara! What's wrong with a tiara?"

But neither Flora nor Fauna even glanced her way. That made Merryweather mad.

"It's settled. We're giving her a dress," Flora said.

"Doves," said Fauna.

"Why can't we give her a –" Merryweather began but, as she waved her arms, trying to get the other fairies' attention, she lost her balance and fell right into the big box. Flora and Fauna did not notice.

"We'll give her both!" said Flora.

They pointed their wands at the box, showering it with sparkles. A huge piece of satin ribbon appeared, wrapped itself around the box, and tied itself into a big bow.

Flora and Fauna put on their capes, ready to deliver the gift to Aurora. But where was Merryweather?

"Oh, well, perhaps she went on ahead," said Flora. "Let's be on our way."

At the palace, Flora and Fauna placed the gift before the Princess. When Aurora untied the ribbon, Merryweather burst out of the box. She presented the Princess with a beautiful tiara that sparkled with red, green and blue jewels.

"Oh, thank you, my dears! It's perfect!" Aurora said with a gasp.

Merryweather smiled. "That's exactly what I thought!" she said.

November

10

A Silver Lining

It was a rainy day on the mainland and Lizzy, the fairies' human friend, sighed as she looked out of her window. Tinker Bell fluttered in the air next to her.

"We can't go outside to play," Lizzy said sadly. She hated being stuck indoors!

Tink felt sorry for her friend. "Maybe I can find a way to cheer you up." She fetched Lizzy's tea set, and together they had a pretend tea party.

"Would you care for a cup of tea, Miss Bell?" Lizzy asked in a posh voice.

"Yes, thank you," said Tink. "It's delicious!" They giggled.

But Lizzy was soon feeling sad again. "Oh, it's still pouring! Why does it have to rain in summertime?"

Tink thought of something else. She used Lizzy's crayons to draw pictures of her adventures. Lizzy gasped as she saw the picture of Tink flying away from the hawk. "Scary! That hawk almost caught you!" She sighed. "If only the rain was as much fun as your adventures."

"Aha!" said Tink. "I think I've got it!" Quickly she made herself an umbrella out of newspaper and a pencil. She needed some help from her friends to make this idea work!

"Come back soon!" Lizzy begged as Tink flew off to the fairy camp, dodging the raindrops as she went.

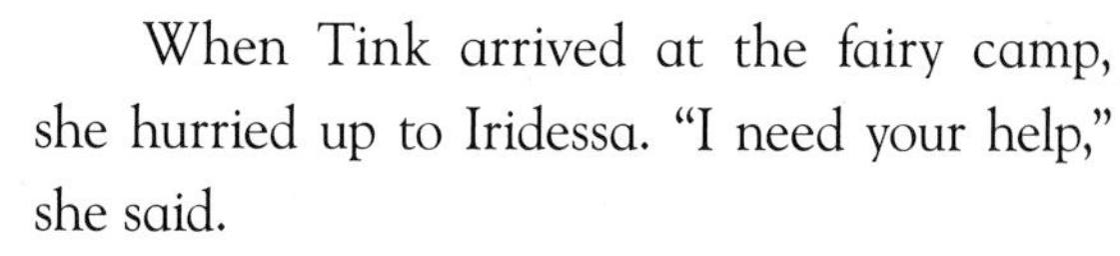

When Tink arrived at the fairy camp, she hurried up to Iridessa. "I need your help," she said.

"Sure!" Iridessa said. "What's wrong?"

"We need to make Lizzy smile again," Tink told her. "Have you seen Silvermist?"

But Silvermist had gone with Fawn to teach the frogs to croak and she wouldn't be back for ages. Tink frowned. She'd have to adapt her idea....

Back at Lizzy's house, Iridessa and Tink searched through the kitchen for things they could use. "This whisk will do the trick!" said Tink.

"And this bowl will be perfect," said Iridessa. Together, they took their findings up to Lizzy's room.

"What are you doing?" asked Lizzy, as the two fairies filled the bowl with water and set it on top of her wardrobe. Using the whisk to whizz the water into the air, Tink laughed in delight. "Water droplets!"

"And now, I'll bring out a sunbeam!" Iridessa reached into her bucket and threw a handful of light into the air. Where the light struck the water droplets, it created a beautiful rainbow – right in the middle of Lizzy's room!

Lizzy was thrilled. Rain wasn't so bad after all – because with rain you could also have a rainbow!

Disney THE JUNGLE Book

Dawn Patrol

One day, Mowgli went to the jungle to visit his old friend Baloo the bear.

"Why so sad, Mowgli?" asked Baloo.

"It's the dry season, and the river is getting low," said Mowgli. "My friends in the village are worried about running out of water."

"Oh," said Baloo. He scratched his head. "But what about the spring in the jungle? It never goes dry."

Mowgli shook his head. "The spring is much too far inside the jungle. It would take all day to get there from the village."

Just then, Bagheera the panther padded over. "Mowgli, I might have a solution for you – Dawn Patrol."

The next morning, Bagheera, Baloo and Mowgli all waited by the spring. Before long, the ground shook with the approach of Colonel Hathi and his herd of elephants.

"Hup, two, three, four. Hup, two, three, four," chanted the Colonel as the herd marched behind him.

"Here they come," announced Bagheera. "Dawn Patrol."

Quickly, Bagheera, Baloo and Mowgli hid in the bushes. They waited for the elephants to stop at the spring and take a long drink.

"Ready to try my plan?" Bagheera asked Mowgli. The boy nodded, then the two sprang from the bushes crying, "To the river! Quick! Everyone, as fast as you can!"

The elephants looked up in alarm.

"W-what's the m-m-meaning of this?" stammered the Colonel.

"Shere Khan is coming! Everyone run for the river!" called Mowgli.

"Company ... RUN!" cried the Colonel, and the elephants stampeded through the jungle.

Bagheera and Mowgli watched the herd knock down every tree between the spring and the river. When Mowgli reached the river, he turned round and saw a clear, easy path straight to the big spring!

Now it was time for Baloo to play his part.

"Hey, whoa!" cried Baloo. "False alarm!"

"What's that?" asked Colonel Hathi.

"Shere Khan isn't coming after all," said Baloo. "Human hunters are after him, so he's heading far away. We're all safe!"

The Dawn Patrol sighed with relief. Then Colonel Hathi called, "Forward, march!"

As the elephants marched off, Mowgli grinned. "With this new path to the spring, my friends will never run out of water."

Bagheera nodded. "Good work," he said.

"Yes, it was," said Baloo with a laugh. "And you know what was good about it? Somebody else did the work for us!"

November
12

Disney Princess
Beauty and the Beast

A Friend for Phillipe

Belle loved life in the castle with her Prince, and she loved her faithful horse, Phillipe. Lately, however, Phillipe had been acting strangely. One morning, Belle decided to try and cheer him up. She asked her friends for some help.

First, Lumiere helped Belle brighten up Phillipe's stall. They covered the walls with wallpaper and trimmed them with gold. They piled pillows in the corners and hung a huge chandelier from the ceiling.

"*Voilà!*" Lumiere cried, when they were done. "What more could a horse ask for?"

But Phillipe just stared sadly out of his stall's window.

"I wish I knew," replied Belle.

Next, Belle saw to it that Phillipe was treated to a bubble bath fit for a king. "If this doesn't make him smile," Belle told Chip, "I don't know what will!"

But in the end, although he was shiny and sweet smelling, Phillipe was just as glum – and Belle was just as puzzled. She asked the Prince if he had any suggestions.

"A good walk always used to cheer me up," the Prince said.

Belle thought that was a wonderful idea. She rode Phillipe to a wide, open meadow, but he wasn't interested in galloping.

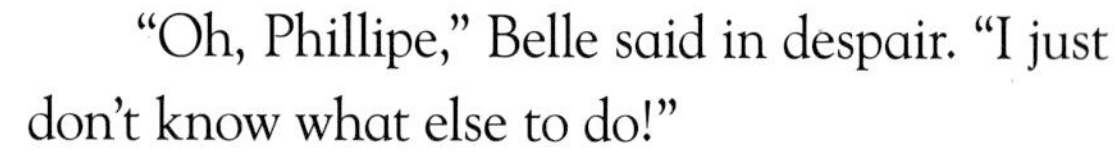

"Oh, Phillipe," Belle said in despair. "I just don't know what else to do!"

Then, all of a sudden, Phillipe's ears pricked up. Belle barely had time to sit up before he charged off!

Before long, they emerged into a clearing filled with wild, beautiful horses! Phillipe whinnied, and several of the horses answered him.

Finally, Belle realized what Phillipe had wanted – to be with other horses!

All afternoon, Belle watched Phillipe race around and play.

Soon, Phillipe had even made a friend. The two horses grazed, chased each other around the clearing, and dozed together in the warm sun.

All too quickly, the day was over, and the sun began to set. Belle put Phillipe's saddle on and they started back towards the castle.

Soon, Belle heard the sound of hooves behind them. Phillipe's new friend was following them home!

"Welcome to our castle!" Belle told the new horse when they arrived. Then she hurried off to fix up the stall next to Phillipe's.

"There," she said when she was finished. "Now this looks like a stable where a horse (or two!) could really live happily ever after!"

And that is exactly what they did.

Disney MINNIE

Where's Leonard?

When the latest episode of *Wizards & Fun* had finished, Minnie logged onto her computer to chat about it with her friends. Macy, Konnie, Daisy and Tom were already online. But someone important was missing – Leonard! Instead of a little picture of Leonard's face, there was a spaceship – how strange!

The next day at school there was even more strangeness. Minnie overheard Leonard on the phone talking about balloons – but as soon as he saw her, he stopped talking and ran away! They couldn't even catch him after class. What was going on?

Over the next few days, Leonard proved impossible to find. And it was nearly time for the special anniversary episode of the TV show. They couldn't watch it without him! Minnie decided it was time to do some investigating. They had two clues – the picture of the spaceship and the reference to balloons. "Konnie and Macy, you two find out what spaceship it is," Minnie instructed. "And Tom, you look for the balloon shop."

The friends split up, each carrying out their special mission!

Minnie and Daisy questioned their teacher. "Leonard seems to have been really busy organizing something lately," he told them.

Konnie and Macy searched online for the picture of the spaceship. Suddenly Macy spotted it. "Hey, it's the spaceship from the special anniversary episode of *Wizards & Fun*!" she cried.

And Tom finally tracked down the right balloon shop, too. "Yes," the shopkeeper told him. "I delivered a thousand balloons to the house of someone called Leonard."

The friends set off towards Leonard's house to see what was happening – but what they found made them totally speechless.

Leonard's house had been turned into a party venue! A huge model of the anniversary spaceship hung from the ceiling, surrounded by hundreds of colourful balloons! And in the middle of it all....

"Hey guys!" cried Leonard. "I knew you'd make it! Let's celebrate! It's the second anniversary of *Wizards & Fun* ... and our friendship! It's thanks to the show that we met each other!"

"This is amazing!" cried Minnie, running to hug Leonard.

"What a great idea!" Daisy exclaimed.

"Hooray for Leonard!" said Macy, giving him a big hug.

Leonard smiled happily. It was great to show friends you appreciated them!

November

14

Disney Princess

Tangled

The Princess Jewels

Freed from her tower and Mother Gothel, Rapunzel and her friends were travelling back to the kingdom. Soon she would meet her true parents, the King and Queen.

"I can't believe I'm really the lost Princess," said Rapunzel.

Flynn smiled. "You'll be great as a princess. All you have to do is wear a huge, heavy crown...."

"Oh!" Rapunzel cried.

"Let me start over," Flynn said. "Remember that tiara from my satchel? Well, I'll tell you a story....

"When I was a kid in the orphanage, I read a book about a princess who said a tiara symbolized everything a princess should be. The white crystals stood for an adventurous spirit, green represented kindness, red stood for courage and the round golden crown itself stood for leadership.

"For years, I thought of that tiara, and then one day, I actually met a gal who could wear it. She certainly was adventurous. She also showed kindness towards everyone, courage and definitely leadership. She turned every bad situation into something wonderful!"

Rapunzel was puzzled. "Flynn, who are you talking about?"

"You!" Flynn exclaimed. "I'm talking about all those amazing things you did when you left your tower in search of the floating lights."

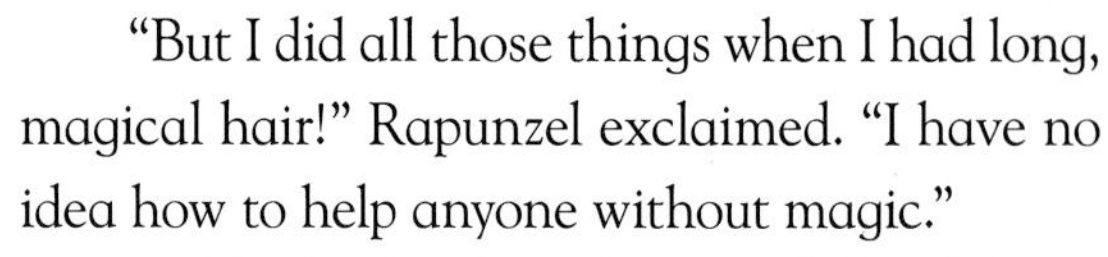

"But I did all those things when I had long, magical hair!" Rapunzel exclaimed. "I have no idea how to help anyone without magic."

Suddenly, they heard a noise behind them.

"Nobody move!" an angry voice yelled. "Hand over your horse!"

"Rapunzel!" Flynn shouted. "Run away!"

But Rapunzel did not run away. She ran right in to rescue Maximus. When it was over, Rapunzel scolded the bandits.

One of the men stepped forward. "It's all my fault," he replied. "I need your horse to take my son to the doctor."

"Oh, my! Where is he?" Rapunzel asked. Within minutes, Rapunzel was tending to the boy's injuries. He smiled as he was hoisted onto Maximus for a ride to the kingdom's doctor.

"How can you ever forgive us?" the men asked Rapunzel.

Rapunzel thought of the princess's tiara – adventure, kindness, courage and leadership. Suddenly, she realized she didn't need her magical hair.

"Come with me," she said.

At the kingdom, Rapunzel received her crown. But as she waved to the crowds, she knew that no one was as supportive as her faithful new friends!

And they always would be, too.

Disney Princess
The Little Mermaid

Ariel's Royal Wedding

Ariel loved Prince Eric from the moment she first saw him. And Prince Eric loved Ariel from the first time he heard her sing. And now they were going to be married!

At home in the castle, Ariel realized that there was a great deal of work to be done. The royal workers started showing Ariel lists and books and plans. She began to feel nervous.

I've never even been to a human wedding before, she thought. *How do I begin to plan for one?* Ariel knew she would need a lot of help.

Ariel asked Carlotta, the friendly maid, to help to make her dress. They worked through the night and made Ariel's dream dress.

"It's so beautiful!" cried Ariel. "I wish my sisters could see it."

The next morning, Chef Louis drew Ariel a picture of the wonderful wedding cake he would make. "It's perfect!" cried Ariel. "I wish my father could see it when it's done."

As Ariel thought about all of the wonderful wedding plans, she began to think about her family. It was Ariel's dream to spend the rest of her life as a human and as Prince Eric's wife, but she wanted her family close by on her wedding day. She began to feel sad.

Later, Prince Eric noticed a tear in Ariel's eye. "What's the matter?" he asked.

"I just wish – I just wish that my family could be at the wedding," Ariel replied.

"Hmm, I thought you might want that. So, I thought, we should have our wedding at sea!" Eric grinned. "It's all planned – we'll be married on the royal ship."

"That's perfect!" Ariel cried. "Thank you!"

Soon, Ariel met her sisters near the shore. She asked all of them to be her bridesmaids. She asked Sebastian to be the ring bearer. And she asked her father, King Triton, to give her away.

The day of the wedding finally arrived. The ship was covered with beautiful pink and white flowers. The human wedding guests were all seated on deck. Ariel's father used his trident to magically lift him and Ariel's sisters up to the side of the ship. The rest of her merfolk friends looked on from the sea.

King Triton led Ariel to meet her handsome prince. The vows were read and the rings were exchanged.

"Kiss the girl!" cried Sebastian. And at last the Prince and Princess were married!

Prince Eric and Princess Ariel knew that their lives would be a joining of land and sea – this was the beginning of a life filled with joy and laughter, shared with family and friends of all kinds.

Disney 101 Dalmatians

Special Delivery

Now that their family had grown so large, Roger, Anita, Nanny and the Dalmatians had moved to the country, or to the 'Dalmatian Plantation', as Roger liked to call it. A weekly delivery of dog food came from the city. It arrived every Thursday at 3pm, and Rolly looked forward to it with keen anticipation.

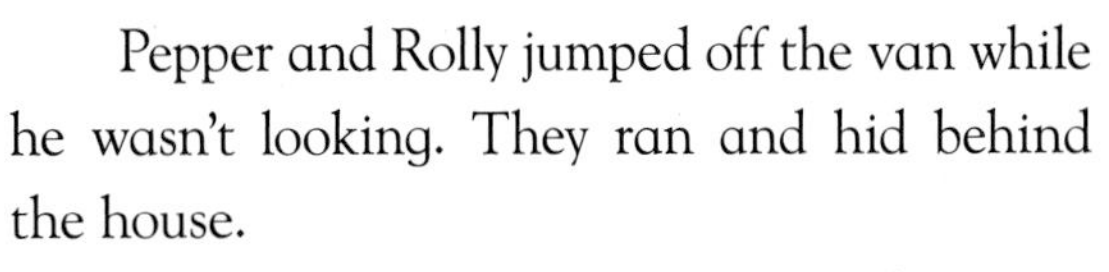

One Thursday, Rolly and Pepper noticed that the back of the van had been left open. "Are you thinking what I'm thinking?" Pepper asked Rolly.

Rolly nodded. "Snack time!" Rolly and Pepper made a dash for the van and leaped into the back. Pepper clambered up onto the pile of bags and sniffed around. There had to be some loose food somewhere....

"Bingo!" Pepper cried. "Rolly, up here!"

Rolly was there in an instant.

SLURP, SLURP, CRUNCH!

The two puppies were so busy eating that they didn't see the van driver come out of the house.

SLAM! He closed up the back of the van. A second later it was rumbling down the drive.

"Uh-oh," Rolly whispered.

Finally, after what seemed like a very long time, the vehicle lurched to a halt. The back door opened, and the driver began unloading bags of food.

Pepper and Rolly jumped off the van while he wasn't looking. They ran and hid behind the house.

"What do you two think you're doing?" a gruff voice asked.

The puppies spun round to see a big bulldog looking down at them. "This is my property," the dog said. "It's time for you to scram."

The two puppies stared at him.

"Now!" he barked.

"You don't scare me," Pepper said boldly. "You're not half as bad as Cruella."

The bulldog's mouth fell open in shock. "You mean Cruella De Vil?" he asked curiously. "You must be Pongo and Perdita's puppies! I heard about your adventures over the Twilight Bark! You live on the Dalmatian Plantation?"

"Yes!" cried Rolly. "Can you take us there?"

"You bet!" the bulldog said. "Let's go!"

Luckily, Pongo and Perdita were out that day and didn't realize what a pickle Rolly and Pepper had got themselves into. But there were 97 puppies waiting in the garden as Rolly and Pepper arrived with their escort.

"Wow," said Lucky, after he had heard their tale. "Were you guys scared of that big mean bulldog?"

"No way!" Pepper spoke up. "That bulldog was all bark and no bite!"

Disney Princess
Cinderella

The Sapphire Ring

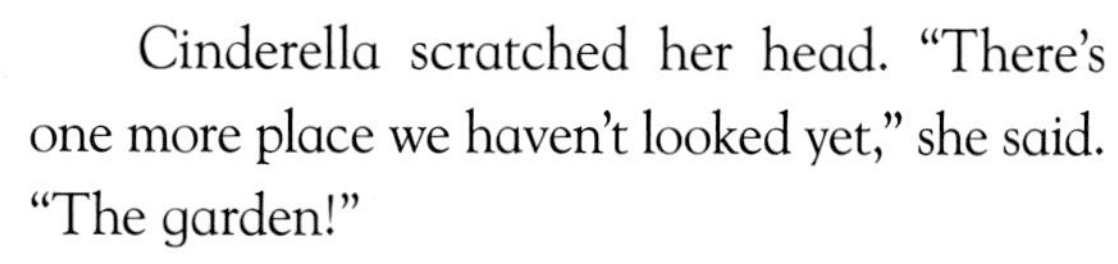

It was one year since the Prince and Cinderella had married. To celebrate their anniversary, the Prince was to hold a ball, and he gave Cinderella a gold ring set with a blue sapphire – Cinderella's favourite stone.

However, the ring was too large and somehow it had slipped off her finger.

"Oh, no!" Cinderella cried. "My ring! Where is it?" She checked inside her gloves, but it was nowhere to be found.

"Don't worry about it, Cinderelly," her mouse friends Jaq and Gus piped up. "We'll help you find it!"

"Where have you been today?" Jaq asked.

Cinderella thought. "The first thing I did was go to my bedroom to write in my diary." So, they hurried to Cinderella's room.

"No ring," Jaq said with a sigh.

"Let's try the kitchen," said Cinderella. "I went there next to make a pot of tea." But the only ring in there was a day-old doughnut.

"Perhaps we should try the library. I read there this afternoon," said Cinderella. They searched high and low, but they could not find Cinderella's sapphire ring.

"I also went to the stables to feed Frou. Perhaps I lost my ring in his stall." The three friends sifted through piles of straw. But there was still no ring.

Cinderella scratched her head. "There's one more place we haven't looked yet," she said. "The garden!"

The friends searched under every blossom and leaf until Gus exclaimed, "Cinderelly! I see it!" He picked up a shiny, blue object.

"Is this your sapphire, Cinderelly?" Gus asked. Cinderella shook her head. It was just a marble.

"Wait a minute," she said as they stopped by the well. "After I drew some water from the well, I noticed my ring was gone. Could it have fallen in there?"

"I hope not," said Gus, trembling.

Jaq rolled his eyes at Gus. "Don't be such a scaredy-cat. Get into this bucket!"

Cinderella lowered Jaq and Gus into the well. "Do you see anything?" she called down.

"Eek!"

Cinderella pulled up the bucket as fast as she could. "What did you see?" she cried.

"Oh, nothing," said Gus slyly. "Nothing but Cinderelly's ring!"

"My heroes!" cried Cinderella. "Wait until I tell the Prince how you saved our special day!"

At the ball, Cinderella and the Prince raised their glasses to Gus and Jaq, their guests of honour, and thought how lucky they were to have such wonderful friends.

Winnie the Pooh

Eeyore's New Old House

One blustery, cold November day in the Hundred-Acre Wood, the blustery, cold November wind blew so strongly that it knocked Eeyore's house right over!

So Eeyore went to Pooh's house. "Well, Pooh," Eeyore said, "it seems that November just doesn't like me. Or my house. So I'm afraid I will have to stay here with you. If you don't mind, that is."

Pooh assured Eeyore that he didn't mind and offered him some honey.

"I'd prefer thistles, if you have any, which you probably don't," Eeyore said. Pooh shook his head. "Oh well," sighed Eeyore. "Perhaps Rabbit has some."

Well, Rabbit did have some thistles, so Eeyore settled down to stay with Rabbit. But Rabbit's house was so full of vegetables and gardening tools – rakes and spades and baskets and twine – that there was scarcely room in the burrow for Eeyore.

"I suppose Piglet might have more room, though I doubt it," said Eeyore.

Piglet told Eeyore he was welcome to stay with him, and even made Eeyore a little bed next to the pantry, which was full of haycorns. But Eeyore was allergic to haycorns, and soon his sneezing almost knocked Piglet's own house down.

"One house knocked down today is more than – *AH-CHOO!* – plenty," said Eeyore. "I'll just have to try Kanga and Roo."

Kanga and Roo were happy to put Eeyore up in their house. Roo was so excited to have a guest that he couldn't stop bouncing. Soon Eeyore was feeling dizzy from watching him. But, just as Eeyore was about to try Owl's house, Piglet, Rabbit and Pooh arrived.

"Eeyore, we've found you the perfect house to live in!" Piglet cried.

"I doubt that," Eeyore said as they led him through the Wood. "The perfect house would have thistles, and enough room, and no haycorns, and, above all, no bouncing. Where will I find a house like that?"

Soon, they arrived at a snug little house made of sticks, with a pile of thistles in it. "Here it is, Eeyore," said Piglet.

"That's *my* house," said Eeyore, hardly able to believe his eyes. "But my house got knocked down."

"Piglet and I put it back together again," Pooh said, "and Rabbit donated his thistles. Now you have a house with thistles, enough room, no haycorns, and ... no bouncing."

Eeyore looked at his house, and then at his friends. "It looks like November doesn't dislike me so much after all," he said. "Maybe, that is."

Tinker Trouble

The fairies had set up camp on the mainland for the summer, and everyone was busy. Tinker Bell looked up to see a bee happily flying through a polisher – one of her own inventions. "Are you sure that bee-liner is working okay?"

The animal fairy in charge smiled back at her and replied, "Of course! It's perfect!"

Tink nodded and walked on. Further off she spotted a garden fairy holding another of her inventions. "Hey you, wait!"

The garden fairy gulped. Had she been doing it wrong?

"I bet you're having problems with that flower-sprayer," Tink said hopefully.

"Who, me?" asked the garden fairy, surprised. "It seems to be working like a charm!" She sprayed a nearby flower to demonstrate.

Tink sighed. Everyone had a job to do except her! She was only useful when something needed making or fixing – and everything was going far too smoothly for that! How boring!

Then she had an idea. Maybe someone else might need her tinkering skills?

Lizzy, her human friend, was delighted to see Tinker Bell. "You want a little work to do?" she asked. Then she pulled out a box full of broken things – a teddy with stuffing coming out, a clock that had stopped and more....

Tinker Bell clapped her hands. "Wow! I'll get straight to it!" This was more like it. Finally she was being useful.

It took Tink all of the rest of the day to mend Lizzy's toys. When the sun had set, she flew slowly back to the camp. "That was flitterific!" she said to herself, yawning. "But I can't wait to get some rest."

"Thank goodness you're here," said a voice.

"Huh?" Tink looked up to see Bobble and Clank.

"While you were gone, everything fell apart!" exclaimed Clank.

"The bee-liner broke and the pulley stopped working," added Bobble. "Plus the painter fairies needed new brushes." He held up the worn-out ones for Tink to see.

"We would've taken care of it," Clank said, "but we know how much you wanted to work."

Tinker Bell felt suddenly dizzy. More work? But she just wanted to sleep! "Th-thanks, Clank," she said in a voice that wobbled.

Clank and Bobble grinned happily at her. "You'll be busy all night long," they said.

THUMP! Tink had fainted.

"She's out cold!" cried Clank.

Bobble smiled. "Tink was so happy at the thought of working that she fainted from joy!"

Poor Tink. She was always making more work for herself!

November

20

Disney MICKEY & FRIENDS

Minnie's Missing Recipe

One day, Mickey opened his door to a very worried Minnie. "What's wrong?" he asked.

"It's the annual Bake-off and I can't find my cinnamon swirl cake recipe!" Minnie cried.

Pluto dropped a rolled-up paper at Mickey's feet.

"Thanks, Pluto," Mickey said. "But I haven't got time to read the newspaper now. We have to help Minnie. Come on!"

Mickey searched Minnie's kitchen and found a postcard on the floor. "What's this?" he asked.

"Donald came over this morning to show me his postcard collection. He was so excited that he dropped them all," Minnie giggled.

Mickey had an idea. "Did Donald pick up your recipe with his postcards? Let's see!"

When Mickey, Minnie and Pluto got to Donald's house, Donald wasn't happy.

"What's wrong, Donald?" Minnie asked.

"It's my new postcards," Donald told Mickey and Minnie. "Five of them are missing!"

"My recipe is missing, too!" said Minnie.

"We were wondering if you accidentally picked it up when you were at Minnie's this morning," Mickey added.

Pluto dropped the rolled-up paper on the table, but Donald was too upset to notice.

"Where did you last see your postcards?" Mickey asked.

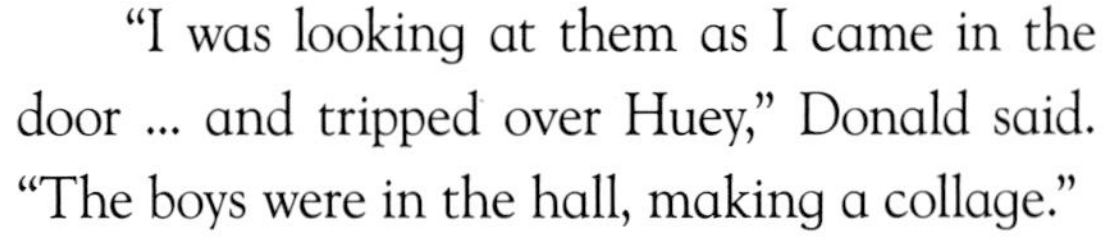

"I was looking at them as I came in the door ... and tripped over Huey," Donald said. "The boys were in the hall, making a collage."

"Perhaps they used some postcards in their collage," said Minnie.

Pluto dropped the paper at Minnie's feet.

"Thanks, Pluto," said Minnie. "But we have to solve this mystery!"

"Did you use my postcards in your collage?" Donald asked when his nephews got home.

"Maybe ..." Dewey said.

"Where's the collage now?" Minnie asked.

"I rolled it up and put it in my rucksack this morning," Louie said.

"But when we got on the bus, it was gone," Dewey added.

"It must have fallen out between Donald's house and the bus stop," Minnie said.

Everyone searched the route, but they couldn't find the collage anywhere.

Pluto barked and dropped his rolled-up paper at Huey's feet.

"This is it! We must have dropped it in Mickey's garden," Huey shouted.

The boys unrolled their collage, complete with the postcards and Minnie's missing recipe!

"You were helping us, Pluto!" Minnie said. "I'm going to bake two cinnamon swirl cakes – one for the Bake-off and one for you!"

Disney Princess
Tangled

Rapunzel's Winter Adventure

Rapunzel woke with a shiver. There was a distinct chill in the air, making her toes curl with the cold. Pascal jumped onto her pillow, gesturing to the window with his long chameleon tail at its full, glorious length.

"What is it, Pascal?" Rapunzel yawned. She crossed the cool floor. When she opened the window's shutters, she was met with a wonderful sight....

"Snow!" she cried.

The forest around her was whiter than the moon. Covered in a thick layer of snow, the trees looked like fluffy clouds on sticks – as if they'd fallen from the sky and settled around her tower. It was a new world outside. A cold, sparkling wonderland with snowflakes dancing on the breeze.

Rapunzel caught a snowflake in the palm of her hand and admired its unique pattern before it melted against her skin. "Beautiful," she sighed.

Pascal was itching to play as he caught snowflakes on his quick, curly tongue. He wanted a snowball fight.

"You know I can't leave my room," Rapunzel said. "But we can make the tower into a winter wonderland instead!"

Pascal disappeared from the tower and returned with juicy berries and sprigs of green holly. Rapunzel threaded the berries and holly together to make splendid garlands that she and Pascal hung all around the room, giving it a festive touch. It made Rapunzel feel closer to the world outside her window – a world she couldn't quite reach.

"With imagination," she said, snatching up her paintbrush and some silvery-white paint. "We can make it snow inside as well."

Rapunzel covered the walls in painted snowflakes, each one different to the last ... just like the real things. As she painted, Pascal pointed to the icicles hanging from the window. They were spiky and freezing to the touch.

"You'll be cold if you go outside now," Rapunzel told him.

Pascal looked sad. He wanted to enjoy the snow while it lasted. Tomorrow the sun or rain could come and all of it would have been a dream, washed away or melted into puddles.

"I have an idea," said Rapunzel. She rushed to her chair by the warm fire and pulled out her needles and wool. "I'll knit you a jumper!"

Pascal squeaked in appreciation. Wearing his new jumper he was back outside in no time, making snowmen for Rapunzel to admire from the window. Little did she know, one day she would be able to join him ... touching the earth with her bare feet – knowing what it was like to be free of her tower.

Disney · PIXAR
FINDING NEMO

A Real Sleeper!

"Time for bed, Nemo," said Marlin. "It's a school day tomorrow," he added. "You need to get your rest."

"Okay," said Nemo. "But can you tell me a story? How about one from when you were younger?"

"Well, just one then," said Marlin, swimming back over to his only child. He thought for a moment, then smiled broadly. "Did you know that when I was younger – much younger, actually – I wanted to be a comedian?"

Nemo's eyes widened with surprise. "*You?* A comedian? Aren't comedians supposed to be, umm, funny?"

"Well, you see, son," said Marlin, "life is not easy for a clownfish. You may as well realize that right now. See, when you're a clownfish, everyone you meet assumes that you are funny. It's a common mistake. Anyway, years ago, I figured that as everyone expected me to be funny, I would try being funny for a living."

"But Dad," said Nemo, "you aren't funny at all."

"Hey now! Wait just a minute!" Marlin said, a bit huffily. "In my day, I was known as quite the crack-up! Let me see. I'm sure I can remember some of my old routine, if I just think about it for a minute." He paused for thought. "All right, it's all coming back!"

He cleared his throat. "Good evening, ladies and jellyfish! The ocean sure is looking *swell* tonight. Would you like me to give you a coral report about the latest happenings on the reef? Get it?" he said, looking down at Nemo. "You see, there's something called an oral report, and the words coral and oral sound quite a bit alike."

Nemo gave his father a pained look.

"So, the other day my appendix nearly burst," Marlin went on. "So I decided I'd better go to a sturgeon!"

Nemo blinked. "Dad, these really aren't that funny," he said with a yawn.

"A *sturgeon*. Get it? Rather than a surgeon?" Marlin sighed and continued his routine. "A funny thing happened on the way to the show tonight. I met a guy, nice fish and all, but he seemed to be a bit down on his luck. He told me he was living on squid row."

Nemo's eyes were starting to droop sleepily.

"Do you know why the whale crossed the ocean?" Marlin continued. "Now, don't try to guess. I'll tell you – the whale crossed the ocean to get to the other tide. The other *tide*."

Nemo's eyes were now completely closed, and a tiny snore escaped from him. Marlin smiled at his sleeping son.

"Works every time," he said with a chuckle.

Disney
DUMBO

A Talented Mouse

"Look, Dumbo," Timothy Mouse said, pointing to the newspaper. "There's another article about us in here!"

That wasn't unusual. Ever since Dumbo had become famous for being able to fly, everyone was interested in him.

Mrs Jumbo, Dumbo's mother, peered over Timothy's shoulder. "What a nice story," she cooed. "Too bad the picture isn't better – why, I can hardly see you, Timothy!"

Timothy peered at the paper. "Hey," he said, scanning the story. "This article doesn't mention me at all!"

"It's all right," Mrs Jumbo said soothingly. "Everyone knows how important you are."

Timothy puffed out his chest proudly. After all, he had taught Dumbo to fly!

Then he sagged again. "Am I really that important?" he said. "It's Dumbo who has the talent – not me."

Mrs Jumbo and Dumbo tried their best to comfort Timothy, but he wandered away sadly. He was so smart, so talented – he should be famous too!

"I have to figure out a way to get famous on my own," Timothy muttered. "But how?"

Suddenly he snapped his fingers.

"I've got it!" he cried. "I'll learn to fly too! Then Dumbo and I can be famous together!"

He quickly climbed to the top of the tallest circus tent. Dumbo learned to fly by jumping off things. Timothy just hoped it would work for him too. He rubbed his hands together.

"Here goes nothing ..." he muttered. He leaped off the tent and looked down. The ground seemed very far away.

"Uh-oh!" Timothy gulped. What had he done? The ground got closer and closer. Timothy squeezed his eyes shut....

Suddenly, Timothy felt himself being whisked upwards. Opening his eyes, he saw that he was clutched in Dumbo's trunk.

"Whew!" he gasped. "Thanks, chum!"

Dumbo smiled at his little friend. He set Timothy in his cap.

Timothy decided flying was much more fun when Dumbo's ears did all the work!

Soon they landed beside Mrs Jumbo.

"Oh, Timothy!" she cried. "You're safe! When I saw you fall, I was so worried ... Dumbo and I don't know what we'd do without you."

Timothy blinked. "Never thought of it that way," he mused. "Maybe I'm not front-page news every day. But who cares? I know I'm important, and my friends know it too. That's what matters!"

He smiled. He had plenty of his own talent, and that was good enough for him!

Disney Princess Cinderella

Scarves for Everyone

Snow was falling outside and the world was icy cold with winter's spell. In the palace, Cinderella sat by a warm fire. It was almost time for the Ice Ball and even with the fireplaces roaring in every room of the castle, the cold was almost too much to bear!

"The Prince is always so busy," Cinderella said. "And whenever I see him, he's blue with cold."

The birds at the window agreed, nodding. They often saw the Prince leaving the palace on royal business and, with the heavy snow flurries, he was chilled to the core.

"I shall make him a scarf," Cinderella decided, reaching beneath the armchair to pull out a basket. Her friends, the mice, had been sleeping on the balls of yarn cradled within.

Cinderella chuckled, moving them aside so she could gather her knitting needles. "You can sleep on this cushion instead." She set a cushion down in front of the fire and the mice scurried over to get comfortable.

"Now, where should I start?" Cinderella wondered. She had three different colours. Blue, yellow and red.

Beginning with the red, she knitted while humming and singing to herself. But as she worked, she couldn't help but notice the birds were shivering.

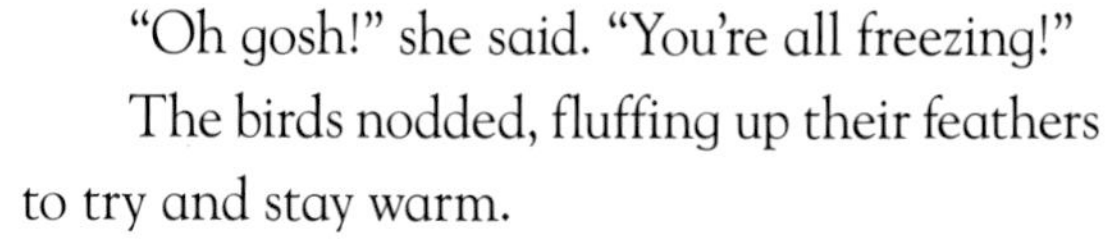

"Oh gosh!" she said. "You're all freezing!"

The birds nodded, fluffing up their feathers to try and stay warm.

Cinderella felt sorry for her friends. With skilful fingers, she made each bird a red scarf.

"There! That'll help you stay warm," she smiled.

Picking up the blue yarn, she began the Prince's scarf once more. But as she was getting into the flow of things, she noticed her mice friends shivering.

"Oh, my! Are you cold too?" she asked them. The mice nodded slowly with a chatter of their teeth.

Cinderella set to work, making the mice the perfect gift of little blue scarves.

"There!" she said when the mice were toasty and snug at last. "Now, my Prince's."

Having had a lot of practice already, Cinderella knitted a long, sunshine yellow scarf.

"My love!" said the Prince, when he'd returned from work with snowflakes in his hair. "What a magnificent gift."

Cinderella helped to wrap the scarf round his neck. The Prince kissed the top of her hand when she was finished.

"You are so lovely," he said.

And together the Prince, the mice and all the birds stayed warm and cosy at the Ice Ball, thanks to the kind-hearted Princess.

Mysterious Disappearances

The fairies were always busy on the mainland, but today Rosetta and Fawn were doing something unusual. They were parting the grass, turning over leaves and looking under flowers.

"Hi guys!" called Tink as she flew over. "What are you looking for?"

"I've lost my compact mirror," Rosetta said.

Tink knew how much Rosetta's mirror meant to her. Without it, how could Rosetta be sure she looked stylish? "I'll help you find it!"

Soon, all three of them were busily searching, but with no luck.

Tink looked up to see Terence flying towards them. "Hi Terence!" she called.

Terence was worried. "Have you seen my satchel of pixie dust? I dropped it and I can't find it anymore."

"So I'm not the only one who's lost something today," said Rosetta.

"My guess is you've left your mirror back at camp," Fawn told her.

Then Tink remembered something. "Come to think of it, I just lost a nice silver button. I thought I left it by the camp entrance, but I can't find it anymore."

Terence frowned. "Do you think someone's stolen our things?"

The fairies looked at each other uncomfortably. It wasn't a nice thought.

"Maybe we just forgot them somewhere," Tink said uncertainly. Then something up in the air caught her eye. "Look!"

The fairies gazed up at a collection of floating objects!

"There's my mirror!" exclaimed Rosetta. She flew up and hugged the compact. "At last I've found you!"

"They're covered in pixie dust," Tink said, examining her silver button.

"That's why they're flying around on their own," realized Fawn.

Terence grabbed a spoon as it floated past. "But who sprinkled the dust on them, and why?"

"Maybe it was an accident," suggested Fawn. She glanced up. "The things are coming out of that tree. Let's go take a look."

The fairies peeped through the hole in the trunk. "That's who stole our things!" cried Fawn.

It was a magpie nest! Magpies loved shiny, sparkly things, and this nest was full of them. But this magpie hadn't reckoned on dropping a bag of pixie dust over his treasures! He hopped around, trying to catch the floating objects.

"Let's help him collect them," Fawn said.

"Good idea," agreed Rosetta, putting her compact safely in her pocket. Spoons and buttons could be replaced, but Rosetta's mirror was her most precious possession and no magpie was going to take it from her again!

Winnie the Pooh

Pooh Welcomes Winter

Pooh had heard that Winter was coming soon, and he was excited about having a visitor. Pooh and Piglet decided to welcome Winter to Hundred-Acre Wood with a party. The two friends set off to tell everyone.

Outside, it was starting to snow. They met Tigger along the way, and they walked to Kanga and Roo's house together.

They all decided to go by sledge to the party. Owl landed on a branch overhead.

"Winter has arrived!" he declared. "I heard Christopher Robin say so."

Pooh told Owl about the party, then they all jumped on the sledge and slid down the hill towards Christopher Robin's house.

"There's Winter!" Tigger cried. "Tiggers always know Winter when they see him. That big white face – that carroty nose. Who else could he be?" said Tigger.

"Well," said Pooh, "he looks shy. We should be extra friendly." He walked right up to Winter. "How do you do?" Pooh asked. "We are giving a party in your honour."

Winter did not say anything.

"Oh d-d-dear," said Piglet. "He's frozen!"

"Quick!" cried Tigger. "We'd better get him to the party and warm him up." They hoisted Winter onto the sledge.

When they slid up to Pooh's house, the others were already there. Owl had hung a big friendly sign over Pooh's door – WELCOME WINTER. Pooh and Tigger wrestled Winter off the sledge.

"Give him the comfy chair by the fire!" Rabbit instructed. Still, Winter did not say a word. His carrot nose drooped.

Just then, Christopher Robin tramped up to the door in his big boots. "Has anyone seen my snowman?" he asked.

"No," said Pooh glumly, "but we brought Winter here for a special party. He doesn't seem to like it."

"Silly old bear!" Christopher Robin told Pooh that Winter was not a person, it was a season. A time of year for cold snow, mistletoe, warm fires and good friends.

Pooh scratched his nose thoughtfully. "Yes, I see now," he said. "Of course, I am a bear of very little brain."

"You're the best bear in all the world," said Christopher Robin. "Come on, we'd better get the snowman back outside before he melts completely."

They undrooped the snowman's nose and put him back where he belonged. They decided to have the party anyway, to celebrate Winter. So everyone sang songs and danced around the snowman until they couldn't dance any more.

November

27

Disney Princess

Tangled

Rapunzel's Royal Wedding

It was a beautiful day, and Flynn had a wonderful surprise for Rapunzel. Maximus kept guard, and Pascal went along to play. But Flynn wanted to be alone with Rapunzel.

Finally, dusk fell, and Flynn took his chance to jump into a boat with Rapunzel. The lovely night reminded them of times past. Flynn wanted to propose! He put his hand in his pocket, but – oops! He did need Pascal and Max, after all. They had the ring.

"Will you marry me?" Flynn finally asked his love, Rapunzel.

"Yes," Rapunzel said happily.

On their way home, Rapunzel wanted to tell everyone their wonderful news!

The pub ruffians were delighted. It turned out they had been waiting for a wedding to organize for years!

Of course, Attila helped Rapunzel to design a cake. They baked, iced and created the wedding cake of Rapunzel's dreams!

Rapunzel looked at lots of different flowers for her bouquet, but it took a field of wild flowers to please the Princess!

As for ring bearers, the choice was clear – Maximus and Pascal could not have been prouder to accept!

When it was time to find a dress, Rapunzel was determined to design her own.

She sketched and sketched ... but simply could not make up her mind!

The pub thugs tried to help, but their dresses didn't seem right either. Luckily, the Queen arrived. "Darling," she said. "I want to help you find the perfect dress."

And she did!

On the morning of the wedding, bells rang through the kingdom. Everyone was excited to see the King and Queen happily riding in the royal coach. And Max and Pascal were thrilled – until Max sneezed and the rings flew into the air!

Max and Pascal chased the rings out of the church and up and down the streets. They finally caught them ... but then went crashing into a tar factory!

Max and Pascal made it back to the wedding just in time for the exchange of the rings – but they looked rather strange, covered in black tar!

Luckily, Rapunzel and Flynn didn't mind one bit.

Everyone helped out to make the reception as perfect as Rapunzel had planned. The newlyweds danced their first dance. They had their first taste of the wedding cake.

And as they rode away in their wedding coach, Rapunzel cried out happily:

"Best. Day. Ever!"

Disney Princess
Beauty and the Beast

The Father of Invention

There was never a dull moment in the castle of Belle and the Prince. Friends came and went, Mrs Potts and the other members of the household bustled about, and Maurice, Belle's father, was always tinkering away on a new invention.

One morning, Maurice wheeled a rather complex-looking machine into the kitchen and presented it to Mrs Potts.

"Just a little something to make your life easier," he said proudly.

"Thank you, Maurice dear, but ... what is it?" the housekeeper wondered.

"I call it a 'plate pitcher'," replied Maurice. He took a pile of clean plates and loaded them onto a mechanical arm. Then he positioned the machine in front of the open china cabinet. He pressed a button and stood back proudly. With a couple of loud clangs, the machine sprang to life.

The plate pitcher began to hurl plates this way and that. They smashed onto the floor.

"Look out, Mrs Potts!" shouted Maurice as a plate whizzed by her head. He crawled along the floor, reached up and hit the off switch. "I'll just go work out the kinks," he said, wheeling the machine out of the room.

The next day, Maurice had another surprise for Mrs Potts. "It's for cleaning the carpets," he explained, pointing to a large metal box with a big hose coming out of it. "No more beating heavy rugs for you!"

"Well, it looks harmless," Mrs Potts decided. "How does it work?"

"Like so!" said Maurice. He picked up the hose and flipped a switch. Instantly, curtains, pillows and lamps were sucked into the nozzle. It even looked as if Maurice himself was in danger of disappearing! Luckily, Mrs Potts came to his rescue and turned off the machine.

"I must have made it a little bit too powerful," Maurice admitted.

The following day Maurice had yet another time-saving device for Mrs Potts. This one was a laundry machine that flooded the entire ground floor of the castle with water and soapsuds.

"Maurice," Mrs Potts said gently, "it is very sweet of you to want to make my job easier. But I enjoy it. By taking care of the castle, I'm taking care of the people I love." She looked thoughtful for a moment, then added, "But I have to admit, the one thing I would love is something that would make me a nice, hot cup of tea at the end of the day."

"I have just the thing!" Maurice replied with a twinkle in his eye.

Mrs Potts looked slightly worried. "You do?" she asked.

"Yes," Maurice answered. "Me!"

Disney Princess
The Princess and the Frog

The Secret Gourmet

When the sun shines in New Orleans, the whole town feels like celebrating. And it's reason enough for Charlotte's father to want to share a meal with friends.

"Charlotte, darling," he said to his daughter one sunny evening, "what would you say to going to eat at Tiana's restaurant for dinner tonight?"

"Fantastic!" cheered Charlotte happily. "I'll go put on my pink silk dress and get ready!"

The young woman never missed a chance to go and visit Tiana. They were very fond of each other. And now that Tiana had married Prince Naveen and they had opened a restaurant together, it was even more fun to visit her!

"I hope Naveen's parents will be there!" Charlotte exclaimed shortly after getting into the car with her father. "I always enjoy chatting to a king and queen!"

As they drove down the road, no one noticed Stella, Charlotte's dog, fast asleep on the back seat.

Stella woke with a start when the car pulled up in front of the restaurant. Usually, Stella didn't like to leave the house. She was about to bark and make her presence known, but then she recognized the delicious smell of Tiana's cooking!

Suddenly Stella didn't want to go back to the mansion after all. She sneaked quietly into the restaurant kitchen at the back of the building.

Meanwhile, Charlotte and her father were sitting down to join Eudora, Tiana's mother, who was dining with Naveen's parents.

"I'm going to serve you all the new House Gumbo!" Tiana announced.

At the back of the room, Louis the alligator and his band were playing jazz music. The atmosphere was fantastic.

Charlotte clapped her hands with joy. "We're going to have an amazing evening! All that's missing is Stella. What a shame she doesn't like going out."

Poor Charlotte! She had no idea what was happening in the kitchen....

Stella was so happy to be there and was simpering and begging so much that the chef gave her lots of food!

"We have a secret gourmet in the kitchen," he laughed. "Her appetite does me proud! Serve her as much as she wants, she's my guest!"

Stella barked with happiness. A secret passenger in the car, and a secret gourmet in the kitchen – it was good to get out of the house after all ... but only if you're a secret guest!

November

30

Disney THE JUNGLE BOOK

Hey, Hey, We're the Vultures!

"Nothing exciting ever happens around here," Buzzie complained to his vulture singing buddies.

"That's not true," said Flaps. "What about that fight we had with the tiger Shere Khan last week?"

"Blimey, you're right," said Ziggy. "That was pretty exciting."

Buzzie sighed. "What are we gonna do now?"

"Well, we could sing," suggested Ziggy.

"Hey, good idea!" said the other three vultures.

"One problem," said Dizzy. "We need a tenor."

"Awww, you're right," said Ziggy. "That little Man-cub fellow, Mowgli, would have been a great tenor. Too bad he left the jungle."

"So, what are we gonna do?" asked Buzzie.

"How 'bout we hold an audition?" suggested Ziggy.

"Good thinking," said Flaps.

So the vultures put the word out in the jungle and, a week later, there was a line of animals ready to try out for the group.

"Name?" Buzzie asked the first applicant.

"Coconut," the monkey replied.

"Alright, Coconut, let's hear ya sing," said Flaps.

Coconut shrieked for a few minutes, and the four vultures huddled together.

"He's not very good," said Buzzie.

"And he's a monkey," added Flaps.

"Next!" said Dizzy.

The vultures auditioned a lemur, two sloths, a wolf, a hippo, a toad and an elephant. None seemed like the right fit. Finally, the last animal stepped up.

"Name?" asked Buzzie.

"The name's Lucky," said the vulture. "Hey, aren't you the four fellows that helped that little Man-cub scare away that tiger Shere Khan?"

"Yeah," said Buzzie. "We are."

"Then I guess you four might be called 'lucky' yourselves!" cried Lucky. He began to laugh at his own joke.

"Go ahead and sing," said Ziggy, rolling his eyes.

Lucky sang for a few minutes and the four vultures huddled together.

"He's not bad," said Dizzy.

"Plus, he's a vulture," said Ziggy.

"And he's the last one left," pointed out Flaps. That settled it.

"You're hired!" the vultures sang.

"See, told you I was Lucky!" cried the vulture.

"But only with auditions," said Dizzy.

"Yeah," said Buzzie. "When we meet Shere Khan again, we'll see how lucky you really are!"

Disney · PIXAR
TOY STORY 3

Toys on Ice

Poor Bonnie was stuck in bed, recovering from a nasty case of the flu. She was feeling a little better, but still needed lots of rest.

"I'm sorry, honey, you can't go and see *Songs on Ice*," said her mum, stroking Bonnie's head.

"But my whole school is going," whimpered Bonnie. "It's a musical!"

Bonnie's mum told her that getting some rest was more important. But she needn't have worried – Bonnie had already fallen back asleep.

"Poor Bonnie," said Woody, when her mum had left. "She looks so sad. We must do something for her."

"Do you have a plan, Woody?" asked Buzz. Woody smiled. He always had a plan! The sheriff set about explaining it to the others, then they all swung into action.

The snow was falling as the toys all sneaked out into the garden, carrying a large plastic tub. Mr Pricklepants the hedgehog shook his head. "Get a lot of snow and take it inside?" he said. "It's absurd."

"Trust me," said Woody. "Bonnie will play the musical 'Toys on Ice' with us, and she'll be happy again."

Rex thought it was a great plan, but before he could tell Woody, his feet slipped on the ice. Rex spun in a circle, his tail sending the other toys flying in all directions. They crash-landed into the snow, face-first! This was going to be harder than Woody thought.

Buzz sat up, looking around. The aliens were nowhere to be seen. Where could they have gone?

"Surprise!" cheered one of the little three-eyed creatures. The other two popped up beside him. "Let's have a snowball fight!"

Woody shook his head firmly. "Guys, we have no time to play," he began, but then a snowball hit his face and he remembered that toys always had time to play. "So, it's war, huh?" he said, reaching for the powdery snow. "My snowballs are the fastest in the west!"

After a fun snowball fight, the toys filled the tub and carried it back into the sitting room. They were about to celebrate another successful mission when something terrible happened. The snow began to melt!

Woody's shoulders sagged. There was no way Bonnie could play 'Toys on Ice' now. Buzz patted him on the back. "I'm sure Bonnie will find a way to play with us anyway, Woody."

And Buzz was right! When Bonnie woke up she felt much better, and the big tub of melted snow was just the thing she needed to create her very own version of the musical – 'Toys on Water'!

Disney Princess
The Little Mermaid

The Mysterious Necklace

It was a fine morning, just right for a walk along the seashore.

With joy in her heart, Ariel strolled along the beach and soon found herself a long way from the castle.

Suddenly, she stumbled against a hard object buried in the sand.

"Ouch!" she cried, discovering a shiny object. She dug it up.

"It looks like one of those delicious things that humans are so fond of," said her friend Scuttle the seagull, licking it.

"Do you mean a 'sweet'?" Ariel giggled. "No, it's a jewel! Scuttle, go and find Sebastian. Tell him to call my father!"

A moment later, Ariel's father, King Triton, emerged out of the sea.

"Father," said Ariel. "I've just found this wonderful jewel and –"

King Triton was amazed. "Where did you find it?" he asked.

"On the beach," explained Ariel. "Do you know where it comes from?"

"I'm going to show you something," said her father solemnly, before transforming her into a mermaid.

Holding the jewel in her hand, Ariel dived into the water after her father. Soon, they arrived at the throne room.

"A tidal wave carried off the treasure of Atlantica," explained the king. "I fear this jewel is the only one that's left."

"I'll help you find the others!" said Ariel.

First, the Princess searched the wreck of a ship and collected almost a dozen jewels!

Then, with the help of Flounder and his friends, she found even more gems in the coral reef.

Hidden among the seaweed, which was every imaginable colour, the jewels had gone unnoticed!

Soon the Atlantica treasure chest was full to the brim once more, thanks to Ariel.

"Ariel, on behalf of the kingdom, thank you," said King Triton, opening the chest to take out the wonderful precious stone that she had found on the beach that morning.

And, giving her a kiss on her forehead, King Triton fastened the necklace round her neck.

Soon it was time for Ariel to turn back into a human and return to her castle, where Eric was waiting for her.

That night, Ariel looked out at the ocean while touching the jewel hanging from her neck. Her family was never very far away, but she found it reassuring to have a little piece of Atlantica with her forever.

Disney
Bambi

The Winter Trail

One winter morning, Bambi was dozing in the wood when he heard a thumping sound nearby. "C'mon, Bambi!" his bunny friend Thumper cried. "It's a perfect day for playing."

Bambi followed his friend through the forest. The sky was blue and the ground covered in a blanket of new snow.

"Look at these tracks!" Thumper said excitedly. He pointed to a line of footprints in the snow. "Who do you suppose they belong to?" Bambi didn't know, so they decided to follow the trail. They soon came to a tree.

"Wake up, Friend Owl!" called Thumper.

"Have you been out walking this morning?" Bambi asked.

"Now why would I do that?" Friend Owl replied. "My wings take me everywhere."

Bambi and Thumper continued on. Next, they spotted a raccoon sitting next to a tree. "Hello, Mr Raccoon," Bambi said shyly. "Did you happen to see who made these tracks in the snow?"

The raccoon shook his head and began tapping the tree. "I know!" Thumper cried. "He thinks we should ask the woodpeckers."

Soon, Bambi and Thumper found the woodpecker family. "Did you make the tracks in the snow?" Thumper called up to the birds.

"No, we've been here all day," the mother bird answered.

"If the tracks don't belong to the woodpeckers or the raccoon and they don't belong to Friend Owl, whose can they be?" Bambi asked.

"I don't know," Thumper replied.

They soon reached the end of the trail, and the tracks led all the way to a snowy bush, where a family of quail were resting.

"Did you make these tracks?" Thumper asked.

"Why, yes," Mrs Quail answered. "Friend Owl told me about this wonderful bush. So this morning, my babies and I walked all the way over here."

Thumper and Bambi happily joined the quail family for a snack. Soon, it was time for the friends to go home. They'd spent all day following the trail. When they turned to leave, a big surprise was waiting for them – their mothers! Bambi bounded over to his mother and stretched his nose up for a kiss.

"How'd ya find us?" Thumper asked.

Thumper's mother looked down at the tracks in the snow.

"You followed our trail!" Bambi cried. His mother nodded.

"Now, let's follow it back home," Bambi's mother said. So that's just what they did.

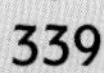

Disney Princess
Beauty and the Beast

Belle's Royal Wedding

Belle's wedding was just days away, and everyone at the castle was busy preparing for the special celebration.

"The Prince has done so much for me," Belle told Mrs Potts. "We need to show him how much we appreciate him, and how well loved he is."

Belle thought back to when she first arrived at the castle. It was so frightening and everyone was under a magical spell. The Prince had become an angry Beast and the servants were enchanted objects. But over time, Belle became friends with the staff. Then she and the Beast fell in love.

Meanwhile, the Prince was preparing for the wedding, too. "I am the happiest man in the world!" he said to Lumiere and Cogsworth. And I want Belle to be the happiest woman!"

When they first met, the Prince thought Belle could never love a hideous Beast. But she spent time getting to know him. When she declared her love, the spell was broken!

"How can I show Belle how much I love her?" the Prince asked. "I know! Let's find a special gift for her in the village!"

Lumiere and Mrs Potts wondered how they could show their love and appreciation for the young couple, too....

The wedding day finally arrived!

During the ceremony, the Prince gave Belle his gift – a blank journal. "You can fill it with all the adventures we will have together," he said.

After the ceremony, the newlyweds walked into the ballroom. The staff had laid out a huge banquet!

"Thank you!" said Belle. "But there is so much! I'm not sure even our whole household can eat all this food!" she joked.

Mrs Potts and the other servants smiled, and led the couple into the garden ... where the entire village was waiting to surprise them!

"I took the liberty of inviting them, on behalf of the household," said Lumiere. It was the staff's gift to Belle and the Prince.

"It's a magnificent gift!" the Prince said. "Thank you for coming!" he repeated over and over. He couldn't stop smiling. He and Belle were both thrilled to welcome everyone into their home.

When the couple shared their first dance, a shout went up from the crowd:

"Congratulations!"

As fireworks lit up the night sky, Belle and the Prince knew that their wedding had been a perfect celebration – for everyone. With so many friends gathered around them, it had been the most magical day of all.

December
5

Disney Princess
Snow White and the Seven Dwarfs

A Visit to the Castle

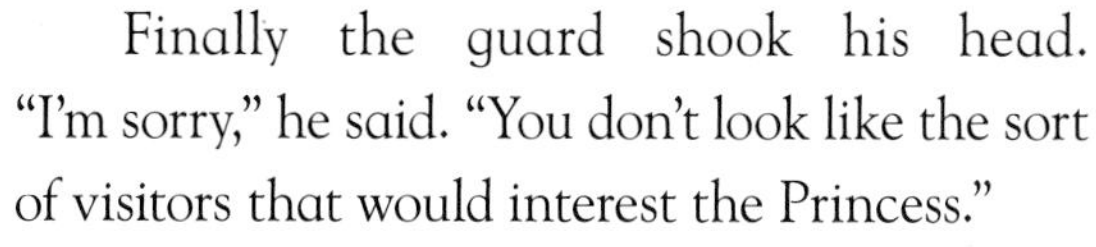

"Gosh," Bashful said bashfully. "Do you think the Princess will be glad to see us?"

"Of course!" Happy chuckled.

"All right, men," Doc said. "Here we are. Now, all we have to do is go up and dock on the floor. That is – knock on the door!"

The Seven Dwarfs had just reached the castle where Snow White lived. They had been so busy in the mines that this was the first time they'd had a chance to visit since Snow White had married the Prince.

Sneezy looked up at the beautiful castle. "*Ah-choo!*" he sneezed. "Wow. This place sure is pretty."

"Time's a wastin'," Grumpy muttered.

He knocked firmly on the tall wooden door. A moment later a guard opened it.

"Er, good day," the castle guard said. "New servants around the back, please."

"Oh, we're not flu nervants," Doc spoke up. "Er, we're not new servants. We're here to see the Princess!"

"Yes! The Princess!" the other Dwarfs agreed. Dopey nodded eagerly.

The guard looked doubtful. "*You're* here to see the Princess?"

He looked them over. The Dwarfs stood up straight, glad that they'd remembered to wash that morning.

Finally the guard shook his head. "I'm sorry," he said. "You don't look like the sort of visitors that would interest the Princess."

"Oh, but we are!" Sleepy yawned. "She'll be interested in us."

"Sorry," the guard said. "You'll have to go."

But Grumpy held the door open. "Mark my words," he growled. "If you don't tell the Princess we're here, there'll be trouble."

"Who is it?" a sweet voice called from inside the castle. "Who's at the door?"

"Never mind, Princess!" the guard called. "Just some strange little men who claim they know you."

"Little men?" Snow White cried, rushing forward. She peered round the door past the guard, and her lovely face lit up with joy. "Why, Doc – Grumpy – Sleepy – Dopey – Happy – Sneezy – even dear Bashful!"

Bashful blushed deeply. "Gosh," he said. "Hello, Princess."

The guard looked surprised. "You mean you know these fellows?" he asked the Princess. "I thought they were just riff-raff."

"Riff-raff?" Snow White cried. "Why, no – they may look a little different, but they're just like royalty to me! They're my very best friends!"

The guard apologized to the Dwarfs. Then Snow White invited her friends into the castle for a nice, long visit.

Disney Princess Sleeping Beauty

Aurora's Royal Wedding

Princess Aurora dreamed many times that a handsome prince would find her, and he had! Even though their royal parents had decided years earlier that Phillip and Aurora would marry, the pair had fallen in love not as prince and princess – he was just a boy in the forest and she was a girl from the glen.

Phillip asked for Aurora's hand in marriage and she said yes. The wedding would be soon, and there was a lot to prepare!

"Everything seems well in hand, Your Majesty," said Flora.

The Queen smiled. "Yes, it does, and I couldn't be more delighted. I'll leave you now, Aurora, to enjoy the fun of choosing a dress."

"Thank you, Mother," said Aurora, but she was feeling nervous. She had yet to make any royal decisions on her own.

Just then, the dressmakers burst in with huge, lavish dresses. Aurora looked worried.

"What is it, dear?" asked Fauna.

Aurora sighed. "I don't know how to be a princess. What if I'm not a very good one?"

"Nonsense," said Merryweather. "You'll be the finest princess this kingdom has ever seen."

When Prince Phillip came by later, he had a splendid idea. "Would you like to go for a walk to get away from the wedding planning for a bit?"

"That would be wonderful!" said Aurora.

On their walk, Aurora confided in Phillip. "I'm not sure I know how to act like a princess. I can't even choose a dress!"

Phillip looked at her with love. "My dear, you will be a wonderful princess. But if you're worried, I think I may know someone who can help."

Back at the palace, Phillip spoke to the Queen.

"Your Majesty," he said, "I think Aurora would like some help – from you, her mother."

The fairies overheard and smiled. Phillip was a perfect husband for their Briar Rose. They led the Queen to Aurora.

"Dear Aurora, I understand that you are worried, but being a princess isn't about what you do. Rather, it's about who you are. A princess is honest, thoughtful, clever and kind. And there is no doubt that you are all of these things."

"Oh, thank you, Mother!" Aurora said. "And I just had an idea about a wedding dress. Would it be possible to wear yours?"

The Queen smiled. "I married your father in a simple but beautiful gown. I think it will fit you perfectly."

On her wedding day, Aurora looked every bit a princess in her mother's dress – and she was starting to feel like one, too.

Once Upon a Time....

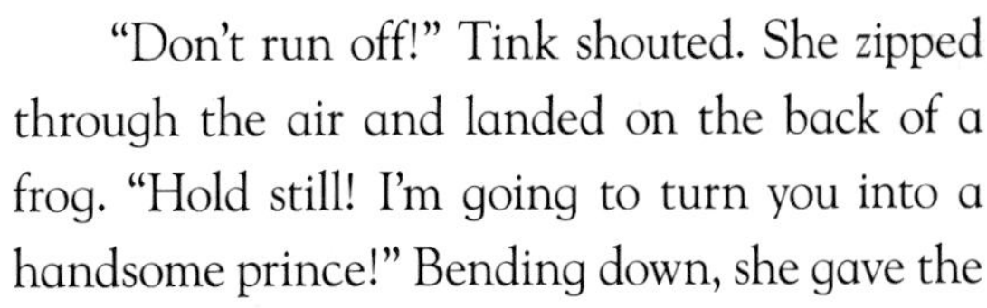

Tinker Bell was on the mainland. Visiting humans was so interesting! Trying to stay hidden, she was listening to a child's bedtime story through a keyhole. A little girl, her hair in ringlets, clutched her teddy as she watched her mother with sleepy eyes.

"And so," the mother said, turning the very last page of the book, "the princess kissed the frog, who turned into a handsome prince. And they lived happily ever after."

The little girl's eyes closed, and she was asleep. But outside the door, Tink was very excited. What a wonderful story! She couldn't wait to get back to Pixie Hollow! "Where can I find a frog to turn into a prince?" she wondered as she flew as fast as she could.

Once home, Tink began her search straight away. Crashing through the grass on the riverbank, she called loudly, "Froggieees! Where are youuuu?"

Iridessa and Rosetta were startled by Tink's odd behaviour.

"What is she doing?" asked Iridessa.

"Looking for frogs?" replied Rosetta in a confused tone. "But why?"

Then Tink let out a loud cheer. "Hooray! I found them!"

Frogs leaped in all directions, frantic to get away from the excited fairy.

"Don't run off!" Tink shouted. She zipped through the air and landed on the back of a frog. "Hold still! I'm going to turn you into a handsome prince!" Bending down, she gave the frog a big kiss!

SMMMACK!

Nothing happened, apart from the frog looking shocked. Tink peered at it. Hadn't she done it right? Why was the frog still just a frog?

Rosetta asked kindly, "Why are you going around kissing frogs, sugar?"

"On the mainland, they say a kiss can turn a frog into a prince," explained Tink.

Iridessa laughed. "They tell lots of stories like that on the mainland."

"But they aren't all true," Rosetta said, taking Tink's hands. "Lots of them are just fairytales to amuse children, dear."

Tink's face fell. "Oh. It sounded so real!"

"Don't think about it anymore," advised Rosetta, as the three of them flew off towards the Pixie Dust Tree.

Tink couldn't help glancing back.

Somehow, deep down, she still felt that fairytales could come true!

Behind a patch of long grass, safely hidden from view, a frog wearing a crown gazed into the water and wondered how long he would have to wait for a kiss to break his spell....

A Snowy Mission

One snowy winter morning, Jessie looked out of the bedroom window and gasped. A little bird was hopping about in the snow, searching for something to eat.

"That bird seems so hungry," she said.

"Yeah, I guess it's hard to find food in the snow," said Buzz.

The friends decided to help the bird. "We could get some crumbs from the bread box and feed it," suggested Woody.

"That's a galactic plan, Woody!" said Buzz, and Jessie quickly agreed.

The toys headed to the kitchen. Jessie and Woody held a bag open on the floor, while Buzz climbed up to the bread box to gather up the crumbs. "Are you ready, guys?" he asked, then he quickly swept the crumbs off the shelf ...

... and missed the bag completely! Woody sighed as the crumbs rained down on his hat, then he and Jessie set to work scooping them all up into the bag.

Finally, when the bag was full, they pushed open the door and ventured out into the garden. The front step was slippery, and the garden was full of deep snow.

"Hold on!" said Jessie. "I don't want to get wet."

The others agreed. If they got wet, Bonnie would know they'd been outside. "We need some waterproof garments," said Buzz, spotting Bonnie's welly boots beside the door.

Jessie knew just what to do. "Ta-da!" she said, bringing a roll of cling film from the kitchen.

"What do you want to do with that?" Woody asked, confused.

Jessie winked. "You'll find out," she said, and she set to work wrapping each of Buzz and Woody's legs in the clear plastic wrap. She did her own legs next, and soon all three of them were wearing a home-made waterproof outfit.

Safe from getting wet, the toys stepped out into the snow. It was hard to walk, and by the time they reached the middle of the garden their legs ached.

As they began to spread the breadcrumbs, Jessie spotted the little bird swooping down. The bird chirped with delight as it spotted the crumbs, and began to hungrily peck at them.

The toys smiled at a job well done when they saw the little bird happy.

"Finally, we can go back inside and get some rest," said Buzz.

"Um ... yeah, about that," said Woody, looking up. He could see that the branches of a nearby tree were full of birds, all cheeping and chirping hopefully. "But first, we've got to feed some more friends!"

Disney Lady and the TRAMP

Sledging

Lady stood on the porch as Jim Dear and Darling walked up the front path. Jim pulled a sledge and Darling held their son. They were all covered in snow, rosy cheeked and smiling from ear to ear.

"That was fun! Wasn't it Darling?" Jim asked.

"I don't know the last time I had so much fun," Darling agreed, patting Lady on the head.

"But we should get out of these wet clothes before one of us catches a cold," Jim said, leaning the sledge against the side of the house.

"I agree," Darling said. And the three of them hurried inside.

Just then, Tramp came walking up the front path. "Hey, Pidge," he said to Lady. "What do you say we take this old thing for a spin?"

"What is it, anyway?" Lady asked him curiously, walking up to inspect the strange object more closely.

"A sledge!" Tramp told her.

"What do you do with it?" she asked.

"You ride down hills," Tramp explained.

Lady looked worried. "That sounds dangerous," she said hesitantly.

"Nah, it's fun!" Tramp cried. "So, what do you say?"

"It's awfully cold out here," Lady said. She wasn't convinced at all.

"Oh, come on," Tramp said. "It'll be great! You saw how much fun Jim Dear and Darling had." Tramp grabbed the rope in his teeth and pulled the sledge across the porch and down the steps.

Lady took off after him. "Wait for me!" she cried anxiously.

"Come on, Pidge!" Tramp encouraged her. "Jump on!"

Lady jumped onto the sledge, and Tramp pulled her down the snow-covered street and up to the top of a nearby hill. "What a view, huh?" he said.

"What a view indeed," Lady agreed. "What now?"

"Now, we ride," Tramp said. He pushed the sledge forward and took a running leap onto it, sending them racing down the hill.

"Oh, dear!" Lady yelped as they went down the hill, the wind blowing her ears back.

"Just hold on!" Tramp instructed.

Lady squeezed her eyes shut, and Tramp barked with excitement. But suddenly they hit a patch of ice, the sledge spun and they went flying – right into a snowbank!

Tramp jumped to his feet. "Pidge, are you okay?" he asked anxiously.

"Okay?" Lady asked. She was already pulling the sledge back up the hill. "Hurry up, Tramp! Let's do it again!"

Winnie the Pooh

A Bounciful Friendship

Tigger was having a bounciful day in the Hundred-Acre Wood. He decided to bounce over to Winnie the Pooh's house. Pooh was cleaning out his cupboards and carrying his honeypots outside. As he was placing a full honeypot on the ground, Tigger bounced straight into him. Pooh lost his grip and the honey spilled!

Tigger looked at the mess. "Would you like some help? Getting out of sticky situations is what tiggers do best!"

Pooh decided it would be better to clean up the mess himself, so Tigger bounced off.

Tigger bounced over to Rabbit's next. Rabbit was busy in his garden. Tigger didn't notice the rake right in front of him – until he bounced on it and fell on Rabbit's plants!

Next, Tigger bounced straight into Piglet and knocked him right off his feet – making Piglet spill all the haycorns he'd collected. Then Tigger bounced to Owl's house and ended up knocking Owl's teapot to the floor.

Next, Tigger bounced off to see Eeyore. But Tigger bounced in so suddenly and loudly that Eeyore fell into the side of his house.

Tigger helped Eeyore up. Just then, Rabbit, Pooh and Piglet arrived.

"Tigger, your bouncing is out of control!" cried Rabbit.

"But tiggers are bounciful when they're happy to see their friends!" Tigger explained.

Rabbit knew that was true. But he was still annoyed. "You need to be a little more careful with others and their things!"

Tigger looked at his friends. He couldn't understand the idea that his bouncing could made them unhappy. He walked away so he could think.

Tigger soon came across Christopher Robin. Tigger told the boy about what had happened.

"I'm sure you can fix whatever needs fixing," said Christopher Robin.

Suddenly Tigger bounced up. "That's it! I'm going to fix everything!"

Tigger gave Pooh a new pot full of honey. He collected a basketful of haycorns for Piglet and planted new seeds for Rabbit. He carefully glued Owl's teapot back together and rebuilt Eeyore's house all by himself.

"I must say I am feelin' pretty tiggerific!" said Tigger, seeing his friends' happy faces.

"Why aren't you bouncing then?" Christopher Robin asked.

"You want me to bounce?" asked Tigger.

"Wouldn't be you if you didn't," Eeyore said. And so Tigger bounced – because it turns out that bouncing *and* being careful is what tiggers do best!

Disney MINNIE

The Revolutionary Solution

"I woke up this morning," explained Daisy Duck to her friend Minnie Mouse, "with the feeling I was forgetting something, but I can't figure out what!" Then she gasped. She'd completely forgotten about the science fair project! The models were all due to be judged tomorrow – what was she going to do?

Minnie had an idea – Leonard! He had all kinds of gadgets and projects at home. The two friends went straight round to ask him to help. Luckily, Leonard had a model that Daisy could borrow. Daisy was speechless. "Oh wow! This is just what I need! Thank you so much!"

There was just time to get the model to school before the science fair opened. Daisy breathed a huge sigh of relief – she wasn't going to fail the project! And there were certainly some interesting ones on display....

Abigail had made a volcano in shocking pink to match her shoes! She sneered at Daisy's model. "Oh look, Daisy made a model out of sweets and lollipops!"

But the guest judge, an important teacher from the Mouse Biology Department, was amazed by Daisy's project.

"This flash of genius could cause a scientific revolution!" he shouted. "This model could change scientific thinking forever!"

Daisy felt terrible. Her picture was on the front of the paper and people were congratulating her everywhere – but it wasn't her model! And she knew that Leonard wouldn't own up to helping her because he didn't want to get her in trouble.

When she was asked to present her model to the whole school, Daisy knew it was time to confess.

"I cheated," she admitted. "The credit belongs to our school's real genius, Leonard!"

But Leonard shook his head. "That's not the project I gave you!" he insisted.

Daisy was confused. "I don't understand."

Abigail stood up and flicked her hair, "I can explain!" She had sneaked in after school and rearranged Daisy's model to mess it up! "The credit belongs to me!" she smirked, reaching for the project.

Daisy jumped for it at the same time – and the model fell to the floor and smashed!

The teachers from the Mouse Biology Department shook their heads in disappointment. A great scientific discovery, created by accident, and now lost forever!

Abigail tried to gather the pieces off the floor while Minnie, Daisy and Leonard couldn't help laughing. Abigail needed to learn that being mean to others gets you nowhere.

False Alarm!

KNOCK, KNOCK!
Tinker Bell yawned as she sat up in bed. Who could that be at this time of the morning?

"Fawn?" she said when she opened the door.

Fawn was carrying a large green basket. "Hi Tink! I need to ask you a favour. This is a present for Rosetta." She held it out. "Would you keep it for me? I'll be with her all day, and I don't want to ruin the surprise."

"Anything for a friend!" said Tink, smiling. She waved Fawn off and placed the basket on her table. There was lots of work to do before the delivery run later that morning. "Remember, sweetie," she told the cricket that lived in her clock. "Sing at exactly 11 o'clock!" She didn't want to be late for Bobble!

The cricket nodded and hopped back inside the clock.

Tink settled down to work. It seemed like hardly any time had passed when....

CHIRP! CHIRP! CHIRP!

"Is it already time to go?" Tink said, surprised. She flew to the depot in Tinkers' Nook, where she found Bobble was still packing.

"Here I am, Bobble," Tink said, saluting.

Bobble grinned. "I'm happy to see you, Tink, but you're too early! I'm not done getting the deliveries ready yet."

Puzzled, Tink flew home again. She was sure she'd heard her cricket clock go off! Had she imagined it?

Never mind. She could get on with some more work before....

CHIRP! CHIRP!

"My cricket clock!" Tink said. She'd definitely heard it that time! It must be 11 o'clock.

But Bobble shook his head when Tink arrived back at the depot. "You're still too early!" he told her, laughing.

Tink was baffled.

"There's something funny going on," she said to herself. Determined to get to the bottom of it, she flew home again.

Opening up her cricket clock, she smiled at the little creature. "You were playing a trick on me, weren't you?"

The cricket shook its head.

"Wasn't it you I heard?" Tink asked.

With a leap, the cricket landed on the table and pointed to the basket Fawn had left.

Curious, Tink lifted the lid of the basket – and now it all made sense! Inside the basket was another clock with a chirping cricket! This was what she'd heard instead of her own clock!

The two crickets chirped happily to each other. Tinker Bell laughed. Well, if nothing else, having two clocks in her house had made sure she wasn't late!

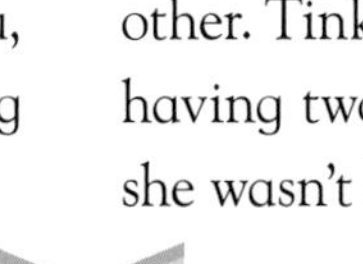

Disney Princess
Cinderella

Cinderella's Royal Wedding

Prince Charming had found the woman he loved, and he wanted to marry her. He asked, "Will you marry me?" and waited for the answer. Of course, Cinderella said yes!

The King was thrilled. In the hall, he pointed to a portrait of a beautiful woman. "This was my wife on our wedding day. And Cinderella shall wear the same thing. It is royal family tradition," said the King. "There is nothing more important than family traditions!"

Cinderella quietly looked at the Queen's portrait. She didn't want to disappoint the King, but following family tradition wasn't easy! The Grand Duke brought her a huge pile of books about royal traditions. She read until eventually she fell asleep and began to dream.

In the dream, Cinderella's mother gave her a special gift. "Cinderella my love, this necklace will remind you that whenever you have a problem, if you listen to your heart, it will lead you to the answer."

When Cinderella awoke, she began to search through some of her old trunks. She soon found what she was looking for – a portrait of her mother on her wedding day.

Cinderella showed the portrait to the royal dressmaker. "Would it be possible for you to make me a dress like this?"

The dressmaker bowed his head. "I would be honoured."

Next Cinderella visited the royal jeweller. "Do you think it would be possible to work with my mice friends and combine two necklaces into one?"

"For you I shall create the finest necklace in the Kingdom," he replied.

The royal wedding day arrived. The King came to see Cinderella.

"I hope you don't mind. This is a copy of my mother's wedding dress," said Cinderella. "It honours my family tradition. And with my necklace and veil, I also honour yours, your Majesty."

The King saw that his Queen's pearls had been used to make the wedding necklace and veil. "Oh my dear girl, this is a great honour. You have blended the treasures of two families – and created a new tradition for our family."

The King proudly led Cinderella down the aisle. The guests were thrilled. The Prince was entranced. Even the Grand Duke wiped a tear from his eye.

The Prince and Princess answered the question that all brides and grooms must answer. "They do! They do!" shouted Gus-Gus.

And so, by following tradition – and her heart – Cinderella had the wedding of her dreams!

December
14

Disney Princess
Tangled

Rapunzel's Heroes

I remember the day started nicely enough. It was the morning of my 18th birthday and the birds were singing. Just the day before, I'd taken a huge step – I had left the tall tower that had been my home all my life! And soon, if all went well, I'd be at the kingdom for the first time, watching the floating lights that were released there every year on the same date ... my birthday.

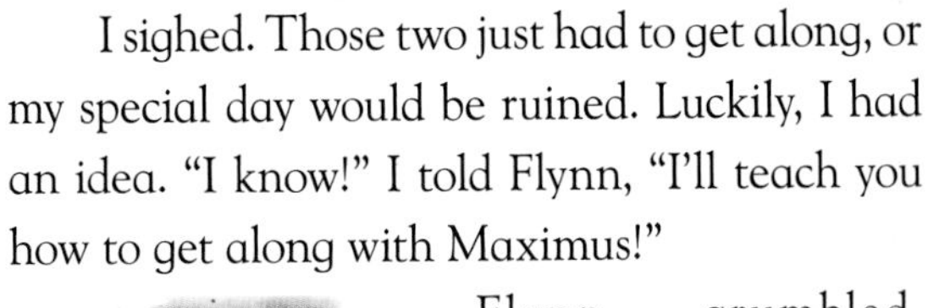

It should have been a lovely morning. But instead, there I was, trying to rescue my guide from a horse!

I'd only known Flynn a short while, but I already knew he was trouble!

After I yanked Flynn free, I stepped in front of the horse and stroked his nose. The name on his chest plate read MAXIMUS.

Maximus thought Flynn was a thief. Still, I hoped the horse wouldn't turn him over to the guards.

"Today is kind of the biggest day of my life," I explained. "It's also my birthday, just so you know."

Together, we set off for the kingdom. Maximus wouldn't let Flynn ride on his back – he threw him off, into a puddle!

"I don't like this horse!" Flynn howled. "And this horse doesn't like me!"

As we walked, Maximus and Flynn wouldn't stop annoying each other.

I sighed. Those two just had to get along, or my special day would be ruined. Luckily, I had an idea. "I know!" I told Flynn, "I'll teach you how to get along with Maximus!"

Flynn grumbled, but watched as I stroked Maximus under his chin.

"See?" I said, nuzzling Maximus's face. "Now you do it."

"Ugh! No way!" Flynn protested. But I asked him to try.

Getting into the kingdom was a little tricky, because Flynn was wanted by the palace guards. Maximus and Flynn managed it, though, by working together. Those two were making good progress!

I think Maximus was a little surprised as he watched Flynn that day, being kind and gentle. Maybe he realized Flynn wasn't so bad after all....

That evening, Flynn gave a bag of apples to Maximus! I was proud of them for making an effort to be friends.

That night, Flynn was put in prison and I was captured by cruel Mother Gothel! Maximus raced to free Flynn. The two of them then hurried to my rescue! They were a team.

After they saved me, I told them how grateful I was. Flynn and Max were heroes. But just as important, they were friends.

Disney 101 DALMATIANS

Having a Ball!

"Ten days until Santa!" the spotted puppies barked, bouncing into one another as they tumbled down the hall.

"Ten days until presents!" Penny barked.

"And ten days until Christmas dinner!" Rolly added, licking his lips.

"Ten days to stay out of trouble!" Pongo said with a smile.

"Do you puppies know what comes before Santa and dinner and presents?" Perdita asked.

"Umm ... stockings?" said Lucky.

"No," Perdita said, laughing. "Before that."

Patch wasn't sure. He sat down on the hall rug to think.

"We have to decorate and sing carols," Perdita said, wagging her tail. At that very moment, Roger and Anita threw open the door to the study and invited all the dogs inside.

Patch blinked. He couldn't believe his eyes. "What's a tree doing in the house?"

"Just watch." Perdy gave Patch a quick lick.

While the dogs looked on, Roger and Anita began to decorate the tree. They hung lights and angels, snowmen and tinsel. Of all the decorations, Patch liked the glittering glass balls best. Balls were one of his favourite things! He could not take his eyes off them.

When the tree was ready, Anita brought in hot chocolate and dog biscuits. Munching on a biscuit in front of the fire, Patch didn't think the evening could get any better. Then Roger sat down at the piano, and everyone began to sing.

Patch howled along with the others, but he could not stop looking at the balls on the tree. A large red one was hanging near the floor.

Patch reached over and gave the ball a pat with his front paw. It swung merrily above him. Looking at his reflection, Patch started to laugh. His nose looked huge!

"What are you doing?" Penny stopped singing to see what was so funny. Then Freckles joined them, then Lucky. The puppies took turns knocking the ball and watching it sway, then – *CRASH*! – it fell to the floor, shattering.

The singing stopped. Poor Patch was sure the special evening was ruined.

"Oh, dear." Anita scooped the puppies out from under the tree. "Careful, now," she said. "Those balls aren't for playing with."

While Roger swept up the glass, Patch cowered. He knew he was in trouble.

"Maybe I should give you all one gift early," Anita said with a grin. Patch couldn't believe his luck. Instead of a firm talking-to, each puppy got to rip open a small package. Patch tore off the paper. Inside was a brand-new red rubber ball!

Disney Princess Sleeping Beauty

Aurora's Home-made Holiday

Wrapped up warm, Aurora and Prince Phillip went for a walk on a snowy December's day. The world glistened as snow fell gently all around them.

"It's very romantic," Phillip said, but Aurora was very quiet. "Is something the matter?" he asked.

"I miss how the fairies and I used to get ready for Christmas," she confessed.

Phillip and Aurora picked out a tree they could take back to the castle to decorate. Aurora even sang a festive carol as they made their way home.

As a surprise later that evening, Prince Phillip sent an invitation to Flora, Fauna and Merryweather for a holiday reunion with his beloved Aurora. Aurora was positively over the moon when the fairies arrived soon after.

"Oh, how wonderful!" Aurora cried. "Now we can have a Christmas like the ones we used to share!"

"That means we can't use magic," Flora decided, for when Aurora was a little girl, the fairies had kept their powers a secret.

Aurora agreed and took their wands ... though they were difficult to catch!

Together the fairies set to work, decorating the Christmas tree with bows and baubles. It was a magnificent vision, with flashing twinkle lights and colourful bursts on every branch.

Then it was time to cook.

"Phillip will love your cakes," Aurora said.

"We'll use red icing!" said Flora.

"And green!" added Fauna.

The next day, Aurora decided it was time to prepare the gifts. "I'd like to give Phillip a homemade shirt," she said, "but I don't know how to sew."

"We'll help!" said Merryweather.

The fairies guided Aurora as she cut and stitched. Aurora preferred to make something instead of buying it, because she felt it made it more special.

When the shirt was complete, they wrapped the gift and placed it under the tree.

Prince Phillip was amazed by the festive beauty of the castle on his return. It was a Christmas delight!

"I understand why you find the fairies so special," he whispered, with a wink.

Aurora led him to the tree in her glittering purple gown and offered him her gift.

"A shirt!" he cried, putting it on at once.

They all burst into laughter.

The shirt was so enormous its sleeves brushed the floor.

"Oh dear," said Aurora. "It's far too big!"

Phillip kissed her. "It's perfect," he said. "And this is the best home-made holiday ever!"

December

17

Disney MINNIE

Who Ate the Brownies?

Minnie had just baked a batch of butterscotch brownies because Daisy was having a party. "The gang will gobble these up," she said, wrapping the brownies in tinfoil and tucking the package into a bag.

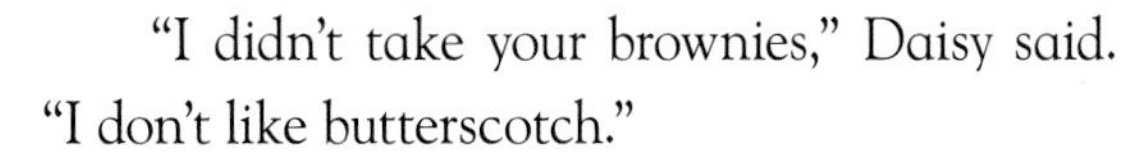

When Minnie arrived at Daisy's house, the others were already there. Daisy was taking food out of the fridge while Donald looked on hungrily. Goofy, who had bandages on both thumbs, was carefully petting Pluto.

"I was trying to hang up some pictures," Goofy explained to Minnie.

"Want to dance, Minnie?" Mickey asked.

"Yes!" Minnie said, putting her bag on the table and following Mickey to the living room.

Minnie was still dancing with Mickey an hour later when she remembered the brownies.

"The butterscotch brownies!" she cried. "I forgot to unpack them."

"Great! Let's eat!" cried Goofy.

Minnie ran to the kitchen and found the bag empty. The brownies were gone!

Minnie went back to the sitting room. "My brownies are missing!" she cried.

"I haven't seen them!" said Daisy, Donald, Goofy and Mickey, one after the other.

"Well, they were in this bag when I got here," said Minnie. "One of you must have sneaked out to the kitchen and eaten them."

"I didn't take your brownies," Daisy said. "I don't like butterscotch."

"Really?" Minnie asked.

Mickey laughed. "Daisy would sooner eat some spinach than butterscotch," he said. "And it wasn't me. You and I have been dancing."

"True," Minnie said.

Goofy gulped. "Well, I sneaked out to the kitchen and ate a few things. But I didn't touch that bag."

"I know it wasn't you, Goofy," Minnie realized. "You couldn't have unwrapped the tinfoil with your thumbs in bandages!"

Then Minnie turned to Donald.

"It wasn't me!" he squawked. "I might have unwrapped the tinfoil to take a peek. But I did not taste your brownies, not even one crumb."

"Come on," Minnie said, deciding to trust Donald. "Let's look in the kitchen for clues."

"Hey, I found some footprints," called Mickey, pointing at the floor below the table.

They followed the trail of footprints up the stairs and into Daisy's bedroom. They disappeared beneath the bed....

Pluto let out a groan. He had butterscotch crumbs all around his mouth.

Minnie smiled. "We shouldn't be too tough on him," she said. "Looks as if he's already paying for it – with tummy ache!"

Disney
DUMBO

The Show Must Go On

The wind whistled around the Big Top, pulling the canvas tent that Dumbo was holding out of reach of his small trunk. "I'll get it," Dumbo's mother said as the tent flapped over their heads.

If the weather hadn't been so terrible, Dumbo thought, *I could have flown up to grab the edge of the tent*. But the whipping wind was too much, even for Dumbo's wing-like ears.

At last, standing on her back legs, Mrs Jumbo caught the canvas in her trunk. She pulled it taut and let the roustabouts tie it off. But Dumbo noticed several new rips in the fabric.

"Quit your clowning!" the Ringmaster barked at the clowns. He noticed the rips too. He ordered the clowns to sew them up. "The repairs must be finished by showtime!"

Dumbo felt terrible. All the circus performers, animals and roustabouts were working hard in the storm. He had gone and made even more work, by letting the canvas get torn. And now the Ringmaster's mood was as foul as the weather!

Just then, Dumbo noticed another blast of cold air whirl the Ringmaster's black top hat off his head.

"That does it!" the Ringmaster shouted. "There will be no show tonight!"

Dumbo could not believe his ears. The announcement was even enough to wake Timothy Q. Mouse from his nap in a nearby bale of hay.

"No show? I can't believe it!" Timothy cried. The rest of the circus folk couldn't believe it either. They silently continued to set up.

"What a fuss over a hat." Timothy shook his head. "The show must go on."

Dumbo nodded. Then something caught his eye. The Ringmaster's hat was caught on the flagpole, high over the Big Top. Perhaps he could get it for him?

Bravely, Dumbo took off. The wind was strong, but he tucked his head down and flapped his ears hard. When the wind calmed for a moment, the small elephant saw his chance. He grabbed the top hat and flew quickly to the ground.

Shyly, Dumbo held out the hat to the Ringmaster.

"Thank you, Dumbo." The Ringmaster took his hat gratefully. He looked around at all the people and animals still hard at work. He looked embarrassed. Then, as he placed the hat on his head, he shouted, "The show must go on!"

Everyone cheered.

"What'd I tell ya?" Timothy asked, winking at Dumbo.

Disney · PIXAR
FINDING NEMO

Old Man Octopus

"You're it!" Nemo tagged Sheldon, who was hiding next to a mollusc.

"Aw, man!" Sheldon swished his tail. "I'm going to get you next time, Nemo."

"Only if you can find me," Nemo teased. Then he called louder, "Ollie, ollie, all swim free!" The rest of the fish, who were playing hide-and-seek, returned to the giant barnacle they were using as base.

When they were all there, Sheldon began to count again.

Nemo swam away, scanning the reef for a good hiding spot. Sheldon would be out to get him for sure. Nemo swam past a large empty abalone shell. "Too easy," he muttered. He darted into an anemone. "Way too obvious." Finally he came to a dark cave in the coral. "Too dark," he shivered, looking into the spooky opening. "It'll be perfect."

Mustering his courage, Nemo swam inside. At first he couldn't see anything. Then, as his eyes adjusted to the dark, Nemo saw a large eye open on the cave wall. What could it be?

Another eye opened. Then the entire wall began to move.

"O-Old Man Octopus!" Nemo stammered as eight long arms oozed off the cave wall. Nemo and his friends swapped stories about Old Man Octopus at sleepovers.

In the stories, Old Man Octopus sneaked up on little fish and gave them a terrible scare.

"Sorry to disturb you." Nemo swam towards the cave entrance. Then he noticed something amazing. The octopus's arms were changing colour and texture! Instead of matching the brown bumpy cave wall, now they looked more like the reddish coral at the bottom of the cave.

"You didn't disturb me. What brings you to this corner of the reef?" The octopus's voice was kind. Nemo's fear melted away.

"Hide-and-seek, sir," Nemo answered politely. "But I wouldn't need a cave if I could camouflage myself like you!"

"Hide-and-seek, eh?" Old Man Octopus laughed. "One of my favourites. The camouflage does come in handy, but nothing beats a cloud of ink when you want to make a break for the base!"

"You can shoot ink clouds too?" Nemo was so excited, he forgot to be quiet.

"I hear you, Nemo!" Sheldon shouted.

"Are you ready to swim for it?" Old Man Octopus whispered with a wink.

Nemo nodded. He high fived one of Old Man Octopus's tentacles. Then, in a burst of inky blackness, he darted out of the cave, past Sheldon, and back to the barnacle base. Safe!

Disney Princess Snow White and the Seven Dwarfs

The Magic of Friendship

One day, the Seven Dwarfs were visiting Snow White and the Prince at their palace. They were all having a picnic.

"Please, help yourselves," said Snow White, as she passed out china plates. "One for you ... and you ... and ... oh, my! Where is Dopey?"

Snow White and the Prince and all six Dwarfs searched everywhere for Dopey. Finally, Snow White spotted him – he had found a caterpillar! Everybody came to look.

"Enough lookin' already," huffed Grumpy. "The Princess has made us a picnic. Besides, caterpillars ain't nothin' but trouble, if you ask me."

"Oh, Grumpy," said Snow White sweetly. "I don't think this caterpillar will be any trouble. Come," she told the Dwarfs. "Let's go back to the picnic. And Dopey, why don't you bring your new friend along?"

Everyone enjoyed the picnic, and ate and ate and ate, until every crumb was gone. Then it was time for the Dwarfs to go. Dopey took his new friend with him.

Before long, Snow White visited the Dwarfs at their cottage. She found poor Dopey in tears! Sadly, Dopey took Snow White's hand and led her outside. Then he pointed to a hard, shiny shell hanging from a branch.

"That old caterpillar went in there a few days ago," said Doc. "But he won't come out."

Snow White shook her head and then wrapped Dopey in her arms. "Oh, Dopey," she said gently, "didn't you know? The caterpillar is changing!"

"Er ..." Doc began. "Changing into what?"

Snow White saw a pair of bright-coloured wings flutter by. She pointed to the butterfly and smiled. "Into that!"

Sure enough, the Dwarfs turned and looked just in time to see the little shell crack open. A creature – Dopey's caterpillar – began to push out. Slowly, but surely, the small wings began to open.

"It is a butterfly!" cried Happy.

Dopey smiled a big smile and held out his finger to his caterpillar friend, now a fancy-looking butterfly! But instead of climbing on to it, the butterfly flew away!

Snow White tried her best to comfort little Dopey. "Don't worry," she assured him. "Remember, I went away, too. But I still come back and visit. Being a good friend sometimes means letting your friends go ... and letting them return for lots and lots of visits!"

Just then, the butterfly landed right on Dopey's nose!

Disney THE LION KING

All Wet

Timon pounded his tiny chest and gave a mighty yell as he swung out over the lagoon. He let go of a vine and threw his arms out wide, hitting the water with a small but very satisfying smack. He popped to the surface, shouting: "Ta-da!"

Pumbaa was next. "Look out below!" he called. He backed up on the rock ledge, then charged. The warthog's splash sent water flying high into the air. The lagoon was still rippling when he surfaced.

"Not bad," Simba said. "But I bet Nala could do better." The Lion King looked up at Nala, who was sunning herself on a rock as far from the water as possible.

"Ha!" Nala laughed. "You know I don't like to get wet."

"Oh, come on, Nala. Give it a try. The water's fine!" Simba said.

"I'm sure the water *is* fine ..." Nala replied slowly, rolling over and licking her paw "... for drinking."

Pumbaa and Timon sniggered. Simba frowned. Nala was making him look silly in front of his friends. Was he King of the Pride Lands or not?

Using his most commanding voice, Simba gave Nala an order. "You will come swimming with us right now, or else!"

Nala did not even lift her head. She closed her eyes. "Or else what, Your Mightiness?"

Simba couldn't come up with anything, so the argument was over. And Nala, as usual, had won.

Accepting his defeat, Simba ran to the edge of the rocky ledge, sprang high in the air and tucked his paws in for a royal cannonball.

Pumbaa and Timon were drenched. Slinking slowly out of the water, Simba signalled to them. He pointed at his dripping mane, then at Nala's rock.

Timon winked, and he and Pumbaa began a noisy mock water fight to distract Nala. While they hollered and splashed, Simba climbed up to Nala's warm spot in the sun. He walked quickly but silently. Drawing closer, he crouched, his legs coiled to pounce. Nala did not move.

Then, with a triumphant roar, Simba jumped onto Nala's rock and gave his sopping mane a mighty shake. Nala was drenched.

Nala leaped to her feet with a snarl. Simba rolled onto his back, laughing.

"You're all wet, Nala!" Timon guffawed. Pumbaa was laughing so hard, he could barely breathe.

Nala tried to glare fiercely at Simba, but she couldn't. She had to laugh too. "King of the practical jokers," she said.

December

22

Disney

Bambi

Night-time is for Exploring!

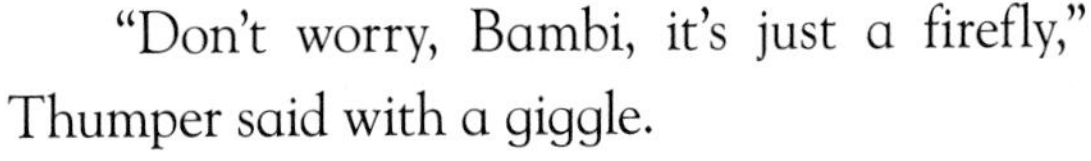

As the moon rose above the forest, Bambi snuggled close to his sleeping mother. What a day it had been! Exploring new places, learning new words and meeting new friends. Bambi yawned and closed his eyes....

"Bambi! Oh, Bambi!"

Bambi slowly opened his eyes. "Thumper?" he whispered. "Why aren't you asleep?"

"Asleep? Come on!" cried Thumper. "Sleep is for the birds! How can you sleep when there's so much to see and do at night?"

"But everybody knows that night-time is for sleeping," Bambi said.

"Oh, brother," Thumper said. "Do you have a lot to learn! Follow me, Bambi, and I'll show you how the night is a whole new day!"

And suddenly, at the prospect of a new adventure, Bambi's sleepiness disappeared. Quietly, he stood up and let Thumper lead the way.

Thumper was right – the forest was as busy at night as it was during the day, but with a whole new group of animals. Owls, opossums, raccoons and badgers – all those animals that Bambi thought spent most of their lives asleep – were now as lively as could be.

"Wh-wh-what's that?" Bambi exclaimed, as a dot of light landed on his nose.

"Don't worry, Bambi, it's just a firefly," Thumper said with a giggle.

"'Firefly'," Bambi said. Then suddenly, the little light disappeared. "Hey, where'd it go?"

"There it is!" cried Thumper, pointing to Bambi's tail. "No, wait. It's over there."

Happily, Thumper and Bambi chased the firefly as it flitted from one friend to the other. "I think he likes us!" Thumper cried.

But their game was soon interrupted by a flurry of sound. Thousands of leathery wings were suddenly beating overhead.

"Duck, Bambi!" hollered Thumper, just as the whole group swooped around their heads.

"Boy, that was close!" said Thumper.

"Were those fireflies too?" Bambi asked.

"Naw," Thumper laughed. "They didn't light up! Those were bats."

"'Bats'," repeated Bambi. "They're really busy at night."

"You can say that again," agreed Thumper, trying to stifle a yawn. And, since yawns are contagious, Bambi's own yawn was not far behind.

"This was fun," Bambi told his friend. "But what do you say we go home and go to bed?"

But there was no answer ... for Thumper was already fast asleep!

Disney Princess
Tangled

Rapunzel's New Friend

Long before Rapunzel knew she was a princess, before she left her tower for an adventure across the kingdom, she was a lonely little girl.

Mother Gothel often left Rapunzel alone. And the only creatures that crossed her path were butterflies, bees and the occasional bird.

But butterflies are notoriously skittish, bees do not like hugs and no matter how many seeds Rapunzel gave them, the birds never stuck around very long.

Since friends were scarce, Rapunzel did the next best thing. She filled each day with an exciting new activity.

She tried painting, but her artwork never looked as good as what she had imagined.

Then she tried baking, but her cakes came out burned and black.

Finally, Rapunzel tried gardening, but her seeds weren't sprouting.

"That's it!" shouted Rapunzel. "I can't paint, I can't bake and I can't even grow one strawberry. I give up!"

But just as she was about to throw away her gardening gloves, Rapunzel noticed a strange pattern in the dirt. Taking a closer look, she realized they were footprints.

A few days later, the same prints showed up in her paint!

When the prints appeared in her flour, Rapunzel knew something was up. "This is a mystery," she said. "I love mysteries!"

So, from then on, whenever Rapunzel painted a picture, she spilled a little paint on purpose.

Whenever she baked, she scattered a little flour.

And whenever she gardened, she sprinkled a little dirt.

She wanted to see if the prints would reappear ... and they always did! But Rapunzel still didn't know who was making them.

Meanwhile, she got really good at painting, baking and gardening!

One day, as she was picking strawberries, Rapunzel spotted an odd-shaped berry.

As she reached for the berry, it changed colour! Before her was a small green chameleon, curled in a ball and frozen with fear.

"So you're the one who's been leaving the funny little prints!" said Rapunzel.

The chameleon seemed to nod. Rapunzel hadn't been alone in her tower after all! But how would she convince him to stay?

"My name is Rapunzel," she said. "I'll call you Pascal. Would you like some cake?"

Rapunzel learned that Pascal never said no to cake. And Pascal learned that Rapunzel was the best friend a chameleon could ever ask for.

Disney Princess
The Princess and the Frog

A Magical Feast

When their first holiday season as a married couple arrived, Tiana wanted Prince Naveen to experience the traditions she knew and loved. So for Christmas Eve, she invited their family and friends to her restaurant.

"How many are we cooking for?" Naveen asked, as he struggled with a tower of boxes full of ingredients.

"As many as want to join us!" Tiana smiled. "The more the merrier!"

Tiana and Naveen spent the next few days cooking and baking away – preparing a magnificent meal for their guests.

"Before everyone arrives," Tiana said, as they were drawing to the end of their food preparations, "I have a surprise for you."

She led Naveen by the hand into a canoe and paddled out to the bayou where huge bonfires lined the river.

"The fires are for Papa Noel," Tiana explained. "He travels on a raft pulled by alligators."

As the fog rolled in, the people on the river bank mistook Tiana and Naveen for Papa Noel himself! They pointed and called to them in excitement.

"Have you seen Papa Noel?" a stranger in a crowd asked, when Tiana and Naveen had reached the dock.

Tiana stifled a laugh. "No we haven't! But would you like to join us at our restaurant?"

When Tiana and Naveen walked to the restaurant, the guests had started to arrive. Louis the alligator was standing outside and a woman cried, "Look! It's one of Papa Noel's alligators!"

Tiana glanced at the guests. Her best friend Charlotte was there, plus Naveen's parents. And a man with a white beard and red coat.

"He looks awfully like Papa Noel," Tiana whispered to Naveen.

Later, dinner was served. When everything had been gobbled up, Naveen and Louis played Christmas carols to keep everyone's spirits up.

Tiana, in the meantime, pushed a trolley full of puddings from the kitchen.

"Let me help you with that," came a voice. It was the white bearded gentleman ... the one who looked like Papa Noel!

He winked and pushed the trolley into the restaurant. Tiana stared after him, amazed.

"I think it's Papa Noel!" Tiana told Naveen, when he was finished playing his songs.

"It could be," he said. "This night has been oh so magical!"

Tiana giggled. She was delighted that Naveen's first Christmas in New Orleans had gone so well. For her, that was magic enough.

Disney Princess The Little Mermaid

The Holiday Treasure Hunt

It was almost Christmas and Ariel was trying to decide which presents to buy everyone. In the ocean, they gave gifts of seashells and clams with pearls hidden inside, but the human world was very different.

On the beach one morning, Max bounded over with a boot dangling from his mouth. It was dirty and worn looking.

"I've been looking for that for months!" cried Eric.

"Max loves to hide things." Ariel chuckled.

This gave her an idea about what to get Eric.

At the castle, Ariel noticed Grimsby the butler was shaking his broken pocket watch in frustration and Carlotta the maid was admiring the red and gold decorations. Now she knew what to get them for Christmas too....

The next day, Ariel bought new boots for Eric as well as a secret surprise. Then she picked out a pocket watch for Grimsby and a red and gold pendant for Carlotta.

Before heading home, Ariel noticed some heart-shaped crystals in the window of a shop. "They'd be perfect for my father and sisters," she said excitedly.

All wrapped up and placed under the tree, Ariel was happy with the presents she'd bought and went to find Eric. Little did she know, Max had spied the pretty gift boxes with their bows and labels on top ... and it had made his tail wag mischievously.

On Christmas morning, Ariel put on a pink gown and joined everyone at the table for a grand breakfast. She couldn't wait to share her presents, but when she left to fetch them they had gone missing!

Flustered, she returned to the dining room. Eric wanted to give Ariel a present but she convinced him to take a walk along the beach first. "I can wish my family a Merry Christmas," she explained, stalling for time.

On the beach, King Triton and his daughters waved from the ocean.

"We knew you'd come," said one sister. "You never forget our traditions!"

Then, Max appeared with a familiar new boot in his mouth. Ariel realized the naughty dog had buried her gifts. "Surprise!" she cried, thinking quickly. "It's a holiday treasure hunt!"

Eric laughed and was the first to start digging. Soon, all the gifts that Max had buried were with their rightful owners and everyone agreed how beautiful and thoughtful they were.

That evening, sat by the Christmas tree, Ariel gave Eric his secret surprise present.

"A ship in a bottle!" he said. "You're truly special, Ariel."

"It's our love that's special," she replied.

Love was truly the best gift of all.

December

26

Friends Forever

The fairies had returned to Pixie Hollow after a summer working on the mainland. But Tinker Bell was very sad. She'd made a human friend over there and, now she was home, she missed Lizzy terribly. She sat on a branch over the river and stared miserably into the water.

Rosetta and Fawn tried to cheer her up. "You can go back to see her on the mainland next summer," Fawn said.

Tink shook her head. "I'm afraid Lizzy's going to forget about me."

"Impossible!" said Fawn. "Come with me. I'll show you something." Taking Tink's arm, she dragged the reluctant fairy to visit her friends the squirrels. "Look how happy they are to see me again," Fawn said, as the squirrels bounded round in delight.

Tink wasn't convinced. "They remember you, but Lizzy isn't a squirrel!"

Rosetta tried next. "Let me introduce you to my friends," she said, showing Tink all the beautiful flowers in her garden and how they waved at her in the sunlight. Rosetta's flowers bloomed every year under her care, and she knew they would always be there for her.

"Thanks for trying to help me," Tink said, "but Lizzy isn't a flower or a squirrel." A sob burst out of her. "She'll grow up and forget all about me!"

Rosetta and Fawn stared in dismay as Tink flew back to the river to stare unhappily into the water. What else could they do?

"Hey, Tink!" called a voice. "Tink!"

"Look, it's Bobble!" exclaimed Rosetta.

In his arms, Bobble carried a large parcel. "I've been looking for you all day," he told Tink, panting. "This is for you."

"Thanks," said Tink, puzzled. "Where'd you find it?"

"The last fairies to come back from the mainland brought it with them," explained Bobble.

Tink took the parcel from him and shook it. "I can't hear anything." What could be inside?

Tink's friends gathered round as she unwrapped the parcel. Inside was a large peppermint cake and a note. Tink's expression brightened as she read the note. "It's a present from Lizzy! She says, 'Even if you're far away, we'll be friends forever.'" Happiness flooded through her. Lizzy wasn't going to forget her!

"How flitterific!" cried Rosetta, clapping her hands.

Together, the fairies sat down on a picnic rug to eat the cake. Tink felt so happy she thought she might burst. Her friends had been right. Friendship was the most wonderful magic there was!

December

27

Disney MINNIE

The Pesky Pet

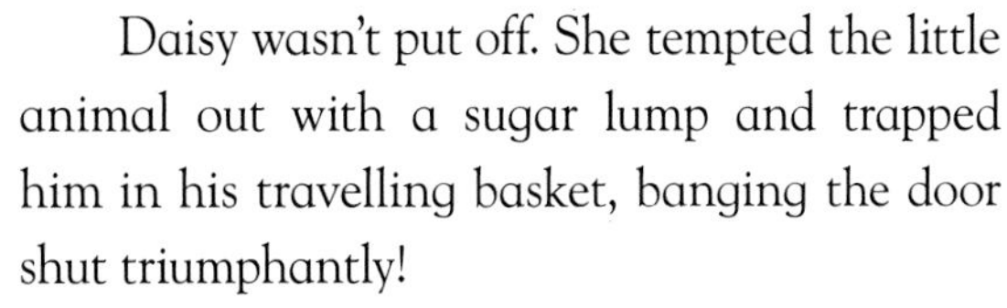

Daisy Duck was saving up for a fancy new surfboard. "I'm getting close!" she told her best friend Minnie Mouse.

And Daisy had the perfect idea for how she could raise the rest of the money – pet-sitting! "But Daisy, you've never even had a pet goldfish," Minnie pointed out.

"That's not a problem," Daisy shrugged. "Mrs Flamingo wants a pet-sitter next weekend!"

Minnie wasn't sure her friend knew what she was taking on.

Sure enough, when she went to visit Mrs Flamingo, Daisy was surprised to discover that the small furry pet was a sugar glider – a really unusual animal, like a flying squirrel!

"My little sweetie's name is Sugarplum," Mrs Flamingo told her, stroking him fondly. "Remember – he's a nocturnal animal and he doesn't like light. And make sure you never give him sugar during the day."

Daisy promised faithfully to look after Sugarplum and Mrs Flamingo swept out of the house, saying, "See you Monday!"

Daisy had no idea what to do with a sugar glider. "Come here, cutie!" She reached out to tickle Sugarplum under his chin – but the glider leaped off his cushion and dived under the dresser!

Daisy wasn't put off. She tempted the little animal out with a sugar lump and trapped him in his travelling basket, banging the door shut triumphantly!

Sugarplum didn't like being shut up – and he'd had sugar now! He hit the bars of his cage, driving Daisy mad! She rang Minnie and begged her to come over.

"What did I tell you?" said Minnie. "You can't take care of him, can you?"

They took Sugarplum to Leonard's house, but he escaped again and tried to steal Leonard's precious treasure chest!

Desperate times called for desperate measures – Donkey Donuts! Even there the sneaky glider was up to more mischief. An ice cream tub flew through the air and landed on their classmate Abigail! Minnie and Daisy tried not to laugh but Abigail was always so mean to them, it was funny to see her covered in ice cream.

The glider looked sad. "He needs a friend to play with!" Daisy suddenly realized.

Leonard knew just what to do. He found a toy to keep Sugarplum company. The little creature beamed happily as he played with it.

Minnie and Daisy breathed a sigh of relief. "Next time," promised Daisy, "I'll think things through a little more!"

Winnie the Pooh

Roo's New Babysitter

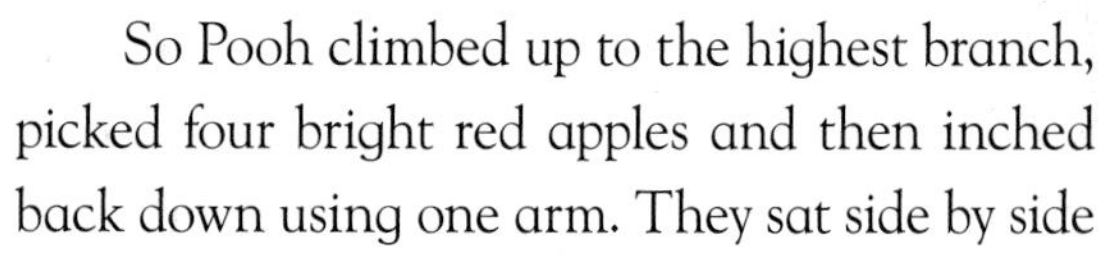

"I don't want to be babysitted!" cried Roo. Roo's mama, Kanga, was going shopping and Pooh was going to babysit.

"I want to go shopping!" cried Roo to Kanga.

He had a large bag and was filling it with items from the kitchen when Pooh arrived.

"Hello, Pooh," said Roo. "I'm shopping!" He put more tins in his bag, partly because he didn't want his mama to see how much he minded being left behind.

Roo and Pooh said goodbye to Kanga. Then Pooh gave Roo a hug and tried to feed him a nice smackerel of honey.

"I want to go shopping," squeaked Roo. "I don't want to eat."

"Hmm," said Pooh. "Now what do I do?"

"You don't know how to babysit?" asked Roo, with a mischievous look on his face. "I'm good at babysitting. I'll tell you how. The first thing a babysitter does is climb!"

Pooh, who was starting to think there was not much *sitting* involved in babysitting, said, "Okay, let's find a good climbing tree."

They climbed the old apple tree in Roo's back garden. Roo hopped from branch to branch, and Pooh climbed up behind him.

"Mmm," said Roo. "Look at those apples. Babysitters always pick apples for supper."

So Pooh climbed up to the highest branch, picked four bright red apples and then inched back down using one arm. They sat side by side and swung their feet and ate the sweet apples.

"This is the best supper ever!" cried Roo.

Next, Roo showed Pooh how babysitters pour a whole bottle of bubble bath into the bathwater. Roo disappeared under the bubbles. Pooh blew on the bubbles but he couldn't see Roo anywhere!

"Look at me jumping," squeaked a little voice.

Roo was jumping on his bed, all wet! Pooh dried Roo off, then helped put on his pyjamas.

"Time for your Strengthening Medicine," said Pooh, a little more sternly than when poohs usually say such things. But Roo didn't want it. He folded his arms across his chest.

"Oh well," said Pooh, slumping in a chair. "Why don't you give *me* a spoonful? I think I could do with it!"

"Now, Pooh, dear, here's your medicine," said Roo in a cheerful, grown-up sort of voice.

"Ahhh!" said Pooh. "Thank you, Roo. You are a good babysitter."

Just then, Kanga opened the door and saw Roo and Pooh snuggled together in the chair.

"Mama!" cried Roo. "I'm babysitting Pooh!"

"Of course you are, dear," said Kanga.

Disney Princess Snow White and the Seven Dwarfs

Snow Dwarfs

On a cold winter's day, standing by the frosted window pane, Snow White leaned on the warm shoulder of her Prince Charming, as they watched the snow falling outside.

"I think we should visit the Dwarfs' cottage," she suggested. "I'm sure they'd enjoy some of my hot soup on a cold day like this."

Prince Charming admired Snow White's caring heart and agreed, taking her through the forest and smiling as the ice crunched under their feet. But at the Dwarfs' cottage, there was no one to be seen.

"They're probably working in the mines," Snow White said and prepared the soup for them as a surprise.

As time went by, Snow White started to worry. The Dwarfs still hadn't come home and it was getting late.

"We should go look for them," she said, wrapping up warm again. "The snow is very deep now and they're so little."

She and her Prince mounted their horses and set off for the mine, only to pause in surprise.

"There are seven frozen little men!" Snow White gasped, staring at the row of snowy white statues. "Something terrible has happened here!"

Prince Charming helped her down from her horse and as she rushed to the snowmen shaped like her friends, Happy emerged from the entrance of the mine. His arms were open wide in greeting and his skin looked rosy and warm beneath his many layers of clothes.

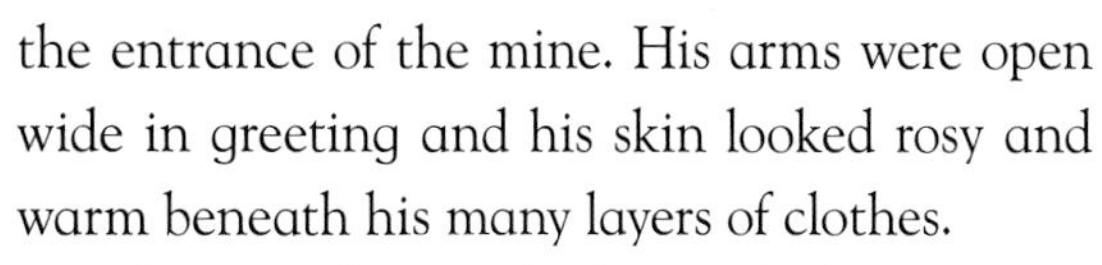

Snow White sighed in relief, as Prince Charming's arm wrapped round her shoulder.

"We were playing in the snow," Happy said cheerfully. "Do you like our snowmen?"

"They look just like you all," Snow White admitted, blushing slightly. She'd truly thought her friends had frozen in the winter weather!

"We call them Snow Dwarfs!" said Grumpy, as he left the mine carrying a bag of gems. The other Dwarfs soon followed close behind him, all bearing bags of diamonds and pickaxes balanced on their shoulders.

Snow White gave each Dwarf a warm hug and together they made their way back to the cottage, throwing snowballs, laughing and making snow angels on the ground as they went.

When they were home safe and warm, Prince Charming stoked the fire to get the flames to roar and Snow White served a magnificent soup to warm her friends from the inside out.

The Dwarfs were so happy! Even Grumpy had a smile.

Winter could be hard sometimes, but it was always magical when there were friends to share it with....

Disney Princess
Beauty and the Beast

A Wintry Walk

"It's so beautiful," Belle murmured as she gazed out of the castle window. Snow had been falling for hours and hours, covering everything in a deep blanket of white. "You know what would be nice? A wa –"

Suddenly, a heavy red cape was draped over her shoulders. "How about a walk?" the Prince asked.

Belle smiled into his blue eyes. "I was just thinking that!" she said.

"Aha," he replied mischievously. "But were you thinking of a walk on these?" He pulled a pair of large snowshoes out from behind a chair.

"Snowshoes!" Belle cried, clapping her hands together. She and her father used to go snowshoeing together in the woods when she was a little girl, and she loved it. No matter how deep the snow was, the special shoes allowed her to walk over the huge drifts.

Minutes later, the pair were in the castle courtyard, strapping the snowshoes onto their boots. Belle walked forward gracefully, heading through the gate towards the forest, pausing to scatter birdseed for the neighbourhood birds.

But the Prince was having trouble, tripping over the giant shoes with every step.

"When I was a beast, I just walked through the snow," he said, panting. "I didn't have to bother wearing silly contraptions like these!" He stepped forward and tumbled headfirst into a deep snowbank.

Belle laughed. At first, the Prince scowled but soon he was laughing too.

"You're thinking too much," Belle said. "It's a lot like walking in regular shoes. You just have to keep your feet a little further apart so they don't get caught up in each other."

The Prince stepped forward. But, when he lifted his other foot, it caught on the icy top layer of snow, and he fell again.

Belle stifled a giggle as she helped him to his feet. "Try to step lightly," she suggested.

"I'll say," the Prince grumbled. He stepped more lightly this time, and moved easily across the snow. Soon he was keeping up with Belle, who led him through the forest. It was a wonderful, wintry walk. And, when they got back to the castle, they found hot chocolate and biscuits waiting for them in front of the fire!

"Oh, good," said the Prince. "Eating! This is one thing I'll always be good at." He picked up a biscuit, which broke and fell with a *PLOP!* into his cup.

"Aw," he said, crestfallen.

"You know," Belle said with a teasing smile, "you aren't so different from the clumsy beast I fell in love with!"

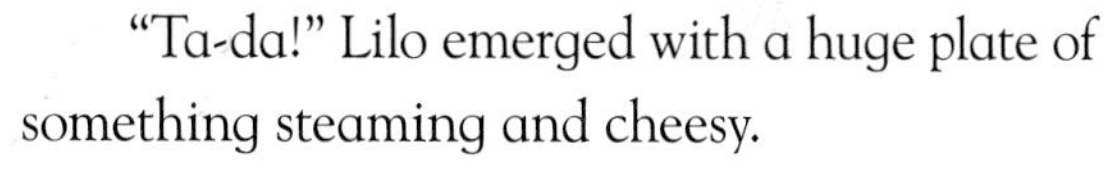

Countdown to Midnight!

"No sleep till midnight!" Lilo and Stitch chanted, bouncing up and down on Lilo's bed. It was New Year's Eve, and Nani had agreed to let them stay up late.

"Okay, okay." Nani held her hands out to calm them. "It's only five o'clock now. Don't wear yourselves out. You still have seven hours until the new year."

Lilo and Stitch looked at each other. Wear themselves out? Impossible!

"Look, Stitch," Lilo said. "We only have seven hours. What do you want to do first?"

"Surfing!" Stitch cried.

"Sunset surfing it is!" Lilo gave the little alien a high five before turning to Nani. "Okay?" she asked sweetly.

Nani shook her head again. *I must be nuts*, she thought. "I'll go get my suit." She sighed.

The three surfed until sundown. Then they headed for home.

"So, what's next?" Lilo asked Stitch.

Stitch smacked his lips. "Dinner!"

"Don't worry," Lilo said. "We'll cook."

"And I'll clean," Nani muttered.

When they got home, Nani lay down on the couch with her arm over her eyes. Five hours until bedtime. She switched on the TV and tried to ignore the crashing noises coming from the kitchen.

"Ta-da!" Lilo emerged with a huge plate of something steaming and cheesy.

"What is it?" Nani asked cautiously.

"Pizza, Stitch-style!" Lilo said. "With anchovies, peanut butter and fruit cocktail!"

Nani cringed. "Don't worry, Nani," said Lilo. "We left the toothpaste on the side this time. Plus, there's a milkshake for pudding!"

The three ate the gooey mess, while Lilo and Stitch discussed what was next.

"How about that milkshake?" Nani suggested before Lilo could come up with a noisier, messier or more dangerous idea.

Stitch grabbed the blender and dumped the milkshake on his head. Nani shooed the two into the sitting room and began to tackle the mess in the kitchen.

The washing-up took forever. Nani could not figure out how they'd managed to use so many pots and pans. She was still elbow deep in suds when her eyes grew wide with alarm. Something was wrong. It was too quiet! Nani rushed into the living room. Lilo and Stitch were sound asleep! Nani looked at her watch.

"Five-four-three-two-one," Nani counted down. "Happy New Year," she said softly, as she covered the pair with a blanket.

She smiled as she looked at the clock. It was only 10pm!

See you
next year!